"You are a fool, Melissa. I am your husband, and I want you."

He went to the door of his dressing room, opened it, passed through, and closed the door behind him.

After a very long time, shivering and exhausted, she crept into her bed and blew out the light. When, in the darkness, she felt the tears on her face, she was amazed, and said aloud in a voice of distressed wonder: "What is the matter with me?"

It was Melissa's wedding night, the beginning of an infernal battle for her besieged heart.

"The lofty peaks of best-sellerdom are traditionally difficult to scale. . . . But there are three American novelists who have climbed to the top not once or twice but over and over again. In so doing they have established themselves as an elite among U.S. fiction writers. . . . All three are women: Edna Ferber, Frances Parkinson Keys and Taylor Caldwell."

Life Magazine

Novels by Taylor Caldwell in Pyramid edition

MELISSA
Taylor Caldwell

PYRAMID BOOKS • NEW YORK

MELISSA

A Pyramid Book

Copyright, 1948, by Reback and Reback. Copyright, 1948, by
Crowell-Collier Publishing Company. All rights reserved.
No part of this book may be reproduced in any form without
the permission of Charles Scribner's Sons.
Published by arrangement with Charles Scribner's Sons.

Printed in the United States of America

Pyramid edition published July 1973
   Tenth printing, August 1973

ISBN 0-515-03114-3

Pyramid Books are published by Pyramid Communications, Inc.
Its trademarks, consisting of the word "Pyramid" and the
portrayal of a pyramid, are registered in the United States
Patent Office.

Pyramid Communications, Inc.,
919 Third Avenue, New York, N.Y. 10022

To Alice and Whitney Darrow

CHAPTER 1

THE DAMP AND WRINKLED GLOVES lay in a little heap on the hall table, where they had been dropped in gestures of complete desolation.

Melissa removed hers from her cold hands and added them to the heap. She stood a moment and looked emptily down at the gloves, lying one on top of the other, and they seemed to be external manifestations of her own stupefied hopelessness. Her mother had gone into the drawing-room before her, and her young sister, Phoebe, and her brother, Andrew, and Mrs. Arabella Dunham Shaw and the latter's brother, Geoffrey Dunham. They were all sitting there, in the utter silence that follows calamity, while she remained behind in the dark cold hall, this late November afternoon. None of them had glanced at her, except Geoffrey Dunham, and he had stood near her for a few moments, while she had fumbled at her gloves. But she had indicated that she wanted him to leave her, with a motion of her hands so abrupt and repellent that he had obeyed automatically. She had watched him go; she believed she saw him shrug as if in indifferent contempt. It was no more than she expected of him; everything he did increased her distrust and detestation. Suddenly, in the midst of her dreadful anguish, she felt a sharp and vivid thrill of hatred, an emotion that was alive for the first time in three stunned days.

She could not look away from the wrinkled gloves, lying there in a heap on the table. It had begun to rain again, and Melissa heard the dolorous running of the eaves and the forsaken voice of the wind against the great oaken door of the old house. What little light remained in the narrow hall faded; what little warmth had seeped into the hall from the drawing-room was sucked away. Now there was only dimness and chill, and herself alone in the hall. Melissa could hear her mother's sobbing, which became part of the wind and the rain. There was no other sound, not even from the kitchen, where old

Sally and the Dunhams' cook, Hulda, were preparing the funeral baked meats.

The Dunhams had filled the parlor with armfuls and baskets and vases of flowers from their conservatories. The flowers now lay on a raw grave in St. Margaret's Cemetery on the slope of a hill, yet Melissa could smell their horrible sick ghosts in the hall. Strange that funeral flowers smelled as no other flowers ever smelled! There was a deathliness about them, a sickness, a miasma. O Papa, Papa! Melissa cried in herself. She wrung her hands together. The merciful stupefaction drained away from her, leaving her open and naked and anguished in the swirling waves of her grief. Her mouth parted in a kind of suppressed gasp, as if for air. But no tears came. Her mother had wept, little Phoebe had cried with the faint and mewling sound of a wounded and innocent animal, Andrew had sobbed drily a few times. But Melissa's eyes had remained glazed, burning, stark, completely sleepless and parched, since her father's death three days ago. She knew that her mother thought her heartless. It did not matter; it had never mattered to her what her mother, Amanda, had ever thought about her, or, for that matter, what anyone else thought. Wherever lay the source of tears, that source in Melissa remained dry. Arabella Dunham Shaw, that sharkmouthed, sentimental and emotional fool, had throbbingly urged her to "give way; do, my poor child." But there was no "giving way" in Melissa. She had looked at Arabella with disgust and bitter loathing, and had confirmed in Arabella's mind the opinion that she lacked sensibility and true female sentiment. How was it possible—Arabella had plainly revealed her thought—that the favorite and most beloved daughter of Charles Upjohn could refrain from the slightest expression of sorrow, could maintain an attitude of subdued calm and glacial dignity in the face of his death?

A fog floated outside over the brown drenched earth. Wisps of it appeared to penetrate the hall, so that faint scarfs and whitish shadows filled every oaken corner. The round drum table where the gloves and the cards lay gleamed like water in the gloom. Above it was a mirror. Old Sally had removed the cloths from the glimmering surface. Melissa lifted her head and saw her own face in the dark and fitful depths, and it was the face of a ghost. Her face stared blindly back at her from the glass, a rigid and emotionless face, all bleached contours and hard delicate planes, like dull marble. When she had been young and helpless, her mother, Amanda, had forced her to swallow iron concoctions, in the belief that she was anaemic and afflicted with the "green sickness," not understanding, then, that the pure and colorless pallor was no indication of weakness, but rather of an indomitable constitution.

"A New England old maid," Arabella Dunham had once said to her brother, Geoffrey. "Oh, believe me, dear Geoffrey, it is not that I truly dislike Melissa Upjohn! I'm sure you'd never accuse me of such uncharitableness, for you know how readily I believe the best of everyone and how far malice is from my nature. But you must admit that Melissa can be very odious at times, most repulsive. She is so cold and without sensibility, and has such a high, hard face. There is nothing attractive in her, though you insist, in your kindness, that she is a true beauty. No one else shares your opinion, dear Geoffrey.

"What did you say, Geoffrey? Melissa is a grande dame? Oh, how absurd, how completely ridiculous! She is nothing but a bluestocking, utterly without heart and sweetness, priding herself on her knowledge of Greek and Latin, and on her scholarly accomplishments! What does a woman need of these?"

"She needs me," Geoffrey Dunham had replied with a smile. He laughed when his sister uttered a shrill wail of horror. "And, what's more, she's going to have me, though she does not know it yet. I may have to wait a long time, until poor old Charles is dead."

Melissa stood unmoving before the mirror, which steadily darkened until her face and figure were lost in it and there remained only a ghostly blur. Now she heard Geoffrey Dunham's strong grave voice consoling her mother, and her white mouth became more tense, harder. The wound in her chest throbbed and pulsated. "Papa," she said aloud, in a low and searching voice. She pressed her hands down on the wet gloves, dropped her head, and leaned heavily against the table. Her father's last words came to her: "I know I can trust your strength and your calmness, Lissa. Your poor mother and your little sister will need you. I know now that it was wrong to have taken you so far from them, to have absorbed you in my needs and my dreams and my hopes. Your brother cannot be the man of the family when I am gone. That is left for you, and I know that I can trust you."

"You never took me away from anything, Papa," she said, in her heart. "I never cared for anything but you. You were all my life. We understood each other so completely. How can I go on without you?"

For the first time there was an acid moisture in her eyes,

which burned and stung. But it did not spill over. After an instant it was gone. But she felt weak and faint, and she clutched at the smooth edges of the table. Her mind became dim and blurred, the rough thick carpet under her feet began to slide away from her.

Someone was holding her, someone strong and steady. Without that grasp, she would have fallen. Her eyes were blind. She murmured: "Andrew. It's perfectly all right. Just a moment of faintness." She tried to pull herself away gently, but the arms held her.

"And no wonder," said a man's voice in reply. "I hear you haven't eaten anything in three days. There, don't move; just lean against me for a while."

But the sound of that hateful voice aroused Melissa, invigorated her. She pushed the arms away with new strength. She could still see only dimly. Geoffrey Dunham's figure swayed and floated and expanded and retreated before her like a dancing shadow. But her detestation made her strong again. She pressed her hands to the sides of her head and muttered: "I am perfectly well now, thank you." All the spots on her body where he had touched her became acutely aware.

"Good," said Geoffrey Dunham, and under the tone of friendly sympathy she heard the old good-natured jeer in his voice. "We've been waiting for you. I am about to read your father's will, and then we'll have our supper. May I assist you, Melissa? My arm——"

But she was already walking away from him, her quivering knees held rigidly, her thin and slender back as hard as stone. Her black-and-rusty gown trailed on the floor; it was an old gown, and completely without taste or fashion, yet it gave to her figure an air of cold elegance. There was only a suggestion of crinoline under it. Not for Melissa the hoops and draperies and ruffles of other women, the soft beguilements of lace and of bows.

Geoffrey reached the door of the drawing-room before her, however. He waved her through it with a bow, in which she felt was his old mockery and amusement. Her flesh tightened and cringed away from him, and she sped into the drawing-room almost precipitously. It was too much! But she must endure this, for the last time. One had only to be calm and composed. One must be steadfast, for Papa's sake. Oh, Papa, Papa!

CHAPTER 2

MELISSA HAD always hated the drawing-room, and had frequented it as little as possible. It was her mother's sanctuary, pride and throne-room, filled with a hundred relics of a New England past. Long and narrow like a huge coffin, dark even on a summer's day, it was faintly lighted by six high and slit-like windows, three in front, three in the rear, all darkly and heavily draped in crimson embossed curtains. A yellow marble fireplace stood in the center of one wall, and now a fire twinkled feebly on the hearth, sending its wavering tongues of little flame in pale reflection on the brass fender, the brass fire-screen, the brass andirons. Small heat came from it; the room, as usual, smelled of wax, earthy chill, ancient wood and potpourri. These odors were overlaid, just now, with the scent of Amanda Upjohn's lavender-water and the old sickening ghosts of the flowers which had lately filled the room.

When Amanda as a bride had accompanied her husband to this house some twenty-seven years before, she had brought with her the cherished furniture of her dead mother, her grandmother, and her great-grandmother, still shining from the wax of one hundred years. There, at the right of the fire, stood the great mahogany highboy, flanked on the left by a huge break front. From the Goodbody family of Boston had come those low, armless chairs, upholstered in faded greens, russets and yellows, and those two love seats in a sallow shade of ancient gold. Drum tables, parquetry tables, tier tables and tiny square tables had been scattered about the room profusely, bearing upon them china and brass lamps over which there perpetually hovered the odor of old oil. Against the wall, facing the fire, stood Amanda's authentic Queen Anne sofa, upholstered in black tapestry over which had been superimposed nosegays of tiny red flowers. Only one thing had ever aroused Melissa's admiration, and that was the fine old Aubusson rug, all delicate and shadowy grays, pinks, blues and yellows. This rug had been Charles Upjohn's single contribution to the room, and Amanda had admitted it chillily.

Her preference was for polished bare floors and a scattered rug or two. But one must make a concession to one's husband, even if he was only a New Yorker, and Amanda had endured the rug during all her married life, though she was often heard to comment on the fact that it was a dust-catcher.

A portrait of Amanda's grandmother hung over the fireplace, the colors changed by time to a dull sienna, a vagrant brown, a touch of old blue. Charles had once insisted that the portrait resembled his daughter, Melissa, but when he discovered that Melissa was coldly infuriated by the remark, he did not repeat it. However, that white cold face, so narrow, so strong, and yet so fragile in its contours and planes, those large, faintly grim and steadfast light-blue eyes, deepset in hollow sockets which were tinged with mauve, that sharp, slightly tilted nose, that colorless yet beautifully molded mouth with the almost imperceptibly protruding lower lip, and that sleek mass of pale gilt hair, might have been Melissa's own. The hair shone from the canvas like something alive, though nearly all the other colors had become murky.

One lamp had been lighted to lift the damp gloom this evening, but an obscure and cloudy duskiness still lingered outside and pressed against the windows, which streamed with rain. Three great elms stood on the dying lawns, their tattered rags of yellow foliage fluttering in the wind. Heaps of leaves, sodden and blackened, had piled themselves about the furrowed trunks. One could see the sky, torn, gray, marbled with black mist looming above and beyond the trees. A drifting fog shut away the long meadows that flowed from the lawns to a low line of hills. The rear windows looked out on wide gardens, ruined by autumn, and fenced away from the barnyard by a squat wall of rough gray stones.

Old Sally Brown's half-idiot son, the Upjohns' "hired man," had brought in the cows from the drenched fields. Now, mingling with the sound of wind and rain, could be heard the desolate lowing of the cattle, and then, for a moment or two, as the wind swept towards the old tall house, there came the long and melancholy howl of a train leaving the village half a mile away.

Melissa walked steadily, and with her usual proud dignity, to a chair far from the fire. She sat down and folded her long pale hands on her knees. Her face, never mobile, remained expressionless, almost blank in its rigidity. The lamplight shone on her hair, which had the patina of satin. No agitated breath moved her high and molded breasts under the rusty dark-brown wool. She turned her head slowly, looked at her sister, her brother, and waited. She might have been gazing at painted statues, for all the emotion she revealed, though Geoffrey Dunham, seating himself with his usual careful grace, thought that for one moment Melissa's eyes had lingered on little weeping Phoebe, and had melted as if with mournful pain.

Amanda Goodbody Upjohn sat in her favorite armless chair near the fire. In her black gown, in the posture of her slender body, in the arrangement of her narrow feet crossed discreetly at the ankles, in the very set of her wide thin shoulders, she might have been Melissa herself, especially now that she had covered her face with her white handkerchief. But she had none of Melissa's youth, which still blurred the outlines of the girl's harsh rigidity. Amanda had once possessed hair the color and texture of Melissa's; now frustrated and embittered years had grayed and coarsened it. She wore a cap of white linen and lace, which only partly softened the effect of the hard twists rolled high on her head.

She was weeping soundlessly, but she had heard Melissa and Geoffrey enter and she removed the handkerchief from her eyes. Now Melissa's astonishing resemblance to her mother could be seen. It was a resemblance blasted and changed by the years, so that where, in Melissa, the pallor and clarity of feature were still beautiful and delicately austere, in Amanda they were blanched and grimly withered. Melissa's flesh still retained its fresh smoothness, but her mother's skin resembled the surface of finely cracked china. Yet both women had that high and petrified calmness of forehead which testified to their distinction of race, and not even time could take that from Amanda. Amanda was the prophecy of her elder daughter, and Geoffrey did not find this too pleasant. But then, as he had told his sister, Bella, he himself was not gentle, dreaming Charles Upjohn, who had been as unworldly as a newly laid egg and just as blandly impervious. For all his affection for old Charles, Geoffrey pitied Amanda.

Charles had once told him of Melissa's umbrage on the occasion of his regrettable mistake in calling her attention to her resemblance to her great-grandmother's portrait. "How is it possible for a child to hate an ancestor she never saw, and if so, why?" he had asked in his bewildered innocence. But Geoffrey knew that it was not the ancestress whom Melissa hated. It was her mother, who resembled the portrait even more than did Melissa.

Crouched in a big wing-chair on the other side of the hearth was little Phoebe Upjohn, mewling like a sick kitten, not entirely with grief, for her father had been aware of her existence only occasionally, but with fear and the horror of death. In speaking of Phoebe everyone used the adjective "little," though she was all of twenty, and no longer a child. All her life she would be known as "little Phoebe," not so much because she was very small and slight but because of some indefinable quality of character. Geoffrey was always reminded of a fluffy chick when he saw her, for she had a mass of bright gold ringlets, perpetually dishevelled, apparently always uncombed, and carelessly bound with a childish blue ribbon. (There were times when he suspected that Phoebe was only too well aware of her appearance of frail helplessness and engaging dependence, took ruthless advantage of it, and exploited it to the full. But it was impossible to be hard with her on this account; she was so charming, so soft, so full of adolescent appeal.)

No maturity of body would ever change that school-girl's little figure, all slender waist, all budding breasts, all round white neck, all Dresden-china arms and curved soft shoulders. One of Melissa's black gowns had been hastily reconverted for Phoebe three days ago by the village dressmaker, and she looked exactly like a child who had arrayed herself in her mother's garments. She sat in her usual position in the chair, tiny feet tucked under her, so that she appeared smaller than she really was. This was one of her conscious, or unconscious, tricks, to melt the heart of the beholder but, again, no one could be impatient with her for this. Her brilliant ringlets and curls spilled over the black bombazine of her funeral dress, and Geoffrey thought the effect exceedingly pretty. Even tears, blotches and swollen patches could not conceal her artless loveliness.

In grief and fear, Phoebe was still delightful. Red-rimmed though the eyelids were, the eyes themselves amazingly darkblue and shining, tilted at the corners and swept by bronze lashes, looked out with the shining innocence of an infant. "She has her father's eyes," friends would say fondly and, indeed, there was much of Charles Upjohn, not only in her eyes, the sweetness of her expression, the round and dreaming fullness of her red mouth, her classic nose and full dimpled chin, but in her character, though only Geoffrey Dunham suspected this.

"There is none so dangerous as the weak or the deliberately weak," Geoffrey would think, "none so ruthless, so cannibalistic, so devouring." And none, in the case of Charles and Phoebe, so guiltless, so innocent, so inculpable. Perhaps the strong, almost inevitably destroyed by the weak, brought their own victimization upon themselves, sublime fools seduced by their own strength, their own delusion of power. One could only laugh at them, not pity them.

Geoffrey looked at Andrew Upjohn, who sat far to the right of his sister Phoebe, and the older man felt compassion for the younger. Andrew fitted nowhere in this family of cold passion and dainty and beguiling weakness. In fact, thought Geoffrey with pleased surprise, Andrew is just a normal fellow, the salt of the earth, a sound rock, as wholesome as a crisp apple, as mild and fresh as cider. Funny I never saw it before; the others obscured my perceptiveness, I am afraid.

Big, sturdy, robust, Andrew sat awkwardly, as a farmer sits, and was all heavy and distressful gloom, in this atmosphere of women. Yes, women, even when old Charlie was alive, thought Geoffrey Dunham. Charlie was the biggest woman of them all, poor old devil. The air of this house had always been abnormal and grotesque, yet Andrew Upjohn, healthy, sane, rugged, had retained his earthy integrity. His massive shoulders were the shoulders of a man of the soil; his hands had been created for the care of crops and animals, and even though they were rarely concerned with either, the flesh had the brownness and darkness of a farmer's, the knuckles were large and powerful, the nails broad and flat. His tight black broadcloth trousers strained over his big powerful muscles; the waistcoat appeared about to burst over his enormous chest. His elegant clothing almost concealed the might of his heroic body, the simple majesty of his arms and legs, and gave him a clownlike and ludicrous appearance, like a farmer sheepishly arrayed in his Sunday best.

Andrew's head was round, larger than the average man's, and covered with a mass of auburn hair, which all the brushings and the macassar oil could not restrain to a gentlemanly sleekness. At the slightest provocation the ends rose up roughly and stiffly above a low wide forehead, as brown as a nut, though he was almost never exposed to the wild hot sun of midsummer. Below that forehead were a pair of small, dark-blue eyes, calmly passionate, yet shy and steady, the eyes of one too patient, too indestructible, too understanding to hurry and to fever after insignificant things. Their intelligence was not the intelligence of a townsman who makes epigrams and converses with shallow sophistication with his replicas; rather, it was an intelligence rooted in profound instinct and knowledge.

Andrew had his father's classic nose, but where Charles'

had been all attenuated delicacy, Andrew's was big and jutting, the nose of puissant man. Below it were folded his big tranquil lips, wholesomely sensual but kind, and a rocklike chin.

Acquaintances were apt to say that Andrew, for all that he was studying law at Harvard, was a mindless, slow dolt, an anachronism in this intellectual family, a misfit, a peasant. Apparently he was no scholar, for, at twenty-three, he was the oldest student in his class, and much derided by the elegant youths in the chairs about him. But Andrew studied law, and no one had ever heard him object. Not that it would do him much good, thought Geoffrey, when faced with Charles and Melissa, who had decided this career for him. No one had ever heard him express a desire for the life of a countryman, but all at once Geoffrey knew that this desire lived vividly in the young man. Why, then, with this strength of mind and body, had he surrendered to Melissa's will? Why had he been persuaded that law was his forte?

Melissa had usurped the power of her mother, had become the dominating tyrant of the household. But, thought Geoffrey with acute surprise, perhaps I am wrong. I have a suspicion, a very nasty suspicion, that it was Charles who was the power and the tyrant—gentle, smiling, philosophic Charles, with his wry and subtle humor, his immured and cloistered life, his bending before anything which might disturb his meditations, his pacific yielding to apparently stronger wills, his desire to be left alone in his study with Melissa his amanuensis and student and idolator. He had yielded, in order to get his inexorable way; he had surrendered, in order to become invincible. The image of Charles, in Geoffrey's mind, suddenly became rearranged into other planes and expressions. The apparently weak and pliant had a secret terrible strength. They allowed the strong their delusion of power in order to get their own implacable will.

Charles! Charles! thought Geoffrey, inwardly smiling. I am afraid you were considerable of a rascal, a lovable, compromising rascal.

Geoffrey looked at the three woman and the young man. He looked at the sallow and shadowed lamplight, the fire which did not warm, the pieces of furniture which were the memories and the childhood of Amanda Goodbody. They were waiting for him to read Charles' will, for Geoffrey was originally a man of law though he had long abandoned that profession. Moreover, he had been Charles' one and only intimate; perhaps it was this, unsuspected until now by

Geoffrey, which filled Melissa's eyes with hatred when she looked at him.

Amanda had momentarily done with expressions of sorrow. Geoffrey was certain she was no hypocrite, and that her tears had been genuine, but how much had been shed unconsciously for her own buried youth brought so clearly to memory this day, and how much for Charles, it was impossible to conjecture. Amanda was a New Englander. Everything in its time and season, and let any irrelevant emotion show itself at its peril! This was the time for the will; all else must wait. Then she would eat, in her stately fashion, for she had the Puritan's innate good sense, and then she would retire to her cold and dismal room, which Charles had not shared for fifteen years. What her thoughts would be there, as she lay in her chill tester bed, would be her own, never to be revealed. Geoffrey studied her with admiration. He had the highest respect for Amanda Goodbody.

Geoffrey had opened his leather brief case, and the will, a simple one of only two pages, was already in his hands. For some reason he was reluctant to begin. Amanda was waiting, composed and majestic. Melissa stared at a point near her crossed ankles, and enigmatic, almost expressionless though her face was, Geoffrey instinctively knew of the slow swell of agony which was rising in her. She, like her mother, would listen and, like her mother, would make little comment; and then, like Amanda, she would rise proudly and leave the room. To think I believed you a tyrant, my darling, he thought. You'll never be one: you are too strong.

Phoebe, docile and childish as always, had hushed her mewling, probably at a stern glance from her mother. She sniffled pathetically into her little white handkerchief, and her riot of bright ringlets fell over her forehead. The will meant nothing to her, but she knew she was expected to stay.

Andrew sat impassive and serene as always. He had been twenty, and a lieutenant in the Pennsylvania Third Infantry, when the War had ended. He had been captured about six months before the end of hostilities, but he had remained in the prison camp in Virginia for two months longer. What had he thought, felt, conjectured, about this fratricidal war? Had some ideal sustained and invigorated him? He never spoke of his war experiences, yet he had been full of admiration for the way the beset Virginians had sedulously cultivated every available acre of ground. He could discourse with shy eagerness about this. Now he was twenty-three, and he still never spoke of the war. It was impossible to know if, or what, he thought about anything.

The dismal wind groaned at the old tall windows, then furiously assaulted the ancient house. One felt the quivering of its long gray clapboards, the trembling of its sturdy oaken doors. The light outside had faded suddenly away and the elms had vanished in the darkness. The meager lamplight flickered.

O God! thought Melissa, in anguish, why doesn't the fool read the will and be done with it? But there he sits, venomously enjoying the dramatic and important moment, revelling in the whole sordid atmosphere of this hateful room. I shall rise in a moment and leave, if he does not speak. The white hands in her lap tightened with almost unbearable pain.

Geoffrey cleared his throat, for Amanda's face had become forbidding. He ruffled the two sheets of foolscap. "It is very short," he said, unnecessarily. Amanda inclined her head. Melissa stared before her.

Geoffrey began to read. Charles had left to "my beloved wife, Amanda Goodbody Upjohn," the farm of two hundred and ten acres, all the contents of the house, except those of his study, and "all present and future royalties accruing to me from books published prior to my death by the publishing house of George Dunham's Son." He politely urged his children to be in accord with this will. He then directed that all unfinished and finished manuscripts, unpublished at the date of his death, become the property of his dear daughter, Melissa Goodbody Upjohn, to dispose of in any manner she desired, any royalties accruing to her, "in part recompense for her devotion to my work, which has made all my writing possible." Melissa was also to have all his books, the furniture in his study, and any "personal effects" not urgently desired by his wife. In particular, Melissa was to have his gold watch, inherited from his grandfather, which had been a present from General Washington himself. The will was dated two years before, January 15, 1866.

No one spoke after the reading of the will, and there was only the sound of the wind and the rain, and the subdued clatter of china being laid on the table in the dining room beyond the folded doors. Then Amanda uttered something which, for a moment, Geoffrey incredulously believed was a wry laugh. But Amanda's white and withered face, though haggard and strained, was as composed as ever, and entirely mirthless.

"It is an expected will," she was saying, in her hard slow voice, which even yet had something of Melissa's strong overtones. "But it means nothing to me unless I know all the facts. You have them, Geoffrey. I should prefer that you let us know, immediately, the worst and the best. You are my husband's executor. You know what there is to know. Let me hear it."

Again Geoffrey admired that granite good sense, that realistic desire not to be deceived, which was Amanda's racial heritage. But, out of his compassion, he hesitated. Amanda said again, inexorably: "I demand it, Geoffrey. You will be doing us no service if you refrain from revealing what must eventually be known."

"Yes. Of Course, Mrs. Upjohn," said Geoffrey. (Oh, that despicable smooth voice, that polite and hypocritical deference! thought Melissa, in her twisting pain.)

Geoffrey Dunham removed some papers from his brief case, and frowned over them, dreading the moment when he must speak again. Well, there was nothing else he could do.

He said: "Your husband, Mrs. Upjohn, has, at the present time, some three hundred dollars in accrued royalties." (Impossible! thought Melissa, with cold and protective rage. I never trusted you, though my poor father did. I would not put it past you to have stolen his rightful money. Why, my father had hundreds of letters about his books from the most distinguished men, and the critics unanimously praised them! I am certain you are a thief.)

Geoffrey went on, cursing to himself: "As you know, Mrs. Upjohn, we intend to publish the sixth volume of Charles' *Phoenician Influence on Greek Philosophy* next summer. I think—I hope—that this will receive—greater—recognition than did the other five volumes. Scholarship is not much admired in these parlous days," he added, disingenuously. "From past sales, I should judge this will bring you at least two thousand dollars in royalties. As this book was contracted for before Charles'—death—the royalties belong to you."

Amanda's hands gripped themselves together. "Are the other volumes still selling, Geoffrey?"

This was the opportunity for which Geoffrey had been waiting. He said, with an uncandid smile: "I am glad to tell you, Mrs. Upjohn, that we expect to go into another edition next fall, and doubtless there will be considerable money accruing from that." He thought to himself: Three thousand, four thousand dollars? It means nothing to me; it means everything to these poor creatures, and though I could never be accused of having a philanthropic nature, a slight juggling of the ledgers will do little violence to my instincts as a publisher!

Amanda coughed; she touched her lips with her handkerchief. Then she raised her head with her old pride. "This is good news, certainly, Geoffrey, and unexpected. But what of the farm, and Charles' accounts in the bank?"

Geoffrey removed other papers from the brief case. "Mrs. Upjohn, I am afraid the news is not so good about the farm and the banks. There is a mortgage of some three thousand dollars on the farm, a payment is due the first of December in the amount of six hundred forty-five dollars, including interest. Charles had two bank accounts. The deposits, as of today, total five hundred dollars and thirty cents."

Amanda gazed at him steadily, while she rapidly calculated. Then she said in her clear hard tones: "It seems, then, that we are beggars."

Geoffrey opened his mouth to speak, but Amanda went on, without emotion: "This comes of neglecting the farm over a period of many years, of allowing the stock to diminish, of hiring uncouth and incompetent hands, of ignoring the necessity for proper supervision." She paused, then added, grimly: "But I shall keep the farm, come what may, say what anyone will. It was bought with the money my papa left me. It is morally, and legally, mine. I shall keep it. How, I do not know as yet, but keep it I shall."

For the first time, Melissa looked at her mother, and her pale-blue eyes blazed in contempt and scorn. But she said nothing. How she must have hated the farm, as Charles hated it, thought Geoffrey, having intercepted Melissa's stabbing glance at Amanda.

Geoffrey said: "I think it can be arranged that payment on the mortgage be deferred for another six months, Mrs. Upjohn. By that time there will be more royalties, though I am afraid you will have more interest to pay," he continued, knowing his New Englander's pride. As he expected, Amanda inclined her head proudly.

"Certainly, Geoffrey. I can rely on you to arrange the deferment. Beggars cannot be choosers about the rate of interest. I shall make no objection to any terms you arrange."

"There will also be the crops next summer," said Geoffrey, gently. "Let us hope we may have a good year." He would juggle the ledgers in the amount of four thousand dollars, or deposit the money in Charles' name, out of his own accounts. "I have a very optimistic feeling about your prospects, Mrs. Upjohn," he added, "so I'd not worry too much."

Amanda smiled grimly. "I have never worried too much. Now, having the facts, I shall worry less. I am on firm ground at last."

Her pale and watery eyes moved away from him, and fixed themselves in bitter contemplation on the fire.

"My papa left me twenty thousand dollars. He, like you, Geoffrey, was a publisher; he had eight children, and his estate was divided equally among us. The family lived in Boston, but Papa had his small residence in New York, and he returned home each month for a visit of several days. Sometimes a daughter accompanied him back to New York, for a short time, for shopping purposes."

Geoffrey listened with acute sympathy, for Amanda was speaking as if meditating. Poor old soul! She must indeed be stricken almost beyond endurance, to have lost so much of her natural reticence. Her children, even Melissa, were attracted by her new intensity of voice, her new, almost distraught, manner. Her tone, though quiet, had a quality of passion.

"It was in Papa's office that I first met Charles Upjohn. Papa had accepted a small manuscript. We were introduced, and, I believe—there was some attraction between us from the very beginning. I was considered a handsome young lady, Geoffrey," and she smiled bitterly.

"I can well believe that, Mrs. Upjohn," he answered, with gentleness. Had Melissa moved ever so slightly, lifted her hand?

Amanda went on as if she had not heard his remark: "Papa opposed the match. I was twenty-six years old, however, and Mama was considerably worried. However, I was exceedingly fond of Charles, and I would have my way. Papa told me he was not the man he would have chosen for me, but Papa had seven other daughters, and Mama was quite agreeable.

"Charles was a New Yorker, born and bred. He was very poor, Geoffrey, for he wrote books only a few scholars could understand. But he was a gentleman—even Papa admitted that —and his background and family were impeccable. He loved his native city. I despised it. When we married, and Papa died shortly thereafter, I convinced Charles that if he desired quiet and isolation in order to write, we must not live in the city. He had too many distracting friends. He agreed. We could not afford a stony New England farm, and the best land was already owned. I spent a few months exploring the country, and found this place. It is only ten miles from Philadelphia, so that Charles could have his urban atmosphere and refreshment whenever he desired. He had a number of friends in Philadelphia. They were near enough for occasional visiting, but far enough away so that they would not intrude upon him too often.

"I paid twelve thousand dollars for this farm, and I was exceedingly happy. There were eight thousand dollars in the banks in Philadelphia. The future seemed very auspicious." She smiled convulsively.

"I have never believed that females should manage business matters, Geoffrey, and that is where I made the gravest error. Charles admitted that the farm was conducive to study and reflection, and he began to write steadily. But I can see now that, for all the security it had given us, he truly detested the farm. I believed I was very shrewd, Geoffrey!

"It was not until ten years ago that I discovered that the farm was not even paying for itself, that my remaining eight thousand dollars had been swallowed up in debts. It seemed very strange to me, for our crops were almost uniformly good. Of a certainty, however, I understood that the men we were hiring were dolts and incompetents, and not too honest. Still, I did not worry overmuch. Charles was writing, and his books were being published, and he always assured me that our affairs were in splendid condition. Charles himself was always serene, and I believed, in my folly, that if our affairs were in a desperate state he would reveal some perturbation. I see now that nothing ever perturbed Charles very much, provided he had his writing, his study, his walks, his occasional visits to Philadelphia, and his books. I ought to have known!"

You ought to have known that Charles was utterly irresponsible, undependable and childlike, thought Geoffrey. But you must have known, and, like a good wife, you forced yourself not to see. Then, too, there is a fatalism in you New Englanders.

Amanda threw out her hands in a quick distracted gesture. "And now we are beggars. I have two unmarried daughters, and a son."

She turned her head and looked at her children. She touched Melissa with her eyes, and those eyes became stony. But they softened when they glanced at Phoebe and Andrew. "Tomorrow, we shall have a family conclave, and we'll discuss what is best to be done. But in all events, I shall keep this farm. It is part of me, part of my life and very flesh."

"Yes, of course," murmured Geoffrey. He said: "I am at your service for advice or assistance at any time, Mrs. Upjohn."

She inclined her head with stiff graciousness. "Thank you, Geoffrey. It is very kind of you. I shall remember your offer.

Now that I have the facts, I have no fear. I can manage very well, with the assistance of my children."

The folding doors near the far end end of the room opened, and Arabella Shaw appeared, smiling dolefully. "Tea is ready, my poor dears," she said, "and you *must* force yourselves to partake of a small repast, even on this sad occasion."

Geoffrey rose, as did the others. Indomitable as always, Amanda darted a glance at her children. "It is only intelligent to prepare strength for tomorrow," she said.

But, without a word, Melissa turned and left the room, her black skirt swaying. They watched her go in silence. Her face and gilded hair were a sudden vivid flash as she passed the lamp.

CHAPTER 3

SOMEONE HAD lit the wrought-iron lamp which swayed on its black chain from the hall ceiling. The light flowed dimly on the oak-panelled walls, on the long mirror over the drum table, on the stiff, carved oaken chairs, on the dark-brown carpet, on the ancient grandfather clock. But the shadowy light only enhanced the chill and desolation of the hall. Beyond the clock rose the abrupt oak staircase with its wooden balustrade and polished steps. The upper part of the house lay engulfed in darkness.

Melissa stood alone in the hall. She quietly wiped her forehead, the palms of her hands. She did this mechanically, and without hysteria, and her breath was controlled. She climbed a stair or two, then stood there, listening. The wind beat against the house like an attacking army, and the hanging lamp shivered. Every board, every beam, trembled. A shutter or two banged somewhere. The sound of the rain was the sound of a cataract, washing and flooding over the old four-storey house. But it was very tall and very narrow, and sound; it had seen a thousand storms like this, and it would hold firmly and strongly. Nothing could shake its graystone chimneys; nothing could shatter its thick oaken doors. Its clapboards might quiver, its shutters might tear themselves away from their iron hinges, its windows might rattle, its floors might vibrate. But it would stand, its cellars deep in the black earth.

Melissa leaned against the balustrade. Faintness had come over her again. She clenched her teeth, threw up her head. In a moment, this silly weakness would pass, and she would be able to go up the stairs to the study—and her father. He was waiting there, surely. She did not see his light, for he must have closed the door. But his fire would be burning, as it always burned, and she would see him there under his lamp, his thin gray head bent over a book. Or perhaps he would be at his old desk, writing, the scratching of the pen louder than the storm outside. She would come in softly, and he would look up, smiling fondly, and the lamplight would gleam on his spectacles. "Come in, my dear," he would say. "This last chapter is not going well, I am afraid. Please glance over it and tell me what is wrong."

She would sit on the hassock near him, and begin to read. She would be overwhelmed, as always, by his pure felicity of phrase, by his beautiful carved paragraphs, by his scholarly quoting of ancient philosophers in their native Greek and Latin. O dull and hideous world that did not appreciate such grandeur, which filed away on dusty shelves the few books it bought, and forgot the glorious intellect which had conceived them! She would return the chapter to her father, and she would say with passionate strength: "Papa, it is perfect. Not a line must be changed." Then he would beam at her, touch her cheek with his long thin fingers, and say: "Let us ring for tea, shall we, my dear?"

Old Sally would come up, fat, waddling, grumbling at being disturbed so late in the evening, the silver tray rattling in her hands. There would be sliced seed-cake, or fruit-cake, and hot tea, thick cream and loaf sugar. They would sit together and drink and eat, and laugh softly, and discuss the next chapter. The wind might howl, the rain might run in rivers through the eaves, the shutters might bang, but here, in the quiet house, before the fire, in the warm lamplight, daughter and father would sit in complete content and the richest and sweetest companionship. Above and about them the others would be sleeping. They would hear old Sally climb to her attic room, two storeys above, under the slate roof. Then there would be no other sound in this lamplit sanctuary except for their own voices and the chuckle of the fire. They might sit there until long after midnight, until the chiming of the clock below would startle them to an awareness of the hour.

Melissa came to herself, and was dully surprised to find herself sitting on the stairs in the hall, whereas she seemed to remember having climbed those stairs. A deathly chill made her shiver violently. She felt mortally sick and leaned her head against the hard balustrade. I must have fainted for a moment, she thought, abstractedly. She looked about her, her eyes swimming. How had she come to be here, when her father was waiting for her in his study? But, said her mind clearly and coldly, he is no longer there.

"No!" she said aloud, with fierceness. "It is not true. It is not true that he is—dead!"

She heard her own voice uttering the terrible word, and she put her hands to her throat as if to choke away the horror of her own speech. The pulses throbbed under her fingers as if they would burst the flesh. Now something opened in her breast, wide and bleeding, running with dark and dying blood. She felt the thick and failing current in her veins. Her arms and legs grew numb. She bowed her head on her knees.

The old walnut clock, its face faded and almost obliterated by the years, struck a dolorous series of notes. Eight o'clock. The oaken walls echoed the sound, humming under the vibrations. The wind grew louder, and the rain.

Melissa pulled herself to her feet. The steps below her tilted and swayed. The clock leaned at an impossible angle. In a moment it would fall with a crash, and they would all come running. She must get away before they came. It would amuse them so, to see her standing there like a black statue, the shattered clock below her.

She put her hand on the smooth balustrade and dragged herself up the stairs. They were a nightmare flight, going on up forever and forever into the cold darkness, touched, here and there, by a ghostly shadow from the hall light below. But one had to climb the flight, no matter how one's knees bent or how one's breath came in long painful gasps. Her father was waiting for her.

The study door was unlatched. She could not understand why it was so enormously heavy, and why it took all her strength to push it open. No lamp had been lighted in the study and it was completely dark. The fire had not been lit and a cold blast of air struck at Melissa's damp face. She pushed the door closed behind her, leaned abjectly against it, in order that she might not fall, her shoulders bent desperately against the cold wood. How loud the wind was, and the rain! The shutters here had not been closed, or had been latched carelessly. They banged and pounded against the clapboards, swinging and creaking. The rain hissed and rushed against the windows. The room smelled of old ashes, of old

tobacco, of old pipes and wool and books and wax, of dampness and decay.

Melissa leaned back against the door. She had pressed her
palms against it for support. She listened to the roaring of
wind and rain, the pounding of the shutters. In a moment, she
would be strong enough to go to the windows and do something about the shutters, and she would light a lamp, and make
a fire.

Now the faintest and most crepuscular dimness pervaded
the room, not really a light, but a glint from the drowned full
moon beyond the clouds. She could see the windows now; they
ran with swift black streams of water. She pushed herself away
from the door, went to the windows, threw them open. Immediately the roaring became a deafening thunder. She leaned
out into the rain and tugged at the flailing shutters. Her
strength, already spent, was almost unavailing, and she felt
the water lashing into her face and battering her head. It was
deathly cold, and where the rain soaked into her bodice and
shoulders it was like the drip of ice. Finally, she was able to
pull in the shutters and latch them, and close the windows.
The roaring subsided to a dull and threatening mutter.

She went to the fireplace, groped for the tapers and the box
of lucifers. Her hands were completely numb, and she had to
try several times before she could strike a light. She lit the wax
taper, found her way to the lamp on her father's desk, and lit
it. Immediately the room was flooded with a wan and dusty
light. She returned to the fireplace, knelt down, and put the
taper to the crushed newspaper under the kindling. It smol-
dered and smoked; finally the short apple logs took fire, and
a blaze of sparks gushed up the blackened chimney. Melissa
crouched on the gritty hearth, shivering uncontrollably, pushing back her wet and disheveled hair. Now the logs caught,
crackled sullenly, and a tongue of flame flashed upwards. She
pressed closer to the fire, feeling nothing but her deathlike
coldness, her passionate desire for warmth. The wind battered down the chimney, blew out a cloud of smoke. But
Melissa did not retreat. The necessity for warmth was too compelling.

She crouched there, shaking and trembling, her chin on her
wet black knees, her dress flowing about her stiffly, spread out
in heaps around her body. Her hair still dripped; she felt the
cold drops running down her neck into the hollows of her
breast. Wherever they touched, they numbed, like pellets of
snow. The heat of the new fire beat out at her, but she could

not get warm, and all her body ached. Then she turned her head and looked at the room.

She knew every inch of the study, but now it was strange, an alien room, belonging to no one, abandoned and shut away. Charles had occupied it only four days ago, yet years must have passed, for it was no longer familiar. She knew all those oaken bookcases which lined the walls; she knew those books, in their dim brown and crimson and blue bindings, their faded golden titles glimmering in the lamplight. She knew this black marble fireplace, this flagged hearth, that mantelpiece which held Charles' rack of pipes, the hobnailed glass which held the wax tapers, his metal box of tobacco, which had come from China, the old pink seashell which someone had given him when he was a child. There, against the far wall, stood his horsehair couch, with its untidy heap of blankets and the mussed pillow, where he slept at night. There stood his old high desk, with the cubbyholes full of bills, papers, memoranda; she knew each of the quill pens on the scarred desk, the ink-pots, the blotters, and the old-fashioned sandbox which he never used but which had belonged to his father. There was his old black-leather chair with the foot-stool, her own black-leather hassock drawn near it, his large oaken table where the manuscripts were assembled, and which was still covered with heaps of papers inscribed with his meticulous and beautiful small writing. On the little table beside his chair stood the brass lamp Melissa had lighted. A pipe still lay there, where he had left it on the terrible night when he had died so suddenly, alone before his fire, just after Melissa had left him for bed.

Another Aubusson rug covered the floor, its colors almost obliterated with grit and dust, for Charles would permit no one in to clean his study and what housework Melissa had ever done had necessarily been so careless and haphazard as to make little difference in the general confusion and dust. Dust lay thickly on the tables, on the desk. It lifted into the disturbed air, with a dry powdery smell. The fire and the lamplight shone on all the shabbiness and disorder. The draperies at the windows, of an old blue discolored cloth, bellied in the wind that came through the cracks.

The fire burned high, but the room remained as damp and cold as a vault. Melissa crouched closer; she felt the burning on her forehead and on her cheeks, but she could not feel the warmth itself. Her head was turned over her shoulder; she looked slowly and heavily at every object in the room.

Oh, surely Papa was coming into the room now! She

strained her ears, held her breath, waiting for the soft shuffle of his footsteps. She looked at the door. It must open, if only she willed it strongly enough. It did not open. It gleamed in the lamplight, and remained closed.

Then, for the first time, she knew, inexorably, that he was dead. Dead. He would never enter this room again. He would never take down a book, and glance through it, commenting wryly on a certain passage, his spectacles sliding down his long thin nose. He would never again pass his veined and mottled hands, which looked like the hands of ancient marble saints, over his white and narrow skull, and turn to her with a soft laugh of mingled perplexity and amusement. Never again would he regard her with his vague but brilliant blue eyes; which seemed to stare beyond her at serene and dazzling landscapes. Never again would she see the smile on his wide full lips, with their crooked corners, a smile that combined ruefulness and satire, gentleness and profound meditation. She would never see his profile again, outlined by the fire. All his features had been clear and salient, acute even, yet they had given the impression of too much pliability and mildness, and this, at times, had puzzled even Melissa, had made her dimly uneasy. But she had explained it by telling herself that it was because her father had such subtle mobility of mind, such sensibility, such intellect, and that it had softened and changed the original mold of his features.

She pushed herself to her feet and wandered over to her father's desk. She touched the papers, the ink-pot, the pens. They felt cold as ice. They would be moved and tidied, but never again by her father. She saw the little thin sheaf of paper to the right, near his reference books. She had forgotten. It was a sheaf of little Phoebe's poems. She picked them up, and her aching eyes scanned them. How surprised she and Charles had been when they had discovered that Phoebe, small, shy, smiling Phoebe, wrote poetry! The girl had come into the study, simpering like a bashful child, and they had looked up at her in courteous and affectionate expectation, for Phoebe never came here—they could not remember her ever entering this room before. She had not looked at Melissa. She had just run lightly over to Charles and had dropped her pathetic little sheaf on his knee, and had blushed, and exclaimed softly and breathlessly: "Papa, I wrote these poems! I've always written poems and then thrown them away. But I—I—thought these weren't bad, and I do wish you'd just look at them, and then tell me!"

She had stood there, in her blue cotton frock, her pretty

hands clenched tightly before her, her face bright with blushes, her eyes filled with glittering tears, and there had been something both defiant and touching in the glance she had given Melissa. Charles was always gentle. He took his pipe from his mouth and smiled at his younger daughter indulgently. "Well, this is a surprise, my darling," he murmured. Out of the corner of his eye he had pleaded with Melissa to be patient, for she was frowning, and for a moment he thought how odd it was that Melissa could frown without a single line invading the frozen expanse of her brow. He had cleared his throat, and he began to read the poems aloud.

Melissa had listened, at first impatiently, then with startled astonishment. The poems were perfect, exquisitely composed, without a flaw. Their sentiments were childish, immature, almost inane. But the talent was there, smooth as rippling silk, faintly luminous like Dresden china. Charles' own face, too, began to express surprise. Now his voice lost its indulgent quality. He read with seriousness, on and on, poem after poem, while Phoebe stood there so stiff and childish and tense, her golden ringlets spilling on her shoulders and over her forehead, her eyes tearful.

Then, at last, Charles had slowly dropped the sheaf onto his knee again, and looked at Melissa. They gazed at each other steadily, in silence. Finally Charles said: "The child has talent, Melissa. It is authentic, yes. The meter is perfect. How strange it is that we've never known this before." And all the time Phoebe had stood there, but now she had uttered a whimpering sound and had begun to cry, her hands over her face.

Melissa had stood up and put her arm about her little sister's shoulder. For a moment or two something ignoble had burned in her, like an ugly jealousy, because Phoebe had put her little soft fingers like a wedge between herself and Charles. The swift thought had run through her mind: Now Papa and I shall never really be alone again. But she had pushed the thought away, and she had spoken with an alien richness in her cool and neutral voice: "Dearest Phoebe! And you never told us before!" Phoebe, overcome, had buried her head on Melissa's shoulder and had sobbed, while Charles and Melissa had looked at each other over that shining head.

Later, Charles and Melissa had made their plans, with a touch of unusual excitement. Phoebe would write a number of poems, enough to make a slender volume. Then Charles would approach Geoffrey Dunham, and urge their publication. "Pure, limpid water!" Charles had cried, his blue eyes very brilliant. "Dew on the grass! It is a true talent, Melissa, and with cultivation, with caution and guidance, our little Phoebe will emerge as an important and significant poetess. It is our duty, our privilege, Melissa, to guide and cultivate her. I am afraid, my love, that your obligations have now increased and must embrace your sister as well as myself."

He had expressed a courteous and affectionate anxiety for Melissa. Dear Papa, she had thought. He does not know that I am quite adequate to all "burdens," for they are not really burdens at all. They are a delight, and a joy.

For the first time in their lives, they began to observe Phoebe acutely. In truth, they had hardly noticed her before, and only with that vague fondness which an adult bestows on an engaging child or on a lovable domestic animal. Now they saw that Amanda was quite ruthless with the girl, that she kept her busily absorbed in household duties, as a sort of assistant to old fat Sally, that her days were full of bed-making, silver-polishing, cooking, mending and dusting, from morning until night. She must have been doing this for years, though they had never noticed it before, and it seemed unbearably pathetic to them that Phoebe bustled about her tasks so cheerfully, with such pink cheeks, with so many amiable smiles. How she must be suffering, in her sensitive heart, at being forced to perform so many mundane, dull and ugly tasks, yet how amicably, and with what docility, did she obey! Charles and Melissa suffered with her, but they respected her courage and delicacy, and did not offer sympathy. However, she was often invited into the study, while Charles gravely discussed the nuances of poetry with the child, as she sat near him, and Melissa nodded her head at intervals. She was theirs to cultivate. They must be prayerfully careful and devoted.

Naturally, it was not long before Amanda became aware of the defection of her younger daughter. It was Phoebe's custom to join her mother in the drawing-room in the evenings, with her basket of mending, her knitting needles, or a book of essays which she would read aloud. Now Amanda was left alone before the grudging fire. Andrew was at Harvard, Sally was in bed, and Charles, Melissa and Phoebe were engrossed in the study, while Amanda had nothing but the autumn wind for company. She made her investigations, and when she discovered how the land lay, she was grimly and coldly outraged.

One morning, at breakfast, she attacked. She had fixed her pale hard eyes on Charles, and had said: "What is this nonsense about Phoebe and poetry, Charles? I never heard of it before, until the silly child confessed to me last night, after questioning."

Charles had looked up from his ham and eggs, and had smiled that soft and beguiling smile of his. "My dear Amanda, it isn't nonsense in the least. To use a rather coarse expression, we have struck gold in this house, unsuspected gold, pure and shining. How could it have escaped you so long, my dear? You and Phoebe have always been so very close, this ought to be no surprise to you."

As always, his gentlest rebuke threw Amanda into a furious, defensive mood. She exclaimed: "Absurd! Yes, I have often seen Phoebe scribbling, but young girls are always scribbling romantic nonsense, lilies in the dell, moonlight and roses, dew in the morning. I indulged her, for she was always competent and dutiful in her tasks about the house. I have not forgotten my own youth," she added, her lined and parched skin flushing. (As always, she never looked at Melissa when engaging in any dispute with Charles, but she felt again that thrill of hatred and rage at the knowledge that Melissa was regarding her with remote coldness, as if she were only a rude and inconsequential intrusion in the room.) "No, Charles, I have not forgotten my own simpering and vaporous girlhood, and so I was indulgent with the girl. I knew that upon her marriage to John Barrett she would forget her scribbling; I knew that poetry often afflicts young girls just before their marriage. It is natural. But once married, once settled in her own home, once engaged in wholesome household duties, all this nonsense would be forgotten. You can imagine my alarm, then, when I discovered that you and—and—when I discovered that you were deliberately cultivating the girl's romanticism, and taking it seriously, to the disruption of her normal way of life and the jeopardy of her expectations. Then it became my duty as a mother to settle the matter once and for all."

Phoebe had sat there, mute, very small, her eyes swimming with tears, her pink cheeks whitening. She had looked helplessly at Charles and Melissa. Charles stirred his coffee thoughtfully, while his daughters waited. But he seemed loath to speak. Then Melissa had lifted her chin, fixed her mother with her eyes, and had said coolly: "Mama, perhaps Phoebe does not wish to marry John Barrett and become part of his farm. We have had discussions over the matter, in the evenings. She is convinced that her destiny is poetry, not a dull and lightless marriage with a farmer, however prosperous."

Charles glanced up quickly, frowning just a little, distastefully. There were times when he wished that dear Melissa were not so direct, so crude, so like a marching grenadier with big clacking boots. Diplomacy, reason, were so much more effective, so much more civilized. But for all his admonitions, all his teaching, there were times when Melissa broke through courtesy and the ring of subdued voices like an armored and warlike young mare. Brunhilde was doubtless very stirring and majestic but a little too incongruous at a polite breakfast table in the palely bright autumn morning of a Pennsylvania countryside. Harsh trumpets caused blue Spode china to rattle, and threw quiet air, redolent of ham and coffee, into turmoil.

It was Amanda's custom, for many years now, to ignore Melissa as much as possible, to pass over her with eyes faintly glazed, as if unseeing, to speak rarely to Melissa and only when necessary. But too much was now at stake to pretend that she did not exist, to wave away her words with a slight motion of the wrist. Melissa was placing Phoebe in danger, in serious jeopardy, and Phoebe was the soft core of Amanda's stern heart. Yes, it was Melissa who was doing this, and only Melissa. Whatever evil, fruitlessness, frustration and despair lived in that house, unsuspected by Charles, it all stemmed from Melissa. But she must not touch Phoebe! Never, never, must she ruin, seduce, defile and destroy Phoebe!

So it was that for the first time in a long while Amanda looked at her elder daughter with wild hatred and fury and defiance. "Hands off my child, my girl!" she cried, and there was something ominous and threatening in her low hard voice. She stood up, stately, if trembling visibly, like a tall, beset tree, and she clenched her thin hands at her side. She regarded Melissa with an expression so terrible that Charles, slowly rising, was caught in the very act and paralyzed; he remained crouched in a most ludicrous position, half in and half out of his chair, his napkin clutched to his breast, his spectacles sliding down his nose.

"You've done enough wickedness in this house!" Amanda went on, seeing nothing but Melissa. "You have schemed enough, and plotted enough, in your silent secret way! But you shall not touch my child! She is not yours. Hands off!"

Melissa had not moved. Her still white face remained immobile, though her eyes became enigmatic. One long, slender hand was stretched beside her cup. The fingers did not curl. They remained like marble fingers, smoothly relaxed and quiet.

For a long and awful moment mother and daughter regarded each other in a sudden and malignant silence. Then Amanda, paler than ever, turned to Phoebe and, though her voice was firm, it broke a little at the last as she said: "Come, my child. We have work to do, and it is getting late. It is the day for polishing the silver."

Melissa's mouth opened slightly, but Charles, who had fallen back in his chair, had laid his hand over hers, warningly. Phoebe had peeped at them both in a frightened and meek sort of way, then had slipped from her chair and scurried after her mother like a yellow chick following a hen.

The silence remained in the room for several moments after Amanda and Phoebe had left. Then Melissa stirred. She lifted the coffeepot and poured more coffee into her father's cup. She gave him the cream and the loaf sugar. He took them with a courteous inclination of his head. When he glanced at Melissa, she was smiling with her mother's own grimness, and Charles was disturbed by it.

"Would you like some more biscuits, Papa?" asked Melissa, her hand reaching for the little silver bell.

"No, thank you, my dear." Charles paused. He seemed very thoughtful. Altercations of any kind annoyed and distressed him.

Melissa said quietly: "Shall we go directly upstairs, Papa? We were to go over Phoebe's last poems, if you remember."

It was settled. Charles was relieved. The incident would be forgotten. But Melissa would not forget that she had a duty towards Phoebe. He could always rely upon Melissa. They went upstairs to the study, and Melissa ordered that trays be served to her and to her father in that room.

The first skirmish had been won by Amanda. Melissa was not disconcerted. *She* always won in the end. She would win this time, too, thought Charles contentedly. One had only to leave it to Melissa. He hoped the struggle would not be too distracting. Why could not everything always be serene and pleasant? He dreaded the morrow and prayed that Melissa would not involve him too much.

But there was to be no tomorrow for Charles Upjohn. He had died that night, after Melissa had left him.

Melissa was remembering all this, as she stood tonight in that cold and disordered study, the sheaf of poetry in her hands. She laid down the sheaf. Her struggles, then, must be renewed, to save Phoebe from the lightless and wretched state to which her mother had condemned her. She would save Phoebe, as she had saved her father.

"I won't forget, Papa," she said aloud. She squared her

shoulders, as if taking up a burden she had momentarily dropped. And then, all at once, it seemed to her that her heart broke. She pressed her hands to her eyes.

With heavy, dragging foosteps, she went back to her father's chair. She fell down upon the hassock beside it. She laid her head upon the worn black leather of the arm and, for the first time, she wept, utterly desolate and forsaken. She wept on and on, but it brought her no surcease, no relief from the tortured wound in her heart. The tears streamed down her cheeks, and they were as hot as fire. The wind pounded at the shutters, tried to tear them loose, then, frustrated, went on howling over the fields and the hills. The rain streamed and gurgled in the eaves.

"Papa, Papa!" she whispered, rolling her head upon the arm of Charles' chair. "I can't bear it, Papa. Come back, come back."

She heard the slightest sound near her, the creaking of the door. Slowly, painfully, she lifted her head. Geoffrey Dunham stood there, with a tray in his hands. He shut the door behind him with his heel.

"I thought you'd be here," he said. "And now I've brought you some food, and I'm damned if I'm going to leave until you get it down."

CHAPTER 4

MELISSA PUSHED her loosened hair from her wet face, and Geoffrey saw that face, haggard, torn with anguished emotion, wet with tears. There was a shrunken gauntness about it which alarmed him. But cheerfully, and quietly, he pushed aside Charles' pipe and papers and put down the steaming tray.

Melissa struggled to her feet. "Go away. Oh, go away!" she said, hoarsely, her voice hardly above a whisper.

But he was arranging the dishes, while she stood there, shaking, futilely pushing at her hair, regarding him with detestation and hatred, with mortification that he should have found her so abandoned. Never had he appeared so despicable and loathsome to her, so repellent. She was seized with a rage against him. All his faults of feature, figure and manner seemed to her grotesquely enlarged, so that she shut her eyes in order not to see him. Desperately, with all her will, she attempted to thrust him from this room, which he "desecrated" with his very presence. She had a wild impulse to run out and leave him. But it was as if she would then have left her father to the attack of this hateful man, and Charles must be protected from such as he.

She had always despised Geoffrey Dunham, even when she had been a young girl of fourteen and he a man of thirty just inheriting his lately deceased father's publishing business. She had never seen Geoffrey before that time, for he had been in charge of the firm's London establishment. Now he had come back home, and he had called upon Charles to renew an old acquaintance. Charles had expressed soft, unfeigned pleasure, had forgotten his daughter, had clasped the young man's hands with affection.

It was a summer day, and she and Charles had been together in the gardens hidden from the house by a clump of old plum trees. She had just recited her Latin to him, and he was going over her papers. How serene was the sunshine then, warm and mellowed, with butterflies falling and rising in the soft air and the bees busy over the tangled roses! Then there had been the barking of old Chief, the collie, and Geoffrey Dunham had come, like the devil himself, into that garden.

She could never tell why she so hated him on sight. Perhaps it was because he was so urbane, so polished, so patronizingly at ease, for all his friendly and pleasant greeting. He had worn strange London clothing, with light gray pantaloons strapped under his gleaming boots, and a flowered waistcoat, a darker gray coat with long tails, and a brilliantly white stock with a pearl pin. He held his tall gray hat in his left hand while Charles shook his right, and he had laughed genially, all his big white teeth flashing in the sunlight.

He had looked down at Melissa, and had said, pleasantly: "This is your daughter, I presume, Charles. A pretty little minx." And then he had lifted a lock of her straight pale hair, which hung far below her waist like a shawl, and had tweaked it. Yes, she had hated him then. That was the beginning, dismissing her as though she were of no consequence, only a tiresome child! He had gazed at her, smiling in amusement, for she had jerked her head away and had glared at him in her cold and almost malefic fashion.

She would never forget how he looked then, tall, very broad of shoulder, debonair and sleek in his disgusting London finery, with the heavy gold chain across his lean middle, and his shining hat in his hand. He had a large and shapely head, with the dark crisp hair cut affectedly long, and a face astonishingly brown from Riviera sunshine. He had somewhat small gray eyes, penetrating and satirical, and without any softness or kindness. His nose was Roman, and, to Melissa, gross, with its flaring nostrils and blunt tip. He had a big and heavy mouth, and the most enormous white teeth, and his smile, though now so agreeable, was hard of outline. There was something about him too assured, too shrewd, too competent; it emphasized all of Charles' unworldly gentleness and made her father appear old and defenseless in the warm summer sunlight. He had thrown into contrast Charles' shabbiness and vulnerability, made him appear unshielded and unarmed, prey for any expedient and ruthless man. And, indeed, Geoffrey Dunham was everything that was expedient and ruthless, and he made no attempt to conceal the fact, not even from competitors, not even from valued authors.

The Upjohns sometimes did not see Geoffrey Dunham for months, and then again he would return weekly from his city lodgings in Philadelphia. He preferred the country, he would say, and now that his newly widowed sister had come to manage his house for him, he "had a home." Melissa was seventeen when the weeping Arabella had arrived from Boston, and now Melissa had another object to hate almost as much as she already hated Geoffrey. A few times, upon her father's pleas, she had accompanied him to the great house half-way up the hillside, but she had gone with shrinking and disgust to endure Geoffrey's amused banter and Arabella's maudlin ministrations and hospitality.

The years had passed, and she never saw that repellent man without a shiver of abhorrence. Worse than anything else was Charles' obdurate and insistent affection for him and trust in him. She saw the meager royalty reports, and was positive that her father was being cheated. But Charles only laughed at her gently. She never guessed that he derived a secret and malicious satisfaction from the sight of her young and ingenuous jealousy, for there was something in Melissa which blinded her to anything ignoble or devious. Nor did she even know that she was jealous. She knew only that Charles was excessively affectionate when Geoffrey appeared; she did not know that the display was deliberate, though it was not long before Geoffrey realized it, and with contempt.

Geoffrey had seen too much of the world not to recognize what was revealed to him, and he was alarmed for Melissa. This, then, was what had compelled him to suggest to Amanda that Melissa be sent away to school. Amanda had inspired him with admiration and liking for her integrity and her common sense. He also shrewdly suspected that Amanda was well aware of what she saw, for she had insight and a wide clarity of vision. She had listened to Geoffrey's quiet suggestion, and then she had said, without apparent emotion: "I have already spoken of it to Charles, Geoffrey. He will not have it."

Things had not adjusted themselves, and when Melissa was twenty years old he suddenly, and with consternation, understood that he was in love with her. He forced himself to remain away from the Upjohns for a whole year. But it was no use. Now he began to feel, and to know, acutely, the morbidity and unhealthy atmosphere in that old tall house. He must rescue Melissa before it was too late. After five years, he was still trying to rescue her.

Though he was now forty, the years had not changed Geoffrey much. The crisp dark hair had grayed at the temples, the dark face was a little fuller, the upright figure not quite so svelte and suave as it once had been. But his urbanity and polish had become more mellow with time, and his innate ruthlessness had carved thicker lines about his level mouth and his small shrewd eyes, giving him a strong and invincible look.

He had always appeared gross and insensitive to Melissa, and now, as her aching and tormented eyes regarded him with such abomination, she felt a sharp nausea and loathing for him, which, for a moment, even made her forget her grief.

"I will not eat," she said, her voice coming painfully from her tight throat, "and I ask you to leave me alone in this room, Mr. Dunham."

Geoffrey lifted a silver lid from the top of a small bowl. "Ah, our Hulda makes the best broth in the township!" he exclaimed. "Delicate, yet rich, with those tiny dumplings of hers. A breast of chicken here, too, I see, and hot bread and good butter. What is this? Ah, yes, a slice of Arabella's own fruit-cake, and our own China tea. It smells like all the gardens in Pekin."

He set the dishes on the table, after first smoothing out a fine white tray cloth on it. Melissa watched him with red-eyed scorn and comprehension. He was such a powerful and cunning wretch. He knew, from her father's will, that Charles had left several unfinished manuscripts, and he was already plotting to seize and publish them for a pitiful royalty. So it was necessary for him to pretend to be placating and thoughtful of her. Only she could complete the manuscripts, from her father's copious notes. Without her, the two next volumes would never be completed. And then Melissa had another thought. She glanced down at Phoebe's sheet of poems, and a quick flash passed over her sunken eyes.

She tried to make her voice more courteous: "Truly, Mr. Dunham, I want nothing to eat. The thought sickens me. I think I should prefer to go to bed." She took a tentative step towards the door. Geoffrey sat down, but not in Charles' chair. He sat down nearer the fire and lit a cheroot, all his movements thoughtful and precise. He actually had the ill-breeding, the monster, to sit while she stood! That betrayed the full measure of contempt he had for the Upjohns, revealed the low esteem in which he held Charles' daughter!

"I said, Mr. Dunham, that I am going to bed," she repeated sternly.

"Good. Probably an excellent idea." He glanced at her kindly. "In the meantime, I think I shall eat this delightful collation myself. It is a wicked thing to allow good food to go to waste. Good night, Melissa."

She could not leave him here, desecrating her father's study, enjoying himself in the very room where Charles had died. Yet she did not know what to do. She was exhausted, and now she knew that she was famished. Her common sense told her that if she allowed her strength to deteriorate, she would betray Charles. The smell of the broth and the tea did strange things to her. Besides, she thought, the more rapidly she ate, the sooner she would be rid of this man.

It was an effort to speak out of the depths of her sinking weariness. "I suppose I must thank you, Mr. Dunham, for this kindness of yours. It would be rude of me to refuse, would it not?"

"It would indeed," he assured her, examining the glowing tip of his cheroot.

"But it would also be rude if you remained away from the others, downstairs."

"Your mother," said Geoffrey, "has already retired, and your sister. Arabella and Hulda are 'clearing up.' Andrew, I think, has gone into the library, and shut himself up there. Evidently you do not know how late it is."

Just then the clock below chimed ten, and Melissa started. "It is not in the best taste, I am afraid, for you to remain alone with me, Mr. Dunham."

He took the cheroot from his mouth. "Best taste be damned, Melissa. Don't be a fool. Sit down and eat, or I shall eat it myself. I am going back to Philadelphia tomorrow, and then I am going to New York for several weeks. Though I quite understand that your father is just lately dead and that this is a sad occasion for all of you, there are matters I must discuss before I leave. I shall have no other time after tonight."

Melissa sat down slowly before the food, and stared at it. "You have discussed them with my mother?"

"No. I am afraid she knows very little about your father's affairs."

New strength came to the girl. The battle for her father had begun. She must not betray him by the pampering of her own grief. Her hand shook as she lifted the spoon to her mouth. The hot soup filled her with warmth, and she ate quickly. Geoffrey did not watch her. He looked at the fire. He smelled the dankness and decay in the room, saw the dusty disorder. His nose wrinkled distastefully. He heard the subdued clatter of the china. The poor dear fool! Only once, after ten minutes had elapsed, did he glance at her out of the corner of his eye. She had cleared away all the food, down to the last morsel, and sat there, straight and stiff, sipping her tea. She seemed very pathetic and young to Geoffrey, in her austere and coldly defiant strength, too thin, and with such a chaste modelling of forehead and chin—a white-faced but dauntless and bewildered nymph, who fancied herself a Valkyrie, challenging a formidable world in the name of her father. My dear, he thought, today a special Emancipation Proclamation was delivered for you, and some day you will know it.

Melissa set down her teacup, then sat in her chair like a ramrod, her hands in her lap. Geoffrey knew that she was gazing at him commandingly. He said, reflectively:

"I understand that there are two more volumes, almost completed. Doubtless, you can complete them, Melissa."

"Yes," she said quietly, "I can. But not for the old royalty, Mr. Dunham. I always thought that unjust and beggarly. Now that my father is—is—not here"—and for a moment her voice broke and her head bent—"I must protect the rights of the family."

"What royalty would you suggest?" asked Geoffrey, frowning at his cheroot. He took his gold penknife from his waistcoat pocket and cut off one end of the cheroot, drew on it again, and murmured in satisfaction.

Melissa's heart was beating too hard, but she said defiantly:

"Twice the customary royalty, Mr. Dunham."

"Impossible!" he exclaimed. But he said to himself: I should have thought of that before, then there would have been no twinges of my publisher's conscience, no squirmy contrivings as to how to increase their bank account.

"Yes," said Melissa, in a loud, hard voice.

He turned his head and looked at her over his shoulder, he could hardly keep himself from smiling at the ridiculousness of the situation. There sat the poor girl, her face a pale flame, her chin resolute and lifted, her eyes fanatical. Let her fight a little. It would do her good.

"You are trying to take advantage of my friendship with Charles," he said, striving to make his own voice bellicose, even blustering.

"I am trying to right an old wrong," she said, with trembling courage.

She waited, but Geoffrey only sat and smoked. Her fingers wound themselves tensely about each other until the knuckles sprang out. Geoffrey let her wait. He appeared to be reflecting.

"You have never lost any money on my father's books," she said, when she could not endure the waiting any longer. "In fact, I am certain that you have made a fortune," and her tone was bitter.

O my God, thought Geoffrey, recalling the Upjohn account. He scowled. "I am admitting nothing, Melissa. The publishing business is no esoteric venture. I, like all other publishers, am in business for a profit, and not for spiritual exaltation. I might be selling stoves, or brooms, or blankets. Books are a commodity. If they sell well, we all make a profit. Now, I am not saying that Charles' books were a complete failure—"

"You dare not!" she cried.

Geoffrey waved his hand impatienly—"I am merely saying that they had a modest sale, for they did not appeal to the less cultivated taste."

But Melissa had not heard him. She was considering what he had said just before his last words, and now she shook with outrage and anger. " 'A commodity'! You dare call my father's lifework a 'commodity,' as if it were only a cake of soap, a washtub, a pot or pan! You dare—blaspheme—it like that!" She sprang to her feet and, even above the noise of the storm outside, her breath was fierce and loud.

Geoffrey rose slowly and looked at her, at her eyes which threw off pale blue lightnings of wrath and affront. Again, he had a difficult time to keep from smiling.

"Perhaps I was a trifle—coarse, shall we say, Melissa? I was oversimplifying the situation. But I was merely trying to say that the law of supply and demand extends even to the publishing field."

"My father's soul, his life, his learning, his studies, his reflections, his scholarship, were in his work!" she cried, almost beside herself. "You never knew that; you never realized it. To you, he was only a manufacturer of commodities from which you would take an unjustly large share of the profits!"

Rage had exhilarated her. Her color was less ghastly, there was even a hot coral in her lips, and her disordered hair was a bright flutter over her forehead and about her cheeks, as if a wind had touched it. Good, thought Geoffrey. There was no passion so devastating, so tremendous, as the passion of a repressed woman. He saw how her breasts seemed to pound against the black fabric that covered them, how a large violet vein throbbed in her long throat. The energy of fury poured out from her, the single-hearted, powerful fury of an innocent and aroused spirit.

"My dear Melissa," he said, in a conciliatory tone, "I apologize again. I did not mean to offend you. I forgot that you are not an ignorant woman who must be presented with prosaic words in order to simplify a discussion. Let us say that Charles gave the world works of great scholarship which may gain greater appreciation over the coming years. After all, the war disrupted many minds, made reading and study and scholarship temporarily irrelevant things. The situation will improve, now that there is peace again.

"I am quite willing to discuss, amiably, the subject of your father's future royalties, or, I should say, the family's. I must study our books. But I can assure you that future royalties will be at a higher rate."

His manner, his calmness, quieted Melissa to some extent. Now her whole face glowed with triumph. She had forced this robber, this despicable man, to consider her terms. She would compel him to accept them!

Geoffrey knew her thoughts, and smiled to himself. Now he knew fully, for the first time, that emotion was the secret force which would conquer this poor girl. He had always suspected it, but then, she had always been so controlled, so frigid, whenever he had seen her before.

He extended his hand with a frank air. "May I again express my sorrow over the death of a dear friend, Melissa? Though your own loss is so immeasurably greater, believe me when I say that Charles'—passing—has left a deep gap in my life."

She was still aglow with her grim elation, and it was with absentmindedness that she gave him her hand. It was not until she felt his kiss upon it that she came to herself. With a

faint cry she snatched her hand away, shivering. He pretended
not to notice. He bowed deeply and went out of the room.

She watched him go, her left hand clasped convulsively
over the back of the right. Her mouth had fallen open, and
her eyes stared intently at the door even after it had closed
behind Geoffrey. Then she looked down at her hand. The
place touched by his lips burned and tingled unbearably. She
rubbed it with fury and revulsion, as if in some way her
flesh had been violated. He had dared to do this disgusting
thing to her, right in this room where her father had died!

She started for the door, and her own room, where there
was water and soap. Then, with her tingling hand on the knob,
she stood still, blank and motionless. She stood like that for a
long time, listening. Finally she heard the grating of the Dunham carriage on the gravel drive below. Hardly knowing what
she did, she ran to the window, threw it open, tore frantically
at the shutters.

The rain had stopped, but the wind still surged against the
house like an unseen surf. It had torn the clouds into streamers
of milky vapor which blew against the black sky. The moon
rushed out from behind them, leaping like a silver ball through
space, and its light poured down on a dark and somber earth.

The Dunham carriage lights blinked with a yellow blur on
the road beyond the house. Its polished top gleamed in the
moonlight, dripped with silver drops. Leaning on the window-
sill, the wind tearing at her hair until it streamed like a banner
in the gale, Melissa watched the carriage until it was
swallowed up in the night. Then she bent her head on her
arms, and wept again, wildly, desolately, and did not know
why she wept.

CHAPTER 5

THE DUNHAM CARRIAGE wound its way over the
sodden mud road that led from the Upjohn house to the
great Dunham house on the slope of the nearest hill. Now
all the countryside was washed in wet silver, and the dying
trees groaned in the heavy gale. Sometimes a cloud rushed
across the face of the moon, and the yellow lights of the carriage splashed on the rivers of water that rippled over the

road. Sometimes the carriage lurched over softened mud, and the wheels sucked protestingly at the glue-like substance. Now the carriage began to rise slowly towards the twinkling lights on the hillside. But the countryside behind it, and beyond each side, floated in moonlit mist.

It had turned cold. Geoffrey and his sister, Mrs. Arabella Shaw, pulled the fur lap-robes closer about themselves. Arabella said, sniffing: "I think we shall have snow, Geoffrey."

She could not see her brother's face, but she knew he was leaning back in the carriage. She could smell the rich aroma of his cheroot, and she surreptitiously let down the window a trifle. Her husband had been an enemy of "the wicked weed" but there simply was no use in mentioning the matter to Geoffrey. She was on his partial bounty, which had been very cruel of Papa, who had had a reverence for the English law of inheritance. After all, there was no sense in Geoffrey's hinting that she ought to remarry. She was a widow of forty-five, and husbands of the proper age and affluence were practically nonexistent. Fortunate for her, indeed, that Geoffrey had so far refrained from the folly of introducing a slip of a stupid girl into Dunham House, and for the past year or so she, Arabella, had begun to breathe easier. Geoffrey was slightly past forty now, he had not spoken of Melissa as a possible wife for nearly two years, and he had seen very little of the Upjohns in that time. She, then, was almost completely safe; she could look forward to long and pleasant declining years as sole mistress of Dunham House, and the weekly, or monthly, brief companionship of her brother. She asked no questions of him, and about once or twice a year accompanied him to his Philadelphia quarters and entertained his few friends, who were also in the publishing business.

But almost all the entertaining in which Geoffrey engaged was done at Dunham House at Christmas time, and in the summer, if he did not go abroad then. The war was over, thank Heaven, and Arabella could anticipate a goodly list of house guests at Christmas and New Year's, and perhaps a pleasant party at Thanksgiving. She did so adore the Littlefields of Philadelphia, who had no marriageable daughters, and the Sheridans of New York. It had been a most delightful Thanksgiving last year, with the Littlefields and the Sheridans and the Bertrams. She must begin, almost immediately, to set about her preparations. The Christmas list was completed too.

She busied herself determinedly with her thoughts, for she knew, with anxiety, that Geoffrey was thinking of the Up-

johns. It would be inappropriate just now to talk of Thanksgiving and Christmas, so soon after the funeral, and so soon
after leaving that dreadful old house in the valley. Yet Arabella felt a compulsion to speak, in order to distract Geoffrey
from his thoughtful brooding. Danger lay there. But what to
say? No one could accuse her of being insensible, of dismissing
Charles' death as a matter of no consequence. After all, had
she not permitted Hulda to remain with the Upjohns until
tomorrow in order to relieve poor Amanda of the need to
assist old Sally, and to permit the girls a period of rest for
proper mourning? Had she not filled their larder with baked
hams and cold meats and loaves of bread and pots of preserves? No one could say that she was not the most tender-
hearted of neighbors, for all the Upjohns were so impossible,
so morbid, and such unpleasant company. But no wonder
people in the country and in Midfield "talked." The Upjohns
were recluses, and engaged in practically no entertaining, and
were seen very seldom by their neighbors, or in the village. It
was true that they were quite poor; even she, Arabella, had
not guessed until tonight how desperately poor they were. But
it had been the opinion of the neighbors that it was a deliberate austerity, and not one actually based on real poverty.
"High thinking and plain living, humph!" said Arabella to herself. It was very evident that high thinking was only an
apology for poor, rather than plain, living, and a necessity.
What a silly affectation! What hypocrisy!

There were some who still pretended that money was less
valuable than tradition, learning more to be desired than
good fires and excellent tables, and family much more important than bank accounts. Thank Heaven, this nonsense
was falling into disrepute in America. If a man were not
prosperous, his tradition, learning and breeding were of no
consequence whatever, and he had forfeited the respect of
his associates. After all, in free and republican America, where
any creature worthy of his salt could pile up a fortune, was
not money truly the measure of a man's worth? It was so silly
of the darling Sheridans to say that one such as Charles Upjohn represented the only true aristocracy in America, and
that with the passing of that aristocracy the country would
become a dreary wilderness of money-grubbers and animalistic
workers. She, Arabella, could not suspect the Sheridans' kindness in the slightest, and their eyes had always been clear
and without guile when they would say this, and surely they
were not thinking that the Dunham fortune was based on the
money poor dear Mama, whose father had manufactured

pottery in Syracuse, had brought to Papa at a crucial moment in the Dunham affairs. After all, there had been three generations of male Dunhams in the publishing business, the first in England. No, she could not suspect the Sheridans, who were distinguished for their breeding. Besides, who knew of the dreadful cheap pottery, anyway? Family records were never kept in America, and that was a sensible thing.

They were less than a quarter of a mile from Dunham House now, and perhaps she could pretend to be absorbed in sorrowful meditation, and Geoffrey would not speak. After all, he would expect her to be subdued by the events of the day. She had only to keep quiet and endure the smoke of the cheroot, and then they would be home and a cosy fire would be burning in the hall. It was very late. Geoffrey would not expect her to linger and discuss the Upjohns with him. And tomorrow he would return to Philadelphia, and go on to New York for several weeks, and by the time he returned the Upjohns would be almost forgotten by him. She wished she had not sent a messenger to Midfield to inform Geoffrey by telegraph that his old friend was dead. It might have been better if she had written him later, after the funeral. But then, Geoffrey was so capricious and unpredictable, and it was just possible that he would have been furious with her. She had done the best she could, and now she had only to keep silent.

She wished the coachman would hurry. He was driving much too slowly, in spite of the awful road and the gushes of water that flowed over it. Then, to her horror, she heard herself saying in a sighing voice: "I cannot believe that poor Charles is dead. And that the family is really so penniless. Whatever will the poor creatures do, Geoffrey?"

Geoffrey smoked calmly. Arabella upbraided herself for her words. She wished she could see Geoffrey's face, but she could see only the firefly that was the burning end of his cheroot. Then Geoffrey chuckled. "I have an idea that Amanda will now manage the affairs of the family very competently. There is iron in the soul of that indomitable woman. Do not worry too much about them, Bella."

Arabella felt a profound relief, for Geoffrey's voice had been cheerfully indifferent. But still, she had to probe the dangerous area in which Melissa's name lay, like a festering abscess.

"Perhaps you are right, dear Geoffrey, but it is very hard not to be concerned with the sorrowful affairs of old friends. Of course, Phoebe is to be married to young John Barrett in June, and an excellent marriage it is for her, too, and Amanda will probably contrive to keep Andrew at Harvard." She paused, then went on resolutely: "It is evident that Melissa is a confirmed spinster, and it is her duty to remain with her mother and complete her father's lifework."

She waited. But Geoffrey merely puffed, and then he yawned. Never had a more delicious sound come to Arabella's ears. She let out her tight breath in slow exhalations. She continued, with confidence: "A most unpleasant and disagreeable woman, Melissa. And so—so unattractive, and wild-looking, for all that stony expression of hers. There were moments today when I thought her completely insensible. She offered no comfort to her mother, and seemed to have detached herself from all the members of her poor family. When she was younger, there were times when I thought her not unhandsome, but now that she is definitely a spinster, and no longer young, she is most unprepossessing. Fortunate, indeed, it is that she never desired to marry, though I have not heard that any young man has ever proposed to her."

Geoffrey still did not answer. Arabella could not see her brother's face. She waited, and felt a prickling of dampness along her hairline. Why did he offer no comment? And then, when her alarm was at its height, he said, yawning: "I must leave on the seven o'clock train tomorrow, and I urge you, after these exhausting few days, not to rise to see me off. It is too early, and you are too weary."

Arabella drew a deep breath that was like the inhalation after a prayer. Her eyes filled with grateful tears. She sought her brother's hand under the robe, and said, just a little incoherently: "O Geoffrey, how can you ask me to lie abed while you prepare to leave in the cold dark morning! It is my duty, no, my pleasure, to say goodbye to you, and to see to it that you have every comfort, and to pour your coffee! No, I insist upon it, my dear, and will hear nothing to the contrary!"

In the darkness she did not see Geoffrey's smile, but she felt the returning pressure of his hand. To her joy, the carriage was now turning up the smooth gravel path of the drive, and the pile of Dunham House lay before her.

They stepped out of the carriage under the carriage porch, and Geoffrey assisted his sister up the wide stone stairway to the door, which immediately opened and emitted a gush of warm candle- and firelight. The ruddy flare splashed on the granite steps, so that they had the quality of wet marble. Indeed, the whole great house loomed in the night as if built of that substance, though in fact it had been constructed of special white granite, very costly and smooth, somewhat incongruous in that region of fieldstone. Three stories tall, with deep wide cellars, it presented an austere Georgian front to the long and wandering valleys below, and could be seen, on bright days, by the villagers of Midfield, two miles away, while on clear nights its windows would twinkle like stars on the hillside. Elms and evergreens surrounded it, but at some distance, so that it was encircled by vast stretches of clipped lawns, and open to the sun. Behind it lay terraced gardens, with flagged paths, grottoes, tiny glades, rose-gardens, vegetable gardens, a large hen-house, a carriage house, and the stables. There was a spring at the end of the main garden, which had been dammed, and in the summer a lily-covered pool filled with thumping frogs made the warm nights deeply sonorous. The pottery fortune was, in the main, responsible for the beauty, entrancement and serenity of the gardens, as well as for the house itself.

Wind tore and battered at Geoffrey and Arabella Dunham as they alighted from the carriage. Geoffrey assisted his sister over the slippery wet steps, while she gasped for breath and tried to keep her fur hood over her head. The carriage grated back to the stables, and, breathing a word of gratitude at being "safe at home once more," Arabella scurried into the hall, sweetly greeting the butler as the latter closed the door behind her and Geoffrey.

The immense square hall was paved with dark red-and-black marble squares, which gave a baronial atmosphere to it, as did the vast walnut stairway curving up to a great arch and leading to the second floor. The walls, of darkest walnut, were gracefully and heavily panelled, and had no other ornament than the darkened portrait of Geoffrey's grandfather over the mantelpiece. The fireplace was of pillared black marble, polished, vast, and glowing with mighty logs, and furnished with the brightest brass andirons and other equipment. On the mantelpiece were set three crystal and gilt candelabra, shining with bending and flowing candlelight which illuminated the portrait above it. A very monolith of a grandfather's clock, of walnut intricately carved, loomed against the stairway, sounding each quarter hour in a majestic Westminster peal of measured notes. Against the right wall stood a long dark table bearing a blue Chinese vase full of flowers from the conservatory, and here and there were scattered tall carved chairs of walnut with red velvet seats.

To the left opened the library, to the right, the spacious,

dark, double drawing-rooms, and behind the drawing-rooms, the dining-room, and others.

The fire rose higher at the gust of wind which followed Geoffrey and Arabella. The candle flame bent and flowed in banners of soft yellow light. The hall was pervaded by the mingled odors of warm smoke, tallow and the fresh sweetness of the flowers. Two English setters rose from the Aubusson rug before the hearth and came leaping and barking joyously at their master. Geoffrey bent to their greetings, while the butler assisted Arabella with her hood and cape. "Any important messages or letters, James?" asked Geoffrey as he fended off the vociferous affections of the dogs.

"Oh, what a relief to be home, dear Geoffrey!" exclaimed Arabella, in her sweetly whining and sentimental voice. "James, please see about some tea and perhaps some cold meat and a pastry for Mr. Dunham."

"No, thank you, Arabella. You'd best go to bed. I'll stay only a short time in the library, while I look over my letters."

But Arabella did not want to leave her brother alone in the library, "with his thoughts." Gentlemen often had dangerous thoughts which boded no good for those dependent upon them. She said, with an arch smile: "I think I'll join you in a glass of mild port, Geoffrey. There is such a lovely fire in the library, I see, and I must just toast my toes for a few moments before it. And then to bed for both of us!"

James was an elderly, short and very fat little man, and he knew all Geoffrey's moods, so he only needed to see one of Geoffrey's eyebrows lifted in a certain way for him to say smoothly: "There is a fire in your own chamber, Miss Arabella, and I believe that tea things are prepared. I shall bring up the kettle at once, as the maids have all gone to bed."

Arabella flashed one of those glances at James which Melissa had aptly called "shark-like," but her sweet smile, though stiffening somewhat, remained fixed. Geoffrey said, quickly: "Dear Arabella, you look exhausted. Please go upstairs. I must look over my letters, and I shall be very dull company." He held out his hand to her, bent and kissed her forehead, for she was a rather small woman. "Good night, dear Arabella, and sleep well."

Arabella, still fuming, still smiling, hesitated. Her shortness of stature was emphasized by her broad plumpness, now straining at the dark purple silk of her widow's garb. Arabella believed she had considerable French chic, and had not the gown indeed come from Paris? But she inevitably wore gowns a size or two too small for her, their elaborateness of ruffle, drape and bustle calling attention to her stocky and over-nourished figure with its thick short arms and tiny, fat white hands. Arabella wore jewelry in great quantity, many winking rings, bracelets and chains, which she had not been able to relinquish even on this day of dolor for the Upjohns, a commonness which Geoffrey had noticed. But there is no use ever talking to Arabella, he thought. She just has no taste, poor thing, and he thought how much she resembled their mother, of pottery fame. It was unfortunate that their father had had to espouse Miranda Bolt for the sake of his sacred publishing house, and Geoffrey suspected that old Mr. Dunham understood that thoroughly and never quite forgave his wife for the necessity.

Arabella's face was an anomaly. She had the fat and ruddy fullness of her dead mother's face, heavy and round, glistening, and giving evidence of an untrammelled appetite for the richer things of the table. With that countenance, she ought to have had rotund and jolly features, radiating good-humor and a placid disposition. But, on the contrary, she had acquired the contour of old Geoffrey Dunham's features, without their aristocracy. Her nose was sharp, bent and pointed, and very large, almost a parrot's beak, and under it was a tiny, slit-like mouth, which, when opening to speak and smile, lost every vestige of lip. This made a rather unpleasant orifice, round and hard, filled with long, narrow, and quite yellow teeth. Again, Melissa's description of "shark-like" was very apt, and Melissa did not know which was the more unpleasant: Arabella's mouth in tight repose, or Arabella's smile, thought by the poor woman to be very engaging, and which she was at pains to practice constantly.

Her eyes, a hard, slate-gray, quite indicated her character, which was acquisitive, suspicious and disingenuous, for they never were lit up by the almost constant smile beneath them. In fact, they were well-nigh expressionless, except when a shrewd flash would light them, or a chambermaid on the occasion of some dereliction would find them fixed upon her like granite points. Her brows were light and sparse, though above them was piled a mass of gray-streaked lightish hair, always dressed in the most elaborate puffs and ringlets. She was Geoffrey's senior by several years, yet she maintained a great vivacity of movement, a great youthfulness of lavish gesture and bounce. Geoffrey would wish she would not so over-work herself in order to acquire a reputation for being remarkably well-preserved, and for being his junior when among more casual acquaintances; he was sure that it must be an enormous strain upon her and her health. He was fond of her, in a careless way, for she was always devoted to his interests, though he was not in the least deceived that she had any charity of nature, any real kindness of heart, or any appreciable amount of brains. Sometimes her constant sentimental babble, her overripe sweetness, and her trilling, hackneyed phrases irritated him beyond endurance, yet he was invariably courteous and affectionate to her. After all, the poor woman was only a silly fool who had been indiscreet enough to marry a very bad artist. (That was during the years when Arabella had taken up "Art" at her papa's expense in Philadelphia.) Adelbert Shaw had run through Arabella's private fortune very quickly, in less than twelve years, to be exact, and after his death she arrived home at Dunham House with less than two thousand dollars.

Arabella, however, had not recovered from her attack of "Art." During her spare moments, she painted lavishly in her "studio" on the third floor, the room with the north light. Her canvases, always of "sweet pussycats in the most beguiling attitudes," or of summer flowers, or a "most entrancing aspect of the garden," were stacked five deep all around the walls. They were most atrocious. Geoffrey did not pity her for her folly in marrying Adelbert Shaw, or for her loss of fortune, or for her widowhood, but he did pity her for the terrible works of art which she endlessly produced.

Geoffrey, looking at his sister tonight, smirking under the candlelight, and wearing a yellowish reflection on her face from her purple gown, was suddenly impatient. He knew what she was thinking, and he frowned a little. He repeated: "Good night, dear Arabella," and turned away and went into the library, closing the walnut door firmly behind him. A few more of Arabella's platitudes, and he would have been rude to her. When she was out of his sight he invariably forgot Arabella, and he never remembered her spitefulness when he had been a child, or her tale-bearing, or her sanctimonious sweetness of expression while she had watched him being punished. Her mother had favored her, for they had been much alike, and Mrs. Dunham had never had that devotion to her son which was almost axiomatic between other mothers and sons.

The dogs had followed him into the library, and he let them lie at his feet while he absently pulled at their ears. He liked the peace of the enormous library, away from Arabella. Here, too, everything was of walnut or black marble, the walls ponderous with many hundreds of books, the walnut ceiling vaulted. From that ceiling, on a chain, hung a huge crystal chandelier, unlighted tonight. But James had lit one of the polished brass lamps on a table near the fire, and the firelight and lamplight made a warm and ruddy circle surrounded by soft and shadowy gloom. The long sofa against the wall was of black leather; the deep chairs, scattered throughout the library on the dark crimson carpet, were either of black or green or red leather, and very restful. Each chair had its round, square or octagon table of walnut, and its individual lamp. The room had been designed for comfort, for reading, for thought, for work. In a corner, near one of the wide, enormous windows draped in dark-green satin, was Geoffrey's large walnut desk, closed now.

Two heavy bronze candelabra stood on the mantelpiece, and between them ticked an old black marble clock with a gold face. The great walnut clock in the hall boomed out eleven notes; it was like the striking of a weighted stick on a velvet drum. The fire hissed and flared. The wind rolled impotently against the windows, against which the draperies had been drawn. Geoffrey took a cheroot from the silver box which lay on the table beside him, lit it, leaned back in the chair, and continued to stroke a dog's head absently. There was a tap at the door, and James entered with a silver tray on which stood two bottles and a glass. He put it down on the table.

Geoffrey said, smiling: "James, are you clairvoyant?"

James' round and rubicund face was grave, but his eyes twinkled. "Oh, no sir, Mr. Dunham. But you left word, if you remember, that you would return tonight."

Geoffrey still smiled through the smoke of his cheroot. Someone had once told him that he had none of the attributes of a gentleman, and he had replied: "Gentlemen are invariably fools, and unless they have had the good sense to endow themselves with ancestors who were not gentry, they also invariably starve." One of the inflexible rules of gentlefolk was not to discuss equals with inferiors, especially not with servants. So Geoffrey said: "Wait a minute, James. I want to tell you something. Please give orders that fresh flowers are to be sent to the Upjohn house twice a week, from the conservatories. Our best flowers," he added, thinking of Arabella.

"Yes, sir," said James, without expression, but with a flicker in his eyes.

Geoffrey leaned back and smoked with a pleasant expression. "Do you often see old Sally in Midfield, any of you, James?"

"The Upjohn Sally, Mr. Geoffrey?"

"Tut, tut, James. Let's not start being so definite now. Who else?"

James allowed himself the twinkle of a smile. Goeffrey nodded at the whiskey bottle. It was a familiar gesture. James, with a bow, picked up the bottle and tossed down a neat swig. Then he carefully cleaned the top with a very white handkerchief, wiped his lips, said: "Ah." He looked at Geoffrey, and lowered his voice:

"And what'd you like to know, Mr. Geoffrey?"

"The Upjohn larder, James. Full or lean?"

"Lean, sir. Not mean, but lean."

"You'd say adequate?"

"Monotonous rather, sir."

"Wine?"

"It was kept just for old Mr. Upjohn."

"Well, James, once weekly there must be carried a fine ham, a hamper of wine, a side of bacon, and some other delicacies from our larder to the Upjohn household, in addition to the flowers. It must be done discreetly. I'll leave the wording to you."

James pondered. "Mrs. Upjohn has the reputation of being a very proud lady, sir."

"I think, after a certain conversation I had with her tonight, alone, that she will accept, with understanding."

The servants had heard, through James, of Geoffrey's conversation with his sister, two or three years before, about Melissa, and had been disappointed that the occasion of Arabella's discomfiture was being so long delayed. James' little eyes sparkled. He would have a morsel to tell 'em in the servants' dining-room tomorrow morning!

Geoffrey continued: "I know the reputation of the Upjohns which my friends hold, James. But what do the servants say of them?"

James was beginning to enjoy himself, and he said, without reticence: "Mrs. Upjohn is very proud, like I said, sir, and hoity-toity, but everybody respects her. She is a lady. Miss Phoebe is very pretty, and we all think she is making a good match with Mr. Barrett; she's a nice little creature. Mr. Andrew—well, somehow Mr. Andrew don't figure in things much. Kind as if he was just someone goin' in and out occasionally. And there's Miss Melissa." He paused, peered uncertainly at Geoffrey. "They say Miss Melissa don't know she's alive, poor young lady."

Geoffrey nodded gravely. "I see."

James went on: "Nobody among the servants ever thought highly of Mr. Upjohn."

Geoffrey said nothing, but stared at the fire. James waited. He became a little uneasy. Sometimes he wished the master was a little less "familiar." A man knew where he was in a proper household, and besides, when certain amenities were observed and certain taboos respected, there was "dignity." Yet, thought James, we all love the master, and there's none that pays better, even in Philadelphia, none more careful of his servants' comfort and health and fortunes. A hard man he is, and that's a fact, but behave yourself, and don't slack up on your work, and there's none better. He's worth a hundred great "gentlemen," with their high airs and their cruel ways. James pondered while he waited. Let them talk! Mr. Dunham was a gentleman in the real meaning of the word, even if there were no portraits of old ancestors in the house, and no crested silver, even if there were funny rumors about his fancy women in New York, given out by that silly girl who was lady's maid to old Mrs. Sheridan. Hadn't Mr. Dunham been a colonel in the war, and didn't he have a medal? That's how families were built.

Geoffrey was speaking. "What do the servants say about the late Mr. Upjohn?"

James hesitated. "We didn't know much about him, sir, never having seen him much. But old Sally once told Hulda that he—he was a devil, sir. A real devil."

Now Geoffrey was silent for so long that James felt he had been dismissed. He tiptoed from the room, closing the door softly behind him.

Geoffrey sat, smoking and abstractedly listening to the wind that had increased its voice to a somber and threatening roar. He could hear the threshing and beating of the trees. A gush of smoke belched out into the room. The dogs stirred uneasily. Despite the noise of the wind, the house stood engulfed in a private silence.

Geoffrey refilled his glass, returned to the fire. He watched the logs fall apart in a golden rush of sparks.

So, Charles was "a real devil." In a way, thought Geoffrey, I was almost as completely deceived as the others. I was almost as deceived as poor old Charlie himself who, had he been accused of malignance, would have been appalled and stricken, and would have denied the accusation with a rare and trembling passion. Can a man be guilty and believe himself to be innocent of the slightest vileness? Yes, it was possible. It probably happened every day, in every family, and the silent victims of such people were legion.

Charles Upjohn had been a very subtle and perceptive man. Such men are not simpletons. Geoffrey's thoughts grew darker, and he scowled. He began to doubt whether Charles would have been aghast at the accusation that he was "a real devil." What a damn fool I was! said Geoffrey to himself. I'll wager there was many a time when Charlie laughed at all of us. What an idealist he appeared to be, what a gentle, ingenuous saint, dreaming, scholarly, cloistered! But I'll bet he was no idealist at all. He was too pleasant and agreeable, in the first place, and idealists are invariably the most repulsive and obnoxious animals under the sun. I'll have to give that reflection more time, later on. It has possibilities.

In the meantime, there is the enigma of Charles Upjohn. He may be dead. But he is still as potent as ever, perhaps more so. Funny that I never thought that old Charlie was potent. Now I see that he was. Of all those poor creatures in that household, Charlie alone had an inexorable will to live, was determined to order his life as he desired. There are always a thousand obstacles in the path of that fascinating idea, and the ordinary man compromises, for the sake of those others who are involved with him in living. But Charles did not compromise. He first convinced Amanda, and then the others, that he was defenseless, unworldly, a great child, needing protection against such a harsh world. So they took upon themselves all the burdens he ought to have carried, and which were his own responsibility, and left him free, free to study, to reflect, to suck out his family's juices like a parasite, to continue to delude them that he was a mighty scholar.

What a conscienceless wretch he was, and how implacable in his exploitation! Did he ever have a pang of remorse, of regret? I doubt it. He enjoyed life to the very last essence. It must have been hard for the old devil to die and free his family. But did he free them? I think not. I am afraid not. His hold on them is stronger than ever. He created a legend about himself when he was still alive. His family will add to that legend. Melissa will add to it.

Geoffrey took the poker and plunged at the logs. He thought of the moment's private conversation he had had with Amanda just before leaving. He had taken her hand and had said softly and hastily: "Dear Mrs. Upjohn, I know that this is a somewhat odd time to speak of this, but I am to be absent for a few weeks and I wish to give you plenty of time to consider. I should like your approval of my suit for Melissa."

Poor woman, how she had strained back from him in a very stupefaction of incredulity and amazement! Her colorless eyes had protruded and blazed, and she had put her hand to her heart, and her gasp was loud and audible. Then she had whispered:

"Melissa! You are speaking of—Melissa—Geoffrey?"

"Yes, Mrs. Upjohn, Melissa." He was concerned at her appearance, her sudden blanching, and her trembling, which became almost violent.

She had stared at him, utterly speechless, then. Her hand was shaking in his. She moistened her dry lips, and her eyes moved helplessly in their reddened sockets. She could not believe it. Her gaze fastened on him, searching for mockery, for some explanation of this incredible thing.

"Melissa," she whispered, and there was a stunned sound in her voice. "I cannot understand—Melissa."

Now something flashed over her face, suspicious, dark and somber. Her voice was low but clearly audible when she said:

"I do not understand. You—and Melissa. There are things I do not understand! Geoffrey, you do not know Melissa. I am her mother. She is my daughter. How is it possible for you to want Melissa?"

Geoffrey considered. Her eyes searched his almost feverishly. She went on: "My conscience will not permit me to be silent. There are evil things about my daughter. She has brought grief and misery to this house. She robbed me of my husband, with her guileful ways. Charles was always so innocent, so easily deceived. Melissa is a bad woman, Geoffrey. My conscience compels me to tell you, so that you may reconsider, put aside this most unfeasible thought—"

When he did not speak, she went on, in a louder and wilder tone: "You are a good and illustrious man, Geoffrey. I cannot permit you to destroy your life."

"You refuse, Mrs. Upjohn, to consider my suit?"

She caught her breath, withdrew her fingers from his. She clasped her hands together, as if wringing them. She said: "Melissa hates you, Geoffrey. She was jealous of her father, and hated you because she loved you. She will not accept you."

He smiled, bent and touched her damp forehead with his lips. "Let me worry about that, dear friend. I shall need your help. Please help me." He had left her then, and she had watched him go, dumbfounded.

Geoffrey thought of Melissa for a long time, Melissa whom he had loved since she had been a child of fourteen and he a man of thirty. He thought of her quite dispassionately. He had always wanted her. He had wanted her even when he had not known he had loved her, five years ago, that drugged, sleeping girl with the chaste and lifeless face of an unawakened Psyche. But now, as he sat before the fire, and the clocks struck midnight, he saw there were formidable ghosts in his path, and the most formidable was the sinister ghost of Charles Upjohn. Geoffrey rubbed his big hands over his face, pressed his fingers against his eyes. The Psyche slept in a stone chamber which had no door, and she was guarded by an evil spirit who possessed her more in death than he had in life.

Geoffrey got up and began to pace the room, back and forth, while the fire fell lower, the dogs snuffled in their dreams, and the wind, falling away, was only a faint thunder in the far hills.

CHAPTER 6

THE WIND BEAT against the old gray clapboards of the Upjohn house, swirled around the chimneys, and howled along the eaves. But the house was quiet and dark. However, those within it were not asleep. They lay and stared blindly into the darkness and listened to the wind, and each knew his own particular desolation.

Andrew's room was the smallest and darkest in the house, hid away at the end of the narrow and creaking corridor which had no windows, so that even on the brightest day it was necessary to grope to reach the door of that room. He had always had that room. It was not consciously chosen for him. But always Andrew had been a stranger in that household and had been given a stranger's room, forgotten and isolated. Even his mother, Amanda, had a way of sometimes forgetting her son's existence, though she often smiled at him and spoke to him affectionately. Charles had always been courteous towards his son, Melissa had consulted him, during his visits, about his studies, and Phoebe had expressed her admiration for his handsomeness. When he was absent, no one thought of him. It was not that he was the victim of his family's indifference or coldness or deliberate neglect. But from his earliest childhood he had not impinged too vividly on the consciousness of his parents and his sisters. Perhaps it was because he was always so silent, so giving to wandering through the woods and over the hills for long hours, and because he gave no one any trouble and was never known to have been a participant in any quarrel. Charles had vaguely thought of him as "amiable," Amanda was once heard to say that "he never gave me a moment's trouble," Melissa had carelessly remarked that he was "such a nice boy," and Phoebe observed that the farm always seemed to take a brisker and more prosperous air when Andrew was home.

He lived on the periphery of the Upjohn family, his quiet orbit never quite touching the discordant edge of the family's intense solar system. He revolved alone, in sight, but not in contact. He seemed always to be as unaware of the others as they were of him. No one ever conjectured whether Andrew loved this member of the family or that, or what he thought, or what he desired. Andrew was there, a tranquil and amicable body, easy to forget.

Charles had been his tutor for several years, devoting three hours a day to the boy's studies, until he had gone away to school. Yet Charles never quite remembered whether there had been any discussions about the history he had taught his son, or whether they had engaged in any of those spirited arguments so common between himself and his daughter Melissa. Andrew simply accepted his lessons without comment. He had been dull, rather than a dullard. He was, Charles had thought, the very essence of comfortable mediocrity, for all his shrewd, dark-blue eyes and the way he had of suddenly looking at his father with a kind of still intensity. Perhaps Charles had not been aware of that intensity, or he had dismissed it immediately from his thoughts, as he always had a way of dismissing that which made him even vaguely uncomfortable.

In school, though no one of the Upjohns knew this, Andrew had become very popular with his teachers, and had made a few fast and devoted friends. When at home, he carried on a steady correspondence with these strangers. It was typical that no one in the family remarked on the many letters he received, or asked him about those who had sent them. They never expected to see Andrew display temper or umbrage or resentment or petulance, for he never had displayed them, even when a baby. They never exploited him, as good-natured people are usually exploited, just as they never quarrelled with him. When he had gone away to war, they were not overly concerned. Nothing ever happened to Andrew. Whenever his mother received a letter from him, she would examine the envelope with bewilderment before opening it, and then would exclaim: "Oh, it's from Andrew," with a note of surprise in her voice. In order that they might remember to write to him, the members of the family would be forced to make a note in their diaries or account-books.

On a certain day, Charles, upon receiving a letter from Andrew's headmaster, had ejaculated: "Good God, it seems that Andrew is finished with that school, and will return home next week! Whatever are we to do with him now, Melissa? Sixteen years old! Is it possible?"

It was Melissa who had decided that Andrew must be a lawyer. Charles then learned that Melissa had given the subject of Andrew considerable thought during the past year. Charles had looked at his daughter with admiration and amusement. Imagine thinking of Andrew! Melissa had said: "I have been studying Andrew's school reports this last year or so. He has a very analytical and logical mind, perfect for a lawyer. Of course, Papa, he could never qualify as a trial lawyer, for he has no brilliance or imagination, and no originality. But he has the qualities of doggedness and perseverance invaluable for legal research, which requires complete and meticulous attention to detail."

Charles had laughed with that indulgence invariably displayed by the vivacious of mind for the plodder. "Well, my dear," he had said, "I trust your judgment. Andrew shall be a lawyer. He will never send home any enormous amounts of money, but perhaps we can rely upon a certain income, and he will be off our hands."

They "consulted" Andrew about his proposed career. Charles was never quite certain whether they had really consulted him, but he did remember that Melissa had brought Andrew into her father's study, had outlined his gifts of mind to him, and had announced that Andrew was to go to Harvard the next autumn to begin his legal studies. Andrew had just sat, gravely smiling, occasionally nodding, and then had gone away. Neither Melissa nor Charles ever questioned themselves as to what the boy had really thought, or wanted. But then, no one ever questioned this. Andrew was someone to be disposed of neatly, filed away, and forgotten. Neither of them saw his last, uncertain, and imploring glance.

Amanda had been aghast at her husband's decision. "And where, pray, Charles, is the money to come from? Harvard, indeed! A lawyer, indeed! It has been my belief that Andrew would assume the burden of managing the farm after his school-days were over. He is a man now, and quite capable of managing the land."

Charles had talked to her gently and persuasively. Amanda never knew how the mention of money, and the need for it, disturbed and irritated him. But Charles knew that he could always appeal to Amanda on the basis of "good sense." It was "good sense" to educate Andrew for the law. He would make considerable money, and help support the family beyond the value of his presence on the farm. The money would be "found" in some way. Amanda was not to distress her "little head." Amanda, overcome as usual by her husband's smooth and specious arguments, might have been content had she not seen the sudden triumphant flash of Melissa's eyes. But it was no use to argue with Charles. He always managed to get his way, either by an air of exhausted and gentle weariness which it would be cruel to aggravate, or by his charming smile or his affectionate glance. Amanda retired from the argument, feeling, as always, that she had tangled with an invisible, soft, yet inexorable web, and that its filaments had choked her judgment.

So Andrew had gone to Harvard. Here, in the company of more gifted and more agile minds, he was lost, as he had not been lost in his country school. He lumbered through his classes. He had to repeat, and repeat again, for the next four years. Then, on the outbreak of war between the States, he had enlisted in the army. Some way—and this always remained a dim mystery to his family—he had received a commission. He had returned from the war, and the prison camp, as serene, impassive and unmoved as ever. No one bothered to question him about his experiences. It was taken for granted that Andrew's experiences would always be dull and uneventful. And, indeed, Andrew showed no marks of the war years. Rugged and quiet, rarely speaking in his slow, deep voice, he returned to Harvard without comment. He never showed even his mother the long and ugly bayonet slashes on his chest, the badly healed wound on his right leg. He never spoke of them. Again it was taken for granted that nothing had happened to Andrew.

Andrew's room was not only the smallest and darkest in the house, but the narrowest. It had one tiny window, high in the knotted-pine wall, which overlooked the roof of the kitchen below, a small segment of the kitchen garden, and the rear of the big gray barn. He had no view of meadow or hill. Views were not considered necessary for Andrew, who would probably not appreciate them. No one in the family knew that Andrew, when at home, would always arise at dawn and go outside to watch the morning skies. He moved silently, and always returned to his room unobserved, to the chorus of the fowl and the hosannah of the birds. Then he would lie on his hard and narrow bed, remembering, with a still glory on his big and rugged face.

He lay on his back tonight, his big arms folded under his head, his eyes staring at the dim rectangle of the high little window, which no one had ever thought to soften with curtains. His large straight body was covered with a thin, frayed patchwork quilt. The straw mattress creaked faintly with his slow, heavy breathing and his slight movements. He listened to the enormous howl of the wind as it rattled his unshuttered window. The room was very cold and dank. But he did not feel the chill. His body was always so warm, so deeply pulsing.

Through no one ever believed that Andrew "thought," he was thinking. His thoughts were like the quiet strong beatings of his heart, sonorous, steadfast and calm. They were grave thoughts, but not somber, for Andrew was naturally attuned to the immense inevitabilities of life. He was thinking of his father.

He had been afraid of Charles, for something in him, pure and uncorrupted, had recognized corruption. But he did not know why he was afraid, for his fear was instinctive. Andrew had never been "clever" with words. He had no words for his fear and his doubt and, as he was so intensely loyal and devoted, he had quelled the voice of warning. He thought his shrinking was the result of his recognition of his own dullness and nothingness and inferiority.

He had always been afraid of Melissa, too, because she reflected so much of his father's light, and was always so assured, so cold, and so definite in her decisions. He had accepted their decisions about his life as he always accepted everything about them. They knew best. His own passionate yet slow cravings, his own desperate hunger, were stupid things, too shameful to mention. They knew all the wise decisions; they knew him better than he knew himself. This he believed with complete faith.

He hated his thick and unresponsive tongue, which could never express his thoughts. He thought of himself as dumb and ignorant, heavy of movement, amorphic, sluggish of comprehension. The vast tides that rolled and retreated and surged in him were too enormous for words, and so he condemned them as foolish and shameful. Sometimes he had lingered on the edge of a conversation between Melissa and his father, and had listened to them, wondering, vaguely exalted, and deeply moved. He did not understand a word they said, but he was convinced that it was splendid beyond all understanding. Finally, becoming aware of him, they had flung him the half-amused, half-impatient, glance which one casts at a big puppy lurking in the background, and he had felt himself dismissed, and had slunk away.

He was thinking of all this as he lay in his bed, staring into the darkness. He was thinking of the splintering thought which had come to him when he had watched his father being lowered into his grave. He had thought: I am free at last.

His thoughts had always come to him slowly. They had been like thick-husked seeds planted in the ground. A day would come when the husk would split, and a thin frail tendril would emerge, green and seeking. Then the dark and heavy earth of his mind would be pierced by the delicate stem, and a hopeful leaf would be put out. But it would take a long time before the thought became a rooted and steadfast tree, matted in invincible branches beneath the sun. So he could not understand the suddenness and violence of the thought at his father's grave. He did not know of the seed which had been planted in his slow and solid mind years ago, and which only now, as the darkness rolled away, was revealed as a full-grown tree.

I am free at last, he had thought. And he had looked at his mother, standing there in the gray drizzle near the raw earth. He had looked, and thought: We are all free. He had loved his mother, as an animal loves its dam, but he had never thought much about her. Now he saw her, and for the first time a quiet and angry bitterness came to him against his father. No expression showed itself on his large and impassive face. Andrew thought with his instincts, and his instincts were awakened now; emotions, rather than true and relentless reflections, marched through his mind. He had looked at Melissa, and his small blue eyes had darkened, partly with pity, partly with disgust. He had looked at little mewling Phoebe, whose golden ringlets were the only bright color in the foggy grayness, and his dark-auburn brows had drawn together in a thick knot.

He thought: Why have I done this thing to my life, and allowed it to be done? I saw his face this morning as he lay in his coffin, and I knew he was a lie. I let him do what he wished with me, because he had deceived me, just as he had deceived my mother and my sisters. How was it possible I did not know until this afternoon when I saw his face for the last time before they closed the lid down upon it? I knew it all at once, suddenly, like lightning.

But it had not come like lightning, and Andrew's mind, moving like a belated sun over a dimmed landscape, began to pick out hidden landmarks and the shapes of his tree-thoughts. He had forgotten, but now, involuntarily, he thought of a certain morning in spring when he had been fifteen years old, and home for the Easter holidays. It was the morning when the hard lifeless seed had been dropped in the earth of his mind.

He saw that morning so clearly now. Yesterday it had been cold and bitter, winter lingering in slabs of white ice, like fallen gravestones, under the bare trees. The wind had been a lash, the rain, drops of ice. But this morning had come, and with it the long sweet breath of spring, like a smile, like a soft, triumphant chorus hardly heard, only felt. Never had there been such a sky, so pure, tinted like a robin's egg, across which moved thin drifts of clouds radiant before the new sun. The brown wet earth lay under the light, still naked, but softened with mist and exhaling a thousand strong and fertile scents too intoxicating for endurance. The hills floated in mauve radiance. The trees were still empty, yet there was a pliability about their branches, a gentle blurring; no longer were they stark and hard and rigid as they had been only yesterday. A faint greenness, like a haze, touched the distant fields, which had lain like rutted iron the other morning. The fowl in the barnyard, the pigs, the horses in the stable, the cattle in their stalls, lifted their voices excitedly as if they had slept all winter and had come awake only at this hour. Robins hopped over the ground, their red-umber breasts bright in the sunlight, and sparrows twittered noisily in the eaves and over the slate roof of the house, which, damp from the rains of the night, now flowed like water with the blue reflection from the sky.

Andrew had seen Charles and Melissa in the wet brown garden. They were listening, and seeing, standing hand in hand like lovers, with the sunlight on their faces. Charles was wearing his old black cloak, which fell about him in lean shabby folds. His heard was bare, and the sunlight had turned his gray hair to a flat silver. As always, his shoulders were bent, and he was the delicate and attenuated scholar delighting esthetically in the young morning. Melissa was clad in one of her somber and bunchy brown frocks, careless, as always, of her seventeen-year-old virgin beauty, unaware of the slender elegance of her figure, which even her garments could not destroy. She had thrown a gray shawl over her shoulders; it fluttered in the wind. Her profile was turned towards Andrew. and for the first time he knew that his sister was beautiful. Her pale gilt hair shone and glittered in the sun, like a gold piece fresh from the mint, and Andrew thought that her profile, too, resembled the profile on a new coin, so clearly cut was it, so sharp and intense of feature, so unworn by ugly hands.

Andrew had left the house with his usual careful silence, and now stood behind his father and sister. He was content to be near them, without their seeing him. He wanted to hear their voices speaking about the morning. He felt the earth under his feet; all at once, it seemed to pulse against them like a deep, awakening breast. He stood on the breast of the earth, and he knew it was alive, that it had cognizance, that it was a huge sentient being. He must have always known it, all his life, but now he knew that he had known it forever.

Charles began to speak, in the dreamy voice he affected when he wished to inform his audience that he was poignantly moved:

"Melissa, I feel, this morning, that the earth is a living being, personally alive, a huge creature with a soul and a consciousness of its own, apart from the creatures who live upon it."

Melissa looked at her father breathlessly, and now her face became fluid with quiet rapture, and she murmured incoherently. But Andrew did not look at her. He stared at the earth under his feet and felt its pulse. It lived. But then, he had always known it. The earth was alive; it had a spirit. He had always loved it. Some time, during his school years, he had read that men had once worshipped the earth. He remembered how the schoolboys had laughed scornfully at the idea. They were wrong! The great mother earth was a Being, with an enormous heart forever beating, with a pulsing so huge, so ponderously living, that the little hearts of men must stir in answer, however feeble.

His father's graciously approving voice echoed in the boy's ears, and suddenly Andrew could not bear to hear it, though he did not understand why. But he felt that something blasphemous was being uttered, something loftily and indulgently patronizing, as if Charles believed that the earth, great Mother Earth, ought to be pleased that one of her minute children had recognized her, had granted her sentience, from some celestial throne set far above her grossness.

Andrew ran back into the house and shut the door of his room with a rare vehemence. He sat on the edge of his bed, and his hands were sweating, and his face was flushed, as though he had been witness to some scene of desecration. He was young, and his emotions, though vast, were always formless, and at last he did not know why he had felt this thing. He knew only that something alien had salted his mouth; he did not know it was hatred.

But now he knew it as he lay in his bed and stared at the gray patch of little window. The seed had been sown that morning, the seed which would be revealed as a mighty treeshape in the hour when he stood by his father's grave.

He thought to himself, moving his large head on his strong, muscular arms: The earth was always mine, and I always belonged to the earth. There was nothing, ever, between us. How dared they stand there, that morning, and be condescending to the morning, and ethereally enraptured over it, no doubt feeling in themselves a mean, exalted self-approval because they had allowed the everlasting earth a little measure of consciousness! Like angels affably acknowledging the wagging tail of a dog! I hated him then, though I did not know it. I know it now. It was my knowing it was hatred that set me free. It was my knowing all about him, and despising him. Melissa? She is a fool.

He thought of the earth, and he said to himself: Mine! There is nothing to keep me from it now. What kept me from it before? My own stupidity, my own wicked and senseless humility. In some way, a corrupt mind took hold of my mind. I can see now that a corrupt mind can enslave and injure more than a corrupt act. But his was a very peculiar corruption. I wonder if he ever knew that he was a fraud? I wonder if he deliberately set out to destroy us all, or whether he, too, was helpless?

Andrew listened to the wind, and smiled deeply to himself. It was the voice of promise and deliverance, of freedom and peace. It was the voice of the holy earth. He had never experienced any spiritual reaction in church, or in his Sunday school, and had hardly listened to the sermons. But now he remembered something: *Be still, and know that God is.* He was not certain if this was the exact quotation, but he understood it. *Be still, and know that God is,* and knowing, know that the earth is one with Him, and He with the earth.

CHAPTER 7

NEXT DOOR to Andrew's room was the linen and storage room, beyond that a "guest chamber," which no guest had ever occupied, and beyond the guest chamber was Phoebe Upjohn's room. In some way—though it is doubtful whether Phoebe had ever asked for it outright—the room was one of the best, if not the best, in the house. Phoebe always managed to obtain the nicest thing available, whether it was food or clothing, a piece of jewelry or a delicate length of lace, even if no one ever recalled that she had demanded it. Agreeable gifts, and events, appeared to flow toward Phoebe involuntarily. She had a sweet selfishness, which had a hypnotic effect on the others, and made them strain to give her her spoken, or unspoken desires.

So Phoebe had the best room in the house, if not the largest. It was not afflicted by the long, narrow aspects of the other rooms, so gloomy, chill and depressing. In contrast, it was square, and faced the south, so that any wandering beam of sunlight always found its way there. Amanda's girlhood furniture filled it, a pretty rosewood desk inlaid with ivory, a small handsome commode, whose doors were painted with a delicate scene of sporting cupids and flowers, a rosewood bookcase, two graceful little damask chairs, a handsome tapestried wing chair, a carved wardrobe of mahogany, and a beautiful canopied bed, draped in pale yellow satin with a white fringe. Here and there dainty little footstools, worked in the most meticulous petit-point, were scattered about the room, available for Phoebe's small feet. Pale yellow rosebuds were scattered on the soft green wallpaper, which Phoebe had especially chosen in Philadelphia, and there was a wide dim green rug, scattered with yellow roses, also unaccountably purchased on the occasion of a visit to that city. Two large windows, close together, had been draped with yellow satin to match the canopy of the bed. The satin was old and cracked, but this was hardly visible. All in all, it was a charming room, and Phobe nestled in it like a bee in a flower.

Phoebe, like all the others in the household, was not asleep tonight. She lay, curled cosily under her mother's best quilts and eiderdown puff, and listened contentedly to the wind. She was a luxurious little creature, sedulously careful of herself, and she liked to hear a storm outside while she was here so snugly sheltered and warm. Her head, pressed deep in the warmth of the pillows, hummed with thoughts. They hummed with thoughts of her father, Charles.

Poor Papa. She was so very sorry that he was dead. She pictured him lying in the cold earth, so yellow and so wet, while the wind howled over him. She curled herself more closely together under the heap of quilts and puffs, and loved the cosiness with a voluptuous enjoyment. How dreadful it was to be dead! It made being alive and safe so wonderful, so delightful. She could feel the contact of the smooth linen on her arms and feet, and against her cheek, and revelled in it.

Her eyes smarted a little, and she remembered the tears she had shed. She had cried because she was emotional, and because she knew she looked so helpless and pathetic when she wept, and that everyone's attention would be turned to her in consolation. But really, poor Papa! It was sad he was dead. He must hate it so, if he knew. Phoebe, always so pious in church, always ready with an appropriate text, sincerely doubted whether her father had any conscious existence now. She wished, for an instant, that he knew he was dead. In a way, it would enhance her own cosiness under the quilts. She ran her hand gently over the swell of her young hips, and smiled in the darkness.

Poor Mama. It was so silly that Mama had never known anything at all about Papa, Papa with his worn, greenish cloak, and his eloquent gestures, and his precious way of speaking. Phoebe giggled softly, then stifled her mouth with the edge of the quilt. Stupid Melissa, who looked at her father with the shining eyes of a saint. If she, Phoebe, had had only a little more time, then Melissa would have been quite out in the cold. Melissa was growing old now, and no one but Phoebe knew how Charles had hated age, wrinkled and dry skins, and how he delighted in fresh beauty.

Again, Phoebe giggled. She thought how clever her papa had been, and she, his little daughter, was just like him. They knew how to get their way, how to make fools do their bidding gladly, without even a lift of the voice, or a struggle. Only imbeciles fought for what they wanted, shouting, and getting upset over the slightest object, when all that was necessary was to keep the voice soft, to remain helpless and touching, to smile sweetly and affectionately. Papa was so clever; Phoebe had very early learned her lessons from him.

She had really liked Papa. He was so amusing, but not in the way he had seemed amusing to others. It quite diverted her to watch him getting his way with silly old Melissa and Mama, though he had lately left Mama to her, just as she, Phoebe, had rarely encroached on Melissa. Yes, she had liked Papa. It was better than a play, watching him. He was such a wonderful actor, so much more clever than all the stupid rest of the world. She had learned many adroit things from him. She had learned to be cheerful and sweet-tempered, to appear to bow before the will of "stronger" people, to pretend to be pliable and helpful and eager to please. By obeying Mama with soft smiles, by displaying an anxiety to be useful, by acceding with a "yes, dear Mama," she had gotten this lovely room, a wardrobe full of dainty gowns, three gold bangles, a spangled net for her hair, eight pairs of the prettiest slippers, and a whole commode full of dainty petticoats and chemises.

Phoebe had known her own power, as Charles had known his. She frowned now in the darkness. She had not possessed quite all of Charles' patience. She was not always content to allow the stupid "strong" to believe in their strength. There were times when the very sight of Melissa, competent, haughty and severe, going about Charles' affairs as if only she were important to him, had irked Phoebe almost beyond endurance. She had longed to "take her down a peg," just for the sake of demonstrating her own secret potency.

Phoebe was no fool, nor had she ever been the sweet little idiot the others in the household had believed her to be. She had a certain flair for the lovely word, a certain frail perceptiveness of beauty. Her isolated life had compelled her to read widely and, as she was of a very superficially romantic temperament, she liked the more airy poetry. A few years ago she had, for her own pleasure and self-satisfaction, begun to string fragile and colorful words together. Then, too, she was very deft. She could take one of Keats' or Shelley's lesser-known poems, rearrange, alter a word or two here and there, rephrase a certain line, and have quite an artless little poem of her own. It was part of her cleverness that she could plagiarize without detection, and a tribute to her remarkable cunning that she could remain unexposed. She had no true inspiration of her own.

A year before, love had come to Phoebe, in the narrower

sense of the word, for young John Barrett, a childhood friend, had suddenly, with Phoebe's assistance, been made aware of her beauty. John was the grandson of old Mr. Barrett, who owned one of the richest and most prosperous farms the other side of Midfield. No one, least of all John, had expected that old Mr. Barrett would leave the farm to the young man, for John was the son of Mr. Barrett's only daughter, whom he had hated. Upon her death, and her husband's in Philadelphia, John had been brought to the farm with the grudging consent of the old man; who had immediately set him to work from dawn to sunset and had treated him so cruelly that indignation had been widespread in the community, even at a time when it was considered wise and proper not to spare the rod in the bringing up of a child. John was not allowed to eat with his grandfather; he must eat with the surly housekeeper in the kitchen and be subject to her blows. He slept in a cold attic, among ancient trunks, discarded furniture, and rats. His clothing was rags. But somehow he had been able to acquire an education of a sort and had grown up to be a dignified and gentlemanly young man. He had eventually gained admiration for his own sake, in spite of the pity of the community. When his grandfather died, and it was discovered that he was the heir to all that rich nest, the money in the bank, the fine old house, the fat acres, the shrewdly bought stocks and bonds and the excellent horses, admiration and pity had become respect and approbation.

He had always peeped at Phoebe in church, though she had never turned a direct glance on his frayed shabbiness, big red hands and big muddy boots. But his grandfather had not been dead two weeks before she was peeping at him in return, and blushing all over her pretty bright face.

Before the year was out, Phoebe, to her own immense satisfaction and Amanda's joy, was formally betrothed to John Barrett. The others in the family had merely smiled vaguely, had not given the matter much thought until Phoebe had produced her poems.

Then Melissa had begun to speak with passionate scorn of John Barrett, "that soulless farmer, that clod, that lout!" Phoebe must live a transcendental life of poetry, dedicated to the service of something beyond herself. She must abandon the very thought of marriage to John Barrett. Melissa took Phoebe's life competently into her hands and daily, impatiently, urged that Phoebe send John packing. Phoebe had promised, in a small soft voice. For the first time, fear came to her, fear that Melissa might, after all, really be strong and dominant. But it was a passing fear, and after a while Phoebe was merely amused and contemptuous.

She knew a crisis would soon arise. Then Charles had died.

Again, Phoebe, remembering, smiled luxuriously in the dark. It was very thoughtful of Papa to die so conveniently. There would be no need, now, of engaging in distasteful combat with Melissa. Even silly Melissa would know that it was necessary for Phoebe to marry, to marry at once, and to marry John Barrett. So Phoebe would be spared a contretemps, and, like her father, she always avoided a contretemps whenever possible. It was much pleasanter to get one's way by apparent compliance.

She thought of John Barrett, and now a glow moved over her body. I am truly fond of John, she thought. He must never be sorry that he chose me. Thanks to dear Mama, I am a most excellent housekeeper. I shall, of course, make many changes in that old house, and we are going to be very happy indeed. Doubtless, John will take me to New York often and, later, we shall travel.

She was so pleased with her thoughts and with the visions they had conjured up that she began to cry into her pillow. Softened and happy, she wept for her father, and thought how frightful it was that he was dead. Of course, silly Melissa would have no one at all now, and it was what she deserved, with her haughty ways and her overbearing manners. She would discover that she had no power at all, really. It served her right.

The wind groaned somberly in the eaves, and Phoebe slept, a smile on her face.

CHAPTER 8

AMANDA'S ROOM, which she had once shared with Charles, overlooked the wide bleak lawns and the torn elms, also the distant road, the flowing meadows beyond, and the great brown hills. Narrow and long, it lay over the drawing-room below and was lighted by a thin tall window at each end. Here Amanda had hung her mother's somberest draperies of dark crimson, now threadbare but still elegant, and here she had placed her mother's own bedroom furniture, all heavy black walnut of ponderous size and weight; with dim narrow mirrors reaching almost to the ceiling. Handmade rugs, also dark of hue, had been scattered over an oaken floor so polished and so old that it appeared made of dusky glass. Amanda had hung dimmed portraits of her parents, her grandparents, her great-grandmother and one illustrious great-grandfather on the faded gray walls. Against a far wall, near her great-grand-father's black and enormous desk, her father's and her grandfather's fine old books stood in a black walnut bookcase with glass doors.

From the very beginning, Charles had hated this room, and had expressed himself eloquently about it. So it had been no great shock when, fifteen years later, he had withdrawn from it and had taken to sleeping in his frowsy study. Amanda had not commented on this abandonment, but sharp lines began to appear about her stern mouth. Modesty, delicacy, self-restraint, kept her silent. Later, marks of suffering would shadow her pale eyes when she saw Melissa with Charles and observed how the girl spent long hours with her father in his study. So it was that Amanda, always known for her good sense, her practical and realistic outlook, began to be blinded by her emotions. She did not blame Charles; she had never been able to blame him. She blamed Melissa.

She lay, rigid and ice-cold, in her wide hard bed, and stared at one of the shadowy windows. She listened to the wind and the rain. Her worn hands under their cambric ruffles were clenched together. All her body seemed clenched, every muscle drawn like hard rope, as she silently struggled against her desolation and despair.

How starkly vivid her life lay before her, like pinnacled rocks on a desert! She remembered so many things now. She remembered the anxious face of her father when she had told him of her coming marriage to Charles. "My dear girl," he had said, "you know nothing of this man. Yes, I know that we are well acquainted with his background and family, which I admit are impeccable. We know he is considered a very erudite scholar and writer. But we know nothing else. I have known him for many years, yet still I do not know him. Why? Because he will not let himself be known! Why? He is of a good reputation; they speak highly of him in New York, elaborating on his good temper, his education, his brilliant qualities of mind. There is nothing murky or reprehensible in his history. Yet he hides himself. Is it shyness? No. I know shyness. Is it reserve, which we have always admired? No. It is not reserve. It is something else, and I fear it for you. There is something dangerous and wrong in a man who will not let himself be known even by those closest to him, even by those he professes are his friends."

Amanda could see her father now, so clearly. Tall, lean, clad in black broadcloth, he stood before the black marble fireplace in their home in Boston. He had a thin gray beard, meticulously cut and shaped, and he had pale bright eyes, penetrating yet kind. He stood with his back to the fire, his coat-tails draped over his arms, leaning towards his daughter, with trouble on his narrow white face.

Nevertheless, she had married Charles, and had loved him, and still loved him. Her father had been wrong. Never once had Charles used an ugly word to her; never once had he displayed angry impatience or lack of consideration or cruelty. He had always been full of gentleness and reason, always courteous, always pliable and considerate. He had striven to shield her from every anxiety, had invariably displayed fondness for her, his every word had been humorous and kind. Yet she had been most desperately unhappy.

But why? she cried out to the wind and the darkness, with anguish in her heart. Charles had been perfect. There had been no flaw in him. The reason for her misery lay elsewhere, as she had always known. The misery lay with Melissa, who, from earliest childhood, had seized upon Charles, had appropriated him, had turned him away from his other daughter, his son, and his wife. (Oh, Charles! Charles!)

Amanda's heart beat with thick violence and pain, with dark emotion. It was as if a black obliterating hand were moving over her struggling mind, which tried to see something she most enormously wished to deny. She felt the denial in herself but, in her agony, gave it another name. She called it hatred for Melissa, who had taken Charles away from his wife.

When had Melissa begun to haunt her father's study? It must have been when she was ten years old or so. Charles had first taught her her lessons in the dining-room, by candle-light and firelight, in the long winter days. Then they had gone up to his study, where "there was more quiet," to quote Charles. Phoebe and Andrew were young and noisy, and Charles had claimed, with an affectionate smile, that it was impossible to conduct lessons in that atmosphere. Thereafter, Melissa and her father had immured themselves upstairs, with the shut door like an immovable barrier. But, strangely, he continued to teach Phoebe and Andrew in the dining-room.

Amanda had not complained. It was not in her nature. Besides, on the surface, it was "reasonable." As early as twelve, Melissa had become her father's amanuensis. She answered his letters in her sharp and angular handwriting, so clear and un-compromising. Yes, it had all been very reasonable, and Amanda had been taught by her New England father to respect reason above all other things. She had told herself firmly that she was absurd, when she began to repine at her loneliness and isolation, at the long empty hours. She saw Charles less and less. He was always in his study with Melissa, and when she passed the door she could hear the murmur of their voices, Charles' rich humorous tones, Melissa's quiet firm answers. There was an intimacy in the sounds which vaguely frightened Amanda, she did not know why. She did not know that she was afraid.

Remembering, her face grew damp again, as if with terror. She thought: I should have rescued Charles from her. I ought not to have been so restrained. I let Melissa destroy him, close him away from his family, deny him the warmth of a family life. He was always so compliant, my dear husband! Always so generous, so afraid of giving pain, so soft in the hands of a firm character! He would not hurt Melissa.

I have never been able to love Melissa. Even when she was a very young child she was cold and insensitive, turning from every proffered affection save that offered by her father. She never had a friend; she repulsed the friendly gestures of other children. She haunted her father, until she utterly conquered him. Never have I had a tender word from her; never did she consider her little sister, or her brother, until the day she laid her wicked hands on my Phoebe's life, until she sent Andrew from his home for an education he does not want. One by one, she eleminated us from Charles' life and absorbed him unto herself. Now she is trying to destroy my son and my daughter, and this time, Papa, I shall fight to the death, as I ought to have fought before.

Amanda flung aside her sheets and her quilts, and sprang to the floor. She walked up and down in her bare feet. She moaned a little.

The sound of her feet was dull and feverish below the voice of the wind and the rain. She wrung her wet hands; her throat ached from her harsh and rushing breath. The black hand moved away from her mind and now, suddenly, she saw everything!

"My God!" she cried aloud, in wondering torment. "How could I have been so blind? How could I have allowed my life to be destroyed so, and my children's lives? How could I have let Melissa be destroyed before my very eyes?"

Horror seized her, and she covered her face with her hands.

Melissa! Charles had first destroyed his wife, and then had destroyed Melissa! But such a small and obscure triumph, such a tiny field for cruelty and malignance! He was a man of gifts; he could have broadened his destruction had he wished. Yet he was content with this poor, small conquest, this conquest of a lonely woman and a girl. Had he so base a heart, so narrow a mind, that this contented him? Or did he know that he did not possess the power to do harm to more than us?

Shame for Charles filled her, as well as horror. She sat down in a chair near a window, and shivered violently. She thought of the web that always seemed to smother her whenever she had tried to enter into a contest with Charles. She saw that Melissa was completely swathed in that web. Was Melissa lost? Was it too late?

Geoffrey Dunham had asked her consent in his suit for Melissa. Again, Amanda's face was wet; she sat up, stared urgently into the darkness. And she had warned him against the girl! Amanda pressed her clenched hands to her lips as if to try to recall the words she had spoken. She remembered Geoffrey's faint, enigmatic smile. Had there been compassion in his eyes, wonder at her blindness? Yes, she was sure of that. He had known. He had always known.

"Melissa!" she cried into the darkness, the tears spilling over her face. "My child! My child!"

She stood up again, returned to her bed, and threw herself upon it in utter and despairing abandon. She thought, incoherently, how she had been deprived of even an honest widowhood, for she could not mourn her husband. She could not remember him with pride and with trust. She thought of the women she knew who had lost their husbands, and she remembered their tears, their proud words of love. They had their consolation in their memories. She had nothing. How innocent she had been, how ingenuous! Her husband's face swayed before her, benign, gently smiling, and now she saw how inscrutable and hooded his eyes had been. He had lived a secret and ominous life of his own, yet he had put out a silent and corrupting finger to destroy others, others who never knew they were being destroyed. She squeezed her own eyes together to shut out his face, she cried aloud: "No, Charles, no, no!" All her robbed heart raised itself like a shield before the memory of him.

After a long time, weak and trembling, she pushed herself to her feet, threw her woolen wrapper over her nightdress, and crept out into the hall. The scent of the funeral flowers lingered there and she closed her nostrils against it. The dark hall was silent; somewhere a mouse gnawed, she heard the running of the water in the eaves, the forlorn crying of the wind, the strident ticking of the clock below. The old house creaked as if a legion of ghosts were walking up and down the stairs and over the ancient floors. A spectral chill blew over Amanda, fluttered her garments about her feet. She felt, rather than saw, the cold doors shut against her as she stood alone in the hall listening to the faint sounds all about her. She crept on, reached Melissa's door. No light showed through the crack. Amanda pressed her trembling palm against the icy wood and all her spirit went through the door to her daughter.

She stood there a long time, until her flesh was heavy with cold, and her heart too numb with pain to feel anything.

CHAPTER 9

MELISSA'S BEDROOM windows, two of them, narrow and tall like slots, looked out at the dreary side garden, the long road that wound down to Midfield, and a series of stark brown meadows. The room was furnished with Spartan austerity; in fact, so bleak was it that one of discernment would have suspected that there was just a little innocent pretension, a little preciousness, in the meagerness of furniture, the uncarpeted floor, the skimpiness of draperies, the lack of decoration and feminine prettinesses. Large, cold, filled with a glare of hard north light during the day, and with a crepuscular shadowiness in the mornings and early evenings, not even a fire could heat it adequately. Melissa herself had painted the walls a dull gray, making them resemble the walls of a monk's cell. Over the brown marble fireplace, itself a miserable monstrosity, she had hung a fairly good print of the Mona Lisa, a present from her father. There were no other pictures or portraits on the bare walls, nor did the mantelpiece boast more than a pair of large pewter candlesticks filled with fat candles. The fireplace equipment was rusted steel, even the fender. Near the hearth was a Boston rocker, innocent of cushion, its legs splintered and worn. A great rickety wardrobe in a far corner held Melissa's few garments and her other pair of shoes. The commode was innocent of linen scarf; two dingy towels hung on its rails. Its china pitcher and bowl, without decoration, stood on the top, scrupulously clean if well cracked.

Beside them lay Melissa's comb and brush, her soap in a white dish, and above it hung a small distempered mirror in a wooden frame. She had no bureau. Between the two windows was her desk, wide flat, stained, at which she examined and corrected her father's manuscripts and prepared them for postage. She had a single inkpot, a blotter, and an old quill pen. In the center of the bare room stood her hard, narrow, tester bed, starkly made, and covered with a quilt. Not for Melissa any counterpane, fringed or draped.

One whole wall was occupied by a long bookcase, literally jammed with books, classics, reference works, poetry, travelogues, Roman poets in the Latin originals, French books, German books, an ancient encyclopedia, and, on a shelf by themselves, Charles' books, in fine calf with gold tops.

Melissa believed passionately in views, and in order not to obstruct her view of the countryside below she had resisted Amanda's suggestions for full and heavy draperies at the windows. Consequently, the girl had hung thin sparse curtains of pale brown linen at the windows, and had thrust them so far back that they were hardly more than crumpled ropes. Melissa never closed her shutters, even on the coldest nights. She liked to watch the desolate moon rising in the midnight winter skies, and to catch the first shallow morning light as it crept over the earth.

Charles called it affectionately "my nun's cell." He hated fripperies, he had said. Frivolities were not for Melissa, with her Greek mind and stern, dedicated life. So Charles said. He had begun to deride feminine trappings and conceits to Melissa during her very earliest childhood, so that any secret longings beginning to arise in her child's mind for pretty garments, handsome rugs or delicate colors had been effectually crushed. Once he caught her furtively embroidering a scarf for her commode and tatting lace for her pillowcases, and he had expressed such a gentle disgust, such a soft derision, that she had instantly thrown the things into the fire and had remembered them thereafter with flushings of shame.

It was at Charles' suggestion that Melissa had pulled back her hair so severely from the hard if noble planes of her face and knotted it grimly at the nape of her neck. Once she had tied it with a blue ribbon. Charles had given the ribbon one hurt and disappointed glance, and it, too, was tossed into the fire. Later, he had said gently, as if grieved: "Would you tie a ribbon about the head of a Greek statue, my darling?"

It was Charles who early had told Melissa that he despised the trumperies of silly females who had nothing but vapid thoughts in their heads. It was Charles who said that the man and woman of "true mind" thought of garments as necessary coverings only and protections from inclement weather. Melissa had gravely agreed with him, and had quelled any wistful yearnings of her own.

Once Amanda had looked Charles squarely in the eye and had said in a low tone: "One would suspect that you desire that Melissa may never marry, that she present herself as an ugly spectacle in the eyes of gentlemen. Assuredly, she dresses to please you, and as a result she is hideous." But Charles had returned Amanda's look with one of astonished bewilderment and had left his wife with a very visible quivering of his full mouth. Later, he had condescended to say: "My dear Amanda, it is regrettable that you do not discern that Melissa has a statuesque beauty of her own which should not be marred by stupid ruffles and laces, bangles and hoops. If you do not see that, then I am truly sorry for you. As for marriage, it will delight me if Melissa obtains a man worthy of her. Unless she does, it would much better for her to remain a spinster."

What Amanda did not know (if she had known she would have struggled with Charles long ago for the girl's soul) was that Charles had begun a sinister campaign against marriage for Melissa when she had been but fourteen years old. He had opened his campaign with wistful hints of the misery one of mind must endure when mated with one who has no eye above material and mundane things. His hints were accompanied by sighs, by martyred but resigned gestures, by smiles that implored sympathy and understanding. Melissa's single heart, intrinsically so passionate, so trusting and so pure, had understood, and the intense tenderness she felt for her father in his wretchedness began to grow into an intolerant hatred for her mother who so afflicted him.

From the particular, Charles moved on to the general. Marriage at its best was a wearisome thing, enchaining, stultifying, frustrating. It was for those who had no aim but the aim of an animal. The cultivated mind bogged down in the marsh of matrimony, became overlaid with slime and, finally, was choked to death. Matrimony, then, was the final refuge of mediocrity and dullness; it rusted the bright sword of spiritual or objective adventure; it murdered the winged soul; it hung weights of lead on the leaping feet; it substituted for the lustrous pages of poetry the dead ledgers of the commonplace. It was not for the man or woman of sensibility and refinement, and certainly not for those who looked at radiant horizons.

All this was for Melissa's pre-adolescent stage. Charles had considerable acuteness; he knew that an essential purity lived in the very young and innocent. He knew that the virgin mind quivered like a butterfly in the wind, that is was horrified at grossness, violently repelled by any obscene suggestion, that it shrank from the touch of hot coarse hands. Now, with the utmost delicacy, Charles began to suggest to the girl that marriage in itself was a loathsome and obnoxious thing. How frightful it was, he suggested, that one of sensitiveness should willingly allow herself to be despoiled. He used no words that even Amanda might have objected to, but he was a master of innuendo, of gesture, of expression. Melissa felt herself burning with shame and horror and disgust.

She was appalled that she could bring these visions to her mind, and felt in herself a sickening sense of guilt and aversion. After a while, she could not brush against a young man's arm in church, could not even look upon a young man, without that flaming sensation of guilt, without that overpowering aversion. When a young man of the neighborhood dared suggest that he call upon her, she would glare at him with such repugnance and with such a fire in her eyes that he would shrink away and carefully avoid her in the future. When Amanda began to refer pointedly to the fact that Melissa was in her twenties, that she was already a confirmed spinster and ought to be considering a husband now if ever, Melissa would flee the room as if in fear of open violation, and, finding her father, would throw herself into his arms with a burst of terrified weeping.

At twenty-five, Melissa still had the innocence of a child, but it was now a cold warped innocence corrupted by lies. It was an innocence which had been seduced into a kind of perversion, an innocence wholly unnatural. To her, all men but her father were polluting monsters, gross and abominable, from which all women should flee in dread and abhorrence. Just how any man could "pollute" her she did not know. She only knew that the experience would be beyond endurance, as her father had so subtly suggested.

In her strange innocence it never occurred to her to question how her father had brought his delicate soul to the point of begetting children. She was immured in her virginity like a nymph in a tree, her spirit daily growing more fibrous, her gestures turning to wood.

Melissa lay in her bed, listening to the wind, listening to the rain lashing her windows. She lay there, cold and rigid as frozen earth, her breath slow and shallow against the beating onslaught of grief, unable to move for fear of again precipitating a violent and shaking chill.

She cried out in herself for her father. She was alone now, forever. Her loneliness, her desolation, were chains that held her stiff and icy upon her bed. She caught herself listening for her father's step, even while she knew she would never hear it again. She listened for the crackle of his papers in the study next door, the stabbing of the poker against burning wood, the creak of the musty couch, the closing of his shutters against the night. But she heard only the wind and the rain.

"Papa, Papa," she whispered, and her voice was a dry rustle in the dank silence of the room. The sound increased her anguish. She gripped the edge of her quilts with straining hands.

"What am I to do now, Papa?" she whispered. "Papa, how am I to live without you? You interpreted everything for me. Now I am left without a tongue, blind and deaf. I never had anyone but you."

The silence thickened about her, became smothering water. She gasped, feeling herself about to choke. Her heart palpitated, faltered, sank to a heavy, dull beat. Suddenly she saw the raw open grave again and the coffin being lowered into it. She cried out feebly, flung her hand over her eyes as if to shut away the vision. Now her bed shook with her trembling. "No, no," she said aloud, while her mind answered: "Yes, yes."

If I were only dead, she thought. Dead and sightless and senseless. Anything was preferable to this torture, this knowledge that for her all life had died. How was it possible ever to sleep again, knowing that she would awaken each morning to fresh desolation and pain, knowing that no matter where she walked she would never see her father, no matter how intently she listened she would never hear his voice? The dreadful days lay before her, the dreadful years, of emptiness. For her, there would never be another morning, another sunset, another spring. She would walk in grayness, in perpetual winter, until the day when she would gratefully die. She would never again see beauty, for her father had been her eyes. There would be no music in the wind or in the sky, for he had been her ears. She would move mutely in shadows, her outstretched and searching hands touching nothing. Until the day when she would die.

I cannot go on, she thought. Surely, one did not have to live if one wished to die. There was no law compelling her to endure the sightless and the soundless years.

I have only the past to remember, she said to herself, and in remembering the past my life will be unendurable.

She and Charles had hated the farm. It was to him a prison, he had told her mournfully, a prison which he must endure because his wife had willed it. He hated the long empty road which led to the "horrible, stupid village," as he called it. He hated the motionless days, he who had been accustomed to the bright and seething life of a great city. He hated the nights, in which nothing ever happened, in which there were no friends to gather about the fire and laugh and talk and sip wine. He hated the way the weeks glided into one another, faceless, eventless. He had been condemned to this, condemned to look at the uninspiring earth, condemned to exile because of the hard resolution of a woman without sensibility. He had not said this in so many words, for Charles was too expert in insinuation to be so tactless and so brutal. But he had conveyed it all to Melissa, who, through him, had hated their life and the farm, had guessed his misery though she had not heard it in so many words. Charles had trusted no one. He was not a man to commit his security to any hands, even the hands of one who loved him. He did not want to wait uneasily for the possible day when Melissa might, in a passion, quote him to Amanda, either in a moment of championing him or while deliberately betraying him in a bitter disillusion. He had a very healthy respect for Amanda, and knew just how far he might go with her.

He had often talked to Melissa of New York, Boston and Philadelphia, conveying to her credulous mind scenes of excitement and sophistication and charm which did not exist, and which he knew did not exist. But it had been agreeable to him to watch her face darken or glow with longing and wistfulness, and he had smiled to himself a little as he understood how she ached, despairingly, to be off this farm and among the scenes he had invented. She did not know that she was being cruelly tantalized; she thought her father was merely trying to enliven her miserable and isolated life. When he described balls, and splendid parlors, and assemblages in which he had shone and had been courted and flattered, the poor girl bridled with pride and joy. Then, though she did not detect it, Charles would look at her inscrutably under his full and heavy lids, and would smile curiously to himself, as in some secret contempt.

"One of these days, my love, when I become truly rich and

famous, you and I shall go off together to New York, perhaps
to live there for the rest of our lives," he would say, touching
her cheek tenderly with the back of his hand. Melissa would
look at him with pale but strong ardor, and catch her breath.
Even at twenty-five, she had still believed this might come
true. There was no end to her innocence.

And now, she thought, as she lay in her bed, it is all over
before it ever began. My father will never live in the places
he longed for. Even if he became famous—now—it will be too
late for him and for me.

It was all her mother's fault! Why had she clung so obsti-
nately to this appalling and wretched land, to this hideous
house so utterly without graciousness, beauty, or even warmth?
If it had not been for Amanda, Charles might still be alive.
He had died of a broken heart, having been denied what he
desired by an unfeeling and arrogant woman.

Melissa turned her head and pressed her shaking mouth into
the pillow, while all her body arched and trembled with hatred
for her mother. How often had Amanda begged, even insisted, that Charles write the disgusting "popular" articles
requested of him by various newspapers and periodicals!
Charles had always gently refused, and Amanda had thrown
up her hands in despair. She never knew him, she never understood him. Melissa sobbed incoherently into her pillow. She
broke his heart with her stupidity; she killed all his ambition;
she made a mockery of what was so sacred to him. What could
she, Amanda, know of beauty and loveliness?

As clearly as if it were happening again, Melissa suddenly
remembered a certain twilight of the last winter. She and
Charles, jaded after long hours of work over his latest manuscript, had thrown on cloak and shawl and had gone out into
the air. It had been a wild and stormy day of wind and snow,
but now a great stillness lay over the white land and seemed
caught in the empty branches of the trees. Charles and Melissa
moved slowly over the soft and soundless earth, and then had
stood quietly, hand in hand, looking out over the marble desolation of meadow, field and distant hill. There was no sound
at all, no movement.

Then, very slowly, very subtly, the sky changed. It turned
to a dark grayish-lavender, deepening to a smoky purple towards the west. And now a weird, mauve light fell on the snow,
darkened to somber heliotrope on the hills. It appeared to
become translucent, that mauve light, so that everything took
on a dreamlike transparency and unreality. It was not beautiful, though Melissa told herself that it was. There was even

something nightmarish about it, something portentous, something that struck on her heart with overwhelming depression.

"It is like my life," Charles had said, very softly. The curious dead radiance lay on his face, so that there was a suggestion of death in the hollows of his eyes and about his mouth.

Melissa had clutched his hand almost convulsively. She said: "Yes! Yes, I know. How terrible it is."

She had looked at her father, then, in her depression. And she saw that he was smiling at her tenderly. She remembered that smile very clearly. But now she remembered something else, and her mouth left the pillow and she stared into the darkness. Charles had looked at her, and his eyes were oddly bland and secret, as if he had momentarily peeped from behind a disguise and was laughing at her silently.

Melissa sat up abruptly in her bed, still staring emptily before her. It was at that moment that Amanda put her hand on her daughter's door and sent her searching despair into the room.

No, no, thought Melissa confusedly, pushing back her hair from a damp forehead. It was that horrible light. I didn't remember it then. I am imagining it now. It was certainly the light—Or my imagination. Why should Papa have been laughing at me?

She fell back on her pillows. Her heart was beating in the strangest way, as if it were frightened, straining to drag her away, on a long flight, from some great danger. She pressed her hands to her breast to quiet that terrified beating. I am sick, she told herself. I am half out of my mind with grief.

The wind surged against the windows, seemed to force itself into the room and beat down against the girl's breath. Her eyes grew dim; the lids fell. Her breathing became slower, and she dropped into the sleep of exhaustion. Her last thought was: Phoebe, Andrew. I must get them away from this awful place, for Papa's sake. And then, in her dreams, uneasy and broken, she imagined she was running away, running into darkness from something that threatened and followed her.

CHAPTER 10

AMANDA UPJOHN sat in her dim cold parlor and looked at her children sitting in a semicircle before her.

The rain had stopped with the wind, at dawn, and now,

at ten o'clock in the morning, a dull brownish light lay over the barren landscape and stood at the tall narrow windows. Again a meager and comfortless little fire burned on the hearth. In contrast with the thundering storm of last night, the silence seemed breathless and pent. Amanda wore her heavy black shawl over her mended black bombazine. Phoebe was wrapped in woolly white depths, Andrew had dressed himself in his stiff Sunday best, as if realizing that this family gathering was very important. But Melissa sat stiffly in her own funeral black, shawlless, her hands folded in her lap.

Amanda's dry-rimmed eyes moved slowly from one to another of her children. They became mournful as they touched Phoebe, somberly thoughtful as they reached Andrew, and strange and intense when they finally fixed themselves on Melissa, who stared motionless at the floor. Yet still as the girl sat, almost without breathing, wrapped in her own heavy torment, she had about her an enigmatic vigilance, and Amanda knew that she was waiting, inexorable as always. However, Amanda was not infuriated, as she might have been a few days ago. For now she saw that there was something unbearably pathetic about her elder daughter, and she looked away from her with a sick pang.

Then her lips tightened sternly, and she said in a low firm voice: "I have asked you all to come here, Phoebe, Andrew, Melissa, because, as you realize, we find ourselves in a very desperate state. We all know the extent of the fortune your father has left us, or, I should say, the lack of fortune." She stopped, because she could not speak of Charles now without a hard catch in her throat. She pressed her hands together very hard, reminded herself that this was no time for emotion, however bitter, and went on:

"As I told Geoffrey Dunham yesterday, it seems that we are practically beggars. We must look at our affairs without flinching or self-pity. We know what we have. We must plan what is best to do."

Melissa stirred, but very slightly, and her pale dry mouth opened a trifle, then closed again. She did not look at her mother, however.

"Had our position been less ominous," continued Amanda, "we might have allowed ourselves a quiet period of—mourning. But mourning, like almost everything else, is a luxury reserved for the secure and for those who have no pressing problems.

"Yes, desperate as is our plight, and though our debts are tremendous, we are not without hope, and for that we can thank God. Phoebe will be married in April to John Barrett, a most worthy young man, who can give her an excellent home and very adequate security. I regret, Phoebe, that you did not allow him to accompany us home—yesterday—when he desired it."

Phoebe peeped at her mother from under her bright ringlets, sniffled pathetically, and dropped her head. Her eyes were quite dry. Melissa lifted her own head sharply and fixed her eyes steadily on her mother.

Amanda sighed. "Well, Andrew, we must next come to you. We have this land, this farm, which is in a deplorable condition. But I have long thought that it needs only expert attention and care to provide for us quite comfortably. I am sure you can give this attention and this care, for I have often observed in the past that farming attracted you. You have your opportunity now, my son. You will not return to Harvard, and something tells me that you do not regret this."

Melissa lifted her right hand with a strong jerky movement. "May I speak?" she asked, and her voice was loud and harsh.

She expected a refusal from her mother, and moved to the edge of her seat as if to stand. She was extremely agitated, and now her breast rose and fell rapidly. But Amanda only looked at her and waited, and Melissa sat, one leg still in a rising attitude.

Melissa spoke again, and her voice broke: "There is something you have not considered, Mama, and that is Papa's wishes. You know that he has—had—great hopes for Phoebe, and it was settled among us that she was not to marry John Barrett, but to pursue her studies and her poetry."

She wrung her handkerchief between her hands in the extremity of her passionate determination to win her father's way.

"As for Andrew, it was completely understood that he was to finish his studies at law and obtain a post in Philadelphia, which was practically offered him by some of Papa's friends. You cannot, you must not, interfere—" She could not speak again, but could only sit poised on the edge of her chair, her head flung up, her pale face turned with implacable insistence upon her mother.

She expected Amanda's cold fury to pour over her. But Amanda merely gazed down at her hands as if in deep and heavy reflection. Then Amanda answered her daughter, and there was something sadly gentle in her tone:

"Melissa, there are many things I can tell you. The years are full of them. But this is not the time. Later, you will understand. I understand, and that is why I cannot listen to you or give consideration to any of your demands. You must all trust in my wisdom."

Melissa turned to her sister with a gesture of despair: "Speak, Phoebe. You know what you wish. You remember our talks with Papa. Tell Mama, now."

Phoebe bent her head lower. Her little red tongue touched her lips. Stupid, silly old Melissa! Of course I am going to marry Johnnie. It's time Melly was put in her place, and perhaps Mama, too, both of them deciding what I'd to do with my life! No, I won't give Mama that satisfaction now. I'll let old Melly believe that she can probably get her way. It will be all the more amusing when things topple over on her a few months from now.

Phoebe sobbed touchingly, covering her face with her handkerchief. "I don't know, truly. Papa said that I had such a gift."

A bright spark touched Melissa's urgent and pleading eyes. Amanda sat up very straight in her chair and stared at her younger daughter compellingly. But Phoebe would not look at her.

"Certainly," said Amanda, in a shaking voice, "I cannot force you to marry John Barrett, Phoebe, though you have given him your word. But I beg of you to consider, before you ruin your life with childish folly. We have no money. Unless we struggle very hard we shall not have even a home. Your poetry! What do you expect to do with it, child? Sell it? To whom?" Then the enormity of her daughter's words struck her with horror. "What are you saying, Phoebe?" she cried. "That you are not going to marry John?"

"Oh, I don't know!" sobbed Phoebe. "Oh, can't I be let alone?"

Amanda said nothing. She sat in her chair in a sudden stony silence. Melissa sprang to her feet, ran to Phoebe, knelt beside the girl, and pulled the golden head to her shoulder as if in passionate protection. Phoebe allowed herself to collapse against her sister, and cried.

Andrew had not spoken at all. He just sat there, looking slowly from his mother to his sisters, and his small, dark-blue eyes were very meditative. He wanted to smoke his old pipe; he longed with hunger for a smoke. His hand fumbled at his pocket. A sudden loud burst of sobs from Phoebe made him frown a little, impatiently. A man was out of place among a flock of women. He wished Phoebe would shut up, and he wished that Melissa would not be such a damn fool. He looked again at his mother and was about to speak, when Melissa exclaimed:

"Phoebe, dearest, do go to your room and rest for a while. Lie down, and after a little while I'll come to you and we can talk quietly." She stood up and helped Phoebe to her feet, then led the girl to the door. Phoebe clung to her in the most pathetic way, and Andrew, watching them, felt that something was out of place, false, in the touching picture of the young girl leaning against her sister. He was not a very subtle young man, but he sensed that something was not quite right. He frowned again, and his brown forehead wrinkled.

Amanda did not watch her daughters leave the room. She sat in her silence. She did not look up when, in a few moments, Melissa returned to her chair. She knew, without looking, that Melissa wore an air of proud vindication and determined conquest. But she felt no anger.

Melissa leaned against the back of her chair like a judge disposing of urgent cases. "Andrew," she said, "you haven't spoken. You know what Papa wished for you. You know the money that has been spent on you. Have you nothing to say?"

But Amanda answered for him: "There is no money. There is nothing for any of us but this land."

"We can sell the farm!" cried Melissa. "Papa always hated it, and so do I. We can sell it. We can move away from here, to Philadelphia, or to New York, while Andrew completes his studies and Phoebe writes her poems. I know she will sell them. I have absolute knowledge that she will. We can buy a little house in the city. I can myself, perhaps, obtain a situation as a teacher, or a governess. Papa has friends in Philadelphia who will help me obtain such a post. The money we can get for this farm will support all of us until Andrew has completed his law course and Phoebe has sold her book of poems to—to Mr. Dunham, and I have prepared Papa's last manuscripts for publication." Her voice began to shake with her emotion. "I can work on them at night, after my teaching duties are over. It is our only hope, to sell the farm—!"

She trembled, gripped the edges of her chair with her hands. Deliverance. Deliverance from this dreadful farm, this empty land, deliverance for Phoebe and Andrew and herself. In the stress of her excitement she almost forgot her grief as she fought for her father's wishes. Her face blazed, so that light seemed reflected from every strong delicate plane. A lock of her hair fell over on her forehead, and she brushed it aside with a gesture almost violent, as she stared at her mother, waiting for Amanda's reply.

Amanda said, coldly and clearly: "No. We shall stay on the farm. It is all we have. You must be mad, Melissa."

But Melissa went on, in her loud crying voice: "We can't waste Andrew's life! Papa had such a struggle to pay for this term, for Andrew. It—it is paid up to January. By that time the farm will be sold and we'll have money!"

Andrew thought: Yes, it is paid up to January. It would be a waste not to take advantage of that. I'll go, until January.

He had known very little wrath before in his life, very little anger. But as he looked at his mother, and then at Melissa, straining so wildly on her chair, he was filled with disgust and indignation. Damn women, anyway. They always made such an uproar. They decided everything, pushed themselves into the affairs of men with their clamoring tongues and their insistence. It was enough to make a man vomit.

He stood up, looming high into the dimness of the room like a prodigious presence. He said, and the sound of his own voice, strong and deep, startled even Melissa, and made her turn to him: "Suppose you, Mama, and you, Melissa, let me do a little thinking for myself? Suppose you let me decide what to do? I won't tell you my decision yet. But I can say this: I shall return to Harvard tomorrow, until January, at least."

"Oh Andrew!" cried Melissa, and tears of joy wet her eyes. "Andrew—"

"Andrew," said Amanda.

But Andrew made a gesture of complete weariness and aversion, and went out of the room slowly and heavily. They heard the door close after him. They did not see him shrug, in the hall outside, nor rub his hands together as if to remove something sticky and clinging. They did not see him put on his shabby heavy coat, and his broad-brimmed hat, and go out towards the stables in the rear.

Now there was only a long silence in the parlor. I have won, thought Melissa. I have fought, and won, for you, Papa. It shall all be as you wished. All.

Amanda had been sitting so quietly for so many minutes that it appeared that she dozed. Her dry and haggard face had fallen into lines of complete abstraction. Melissa watched her. It is all over, she said to herself. I have only to go now.

Amanda began to speak just as Melissa began to rise, and the girl sat down again, clenching her hands together.

"Melissa," said Amanda, without agitation or emotion, "you are quite mad. You think you have won. I can only tell you this: We shall not sell the farm. It is mine. Andrew cannot continue his studies. There will be no money. Whether Phoebe marries John Barrett or not is her own affair. She will come to her senses, I believe, when she discovers that there is no other escape for her from poverty and penury. Andrew will return to the farm. He can do nothing else. He will provide for us here. In any event, we are staying."

Melissa's clenched hands opened. She looked at her mother, and the wildest hatred and despair flashed into her eyes. "It is impossible, Mama! You can see how impossible it is. Have you no regard for Papa's wishes, no remembrance of his work and what he strove to do?"

Amanda moved her head ponderously in Melissa's direction. Her expression became somber and very still. "Yes, Melissa, I know now what he strove to do. I have learned all about it, before it is too late. I only pray to God it is not too late."

Stupefied, Melissa could only blink. She hardly heard her mother's words. She could only say to herself: There must be some way. I must find a way. An almost intolerable pain shot through her head.

"As for yourself, Melissa," Amanda continued heavily, "I can only say this: You are twenty-five years old. You are a woman past her first youth. You speak of obtaining a teaching position in Philadelphia. You are inexperienced. How much do you think anyone will pay you? What do you know of the world? Consider a moment. Do you believe that you can earn enough to support Phoebe and yourself and to let Andrew continue his studies, in the event that they go with you? I am beginning to understand Phoebe. I do not believe she takes her—poems"—and Amanda's lip twisted—"seriously. I do not believe she will go with you. Nor do I think that of Andrew, either. If you go, you go alone, probably to starvation and homelessness. You will go in your utter madness, and learn what you will inevitably learn."

A hard stone seemed to have settled crushingly on Melissa's chest. She could hardly breathe. She crouched in her chair. She looked at her mother with eyes hot with despairing hate. Oh, the obdurate, scheming woman, who had killed her husband with her implacability, who was now determined to destroy Phoebe and to deprive Andrew of his very life! There must be something, something, anything, to rescue her brother and her sister from the hands of this woman.

Then, for the first time, Melissa implored her mother: "Are you not going to think of Papa, not even for a moment?" She wrung her hands together.

Amanda's face changed as she heard the break in her daughter's voice and saw the hopeless gesture of importunity. She said steadily: "Yes, I am thinking of him. I am thinking of him a great deal, Melissa."

"Then why do you not remember what he wished for us?" cried the girl.

"I am remembering," said Amanda, and she looked away, and at the fire, and her expression became stern and resolute.

"Then why? Why, Mama?"

Amanda was silent. Melissa stood up. Amanda gave her a swift glance. "I cannot tell you why just now, Melissa. You would not understand. It would be too terrible for you. I can only reiterate: We are staying here, Phoebe, Andrew and I. If you go, you go alone. There is nothing you can do."

Melissa pressed her fingers hard against her eyes. When she dropped them, slowly, her face had become wizened with anguish. She looked exhausted and broken.

And now Amanda could not look at her daughter because of the pain she felt for her. "I hope you will not go, Melissa. I hope you will remain. I think you will, when you have had time to think." She paused: "I even think you will consider what I must tell you. An offer has been made for you."

There must be a way, thought Melissa. There must be some way I can rescue them. Then her mother's words penetrated to her stupefied brain, and she started back, with a look of horror.

"What are you saying?" she exclaimed, with incredulity. "An offer? What are you saying? An offer of marriage?"

She could not believe it. She could not believe this final enormity.

Amanda gazed at her steadfastly. "Yes, Melissa, an offer of marriage. I could not believe it myself, when it came to me yesterday. I can hardly believe it even now. But there it is."

Sick with outrage and shock, with overpowering mortification, Melissa flushed scarlet. She stammered: "It—it is not possible. There is no one who would dare. Who had the effrontery?"

"Effrontery?" Amanda turned in her chair and regarded her daughter with wrath. "You consider an honorable offer effrontery? But then, I ought to have known. Sit down, Melissa. You are trembling so violently that I am afraid you will fall. You are stupid, my girl, and I think the man who offered himself must be stupid, too. It is Geoffrey Dunham."

The silence that fell in the room was like the silence that follows a gigantic explosion. Slowly Melissa sank into the chair she had left. She sat there then, and could only look at her mother. She had become very white.

"Geoffrey Dunham," she whispered harshly. "Geoffrey Dunham!"

Amanda nodded grimly. "Unbelievable, isn't it? I agree with you. What could he want with you, Melissa? What is there about you that he could want? I asked him that myself, and he only smiled a little. Look at yourself, Melissa; think of yourself. What would he want with a woman like you, a foolish, blinded, deluded woman?" She said in herself: My child! My child! "A penniless woman, who knows nothing about anything?"

"He had the audacity," whispered Melissa. She closed her eyes as if to shut away her humiliation.

"He had the imbecility," said Amanda, forcing down her pain, "to want to marry you, to take you to his beautiful home, to surround you with every luxury, to give you whatever you desire, to dress you as you have never dreamed of being dressed, to put jewels about your neck and on your hands, to make you mistress of his house, to offer you all the world. He wanted to give you this in return for nothing. For nothing at all, Melissa. I do not understand it. It does not seem possible. He could not actually want a woman of twenty-five, with the inexperience of a child, totally lacking in grace, deliberately spurning any charm she might have, a woman who had never seen anything or known anything. A completely ignorant and silly woman. He, Geoffrey Dunham!"

"He dared insult me like that!" said Melissa, in a strained and choking voice.

Amanda stood up, flinging out her hands hopelessly. "You are quite mad, Melissa," she said. "I am afraid I can endure your company no longer."

She went out of the room, moving with her stiff stateliness, quietly closing the door behind her. She left Melissa sitting there before the meager fire, as still as if she had died.

Amanda climbed very slowly up to her room. Once there, she lay down on her bed, flaccid and overpowered with sick exhaustion and agony. After a while, she felt as though an iron knife, red with fire, had been plunged into her heart. I have lost, I have lost everything, she thought, before she fell into complete darkness.

CHAPTER 11

MELISSA FORCED herself to move sluggishly to the kitchen. Phoebe had gone to bed with her tears, and begged to be left alone. Melissa had heard her mother's door close while she had crouched in the parlor. She had remained there an hour, shivering, stunned by calamity. But it was nearly noon now. Someone must help Sally.

Old gray Sally looked up, and when she saw Melissa she grunted in a disagreeable fashion and muttered under her breath as she slammed an iron pot on the great brick range. She was extremely obese and untidy and insolent, and only the fact that she would accept very poor wages for the privilege of having her son, Hiram, on the premises, had kept her in the Upjohns' employ. She received eight dollars a month and her lodging, the latter consisting of two tiny slanting rooms under the eaves, which she occupied with her son. Sally was not reconciled to life, for all she was ignorant and gross and had never gone a step beyond Midfield. She had a chronic resentment against all humanity, against the farmhand husband who had deserted her some twenty-five years ago when she had been thirty, against the farming gentry in the carriages who glided by on the roads, against her broad, flat, whitish and bristled face, her uncouthness, her poverty, her homelessness, and most of all, against the Upjohns, who, she felt, had taken advantage of her impotent state. Didn't poor Hiram do all the farming now being done on this farm and receive nothing for it? Was it his fault that he wasn't "too bright"? Didn't she herself work and slave from sunrise to sunset for a pittance?

She hated all the Upjohns, with the growling and malignant hatred of the ignorant and the brutish for their betters. She had hated Charles, with his "fancy" and dainty ways, his air of a grand gentleman for all his shabby and wrinkled clothing; she detested Phoebe because the girl was lovely, Andrew because she believed him no brighter than her own son, "and he goin' off to that collidge," Melissa because of her bemused hauteur and domineering voice, and Amanda because she knew all about Sally and would stand no nonsense. To Amanda, she was obsequious and toadying, though she hated her more than she hated all the others. But she bullied Phoebe, showed her open contempt for Melissa, and had let Charles know, without reservations, that she thought him a pretentious fool and an exploiter of honest women. When Andrew had been reported missing during the war, she had gloated and chuckled deliciously to herself under the eaves. When Phoebe's engagement to John Barrett had been announced, Sally had been beside herself with rage and had spat upon the food she served in the long bleak dining-room. When Charles had died, she had rejoiced secretly, grinning furtively while the family had attended the funeral, rubbing her huge aproned belly with delight. It was "good for 'em," with their high and mighty ways and their hoity-toity voices. Sally had not been unaware of the family's poverty and insecurity, and she knew their desperate straits now. While alone in the kitchen, she had hummed exultantly. With their needin' Hiram for the farm, no fear that she, herself, would be discharged, in spite of their havin' no money. Maybe that grand lady of a Melissa would have to milk the cows now, and help with the garden, and churn butter. She, Sally, would have a talk with the mistress, complaining of her "rheumatism" and her increasing age and suggesting that, now that Phoebe would be marrying in the spring, she would be needing extra help with the chores. "I'll soon be a-milkin' my last cow," Sally had whispered hoarsely to herself, shaking her fist at the door of the parlor where Amanda was discussing the family affairs with her children. "I'll soon be a-doin' my last ironin' and my last emptyin' of their slops." Under Sally's threat of leaving, Amanda would have to accede. Sally knew her value to the Upjohns.

To Sally, as to others of her kind, the only difference between herself and others was the possession of money. Now that the Upjohns had nothing, they were no better than she, and she'd soon put 'em in their places and show that she was "as good as them, maybe better." Their breeding, their education, their books, the old piano which Poebe played with such grace in the dark little "music room" off the parlor, their family traditions, meant nothing to Sally. They were all "pretendings." She had observed Charles' published books and his manuscripts with scorn. "Him, makin' out like he's somebody, when he ain't got a cent," she had muttered to herself. "Puttin' on airs, all of 'em. I'll show 'em, or my name's not Sally Brown."

She looked up when she saw Melissa entering the kitchen with a slow and heavy step, and her tiny pig's eyes narrowed with hate and triumph. She waddled to the table and began to pound dough viciously.

" 'Bout time, Miss Melissa," she growled. "Your Ma's gone to her bed, and Miss Phoebe ain't comin' down to lend a hand, and the butter needin' churnin' over there, and the slops not emptied, and the sittin'-room not reddied up, and the lamp chimneys not washed yit."

"I came to help you, Sally," replied Melissa, in a faint and exhausted voice.

Sally glanced at her sharply. She had always thought Melissa ugly, almost as ugly as herself. Now the girl looked haggard and old, her bunched skirts dragging, her bodice badly buttoned, her hair disheveled. Sally smiled to herself. There was no need of telling Melissa that the tasks she had suggested had always been her own. She'd break this fine miss in well, before the mistress knew anything about it!

Melissa sat down before the churn and looked at it, stupefied. She had done very little about this house, for her work with Charles had taken most of her time. Muttering impatiently, Sally waddled over to the churn and showed how the task should be done. Melissa took the handle, moved it up and down with slow regularity, her stricken eyes fixed on nothing. The sound of the churn made a dull and dolorous swishing in the kitchen.

The brief brownish light had faded outside, and now the clouds hung threateningly low. The kitchen was dark and gloomy, and chill in spite of the brick range. Narrow, like all the other rooms in the house, its high small windows looked out upon the vegetable gardens, now black with frost and full of dead stalks and dank leaves. Beyond them stood the farm buildings, gray and weatherbeaten, streaked with the rain of last night. The walls of the kitchen were of brick, the floor of irregular fieldstone, grimed with the grease of generations. A row of water pails stood under the windows, and, beside them, pails for slops for the pigs, and other refuse. Sally's broken old rocker stood before the range, and there was a stool before the churn. These, with the table, were the only articles of furniture in the kitchen, except for a food "safe" against a far wall. A pantry lay off the kitchen, filled with flour and sugar barrels, its shelves containing salt and spices and slabs of oily bacon. It had a smell of mice and cheese, and was windowless.

Melissa's hands moved up and down on the churn handle. Sally slapped and pounded the dough, greased the bread tins. She watched Melissa with sidelong glances.

She began to grumble. "Too much to do for one lone woman around here. Got to have more help. Not gettin' any younger. I'm a-goin' to tell your Ma that if I don't get more of a hand, Miss Melissa, I'm leavin'."

Melissa did not answer, for she had not heard. There—must —be—a—way, she thought, the words keeping time with the churn. Her numbed mind kept up the refrain; she had already put aside the unbearable mortification of Geoffrey Dunham's "offer." She thought of it no longer; it was like something indecent, to be forgotten as soon as possible.

But where was there a way? There was no money. The only opportunity of obtaining any money was through her father's still unpublished and unfinished manuscripts. She had all his notes. It would not take too long! With the promised increase in royalties, she could save Phoebe and Andrew. She would hoard the money; her mother should get not a single penny of it. It belonged to Phoebe and Andrew. Melissa's hands slowed on the churn. When the work was done, she herself would go to Philadelphia and find a situation. Her mother would not be able to keep up the farm; if she would not sell it, she would lose it. Her hands fell from the churn. What was she doing here, wasting her time like this, when there was so much work to do, and so little time! She stood up, and began to walk with fast irregular steps to the door.

Sally, seeing this, shouted: "See here, Miss Melissa, there ain't no butter, and you got to help, or I'll go to your Ma this very minute and leave!"

Melissa stopped abruptly, then turned about. "But I have work to do, Sally. Miss Phoebe will be down later, and probably my mother."

Sally put her fists on her hips, and stood there glowering, like an immense and quivering obscenity. "Now, looky here, Miss Melissa, I got to have another hand or two. Your Ma's sick; she ain't a-comin' down; she's a-failin', and you might as well know it. Miss Phoebe ain't no good without your Ma on her tail. You gotta help, and keep on helpin' everyday, or I leave now. Now!"

"You can't do that, Sally," said Melissa, coldly. She paused. "Unless I work on my father's books, we'll have no money to pay you."

Sally tossed her head and snorted. "You ain't got no money anyways, and I ain't a-goin' to wait. You help now, ma'am, or I'm through."

Melissa stood and looked at the old woman. But Sally was not to be quelled. With a gesture of bitter resignation, Melissa went back to the churn. I can work at night, she thought. But how slowly it will go then. No matter, I'll work all night, if necessary. There was no use appealing to Amanda. Melissa knew her reply in advance. She would collaborate with Sally in her daughter's humiliation, agree that Melissa must help.

With her heart full of anguish, misery and anger, Melissa continued to churn. When the butter was ready, Sally showed her how to salt and beat it and place it in the molds. Then she must wash all the lamp chimneys in cold and greasy water, which rapidly turned black. She must fill all the lamps, trim the wicks, and place the cleaned lamps on a shelf near the range. The air darkened steadily, and Sally grunted about her own work.

"If your Ma and Miss Phoebe wants to eat, they can come down. I ain't a-goin' to carry up no more trays, with my rheumatism. You better find out, Miss Melissa."

Melissa crawled heavily up the stairs, weighted down with her crushing weariness. She passed the study with averted eyes and a catch of her breath. She knocked on her mother's door, and when she received no answer she opened it a crack. Amanda lay straight and rigid on the bed, apparently sleeping. Melissa closed the door and went to Phoebe's room. But at the sight of her sister, Phoebe turned her face to the pillow and wept loudly.

Melissa went to the bed. "Darling," she said, "shall I bring you a tray? You must eat, you know."

Phoebe sniffled, her face still averted. "Just a little broth, please, and perhaps a poached egg, and some tea." She burst into fresh tears.

Melissa hesitated. "Don't, don't, dearest," she murmured. She knew nothing of tender and consoling gestures, and stood like a young man, overpowered with uneasiness and helpless grief. "Don't cry, Phoebe. We'll find a way for you."

Phoebe only wept, and Melissa went out. She looked for Andrew. His room was empty. Melissa looked through his window and saw the fresh marks of a horse in the muddy path below. Melissa frowned, sighed, went downstairs.

"Some hot clear broth, and a poached egg, with toast and tea, for Miss Phoebe, Sally," she ordered. "I'll take up her tray."

Sally tossed her head grimly. "You'll do more than that, Miss. You'll cook up the whole shebang. You'll find the soup in a kettle in that there pantry, and the eggs, too, and the bread and tea in the safe. I've got too much on my hands just now."

Burning with suppressed rage and tiredness, Melissa awkwardly prepared Phoebe's tray. The soup was greasy, and she winced. The water for the eggs boiled slowly on the sullen range, as did the kettle. The tray was a sorry sight when she had finished, the broth viscid, the eggs hard on the watery toast, a scum on the cup of tea. Sally watched her with furtive satisfaction. Melissa tucked up her skirts under her belt and carried the tray upstairs. Phoebe, rumpled flushed, tear-stained and childishly lovely, sat up and inspected the tray and cried out in horror, "Oh, that terrible Sally! How dare she send up a tray like this to me?"

"I made it," said Melissa, with new humility and wretchedness. "She says I have to help with a lot of the work now." Then she felt some impatience. What did food matter, anyway, except to sustain life? Why this fuss about proper delicate preparation? A hard-boiled egg was still an egg, and bread was still bread, even if burned. It would keep Phoebe alive, and that was all that could be expected. "Eat it, Phoebe. It will give you strength. I have no time to bother."

Phoebe lifted her shining head and stared sharply at Melissa. Then, though she did not smile, a dimple appeared in her pink wet cheek. "You say Sally's making you help?" she asked. A crafty amusement flashed into her eyes, a surprised satisfaction.

"Yes, yes. Do eat, Phoebe. I'll come back for the tray."

Phoebe watched her sister leave the room, and now she smiled broadly, and her small round breasts heaved with suppressed laughter. Good old Sally. She, Phoebe, would slowly but surely relegate all her chores to that silly old Melissa. It would serve her right. She hoped Sally would just make a slave of stupid old Melly.

Melissa sat at the kitchen table and ate dry bread and cheese and water. She was not conscious of what she was eating. When she was finished, she would go at once to the study and begin to work. Her mind busied itself with the uncompleted notes. She forgot Sally and the kitchen.

Her lunch completed, she stood up. Sally said at once: "You better reddy up the parlor, Miss Melissa, and clean up the hearth and bring out the ashes. Your Ma sits there of nights, and she'll not like it if it's still dirty. And then there's the beds and the slops. I ain't asking you to brush up the floors, but I gotta have some help."

Melissa regarded her with dismayed hatred. "I've worked for hours, Sally. Now I must do my own work."

Sally rapped an iron spoon furiously on the range. "Go ahead," she said. She deliberately untied her apron. "I'm a-leavin' now, and Hiram with me, and it's good riddance to all of you."

Melissa clenched her fists. Then, in a shaking voice, she asked for the ash container and dusters. She went into the cold dim parlor and began her awkward work. The ashes got under her nails and into her clothing. She spent an hour in dusting. When she returned to the kitchen, Sally was preparing the evening meal.

She said, not looking at Melissa: "Hiram'll show you how to milk when he brings the cows in. I ain't a-doin' it any more, I can tell you that. You're young and strappin', Miss, and it's on your hands now. Did you make yours and Mr. Andrew's beds and bring down the slops? And you'd better take out those pails to the pigs, when you've done that."

Melissa worked, raging silently and helplessly. All this time wasted, while she, Melissa, did the work of a hired girl! It was not to be borne. The manuscripts waited. Tonight, thought Melissa, blind and staggering with exhaustion, tonight I'll work. She could hardly keep her eyes open when she dragged the pails out to the pigs. Their smell, their gruntings, nauseated her. When she returned to the kitchen, Sally gave her the feed for the chickens. Her shawl fluttering in the cold and acrid wind, Melissa went out again, driving herself with inflexible determination. The chickens scrambled about her skirts and she backed away from them. The sky darkened over her. She looked at the cold brown fields and the dark hills beyond, and smelled snow in the air. A tear or two involuntarily fell over her chilled cheek, and she wiped them away with angry impatience.

In the west, the sky was very gray and heavy. But now, slowly, torn splashes of bright brass appeared through the clouds, and a wan and spectral light fell on the earth, turned the hills to a yellowish brown. Far along, in the distance, the lights of Midfield began to blink. Melissa heard Hiram herding in the cows, and started. Sally had told her she must learn to milk. Sighing, almost groaning, Melissa put down the empty tin in her hands, and went towards the barn, the mud sucking at her shoes.

She hated the barn. She never went there if she could avoid

it. She smelled the manure, the sharp ammoniac stench, heard the stamping of the cows. There was a dry stink of hay and a wet smell of straw. Hiram, seeing her come in, gave her his foolish grin and asked no questions.

"I'm afraid of the cows, Hiram," she said, wincing away from the animals.

"Nuthin' to be 'fraid of, ma'am," he said, with another grin. "Ma sent you out? She be a-gettin' old, y'know." It was probable that he was not as stupid as he looked. He began to pitch feed into the mangers.

Over an hour later Melissa stumbled into the kitchen, carrying the pails of milk. Her hands were burned, aching and sore, and she shuddered at the memory of her milking lessons. She put down the pails. Sally was not in the kitchen. Melissa flung down her shawl, looked at her hands with loathing, and washed them. There were large blisters on her palms.

She heard Sally's lumbering steps on the stairs, unusually hurried now. She turned. Sally's great flabby face was contorted with fright. "Somethin's happened to your Ma, ma'am. Groanin' and makin' funny sounds in her bed. Go out to the barn and tell Hiram to ride like mad into the village and git Dr. Mellon!"

CHAPTER 12

A SCORE OF TIMES a day Melissa said to herself, but aloud, in a faint dull voice: "I cannot go on." And many times a day she climbed up and down the steep back stairs, balancing trays, basins, kettles of hot water, mustard plasters, warmed blankets and fresh glasses. Many times a day she brought them downstairs again, including wrinkled sheets and pillows for airing in the cold snowy wind. The hours became individual nightmares of exhaustion, all alike. The stairs became a treadmill, on which her feet were forever set, so that sometimes she had to pause and wonder, in confused agonies of weariness, whether she had been climbing the stairs just now or descending them.

Her mother lay in her still and darkened room, bolstered up by several pillows, her stertorous breathing, her sighs and gasps an ominous sound in the hushed quiet. A shaded candle burned day and night between her windows. She never spoke, for that was forbidden. She could not lift her hands. It was

Melissa who had to turn her every fifteen minutes. It was Melissa who had to bathe her and change her sheets, comb her whitened hair, hold the glass to her lips, feed her, ease her in a hundred aching ways, rubbing her feet and shrunken arms, wiping the sweat from her pallid forehead and her gray cheeks, administering certain pungent drops to her every half hour by the clock, twenty-four hours a day. It was Melissa who sat up with her at night, sometimes falling into a tormented doze in her straight chair, to come awake with a start so violent as almost to throw herself to the floor. There was no company, no surcease, for Melissa. She could not even read. She had once had a vague thought that she might work on her father's manuscripts during the night watches, but the candlelight was too dim, and that dreadful moaning and gasping from the bed beat into her brain like iron fists.

Dr. Mellon had suggested a woman from the village to relieve Melissa, but Melissa replied simply: "We have no money. Besides, my father would have wished me to stay with my mother." So she sat there at night, rising every half hour to give the poor semiconscious woman her drops in water, to wipe away her sweat, to lift up her pillows. She sat and watched the candlelight, and finally she could think no more, was only a pair of burning eyes and a throbbing heart. She watched the candlelight on the high mouldering ceiling; she watched the shadows flickering on the walls, and chasing themselves in fugitive shapes over the black, lurking furniture. She watched the gray dawns come, and was sometimes so prostrated that she had to watch those dawns for a long time, until they lightened, before she knew whether the morning was coming or it was about to be night again. Sometimes she did not know whether she was awake or dreaming that she was awake, and the clock became to her an evil, clicking enemy who was trying to escape her and carry the dangerous minutes away, and with them her mother's life. Sometimes, when she approached Amanda's bed, she felt singularly light, as if formed only of mist, so that she seemed to drift, and her hands had no substance; and sometimes she felt that every muscle had become weighted lead and that she could not carry her body a single step forward.

The long, dusky brown days crept into December, became white and blinded with snow, became lost in blizzards. The wind howled down the chimney, scattered sparks on the bedroom hearth. The draperies stirred in the gales that seeped through the shutters. At night, the house rumbled and complained in the maelstrom of the storm. But Amanda's glazed eyes hardly moved; she seemed intent only on getting the next breath, and the next; all her being, all her efforts and spirit, were concentrated on that terrible necessity. When she looked at Melissa, she did not appear to recognize the girl. When old Sally crept into the room, or the doctor, she glanced at them blindly, then dropped her lids.

Dr. Mellon had told Melissa that her mother had a very slight chance for life. It was his opinion, though he did not tell this to Melissa, that long years of tension, of strain, of frustration and old grief, had wrecked that indomitable heart. He himself was always amazed to find her still alive when he called; he was filled with respect that a human will could so long defeat inevitable death. He was an old man, and knew the powers of the human will, and he suspected that Amanda would not die until she had fulfilled some mission she had set for herself.

His concern now was for Melissa, and he admired her for her indestructibilty, for her grim determination not to collapse. Always thin, she had become emaciated, and the beautifully formed bones of her face now turned angular, sharp and clear, the flesh refined away by exhaustion. Her light-blue eyes, formerly abstracted and clouded and cold, grew almost vivid with the fever of weariness. Quite often she forgot to dress her hair even in her own rough and careless fashion, and allowed it to hang in two long braids of pale gilt almost to her thighs. Wearing her funeral black, which, though wrinkled and creased, had a sad air of elegance, she reminded the old doctor of some mourning Teutonic goddess, some Freya inconsolable and dark with unreason. No argument to spare herself elicited even a protest; she did not seem to hear. The doctor was not deceived that it was devotion to her mother which kept Melissa constantly in that somber bedroom, for he had known the Upjohns for many years and had delivered all Amanda's children. It was something else, perhaps a rigid sense of duty, or an obscure accusation of guilt, or even hatred. The doctor shook his head. He was old, but there were many things he did not know regarding the hidden places of the human soul, he confessed to himself. Finally, he gave up his arguments with Melissa, which were always one-sided. He began to hope that poor Amanda would soon be at peace and that her daughter could rest.

Even old bloated Sally was subdued by the event of Amanda's fatal illness. She hardly complained: firstly, because in the face of approaching death she was afraid, and, secondly, because she knew that Melissa would not hear her.

All the chores had fallen to her again, and more, for Amanda was not at hand, and Phoebe, protesting hysterically that she would die, "I know I will," kept to her own room and sobbed loudly whenever she heard a footstep outside. She called pathetically for her mother, and could sometimes be detected praying behind her door, but no daughterly solicitude would persuade her to enter Amanda's room. Like Charles, she refused to involve herself in an unpleasant or frightening situation. When she felt she was safe, she sewed placidly on the lengths of new silk and wool which were her trousseau, and embroidered her bridal sheets and pillowcases. She slept easily at night, and dreamlessly as a child. When awake, she thought of her future, hardly emerged from her room, accepted the trays the staggering Melissa brought her, smiled at Melissa's bent and retreating back, and sobbed until her sister was out of hearing. She found all this very agreeable. She was relieved of onerous household duties; she was enjoying Melissa's wretched state. If she thought at all of her mother, it was with indifference. Amanda was now in no position to pamper her, and so her importance in her daughter's life had diminished.

The house, always dank and gloomy, had heretofore been well-kept, for Amanda had been an excellent housekeeper. But now Sally, saddled with all the work, with endless washings of linens to do, and with no supervision, let dust and dirt accumulate. Days would pass without any room receiving the ministrations of broom or duster. Hearths piled high with ashes; grit covered the carpets, and drifted onto the windowsills. The house, once filled with the smell of wax and polish and soap, now reeked with the odors of grease, dust, ashes and unaired rooms. Slowly it fell into decay, each room, each piece of furniture, exuding neglect and hopelessness. The dining-room, as narrow and bleak as a cold slit, was never used now. Melissa ate her brief meals in the kitchen. She never sat in the parlor, not even for a moment.

Andrew had returned to Harvard three weeks ago. He had wanted to remain, but Melissa, gathering the full force of her will, the full passion of her devotion to her dead father, had beaten down her brother's resistance. "There is no use in your remaining, Andrew," she had said, with the old hard ring of authority in her voice. "It may be weeks. It may even be months. Besides, you will be returning home for Christmas. You have your studies. You dare not abandon them now. Papa struggled so hard for you." So Andrew had gone back to Harvard. Women were too much for him, he had reflected somberly. But there would soon come a day when they would dominate him no longer. Poor Mother. Yet she had hardly ever noticed him. He had no dislike for her, and certainly no affection. He was only sorry for her, but he was also impatient. She had allowed her husband, who was, in a way, a woman himself, to ruin and degrade her. Andrew, to his surprise, discovered in himself a disgust for any human creature who permitted another to devour his life, to suck the juices from him. It was not so much Melissa's arguments which persuaded him to return to Harvard as his desire to complete his emancipation, which had begun on the day when he had stood at his father's grave. "I must clear my eyes," he thought. While at Harvard, he would round out his plans. In the home atmosphere of despair and silent decay, his mind would be too confused.

Melissa was alone with her days of nursing, suffering and weariness. She was alone with the candlelight and the gaspings of her mother. She was alone with Phoebe's tears and "vapors." She was alone with the dry bread she ate and the stiff chair in which she dozed.

She dared not think of her father very much now, for if she did she knew her last waning strength would go and she would collapse. But sometimes she felt that he would be proud of her. Long-suffering, patient, self-sacrificing as he had been, condemned by this dying woman to a frustrated and painful life, he would still be all gentle forgiveness, would urge his daughter to minister to his enemy with tenderness and commiseration. Had he not always advocated patience and nonresistance to fate? Had he not always spoken with kindness and tolerance and understanding of everyone, even when Melissa had raged? He would want her to do this thing. She was not serving her mother; she was serving Papa.

Snow piled itself against the doors, heaped itself about the trees, ridged the walls, obliterated the road, whitened the hills against a white sky, covered the slate roofs of the house, the barn and the out-buildings. Soundlessly the days crept towards Christmas, moving over the snow. The windows became blank, covered with frost, so that the house was a prison, shut-in, immured, unaware of any life beyond itself. No visitors arrived; Dr. Mellon had forbidden them. For a little while, the neighboring farmers, and even the gentry in Midfield, had sent messages and vague offers of help. Now these no longer came. Melissa sat in her candlelighted tomb and listened to her mother struggle for one more breath, then another.

CHAPTER 13

ONE NIGHT, as the clock in the hall below struck midnight, Melissa came to herself with a start. She had been dozing. She sat upright and looked at her mother. Amanda seemed to be sleeping. Her breathing was quieter and more regular. Her hands no longer clutched the quilts in a prodigious effort to breathe. They lay slack on the covers, the calloused palms turned upwards in a gesture of utter resignation.

Melissa crept to the bed. Her mother's eyes were closed. Her color seemed better. Melissa returned to her chair, sighing, pushing aside a lock of hair which had fallen against her cheek. She could not doze again. She was conscious of a constant vibration in herself, deep within her bones, and the painful throbbing of her own heart. She was wide awake with the toxins of exhaustion.

She thought: Why, it is only three days to Christmas. Andrew would be coming home in a day or two. He would be coming home to a desolate house, and to fear. Melissa remembered past Christmases. She and her father would go into the woods with a small bright axe, and they would bring back a fresh young fir tree smelling of snow and cold and resin. They would set it up in the drawing-room, while Charles fondly laughed at himself for his sentimentality. Together, assisted by Phoebe, and enlivened by her gay chitterings, they would decorate the tree. Strings of colored paper, twisted together. Balls of molasses popcorn. Candles. Borax to be sprinkled over damp needles. Presents to be hung on the bending and fragrant branches. It would be very gay.

I owe it to poor little Phoebe, and to Andrew, to get a tree for them, thought Melissa. I shall decorate it myself. She swallowed hard against a wave of uncontrollable sorrow and pain. Papa would want it. I must get a tree. I must make every effort to make the house comfortable for Phoebe and Andrew, and to ease their grief. Life must go on for them. They are young. When—this—is all over, then I will direct them again, and do what is best for them. Tomorrow, if Mama seems better, I'll go into the woods for a tree, or send Hiram for one. Who knows? Perhaps in a few days I shall be able to get to work on Papa's manuscripts. I need the money! Andrew's and Phoebe's lives must not be injured by this.

She went to the bowl on her mother's commode, dipped a cloth in cold water and pressed it against her feverish eyes. She smoothed back her hair. She turned around. For the first time in weeks she heard her mother's voice, faint, almost a whisper: "Melissa!"

Melissa started, then began to tremble acutely. She crossed the room to her mother's bed in a sea of wavering shadows. She stood by the bed and looked down at Amanda. Amanda's eyes were wide open now, sunken deeply in their sockets. But they were no longer glazed. They were alert with consciousness and awareness. "Yes, Mama," said Melissa. Her pale heavy braids swung across her shoulders, touched the quilts, as she bent over Amanda.

Amanda looked at them, turning her eyes slowly. Her hand moved. She touched one of the braids, held it a moment in her gaunt fingers.

"You must not talk," said Melissa, in a low tone. "You must not move. Is there anything you want? No, do not speak. Just move your head. Water? It is not time for your medicine. Are you comfortable? Do you need another blanket? It is very cold in here, and I'll stir up the fire at once."

But Amanda's fingers clutched the braid she had taken. "Sit near me, Melissa," she whispered. "I must talk to you. I insist."

Melissa sat down carefully on the edge of the hard bed. Amanda held onto her hair. She could not pull away.

"Only a few words," whispered Amanda. She was not gasping now, but breathing normally. "You have been here a long time. I have known it. Why?"

Melissa said, urgently, but still in a hushed voice: "You must not talk. It is Dr. Mellon's orders. Yes, I have nursed you all this time. You have been very ill. But you are getting better now." She paused. "Papa would have wanted me to take care of you," she added, with the brutal forthrightness of her innocence.

Amanda smiled. It was only a shadow of a smile, bitter and twisted. Her fingers caressed the braid she held, but Melissa was not aware of it.

Amanda murmured: "Your father, Melissa, he devoured you as he devoured me. No, do not pull away. You must listen, if you would save your life." Her face had become alive, fluid with her indomitable will, and she held tighter to Melissa, who had involuntarily arched back against her mother's hold. "Listen, Melissa, and remember. He tried to destroy you, as he destroyed me. He was a man who all his life wanted power, and adulation, and influence over others. He thought he might get it through his writings. He thought he might have admiration that way. But he failed. He failed, because there was no truth in him. He was a liar."

Melissa's eyes flashed in the semi-darkness, and her dry lips parted in a wild protest. Her whole body shook with denial and horror, and with fear. She forgot her mother's dangerous condition. She yanked her braid from Amanda's grasp and stood up. She cried out: "That is a lie! He was everything that was truth! He cared nothing for power. He derided it to me, said the man who wanted it was contemptible. Power! He only wanted to study and work and live in peace—"

She had to catch at the bedpost to keep herself from falling. Her breast rose and fell with anguish and outrage. And Amanda lay on her pillows and regarded her daughter with dying sternness.

Amanda did not move, but her eyes caught and held Melissa's, and finally the girl was silent and only stood there clutching the bedpost.

"Listen, my daughter," whispered Amanda. "He wanted power, and could not get it in the world. It was a disease in him. So he did the next best thing he could. He exercised power over us. If he had lived, there would have been no hope for you. He's dead now. And you are free, if you'll only take your freedom."

Melissa covered her eyes with her hand, and could not speak. Papa, Papa, she thought.

"Be free, Melissa," said Amanda, in a stronger voice, with a ring of warning in it. "Go free, Melissa."

Melissa dropped her hand. Amanda's eyes held hers compellingly. Then the older woman said: "Send for Arabella Dunham. I must see her in the morning."

She closed her eyes, and seemed to sleep again.

Melissa crept back to her chair. She sat there, her clenched hands on her trembling knees, her body bent forward, her eyes staring at the floor. She was one savage storm of grief and rage and bitter agony. Papa! To be so calumnied, so despised, so rejected! To be spoken of so, while he, dead and silent, could not defend himself. She saw him so clearly, asleep in his grave, smiling, pathetic, vulnerable. "No, Papa," she whispered, "you are not defenseless. I am alive, and here. No one shall dare slander you again. No one understood you, Papa, except me. And some day the world shall know what you were, what a genius, what a great man, what a noble man. I shall never forget you, Papa."

Tears began to roll down her cheeks. Her shoulders shook with repressed sobs. The hour for her mother's medicine passed unheeded, while Melissa wept and could not stop her tears and Amanda seemingly slumbered.

CHAPTER 14

MELISSA ADMITTED Mrs. Arabella Dunham Shaw to the house and silently helped her remove the wide sable stole which covered her plump shoulders and arms. She took Arabella's bonnet of blue velvet, trimmed with large purple roses, and Arabella's gloves. During all this, Arabella chattered with hushed vivacity, expressing her regret, her shock over her friend's desperate illness, her constant desire in the past few weeks to force her way into the Upjohn house, "there to give poor dear Amanda my best love and assistance. But all I could do was to send flowers, and the hampers that—I mean, the hampers, and an occasional message. I did not want to annoy you with any insistence, dearest Melissa, for I knew how burdened you were, and how irritating the demands of even the closest friends can be during times of affliction. But I assure you you had all my prayers, and my silent devotions, and my most passionate hopes. How many times did I sit at my bedroom windows and endeavor to strain my eyes to catch your midnight candle! How many times did I clasp my hands in fervent supplication that your period of trial might soon be ended! How many tears have I shed! But then, as Geoffrey often says, I am afflicted with too much sensibility. You should hear how he scolds me when he is at home! By the way, he has not returned since the sad passing of your poor darling Papa, but every letter to me is filled with his affection and his concern for all of you. Dear me, my child, have you a fever? Your face is so flushed and hot."

"I have no fever," muttered Melissa. She added, in a louder tone: "Mrs. Shaw, I sent for you against the orders of Dr. Mellon because my mother insisted upon seeing you. Dr. Mellon finally concluded it would be more dangerous to re-

fuse her wishes than to grant them. I trust you will not remain long."

How utterly without manners, thought Arabella, with a
glint of aversion in her eye as she looked at Melissa. She
sniffed. She caught the strong, acrid odors of the neglected
house, and her sharp glance noted the decay, dust and dirt
in the hall, which was very cold and damp. She added to herself: It is disgraceful. Melissa is nothing more than a dreaming
slut. She put her handkerchief, heavily laden with musk, to
her nose. She said, in a sighing voice of compassion: "Certainly, I shall not remain a moment more than necessary,
dear child."

Her thoughts went on: I wish Geoffrey could see her now!
She is as fleshless as a scarecrow, and her frock is dirty. And
her eyes! They are quite mad. And there is a smudge on her
bony cheek, which looks as though it had been there for days.

She turned about, still sighing, and tried, with the aid of
the clouded mirror over the hall table, to smooth the curled
rolls of her gray-streaked light hair. She peered closer to admire the fit of her plum-colored velvet bodice with its pearl
buttons, its bows at the shoulder, its ruffle of fine lace at the
neck. She smoothed down the folds of the velvet skirt,
plumped out a huge bustle at the back, and rattled her gold
bangles. Long pearl ear-rings hung at her ears, and swayed
against her fat cheeks. She smiled, and her shark-like mouth
opened in a lipless oval. Then she quenched the smile, and
turned again to Melissa.

"I shall write tonight and tell dear Geoffrey of my visit. He
will be so happy to know that Amanda has improved a little.
Did I tell you, dear, that he is practically engaged to the
most wonderful girl in Philadelphia? One of the Biddles, no
less! So charming, so chic, so graceful and aristocratic. She
can play the harp so heavenly! I was quite entranced when I
last saw her. It was easy to observe that she was smitten by
Geoffrey, and now I have such hopes!"

Melissa moved, with a dry rustle of her garments, to the
stairway. "Shall we go up to Mama at once?" She looked at
Arabella from the shadows, and her face was a whitish mask
filled with eyes.

Arabella followed Melissa up the stairs; she heard the
grinding of the grit under her fashionable French boots and
high, tapering heels. Her skirts gave out a sweet silken rustle
and swish, loud in the silence. Her scent followed her like a
cloud. She panted when she reached the top of the stairway,
but she moved quickly behind Melissa to Amanda's room.

That room, observed Arabella, as she tiptoed within, was at least well-kept and clean, and had no unpleasant odors. The candlelight wavered against the musty drawn draperies, and at first Arabella could hardly see the white bed in the center of the room. She approached it on tiptoe, with a soft murmur in her throat. Melissa stood at a distance, with her back to the door.

"Dear, dear Amanda," said Arabella, in a hushed, musical tone, bending over the bed. "How glad I am to see you so well, and able to receive visitors!"

Amanda gazed at her from her pillows. Her mouth was sunken, her face a ghastly color. But her eyes burned indomitably upon her friend. She even smiled a little, and allowed Arabella to press her cold hand. She indicated a chair. Melissa stirred near the door.

"You are permitted only a few minutes, Mrs. Shaw," she said, and her voice was too loud, and a trifle shrill.

Amanda said, not looking away from Arabella: "Melissa, I wish to be alone with Arabella." Her voice was stronger today. Death stood beside her, but she held it off by the sheer force of her inexorable will. Arabella sat down with a crackle of silken petticoats, and gazed at Amanda with her head cocked compassionately to one side. Melissa hesitated, then left the room.

The dim firelight leapt up, and threw a wan light on Amanda's stern face. Arabella touched her scented handkerchief to her dry eyelids. Amanda studied her friend. A silly, frivolous, heartless old fool, a false and crafty woman! Amanda saw the hard slate-gray eyes, the parrot-like nose with its sharp cruel tip, the fat, faintly rouged cheeks, and the rich and gaudy finery. Amanda smelled the strong, expensive but sickening perfume, and she turned her head slightly away. She thought: It is impossible to trust her. I must abandon my plan to plead with her for help for Melissa. I know now I dare not speak to her of Geoffrey's offer, for she would circumvent his desire if she could, and would not send him the message that I must see him at once, for all the lying promises she would give me. She would tell him nothing.

She asked aloud, in her faint but resolute voice: "Have you written to Geoffrey that I have been ill, Arabella?"

Arabella had written one letter to her brother to say that Amanda had had a slight seizure the day after the funeral, but that he must not worry in the least, that she, Arabella, was in constant touch with the Upjohn household, that everything was in good order and that there was no occasion for any undue concern. When Geoffrey had written demanding more details, she had added in a postscript: "Amanda is doing splendidly and will be her old self in a day or two."

She smiled at Amanda tenderly, bent forward from her chair to pat Amanda's icy fingers. "Indeed I have, dear friend, and he is all anxiety. He will return at Christmas, and will come to see you. Though, of course, everything will be very confused, as we shall have eight house guests for the holidays. But I do hope he can spare an hour or so for his old friends." To herself, she thought: Amanda is obviously dying. I doubt whether she will survive until Christmas. And I shall contrive to keep dear Geoffrey so busy with his dear friends that he will hardly have time to visit these dreadful people.

She added aloud: "And when you see Geoffrey, Amanda, I know that you will express your gratification at his engagement to darling Miss Grace Biddle, of Philadelphia." She spoke in a simpering arch voice, and contrived to look extremely coy. But her sharp and malevolent eyes fixed themselves watchfully upon Amanda.

Amanda did not start, did not turn to stare searchingly upon the other woman. She said to herself: It is a lie. She has a motive for that lie, and I know what it is. I must be very careful. She looked at Arabella now, turning her head slowly. She managed a quiet smile.

"That is good news, indeed," she whispered. Arabella drew a relieved breath. She had been frightening herself unnecessarily, filling her life with nightmares. Geoffrey had forgotten that incredible remark of his three or four years ago. Perhaps he had only been teasing his sister.

Amanda went on, and she managed to inject a hint of secrecy into her feeble tone: "I have some news for Geoffrey. He is Charles' executor. Some unexpected money has been found. I wish to put it into his hands, for my children." Amanda had rarely lied in her life, but she spoke this lie with quiet assurance.

"Indeed," murmured Arabella, conveying congratulation. "That is happy news, dear Amanda. Geoffrey will be so pleased." She herself was pleased. She magnified the "money" into a fortune. She would tell Geoffrey that there was no need for his assisting the Upjohns. Perhaps she could tell him that Melissa had gone to Philadelphia to spend Christmas with friends, and had taken her mother with her, and her sister. It would be a precarious falsehood, but she would try it.

"So," said Amanda, "I wish you would send Geoffrey a

telegram tonight, immediately upon leaving here, that I must see him at once."

Arabella said: "But dearest Amanda, he will be at home on Thursday, for Christmas, and this is Monday! Surely business can wait until then!"

"No," said Amanda firmly, "it cannot wait." She turned her head and looked unyieldingly at Arabella, and the power of her will was like a compelling hand on the other woman's shoulder.

She watched Arabella, and when the latter hesitated, her eyes wavering cunningly from side to side, she added: "I am afraid I have burdened you. I shall send Melissa, or Hiram, to Midfield tonight, to send a telegram to Geoffrey." She paused, went on: "One cannot rely upon telegrams. If I receive no answer by tomorrow night from the telegraph office that Geoffrey is returning immediately, I shall send another message."

Yes, she is capable of it, thought Arabella, with enraged dismay. And then, when he returns, he will be furious with me that I have kept the truth from him and have not sent for him myself. She has me in a trap.

"Nonsense, dear Amanda!" she exclaimed. "I shall send Geoffrey the telegram immediately." Her frightened thoughts continued: I shall telegraph him, saying that Amanda has taken a turn for the worse, and that he must come at once. There is slight chance he will ever know that she has been at the point of death for weeks. And there is always the possibility that she may die before he arrives. Oh, how dreadful and irritating fate can be, when one means only for the best!

Amanda smiled grimly, and said: "Thank you." She indicated her medicine on the table. "Would you please, Arabella? Poor Melissa has been constantly at my side. Perhaps she has thrown herself upon her bed for a few minutes' much-needed rest."

Arabella rose with a flutter, administered the medicine. She began to chatter nervously: "Geoffrey will be so upset! With the house guests arriving and everything, and with his engagement to be announced. On second thought, darling Amanda, do not mention this to him. He will be annoyed that I have announced it prematurely. You know how shy gentlemen are about these things."

Amanda nodded gravely, by a supreme effort preventing a smile. "And now, Arabella, if you will be so kind as to lift my pillows and arrange that blanket over my feet. Melissa must be resting."

Arabella obeyed, then sat down by the bed again. Amanda closed her eyes and seemed to sleep. Arabella fixed her eyes upon the older woman's face and willed that she might die at once, before Geoffrey arrived. She had discovered that James, Geoffrey's man-servant, had been sending hampers to the Upjohns at her brother's request. It had been days before she had been able to conquer her fear. And now, as she watched Amanda sleep, she was overcome with dismay and terror and hatred. All her fears returned to her, tremendously exaggerated. Fervently, over and over, she willed that Amanda might die tonight.

CHAPTER 15

WHEN DR. MELLON arrived that evening, he was quite astonished at the change in his patient, and, with gratification, he exclaimed: "Well, now, this is excellent! Practically a miracle, my dear Amanda!" He beamed at her, the kind old man, and opened his bag. But as he listened to Amanda's heart, his wide smile grew less, became grave and concerned. Slowly he straightened up, staring at Amanda keenly and for a long time. Then he repeated, but in a very low voice: "Yes. A miracle." He stroked his white beard in puzzled distress.

"You mean, do you not, that my heart is no better, though I appear better?" asked Amanda quietly. She lifted her hand as if it were heavily weighted. "Yes, I know I have little strength. But God has been good enough to allow me sufficient for what I must do."

She spoke to him for a moment or two longer, then fell suddenly into a deep sleep.

The next morning, when Melissa opened the door for Dr. Mellon, she was surprised to see that he was accompanied by a buxom young woman from the village, carrying a bag and exuding an air of capability. Dr. Mellon said heartily: "This is Matilda Pratt, Melissa, a very competent nurse."

"We do not need a nurse," replied Melissa, peremptorily, and attempting to bar the way. Her dwindled face flushed.

"We have no money. My mother has no money to pay for a nurse."

She caught hold of the newel of the stairway, for she was half fainting with weariness. Dr. Mellon continued to smile heartily: "Nonsense, Melissa. Your mother asked for Matilda. She wishes to spare you any more night vigils, or day vigils, for that matter. She is much concerned about you."

Melissa gave him a hard sardonic smile and straightened up. But she allowed the doctor and the rosy nurse to pass her on the stairs. Dr. Mellon nodded affably at her, and her face became rigorous. Besides the nurse, the doctor had brought a message from the telegraph office for Amanda, as she had requested. Geoffrey Dunham would arrive late that afternoon and would come at once to the Upjohn house. The message had been for Melissa, but the doctor had tactfully refrained from giving it to the girl, for Amanda had warned him.

"There will be a message in reply to one sent by Arabella Shaw," she had said, controlling her laboring breath. "Whether it be for her, or for us, deliver it only to me. You will have no difficulty, I know, doctor, in ascertaining whether such a message has been received."

Melissa remained near the stairway until she heard her mother's door close after the doctor and the nurse. Now she was dully enraged. Her mother was obviously better. There was no need for the night watch; there was no need to waste Papa's precious money, which must be preserved for Andrew and Phoebe! It was intolerable. It was part of her mother's hatred for Papa and herself. Melissa wrung her hands in a gesture of panic.

Then she thrust out her chin in the old, intolerant way. No matter. There was always a way for an inflexible will. Amanda would not defeat Charles. She would not defeat her daughter. When she, Melissa, had a little strength, she would fight only the more ruthlessly. Melissa sat down very suddenly on the stairs, bent her head on her knees, and struggled with her faintness.

After a long time she crawled up the stairs. She peered into her mother's room, then hastily shut the crack she had opened. Dr. Mellon was preparing to leave. The nurse was already in efficient attendance and Amanda was smiling a little. I'll go down to the kitchen and help Sally, thought Melissa. Then she stopped still in the hall. Here was the opportunity she had craved. She could work on her father's manuscripts now. Tiptoeing, so that the alert Sally might not catch her in desertion, she stole slowly down the corridor to the study. She closed the door silently behind her, her heart thumping as if in escape. If that odious nurse was to be paid, there was no time to be lost. She must begin work at once, for the sake of her brother and sister. It was only nine o'clock. She might have some three hours and not a minute must be wasted.

She looked at the study, and her tired eyes filled with tears. No one had cleaned it in weeks. It was exactly as it had been on the day when her father had been laid in his grave, except that a heavy fur of dust lay over everything and a mouldering smell floated almost palpably in the dank, closed air.

She opened the windows and let in the cold snowy wind until the sickening closeness of the room had lessened considerably. She looked at the fireplace. There was no wood; she had burned it on that dreadful night when Geoffrey Dunham had forced his way into this room. She dared not go downstairs for more, for she might encounter Sally who would soon know that Melissa's services were no longer needed in Amanda's room. Shivering, Melissa went to her father's wardrobe and took down his old greenish cloak. She wrapped it about her. It clung to her shoulders and arms like a loving embrace. She burst into deep, subdued sobs, held the folds to her lips and kissed them in an agony of fresh sorrow. She sat down on her hassock, buried her face in the cloak and rocked in her grief, her sobs muffled by the thickness of the fabric. Her father's death, held at bay these last weeks, returned to her with full and piercing reality.

At last she lifted her head, wiped her eyes, and dried her wet cheeks. Her face, softened by sorrow, now hardened resolutely. This was no way to serve her father when there was so little time. She could almost hear his gentle words of reproach. She stood up, fastened the cloak firmly about her neck, and went to his desk. She opened the desk, sat in his chair, took up his pen. The manuscript and its notes lay before her, untouched, waiting.

She ran quickly through the notes, blinking her sore and reddened eyes. Some appeared to be missing. Though she felt that she was trespassing, she opened several drawers in her search. Her father's desk had always tacitly been regarded by all as sacrosanct. Here the notes lay, until he was ready to use them. She came on a large flat notebook of black leather, and opened it with trembling hands. Then she sighed with relief. Not only did it contain the notes he had previously discussed with her, but many more. They were all there, in his exquisite handwriting, and again tears ran down her cheeks as she saw them.

She began to work, correlating the notes, so that she might finish the manuscript. In this she displayed a profound orderliness and trained intelligence. An hour slipped by in that icy room as Melissa in her father's cloak crouched over the desk and wrote firmly with numbing fingers. She lost all sense of time.

She came to a series of notes on the ancient Carthaginians. Charles had written beside them in smaller writing: "To be used for the seventh volume of the series." Melissa began to put these notes aside, then read Plutarch's denunciation of the Carthaginians:

". . . harsh and gloomy, ruthless to their subjects, running to the extremes of cowardice in fear and of savagery in anger, obstinate in decisions, austere and narrow, and insensible to amusement or the graciousness of life."

Under this he had written: "How like my dear Amanda! But how docile she has become, since she has discovered who rules! It is a pleasure to see her despairing abjectness, her attempts to regain her integrity—It is all the more amusing because she does not know how supine she has become. She struggles quite blindly—with her New England instinct not to surrender."

The writing had a gay and humorous flow, a gleeful, dancing tilt. Like a caricatured face, it expressed something evil.

Melissa sat and stared at the comment. She read it over and over. She read it, and sat there, until her cold flesh lost all sensation. She crouched over the book, and could not stir. She bent over it as if stricken by paralysis. Her eyes would not move away from the script; it was as if something was compelling her to remain there, helplessly reading and rereading it, absorbing all its cruelty and gloating derision.

Then, very slowly, she closed the notebook. Methodically, she replaced it in its drawer and closed the drawer. Her hands had no feeling; her mind was empty. She tidied the heaps of notes methodically, straightened the pages of the manuscript. She wiped the pen, put it down, dropped the cover of the ink-pot. She did all this automatically, and from long habit. Then she said, loudly and clearly: "No!"

Her voice aroused her from her dead apathy, and she started up with such abruptness that the cloak fell to her feet. She stood rigid, staring before her. Somewhere there was a dull and heavy pounding; she listened to it, dazed, and did not know it was her own heart. But she felt its most enormous and staggering pain.

She heard her mother's words of yesterday: ". . . he wanted power. He had a lust for it." She clapped her hands over her ears, and again cried: "No!" She flung up her head and clenched her teeth so hard that her jaw-line sprang out like marble under her thin flesh. She gripped her hands together and fought down the terror and the fear as if they had been wolves tearing at her throat and her life depended on the outcome. She knew she must not be overcome, that she must fight for her whole existence in these appalling moments.

She willed her mind to become quiet. She willed her body to stop its anguished trembling. She closed her ears. She was absorbed only in her atempts to rally from some profound shock.

Slowly, at last, she unclenched her fingers from each other; slowly, she became still. She did not move for a long time, for there was no quickened movement of blood in her legs as yet. Then drained, quiet, unfeeling and unthinking, she went out of the room. She said to herself: I must get away. I must leave this house. I must go where there is nobody, so I can think sanely.

She went out of the room, creeping like a fugitive. She went to her own room, took a heavy gray shawl from her wobbling wardrobe, wrapped it closely about her head and shoulders. She went downstairs; the stairway wavered like a tremulous ribbon before her, and she carefully held up her skirts and took each step cautiously. She opened the heavy oaken door of the hall and closed it behind her. The snow had stopped. The whole world was one black-and-white silence. She thought: I will go into the woods and get a Christmas tree for Phoebe and Andrew. She bent as she passed the little windows of the kitchen, so that Sally might not see her. Beyond the house lay the woodshed. There she found the small bright axe, and carried it away with her.

Moving more quickly now, racing like a gray-and-black shadow against the snow, she went across the white-filled meadows, her skirts flowing behind her as if struck by wind. Everything was silent. Not a twig or branch cracked anywhere; not an animal scurried before the girl's flying footsteps. Once or twice an evergreen dropped its load of snow with a faint cold sound. The sky overhead was a lid of motionless mist, and everywhere was the pure and sterile smell of the winter day.

The woods drew her in. Pines and hemlocks and spruce

stood immobile, coated with whiteness. Here and there a huge and twisted black tracery of elm or poplar or oak broke the ranks of the firs, gave, through their skeleton shapes, a view of the skies. Melissa broke the trackless marble with her hurrying feet. Deeper and deeper she penetrated into the breathless and alabaster quiet. She reached a small clearing. A fallen trunk stood in her way. She sat down on it, huddled, the shawl falling from her hair, which was revealed as a pale bright blur against all that frozen whiteness and blackness.

Her feet were enveloped with snow, and the cold made them numb. But she did not feel it. She stared at the ground, and did not move. Now the desperate struggle was resumed; grimly she faced it.

"I must understand," she said aloud, in her quiet and ruthless voice. "I must understand, or I'll surely die."

Her father's notebook lay before her as clearly as it had lain on Charles' desk. Over and over, she reread what he had written. The words were like fire, sharp and bold. With each rereading, something sank away in her, like the withdrawing of blood, like the dying of some innocent virtue. Courageously, she repeated the words to herself, for Melissa had always had a formidable courage, and no deviousness had ever scarred or weakened it.

She did not know that there are some truths which must be denied if one is to live. Her young body defied death and defeat, it clamored that the truth be hidden from it in order that it might survive. Her stricken brain, answering the call of that body, rallied, began to marshal specious arguments, lying consolations, twisted reasonings, until the time when she could endure the truth and not die of it.

Before the deathliness of the face of the truth, her brain spun rapid and concealing webs. A quiet but insistent thought came to her: I must do justice to Papa. I must not come to some treacherous conclusion. As she thought this, her father's face and body rose up before her, as vividly as in life, gentle, benign, tender and humorous. She could even hear his faint voice:

"Oh, Melissa, how can you betray me like this, even for an instant? Have you forgotten our long years together, our years of trust and affection and work and candid discussion? Can you recall a single word of mine that was cruel or harsh or without pity? Did I ever deal treacherously with you, or with anyone else, in all the time you have known me? Yet you balance years of love and understanding against a single paragraph inadvertently read, and which you are now shamelessly misinterpreting."

Melissa could actually hear the strong melodious sound of her father's voice, so that she was certain that he was with her in fact. She was silent. She did not reply to the ghost. But a curious warmth crept over her cold flesh. She melted inside, and her strength drained away. She began to cry helplessly, but with passionate relief, like one who has had a reprieve. Her pardoned and rescued body began to pulse again with rallying life, and the exhausted brain, triumphant over reason, dissolved in emotion and remorse.

"Oh, Papa, Papa!" she moaned. "How can you ever forgive me for thinking such horrible thoughts? If I am so weak, how can I ever complete your work? I'm not worthy to do it, and if I don't do it, how shall I save Phoebe and Andrew?"

Now her heart throbbed with a sense of hurry and urgency as she deserted the truth she had seen in one awful moment. Now her feet were set again on firm ground, but she trembled from her former struggles. Wrapped in a kind of warm blessedness and enclosed in a kind of peaceful but singing sanctuary, she got to her feet. Her way of life, all her plans and hopes, her beliefs and convictions, were safe again. She was no longer thrown adrift into darkness, where there was nothing sure, nothing inviolate, nothing with a purpose, where everything was frightful and lost.

She felt almost rapturous as she went into the woods, carrying the axe. She had no thought now but contentment and peace. She found a perfect little tree, and hacked away at its trunk, close to the snow. It resisted her efforts for a long time, clutching sturdily at life. But finally it wavered, then toppled, and its small snow-filled branches sank down to the white earth.

Melissa seized the trunk, and dragged it through the woods. It wounded the pure snow; it was like a body being hauled unprotestingly to death. Sometimes its frail branches clutched at a hidden stone, or entangled themselves with dense brush. It appeared to have a dying but sentient life of its own, and Melissa's breath came in fast plumes of smoke in the clear, purged quiet. Her exertions restored her depleted energy. Never had pure cold air exhilarated her like this, nor had her blood ever flowed so freely. She was young again, and happy for the moment; once she even laughed a little as she freed the tree from a tangle of blackberry bushes. At times a kind of glad delirium and release seized her. She had come into the woods to fight a terrible fight, and she had won and was returning, joyous with conquest.

She put the axe back in the woodshed, and dragged the tree into the house. Sally was not in the kitchen. Melissa did not notice the station hack at the front door. She lifted the tree in her strong arms and carried it directly to the drawing-room.

CHAPTER 16

A FEW MINUTES before Melissa had returned from her sojourn in the woods, Geoffrey Dunham arrived at Midfield and had immediately taken the station hack to the Upjohn house, sending a message to his sister by a boy in the village to announce his arrival and ask that she send a carriage for him at the Upjohns'.

Now he sat beside Amanda's bed, alone with her, for she had sent her nurse from the room. He was extremely shocked at Amanda's appearance, and asked her at once why she had not sent for him before. Arabella's letters to him, he said, with cold anger in his voice, had told him nothing, had, in fact, reassured him that Amanda was only slightly ill.

Amanda considered. In her good sense, she reflected that one should avoid enemies at all cost. Melissa would soon live in Geoffrey's house, and whether or not Arabella then sought another residence, Melissa would inevitably come in contact with her. Enemies, even the meanest and apparently the most impotent, had a way of suddenly becoming dangerous when least expected. No, it was bad policy at any time to make an enemy, and she, Amanda, wanted no enemies for the vulnerable Melissa, who, because of her innocence, would not recognize a foe when she saw him.

So Amanda said weakly: "Dear Geoffrey, it is I, perhaps, whom you should reproach. I particularly requested Arabella not to alarm you. I did not wish you unduly disturbed. But now that I know I have very little longer to live, I had to send for you."

Geoffrey's anger subsided, but he eyed Amanda with suspicion. She returned his look with quiet equanimity. She repeated: "Reproach me if you must, Geoffrey."

"I do not intend to reproach you, Mrs. Upjohn, under any

circumstances. I am only shocked and hurt that you did not send for me before."

Amanda smiled feebly. She regarded Geoffrey with her sunken and clouded eyes. How strong and assured he was! She was not deceived as to the virtues of the man, but at least he was honest in his brutality, clean in his ruthlessnesses. There were no shadowy deviousnesses in his character, no twistings, no soft capriciousnesses, no blurrings of his outlines. He is a hard man, and perhaps even cruel, she thought, but at least he has mental honor, and there are things he would not do. If his voice was rarely gentle, it would never be treacherous. He had his own code, and though some of the rigorous might denounce it, he adhered to it according to his own interpretation of good and evil. He would not deceive from corrupt delight in deception. He did not lust for power, because he had it and was capable of attaining it openly. He was no benign hypocrite who concealed all enormities under a mild and ingratiating exterior, and therefore he was not dangerous. She could trust him, this man who was not a liar and certainly no weakling.

Geoffrey said: "It is all nonsense, of course, that you are dying, Mrs. Upjohn."

Amanda smiled faintly. "I was dying, and then I knew I could not die until I had seen you, Geoffrey." She looked at him with sudden piercing attention. "It is impossible for me to go on living. I have been dying for a long time, for years, because life was unendurable for me. It hasn't improved, Geoffrey. I don't want to live."

"Nonsense," he repeated. "When one is recovering from a severe illness one has any amount of sentimental thoughts."

She smoothed the sheets restlessly with her worn hand. "Geoffrey, I have always failed. I am on the point of failing utterly. No, please listen to me, for I—I am not strong and every word is an effort. My children: Phoebe, Andrew, Melissa. Melissa, in her awful innocence, and ignorance of the world, has plans for the others. No matter; I doubt they will agree, but it will shock Melissa beyond endurance when they defy her. She will have no one to look to but you, Geoffrey."

"Yes," he replied, gently.

Amanda sighed. "I told Melissa of your offer. She seemed to think that you had insulted her too horribly for any comment from her."

Geoffrey smiled. "I thought that would happen," he said.

Amanda lifted her head from her pillow, and looked at

him urgently. "Geoffrey, you still want Melissa? You will not let her go? I must know that!"

He was alarmed at her agitation. He took her hand, and the fingers jumped against his palm like cold dry bones. He said: "I still want Melissa, and I won't let her go. You can rest assured about that."

"No matter how she refuses?"

"No matter how she refuses."

"You will find a way?"

"Of course. The poor girl!"

Amanda's eyes filled with tears; she let them fall over her face and did not hide them. She could hardly speak, and he had to bend over her to hear her: "Geoffrey, I was a blind and wicked woman. When you asked me for Melissa, I said unpardonable things about her. I said she was bad, that she had brought evil into this house. How can God forgive me for that? I did not know! But I know now. If only I had the strength to tell you everything, to make things clear to you—" She could not speak, but she clutched his hand desperately.

"You don't need to tell me," said Geoffrey, greatly disturbed. "I already knew everything."

She gazed at him for a long time, in silence. Then she whispered: "About Charles?"

"Yes, everything about Charles. He was quite a villain, Mrs. Upjohn."

She turned away from him, and looked at her cold windows. "No," she whispered at last, "he was no villain. The wrong is in us, because of our blindness. It is the innocent who create villains, who perpetuate them and give them power. And the stupid." She paused, labored for breath. "Charles was only a little man. Melissa and I, and perhaps the others, created him. If he ruined our lives, it was because, in our innocence, or our ignorance, we invited him to do so. Charles did not make a legend of himself; Melissa did that. She must be rescued from the legend, Geoffrey."

Geoffrey thought this a very charitable and faulty view of Charles, but he also thought that there was a nucleus of truth in Amanda's words. Perhaps it was true that there were no villains, in the pure sense of the word. They tentatively suggest the idea, others enthusiastically enlarge upon it, give it reality. Still, the kernel of the villainy remained, and Charles could not be exonerated.

"How can Melissa be rescued from her self-deception?" asked Amanda, almost frantically.

"I am not sure that Melissa has completely deceived herself," said Geoffrey. "I think Charles gave her very active assistance. No, please don't speak again. It exhausts you. I only want to tell you this: Whatever happens, I won't desert Melissa. I'll marry her, and as soon as possible. She has no chance against me," he added, with a reassuring smile.

Amanda sighed, and closed her eyes. "I look back at my life, and I see what a fool I was," she murmured. "Why do we have to come to death before we know what follies we have committed?"

"I don't know," said Geoffrey. "It is bad sport on the part of Heaven, isn't it? But then, you aren't dying, dear friend."

He got up, and through Amanda's window he had an oblique view of Melissa, shawl a-flutter, hair uncovered and blowing, dragging the Christmas tree towards the back of the house. "She is such a poor, silly child," said the panting voice from the bed. "She is so innocent, so arrogantly stupid, so open to any calamity."

"The innocent invite calamity," remarked Geoffrey, half to himself. "That is why there are wars and all the other damn foolishnesses. I don't think the world of men is villainous. I think it is just naïve. It amounts to the same thing in the end; catastrophe is none the less complete because it is invoked by ingenuous fools."

He thought of the war which had murdered so many thousands a bare three years ago, had crippled and embittered so many millions more, and had almost irrevocably divided a nation forever. When would men learn that wars never decided any issue, and that if it seemed so it was a delusion? Murder never cured hatred or enthroned justice. The root of wars, of any crime, lay in man's belief that violence could create peace or change human nature. Man's applauded brain, his cherished "reason," had only changed him from a sensible animal into a confused beast who thought dangerous thoughts and filled a perfectly normal world with the phantoms of nightmare, the howling dervishes of mad dreams. Yet, thought Geoffrey, it also discovered, or invented, God. For this vision alone, for that single transcendental passion, it should be regarded with awe and reverence, and forgiven.

Who am I, anyway, to despise or deride or condemn anyone else, thought Geoffrey, as he stood by the window and looked out at the wide white desolation. I have probably never had a thought or a desire that somebody else hasn't had before me, multitudes of somebodies. And most probably all of us, to a lesser or greater degree, have committed the crimes of all men, and, to the same degrees, possess the nobility of the saints and the dreams of the heroes. We are all one blood-stream, possibly all one soul, just as all other animals are linked together with the long chain of instinct and mystery. *Homo sum; humanum nihil mihi alienum puto*—I am a man; nothing human is alien to me. If I want to understand any other man, even such a man as Charles, I have only to look into myself.

He walked back slowly to the bed, and sat down. Amanda had spent all her strength and could only lie on her pillows now and smile at him faintly. He returned her smile, with inner compassion. She was a woman of sense and, above all things, he admired sense.

Amanda, in her turn, regarded him with affectionate approbation. He sat beside her, massive and firm, his shoulders hard, wide and sleek under their black broadcloth. His crisp dark hair, touched with gray, had a vital spring at the temples, and if his small gray eyes were stony and unyielding, they could, at moments, be kind. She thought that under certain conditions they could even be tender. Certainly, they were shrewd and direct and, in their own way, honest. His mouth might be thick and somewhat sensual, but it showed a lust for life, and there was common sense in the heavy lines about it. Melissa considered his dark face and Roman nose gross; Amanda knew them for the marks of a healthy and sensible man. He had good big hands, without delicacy, the hands of a man who had a certain subtlety which did not interfere with his strength.

Amanda liked the way he dressed: richly yet conservatively, his only jewelry the black pearl pin in his full crimson cravat, the signet ring on his finger, and the gold watch-chain that stretched over his black and figured waistcoat. Yes, a level-headed man, intelligent without being intellectual, sardonic but without cruelty, hard without being obdurate. She could trust the fanatical Melissa to him, but for a moment she was disturbed by the thought of what he would have to endure with the girl. However, he was at least fifteen years older than Melissa, and very much wiser.

"You will have a difficult time with Melissa," she murmured.

"Don't worry, Mrs. Upjohn. The poor girl isn't half as thorny as you and she think she is." He paused. "I know what you are thinking: Why do I want Melissa? Because she reminds me of you. You are both devils for personal integrity."

The nurse returned to say that her patient must rest now, and Geoffrey got up to go. He hesitated a moment, then bent

over Amanda and kissed her cold damp forehead. She clung
to his hand briefly, then released him. She watched him leave
the room, and sighed with content. Then she laughed feebly
at his last words.

Geoffrey went down the stairway, frowning abstractedly.
He had just reached the hall when the parlor door opened and
Melissa appeared as abruptly as a jack-in-the-box. She was
more disheveled than usual; her black frock was pricked all
over with green pine needles, and her hair hung in gilt wisps
about her cheeks, which were still flushed from her exertions
with the tree.

She had erupted from the parlor, but when she saw Geoffrey
standing before her in the hall she stopped as suddenly and
completely as though struck in the breast by an iron fist. She
literally swayed backwards, and one of her heels cracked
loudly against the door she had closed. Her color vanished
instantly, and she stood looking at Geoffrey with mingled
shock and outrage and something like hatred and terror.

Geoffrey began to smile at her, then he saw how emaciated
she had become, how ghastly were the shadows her facial
bones cast over her white face. Her clothing, he saw, looked
much too large for her shrunken body, and blue veins protruded in her temples and over the tendons of her thin neck.
He said with consternation: "Good God!"

"What are you doing here?" she cried. Then, remembering
his "offer" and her humiliation, she turned a feverish scarlet.

But he did not hear her. He was too busy looking at her
face. Her expression, always somewhat fixed, had now a
fanatical intensity, a rigor, which dismayed him. He said:
"What the hell has happened to you, Melissa?"

"How dare you come to this house?" she answered, hysterically, pressing herself back against the door and gathering
her skirts about her.

He stared at her, incredulously, then frowned. "What's the
matter with you? Have you lost your mind? What do you
mean, anyway?" His voice was impatient, but his concerned
eyes searched her face and he could not be too angry with this
poor and dwindled young creature. "Don't you remember
me?" he added, trying to smile humorously. "I'm Geoffrey
Dunham."

She could only look at him with a loathing he found unbelievable. Her nostrils flared suddenly. He was making fun of
her again! He had come here to tease her, to ridicule her.
Now she saw it all: he had not been sincere when he had made
his offer. He had been laughing at her all the time, secretly.

He had not only robbed her father, was not only intending to rob all the Upjohns, now that Charles was dead and defenseless, but he had deliberately taunted her mother with his lying offer of marriage with herself. How could a man be so base, so contemptible, so unscrupulous?

It was incredible that she could be thinking this, but she thought it, this immured and ignorant girl. And as she did so she felt such a desolation, such a misery and inarticulate despair, that her lips turned cold and her heart began a long and sickening roll of pain. She shivered and trembled; she shrank back against the door, for her legs had become too weak to hold her. But her eyes, full of a blue blaze, never left Geoffrey's face.

"How dare you humiliate me with your lies to my mother?" she asked, and her voice shook.

He stared at her, dumbfounded. Then, very slowly, he began to understand, and he looked away to hide his compassion, his impatient amusement. He said, quite gently: "I wasn't lying, Melissa." He turned to her again. "Why, you poor, damned little fool! Is that what you thought all the time?"

He took a step towards her, but she shrank back, spread out her arms against the door in an attitude which uncomfortably reminded him of crucifixion.

"You lied! You lied!" she said, and then repeated it breathlessly: "You lied. You always made fun of me. You are making fun of me now." She caught her breath and cried loudly: "Go away! Oh, go away!"

She swung about, faced the door, and buried her head in her arms. She began to sob with such a forlorn and distracted sound that Geoffrey was aghast. Her back was so thin, for all the broad straight shoulders, and her black frock dragged on the floor. He could not stand looking at her and not touching her, yet he knew he must not touch her now. And he knew that whatever he might say would not reach her in her present frantic agony.

Then he heard the kitchen door open down the long corridor to the right, and he turned quickly, swept up his coat and hat and gloves and cane from the chair where he had laid them, opened the oaken door, and went out. The Dunham carriage was slowly struggling up the snowy pathway and he hailed it with a flourish of his cane. He climbed into the carriage and was driven away. Then he settled down upon the cushions and said simply: "For the love of Christ!"

Melissa dimly heard the door closing after him. After a little, she dropped her arms and, overcome with weakness, turned about, her face still running with tears. She heard the crunching of carriage wheels on the snow; she heard the carriage turn about and the sound of it diminishing as it reached the road. Something opened in her chest like a sharp agony. She rushed into the parlor again, and went to the windows. She watched the carriage out of sight, until it was hid in a bend of the road. She waited and watched until it reappeared again on a higher level. She watched until it was only an insect crawling towards the distant house on the hillside.

Then she sat down in the cold and empty parlor and, unable to find her handkerchief, wiped her eyes and cheeks on her ragged petticoat. "He was lying," she said aloud. "Oh, yes, he was lying!" And she began to cry again.

CHAPTER 17

Mrs. Arabella Dunham Shaw awaited the coming of her brother with considerable anxiety and trepidation. She had sent him the telegram requested by Amanda Upjohn, and it had been urgent enough. But now he was with Amanda, and Heaven only knew what he would say to him! As Arabella had had few honest thoughts in her life, and as she always found deception and falsehood expedient, she naturally came to the conclusion that all other human beings were as crafty as herself, and as perfidious. Insincere and sly, chronically suspicious of everyone's motives, she believed in the integrity and honor of no one, and was of the opinion that the apparently upright and single-minded were both liars and hypocrites. She suspected them more than the openly devious and false.

So she hovered behind the curtains of her bedroom and peered with increasing apprehension down the road which led to the Upjohn house. Over and over, she rehearsed her defense. She, herself, had been ill, and had known very little of Amanda's illness. She had not wanted to worry her brother, who would soon be home for Christmas, anyway. She had often visited Amanda, though the latter had been unconscious and was unaware of the visits, and Amanda had not seemed in very great danger. She had been forbidden to see Amanda, by that intolerable Melissa, that vicious Melissa, that inimical Melissa. She had been requested by Amanda, herself, not to trouble Geoffrey.

But what was Amanda now saying to Geoffrey? Was she relating a whole lying history of neglect? Was she appealing to Geoffrey's ridiculous sympathy, as a lonely and abandoned friend? Was she telling him that Arabella had visited the house only once, and then only upon request? Was she picturing herself heart-breakingly as a very sick woman who had no one to appeal to but Geoffrey Dunham? A vivid and repulsive vision of Amanda sobbing on her pillows, upbraiding and denouncing Geoffrey's sister, came to Arabella's infuriated mind. It would be just like that hypocrite, Amanda, just like that cunning and designing woman! Fright mixed with rage filled Arabella, and she twisted the fine lace of her curtains in sweating hands. "No matter!" she exclaimed, aloud. "You'll not get that odious daughter of yours into this house, Amanda Upjohn! I'll not tolerate that repellent baggage for one instant!"

Arabella reflected incoherently upon her status in this house. The servants hated her because she demanded constant perfection and would not allow them to lapse in their duties even for a moment. They hated her for asking them to earn their wages! That was the way with the lower classes. They resented all discipline, and thought themselves as good as their betters. Her life was a constant warfare with the kitchen and the halls. Everyone tried to cheat her, from the shops in Midfield to the gardeners on the grounds. The whole world, from her brother to the very kitchenmaid, was in a conspiracy to deprive her of her rightful heritage, to humiliate her. Her father had been insensible to her proper rights. Only her husband had understood her, and now he was dead. She brought out her rose-scented handkerchief from her sleeve and wiped her eyes. But she never looked away from the road that rose from the valley.

By the time Geoffrey's carriage appeared, she was one seething rage and hatred. She hastily withdrew from the window, bathed her eyes with Cologne water. Her great and frivolous bedroom was filled with the fresh odor of lemon verbena, powder and sachet. She warmed her cold hands for a moment or two at her fire, plucked out the bustle and the draped ruffles on her dark-green silk gown, patted the rolls of hair on the top of her head, shook out the ringlets on her lined and yellowish neck, and tripped down the stairs, a welcoming and affectionate smile on her face. She rustled and bounced girlishly down the massive staircase, her chains and ear-rings and bangles jingling. But she trembled a little when she heard the knocker. She, herself, opened the door, though James, Geoffrey's man, had promptly appeared.

Geoffrey was immediately enveloped in his sister's plump and scented arms, and her voice filled his ears with glad cries: "Oh, darling Geoffrey! How lovely it is to see you again! James, take Mr. Dunham's things. Geoffrey, my love, how well you look, and how fresh! Do come into the library at once; there is such a nice fire waiting, and your own best brandy, and such delicious little cakes!"

Geoffrey reeled under this unusual assault of affection, and he felt a twinge of suspicion. But Arabella did indeed seem glad to see him. At any rate, he was in no mood for accusations against this silly woman. He kissed her heartily, allowed her to link her arm to his and to bounce beside him into the library. There she made quite a violent fuss over him, drawing his favorite chair to the hearth, pouring his brandy, regarding him with vehement affection, then sitting down near him with a crackling of taffeta petticoats and a fresh gush of scent and flurry of ringlets. She clasped her hands together in great anxiety, rolled up her eyes, and cried: "Do tell me at once how dear, dear Amanda is! I must know! I have been dying of concern! But she would not let me send for you. She especially forbade it. I pleaded with her, but it was no use at all. What can one do with such a darling, obdurate but thoughtful woman, Geoffrey? I sent such hampers, larger than the ones you so artfully ordered," and she rolled her eyes at him coquettishly, "and such flowers, and such loving messages! It was all I could do. And then, when I last saw her, I simply insisted upon sending for you, in spite of all her arguments."

As this tallied with Amanda's own account, Geoffrey's suspicion disappeared. He said: "Amanda is very ill, Bella. She is convinced that she is dying, but that is nonsense of course. I doubt, however, whether she will be well again for a long time."

Arabella sighed, then opened her shark's mouth in a round oval of sympathy. She dabbed at her eyes. "Dear Geoffrey, one must be prepared for anything. I, myself, thought Amanda failing very rapidly." She sighed again. She was safe, but she was immediately suspicious of some dark plot on Amanda's part in concealing the truth. She added: "It all comes at such a busy time, too. Our guests will be arriving tomorrow, and the house is in such a confusion. But never mind. Tell me all about yourself and what you have been doing these weeks."

It was pleasant and agreeable in this warm, rich library, with the crimson and blue and brown backs of the leather-bound books glinting in the pale sunlight, with the mighty logs crackling and spluttering on the hearth, and the two setters lying on Geoffrey's feet. The brandy was warm in him; his sister bent towards him with great admiration and affection. There was a faint scent of roasting beef mingling with the odor of smoking wood. The large windows looked out on a white still world, glittering with vagrant sunlight. Geoffrey listened indulgently to his sister's plans for Christmas. He, himself, disliked the holiday, but it gave Arabella pleasure, and God knew she had very little of that. He listened to her, but he was remembering Melissa and her pathetic weeping, and the sharp bones of her exhausted face.

"Now, I know you don't like the Littlefields very much, Geoffrey," Arabella said in a soft, reproachful voice, "but please don't frown so. They are my best friends, and have been so very amiable to me."

"Why shouldn't they?" asked Geoffrey, coming out of his trance. "We have more money than they have, and that is their yardstick of importance." He pulled the ears of one dog, and smiled unpleasantly. "It's very strange. We loftily denounce the caste system in England, and the sharp division of classes, and call it 'undemocratic' because the British value men who have a tradition of breeding, culture, and family. We are so damned democratic, we say, scorning the British system. Yet our vulgar yardstick is immeasurably more contemptible and disgusting. We value a man in proportion to his bank accounts, his stocks and bonds. We do not respect a man for what he is, as the British do, but for what he *has*. And this, when any unscrupulous mountebank, thief or despoiler of the helpless can make a fortune for himself in America in a few years!"

Arabella shook an arch finger at him. "Oh, that comes of the years you spent in England, dear, dear Geoffrey! So snobbish!" She thought of the pottery fortune, and was annoyed. Geoffrey had such a small sense of proportion. He was always remembering that odious pottery, and would never allow his sister to forget it.

Geoffrey smiled. "It is natural that we should suspect gentlemen, for gentlemen are rare in America. I think, too, that we are only too conscious of an inferior heritage and must therefore denounce those of superior heritage in order to preserve our egotism. Values which do not enhance our vanity are values we'll not have knocking about the place at any cost."

He added: "The Littlefields are in cheese, aren't they?"

"Oh, what an uncivil and crude way to put it, Geoffrey! And how unkind; 'In cheese'! One instantly thinks of maggots." She shuddered elaborately.

"Well, the Littlefields are sort of maggoty, aren't they?"

Arabella burst into giggles. The Littlefields were her dear friends, but she enjoyed Geoffrey's remark tremendously. She said: "To hear you, Geoffrey, one would believe that the dear Littlefields were farmers, selling ugly wheels of cheese. And you know very well that they are the largest importers of delightful foreign cheeses in America. 'Importers' does sound so much more genteel."

"A smell is still a smell, foreign or not, rich or not, and the Littlefields bore me," said Geoffrey.

Arabella was annoyed. Something had disturbed her brother, and he was apparently not in a holiday mood. He had always been difficult about holidays, and disliked most of his sister's friends. But he had invariably been gracious, after prolonged and appeasing effusions from her. This time, however, his mood struck her as abnormally distrait. It could only be those awful Upjohns, thought Arabella, with aversion and hatred.

Geoffrey startled her when he spoke again: "It's just occurred to me that our past invitations to the Upjohns for Christmas Eve, or Christmas Day, or New Year's Eve, or New Year's Day, have been lukewarm. At any rate, I suspect it, for only once did Charles come, that was about five years ago, and Phoebe has appeared only twice at our New Year's Eve dance. I don't recall that they enjoyed themselves. As for Amanda and Andrew and Melissa—they never came. We have not only been remiss as hosts, we have been remiss as friends. Why weren't they urged to come here more often?"

He looked at his sister sharply, in a very disagreeable way he had. Arabella felt her lips grow cold and her ready smile more fixed. Would she never be free of those Upjohns? Were they destined to haunt her peace and her pleasures and safety forever? She patted Geoffrey's knee coquettishly, tilted her head at him, and sighed: "But, my dear, they received exactly the same engraved invitations as did our other friends. Did you expect me to go down to them and implore them on my bended knees?"

Geoffrey refilled his brandy glass, and took a very irritating length of time to do it. Then he sipped, and stared at the fire.

Arabella watched him closely, and her heart began to flutter in an alarming way.

She said, soothingly: "Yes, Charles came and, contrary to your remark, he did enjoy himself. He was much admired, though I thought he posed a little absurdly. But everyone was kind, and the next year he was asked for, even if he didn't deign to honor us with his presence." Her long yellowish teeth showed for a moment in her sweetish smile. "And everyone thought Phoebe exquisite, though her gown—her gown, my dear!—was too appalling for words. The seamstress poor dear Amanda employs in Midfield is not only mediocre, she is practically mutilating. But then, the Upjohn females were never distinguished for taste, you will have to admit. The material from which the gown was made was not too bad, Charles having sent for it to Philadelphia, but the color was atrocious, a kind of cerise which ruined her hair and coloring. And the lace at the neck and sleeves! Pure Nottingham. We have better at the windows of our servants' rooms. The next year the poor child appeared in it again, but this time the ruffles were bound in a nasty shade of yellow. The combination was ghastly. That was the time when we were wearing very large hoops, you remember. Phoebe's hoops were the hoops of a serving-girl! She was very ill at ease——"

"No doubt, with all you vicious females staring at her and giggling in a ladylike fashion behind your fans," said Geoffrey.

"Oh, my dear, we are not that ill-bred! I must protest! Everyone received her charmingly and gave her many compliments. But Phoebe knew she was out of place. She was always a sensible girl——"

"Out of place!" exclaimed Geoffrey, and his full dark face became ruddy with anger. "Out of place among the cheesemongers? Charles came of a distinguished family, dating far back before the Revolution. His people were English gentry even then. As for Amanda, I happen to know her history, and my father knew her father well. One of the greatest gentlemen in Boston, in America. You talk like a fool, Arabella. But then, you always were a little more than vulgar. And yet, I agree with you. Phoebe was out of place among the cheesegentry. We ought not to have insulted her by inviting her."

Arabella lost her temper. She did not often do this with Geoffrey, for she was afraid of him. It had always been her part to placate. But the Upjohns had become too much for her, and the dark fear that haunted her days undid her self-control. She cried recklessly: "How can you speak of the

Upjohns as if they were of any consequence whatever, Geoffrey! They haven't a penny! They are as poor as church-mice."

Geoffrey gave her a look which made her wince. He stood up, began to walk slowly about the room, carrying his brandy-glass. He said, heavily: "I hear your echo everywhere, Bella, so I suppose I shouldn't be too hard on you. I see men of distinction despised by nameless boors who have acquired wealth by crime, thievery, quackery, exploitation, filthy politics, manipulation of stocks, horse trading, butchery, downright robbery, cheese-manufacturing, machinery, flour-making, and God knows what else in the way of rascality and plebeian trade, which once were despised by gentlemen of culture and breeding. We are selling gentlemen into economic slavery and social exile, and allowing the faceless hordes, who have contrived to browbeat or swindle their neighbors out of their dollars, to sit on the velvet seats of government and dictate who shall or shall not enter the sacred chambers of 'society.'"

He drank a little of the brandy, while Arabella watched him and bridled with fright and umbrage.

"Tradesmen!" said Geoffrey, with profound loathing. "We are becoming a nation of despicable tradesmen who imitate the gentry as well as an ape can imitate a man. You can't breed gentlemen out of cattle."

Arabella, forgetting herself further, exclaimed spitefully: "Our mother was a peasant, as you would say! But you would not be drinking that fine brandy and walking up and down this handsome room but for her money!"

Geoffrey turned his head and smiled at her unpleasantly. "That is just what I mean, my dear Bella. That's just the disgusting thing about it."

He walked up and down again. "It wouldn't matter so much if the cheese-mongers and the other tradesmen remained humble, and conscious of their source. No, one could tolerate them, then. But they become so damned arrogant! It isn't a matter of race, either. I'd be delighted to entertain a Chinese mandarin, and should consider that he honored me by accepting my hospitality. But I can't bear to see a tradesman in my drawing-room, even if he bears an Anglo-Saxon name, and, by God! I'll soon put a stop to it."

He went to the fire and kicked at a log quite savagely. "What will happen to our country then, with its best blood bred out and squeezed out, despised and rejected, because it has no money? A nation of dolts, fools, and liars, mountebanks and vulgarians, without passion or vision, truth or nobility, degrading everything they touch and relegating art to the dust-bin because they cannot understand it."

He crushed a smoldering piece of wood with his foot. "It happened to Rome. It can happen to America. Rome did very well until the plebe replaced the aristocrat, and out-bred him. The history of the fall of every nation is the history of the rise of the low-bred man and the fall of the gentleman."

Arabella listened with bewilderment and angry malice. "What of our dear Mr. Lincoln? He came of humble parentage, was born in a log-house, and saved our country!"

Geoffrey gloomily turned his glass in his hand. "I doubt very much whether Mr. Lincoln came of peasant stock. His name proves that, if nothing else. But somehow he had acquired the peasant's point of view, and we're going to suffer for it. We are already suffering for it. Look at the carpet-baggers now despoiling the aristocratic South. There are some who blame the Negro, but that is a stupid man's reasoning. The blame lies in the peasant rampant, unrestrained by law or custom."

Arabella stood up, trembling with umbrage. "Geoffrey, you have a singular way of expressing yourself. Our house will be filled with our guests tomorrow, and I do hope you will restrain——"

"They aren't my guests." Geoffrey set down his glass with a thump. He smiled. "Remember that my father was a gentleman, even if my mother wasn't a lady. And now we come back to the Upjohns, who have been ignored by the rich peasantry around here. Or perhaps Charles, with a gentleman's good sense, refused to have anything to do with them."

At the sound of that hated name, Arabella trembled violently. "A gentleman! He was a freak and a nobody, and so are the rest of them, though you refuse to see it. Look at that dreadful Melissa, with her bunched frocks, her milk-maid's hands, her uncouth voice, her big stride, her chapped skin, and her utter lack of style! It would be like having a stable-boy in our drawing-room to admit that creature!" Now all her hatred for Melissa, all her natural venom, spewed out of her. "You should hear what everyone says about your fine Melissa Upjohn! She is a caricature and a byword, a graceless, ugly, frumpish, untidy female, with the manners of a farm-hand."

She stopped, panting. Geoffrey turned and looked at her steadily, at her gaudy gown, her trumpery ringlets, her masses of tinkling jewelry, her fat, suffused face. And he thought of Melissa with her high air of breeding and race, the strong nobility of her features, her disheveled elegance, her pride and heroic carriage.

He said, quietly: "Go away, Bella. I have things to think about and you annoy me."

Arabella uttered a whimpering cry, gathered up her green-silk skirts, and fled the room. He knew that she would go upstairs to her glittering and lace-draped chamber, and would sob and weep and beat her pillows and impotently hate, not only the Upjohns, but himself. Probably me, more than anyone, he thought, and smiled.

He sat down and poured his glass full again. He stretched his big legs out to the fire. He pulled a dog's ear, and the dog, fawning, put its paws on his knees. He looked at the great affectionate eyes, then pushed the dog away.

"Well, anyway, you're honest," he remarked, "and that's something."

CHAPTER 18

Now THAT Arabella had gone, he could light a cheroot and smoke in peace. He was somewhat annoyed with himself. He had not seen Arabella for a month, had written her but three letters, had been greeted upon his return with cries of pleasure, and had immediately quarreled with the poor old fool. "It's the pots coming out in me," he said aloud, thinking of his mother's source of fortune, and grinning. Well, after he'd done a little thinking he would go to Arabella and make his peace. After all, she managed his house expertly, was a good hostess for him. He owed her considerable, even if she almost constantly exasperated him and could not conceal, however she tried, that she hated and feared him. Besides, she was due very soon for a profoundly severe shock; he might as well be civil to the poor silly thing as long as possible.

He had been thinking of Melissa all the way home, and now he resumed his thinking. He was essentially a man of action and directness, and he saw now that he would have to exercise considerable subtlety, a thing he despised. I hate this fiddle-faddling around with women, he thought. But females of breeding must have this pre-nuptial dance, or all their confounded sensibilities were offended. A man could not go to them and say candidly: "I adore you. I love the way your breasts curve out of your bodice, and the glimmer of your thighs under that pretty silk, and I want to bite your white neck, very gently, before proceeding to more ardent familiarities. So, considering that you entrance me, and that I want to go to bed with you, will you honor me by meeting me at the altar? A foolish preliminary, but a necessary one, it seems."

He had said this often to ladies, without, of course, the altar business, and they, not being genteel, had delightedly accompanied him to whatever destination he suggested. They were honest women, and they knew what a man really wanted, even when he spoke of love. But genteel women were not honest; they always pretended that gentlemen wanted only to hold their hands and discourse with them on a high plane. They assumed such an air of delicacy and innocence that it quite sickened a man.

Melissa was worse than genteel. She was ignorant. Geoffrey was quite certain that her life on the farm had not enlightened her in the least. Doubtless she thought roosters existed for the sole purpose of making soup. Their connection with eggs would be a dark mystery to her. As for the other animals, if she had ever seen them in amorous play, she had probably thought it only high spirits, if she gave it a thought at all. Yet Geoffrey was sure that though she was a sleeping nymph she could be awakened to full womanhood. She had her uneasy instincts, buried though they were. It was his duty to excavate them, and he saw now that it would be no easy work.

The first step—and probably the hardest—was marriage. How to browbeat, blackmail or bully her into it? He knew that she was unimpressed by his wealth or position or power; her father had taught her that these were without value. And he was no infernal milksop of a man, who could talk to a woman of spiritual and poetic things. He could not startle her with unsuspected gifts of the mind, for he did not have them. The best way to approach her would probably be with his own translation of Virgil or of Plato, or with a dissertation on the influence of Greek art on the Renaissance. If he appeared before her as a man, she would only look at him blindly. Yet it was as a man that he must eventually appeal to her, for that was the only way to awaken her slumbering soul and arouse her woman's body. The bedroom, he reflected, has cured more women of the vapors than anything else. But how to get Melissa into the bedroom? He would do it some way, but the way was still obscure.

"Curse you, Charles," he said. "You've made it damned hard for me, or for any other man. But you'll not win, you affable old rascal. I'm getting a faint inkling of how you corrupted Melissa's mind, and, knowing that, I know also that I'll be able to drive out the corruption."

As he was a man who rarely deluded himself, he wondered again, as he had wondered a thousand times, just why he wanted Melissa and loved her. He had known handsomer women, and certainly more amiable, complaisant and charming women. He had known women who had amused him, excited him, and pleased him. Melissa had none of these allurements. It was beyond understanding, he thought impatiently. But he had only to bring Melissa's pale fixed face with its clear, fanatical eyes before him, to imagine her walking or gesturing, and he was all a-flutter like some idiot school-boy. In a way, she was the only woman he had ever loved. He could think of her for hours at a time, and not once imagine her naked. If this thought occasionally came to him it was with immense excitement and tenderness, something he had never felt before. She was everything to him: child, woman, potential friend, the dearest thing on earth. And he could not understand why. She had never smiled at him more than once or twice, and it had been a tight, shrinking smile, more like a grimace, and only for the sake of politeness. He could not recall that he had ever heard her laugh, and laughter in a woman was very important. But he had only to see her to be enthralled and touched and moved.

"Just a prancing, middle-aged Galahad—that's me," he thought. "All clad in white armor and riding a white horse. 'My strength is as the strength of ten, because my heart is pure'!" He burst out laughing and stood up, throwing his cheroot into the fire.

Now that he had determined to marry Melissa, and that as soon as possible, he had the naive impulse to look about his house and see it through Melissa's eyes. The servants were well-trained. He rarely saw them, except at meal-times. Yet evidences that they were in the house were everywhere. He went out into the hall. Under the arch of the black marble pillared fireplace fresh logs had been laid on the glowing ashes, and they spluttered heartily. The three gilt and crystal candelabra on the mantelpiece had been lit, and the great square hall was filled with a soft golden glow of mingled fire and candlelight. It danced on the floor of dark red and black squares, on the paneled walls, on the walnut stairway curving up to the room's vast arch. It glimmered on the enormous grandfather clock, and the old gilt face brightened. The clock sounded its deep melodious chimes, then there was a soft booming as the hour, six o'clock, was struck. Fresh flowers from the conservatory had been placed in the blue Chinese vase on the long walnut table against the right wall. The tall carved chairs with their red velvet seats were like bishops' thrones. Everything was silent, except for the crackling of the fire. The flowers filled the warm air with a sweet and poignant scent.

Still seeing no one, for the servants were busy with preparations for dinner, Geoffrey threw open the large double doors that led to the drawing-rooms. They were dark. He lit a lamp. It was cold in these rooms, for no fire burned on the hearths. Only when guests were expected were the rooms aired, the candles and the lamps lit, and the fires laid. The first room was the formal drawing-room, but the one beyond it was used as a ball-room during the holidays. This first room was called by Geoffrey (who "had no sense of elegance or dignity"), "the Yellow Room." Arabella preferred to call it "the Louis Fifteenth Room." The pottery fortune had been used to advantage here. Old Mr. Dunham and his wife had traveled over Europe and had brought back whole cases of treasure. A minor French palace had been sacked for these lovely furnishings. It was an enormous room. Its walls had been hung with yellow silk damask, delicately figured. The wide ceiling had been painted in soft cream, and bright gold-leaf mouldings cast an intricate pattern over it of flowers and birds and twining leaves. The rug was of the softest and dimmest Aubusson, in tints of faded gold and cream. The fireplace itself was of golden marble, veined with delicate brown, as was the hearth. Two golden cupids, over the fireplace, held candelabra filled just now with unlighted, tall, pale-yellow candles. Brass andirons, glittering in the shifting lamplight, held waiting logs.

Over the fireplace was a fine old painting of nymphs, white hounds and cupids at play against a background of dim green forest and pale shining sky. It was a charming picture, but only Arabella could discourse with familiarity on the famous artist. It furnished, in its brighter and different tints, the only relief from the prevailing gold. Endless little carved golden chairs, with gold damask seats, were scattered about the room, and many settees and love-seats to match. Even the delicate and spindling tables had been painted gold, and the tops were of the same golden marble as the fireplace. Here and there were cabinets, on tall golden legs, their curved fronts painted in faded scenes of pillars, gardens and swooning ladies. A golden and cream pianoforte stood between the tall windows, a yellow Chinese vase on it filled with yellow roses and green leaves. The very draperies were of golden velvet, with golden fringes, and hung in massive folds from ceiling to floor. The lamps had golden bases, and their shades were of carved gilt over yellow glass.

Geoffrey, to tease Arabella, frequently remarked that the room gave him the jaundice. Secretly, he admired it, though its golden coldness sometimes oppressed him. He could not remember whether Melissa had ever seen this room. He suspected not. It was never opened except for important guests. Only Charles and Phoebe had seen it in its full, resplendent, and golden New Year's glory, with all the lamps lit and a fire roaring on the hearth.

Geoffrey lit a candle which he had removed from the cupid candelabrum, and carried it through the broad arch into the room beyond, which was used as a ball-room. It repeated the gold decorations from the first drawing-room, but these were scattered, and the Aubusson rug had been removed in the holiday preparations.

He and Melissa, he thought, would be married in the Yellow Room, and there would be a dance in this ball-room in celebration. In imagination he already saw the gay velvets and silks of the women, the sconces lit and shining, the fire blazing. He heard the lilting music, and the laughter.

He returned to the library, went through it to the rear, and opened the dining-room door. Here all was richness, majestic and inviting, from the crimson Oriental rug to the pale-rose damask walls, from the black-marble fireplace to the cathedral-like crystal chandelier that swung from the walnut-beamed ceiling. A shimmer of silver shapes on the immense sideboard greeted Geoffrey's candle, and cabinets winked with their array of glasses.

Now Geoffrey went upstairs and passed the long rows of guest-rooms, the walnut doors brightening as he passed. He stopped a moment at Arabella's door. She was still whimpering behind it. He frowned, hesitated, then passed on. Here were his own apartments, his somber but luxurious bedroom, the dressing-room beyond, and, adjoining the dressing-room, the room which Melissa would occupy. These had been his parents' apartments, and now he occupied them. His mother's room had never been used, not ever for guests. It was tacitly understood that it would belong to his future wife. He opened the door, and stepped inside. Bitter cold greeted him. But it was a charming soft room, large and airy, with a view of the side-gardens and long slopes, spectrally white now in the growing twilight, but green and restful in summer. Here the walls had been hung with the palest blue damask; a rosy Aubusson rug covered the floor. Turquoise glass candelabra stood on the white marble mantelpiece, and were reflected in a huge gilt-framed mirror. The furniture had been covered with dust-sheets, but Geoffrey remembered them well. There was a blue chaise-longue, rose-colored little chairs, a coral-velvet love-seat, white velvet hassocks, and small turquoise and silver lamps on the bed-table and other tables, which had been painted a soft white. Thin draperies of white velvet, patterned with blue, gold and rose, had been drawn closely over the windows to keep out the sunlight. The gilt threads in them danced before the candle in Geoffrey's hands.

He looked at the shrouded chests, which he remembered as white also, at the dressing-table with its long gilt-framed mirror. He recalled that his mother had kept the dressing-table covered with crystal and golden bottles and little jars. He saw them sparkling in lamplight and firelight, and, in memory, he felt the warmth of a fire.

This was Melissa's room, all this delicacy and brightness and charm. Then he remembered Melissa's black and bunchy frocks, her austere face, her long stride, and smiled. Well, he would change that. He saw Melissa, in a blue silken negligée, sitting at the dressing-table, her long pale hair rippling to the floor. He saw the gold and crystal brushes in her hands, smelled the perfume she would use.

Satisfied, and quite excited, he went out, and again passed Arabella's door. He knocked. She sobbed loudly. Impatiently, he called: "Oh, come, Arabella! Open the door for me."

But she called faintly: "Come in." He pushed the door open and found Arabella, as he had expected, weeping on the bed. He put down his candle and looked at her. She was very mussed. He said: "If I offended you, I'm sorry. And now bathe your eyes, my dear, and get ready for dinner. We'll have a little wine in the library, if you wish."

But Arabella was not yet ready to be placated. She sobbed: "To think that you would so insult your sister because of those horrid Upjohns, that very horrid and hideous Melissa! I can't bear it, I can't!"

"It seems to me that it was you who were insulting Melissa. I never mentioned the girl," said Geoffrey, coldly. "I thought the Upjohns were your friends, too, but you attacked them viciously."

Arabella wiped her eyes, as yet at a loss for words. Then, impetuously, she opened her mouth to accuse Geoffrey further, when she saw the candle which he had placed near her on the table. "Where have you been? What is the candle for?" she asked, in a voice hoarse from weeping and anxiety.

Geoffrey sat down in her bed-side chair. "I've been on a tour of inspection. The holidays, you know. Wanted to see if the Yellow Room still gave me the jaundice. And then I looked over Mother's room."

Arabella sat upright on the bed, her ringlets flying in agitation. She stared at her brother, with swollen and reddened eyes, and they became sharp and pointed like marbles of granite. "Mother's room? Mama's room? Why?" Her heart began to pound with dread and panic, and she pressed her hand against the lacy ruffles over it.

Geoffrey shrugged. "Just curiosity, perhaps. I haven't been in there for years. Possibly I just wanted to see whether it was being well-kept."

Arabella regarded him in intense silence, and he looked back at her, smiling amiably. Then at last she moistened her lips and said: "How extraordinary, that you should bother about Mama's room." Her eyes still pierced him.

Geoffrey shrugged again. "Isn't it supposed to be my bride's room? Perhaps I'm thinking of marrying, even at this late date."

He stood up and surveyed the welter of lace and velvet and crystal and flounces in his sister's room. Its thick perfume suffocated him.

"Marrying?" whispered Arabella sharply. "You are thinking of marrying, Geoffrey?"

He scowled impatiently. "Oh, the devil! I don't know. I'm playing with the idea, Bella. Why shouldn't I amuse myself?"

Arabella's panic almost overwhelmed her. She could hardly breathe. She twisted her lace handkerchief in her hands. She could not look away from him.

"Who, Geoffrey?" she stammered.

Geoffrey moved his large head in exasperation. "I didn't say 'who,' Bella. Don't be a fool. The next thing, you'll be announcing my engagement and making an ass of me. Don't go around, for God's sake, making sly comments and giving coquettish hints. There's no one yet. And now, join me in the library and let's have a little peace in this house."

He went out of the room, and Arabella watched him go. Her heart was still thumping in terror. She had to sit still for quite some time before it slowed down and she could move.

She went to her dressing-table and bathed her eyes and patted her hair. She looked at her broad and puffy face, then hastily powdered it. Its color had gone; it was quite pasty. She opened a drawer, brought out a pot of rouge, and applied it skillfully. But her little eyes were strained with fear.

She argued with herself, as she had argued so many times before on similar occasions of alarm. She was frightening herself unnecessarily. Geoffrey was only teasing her, for he knew that she hated the thought of his marrying. But now her panic did not subside. Some instinct warned her. She clasped her hands together tightly. Who? Some girl of good family in Philadelphia or New York, some spoiled and petulant minx who would render her life intolerable? Some chit, with pettish and pampered ways, who would regard Arabella as only a superior house-keeper? The idea was not to be borne.

But what if it were Melissa Upjohn? At this, Arabella uttered an involuntary cry and covered her face with her hands. Not Melissa, dear God! Oh, certainly not Melissa, that horrible creature, that gargoyle, that hoyden and frump! Not Melissa Upjohn in Mama's pretty room, or coming down that noble stairway, or sitting at the foot of the dining-room table! It was not to be endured. She, Arabella, could not remain in this house if Melissa came here. But where would she go? What would she do?

Life could not be that cruel. Arabella rubbed her aching forehead. Feverishly, she recalled Geoffrey's words. She must guard herself, she thought. She must stop putting foolish ideas into his head. He was just at the dangerous age. Men committed such follies. She must keep quiet, and pretend he had not teased her. That was her only safety. Forcing a gay smile, she went downstairs.

CHAPTER 19

THOUGH THE WEATHER remained bitterly cold, it rained in the night, so that gutter and eave rippled and gurgled with water. But at dawn the rain stopped, and everything became curiously still, struck into immobility.

For the last night or two, relieved of her duties, Melissa slept the instant she went to bed, falling asleep as if struck down. She awoke this morning in her cold and fireless room, and went to her windows. The strangest sight lay below her.

Every tree was incandescent in the sunshine, each thin branch and twig plated with bright clear glass, glittering with a thousand prismatic colors under a brilliant sun. The dwindled snow had lost its soft undulations; it had become rigid white fire, straight and stark, like a carpet of stiff tinsel. Now a slight wind stirred, and the glassy branches and twigs of the trees moved, and rattled, and threw off thin waves of tinted light. The sky had taken on an unearthly pale blue, translucent and far. So clear was the air that distance had lost perspective, and Melissa could see the sharp brown hills and the small houses upon them, and even the whitish-brown blur which was Midfield, in the long valley below.

For the first time since her father's death she felt the warmth of an objective pleasure in the bright and crystalline scene. She thought, suddenly: I wish I believed in God!

She was taken aback, and amazed, at her thought. Her father had obliterated God from her universe, as he had obliterated other "sentimentalities" and "errors." The mind of man, he had told her, can take its final step out of the primal ooze only when it understands that it alone is reality, that it alone has power to confer reality. Emotion is man's dark and primitive past; it is an anachronism, and should be discarded as man has discarded his tail, his prehensile toes, his fur. As incomplete man carries in his body vestigial remains of organs no longer necessary for his functions, so he carries in his mind vestigial superstitions and passions no longer necessary for his life. God was not essential to existence. The forest and the jungle had been left behind in man's progress and, with them, the animal fear and terror of the unknown which were marks of the beast. "Animal man is obsolete," Charles had said. "The man of the future is the man of mind."

"There are some who say," he had continued, "that the banishment of 'God' necessarily means the banishment of music and poetry. These people declare that music and poetry are essentially emotions. That is arrant nonsense. They are abstractions, and have a mathematical basis. Only when man's mind is pure intellect, controlled solely by reason, can music and poetry reach their perfection."

But Melissa looked down at the prismatic scene below her windows and felt a deep and aching nostalgia for something mysterious which she had lost, or perhaps had never known. Another thought came to her: I wish I knew how to pray! It was very foolish, she knew, yet only prayer could express beauty. Her thoughts went on confusedly, and with a kind of pain: Perhaps we can experience knowledge only when we interpret the beautiful in the lexicon of God. If God was only a superstition or an emotion, it was still a magnificent one, and human vocabulary was bereft of much of its meaning when it could no longer speak the name of God.

She drew away from the window, strangely oppressed and desolate. And then she felt the flooding sickness of disloyalty. What was the matter with her? Twice before, she had doubted her father and his wisdom and nobility, had thrown a darkness over his remembered face. She felt a silent reproach in the air about her, a sadness, a bewilderment and regret. If she continued to allow herself to be swayed and confused like this, thrown into perplexity, she would be committing a sin against her father and all his work for her would come to nothing. She resolutely turned her back on the cold and brilliant loveliness below. "Nothing exists beyond the mind of man; nothing has reality," he had said. Therefore the beauty of the world was meaningless, without purpose or design. Her father had said this, and he had known.

She dressed and washed, but she could not shake off her oppressed and somber thoughts. They came to her involuntarily, like an alien and insistent voice. Her father had often spoken, sonorously, of the "heroic human mind." But it was heroism in a vacuum, if there was no God. It had no meaning, no point, no compass, no beginning and no end. It had dignity only when it stood in the shadow of God, and it had purpose only when it guided its course by that fixed and spiritual star. Alone in the everlasting darkness, it was only an empty shout without words, and the things which it dreamed had no significance.

"Oh, God may be a lie, but I wish I believed in Him!" she said, aloud.

The sound of her own voice frightened her, and the words revolted her, implying, as they did, her relapse into atavistic folly. She wound up her hair with tremulous hands, and ran out of the room.

But some of the eerie joy of the morning remained with her, false and foolish though she believed it to be. It was a morning to gather red berries to be strung on the Christmas tree in the parlor. It was a morning to think of fruit cake and the turkey waiting in the barn-yard. Andrew would be returning home this evening. There was a bottle of good brandy in the cellar, and cider, and red apples. She would bring them all up today, in readiness for Christmas. Though Papa was dead, he would want his family to forget for a day, and be happy. He had thought Christmas silly, and had spoken indulgently of the Roman Saturnalia, which he had considered much more sensible. Saturn was a less oppressive god than Jesus, and much wiser. But let the people call him Saturn or Jesus: it did not matter. Only the holiday was pertinent. "Thank God for the 'pagan' Romans," he had said. "They have mitigated a little for us, with their appropriated feasts and happy rituals, the horror of Christianity."

Melissa stopped at Phoebe's door. It was nonsense for the girl to hide in her room and cry all the time. This was Christmas! Melissa knocked with peremptory firmness on the door, and called: "Phoebe! Tomorrow is Christmas, and I do want you to help me today."

She put her hand on the door handle, turned it, and entered the room. Phoebe was sitting up in bed, brushing her shining curls. Idleness had plumped out her rosy cheeks, but when she saw Melissa she pulled her mouth down in a doleful expression.

"How can you speak of Christmas, when Papa is dead hardly more than a month and Mama is dying?" she asked, in a quivering voice. "Haven't you brought my tray, Melissa? I think I could eat a little bacon this morning."

Melissa was touched, but exasperated. "I know it is very distressing to you, dear Phoebe, and that you have a delicate temperament. But Andrew will be home tonight, and we ought to make things a little more pleasant for him. It is such a beautiful morning. Do get up, and come out and gather red berries with me. Perhaps we can find some mistletoe. I know where there is some ivy, and it is still green, and we can decorate the parlor with it. And there are popcorn balls to make and dip in molasses for the tree, and red ribbon to twist. It is very sad for all of us, but we need not make it sadder. There is work to do."

Phoebe flung herself forward on her pillows and sobbed alarmingly. "You've always said that odious thing: "There is work to do'!" she cried betwen her gulps. "I hate that expression! It is so dull and dreary and heartless!"

Helpless as always before uncontrolled emotion, Melissa stood by the bed and said feebly: "But, my darling, aren't you interested in living again? There are your poems to complete. I thought that if you saw how beautiful it is outside you would be inspired to write another poem—"

"Send me my tray!" cried Phoebe, clenching the pillows

around her face. "And go away, do, please, Melissa. I—I'll get up tonight, if I can, when Andrew comes."

Melissa felt a surge of some emotion of her own. She wanted to seize Phoebe in a healthy rage and shake the girl out of bed, fling her through the door. She had never felt this before with regard to Phoebe, and she was shocked. Whatever was the matter with her? She was constantly being assailed by the most alien passions; it was dreadful. Ugly thoughts about Papa, and now this hunger to lay hands on her miserable little sister: there was something wrong with her.

She went out of the room, and down the back stairs to the kitchen. Sally immediately attacked her with vigorous threats and denunciations. Christmas! Well, there'd be no Christmas unless Melissa made all the preparations! It was high time, too. She, Sally, would leave at once unless she had help, and no mistake this time, Miss! What with that hoity-toity nurse, and all the sickness, and the trays, and the other unnatural things, it was too much, that it was, for a lone woman. Sighing impatiently, Melissa took the slops out to the hogs, and brought in the filled milk pails which Hiram had left in the barn to catch chaff or any random manure. Melissa had been relieved of the milking job during her mother's illness, but now it was hers again. With a sudden rush of relief she remembered that Andrew liked to milk. During his time at home, then, he could do this abominable work.

She hurried through the endless chores, for she was determined to gather the red berries and find the green ivy. She watched for her opportunity, and when Sally went lumbering out of the kitchen for a few minutes, Melissa caught up her ragged gray shawl, flung it over her head and shoulders, and rushed out. She circled around the house to the gate in the picket fence, and was just about to open it when she saw a string of three carriages driving up the road towards the Dunham house.

They were filled with ladies and gentlemen and their sleek bags and luggage. As the air was so pure and still, windows had been opened, and gay faces peered out. A black-and-gray blot in all that whiteness and clarity, Melissa stood by the gate, too proud to bolt ignominiously, though the carriages came nearer. She became at once the target of every eye, and as she saw the curious glances she felt suddenly old and bedraggled and ugly.

"Do look at that strange, Gothic creature!" a high sweet

voice floated towards Melissa as impertinently as though she had no ears and no understanding. "A farmer's wife, doubtless."

Melissa flushed darkly. She flung up her head and her eyes silently and contemptuously challenged the silly creatures in the carriage, all bedecked in their furs and velvets and foolish little bonnets. The gentlemen were less insolent. They smiled at her. One said, quite clearly: "By Jove, a handsome piece, for all that! Look at that hair, like the old gilt on an ormolu clock. Wouldn't you like to paint her against the background of that lean gray house, Holland?"

The ladies laughed. The carriages went on. The breath of the black Dunham horses flowed back like plumes of vapor in the bright air.

Rage choked Melissa, and furious desolation. A farmer's wife! They had looked at her and had commented upon her as though she were some doltish creature without hearing or sensibility, some dumb brute who could not understand the spoken language. She, the daughter of the distinguished Charles Upjohn whose scholarly works were renowned among men of letters! Melissa gripped the gate in shaking hands, and, full of hate, watched the carriages climb the long and winding hill to the Dunham house. They were going up there for holiday merriment, these empty animals. They would dance and coquette, sing and laugh and drink and eat, and trail their lustrous silks and satins through all those great rooms. She suddenly saw Geoffrey, smiling, bending over the shoulder of one of these worthless and twittering women and peering around her fan. He would flirt and dance with her, and with her sisters. The music would pour out into the snowy Christmas night, and every window would be lit with golden radiance, every fireplace would be roaring. There would be no sadness there, no desperate anxiety about money, no grief for one who had died, no sparse pantry, no small Christmas tree strung with wood berries, popcorn balls and cheap red paper. Melissa remembered Phoebe's ecstatic descriptions of the ballroom and the Louis Fifteenth Room. A mighty tree had stood in the corner, covered with tinsel and colorful glass balls, and had glittered with candles set in silver and gold candlesticks. The ladies had been pictures out of *Godey's Lady's Book*, and *Harper's Bazaar*, and the Parisian *La Mode*. And such music, such gayety, such dancing and singing!

It is because he is rich, thought Melissa, with increasing

hatred and pain. It is because they are all rich and idle, and we are poor.

Because envy was alien to her, she did not know that it was this she felt. She knew only a sense of abandonment, forlorn loneliness and yearning, and she could not understand even these. She pictured vividly to herself the house on the hillside. But through every room, in every firelit corner, she saw Geoffrey, Geoffrey who had laughed at her and insulted her with impunity.

They will speak of me tonight up there, she thought, with a burning ache in her heart. And *he* will answer them and make game of me, and that horrible Arabella will gurgle and chitter, and everything will be fine and high merriment. Oh, how I hate him!

Her hands pressed harder on the gate, until her flesh protested. She went off into the woods and gathered the few berries the birds had left. But she was no longer eager. She saw herself, tall, black and gaunt, trailing her disheveled skirts through the crusty snow, her hair straight and badly arranged. Suddenly she flung the shawl off her head and smoothed her hair, feeling its roughness. She looked at her hands, red and coarsened and chapped. Big, ugly hands!

Started and shocked at her thought, she dropped her hands to her sides and stared emptily before her. What in heaven's name was the matter with her? Who cared if she had no beauty, and her hair was an unkempt mass, and her hands showed neglect and hard work? She was useful; she had a purpose in life. She was no idle and frivolous fool. A woman's appearance was of no consequence. Her father had told her that, and he had spoken with strong admiration of the sensible Spartans, who had loved work and accomplishment. Empty beauty was the goal of fools. It had no significance, no meaning.

She was having so many grotesque thoughts these days, thoughts which would have appalled her poor father. She could not understand herself. She was treacherous and shallow: that was very evident. Without Papa, she could not control her stupid reflections and keep her eye on the strong and resolute future. She pulled the shawl over her head again, filled her little basket with the berries, and tore the ivy from the trunks of the trees. The shining glass silence stood all around her, and her eyes began to smart from the brilliance. Her feet crackled on the tinsel crust of the snow.

The woods were in the general direction of the Dunham house. Now, as she emerged from them, she could see the house, solid gray-white against the blue sky, its red roof bright and vivid. The chimneys smoked. The sun glittered back from the windows of the conservatory in the rear. Now, very distinctly, Melissa could hear the clear, bell-like barking of dogs and the delicate fairy jingle of bells. Behind those doors and those silk-shrouded windows there would be a quick and rustling movement, the high laughter of women, the deep voices of men. And he would be among them all, moving around on his big strong legs and turning his head to answer a quip or some gay remark.

It was only the brilliance of the air and the sun, of course, which forced tears to Melissa's eyes. It was only the stinging cold which numbed her and slowed her blood. She gripped the basket, and turned away, like an exhausted exile.

She had come farther than she had known. She walked slowly, her skirts dragging, the basket heavy in her hand. She was haunted by loneliness, and something strangely like grief and sick anguish and bitter longing. She moved against all that light like a black figure of sorrow and despondency. She was almost at the gate of her home when she became aware that someone was urgently calling her name and waving an arm at her from the doorway. She looked up, bemused, her wet eyes splintering the sunshine like prisms, and saw that it was Sally.

"Hurry up!" shouted the fat old woman. "Your Ma's a-wantin' you, quick!"

Melissa sped into the house, dropping the basket on the hall table. On legs that bent like tallow, she raced down the upper hall to her mother's room. The door was open. Matilda, the nurse, was bending over the bed. Melissa's eyes, dazzled by the sun outside, could not see at first. She groped into the dim and shuttered room and, panting a little, waited, trying to see her mother.

The bright mist lessened. Amanda lay gasping heavily on her pillows, her eyes closed. A change had come over her face. It was intent, drawn together in a kind of austere intensity, and its color was dark. All her being, her life, was focussed on resisting the pull of death. Even before the nurse did, she became aware of Melissa, and opened her eyes. They seemed to peer at the girl as from the end of a long tunnel or from some great distance.

"Melissa," whispered the dying woman, and one of her hands moved.

"Hush," said the nurse, gently. "Be quiet, Mrs. Upjohn. We've sent the boy for the doctor, and he'll be here soon."

But Amanda looked only at her daughter. Melissa, shaking with cold and dread, came closer. She tried to speak, but her lips had turned thick and chill.

"You've not kissed me since you were a child, Melissa," said Amanda, in her rustling whisper. "Kiss me."

Melissa bent. She had to lean on her stiff arms, her palms pressed against the mattress. She kissed her mother's cold damp forehead. Amanda turned her head, and her lips brushed Melissa's cheek. She smiled as if comforted, and closed her eyes.

Melissa did not move for a long time. Her hair fell over her stooping head, and covered her face.

PART TWO

CHAPTER 20

THE COLD AFTERNOON STOOD starkly at the parlor
windows. The fire snarled and flickered. The three young
people grouped near the hearth in a semi-circle stared at
the fire, feeling the weight of the dim silence crushing them
deeper and deeper into themselves.

They had sat like this hardly six weeks ago, in the same
attitudes. But at that time their mother had been with them.
None of the three looked at Amanda's chair. Geoffrey had
gone, though he would have remained longer had he received
the slightest encouragement. He had read their mother's will
to them, and had waited for comment. None had come,
though Andrew had lifted his head and for the first time
Geoffrey had noticed the strong resolute line of his chin
which so resembled Amanda's.

"If there is anything, then, that I can do, in any way, you
have only to call on me," Geoffrey had said. Andrew had
given him a straight and quiet glance and had replied: "Yes.
We know. Thank you." But Melissa had not looked at Geoffrey. She had let him go like the unwanted intruder she felt
him to be.

They heard the harsh and strident ticking of the clock
in the hall, but could not arouse themselves from their lethargy. Even Phoebe was not weeping. She sat in her chair,
huddled together, her plump face white, her eyes full of
fear and misery. They were not red, for she had not shed
a single tear. For once, she was mute.

Melissa moved sluggishly, as if weighted down by iron.
"We have so much to decide and to plan," she said, in a dull
voice. "It can't wait.

"Andrew, the farm is yours, with all its debts. It is a
liability. It always was. It should have been sold long ago.
Now we must put it on the market immediately."

Andrew gazed at her with his small, shrewd, dark-blue eyes.
They narrowed a little as he appeared about to speak. But
he said nothing.

Melissa lifted her heavy hand, then let it drop back on her lap.

"We shan't clear much, that is certain. But it is a little. I have calculated everything. With the proceeds from the farm, after all debts have been paid, and with what is left in the banks, we shall have exactly seven hundred and seventy-five dollars and twelve cents. We can sell nearly all the furniture. Some of it, I have been told, is very valuable. Let us make a conservative estimate and say that we are able to obtain four hundred dollars from the the furniture. None of us will need these things. Then, I understand from Geof—from Mr. Dunham, we have a certain amount due in royalties, in April. Accounting for everything, we ought to have between twelve and thirteen hundred dollars."

Her voice failed. Her overpowering weariness cut off her breath. After some moments she was able to speak again:

"We must put aside four hundred and fifty dollars for your next semester, Andrew. In the meantime, I must arrange for Phoebe and myself to leave here and go to Philadelphia. I shall write at once to Papa's old friends and ask them to secure me a post as teacher or governess. Phoebe and I will live in lodgings temporarily. Of course, I shall take no post unless she can be with me or I am permitted to live outside of any establishment. A room together, under the eaves, will be all we shall need, until Phoebe has completed her book of poems. We shall live quietly, of course, and in accordance with our circumstances. Later, perhaps, when you are practicing law, you can assist us, Andrew. And then there'll be something from Papa's books. A lot."

Andrew looked at her steadily. Why, the poor damned fool! She actually thought she could do these things, and that he and Phoebe would follow meekly where she led! He was very sorry for her, more sorry than he could have believed possible, and therefore he could not tell her outright not to be an imbecile, that he had never wanted to be a lawyer and that he intended to farm his inheritance and make it pay.

No, he could not tell this haggard young woman this, out of his slow compassion. He was two years younger than Melissa, but he felt himself immeasurably older and far more sane. What did the poor thing know about anything, with her airy talk of Philadelphia and a "post" and her silly plans for the lives of all of them? He saw her pale fanatical eyes, the stern trembling of her lips, and he averted his head in pity.

He glanced at Phoebe. She was sitting upright in her chair, fright vivid on her pretty face. She was staring at Melissa with hatred and panic. She began to beat on the arm of her chair with clenched little fists.

"Oh, Melissa, you are so stupid! Do you really think I'll go to Philadelphia with you, and live like a beggar on cheese and dry bread and tea, and sleep in an attic?"

She thought her sister capable of forcing her to this hideous extremity, and her big blue eyes blazed with mounting rage. "You and all your foolishness! My poems! Do you think I'll live like that, with you, just for my poems? I'll never write another one. I'll marry Johnnie Barrett as soon as we can arrange it, and I'm not going to wait until April. He spoke to me right at the funeral, before we came back to this horrid place, and we agreed that we'd be married right after the New Year."

She subsided, panting daintly but ferociously, like an infuriated kitten. But her blazing eyes did not leave her sister, who stared at her, stupefied.

"I want Johnnie!" screamed Phoebe, resuming the pounding of the chair arm with her fists. "I don't want poverty any more! I want pretty dresses, and a nice house, and a carriage of my own, and furs and feathers and jewels. I'm sick of this misery, and hiding like mice in cracked walls, and never having anything or seeing anything!" She bent her head and beat her forehead, too, on the arm of the chair, and wailed shrilly and desperately.

Melissa could not make a sound. She turned ghastly pale and moistened her lips. She wrung her hands together soundlessly.

Andrew thought this the proper moment, while Melissa was in a state of shock, to break his news.

He said, and his strong voice rose over Phoebe's wails: "She is right, Melissa. If there is a way out, we ought to take it. She'll marry Johnnie Barrett, and be off our hands. You've got to remember that there is hardly any money." He paused. Melissa had moved her dazed eyes to him, and he wondered if she could hear him. "Listen carefully, Melissa. I can't go back to Harvard. There's no money. The only thing for me to do is to work this farm and make it produce, for both of us. Of course, I can't prevent you from going to Philadelphia, alone, but I hope you'll stay here with me. We'll have to let Sally and Hiram go, and do the best we can by ourselves."

Did she hear him? Her eyes were so filmed and still. He could not tell.

Melissa thought: It is because we have no money that they are sacrificing themselves. If we only had money, a lot of it, five or six thousand dollars! Then Andrew could complete his law studies, and Phoebe could write her beautiful poems. But they are sacrificing themselves, they feel that they must.

Once or twice she tried to speak, and failed. But finally her voice came, husky and slow:

"Phoebe, please listen to me. You are young, and you have a gift, like Papa's; you dare not deprive the world of it. Andrew, we must find a way to let you finish your studies. We must find a way."

Andrew frowned impatiently. He wanted to say: "Let's be honest. I never wanted the damn law. I want this, the land." But still he could not say it. It would be too cruel.

So he said, instead: "Melissa, for God's sake let's be sensible. There is no 'way.' Beggars can't be choosers. Don't interfere with Phoebe. Don't try to interfere with me. You can't do it. There's no use."

"There must be a way," whispered Melissa.

Andrew shrugged. He went to the windows and glanced out. "Hiram's bringing in the cows. I'll have to go out and milk."

Like something hunted, Melissa glanced at each corner of the room, looking for escape from this horror, this ruin of the dream of years. She saw the little abandoned Christmas tree in the corner. The berries had never been strung for it. The red twisted paper had not been hung on its small boughs. It waited there, dying, its branches outspread like feeble arms.

"Wait, Andrew," pleaded Melissa, in frantic urgency, as her brother started for the door. She looked at Phoebe, she bent towards the wailing girl. "Please, Phoebe. I'll find a way, I promise you both. There is a way. I've never failed yet. Give me a day or two. Just a day or two, and everything will be all right and we can live as you wish. I promise you."

Had she gone crazy with grief and stress, thought Andrew. He stood by the door and regarded his sister with some anxiety. Her face had suddenly become ignited by a secret resolution.

"What do you mean, Melissa?" asked Andrew quickly, moving a step towards her. If she were going to become violent, he would have to be close at hand.

She stood up swiftly, her black skirts swirling with her movements. She had the strangest smile. She put out her hand and caught Andrew's sleeve.

"I know a way, dear. Then Phoebe can have some—pretty—

things, and not be frightened, and she won't need to marry that dreadful farmer. She can live in peace, and write her poems. You, Andrew, can go back to Harvard in a few days, and finish your studies, as Papa planned. Phoebe shall live with me, somewhere—I haven't thought that out completely. But I'll find a way. Just give me a day, two days. I see it now: Phoebe shall live with me. It can be arranged. I know."

He had never seen her like this, so strange, so trembling, so feverish. He put his fingers on the hand on his arm.

"You're tired, Melissa. Please go upstairs and rest. Yes, everything will be all right. Just go upstairs and lie down. Phoebe, won't you take your sister up——"

Melissa snatched her hand from his. Her face was bright with elation.

"Never mind, Andrew! It is all arranged in my mind. Just wait until tomorrow. Yes, yes, go out and milk, if you wish. It doesn't matter."

She rushed to Phoebe, knelt beside her and pulled the girl to her breast. Phoebe had been stricken silent with amazement. She pushed back against Melissa's arms and stared at her shining eyes so pale and brilliant. Something frightened the girl. She tried to wriggle free from her sister's grasp. She whimpered. "Andrew, Andrew, I'm afraid."

Disturbed himself, Andrew pulled Melissa to her feet. "What's the matter with you, Melissa? Look, you've frightened Phoebe. For God's sake, stop shaking. You'll fall down. You act and talk as if you'd lost your mind. Why don't you go and rest a while?"

"Take me upstairs, I'm afraid of her," whimpered Phoebe, crouching as far back in her chair as she could. "Please, Andrew, take me upstairs."

But Andrew was too concerned with Melissa to hear Phoebe. Melissa stood in the center of the room, smiling as if she had gone mad, her hands clenched together before her, her head flung up, her neck high and strained, all passion and fever.

"Please believe me," she pleaded. "I know a way. Phoebe, Andrew, just give me a day or two and I promise you that you'll both have what you want. Please!"

"Of course, of course," said Andrew, quickly, and with alarm. "You can have ten days, Melissa. Just be quiet now. Nothing has to be settled immediately. You're tired out, poor girl. Everything has been too much for you."

He wanted to be angry with Melissa, but he could not. He felt only compassion and consternation. The nurse was gone, but perhaps she had left a sedative behind. If he could only get Melissa to her room, and calm her, he would have gained something. As he considered what to do, he looked at his sister, this brawny, huge young man, and helplessly rubbed the back of his big head.

Melissa controlled herself. The elation did not leave her face, but her voice was less wild when she said: "Please, Andrew, don't be disturbed. I know what I am going to do. I'm not out of my mind. Phoebe, darling, please don't cry. Haven't I taken care of you? Don't cry like that, you hurt me so. Just leave it all to me, and you'll both be happy."

She's surely mad, thought Andrew, with deep alarm. Melissa pushed his shoulder, and smiled. "The cows are waiting, Andrew." She gave a little breathless laugh. "Take them, Andrew. I've been milking them, and I hate it. Phoebe, please go upstairs and lie down, and I'll ask Sally to bring you some tea at once."

Andrew was only too glad to go. He shook his head as if freeing it from cobwebs, and shrugged. Melissa seemed calmer. She had some scheme, of course, but it would come to nothing. He had only to humor her meanwhile.

He said: "Yes, I'll have to change my clothes to go to the barns. That's right, Phoebe, go on upstairs. Don't bother her, Melissa," he added, as he saw Phoebe shrink away from Melissa's offered arm. "Let her go alone."

He went out, and Phoebe fled from the room as though witches were pursuing her. Melissa was left alone. She began to walk up and down, wringing her hands, her head bent in rapid thought. The Dunhams had sent flowers, and the scent still lingered in the cold air. Melissa did not think of her mother, nor even of her father.

CHAPTER 21

GEOFFREY DUNHAM was in a bad humor. He disliked long holidays, and he disliked some of his guests. His nature was inclined to irascibility, and the necessity to be polite for long periods, without intermissions, was very wearing to him. More than once he had found himself on the verge of a quarrel with one or two gentlemen who had been drinking too much, and some of the women were so vapid as to be unendurable for more than an hour or two. He loved and admired his home, but he agreed with Benjamin Franklin that guests, like fish, stank after three days. These people had been cluttering up his household for nearly seven days now, and would not be gone until January the second. Before their departure, there would be the New Year's Eve ball, which he contemplated with temper.

He loved the country. It would have given him delight to have spent these days alone in his house, to have gone for long walks over the crisp and sparkling snow, to have visited one or two neighbors whom he liked. There were books to read in the library, and some interesting manuscripts which had come into his offices. He could conceive of nothing more pleasant than to spend the days in the snowy quiet of his land, in the warm silence of his library.

But how was he spending the days now, days which should be given over to quiet work, contemplation, fires, walks with the dogs, and visits with his friends? He was spending them entertaining fools and bores. Only the Eldridges made the days bearable, and he saw them only occasionally, Mr. Eldridge being quite delicate of digestion, and needing the services of his wife with various palliatives. So, he must entertain his guests, contrive amusements for them in the silence of the snowy countryside. Backgammon, whist, port, whiskey, anecdotes, charades: all the stupid, time-devouring devices to keep the mind in a soporific condition, and coax the hours to hurry by. Dances in the evening, with the hired musicians finally staggering off at dawn to their quarters on the third floor. He despised it all. Each year he had determined that these festivities should be the last, and each year he succumbed to his pity for Arabella, who spent so many long dull days alone in this house.

As always at this time of the year, he was in a bad humor, but now his temper was a fuming rage against his sister. This was enhanced by his sadness over Amanda Upjohn's death. James, his man, hovered near him, very quiet and subdued, for he felt Geoffrey's smoldering anger by the way he thrust the black pearl into his cravat and twitched himself into the coat James held for him. If the master were a gentleman, now, reflected James, he would shout my ears flat, curse me vigorously, and put all his ill humor on my back. But Geoffrey, who was not a gentleman, could never bring himself to discharge his venom upon those who worked for him and who were innocent of any wrong-doing. So he thanked James in a pent voice for his services, and told him to take the evening off. It was really excellent not to work for a gentleman, thought James happily, as he softly closed the door behind him.

Geoffrey pulled at his chin. James had given him a bad shave that morning, probably because the little man had been doing some celebrating on his own. No matter. But the bristles that cropped out here and there did not increase Geoffrey's good temper. He went out into the long warm hall, where the candles were burning in their sconces, and knocked loudly on his sister's door. She called to him to enter. She was putting the last touches to her ringlets and was holding a perfume bottle in her jeweled hand.

Arabella was quite resplendent in rose velvet and lace, with an enormous bustle and much drapery. Velvet roses rested among the puffs of hair on the top of her head. Diamonds glittered at her ears. Her full but raddled cheeks were suspiciously pink, and stiff with powder. The folds of her short neck almost concealed the diamond necklace about it, and her fat wrists sparkled. She flashed her tiny sharp gray eyes at her brother, and smiled a little. "I am almost ready for dinner, dear Geoffrey," she said. "You have never seen this gown before. Do you like it?"

The gaudy bepuffed bedroom was inundated with scent, and very hot. All the crystal lamps had been lit, and they flooded the room with cruel light. Never had Arabella resembled a stout and bedecked harridan so much as she did tonight, thought her brother with aversion. Then the full force of his anger rushed to his head and his face became crimson.

"Why did you refuse, at the last moment, to attend Amanda's funeral?" he asked, in a dangerous voice. "I thought it was understood that you were to go with me. After all, to quote yourself, she was one of your best friends. I demand an explanation."

Arabella stared at him, and shrank a little. "But Geoffrey, I thought I explained. I had one of my headaches. All that death in that terrible house! I have some sensibilities, and I could not endure it, I really could not. Besides, there were our guests. I could not leave them alone with morbid thoughts." She put her lace handkerchief to her lips and blinked her eyes as if to keep back the tears. "Yes, Geoffrey, Amanda was my dear friend, so dear, indeed, that I preferred not to see her—dead—but to remember her living. Is that so hard for you to understand?"

Geoffrey was silent, his face still red and swollen. She could always outwit him, this stupid and malevolent woman. She had long ago guessed his weakness: he was too susceptible to reason. How a woman completely without intelligence could invent plausible excuses had always mystified him. He knew her well, yet he was constantly being put on the defensive by her, constantly being taken in by her lies, even when he knew they were lies.

She was watching him acutely, her little eyes so narrowed that they were almost completely hidden in the folds of the flesh about them. Then, guessing the precise moment for emotion, she exclaimed: "Geoffrey, how can you be so cruel as to suggest I am without heart? I did not expect this tirade, from you, my brother!" Now tears actually came to her eyes, and she let them slide pathetically down her cheeks.

He knew that in less than a minute he would subside into a welter of impotent curses, and he hated her for his approaching loss of self-control, for the way she was diddling him. But before he could succumb, there was a discreet knock at the door and, furiously, Geoffrey pulled it open. James stood respectfully on the threshold. He stepped back a pace, then murmured: "There is a matter about which I must speak to you at once, sir."

Geoffrey wanted to slam the door shut in the little man's face, but, as he was not quite a gentleman, he could not bring himself to do this in spite of his rage at the interruption. He went out into the hall and drew the door shut behind him. "Well?" he demanded roughly.

James glanced at the shut door, and whispered: "There is a young lady down in the morning-room, wishing to see you, sir. Miss Melissa Upjohn."

Geoffrey stared. "Miss Upjohn? In the morning-room?" He stopped. "Take her into the library at once, and I'll go down immediately."

James hesitated. "The young lady refused to go beyond the morning-room, sir, in spite of there not being a fire. She was quite adamant. She must see you without delay, but she would not take a step farther." He coughed a little. "The young lady evidently walked all the way, sir. She is rather—damp. Shall I ask the stables to have a carriage in readiness to take her home?"

"Yes, yes, of course. Do so at once," said Geoffrey. He went swiftly past James and ran down the stairway. Fires were burning in the library and in the opened drawing-rooms, and lamps had been lit. None of the guests had as yet come downstairs. All was lamplight and firelight and soft silence. Geoffrey went through the library, hurried through the little hall beyond it, and reached the morning-room. The door had been shut, and when he opened it he saw Melissa standing in the middle of the cold room, tall, stiff, rigorous, with her shawl wrapped closely about her.

"Melissa! What on earth?" exclaimed Geoffrey. He advanced towards her, then stopped suddenly. Between the folds of her shawl her face was white and very still, and her eyes were filled with motionless lamplight. They had the strangest expression, he saw, and they looked at him steadfastly and with courage.

"My dear Melissa," said Geoffrey, in a gentle voice. "What is the matter? You look very ill, my poor child. What can I do for you?"

Her white lips parted, and she said quite clearly: "I just wanted to ask you a question, Mr. Dunham. Did you mean it when you made your—offer—to my mother, for me?"

She spoke without shrinking or embarrassment and still gazed at him steadily with that constant light in her eyes. Geoffrey was dumfounded. He studied her for a long moment, seeing only how pathetic she was, and how close, in spite of her straightness and calm, she was to breaking.

"Yes, Melissa, I meant it." He wanted to go to her and take her in his arms, this poor girl, to hide that stark face against his shoulder. But he knew that he must not do this yet.

She sighed. It was a loud sigh, almost like a dry sob. "I am glad you meant it," she said, and her voice trembled just a trifle. "I am ready to marry you, Mr. Dunham. I should like to marry you tomorrow. I have thought it all out. Judge Farrell can marry us tomorrow morning, in Midfield."

Geoffrey was silent. He continued to regard her piercingly, and she looked back at him without faltering or glancing away. But her mouth had set itself in straight, intense lines.

Then Geoffrey said, "Please sit down, Melissa. It is very cold in here. I will light a fire."

"No, please!" Her voice was sharp and quick. "I must go at once. I only wanted to know whether you will marry me tomorrow morning."

Geoffrey walked close to her, but she did not retreat. Now he saw fear in her eyes, but still she did not drop them.

"Tell me all about it, Melissa," he said.

White lines sprang out about her mouth. Then, in her terrible innocence, she said: "There is Phoebe, and Andrew. Phoebe says she will marry John Barrett, that farmer. Andrew says he will not sell the farm, that he will work it. He says they can do nothing else. Because we have no money. They are sacrificing themselves—because we have no money. If you marry me, I know you will help me to help them. Phoebe writes such beautiful poetry. I want her to be—here—with me, after I marry you, so she can write in peace. I have a whole sheaf of her poems, and you will want to publish them when you read them. Andrew will go back to Harvard."

Geoffrey could not speak, for he was utterly astounded. And then he could not speak for fear of bursting out into laughter.

Melissa went on, incredibly: "I thought of asking you to lend us a lot of money. But we could never pay you back, and it would be dishonest. And then I remembered that you had asked Mama for me, and I thought this would be the best way."

Geoffrey drew a deep breath. He said: "Have you discussed this—this—proposition with Phoebe and Andrew? Do they know why you have come here?"

Her calm broke, and she cried: "Oh, no! They wouldn't have permitted me to come! You must never tell them, never! They wouldn't allow me to make this sacrifice——"

Geoffrey was freshly stricken dumb. He could only look, in stupefaction, at those wide, strained eyes with the impossible childish artlessness shining so brightly in them. He turned away from her, and walked slowly up and down the room. It was unbelievable. He saw, out of the corner of his eye, that she was watching him with heroic fear. Yes, it was unbelievable, and again he wanted to laugh. She was twenty-five years old—and it was incredible.

But he also understood. He knew very well that Phoebe was quite determined to marry the very worthy young John Barrett, money or no money. He knew that Andrew was probably gulping in long breaths of relief that he need not return to Harvard. In some manner, this poor courageous creature, possibly assisted by her brother and sister in an as yet unknown way, had utterly deceived herself. No, Phoebe might deceive Melissa, but not Andrew.

To marry her would be only to play up to her self-deception, her blind and foolish dreams. He, Geoffrey, wanted her, and never so much as now. Had he not been planning to "get her into a bedroom"? If he enlightened her, there would be no bedroom, not for years, if ever. The first thing was the bedroom, and then her slow salvation.

He stopped abruptly in front of her. He wanted to say, naïvely: "Am I so repulsive to you, Melissa, that you will only marry me for my money?" But, of course, he did not say this childish thing. He said, instead, "Tomorrow, Melissa? But aren't there some conventions to be observed after— death?"

She replied quietly: "I never cared for conventions. They mean nothing to me. And there is desperate need for the marriage to take place at once, so I can save Phoebe and Andrew."

Yes, he had heard what she said, but again he was stunned. He stood and looked at her, and she returned his look with strong and pathetic fortitude.

"It's all wrong," he said, "but if that is how you want it, then so it shall be. I'll call for you tomorrow, Melissa."

"Oh, no," she said, hastily. "I don't want Phoebe and Andrew to know anything, until afterwards. We have a buggy, you know. I'll meet you at ten o'clock in the judge's chambers, in Midfield." She began to twist the fringe of her shawl in her tremulous hands.

Geoffrey sighed. "As you say, Melissa." He tried to smile. "It will create quite a scandal, you know, my dear."

But she walked away from him to the door. He watched her go. Then, as she was about to open it, she turned, very slowly. Her face had changed.

"I almost forgot," she said. "There was just one thing more I wanted to know. Why do you want to marry me, Mr. Dunham?"

He stared, speechlessly, while she waited in artless patience for his reply. He tried to speak, and then had a fit of coughing to hide the laughter that threatened to engulf him again.

In a strangled voice he finally said: "Because I love you, Melissa. Does that astonish you?"

"Love me?" she whispered, as if in wonder. "Love me?" she stopped, and for the first time her eyes wavered, and she looked aside. Then her pale cheeks turned to fire. She flung open the door, and ran out.

CHAPTER 22

WESLEY FARRELL was Judge of the County Court presiding at Midfield, the County seat. He owned a very large fat farm adjoining the Upjohn land and consisting of some three hundred acres. A very popular and jovial and educated gentleman, it was his shrewd affectation, in pursuit of popularity, to pretend to a rough and ready manner of speech pleasing to the ears of the local farming citizenry. He had considerable wealth, and the complete confidence of the electorate and his neighbors. His farm, excellently managed, produced the herds of cattle which invariably received prizes at the annual County Fair.

Though some seventy years old, he was so ruddy, so virile, so active and vigorous, that he appeared much younger, for he had a strong zest for life and an endless curiosity about everything. He was a kind man, though avaricious. His avarice did not inspire suspicion and dislike among people, however. They admired it, for, to them, it demonstrated complete good sense, thrift and conservatism, all traits they admired. They recounted his sharp dealings with the "city" purchasers of his cattle and even with local storekeepers, and their voices would be full of laughter and approbation. No one could best the Judge, God bless him. He was a match for any man, and even in his shrewdest manipulations always revealed his fundamental honesty. He was "agin" charity of any kind, which again did not earn him dislike, for he had always lifted his loud hoarse voice in denunciation of any proposed increase in taxes. He had hated the War between the States, and had been very eloquent upon the subject, even in the darkest days of the Union. Again, this inspired the affection of the local farmers, for like farmers all over the world they detested war and anything else which threatened to disrupt the calm and productive days of the land. He had the farmer's soul: he abhorred waste of any kind and, to him, war was the most unpardonable and barbarous waste of all.

Never reticent on the subject of "shiftlessness," he refused to dispense generosity upon the incompetent. He was also loud in his dislike for the casual and the irresponsible. He had particularly despised Charles Upjohn, while admiring Amanda and pitying her children. He had made it a point to be rude to Charles on every occasion of their rare meetings. Charles had called him a "country bumpkin," an epithet which had highly amused the competent and acquisitive Judge. He had been pleased to learn that the pretty little Phoebe was about to marry Johnnie Barrett, whom he highly respected and for whom he had a deep affection. This showed the Judge's sense of justice, for he had marked John for his own young widowed granddaughter. He had once told Geoffrey Dunham that it was a "damned shame" that such obviously good farm-material was being wasted in Andrew Upjohn, who was "no more a lawyer than I am a Chinaman." For Andrew, he had nothing but kindliness and affection whenever that young man could slip away from his own home during the holidays and visit the Judge's farm. But when he saw Melissa, during the few times he had encountered her near the border of his own land, or in Midfield, he had stared at her with his hard, shrewd, reflective eyes, and had shaken his head with some gravity.

The Judge had been seen in town this morning, and had been noted going into his offices. This was odd, for the New Year had not arrived as yet, and the Judge liked his Christmas holidays. But passersby saw that a fire had been lit within the outer office, and that a lamp was burning against the gray light of the winter day. By peering, one could see the Judge at his desk, sorting over his mail. It was evident that he was waiting for somebody, and an idler or two loitered about curiously. Then Geoffrey Dunham's polished black carriage, with the two black horses, and a coachman, had arrived, and Geoffrey, his fur-collared great-coat swinging from his shoulders, had hurried into the offices. Before an hour had passed, the whole town knew of the visit, and conjectures flew about avidly. By nightfall, a final rumor, incredible and astounding, had made the town a babble of tongues.

The Judge roared when he saw Geoffrey. "Well, now! What the devil do you want? Got your message late last night, and though I ought to have better sense I drove into town and almost broke my neck, just to satisfy you. What the hell's wrong? Got yourself in a fix, Geoff?" He stood up ponderously, grinning, and shook Geoffrey's hand, staring up at his friend keenly and having to tilt back his great head as he did so. His bulging broadcloth coat and pantaloons were dusty and ash-strewn, his cravat sliding to one side, and crumpled, his linen none too fresh. He held his pipe in his hand, and it had a very strong odor. The edges of his mighty white mustache were stained yellow, and his teeth also were yellow, though very sound.

"Have a snort," he invited, pointing to a whiskey bottle on his desk and two smeared glasses. When Geoffrey assented, with pleasure, the Judge poured out a generous three fingers in one of the glasses, and did the same with the other. The two friends sat down in the littered and untidy little office, which stank of spirits and tobacco, and looked amiably at the fire. The Judge began to talk of local gossip, and chuckled. But he watched Geoffrey closely and shrewdly, for Geoffrey kept taking out his elaborate gold watch and glancing at it.

"Waitin' for someone?" asked the Judge, after this had happened for the third time.

"Yes. Melissa Upjohn," said Geoffrey, smiling.

The Judge stared. "Melissa Upjohn? My God! What for? Somethin' about her Ma's will? Poor Amanda. Married all those years to that elegant skunk. Well, well, Melissa Upjohn. What's the poor crazy girl want now?"

Geoffrey frowned, then smiled. "Judge, you are speaking of my future wife. I want you to marry us this morning."

"Marry you—to Melissa Upjohn?" repeated the Judge slowly. Then he blinked, and put down his glass with the utmost delicacy, as if afraid it might slip from his stained hand. He went into a sudden fit of violent and gasping coughs, and his face turned crimson and became wet. He wheezed and panted. Then he looked at Geoffrey, and his little black eyes were a mere jet glint under his bushy eyebrows. "Holy, suffering God!" he whispered. "You, and Melly Upjohn! I don't believe it." And again he went into a spasm of loud and rasping coughs.

Geoffrey waited with casual patience. "When you get through choking, Judge, I'll tell you more about it," he remarked. He glanced at his watch again. "She ought to be here now."

The Judge subsided. He threw himself back in his chair, which groaned. He sat and stared at Geoffrey for a long time, he seemed distressed and very grave. He finally said, in an unusually quiet voice: "Geoffrey, I can't believe it. That girl. What's the matter, boy? Got to make an honest woman of her, or somethin'?"

"You can always be depended upon to add the nice coarse touch," answered Geoffrey, with a smile that indicated his natural annoyance. "Can't you ever think of anything but your damned barnyard? It happens that I've wanted to marry Melissa for a long time, but she wouldn't consent, until yesterday."

The Judge was increasingly distressed. He continued to stare, with mounting anxiety. He rubbed his thatch of white hair until it stood about his head like a ragged halo. Then he suddenly reached for his bottle and poured himself another large "snort." He gulped it down loudly. He put down the glass and shook his head.

"I wouldn't be a friend of yours, Geoff, if I didn't say somethin'. God help us—I never thought you'd think of marryin' that girl! Never thought you even looked at the bag—the girl—or she at you. I've known about you and her pa, of course. He was always writin' books, and I suppose you had business with the family. Geoff," and he leaned forward and earnestly put his dirty hand on the younger man's knee, "you aren't out of your mind, are you? Nothin' wrong, is there, that I can't straighten out?"

"Don't be an infernal fool, Judge," said Geoffrey. "Everything is quite all right. I told you: I've always wanted to marry Melissa."

The Judge got to his feet. He put his hands under his coattails and began to walk heavily up and down the floor, which complained under his weighty step. He stopped to kick off a lump of mud from his boots, but he did this abstractedly. All the good humor and benevolence had vanished from his face, which had fallen into thick red lines and puckers. Then he stopped before Geoffrey, and looked down at him with great somberness.

"Geoffrey, I can't refuse to marry you. I wish to God I could. I'm your friend, aren't I, damn it! I've nothing against the girl, believe me. But I've watched her since she was a child. She don't know she's alive, my boy. That confounded old devil, her Pa, kept her bewitched, or hexed, as they say in these parts. She acts like she doesn't see anythin', nothin' at all, whether it's man or dog. There's some that says she's tetched in the head. I don't think that. But I think you're gettin' yourself into a mess of misery, and I don't like it. No sir, I don't like it at all. Think about it, boy. Here's a girl that's never seen anythin' or been nowhere and walks around in a dream. Can't recall she ever spoke to anybody in town. There's all kinds of stories about her queerness. And you want to marry her, and take her up to that fine house of yours, and introduce her to your New York and Philadelphia friends, and make a lady of her."

"Melissa is a lady," said Geoffrey, coloring.

The Judge shook his head impatiently. "Well. Maybe. Got good blood. But it's a funny kind of blood. She's her Pa's daughter. Now, if it was that little Phoebe you was after, I could understand. Geoff, I can't see you doin' this and not lettin' my tongue wag. Why, I've loved you, my boy, since you were a kid. I knew your Pa well. A fine old gentleman. What'd *he* say about this marriage?"

Geoffrey did not answer. He looked again at his watch, and then stood up and went to the smeared windows. He said, "Ah!" in a tone of relief. The Upjohns' shabby old buggy was just drawing up to the door. Melissa, clad in her one good gown, of a rusty dark-brown color, and with her mother's black shawl over her head and shoulders, sprang out of the buggy. With bare and competent hands she tied the horse to the hitching-post. She turned, with swift resolution, took a step towards the door of the Judge's office, then stopped abruptly. She stood against the background of white, almost deserted street, shop-windows and box-like wooden houses. Her breath rose in pale vapor before her face, and through it Geoffrey could see her wide strained eyes and tense white mouth. A wing of her gilt hair lay smoothly over her forehead, under her shawl. He thought that in spite of her pallor and the gauntness of her cheek he had never seen so beautiful a face, so stern, so austere, so classical. There was such a high and noble purity in every plane, every modelling, such a carved chastity about her brows, with their white and petrified lines.

Poor child, he thought, watching her, unseen, from the corner of the window. She looks as if she were about to mount the gallows but was determined to do it with high courage and fortitude, with invincible pride.

The Judge said, pleadingly: "Think what your Pa would say, Geoffrey. It isn't too late. The girl hasn't come yet. By the way, why the devil is she marryin' you, and you, her? What's between you? If there was ever a woman less likely and less fit to enter the holy state of matrimony, that girl is the one."

"Here she is, now," said Geoffrey. The bell rang with a peremptory sound. The Judge started. "It isn't too late, boy. Think it over. It goes against me to commit a crime like this, against a friend."

But Geoffrey was opening the door with a calm and reassuring smile. "Come in, Melissa," he said, gently. "I've been waiting for you, and the Judge is ready."

Melissa entered, not reluctantly or slowly, but with her old high stateliness. The Judge said nothing. He stood in the center of the room, his hands under his coat-tails, and peered at her formidably, his lips stuck out under his mustache. She ignored him, and let Geoffrey take her shawl. Then, clasping her hands before her loosely and with composure, she waited. She looked at neither of the men.

The Judge sighed, and advanced to her, and held out his hand. "Howdy, Melissa." She regarded him for a steady moment, then gave him her hand. He was shocked at its coldness, and studied her face. And so his voice was more gentle when he added: "What's this I hear about you marryin' Geoff Dunham, Melissa? Are you sure you want to do this?"

"Yes," she said clearly. Geoffrey came to her side, and involuntarily she moved sideways away from him. But she looked only at the Judge. However, he had seen the movement, and frowned deeply.

"Why, Melissa?" he asked, with a note of urgency. "It's my duty to ask you this, for marriage is no light thing, my dear. It is very serious, and holy, and mustn't be entered into without thought."

Melissa's pale lips parted, and she said: "I know all this. I intend to be a good wife to—to—Mr. Dunham. I'll try very hard, so he won't need regret it."

The Judge was silent. He peered into her eyes, which reflected back his own face but nothing else. They were like blue translucent pieces of mirrored glass, without emotion or feeling.

The Judge cleared his throat, and his voice cracked a little when he said: "My dear, what is the trouble that really brings you here? Tell me, and perhaps I can help you."

Geoffrey began to speak, but the Judge raised his hand sternly, and regarded Melissa with much gravity. The girl's eyes dropped; she stood like a statue. Her face was as smooth as some sleeping and noble mask.

"Yes, Melissa?" said the Judge, softly.

She looked at him again, proudly. "I want to marry Mr. Dunham. He asked my mother—before she died. She gave her consent. I have accepted him."

"But think, Melissa!" urged the Judge. "Geoffrey isn't a man of your world. He is much older than you, almost old enough to be your father. I am afraid this marriage will bring you only unhappiness, my child."

Melissa's lips stirred, and she said, very quietly: "Thank you for your solicitude, Judge Farrell. But I know what I am doing. I can only say that I would never marry any other man."

The Judge lifted his shoulders in a despairingly resigned gesture. But he would not surrender yet. He said: "Melissa, are you prepared to marry this man, conduct his household in a good and proper way, perform your wifely duties and bear his children?"

Melissa started very slightly. Her under lip drew in on a long breath. Geoffrey watched her intently. Then, without fear, she looked into the Judge's penetrating eyes. "Yes," she said, very clearly.

The Judge turned to Geoffrey, and said in a cold, dull voice: "I think you can see, Geoff. You are not a fool. You can see what there is to be seen. I don't understand anythin' about this. But if you two wish to be married, I will marry you." He looked at them both for a long and bitter moment. "Take her hand, Geoffrey."

Melissa turned her head and gave Geoffrey a wide and distrait glance. But she lifted her hand and laid it in his. It was as chill and stiff as a dead hand. His fingers closed about it warmly and gently. "Witnesses, Judge?" he asked.

The Judge did not answer. He opened a door in the rear of the office, growled something. Then he went to the window, knocked on the frosted pane loudly, and beckoned to Geoffrey's coachman, who was huddled in his coat on the carriage seat. The man looked up, surprised, then climbed down clumsily, and stamped into the office. The Judge's clerk, a wizened dark little old man, emerged blinking from the chambers beyond the office.

The Judge said loudly: "I am about to unite Mr. Geoffrey Dunham and Miss Melissa Upjohn in holy matrimony, and you are to be the witnesses."

The two men stared in dumb amazement, then glanced at each other. Geoffrey saw the astounded exchange, and bit his lip. But he still held Melissa's hand, and studied the rigid profile. A pale shaft of sunlight touched her pale bright hair, so that she appeared to be haloed.

The Judge picked up his book, and said bitterly: "If anyone knows of any impediment to this—this marriage, let him speak now or forever hold his peace."

The coachman and the clerk gaped, and were silent. Dully and slowly, the Judge proceeded with the ceremony. Melissa's responses were clear and firm. Geoffrey replied quietly. Within a few moments the ceremony had been completed.

The Judge laid his book down upon the desk and stood looking down at it in silence. He knew that Geoffrey and Melissa had not kissed, that the girl still stood there in her frozen silence, as if utterly unaware that she was now a wife. The Judge shook his head.

"Thank you, sir," said Geoffrey. Unobtrusively he laid a large yellow bill on the desk. He tried to scan his old friend's face. But the Judge, obdurately, would not look at him.

The coachman went out slowly, the clerk popped back into his hole, as if frightened. Geoffrey laid Melissa's shawl about her shoulders and over her head.

"Aren't you going to wish us happiness, Judge?" asked Geoffrey

The Judge turned ponderously. He gave his friend a long and level look, but said nothing.

"Thank you," said Geoffrey, ironically. He took Melissa's arm. "Come, my dear," he added.

The girl went out with him. She walked as if asleep. The Judge watched them go. And then he began to curse with such profanity that the clerk behind the closed door put his hands over his ears.

CHAPTER 23

BECAUSE OF THE COLDNESS of the day, and the sluggishness of the holiday season, few saw Melissa Upjohn and Geoffrey Dunham emerge from Judge Farrell's offices. Melissa, walking, as usual, like a somnambulist, moved towards her shabby buggy and the decrepit horse she had hitched to it. Geoffrey said a few words to his coachman, who, still dumfounded, nodded in a dazed way. Then Geoffrey went quickly to the buggy and helped Melissa to climb into it. She did not resist him, and indeed, appeared unaware of him. He looked up at her, as she perched on the hard narrow seat, and said: "Move over, Melissa. I am driving now."

She had taken up the reins in her bare red hands and now looked down at him dumbly. "I said," he repeated, gently but firmly, "that I am driving now. Move over, please."

Mechanically, she obeyed him, and he sprang up into the vehicle. And then she shrank back from him as far as the torn and flapping curtains would allow. She said: "I am quite capable of driving home, thank you." But Geoffrey took up the reins in his fur-lined gray gloves and slapped them on the back of the old horse. He turned the buggy around, and the creaking vehicle lurched and swayed down the rutted street, past the blind little shops, the post-office, the court house, the red-brick school, all roofed with snow, with snow high upon their window-sills. They passed a few buggies and carriages, and the occupants, struck by this strange sight, reined in their horses to stare, too astonished to answer Geoffrey's salute. The empty Dunham carriage followed, the coachman shaking his head and rubbing his chin.

Melissa did not speak, nor did Geoffrey at first speak to her. Under his expert guidance the horse came feebly to life and trotted anciently. Melissa, seeing that Geoffrey did not attempt anything formidable, and observing the amiable serenity of his strong and somewhat brutal profile, let her taut body relax. She huddled in her shawl. After a little while, as the buggy began the slow ascent to the Upjohn farm, she began to peep at her newly acquired husband out of the corner of her eye.

She felt her poverty, the poor brown stuff of her woolen frock, the ragged fringes of her shawl, the redness of her hands and the clumsiness of her boots. These contrasted strangely with the rich light gray of his pantaloons, the thick soft fur that lined his black broadcloth greatcoat, the gray beaver of his tallish hat. His gloves fascinated her. She let her eyes drop to his polished boots. She let them rise, as if against her will, to the large strength of his legs, the bigness of his strong arms, the massive lines of his well-set shoulders. Then they touched his square chin, the wide, somewhat thick mouth, the jutting arrogance of his nose with its Roman hump, and the straight black brows over his eyes. Now she did not try to look away. Geoffrey was quite conscious of her artless and simple scrutiny, the stare of a wondering child, and he had to draw in his lips to keep from smiling. He knew that for the first time Melissa was seeing him objectively, not obliquely, not with jealous bitterness and suspicion.

He kept his eye on the snow-filled road, and was careful not to look at her, as one is careful not to startle a child or a proud and timid animal. He hummed a little, as if to himself, a cheerful note. He saw that Melissa's hands, half folded in the piteous shawl, were no longer trembling. Then he said: "Have you left word for your brother and sister that you were marrying me this morning?"

She shrank again. "No," she murmured.

He raised one brow, as if in indulgence. "Well, I left word for Bella. She will be waiting for us. So we'll stop at your home, and tell Andrew and Phoebe, and then—"

"Arabella?" asked Melissa, sharply. She sat up very straight. "I don't intend to go up—up there, Mr. Dunham!"

Geoffrey smiled humorously. " 'Geoffrey,' if you please, my dear. Remember: I'm your husband."

But Melissa was actually shaking. "I do not intend, I absolutely do not intend, to go to your house!" she cried.

Accustomed as he was to her incredible innocence, Geoffrey was freshly surprised at her words. He turned his head quickly and gave her a swift glance. He wanted to tell her not to be an appalling fool, but when he saw her panic-stricken face, her quivering lips, her look of utter terror, he shrugged, and urged on the horse.

The Upjohn house was in sight now. Melissa drew a deep and audible breath. "I mean," she said, faintly, "that I can't go up there just yet, Mr.—, I mean, Geoffrey," and she said his name with such reluctance that he wanted to smile again. "I can't go there for a few days, until Phoebe is ready to leave with me. There—there are a number of things we must do, together. We'll have to dismiss Sally and Hiram, and put the farm up for sale, and see Andrew off to Harvard, and sell what we must and prepare—prepare our clothes. There are two frocks for Phoebe, to be fitted—"

Geoffrey did not reply. He knew she was gazing at him with imploring fear. Her voice was stronger, and pleading now, when she continued: "This was all so sudden—Geoffrey, and Phoebe will have to be prepared. She—she will feel I am deserting her, or hurrying her too much. She is so delicate, you see."

Delicate, be damned, thought Geoffrey, remembering Phoebe. A sharp iron nail floating in honey, that little baggage. My dear, he thought of Melissa, you are in for a number of shocks, and you won't like what you'll find out about your fragile little sister.

He said, soothingly: "Of course. I understand, my love."

His voice reassured her, though she winced at the affectionate last two words. "You see," she went on more bravely, "everything sudden has always been such a shock for Phoebe. She has always been so protected by all of us. And she will have to accustom herself to the idea of going with me to your —your house. I'll have to persuade her very hard."

She glanced at him hopefully. But Geoffrey was guiding the horse up the road. "You do have an extra room for Phoebe, please?" she said. Then she brightened. "I don't want to discommode you and Arabella, and so I am sure that Phoebe could share a little room with me. We shan't bother anyone very much. We just want a small place in which we can work together—on my father's manuscript, and on Phoebe's poems."

The whole picture she was so innocently drawing struck Geoffrey as profoundly ludicrous, and he had to struggle to keep from laughing out loud at this absurd girl. He wanted to drop the reins and pull her into his arms and kiss away that frozen tautness from her lips, that dreaming mist from her eyes. He wanted to tell her not to be a poor damned little fool, that she was his wife now, and that, by God, he was going to teach her what it meant to be a wife. But he understood what a wild, strange creature he had married, what a pure, fierce innocence, and he had known, before, what patience he must expend, what long and tedious care, before she could shake off the stone shell in which she was encased and crushed, and emerge as a woman. His wooing must come after marriage, for there had been no wooing before, and now, as he thought of it, he was excited and full of anticipation. There would be no forcing of Melissa, for any show of force would forever drive her from him.

"There will be plenty of room for Phoebe," he said kindly. "She can have any room she wishes, and I assure you that we'll do everything we can to make her happy."

Melissa's pale cheeks actually became pink. "Oh, thank you!" she murmured fervently. She paused, then looked at him again, as if she had never seen him before. "You are so kind," she added, in a wondering tone. "I didn't know—" And her color became hotter.

He wanted to kiss her with an almost overwhelming desire and tenderness. His hands tightened on the reins. The horse turned homeward, up the long lane. Then Melissa first became aware of the carriage following.

"I have to get home some way," said Geoffrey, seeing her start.

"Oh, yes, of course," she said. "But Andrew could have driven you." Her hands fumbled with the fringe of the shawl. "Andrew," she faltered, "will need quite a lot of money. He —he will pay you back, later, when he has been graduated and has a post. With interest," she amended, appeasingly.

Once more, Geoffrey could hardly keep himself from laughing, and he was thankful that they had reached the snow-filled path to the house. He looked up at the latter, at its lean, bare grayness, at its dreary roofs and chimneys and frosted windows. He sprang out of the buggy, and helped Melissa to alight. She gave him her hand with a trusting unawareness, and he thought: Well, that's the first step, and it went off splendidly.

Old Sally had heard the crunching of the wheels on the snow, and she flung open the door, a tirade on her lips. But when she saw Geoffrey, and the carriage drawing up behind the buggy, she stood in silence, her mouth falling open, and gaping. Geoffrey took Melissa's arm and led her to the door. She did not resist, and again he felt profound relief. She was about to speak to Sally, but he broke in smoothly: "Sally, I know you will be happy to learn that Miss Melissa and I were married this morning." He beamed down at the fat old woman, who blinked and gaped and fell back. He held out his hand to her, and slowly she dropped her pig's eyes and looked at it. Something yellow and folded showed in the palm, and she gasped. She feebly took his hand, a transfer was made, and she gulped, mutely standing aside so that Melissa could hastily brush past her. "Thank ye, thank ye very kindly, sir," stammered Sally, her eyes sticking out from her face. "Married, did you say, sir? This morning?"

"Yes, Sally." He went past her and gave her his coat and hat and gloves, in the dank chill of the narrow hall. She took them mechanically, not removing her eyes from his face. She was still incredulous and stunned. Melissa had disappeared, but her firm swift tread could be heard upstairs, and her voice eagerly calling for her brother and sister.

Sally curtseyed, finally conscious of the amenities. She stuttered: "I—I can't believe it, sir. You and Miss Melissa!" The idea was still grotesque to her, her eyes blinked rapidly and there was a frightened and subdued look on her broad lardy face.

"It had to be done quietly, Sally, because of the two recent sad bereavements in the family, and so we told no one," said Geoffrey with frank heartiness, rubbing his hands together in the cold of the hall. "By the way, Sally, could we have a little fire in the parlor? I think we shall have a family gathering. Yes, I rather think we shall." He glanced up the steep stairway. Two other pairs of footsteps had joined Melissa's, and she was speaking excitedly: "You must come down at once! Mr. Dunham is downstairs, and we have something to tell you, dear Phoebe, dear Andrew."

The poor artless lamb, thought Geoffrey, following Sally, who scuttled before him. The old woman was in a dither of stupefaction and excitement. She fumbled with the fire, until Geoffrey helped her. In a moment, a reluctant blaze started on the hearth. The room was so cold that Geoffrey's breath rose in a cloud, and he shuddered. He saw the bleak white countryside beyond the windows, smelled the neglected dust in the parlor. The hearth was full of ashes, and the old rug was gritty.

Now Melissa rushed into the parlor, her brown skirts a-swirl, her face a-light and pressed forward like the face of a figurehead on a ship. In her wake came Phoebe and Andrew, more slowly, and very bewildered. Geoffrey smiled at their surprised faces. He advanced, took Phoebe's dainty little hand and bent and kissed her dimpled cheek, which immediately turned pink. He held out his hand to Andrew, who stared at him suspiciously but was polite enough to say: "Good morning, Mr. Dunham. Won't you sit down?" Andrew turned and glared at Melissa, standing there alone in the center of the room with her hands clasped tightly together and such a pathetic shining in her pale and brilliant eyes. What the hell has she been up to? thought Andrew, with sudden angry pride. Is this her scheme: getting Dunham here to listen to our troubles and probably asking him to lend us money? She is such an idiot!

Geoffrey turned to Sally, who waited, avidly listening, and he gave her a friendly gesture of dismissal. She retreated backwards, still watching him, and very reluctantly closed the door behind her. Geoffrey knew that she would remain in the hall, listening, and this annoyed him.

He said to Andrew: "Thank you. And won't you sit down, too?" He turned to Melissa and courteously offered her a chair. This she refused with a fiercely impatient shake of her head, though she looked only at her brother and sister. "Phoebe!" she cried, "I've got——"

But Geoffrey was assisting Phoebe into a chair, was asking her forgiveness for disturbing her so early. Andrew stood upright on the hearth, huge and unrelenting and more and more suspicious. He scowled, and his rugged young face became marked with his slow and gathering anger. He said, without preamble: "Mr. Dunham, what's Melissa been up to? She was out of her mind last night, and full of extravagances, and then this morning she flew off with the buggy as if she had gone crazy. What is it all about?"

He gave his sister a harsh and forbidding glance, and Geoffrey was immediately surprised at his resemblance to his dead mother. He had thought Andrew completely apart from this strange household, but he now saw that Amanda lived as strongly in her son as she did in her elder daughter. Geoffrey felt a deep warmth and kindliness for the young man. He went to him and laid his hand on Andrew's shoulder. Andrew turned his large head slowly and regarded him in obdurate and proud silence.

"Don't blame Melissa for anything, Andrew," said Geoffrey. "She has news for all of you. And ideas, too. They are for you to reject or accept."

Phoebe was upset and frightened. One knew that that odious Melissa would never give up! She was so full of awful schemes, all the time! Just look at her standing there, as if she had gone mad, with such a shining in her silly, stupid eyes! Phoebe, dressed in rusty black too large for her, shrank in her chair, but her little hands doubled with passionate resolution. The look she gave Melissa was implicit with defiant hatred.

"Oh, what has Melissa been doing?" she cried. "I knew it would be something terrible, the way she ran off this morning, with her shawl flying, and taking the buggy, and thinking nobody knew! She is so ridiculous, I just can't bear her any longer, Mr. Dunham! And Mama just dead, and I an orphan, and all alone in this horrible house, and Melissa out of her mind, just as I knew would happen some day!"

"Hold your tongue, Phoebe," said Andrew, roughly, and turning very pale. Phoebe immediately burst into loud sobs and buried her face in the wing of the chair. Melissa took a swift step towards her, and Andrew raised his voice commandingly, and exclaimed: "Melissa!"

Melissa stopped, in the very act of running. She stared at Andrew confusedly. That tone of his was new in this house, so dominant was it, and so strange.

"Sit down, Melissa," said Andrew with hard authority. "I'm the man in this house now, and it's time you left off the trousers. Sit down, I said!"

Incredulously, Melissa, in a daze, looked about for a chair. Geoffrey came forward and helped her into one. She sat down, stupefied, and could only look at her brother, her hands clenched in her brown lap. She swallowed convulsively, and faltered: "Andrew, I only wanted to say——"

"Quiet," said Andrew, still in his hard tone of authority. He glanced at Phoebe, who, taken aback, had fallen into a soft whimpering. "Phoebe, stop acting like a malevolent little fool," Andrew continued. "I know all about you. You're vicious, and mean, like—like—" He stopped, and bit his lip. "Melissa has probably got some folly in her head, but at least it's a good head, if fuddled, and I want to know what she's done."

Geoffrey had been watching and listening to Andrew with admiration. Again, he heard and saw Amanda in her son, and his new affection for his unsuspecting brother-in-law increased. Andrew turned to him, and the skin about his mouth was very white and hard. "And now, Mr. Dunham, perhaps you can tell me what all this is about?"

"I think I can, Andrew," said Geoffrey, gently. "Melissa hasn't done anything silly. I hope you will soon agree with that."

"You don't know Melissa," said Andrew, quietly. "She doesn't know she is alive. She means well, but—well, she hasn't grown up yet. She has all sorts of fantastic notions, and so I must ask you in advance to overlook any of her foolishness." He paused. "She's probably asked you to lend us money, and while it is very kind of you, and I appreciate it, the answer is: No, thank you." He flushed deeply, and his small blue eyes flashed with a formidable glitter.

"Andrew," began Melissa. But he looked only at Geoffrey, who was smiling.

"Well, Mr. Dunham?" he said, peremptorily.

Geoffrey coughed. "I am afraid you are wronging your sister, Andrew. You see, she and I were married hardly more than two hours ago."

Andrew said, softly: "You were—" He stopped. Phoebe's gasp was loud in the room. Andrew put his hand to his forehead, rubbed it, then shook his head with a bemused air. He dropped his hand. "Will you say that again, Mr. Dunham?" His voice had become hoarse and muffled.

"Married!" shrilled Phoebe, starting from her chair. "I don't believe it! It's some scheme! Why should he marry Melissa?" she screamed, furiously. "Melissa!" She swung, half crouched, on her sister, and her pretty face became distorted with rage and spite. "You've done something to force him to marry you—!"

Andrew took one step towards her, caught her by the shoulder, spun her about, and soundly slapped her face. Then, while she still gaped, he flung her back into her chair. His breath came fiercely, and with pent haste. "You dirty little bitch!" he said, in a harsh voice. "Why, you little animal, you! How dare you talk to your sister like that, you, with your filthy mind!"

Phoebe began to shriek faintly, holding her hand against her bruised cheek. Melissa blank and white as a statue, could only sit mutely in her chair and stare at nothing. Geoffrey was alarmed at her expression, and would have gone to her if Andrew had not stopped him. The young man was breathing unevenly, and his face was drawn and stern.

"I think I ought to have an explanation, Mr. Dunham."

"Of course, Andrew," said Geoffrey. "You deserve one. I can only say that though this may be news to you, I asked your mother, right after your father died, for Melissa. I believe Melissa was told the next day. She—she has been considering it ever since, and yesterday she told me she would marry me. I am sorry if you did not know it before, but everything was confused, your mother was ill, and apparently you were not informed."

"Oh, that horrible, scheming, sly Melissa!" moaned Phoebe. "How dared she do this to me? Telling me not to marry my Johnnie, and plotting all the time to marry the richest gentleman in the whole township!"

"Keep quiet!" shouted Andrew, turning on his sister, with knotted fists. "You envious little beast, you. This is the return you give her for her kindness to you, her plans for you, and you letting her slave all alone while Mother was ill, you lying in your bed like a warm slug! I know all about you, Phoebe. It almost kills you, doesn't it, that she married Mr. Dunham, and can have a finer house than yours, and everything she wants?" He advanced towards her, his hand lifted again, and with a louder shriek Phoebe recoiled in her chair. Geoffrey caught the young man's arm in a strong grip.

"No matter, Andrew," he said. "The girl is young, and is naturally startled. She doesn't mean anything."

"Oh, yes she does!" said Andrew, in an ugly tone. "I know all about Phoebe. I know how she and my father exploited Melissa and made her life a hell. My mother and I had a talk, before I went back to Harvard, before she was ill. She told me a lot I already knew, and a lot I didn't. I had intended changing everything when I came home again." He stopped, looked at Melissa, and his infuriated young face softened. "Melly," he said. "Poor Melly. I talked to Mother that morning, just before the doctor came. She was conscious for a little while. You remember? She asked me to take care of you. And, by God!" he added, in a resolute voice, "that's what I intend to do."

He waited for her to look at him, to speak. But she sat as if stricken unconscious, staring before her, her face a stark white blur in the dimness of the room. Her lips were carved and folded like marble, her eyes empty and motionless.

"Please, Melly, listen to me," said Andrew. He bent over his sister and laid his palm gently against her cold stiff cheek. "I ought to have told you before, but I was such a fool. You see, Melly, I never intended to go back to Harvard. Even if there had been money, I wouldn't have gone. I want to farm, Melly. I intend to make this place pay. I always wanted to be a farmer. Nothing in the world will ever persuade me to go on with the law. I hate it. I only went because I was too stupid to resist. It was all wrong."

Melissa stirred just a little, and her mouth opened slowly. In a voice of muted anguish she said: "Oh, Andrew!" It was an effort for her to speak, but she went on, after a dazed and painful moment: "Don't say that, Andrew. Don't. It isn't true. You only want me not to be sorry, not to try—" She could not go on.

Andrew frowned in his pity. "For God's sake, Melissa, try to understand. You must, for your own sake. Melly dear, I want the land. I've wanted it ever since I was a child. I wish I hadn't been such a damned weak fool! But I thought—I thought my father knew what was best for me. He had me hypnotized, just as he had you hypnotized, Melly. But when he was dead, I thought to myself: I am free. And then I understood what it was I had always wanted, and what I now must have."

Melissa lifted her hand and averted her head as if in agony. "Don't, Andrew," she murmured. "Don't speak so of Papa. I—I believe now that you want to keep the farm. It's a terrible disappointment for me, and I'm glad Papa isn't here to know how you've turned against his wishes. And his money, Andrew—he worked so hard for it."

"Oh, Melly!" cried Andrew, in compassionate impatience. "It was never his money. It was Mama's, her dowry, the money her father left her. Our father spent it foolishly; he added very little to it. He never wanted to have any responsibility, Melly."

But Melissa stood up with a frantic gesture, and put her hands to her cheeks. "Andrew, you mustn't talk like that! It isn't true! I know it. You've been deceived, lied to. Believe me, I know. I—I'm sorry Mama is dead. She suffered. But she always opposed Papa; she never understood him, and she made his life a long misery of frustration. He hated it here, but she *would* remain, and he was smothered, and his heart broke." She had spoken with rapid breathlessness, as against a rush of unbearable pain. "But I want you to be happy, Andrew. Papa would want it."

Andrew glanced at Geoffrey with eloquent despair. He said with resolution: "We'd better settle all this now, Melly. Here's Phoebe: she doesn't want to write poems. She wants to marry Johnnie Barrett, and she'll marry him no matter what you try to do, however you try to deceive yourself that she really wants something else. Phoebe," he continued, threateningly, "speak up, and this time don't lie to Melissa."

Phoebe was utterly cowed now by her brother's manner and expression. She pushed back against the chair as if to escape him. She whimpered: "I won't lie, Andrew, please. You know what I want. I want Johnnie, and I'm going to marry him, just as soon as he wishes. Tomorrow, if he says so."

"Oh, no, Phoebe," pleaded Melissa, lifting her bent head

and extending her hands to her sister. "You are just frightened, darling. You mustn't be afraid of Andrew." She caught her brother's arm. "See, Phoebe, he won't hurt you. He is our Andrew. You can tell me the truth, dear, nothing will happen."

Phoebe was silent. She looked up at her sister's white face and desperate mouth, and her own became shut and spiteful. She licked her round pink lips. Now an ugly little triumph gleamed in her eyes, a secret and vivid delight.

"I'll tell you the truth, Melissa! I don't want to write poems. I hate them! I just let you dream to yourself, because you were so ridiculous. Nothing in the world will keep me from Johnnie, nothing. I haven't any 'gift,' as you say, and I'm glad! I made up things, just to amuse myself, and sometimes I copied, and you and Papa never found out! You were so silly, both of you! And Papa used to make fun of you, too. You never knew it, but I did!" Now her expression changed, became strangely malignant. "And you were a liar and a sneak! You went off and married Mr. Dunham, pretending all the time you didn't mind being poor, when you were just planning to be a rich lady and live in a mansion and laugh at all of us. I hate you, Melissa! I always hated you, and I never, never, never want to see you again or hear your awful voice." She was rapidly becoming hysterical in her envy and furious resentment.

She stamped her foot before the dumb Melissa, and then, in a flurry of skirts, she ran wailing out of the room, almost knocking down Sally in the passage.

Be still, Geoffrey commanded himself. It is better this way, for the shocks to come all at once and be over with. But he could not bear to look at Melissa standing so petrified and so still in the middle of the room, and with such a look on her poor face. Apparently Andrew could not endure it either, for he went to his sister and put his arm about her shoulders.

"Melly, dear, this is what you meant, isn't it, when you asked us last night for a day or two more? You intended to marry Mr. Dunham and get the money for us from him, didn't you? Poor Melly, poor Melly. It wasn't necessary, dear. But I'm glad, anyway. You'll have your own happiness, and then you'll forget all about this and live the life you deserve and ought to have. Just remember that you are his wife, that your first duty now is to him."

Melissa did not answer or move. She stood in the utter immobility of grief and exhaustion. Andrew, his arm still over her shoulders, looked at Geoffrey. "I see it all now, sir, and I think that poor Melly, in her ignorance, has hurt you. But try to understand, please. You can make her happy. Be good to her."

"Oh, yes, Andrew, I understand. You can trust me."

Andrew impulsively stretched out his free hand to Geoffrey and the older man took it. They stood with their hands warmly pressed together, much moved, but smiling.

Then Andrew patted his sister's shoulder and led her back to a chair. She sat down, obediently, like one under mesmerism. Andrew went to the door and caught Sally with her ear against the opened crack. She started away when he flung open the door, expecting to be berated. But Andrew merely said, mildly: "Sally, go upstairs and pack some of Miss Melissa's things. She is leaving right away, with her husband."

CHAPTER 24

GEOFFREY TUCKED the fur lap-robes over Melissa, and the Dunham carriage crunched down to the road and began the long ascent to the house on the hill-side. Charles Upjohn's manuscripts, notes and papers, and a few of his reference books, had been wrapped in an old black shawl and now lay in the back of the carriage, together with Melissa's splintered raffia box and battered leather bag. Charles' belongings made a much larger display than Melissa's, for the box and the bag had weighed a great deal less.

Geoffrey did not speak to his new wife as the carriage moved through a white and sunlit landscape. Neither did he look at her directly, in his compassion. He only knew that she sat beside him as speechless as the dead, and as motionless, and probably as unaware. When the carriage swayed, she swayed helplessly; when it lurched, she lurched also. Her hands, and all her body from the waist down, were covered with the lap-robe, but Geoffrey felt that there was no warmth at all under the fur.

The Dunham house grew larger as the carriage approached it, and all its windows sparkled in the sunlight. Its chimneys blew out great plumes of blue vapor; its red roofs were a vivid slash against the white hillside behind it. Geoffrey now believed he ought to speak to Melissa before confronting his sister. He turned to her, and then was surprised.

Melissa had been crushed and stunned in the lean flat

house below, had moved unresistingly in obedience to all the suggestions from her husband and brother. She had left the house without looking backward once. She had walked feebly and slowly, in a dumb, dazed fashion, and had spoken to no one. She had allowed Geoffrey to tuck the robes about her and had not shrunk from his touch. All this had alarmed him. He was prepared to see her as flaccid and stupefied now as she had been only half an hour ago.

But now she sat upright and stiff, looking steadily at the Dunham house. Her shoulders had squared themselves; her strong white chin had lifted itself in an attitude of resolution and fortitude. Her profile was sharply marked against the moving countryside, and the mouth was firm and rigid. Geoffrey was amazed, and pleased. He saw the pale frosty blue of her eyes glinting between their bronze lashes, and they were now completely conscious with a hard awareness. She was the young Amanda, unrelenting and proud, stately and cold, her mouth a line of bitterness and suppressed pain. She must have known that Geoffrey was looking at her, for she said, without turning to him: "Arabella will be very surprised." Her voice was calm and neutral, with all her mother's inflections and strength.

"Yes," said Geoffrey, matching his voice to hers. "It was very early, and, as no one had retired before three o'clock, no one was about. I left a note for her."

A sharp furrow dug itself between Melissa's eyes, and she said, forbiddingly: "That was—evasive. You ought to have informed her before leaving. She has reason to feel slighted and suspicious."

Geoffrey might have been listening to Amanda, Amanda who had had such a rigorous conscience, such forthrightness. For some reason, he was enormously relieved. He said: "I think I did what was best, Melissa. Arabella does not like to be disturbed early in the morning, for anything."

She moved her head stiffly and repellently, dismissing his lame excuse. "Arabella does not like me. She will be shocked. A note was a cowardly thing."

In his relief and delight, Geoffrey wanted to laugh. "I don't like women's hysterics," he said frankly. "Now, I am not going to say that Arabella loves you, my dear, and will greet you with cries of joy. There may be a few moments of—unpleasantness, but Arabella will soon adjust herself to the new situation. After all, she has practically no money of her own and, in her way, Arabella is a very sensible woman."

Melissa turned her head and gave him a cold and contemptuous look, long and piercing. "That must be very disagreeable for Arabella, and it does not reflect creditably upon you." Again, it might have been Amanda who had spoken, thought Geoffrey with thankfulness.

"Perhaps we can make other arrangements for Arabella," he said.

But Melissa had turned away again, and did not answer. The carriage was now entering the sloping and winding grounds. Melissa watched the approach of the house steadfastly, with no sign of particular interest or disinterest. Then, all at once, she exclaimed breathlessly, her mouth shaking: "There is one thing I must know at once! You knew my father well. I—I don't think you will lie to me now, and I must know! You heard what Phoebe said: That my father often laughed at me secretly. You must tell me honestly: Is that true?"

The words were almost incoherent, and had come from her in a rush. He said at once, without considering, and desiring only to ease her iron misery: "Of course it was not true, Melissa! I knew your father for many years and saw him often with you. Why should you believe the jealous words of a spiteful girl who wanted only to hurt you?"

She did not answer, but he saw her clenched hands move under the robe. He went on, bending sideways towards her: "You have all the years with your father to remember. Do you recall any doubt of him, until now? Don't you think you are wronging him by thinking such things?"

The stern mouth softened, and quivered only for an instant, but Geoffrey saw it. Melissa lifted her chin. She said only: "Thank you. Thank you." Her voice was hardly audible.

So, thought Geoffrey, with deep surprise and gratitude, she has been thinking. This is not new to her, this distrust of her father. Each fresh doubt is an agony, but she will be cured through her pain. The evidence will pile up, and she will know. She will discover everything, but the discoveries must not come from me.

The carriage was approaching the door of the house, white and gleaming in the sun. Melissa spoke again: "I have done a wrong thing in marrying you, Mr. Dunham. It was a useless —gesture. For a moment or two—at home—I wanted to tell you that I could not go with you, now that everything—" Her voice shook, broke for a moment. Then she went on determinedly: "But I had made a bargain. It was not your fault that it was useless. There is just one other thing I want to say: You ought not to have married me. I know nothing of your way of life and I know I shall not like it. So, if you wish to send me home again now, I shall understand, and I should prefer it."

Geoffrey answered quietly: "We made a bargain, and I insist that it be kept. I shall not send you away. You are my wife."

The carriage stopped at the door. Melissa turned to Geoffrey swiftly and there was a sudden trembling desperation on her face. "You will not be happy, Mr. Dunham. I ask you again to let me go home, at once."

"And I refuse," said Geoffrey, looking at her directly. "This is your home henceforth. And you must make the best of it."

The coachman was opening the door. Geoffrey swung out, held out his hand to Melissa. But she gathered up her frayed brown skirts and descended by herself. She did not falter. The desperation on her face was gone, had been replaced by a frozen and prideful composure. Standing beside Geoffrey, she looked at her belongings in the back. Geoffrey said to the coachman: "Bring in Mrs. Dunham's bags at once and have them taken to her rooms."

He touched Melissa's angular elbow, and they went up the white steps together. The hall door was opened by James, whose expression was both excited and suppressed. He bowed to Melissa and said: "Welcome home, Mrs. Dunham."

Well, at least the servants know, and that will save awkwardness, thought Geoffrey. Then he became annoyed at James' covert glances at Melissa's shabby gown and old shawl, and he said, peremptorily: "Mrs. Dunham's apartments have been prepared, James?"

"Yes, indeed, sir," said James, quickly. "Miss Arabella left orders." He coughed behind a discreet hand. "She also left word with me that she is indisposed and will not come down until dinner-time."

There was a curious warm stillness through all the house. No one was about. The opened doors of the drawing-rooms revealed no guest and returned no voice. The fires crackled in the library and in the hall and other rooms, and sunlight lay in great bright fans over walls and carpets. The monolithic grandfather clock chimed a melodious two o'clock, and the notes echoed softly. Geoffrey frowned. Arabella, then, had done her work well. The guests were remaining in their rooms until requested to appear. There was no one present to welcome the new mistress of the house, and now Geoffrey's heart began to thud with anger. He must go to Arabella at once, and what he would say to her would never be forgotten by either of them.

He turned to James and said, abruptly: "You will please send a maid to Mrs. Dunham. Also, she will have a tray in her room, at once."

Melissa stood in the hall. She did not look about her. She stood like a statue, wrapped in her shawl. The pink firelight danced over her white features and still mouth. Geoffrey put his hand on her arm. "Shall we go up to your rooms, my dear?"

Silently and stiffly, holding her skirts up about her ankles, Melissa mounted the vast staircase beside Geoffrey. The numbness which had alarmed Geoffrey before had fallen upon her again. Together, they passed the carved and shining doors in the upper hall, which was also voiceless and soundless. Geoffrey opened the door of his mother's room. Here a bright fire had been lighted, all the dust-covers had been removed, the draperies drawn back from the windows. The sunlight, flooding the room, sparkled on crystal and gilt, brightened the soft blue damask walls, the rosy Aubusson rug, the blue, rose-colored and coral velvets and silks of the chairs, the love-seat and the chaise-longue. The white bed, with its raised mouldings of gold-leaf, the white and gold chests, the dressing-table with its gilt mirror and crystal and golden bottles and jars, might have been new, so fresh were they after all these years. The doors of the mirrored and white-and-gold wardrobe had been opened, and a fresh scent of cedar and faint, subtle perfume mingled with the odor of the burning fire on its white marble hearth. Now that the white velvet draperies, with their embroideries of blue, rose and gold, had been drawn back, the windows revealed the dazzling sunlit snowy slopes below, the pattern of a black bare tree. The pure light danced on the prisms of the turquoise candelabra on the mantelpiece, and on the small turquoise and crystal lamps on the white and delicate tables scattered about the room.

If Geoffrey had expected any interest or admiration from Melissa upon seeing this large and sweetly scented room with its lovely furnishings, he was disappointed. She actually did not appear aware of it. She stood in the center of the carpet, waiting, blindly submissive again, and motionless. When Geoffrey indicated a door and said: "My dressing-room is beyond that, and my bedroom," she turned her eyes obediently to follow his gesture. But they were dulled and glazed. Again the gray shadow of exhaustion was on her face, though her mouth was set in rigid lines.

To Geoffrey's thankfulness, a dark-haired and rosy little maid, dressed all in black crisp bombazine and ruffled apron and cap, knocked at the open door and entered with a curtsey. Her bright black eyes stared at Melissa curiously and with repressed excitement, and her pretty cheeks dimpled.

"Melissa, my love," said Geoffrey, "this is Rachel. She will attend to all your needs hereafter. Rachel, this is your new mistress, and I think you understand your duites. You will unpack Mrs. Dunham's bags immediately. She will have a tray in her room, and then rest until dinner."

Rachel curtseyed again, and said, in a subdued tone: "Yes, sir." She hesitated, then said to Melissa, who did not seem to see her: "Welcome home, Mrs. Dunham."

The girl and Geoffrey looked at Melissa in a sudden awkward silence. Her hands were knotted under her shawl. Tall, thin, dressed in her hideous brown and black, she was an incongruity in this charming and graceful room. Rachel disrespectfully thought of a thin black crow among Dresden bric-a-brac. How strange for the master to marry such an odd creature and bring her to this house! Rachel was new; she had been imported only two weeks before from Philadelphia. But she had heard many stories about the Upjohns from James, who had a penchant for her. She had expected some dashing and handsome young woman, a little odd perhaps, and cold, but not this white-lipped creature with the gaunt cheeks and still, unseeing eyes.

Geoffrey, thankful to leave Melissa with Rachel, went out of the room abruptly, in search of his sister. Rachel, who was a very smart and competent girl, was at a loss when left alone with her new mistress. What could one say to one who was obviously both deaf and dumb, for Melissa had not responded to her maid's greetings? Rachel became uneasy as moment after moment passed and Melissa did not stir nor look at anything. Rachel smoothed the ruffles of her pert apron, and felt herself becoming warm and flushed and very awkward. She stammered: "Shall I take madam's shawl?"

Melissa did not reply, and Rachel approached her timidly. She lifted the shawl from Melissa's shoulders and felt its rough texture with distaste. What a horrid, black old thing, with such a musty smell! And then Rachel saw the pale gold masses of Melissa's hair, and she smiled in admiration. She would brush that hair to smoothness and make it glisten like old gilt. She would braid it in two long plaits, and wind it about that small and noble head. It would reveal a long white neck, which would, perhaps, be decorated by a string of opals or turquoises. Yes, Madam definitely had possibilities. Her figure, if too thin, was good. She would look like a queen! Not for her the puffs and curls and chignons of inferior women!

Rachel drew a coral chair to the fireplace, and placed a footstool there. "Will Madam rest until her tray is here?" she suggested, in a soft voice.

Melissa started slightly, and turned to Rachel. She seemed to see the girl for the first time. Rachel smiled courageously, and again her cheeks dimpled. Melissa stared at her blankly, like one coming out of extreme shock. Then she moved to the fireplace and obediently sat down. She did not lean against the back of the brilliant chair; she sat upright, her hands tightly clenched together on her knees. She looked at the fire, which played over her sunken cheeks and large, colorless mouth. The lines of her long thighs and legs appeared through the brown stuff of her frock. How beautiful she could be, thought Rachel, who was kneeling beside the raffia box and the black bag. She opened the containers, and gasped a little. The box contained a rusty black dress, two worn gingham frocks, a quantity of coarse cotton underwear and three pair of black cotton stockings. There were no peignoirs, no laces, no stays, no gloves, jewels or ribbons. Rachel hung up the frocks, where their full dismalness was revealed swinging from the hooks in the wardrobe, and she put away the cotton undergarments, the stockings, and the three white cotton nightgowns, in the lovely chests. The black bag contained Melissa's notebooks, and extra shawl, several weighty books, an inkpot and a number of pens. Rachel hastily hid these in a drawer. Then she turned to the objects in the black shawl, and was surprised to find manuscripts, more notebooks, and thin reference volumes. These she put away also.

James knocked at the door, and entered with a steaming tray, all white linen, delicate china and silver. He and Rachel exchanged an eloquent glance, then James shrugged. Rachel placed a table at Melissa's elbow, and James deposited the tray upon it. He removed the silver covers. There was a delicate broiled squab, some rich pink ham, some hot bread and butter, a crystal dish of preserves, and a pot of fragrant tea. James bowed to Melissa, who had not turned from her marble contemplation of the fire. "Your tray, Mrs. Dunham," he said softly.

Melissa started, turned her head, stared at James dumbly. He indicated the tray. She looked at it without comprehension. James placed the squab on a hot plate, poured the tea. The room filled with delicious odors of marjoram and herbs and the scent of the strawberry preserves. Melissa mechanically watched all James' motions. He meticulously rearranged the forks and spoons, and pushed back the silver vase that held a single yellow rose-bud.

"Mr. Dunham expressly ordered this luncheon for you, Mrs. Dunham," said James, with intuition. "It will please him if you enjoy it."

"Yes. Of course," murmured Melissa. Then she added stiffly: "Thank you." She picked up a fork. A sudden profound revulsion nauseated her. She put down the fork. Her eyes met James' kind and steady eyes and she swallowed. She picked up the fork again. James had deftly divided the squab and dissected the meat from the tiny bones. Melissa began to eat slowly. James hovered over her. He was very sorry for this poor young creature, so starved and white and numb. He placed fresh morsels on her plate, and was pleased that she ate them all. He put cream and sugar in her tea, and she drank it obediently, like a listless child. But now a faint coral began to touch her lips. Rachel, in the background, watched with deep interest. There was something here that she could not understand. Melissa's stricken appearance had mystified her. Anyone less like a bride could hardly be imagined. But the girl saw James' solicitude, heard his quiet voice, and took her cue. James threw her a significant look, and she nodded like a conspirator.

James left with the tray. He was quite satisfied. Melissa might not have savored the delicacies, but she had eaten most of them. She was now actually leaning against the back of the chair. The ghastly tint had faded from her face. She seemed enormously tired.

"Would Madam like to lie down and rest for a while?" asked Rachel, and there was a note of soft pity in her fresh young voice.

Melissa rose, and then moved to the center of the room. All at once, she seemed to become aware of her surroundings. Slowly, her eyes traveled over every object, from the walls to the rugs, from the bed to the dressing-table, the delicate chairs and turquoise lamps. She saw the bright windows and the dazzling slopes beyond them. Like one moving in a dream she went to the windows and stood gazing through them. Rachel watched breathlessly. Moment after moment passed, while the fire crackled in the silence and Melissa's head gleamed in the sunlight. Then Melissa saw the white-and-gold embroidered draperies, and she touched them as if in wonder. Her rough and reddened hand lifted them, flinched, then lifted them again. She examined the rich velvet texture, followed a golden thread with a finger. She rubbed the back of a hand over a fold, let it drop.

Rachel pretended to be engaged in the rearrangement of the dressing-table jars and bottles, but she watched Melissa out of the corner of her eye. Melissa began to wander about the room. She looked at each chair intently. Hesitantly, she smoothed the coral velvet of the love-seat. Rachel went to the other end of the room. Melissa, in her wanderings, reached the dressing-table, saw herself reflected in the long, gilt-framed glass. She sat down on the white velvet seat and continued to stare at her own image. Then, automatically, her hands lifted to her disheveled hair. She smoothed it a little. Her eyes dropped to the jars and bottles, with their gold tops incrusted with blue, green, yellow and red stones. One by one she picked them up, like an absorbed child; turned them about, opened them. She held them to her nose and smelled the perfume and the lotions, concentrated with age. She put them down, studied the backs of her rough hands and red knuckles. She dropped her hands in her lap and closed her eyes. But now thought came to the stilled places in her brain.

It is all frippery and frivolity, she whispered to herself, with quick fever, for as yet she dared not think of that morning in the "parlor" of the Upjohn house where she had been so betrayed, so ruined and so stricken. It is all folly, all the foolishness of people without significance or usefulness. This is how they live, amid velvets and silks, idling away their lives like greedy grubs, demanding and buying gimcracks with colored stones, and filled with revolting odors. Was the world created for such parasites—this world of stern work and sterner thinking? The books of great men stood in dust on forgotten shelves; the music of angels was silent in closed volumes; the paintings of mighty artists waited hopelessly in deserted galleries. The universe of splendor and majesty echoed with not a single step. And all the while the frivolous and the worthless lolled amid velvet color and artificial scents, and slept and ate and laughed and coquetted, a blasphemy in the face of lofty mysteries, of toil and beauty. What did they know of dreams and grandeurs, of passions and heroisms, of dedications and the noble labors of the giants? They did not know, and they did not care. Yet they had power, an awful, ugly power, for they had money. The price of such a folly as this gold-and-crystal bottle would buy bread for an eager and starving poet. These rugs and draperies and chairs were bought with the life-blood of those who worked. These crystal and turquoise lamps could redeem the life of a great pianist. A writer of profound books might perish for want of the dollars which had bought this fretted silver box made for sweetmeats. O Papa, Papa!

The awful grief, that had been held back by her numbness, now flooded Melissa. The scene that morning in the Upjohn house rushed before her eyes. She saw Phoebe and Andrew vividly, and heard their voices. They were lost, their thoughts and ideals perverted, because there had been no money. They had said ugly things, because they had been desperate. They had refused help, for they had been too proud. Hideousness was closing about them, and she, Melissa, could not hold it away. It was too late. It was always too late, when there was no money, money which the wicked and the frivolous held in tight and avaricious hands and which they would not let go to rescue the lives of those who might save the world.

Melissa, forgetting the presence of Rachel, leaned her head on the back of her hand and sobbed aloud, harsh and grating sobs of utter despair and sorrow.

CHAPTER 25

GEOFFREY ABRUPTLY flung open the door of his sister's apartments without bothering to knock. He was not too surprised to see that the draperies had been drawn closely over the windows, so that the room lay deep in drifted shadows, as if one already dead lay there. But he was taken aback at the reek of Cologne water and smelling-salts which assaulted his nostrils with an acrid wave. Arabella lay flat in bed, her plump body a heap under the white silken quilts, and beside her sat her favorite elderly maid, Ellis, fanning her and murmuring hoarsely in a sympathetic manner.

Geoffrey did not like Ellis, for she was tall and lank and sly, with a spade-like chin, dark flesh, long thin features, and little, tilted, and malicious eyes. But she and Arabella were friends as well as mistress and servant. Geoffrey had often played with the amusing idea of writing a monograph on the subject of mental similarities between those who were faithfully served and those who served them. One had only to study the servant to understand all about the master or the mistress. There was such a situation in his own offices between

Eliot Bargette, his chief editor, and the latter's slavish secretary, Wilson Bogerson. Eliot was a thin, slight, and white-faced fox, with drawn, small features, and Wilson was a grave and sonorous-voiced giant, with features like a church-deacon's. Yet they could communicate completely by a single glance, by the slightest lifting of a silent finger, and they both hated and feared Geoffrey Dunham.

Ellis returned her master's dislike with equal vigor, yet she now rose and curtseyed with deep respect and stood by the bed in a servile attitude, giving Geoffrey sidelong and mealy-mouthed glances. He could not endure the woman. He said: "You may go, Ellis."

The woman hesitated, and threw a swift look at the faintly moaning lady on the bed, as if waiting for the order to be countermanded. Geoffrey lost his temper. "I told you to get out," he said quietly. The woman's deep-set eyes flashed at him in fright, and with a rustle of her skirts and a flutter of an apron she literally ran from the room.

Geoffrey sat down in the chair she had vacated. Arabella appeared unaware of his presence. Her face was buried in her pillows; she kept up an incessant moaning. Her brother said nothing as yet. He merely waited, for he knew that nothing is more unbearable than silence. The room was very hot, and its smells were overpowering. Now he detected Arabella's violet sachet mingling with the smelling-salts and the Cologne and the attar of roses she frequently affected. The fire was a brilliant red hole in the gloom. The edges of the drawn draperies were gilded with the bright fingers of the exiled sun. The little ormolu clock on the white mantel ticked gently and the fire crackled.

After a long while, Geoffrey spoke: "You are an unregenerate bitch, Arabella."

During their frequent quarrels he was often given to what Arabella called "uncouth" language, but never had he used such an epithet in addressing her before. She was shocked out of her dramatic moaning; she lay utterly silent and stiff under her quilts, hardly breathing, but not removing her face from the pillows. Geoffrey stood up and began to walk slowly up and down the room, his mouth grim and set. He went on, pausing at the foot of the bed:

"You have behaved like a slut today. Fortunately, and with rare good sense, you chose not to make a filthy display before your guests. Had you done so, you should not have spent another night under this roof. However, you have communicated something to them, some way, so that my wife entered my home as ungreeted as a strumpet, and passed the closed doors of those who have feasted on my hospitality. By God, I shall not forget this, and you'll pay for it, eventually!"

The short thick mound under the quilts moved. Very slowly, rising like a small hill, Arabella sat up in bed. Her full face was raddled and gray; she had become an old woman. Her reddened eyes had swollen to twice their size and her lightish hair sprang out about her head in a ragged cloud. But there was no mistaking the complete sincerity of her aghast and agonized expression as she peered at her brother between crimson lids.

"You are talking like this, to your sister, Geoffrey?" she asked, each word painfully uttered and incredulous.

"I am talking to a woman who has lost every semblance of decency and who has forgotten even the few manners she had acquired," replied Geoffrey with cold violence. "Had you been the veriest drab who ever bent over a wash-tub, or a fishmonger's wife, you would have displayed more feeling, more propriety, more graciousness, than you have done today. You were always very careful to be meticulously correct in the presence of guests and to control yourself with more seemliness. Had you had a single instinct of a lady you would have pretended to some grace, some fortitude, some naturalness, before these people in this house. But that was beyond you. And yet, I wonder. I believe this was a deliberate attempt on your part to dishonor me, to throw odium on my wife, to cause your friends to laugh in ridicule and slyness behind my doors, to punish me by allowing me to enter my own house, with my wife, like some skulking cur with his dam, shamefaced and sheepish and contemptible."

Arabella stared at him speechlessly, her fat shoulders huddled together under her ruffled silk nightdress, her plump arms hugging herself as if she had turned very cold. Then she gasped aloud and put her hands to her throat. Geoffrey made a sound of disgust, and looked at her with inexorable loathing.

Arabella began to speak, hardly above a hoarse whisper: "You say you shall never forget. Neither shall I, Geoffrey. You speak of my 'dishonoring' you. You have dishonored yourself and dishonored me. You ran away early in the morning, leaving behind a foolish and cowardly note, and married a female who has all my scorn and disdain, and who will bring you nothing but misery. Had you had, yourself, 'a single instinct' of a gentleman, you would have come to me this morning and told me—" She swallowed convulsively.

Geoffrey's face changed as he remembered Melissa's re-

marks to him in the carriage about the note he had left for
his sister. But he was too enraged to be reasonable.

"I left you that note because I know you too well, Bella. I
was afraid you would kick up a hell of a stink and arouse the
whole damn household with carefully unmodulated yells and
hysterias. I knew your hatred for Melissa; I have known all
your tricks and your 'subtlety' for a long time. You would
not have succeeded in preventing me from marrying Melissa,
but you would have tried. How you would have tried!"

But Arabella's shrewd ear had caught the note of overem-
phasized rage in his voice, and she took quick advantage of it.
She found her own voice and cried wildly, beating her quilts
with her fists:

"Yes, I would have tried! I would have flung myself down
before you, so that to pass me you would have had to step
on my body! In my misguided affection for you, I would
have fallen on my knees before you, imploring you not to
commit this crime against yourself, this terrible folly! I would
have clung to you, begging you to reflect, to realize, and perhaps I might have saved you from this disgrace and madness.
To marry such a creature, to bring her to this house, to flaunt
her before the faces of gentlefolk in all her ugliness and
stupidity! I would have tried, even with my life, to save you
from that!"

She burst into hiccoughing sobs, buried her face in her
hands, and began to rock back and forth in her bed. The sobs
became deep and genuine groans. Geoffrey's face grew darker,
but he could not speak. Too much had been said now between
himself and his sister. He listened to her groans and, in spite
of his hatred and fury, he felt sick and alarmed.

"What can our guests think?" said Arabella between the
awful sounds she uttered. "Completely unheralded—you run
away from this house and bring back a 'wife'! And such a
wife! What will they say, our friends? They will laugh at you,
until all Philadelphia roars. Worse, they will think the only
thing possible—that you had to marry her, this frumpish coun-
trywoman, this miserable female in her ragged frock and her
tattered shawl!"

Again, in spite of himself, Geoffrey had a sudden vision of
the faces of his guests and his friends, and heard the distant
rumble of their laughter. And again, his fury mounted, in defense of Melissa, Melissa with her poor chapped hands, her
dreadful garments, her dazed bewilderment and innocent sorrow, her crushing grief. Perhaps he ought not to have done
this to her, in her defenselessness. But there had been no other

way possible. Nevertheless, he heard the cruel and delighted laughter at himself and Melissa. He, at least, could combat his enemies. But Melissa had no weapons, and she had been sufficiently stricken already.

He said, brutally, hating his sister afresh: "You know this, and so you abandoned me, deliberately, and exposed Melissa to the hyena laughter of cheese-mongers and tradesmen and other riff-raff. Had you gallantly accepted the situation, had you expressed some sentiment, however false to your true feelings and nature, they would have had to accept what I had done with some pretension to gentility. You planned to make me lose face, to hold Melissa up to the mirth of jackals. That is the way you have returned the charity I extended to you, the kindness, and the generosity."

His face swelled with passion, became suffused with new rage, so that it had a brutish look. A thick and livid ridge outlined his sensual mouth.

Arabella regarded him in silence, though there was an evil glint between her scarlet eyelids.

"Enough," said Geoffrey. "Here are my orders: You shall appear at the dinner-table as composed as possible, and as gracious. You shall pretend that this was no surprise to you. You shall greet my wife with the respect due her, and make her welcome. If you fail in any of these, you shall leave my house forever, as penniless as you came, carrying with you nothing but what you possessed when I gave you shelter, and be damned to you!"

Arabella caught her breath in a loud hiss of terror. She stared at him incredulously, and her large nose jutted out from her sagging face like a vulture's beak. And Geoffrey stared back, implacably, with an expression that was completely bestial.

Arabella knew when she was defeated. She knew that, for her own sake, she must do the best possible with this appalling situation. But she could not immediately surrender, even if her life had depended upon it.

She whispered malignantly: "Do you know what the whole countryside, and even those parts of Philadelphia where the Upjohns are known, say of Melissa? They say she is demented, crazed. They say things of her and her father which cannot be repeated by any Christian tongue——"

Geoffrey turned white. Slowly, he moved to the side of the bed. Arabella watched him come, and shrank back as far as possible, her heart leaping up into her throat. Again, there was silence in the room, as they looked at each other across the sharp deep abyss of their mutual hatred.

"'A Christian tongue'!" said Geoffrey at last, in a very soft tone. "Your tongue, Arabella. That is the 'Christian' tongue which has slavered at Melissa's skirts. Only you could be guilty of such dirtiness. You have been afraid for' years, haven't you, that I might some day marry Melissa? So you deliberately befouled her, whispering your vile lies into every ear that would listen, hoping that one of these days, perhaps, I might hear an echo from another tongue without suspecting the source of the vicious tale. But apparently more decency lives even in your hearers than in you—you, a woman! Where did you learn such things, Arabella? From your husband, from the dregs that haunted your 'salon' before that miserable wretch died? From strumpets and perverts and other horrible monsters?"

Almost fainting from his tone and his words, Arabella crouched away from her brother, not daring to take her eyes from him for fear of physical violence.

Geoffrey went on: "But, in spite of all your efforts, no such tale ever came to me, nor, if it had, should I have believed it even for a single moment. There is no more to say," he added, thickly. "You have your orders."

He looked at the great wardrobes against the far corner of the room. He went to them, his footsteps, even on the thick rugs, loud in the silence. He flung open the wardrobe doors, and his hands riffled through the crowded racks of gowns and dresses which filled the depths. Arabella watched him in stupefied terror, and as she swallowed drily she made a curious series of sounds. She saw Geoffrey tear several of her best gowns from their hangers, a new soft satin which she had never worn, a black silk heavily and richly draped and embroidered with pearls, a deep brown velvet with golden buttons, a dark crimson velvet with pale cream lace. He tossed the garments over his arm. He went directly to his sister's chests, and wrenched out the drawers. He scooped up handfuls of the filmiest petticoats and nightgowns and chemises. He stuffed his pockets with silk stockings.

Then he turned to his sister. "These will be altered at once to fit Melissa. But when I leave this room you will immediately get up and send a list to Philadelphia for an entire and complete wardrobe for my wife, and you will send another list to New York. You will know the sizes to order. And then you will give the list to James, so as to catch the morning post."

Arabella could not speak. She could only look at the precious frippery on her brother's arm, and her face became wild with rage and hate.

"You will also call your maid, Ellis, and gather up all the jewels which belonged to my mother, and you will send them, in an hour or two, to my wife's room. They are hers, now. You wore them by courtesy. You shall never disgrace them again."

He went out of the room. Arabella watched him go in silence. Even when the door had closed behind him she continued to look at it, and her swollen eyes became terrible.

CHAPTER 26

GEOFFREY threw the heap of clothing which he had confiscated from his sister onto his bed, and walked through his dressing-room to the room which had once been his mother's. Here he found that the white draperies had been partially drawn. But there was a fresh sweet scent in the air, and even the fire seemed cleaner than the one he had just left. Melissa lay on the velvet bed, asleep, still dressed in her brown woolen frock. But Rachel had thrown a light blue robe over the girl's feet.

The maid rose as Geoffrey entered, and her pert black eyes were both alert and soft. She whispered: "Mrs. Dunham just fell asleep, sir. She seemed very tired."

Geoffrey nodded, touched the girl's arm, and led her back to his bedroom. He indicated the gowns on the bed. "These are Mrs. Shaw's. She has kindly presented them to Mrs. Dunham, but they are, obviously, of a size that will not fit her. Do you think you could take one of them at once and, by working very quickly, have it ready for Mrs. Dunham for dinner?"

He looked at his watch. It was half-past three. He suddenly remembered that he had had no mid-day meal. Rachel picked up one of the frocks and examined it critically, went to the wardrobe, removed Melissa's black dress, and measured the two dresses together with concentrated attention. Arabella's dresses were short and wide compared with the long and slender lines of the miserable black bombazine, and Rachel's pink face became dubious and hopeless.

"It doesn't have to fit exactly," said Geoffrey, with impatience. "But it is impossible for Mrs. Dunham to appear to-night in what she is wearing today." He felt cheap and fool-ish, for Melissa, in brown woolen, would be far handsomer than the prettiest guest in his house. He was not a man to consider the opinions of others in his own life. But now he must consider Melissa. Damn women. They forever compli-cated a man's existence, made him dance to the organ-grinder's music of the conventions like an infernal grinning monkey. Who was the fool who said that men have power over women? The truth was that men feared women, which resulted in mas-culine arrogance towards the so-called weaker sex, and an eternally futile gesture of dominance. Geoffrey was now quite sure that women secretly laughed at men and well knew who held the balance of power.

He waited irascibly for the result of Rachel's close inspec-tion. She was now examining the soft light-blue silk of the new dress. Now her face brightened. "Look, sir," she said eagerly. "The gown has not been quite completed. The hem is unfinished. Apparently this was to be done by one of the maids, at home. A matter of some six inches has been marked off. This third ruffle on the drapery can be dropped, the bustle lowered a few inches, the bodice lengthened by letting out this seam, the sleeves narrowed by tucking——"

"Yes, yes," said Geoffrey impatiently. "How long will all that take?"

"If I begin at once, sir, I think I can have it ready for Mrs. Dunham by seven o'clock."

She examined the other dresses, with increasing cheerful-ness. "I can do something with these, one each day, perhaps," she added. She looked over the silken underwear and night-gowns, the petticoats and the chemises, and her cheerfulness became somewhat less. "I can contrive," she said doubtfully. She hesitated, and blushed. "Mrs. Dunham has no—no stays, sir. But she has such an excellent figure that it will not matter."

"Well, get to work at once, child. I will remain with Mrs. Dunham. Also, please ask James to bring me a tray."

Rachel gathered up the gleaming blue silk, one or two of the undergarments, and rustled out of the room. Geoffrey re-turned to Melissa. She still slept in the abandoned unconscious-ness of exhaustion. He sat down beside her and looked long and intently at his wife as she slept. Rachel had loosened Melissa's long pale hair. It lay like a shaft of winter sunlight on the white pillows and even fell over the edge of the bed. It caught shimmers and lights from the subdued sun that peered through the half-closed draperies, so that it appeared to have a restless life of its own strangely at variance with the complete immobility of the sleeping woman. Geoffrey gently lifted a strand; its weight and softness thrilled him with tenderness and admiration. It was not hair that curled, yet he imagined that it clung to his hand. He smoothed it over and over.

Melissa's face was turned away from him, but he saw her flat white cheek, the strong angle of her chin, and her beautiful thin throat. What a fierce innocence lived in this young creature! It was not only an innocence of any of the grosser affairs of life but an innocence of humanity in all its teeming and variegated patterns. Geoffrey was suddenly appalled at her extreme lack of knowledge. She had lived a life more immured than any nun's, for a nun has at least a previous awareness of the world, and some understanding. Yet Geoffrey did not doubt that Melissa had very positive convictions concerning life and human activity, and all of them wrong. There was a narrow arrogance in her learning, which was purely classical and smelled of the library. Her life had been spent among the ancient philosophers, whom she read and studied in their dead languages. Yet of the world in which she lived she was as unaware as an infant and had not the faintest notion that she was so unaware. There was, he recalled, never any uncertainty in her voice when she expounded an absurd opinion, to which, in the company of Charles Upjohn, he had listened with gravity. She had discussed the war with authority, and was given to calling bewildered statesmen fools. There was no use in offering her proofs. She had her fanaticisms, based on complete ignorance, and nothing could change them.

Geoffrey, though he was still throbbing with the after-effects of his battle with his sister, could not help smiling. He had married an abysmal child, with a brain packed with Chaldean, Phoenician, Greek and Roman philosophy and poetry. But if he smiled, he was also disturbed. The first doubt came to him as to whether he had done a sane and wise thing. What if he never succeeded in enlarging Melissa's horizon? He knew of what granite she was made. She was twenty-five years old, and by nature repressed and illiberal, strongly intolerant of opinions differing from hers, or rather, her father's. Any views she acquired were immediately cast in iron, to remain forever inflexible, practically indestructible.

Well, I can try to give her other opinions and other convictions, Geoffrey thought. If once I can get her to compromise, to doubt, to consider, the good work will be well on its way.

There was the softest knock on the door, and James entered with a tray. He whispered, as he put it down: "I am sorry, sir, but you were engaged before——"

And you know all about it, all of you, thought Geoffrey, grimly. But he smiled at James, and nodded. The man left the room and Geoffrey ate with good appetite, but with abstraction, his thoughts all with his young wife. From time to time he glanced at her as she lay flat upon the bed. He saw the firm small rise of her virginal breasts, the strong lines of her shoulders. He saw the maltreated hands, so lean and fine, so graceful in spite of their chapped skin and raw knuckles. She lay like a fallen statue, hardly a breath moved her body. Geoffrey became less doubtful as to the wisdom of his marriage. He remembered the women he had known, soft, corrupt, compliant and disingenuous, full of knowledge and sophistication. Even the young girls, for all their demureness and air of retreat before a masculine eye, were quite knowing, full of the decorous disillusion of old Mother Eve. Women were instinctive liars, they knew all about reality and were without true sentiment or shining romanticism. But they understood that men must keep their illusions if women were to have power over them, and so they consistently fostered those illusions.

Here, however, was a young women without hypocrisy or guile, avarice or any of the common female corruptions. She had the mind and soul of a clean young man. Geoffrey knew now that he had been attracted to her from the very beginning by this quality of cleanness and pure virginity. It was good to have a wife without deception or slyness, incapable of falsehood, full of harsh integrity and instinctive honor.

He finished his meal with satisfaction. He drank the last of the tea. He looked up to see that Melissa was awake and that she was staring at him intently, though she had still not moved.

"I hope you slept well," said Geoffrey, uncomfortably wondering how long she had been watching him and to what conclusions she had come. "You were very tired, my dear." He got up and went to the chair by the bed, and sat down. Her wide light eyes followed his every movement, but her immobile expression did not change.

Geoffrey said, trying to keep his voice light: "You were more than tired, Melissa. You were shocked and stunned by everything that happened today. I want to tell you this: You must not think of your brother and sister with bitterness. You must try to relinquish some of your fixed convictions about them and ask yourself whether there is not some possibility that you were wrong all the time. Most of us are, about others, and the sooner we learn to doubt our own opinions the more civilized we become and the easier we find existence."

Melissa's dry lips opened, then closed. She dropped her eyelids, so that a circle of bronze lashes lay on her colorless cheek.

"I shan't speak of all this again, but I want you to think about it," Geoffrey continued. "I want you to reflect on whether you haven't wronged both your sister and your brother, with your preconceived ideas about them and your determination to manage their lives. That is overbearing, Melissa, and unjust, and even impertinent. They have their lives. You have yours. Don't try to manage others; you will have all you can do to supervise yourself. You must let them go to find their own happiness, and you have a duty to find yours."

He paused. He knew that most of Melissa's mind was shut against his words, and that she found them incredible, if not stupid. But perhaps she had heard enough to start her thinking and considering.

"You have also a duty to me, Melissa," he said gently.

Her eyelids flew open, and the girl regarded him unbelievingly, as if she had just heard an inconceivable statement.

"Yes, a duty to me," repeated Geoffrey, with less gentleness and more firmness. "You made a bargain. I expect you to keep to it. Think of your father, Melissa. What if he knew that consciously or unconsciously you did not intend to fulfill your bargain?" He hesitated, then said guilefully: "Your father was an honorable man."

A white spasm of pain tightened Melissa's face.

Geoffrey went on with deliberate falsity: "Your father knew I wished to marry you, my dear." He paused, surprised. (Yes, Charles, you knew I did, and that is why you concentrated upon corrupting Melissa's mind and poisoning her against me!)

Melissa spoke for the first time, in a rusty voice full of disbelief: "My father—knew that?"

Geoffrey answered strongly: "He did."

Melissa raised herself up on her elbow and her long hair fell over her shoulders and breast. She regarded Geoffrey with enormous concentration. And then, in her terrible naïveté, she said on a rush of words: "Then why did he often call you a devious man and infer that you were not to be trusted?"

I see, thought Geoffrey. He was silent for several long moments. Melissa waited stiffly, propped up on her elbow—waited for his reply.

"I think you wrong your father, or misinterpret what he meant," he said coldly. "I was his friend for many years. By 'devious' he doubtless meant that I was a good business man. As for that 'distrust' business, did he ever assert that I had deceived him or given him a false impression?"

"No," said Melissa, still staring at him.

"Then how do you know what he really meant?"

Melissa sat up in her bed and pushed back her hair. She murmured, falteringly: "I don't know."

Geoffrey heard her words with delight, for he knew that she had rarely, if ever, said that before in her life.

He continued: "Your father was, in his way, in a somewhat restricted circle, quite a famous man. If he had thought he could not trust me, he would have taken his books to another publisher, would he not?"

"Yes," whispered Melissa. She bent her head, and her face was hidden by the straight curtain of her hair.

"So, your father trusted me. I ask that you also trust me, Melissa."

She did not answer. He could not see her face.

"I ask that you remember that you have a duty to me, as your husband."

Melissa lifted her head and looked at him bitterly. "What do you wish me to do, Mr. Dunham?"

He said, with firmness: "I never wish to hear you call me 'Mr. Dunham' again. That is my command, Melissa. My name is Geoffrey. Use it, hereafter. You will take your place as my wife, become a proper and competent mistress of this house, entertain my guests, and learn some of the social graces. You are a lady; these things will come naturally to you. I have a position to uphold. I expect you to help me uphold it to the best of your ability. I know that you are in a difficult position with regard to my sister. She did not wish me to marry you; she did not wish me to marry any woman, for she wanted to remain mistress of my house. Perhaps she will desire to leave, and will go to Philadelphia to set up her own establishment. I hope so, but I shall not urge it upon her. She is a widow, she has few real friends, and she was born in this house. Time will settle this. In the meantime, I hope you will try to maintain polite relations with her. It won't be easy, I admit, for Arabella is a naturally resentful woman."

He paused. Melissa tried to look away, but now he held her with his hard direct eyes. "Melissa, I want you to know that nothing will harm you in this house. You need not be afraid of me. I honor you because you are my wife, and I expect you to honor me as your husband. Try to think of me as your friend, even if you now doubt it. I have always been your friend; some day you will realize that. You are free, in this house, to do as you wish. Your father's manuscripts are here. You may work on them, and, if you need my assistance, I shall be glad to give it. But you must not neglect your other duties. That is your bargain, and I shall insist that you keep it."

Melissa had become even paler than before, and her eyes were stark and desperate. "Mr. Dun—Geoffrey, I shall do what I can to please you. But I don't know whether I shall succeed. Our lives have been so different. I am not interested in people." She caught her breath, then cried: "I hate people! I am afraid of them! I don't know what to do! I want only a corner in your house, where I can work——"

Geoffrey stood up. He was very moved by her anguish, but he kept his voice firm and sharp: "You shall have time to 'work.' But I have told you of your duties, and I shall not let you neglect them. You say you 'hate' people, and are 'afraid' of them. That is sheer stupidity and ignorance. You are really a very stupid and ignorant girl, Melissa, and it is time that you tried to improve yourself."

She flung up her head proudly, and her eyes flashed at him in anger. But she said, with quietness: "I will try. If I do not succeed, it will not be because I have not tried."

"That is all I ask of you," he said with more gentleness. "Dinner is at eight o'clock. This house is filled with my guests. You are to meet them. A gown is being prepared for you, and orders for a complete wardrobe are being listed. You will wear my mother's jewels tonight, and you will, I know, conduct yourself as I expect my wife to conduct herself."

He had a sudden vivid idea of what an ordeal Melissa was to be put through downstairs tonight, and he felt pity for this raw and inexperienced girl. She was regarding him with stern humility curiously mixed with hard pride. He had challenged her, and Melissa was accustomed to meeting challenges. He smiled at her.

"I am not afraid that you will disgrace me, Melissa," he said. He paused, then added: "Or your father. These people know of your father, and honor him. I hope that you will not give them cause to think of him disrespectfully."

Her chin rose and her mouth tightened. She repeated: "I shall try to do my best."

·He bent over her; she did not shrink away from him but looked at him steadily. He said softly: "Melissa, you asked me once why I wanted to marry you. I told you, and you did not believe it. But it was true. Think of that, sometimes."

She did not answer. But she watched him leave the room.

CHAPTER 27

RACHEL AND ELLIS carried in a shining bath-tub and placed it on the hearth. Melissa, still sitting in her bed, watched with consternation. She was accustomed to taking her baths on a Sunday afternoon before the kitchen fire, with all doors shut and barred, and the act completed hurriedly. She watched while the smiling Rachel, and the sly-eyed Ellis, poured big copper kettles of hot water into the tub, and scented it with rose-water. She saw the finest of white linen towels laid out, a soap that smelled of spring, an incredible chemise heavily trimmed with silk lace, two taffeta petticoats, and a pair of silk stockings. Only when she saw these did she exclaim: "What is this?".

Rachel beamed at her, as Ellis, her reluctant duties completed, scuttled from the room. "It is time for your bath, Mrs. Dunham, and then I shall assist with your dressing."

Melissa slipped from the bed. The draperies had been drawn back and the last ray of sunshine struck across the rich rugs and the crystal and the gilt. The air fumed with perfume and warm steam. Melissa's mouth was set grimly as she looked down at the waiting tub and the waiting garments. She shook back her hair and looked slowly about the room, then back to the tub and the fripperies beside it. But she would not let herself think too deeply. She remembered Geoffrey's insistence upon her "duties." If this was part of her duties, then she would submit.

Rachel slipped behind her and began to unbutton her bodice. Melissa started like a wild mare, and Rachel, in her turn, fell back, her lips parted in perplexity. "I can undress myself, thank you," said Melissa, with curtness. She had flushed a little, and her hand, reaching over her shoulder, held her bodice together. Rachel exuded cheerfulness. "I am your maid, Mrs. Dunham, and I am supposed to attend you and give you your bath."

At this humiliating suggestion, Melissa's slight color deepened to scarlet. She said, loudly: "I never heard of such a thing! And I shall certainly never permit it, Rachel! I have been bathing myself, alone, since I was five years old, and always in private, I assure you."

The very thought of her nakedness revealed to another made her drop her eyes and a wave of scarlet ran over her neck and entire body.

"It is the customary thing, Madam," murmured Rachel.

"I don't believe it! What nonsense." Melissa indicated the soap with loathing. "Haven't you any good, yellow, homemade soap, Rachel, and some unbleached muslin towels?"

Rachel, baffled, thought this a humorous sally on the part of the utterly unhumorous Melissa, and let forth several bubbles of respectful mirth. But when she saw Melissa's young and indignant face, she put her hand over her mouth very quickly.

"But, Madam, that is kitchen soap, and this is soap for a lady."

Melissa picked up the delicate articles in question, and sniffed at it with elaborate disdain. She dropped it as if it were hot. "Please go out, Rachel. I'll only be a few minutes." Rachel, after another baffled glance, left the room, closing the door after her with a subdued sound.

Melissa's expression of supreme distaste became stronger. She stared down at the soap. She picked it up from its ignominious place on the floor. She turned its oily richness about in her hands. Then she put it to her nose again. A faint look of sheepish surprise brightened her face. Then, sternly, she laid the soap down, shook her head as if in austere denial of her own weakness. She undressed swiftly and furtively, with suspicious glances at the door. She slipped into the scented water, and again that childlike wonder shone in her eyes. Inch by inch, she relaxed against the high back of the tub, and loosened her limbs in the water. They lay, white and sculptured, in an opalescent bath. She saw them, for the first time, and a startled thought came to her that they were beautiful. Her white breasts were lifted by the water, and they were the breasts of a statue.

It was a shameful thought, and she hurriedly began to wash herself. The familiar motions brought her "back to my senses." She was preparing for festivities in a strange and foolish room, when she should be working! She was idling like some soft parasite, even daring to admire herself like some empty-headed female fool, while her father's manuscripts were shut away as if they were ugly objects. No matter, it was just for tonight. Tomorrow Mr. Dunham—Geoffrey—must be made to see that she was a serious and dedicated person, with no time for follies.

"Geoffrey." The soap lay in her hands and she stared at the fire, which warmed her smooth shoulders. She closed her eyes tightly to shut out the face of her husband. It was impossible. She had no "husband." She was Melissa Upjohn and this was an absurd dream, a grotesque nightmare. Husband! She opened her eyes involuntarily and saw her long body like a mermaid's pale flesh beneath green sea water. Now her heart beat wildly, as if with terror. She stood up and began to dry herself with trembling hands. "Oh, no!" she whispered to herself. "No, no, never!" She stepped out of the tub and stood shaking and glancing about her in an attitude of impending flight. O Papa, you'd never ask that of me! Remember what you told me, many times, many years ago!

The pulses beat and throbbed heavily in her throat and temples, even in her breast, so that all her body was quaking and her arms and legs vibrated. Rachel knocked softly at the door; Melissa shrank and wrapped her towels about her. "Not yet!" she cried frantically. Mortification was almost upon her, and she completed her drying in a frenzied rush.

She almost tore the lace-trimmed chemise as she wrenched it over her shoulders. She fastened the strings of her petticoats with hands that felt huge and numb. She looked around the room in desperation, then caught up her old brown frock and put it on. It slipped over the rustling silk with a strange and intoxicating sound, and for the first time in her life she felt against her flesh the sliding softness of a satin chemise. It was like a lewd touch, a lascivious caress. Rachel opened the door and entered, with the blue gown over her arm, and smiling as always. She continued to smile, even when she saw Melissa's distraught face and the desperate fear in her eyes, and the brown frock.

"But, Mrs. Dunham, I have brought your gown," said Rachel, laying that object tenderly on the bed. "And you haven't put on your silk stockings yet."

Melissa, dazed, looked down at her bare feet, bent her knees a little to cover them with the hem of her skirt. "I have no gown! That doesn't belong to me!" she cried, with vehemence. "This is mine, and I shall wear it."

"But Mr. Dunham expressly wished you to wear this," urged Rachel.

Melissa paused. Her "duty" again! She went to the bed,

lifted the lovely blue gown, and examined it scornfully. It slipped through her hands; her rough nails bruised the shining silk. She let it slip, caught it, let it slip again. The texture of it made that half-sheepish, half-childish look flash out on her face once more. Then, seeing Rachel admiringly beside her, she flung the gown down and held out her hands for the stockings, hands stuck stiffly out before her in an attitude of contempt. Rachel gave the stockings to her meekly, but there was a dimple of triumph near her mouth. She knew the words, now, that could subdue Melissa.

Melissa sat down, turned her back, and pulled on the stockings, which were short and much too tight. Then she had her own rather artless triumph. "I have nothing but those old black boots of mine," she announced. "They will show under the blue dress."

Rachel looked at the boots in dismay. Then she said, dubiously: "If you are careful, Mrs. Dunham, they will not show."

Grimly, Melissa fastened the shoes, stood up. She swept up the dress, opened a closet door, and disappeared within. Rachel sighed, and shrugged. She had learned a great deal about Melissa and the other Upjohns while sitting in the sewing-room; much that had puzzled her was now explained. She laughed a little, silently. The poor, frightened young lady! She, Rachel, must do all she could to help her. Ellis was a bad and very mean fool; the other maids had been kinder in their stories about the new wife of Mr. Dunham.

Melissa stalked out of the closet like a grenadier, full of lofty derision for the figure she must cut in this foolish blue silk. In the darkness, she had fastened it awkwardly, and Rachel went to her. This time, Melissa did not retreat. She allowed the buttons to be fastened properly; she watched Rachel's deft fingers at the sweeping draperies, the bustle, the folds. Then she said, suddenly: "Where do you come from, Rachel?" Her eyes were younger now, and wide with simple curiosity, as she felt her first interest for any human being beyond her own family.

"Oh, I'm from Philadelphia," said Rachel, kneeling to straighten the hem, and thanking her private God for the fact that the boots were covered. In order to distract Melissa, she told of her orphan state, of her ten sisters, "all in service," of her dead parents, of her own years of being maid to grand Philadelphia ladies. Melissa listened, mouth parted in wonder and curiosity, to tales of a world quite beyond her previous comprehension.

"How old are you, Rachel?" she asked, when the girl paused to examine a loose thread.

"I am twenty-seven, Madame," replied Rachel, abstractedly.

"And you never wanted to be anything but a lady's maid?" cried the ingenuous Melissa, indignantly, and yet with an unfamiliar compassion. "It was because you never had the opportunity, of course! How cruel, how wrong, how unjust!" She could not conceive of the fact that any woman could prefer such "degrading" service to the lofty climate of the educated mind. "Oh, Rachel, if you only had had a father like mine, so learned, so wise and famous! If you only had had an opportunity to acquire and read books, and gather knowledge! It is wicked that you never had this opportunity, and there is something vile about a world which has denied it to you."

Rachel sat back on her heels and stared up at Melissa in pure amazement. "But, Mrs. Dunham, I like this work. I enjoy it, truly. I don't like books. I can read well enough, but I never had any need or want for them. What would I do with them?" she added, baffled.

"You never wanted an education?" exclaimed Melissa, aghast.

Rachel shook her head. "No, ma'am, I did not, and that's the truth. Neither did my sisters. It was my mother's last, and best, hope, that all of us would find good positions in service, do our work well, save our money, and perhaps marry some respectable man some day."

Melissa blinked. A world of such plebeian and simple aspirations was to her incredible; it was her firm conviction that any man or woman would delight in the dream of release from ugly toil, of admittance to the cloisters of learning.

"We can't all be ladies with books and pianos," pleaded Rachel. "And most of us would rather work like this, for nice people, and save a little money. After all, willing hands and hard work and respect for one's betters is a good thing, too, and maybe God thinks it's just as important as anything else."

Melissa was silent. Then she said: "It's just that you never had an opportunity."

Rachel smiled cheerfully. "Well, ma'am, if that's so, I'm glad. I couldn't be any happier than I am now, and I could be a lot more miserable. That's all that matters, isn't it?"

Suddenly Melissa remembered a saying of William Hazlitt's: "It is better to be able neither to read nor to write than to be able to do nothing else." Her father had quoted that saying to her in gentle derision. "The man was evidently, and self-

protectively, afraid of the aristocrat of learning and letters,"
he had said. "It is always the mark of the fool and the peasant
to scorn one's superiors and to find their accomplishments of
no worth."

Melissa thought, confusedly: Perhaps, Papa, you were
wrong, and perhaps William Hazlitt was right. Rachel is certainly neither a fool nor an inferior. She does her work well and
cheerfully, and finds it good. What more can one wish?
What, in the end, is more satisfying than to have enjoyed
what one had to do, and to take pride in it, whether it be
the writing of a book or the sewing of a dress or the tilling
of the soil?

She listened to her own thoughts, and then was shocked and
horrified. What was she thinking? What was this new corruption which kept whispering in the secret places of her mind,
this treachery and disloyalty to her father and all the glory of
his life, this descending into banality and dangerous stupidity
in the manner of the rest of the world?

She said hurriedly, and severely: "I'm not so sure, Rachel,
that it is well for one's—spirit—to be content with base and degrading things. If you wish, I will lend you books, and teach
you——"

"You are very good, ma'am," said Rachel with a smile, and
with a fervent hope that Melissa would forget the horrid
thought.

Melissa's eyes brightened. "And then you can become a
governess, Rachel. That will be one step forward, and then——"

Rachel was not sure that her young mistress was serious,
but one glance at her face depressingly assured the girl that
she was. She decided not to pursue the subject. As her mother
had said, it wasn't a good thing to submit to vapors.

To distract Melissa, Rachel confided that her one and only
brother had been killed in the war. This brought Melissa's
thoughts to Andrew, Andrew who wanted the land. She felt
a deep pang, but it was less violent than the pangs she had
endured that morning. She turned away from the thought of
Andrew, and found it surprisingly easy to do so.

Rachel had eased her unconsciously to the dressing-table
seat, and Melissa looked up, startled to see her face in the
mirror and the soft blue silk on her shoulders. The bodice was
artfully cut very low, a small contrivance of Rachel's, and
under it Melissa's breasts swelled clearly and unmistakably.
The color enhanced the intense whiteness of her flesh, made it
shimmer like marble, turned the paleness of her eyes to a more
intense blue. Incredulous, she bent forward to stare at her-

self, at this unbelievable transformation. Her loose, unfastened pale hair flowed over her like a long and gleaming shawl. Rachel picked up a length of it experimentally. "It is beautiful!" she said, in a reverent voice.

The eyes of the two young women met in the mirror, Melissa's confounded, Rachel's triumphant and pleased. Then Melissa colored. Her old habit of suspiciously sensing ridicule under the smooth phrasing of a compliment returned, but, to her wonder, she sensed no ridicule in Rachel. "That is very kind of you," she said stiffly, and removed the length of hair in Rachel's hand. She began to braid it quickly, her cheekbones becoming tinted. But Rachel put her fingers on the braid. "Mr. Dunham would prefer that I dress it for you, ma'am," she urged.

Melissa's hands immediately dropped, and she sat like a stone. Rachel lifted a gold-backed brush and began gently to brush her mistress's hair. With deft strokes, she brought out the brighter highlights, then, swiftly, with careful and critical judgment, she wound the mass about her hands and wrists, and swung the hair into a smooth and twisted knot at Melissa's nape. Its large contours outlined her tall and slender neck; the temples gleamed like dim old gold. "That is perfect for you, ma'am," said Rachel, in a hushed tone of reverence. "No waves, no ringlets, no curls."

Melissa could not believe what she saw. She listened to Rachel's admiring comments with a strange thirst. She bent forward to study her face again, and the sleek blueness on her shoulders. She flushed, and the gaunt shadows ran from her cheeks, her mouth turned pink. It was impossible to deny that she looked quite—presentable. Of course, it was all folly, but tomorrow she could forget about it. She turned her head slightly to catch the lamplight on her hair, and something warm and sweet flooded her.

There was a knock on the dressing-room door, which opened. Geoffrey entered, carrying a small box in his hands. At his appearance, Melissa jumped to her feet, almost upsetting Rachel. She blushed violently and showed every sign of acute agitation. Geoffrey immediately observed this, and he thought to himself: She has been thinking of me. Then he saw the transformation in the girl. Slowly, he laid the box on the table, and stood in silence, studying this unbelievable portrait in blue and gilt and white. But I have always known it, he thought, it ought to be no surprise to me.

He said quietly: "Melissa, you are beautiful."

Her color deepened, but now she looked at him shyly.

Then she lifted the hem of her skirt and, with her complete simplicity, she said: "But look at these boots."

Geoffrey studied them gravely. A miracle had taken place. For the first time in her life Melissa was conscious of her appearance. It was a delicate miracle, one that must be nourished and accorded the utmost care if it were to survive.

"The boots," said Geoffrey, "are regrettable. But there is nothing we can do about it just now. Within a week or so, proper ones will arrive for you. I think that, with care, these will pass unobserved."

It did not occur to Melissa to ask from what source the gown had come. Anything could happen in this extraordinary house, and she wondered, confusedly, why the boots were not forthcoming as the gown had been. Geoffrey opened the box and brought out a velvet container. He opened it and showed Melissa the string of turquoises, diamonds and topazes within. "My mother's," he said, as she regarded them with dazed interest. "There are many more, but this is suitable for tonight. It is unfortunate that your ears were never pierced, for there are ear-rings to match. We can change that later. There are also a bracelet, a ring and a brooch here."

He picked up the necklace, and moved behind the girl. She started when she felt his fingers at her neck, and shivered a little. But she held herself as still as possible. The necklace gleamed and flashed in the lamplight.

Geoffrey stood away, and smiled at her as one smiles at a child. Rachel fastened the bracelet on Melissa's thin wrist, slipped the ring, which seemed a bit loose, on her finger, and pinned the brooch at the deep blue cleft of the bodice. Fire now sparkled with Melissa's every breath and movement. Rachel stood off and clasped her hands in ecstasy. Before the two pair of admiring eyes Melissa was again darkly suspicious but, search as she would, she could discover no taint of ridicule in either. Was it really possible that she was not hideous and an affront to others? Was it to be believed that she could arouse admiration, not only for her learning but for her actual physical appearance? Her father had often remarked, in a tone at once indulgent and fond: "There are many women who are beautiful, Melissa, but they are invariably fools. There are rare women who have intellect, but they are seldom graced with beauty. Beauty is evanescent, a mere physical manifestation. But intellect is as durable as a diamond, and its brilliance is increased by polishing on the fine grinding wheel of thought. Be thankful, my darling, that you have a brain, if no beauty. I prefer it so."

A thought flashed into her mind: Papa had discernment. He could find beauty hidden deep within apparent ugliness. If I am beautiful, as Geoffrey and Rachel say, then Papa must have known it, in spite of my appalling clothes. Why, then, did he attempt to deceive me into thinking that I was ugly? There is always a reason for everything, as you often said, Papa. What was your reason in leading me to believe that I was repellent?

In her distress, she forgot her shyness and looked directly at Geoffrey: "My father often told me I had no beauty whatsoever."

Geoffrey's eyes narrowed. More and more he was beginning to understand. He must, he reflected, speak very carefully. He knew what he must do: He must use Charles dead as a weapon against Charles alive. He made himself smile.

"Perhaps your father was afraid that you might become too vain, and so neglect him. But he often asked me, asked me many times in fact, whether I did not consider you the handsomest girl I had ever seen. When I assured him that I did, he was inordinately pleased." He paused. "Your father once expressed his regret that he was unable to clothe you as he desired, to give you the jewels to enhance your appearance. But he was always happy when I promised him that I would do these things for you, myself, some day."

Melissa's tight face softened, and she regarded Geoffrey eagerly.

Geoffrey went on mendaciously: "How pleased your father would be if he could see you tonight, Melissa. He would be enormously proud. You are dressed as he would have dressed you, had he been able. Who knows? Perhaps he is aware of you at this moment, and is all puffed up with pride."

But Melissa frowned at this sentimental childishness. However, she looked at herself in the mirror frankly and openly, without coyness. "I really do seem rather handsome," she observed. "I should not have believed it."

Geoffrey was almost unendurably touched. Involuntarily, he glanced at Rachel. The girl was gazing at Melissa with deep understanding and womanly pity. Geoffrey said, with unusual feeling in his voice: "Rachel, you have done wonders. I cannot thank you enough."

Rachel, moved, could not speak, but she curtseyed in silence. She picked up a bottle and sprayed Melissa's hair with a delicate scent, and gave her a lace-trimmed handkerchief. Melissa examined the latter with her innocent wonder. Geoffrey held out his arm to her. She looked at it, mutely, for she was a stranger to the ordinary courtesies. "It is my pleasure to take you downstairs to our guests," he said gently. She hesitated, then put the tips of her fingers on his arm with awkward timidity.

CHAPTER 28

ARABELLA SAT among her guests, clad in lavender velvet, lace, amethysts and pearls. Her hair was elaborately dressed, with a curled fringe over her wrinkling forehead, puffs at the sides, and a chignon at her neck. Pomade, lavishly applied, had brightened her hair; powder and "tint," equally lavishly applied, had almost removed all signs of her recent tears and rages, though the edges of her eyelids were still raw. A cloud of attar of roses flowed about her.

She had always feared her brother, and she had always disliked him. But now these emotions were hugely increased to terror and hatred. She knew he never spoke idly, and that, if she did not please him tonight, she would find herself homeless. He was quite capable also of sending her away without a penny, she reflected, raging inwardly. She was at his mercy; she must do nothing tonight to arouse him again. Her future was insecure enough, as it was, with that horrible creature now mistress of this house. Any slip on her part would render her situation untenable.

She was very sprightly, very gay and vivacious, as she conversed with her guests tonight, before the fire in the "Yellow Room." She fluttered her handkerchief, she coquetted, she arched her eyebrows with coy meaning, she simpered and laughed. Oh, yes, indeed, she had known for a long time of dear Geoffrey's attachment to Melissa Upjohn! The marriage had originally been scheduled for long before the holidays, but then such calamity had visited dear Melissa! First, her father had died; his death had been followed by the death of her mother, and there had been so much to do, with that dear child Phoebe in positive collapse and Andrew's future to be settled. Then the atmosphere of the house had become so very, very morbid, my dears, and Melissa's health had begun to fail under the strain. So very terrible. She had been so devoted to both her parents. The dear girl had such fortitude, however. She had been the strength of her household. One is sometimes deceived as to the endurance of the female temperament, its supposed lack of stamina. That was very foolish. When need arose, a woman could be at least as strong as a man. Dearest Melissa had proved that.

No festivities could take place, naturally, after so much grief, and so Geoffrey and Melissa had decided to be married with the utmost quietness. She, Arabella, she must confess, had been shocked by this, for she was a very conventional soul and thought the marriage ought to have been postponed for at least six months. But others were not so conventional. Arabella, at this, sighed, and fluttered her handkerchief. However, it was not her place to criticize, she added, with meek pathos. It was entirely the affair of Geoffrey and dear Melissa. She, Arabella, truly, must not be considered, with her very, very foolish ideas of what was proper. Times changed, and manners with them, and one must try to understand, must one not? Things were certainly not the same as before the war. Whether that was a matter to be deplored was beside the question.

The guests listened, murmured sympathetically, and did not believe Arabella in the least. They had heard her wild scream that morning, and then, later, her wilder sobs behind her door. The discreet questioning of a servant, here and there, had revealed a mystery exciting and full of potential interest. But, as they were polite, and guests, they could do nothing but pretend, and they nodded their heads with deep gravity as they contemplated Arabella's air of vivacious hysteria, her drawn and tinted cheeks, so raddled and lined, her reddened eyes.

Mr. Victor Littlefield was little in stature, character and soul, a little black ant of a man with an ant's hidden and murderous pincers and potentialities. He was sixty years old, but no grayness had appeared in his thin black hair or in his strong black beard. His dress was dignified, for he invariably wore black broadcloth excellently tailored and fitted. Little, darting black eyes shone and danced above the forest below, and they had an ant-like tendency to rove, to examine, to seize. His lady was his second wife, considerably younger than himself, and, as she was the daughter of a prosperous blanket-maker of low beginnings, she was very elegant, indeed, and of such a swooning appearance that one was constantly afraid that a single loud word would compel her to reach for her smelling-salts. Her husband was convinced of her aristocratic fragility; once he had had a certain robustness of his own, but his wife had carefully instilled precious mannerisms in him and allowed him in his conversation to use only the most stilted and ceremonious phrases. Like all vulgarians by race and breeding, she was intensely devoted to the more delicate arts, was one of Arabella's most ardent admirers, and was given to indulge in soirées in her mansion in Philadelphia. So clever was this lady, so careful her conduct, so polished her pretensions, that she had been able to deceive even the most astute, avaricious and well-born members of Philadelphia society, and her soirées were well attended by them on every occasion.

Mr. and Mrs. Brewster Eldridge were a fat, short and smiling couple, in their forties. Mr. Eldridge was also a publisher, but in New York. Some thought them brother and sister, for they were astoundingly alike, both possessing round pink faces, blue, twinkling eyes, small white teeth, and humorous mouths. One felt about them the aura of good-temper, shrewdness and an inclination to kindly laughter.

Then there were the Bertrams, of New York, who had no character or outstanding features at all, but merged against every background and were lost. Their aura was thin and rather dusty, and one felt something faintly acrid about them, something dried and attenuated. But, in Arabella's eyes, they possessed the most sterling of qualities: they were rich. Mr. Peter Bertram's father had been very successful in financing opium running into China, and his pedantic son, who patronized all arts and artists indiscriminately, had inherited an enormous fortune. Mr. Bertram and his musty little lady considered Arabella a veritable genius with pencil and paintbrush, and they respected her all the more because she had no need of their help.

It was not in Arabella's nature to revere or admire anyone who did not possess considerable money, not even a real artist. But, though Mr. Erskine Holland was not wealthy, it was quite the thing to invite him everywhere. Of course, hypocrites pretended that they respected his brilliance as a popular portrait-painter and the fact that his father had been a distinguished artist in his own right and his mother the daughter of a former governor of Massachusetts and the descendant of a long line of Puritan aristocracy. She, Arabella, was not taken in by this hypocrisy in the least. But it was the thing, among the established, to have one's portrait painted by Mr. Holland; he was quite "the rage," and hostesses fought for the privilege of entertaining him and his wife. So the Hollands had been invited for the holidays, and they, and the Eldridges, made the occasion almost endurable for Geoffrey Dunham.

Mr. Holland was a very tall, very lean, middle-aged gentleman, with a wide, thick gray mustache and a pair of crystal-line brown eyes, acute, penetrating and gentle. He had a warm handshake, and his glance missed nothing. Mrs. Holland was a tiny woman, like a dainty piece of porcelain, and though she was in her forties, she appeared much younger. She gave the impression of butterfly fragility and color, yet she had much character, whimsicality and sturdy common-sense. She was given, on occasion, to amazingly vigorous exclamations of "Nonsense!" and almost always she was quite right. Her good-tempered and searching brown eyes were kind even when her words were not. But much was forgiven her because of her charm and her warmth of personality,

It could not be said that Arabella truly liked any of her guests, with the possible exception of Mrs. Littlefield, of the cheese and the vast fortune, who was Arabella's one confidante and her "devoted friend." She endured them all, because they were either fashionable or rich, and hardly one detected the fact that she innately disliked them. There was one guest, however, and he almost unexpected until a day or two before his arrival, with whom Arabella had quite fallen in love in a coquettishly aunt-like fashion. This fortunate creature was the son of Mr. Littlefield by his first wife, and his name was Ravel. Mrs. Littlefield the First had been of a poetic tempera-ment and she had conned this name from some languishing and romantic novel written by an English lady. Mr. Little-field had protested, for he had considerable common-sense of a rather crude sort, but his wife had been determined. So Ravel it was, and Mr. Littlefield was sometimes heard bitterly commenting on the fact that it "suited the rascal, damned if it didn't."

When Mr. Littlefield had remarried, his relatives had murmured darkly of future sinister machinations against the peace and happiness of the young Ravel. Stepmothers were notorious for unkindness, if not for outright wickedness and poison-plots, especially when such a fortune was at stake. But to the astonishment of everyone, Mrs. Littlefield became a sincere and devoted second mother to the child. She never bore any children of her own. Strangers were always amazed when they discovered that Ravel was only her step-son, for the two were not only friends in public and in actuality but had immediately formed a deep attachment for each other. It was Mrs. Littlefield who defended the boy against his father and was secretly guilty of turning any weak affection the lad had had for his progenitor into suspicious dislike. Mr. Littlefield liked concrete facts and common-sense behavior, to both of which Ravel had an instinctive aversion, being of a "poetic temperament." It was inevitable that father and son must some day come to actual hatred. Mrs. Littlefield only hastened the process, and was in possession of Ravel's complete trust and fervid love. She understood the boy very well, and brooded over him even now, when he was almost thirty, with something like obsession.

Ravel had winning ways and few women could resist them. He was also his father's chief heir, and this did nothing to turn the ladies against him. With those exquisite manners and all that potential cash, he would have been considered desirable even had he resembled Caliban. But, as he was also remarkably handsome, the whole effect was devastating as far as susceptible females were concerned. Almost always he preferred to stand, usually against something noble like a marble pillar or a frescoed wall, and his attitudes were dramatically wistful, and calculated to set gentlemen's teeth on edge and ladies' hearts to fluttering. He was almost as tall as Mr. Holland, the artist, but much more elegant and fluid. His figure, usually in faultless black broadcloth and white linen, gave the impression of suppleness and languor and almost feminine slenderness. This last was denied by really excellent shoulders and good musculature, which fine tailoring displayed to artful advantage. All his movements were swimming and graceful, and designed like an actor's, and most of his expressions were overlaid with tender melancholy, dreamy abstraction, and poetic but delicate gloom.

The figure, the attitudes, and the cash, would have been quite enough. But infatuated Nature, in a fit of delirium, had tossed all her gifts at Ravel with an astonishing abandon. She gave him a beautifully modelled face, glowingly pale but redeemed cunningly from effeminacy by a fine strong jaw, good cheek-planes and a large chiselled nose. These hid a telltale soft mouth of too much color and of an ungenerously small cut. The underlip had a full and formless pink outline, somewhat pouting, like a petulant woman's. But women found this adorable. It so expressed his "sensitive" soul, his love for beauty, his refinement and delicacy. One had only to look at that mouth, that face, to know he was a poet. Unfortunately, he *was*, of a sort. Otherwise, he was quite intelligent, a flaw he cleverly hid from the ladies.

His adoring female friends quite often quarreled about what constituted his greatest charm. But there was no quarrel about his eyes. These were conceded to be his best feature, even beyond the mop of rich dark waves which crowned his head and which was cut just a trifle too long in order to give him a Byronic appearance. (He also affected the Byronic cravat, full and flowing.) His eyes were full, melting and dark, with white hooded lids and remarkable eyelashes that could sweep his pale cheek. He could make those eyes flash like jewels, glimmer like moonlight with passionate tenderness, gleam with poetic fire. (He practiced these different moods sedulously before his mirror.) No one of the female sex could resist those eyes. They made the older ladies wish to embrace him with tearful maternal love; they made the younger ladies wish to embrace him also, without the maternal ingredient. He suffered both, with equal grace, having had good tutelage in his beloved Paris, where he had been living for the past three years, romantically residing in the Latin Quarter, writing his poetry and cultivating the ladies of the salons and the soubrettes of the theatre.

For the rest, he had a beguilingly musical voice, resonant and full of the most fascinating nuances, and a pair of extremely slender white hands, expressive and fluent.

Gentlemen fervently averred that he "made them gag." They called him "that puppy." He had no friends among his sex. But as he knew his own worth and understood that the hostility was in great part envy and jealousy, he was only amused. His forte was the ladies, and he cultivated them with ardor. His stepmother saw to it that his allowance was enormous, and so he never lacked for money for jewels, for flowers, for a carriage of his own and a beautiful apartment in New York.

He was, at this time, in the doldrums. He was just recovering from his last passionate encounter with a more than ordinarily determined young lady of the New York stage. She had been resolutely set on marriage, a thing which Ravel regarded with natural abhorrence, for, in his way, he had considerable sense. He knew that marriage would greatly inhibit him among the ladies. Moreover, he knew very well that if he ever married (God forbid!), it would not be to any lady who had displayed her thighs to him either in public or in private. Even in passion, he kept his head. He gave all his charm to his current inamorata, but never his heart. Knowing what a fortune would be his some day, he demanded the like in a prospective wife. He was, therefore, quite outraged and honestly indignant when the young lady of the New York stage artlessly informed him she desired to marry him. He had hurriedly parted from her, genuinely wounded at her lack of sensibility and intelligence. But he was not to rid himself of her for months, for she was a girl of considerable character and obstinacy. It cost him five thousand dollars in the end.

He was now in the mood when he longed for "real true love." This mood was not an unfamiliar one, but he distrusted it. It had led him into some sad and expensive débâcles. Nevertheless, he also welcomed it, for it added a gentle melancholy to his temper and made him absolutely irresistible. Moreover, the poetic and creative passion was upon him, and he had decided that he was now ready to begin his magnum opus, a long dramatic poem on the subject of Orpheus and his lute and his beautiful, tragic young wife. The only trouble was that he needed an inspiration, and none was immediately forthcoming in the persons of any of the young ladies he knew. Not one of them resembled Eurydice. So Ravel, during these holidays, was filled with gloom, creative urges, and urges of a more robust nature, hopelessness, and rancor. His father had been particularly obnoxious about the five thousand dollars, and was not yet placated. He had insisted that his son accompany him and Mrs. Littlefield to "this outpost, this utter negation of beauty, this company of dolts and donkeys and hideous women." His stepmother, who was in his confidence, had urged that he seek some "quiet, sylvan spot" where his muse could have its way with him, and he was in a temper to agree, provided Eurydice made a fortuitous appearance in that spot.

So far, she had refrained. He had had to content himself with the adoration of the dazzled old Arabella, his stepmother, the timid Mrs. Bertram, and the shrewd railleries of the unimpressed Mesdames Eldridge and Holland. If these two latter ladies had been young and handsome, he would have been stimulated. But they were too old for him, too obdurately married, and not too pretty. He regarded them with a jaundiced eye, decided that he did not like witty females, though he could be witty himself, and abandoned any attempts to subdue them.

He had never met Geoffrey Dunham before, and he had been jolted out of his indifference by a real surge of active dislike and suspicion. Here, in one person, was a species he hated—the publisher who never appreciated a poet, and a man who could threaten his own adoring kingdom. As Ravel, in spite of his general appearance, was very masculine himself, he resented the masculinity of another man, for quite natural reasons, and very healthy ones. Had he been a rooster, he would have raked the ground with his claws and his wattles would have turned bright red with rage. Eurydice was certainly not present anywhere on the premises, but there was always the possibility that she would put in a miraculous appearance. And females, being the senseless creatures they were, might, just possibly, prefer a Geoffrey Dunham to a Ravel Littlefield. After a careful if furtive study of Geoffrey, Ravel came to the contemptuous conclusion that he was "gross and insensitive," not really a rival. Nevertheless, females were unpredictable, and sometimes they preferred beasts to cultivated poets and gentlemen. Geoffrey, in return, did not manifest any great liking for his youngest guest and did him the injustice of considering him effeminate. But he shrewdly guessed that Ravel was a fraud and a poseur, and often had moments of amusement at the younger man's expense.

Tonight, Ravel leaned against the golden mantelpiece where the ladies could admire him at their leisure, and listened with interest, for the first time in days, as Arabella's false sprightliness of conversation concerned itself with her new sister-in-law. Doubtless a heavy-footed country wench with big breasts and a perfume of manure about her, thought Ravel, with a sudden return of gloom. Just the sort that Dunham would admire. However, he kept glancing at the doorway with some impatience for the appearance of the bride. There was just a possibility that Arabella might be wrong. There was too much venom in her sugary voice as she elaborated on Melissa, and Ravel knew women and their venom. Whenever he heard that tone of voice, from a lady he knew, about another, unknown lady, he was filled with anticipation. He had rarely been disappointed. It was not likely that he would be disappointed tonight. But one could never tell.

Arabella's voice now took on the subtle intonation of courageous regret. She fluttered her kerchief, and her eyes became positively malignant as she arched her neck, tilted her head, and sighed. "Of course," she said, "it is not the poor, darling child's fault that nature has so feebly endowed her with beauty. But one must remember that a man of dear Geoffrey's age often outgrows callowness, and looks for character and family. With both, dearest Melissa has been amply endowed."

Good God, thought Ravel, much dismayed, and despondent. But a sharp glance at Arabella renewed his anticipation. The other guests, too, had become astonishingly interested, and kept glancing at the empty doorway.

However, so engrossed were they with Arabella's spiteful commiserations on the subject of Melissa's lack of beauty that they missed the first appearance of Geoffrey and his bride, and it was not until Arabella sprang to her feet with guilty and fervish animation that they became aware that their host and Melissa were standing on the threshold of the room. They heard Arabella give a lyrical and dramatic exclamation: "Ah, there they are now, the dears!" and they started, every head turned itself to the door.

Every eye fixed itself upon Melissa, with curiosity at first, and then with startled stupefaction.

The gentlemen, fascinated, unable to look away, stood up slowly, and Ravel dropped his elbow from the mantelpiece.

My God! he thought. An ice goddess! A blue Aphrodite! Eurydice!

She was moving into the room now, beside Geoffrey. Dazzled, Ravel could only stare at her in dumfounded wonder. She walks like a queen, he thought. She is Galatea, come to life. I don't believe it!

CHAPTER 29

THE ROOM OPENED OUT before Melissa like a huge golden cave, brilliantly sparkling with crystal, dazzling her eyes, assaulting her senses. She had been frightened. Now she was blinded, overwhelmed. Phoebe had described this room to her, but she had been incredulous. Confusion fell over her. Wherever her terrified eye fell, it encountered fresh and impossible beauties and splendors. She was dimly aware that she was being introduced to strange people and bobbing faces, but she could only give them a bemused glance before she returned to the staggered contemplation of the room. She had been in this house three times in her early childhood and girlhood, but she had entered the library only, never the drawing-rooms.

Someone was leading her to a chair before the fire. She lifted her astounded eyes to the mantelpiece and stared at the golden cupids with their uplifted candles. A glass of wine was in her hand. She gazed at the colorful painting on the wall above the great roaring fire. Someone was speaking to her. She said "yes," in a faint dim voice; she looked at the golden chairs, the golden tables, the golden love-seats, the golden draperies. Her heart was beating strangely, as if with fear and amazement. She felt herself caught up in a blaze of golden light and shadow, and once she put up her hand and touched her cheek in a bewildered gesture.

Finally it came to her that she was behaving like a stunned peasant. Proudly, she lifted her head, forced herself to look at these strangers from whom she instinctively shrank. They knew of her father, she must do him justice. She must shake the golden mist from her eyes and conduct herself as a daughter of Charles Upjohn. When she saw Arabella glancing with mean and smiling significance at a very unprepossessing and pallid lady in black, who reclined languidly in her chair, a hot wave of shame and anger ran over the girl and her face settled in its old expression of rigor and sternness. She must remember that these women were fools and parasites, of no use whatsoever in the world—and that she was the daughter of Charles Upjohn.

"From what gallery did you steal this ravishing creature, Dunham?" a gentleman's soft and admiring voice was saying. "I swear, she is direct from the hand of Phidias himself!" Melissa became aware of the blur of voices about her and what seemed a veritable cloud of faces.

If Melissa was stupefied, the guests were ill at ease. Their lessons in etiquette, while young, had not taken cognizance of how one should behave when a sudden, unexpected and fantastic marriage takes place in one's very midst, especially when all the circumstances are as odd and bewildering as these were. None of them were intimate friends of Geoffrey's; most of them disliked him, or, at best, had only an indifferent regard for him. Even the latter thought him somewhat ruthless, often irascible, sometimes brutal with his tongue, though they admitted that, in his way, he was a forthright and honest man. "In his way," however, covered a multitude of sins.

And now this unpopular man had suddenly, without previous announcement or hint, ambiguously precipitated a bride into their midst, expected them to behave themselves as if such weddings were daily occurrances and ought not to arouse more than a passing comment. They had valiantly done their best, all of them. They had stammeringly scattered congratulations and good wishes right and left, had inspected, with furtive attention, this very extraordinary and very beautiful young bride, and then, seeing that Geoffrey did not encourage them to more exuberant remarks, nor expect them to ask questions, they subsided into uneasy awkwardness. The gentlemen did propose a toast to the bride, but it was obvious that she was not aware of this courtesy. She sat stiffly in her blue silk before the fire and looked at them blindly, as if their antics were not sufficiently unusual to attract her attention. All this convinced the ladies that, for once, dear Arabella had been right. There was something definitely queer about the whole thing. One or two of the women, who had cynical minds, cast side-glances at Melissa's figure, to ascertain whether the solution to the mystery lay there.

The gentlemen were overwhelmed by Melissa's strange cold beauty, by the classic fixity of her features, by her frozen composure and air of austerity. Because she was young, and had such an unearthly loveliness, they were inclined to believe that Dunham had in some way victimized her, and they felt instinctively protective. Their ladies were not so generous. With the exception of Mrs. Holland, they came to the conclusion that the girl might be somewhat handsome but that she had no real fascination or charm. They had not yet heard her voice; she had made no comment. She only sat there like a stiff, life-size doll, and seemed to see nothing. They did not know that she was frightened into a dazed condition, that she feared them as she always feared the stranger. Where the gentlemen saw a mysterious tragedy, the ladies saw stupidity. After their failure to elicit any conversation from Melissa, they began to give Arabella sympathetic glances, and Arabella's eyes filled with tears of righteousness and self-pity.

But now, when Ravel Littlefield made his admiring remark, Melissa came out of her stunned condition. She looked at Ravel, who was again standing against the becoming background of the golden mantelpiece. His wondrous profile was lit up by the fire; his eyes were melting as they gazed ardently at Melissa. Suddenly, the girl blushed, and she hid her reddened hands under a fold of her blue gown. She looked away from Ravel with dignity, and he was freshly enamored.

"Thank you," answered Geoffrey, indulgently. He stood behind Melissa's chair and lightly touched the golden coil near his hand. Melissa started at his touch, a movement which was not lost in the suddenly avid guests. Mr. Holland's kind heart was moved to pity. He advanced towards Melissa and gave her a courtly bow. She looked up at him, shrinking, but when she saw how kindly he was, she managed a rigorous and uncertain smile. Little drops of moisture had appeared on her upper lip.

"Mr. Holland is our most famous portrait-painter, my dear," said Arabella. "Perhaps Geoffrey can induce him, some time, to paint your portrait." She gave the ladies a sly and long-suffering smile, to which all except Mrs. Holland responded.

Melissa found her tongue. She stared at Mr. Holland, puzzled. "My father often spoke of the artists he had known in Philadelphia and New York, famous artists," she said, in her clear, neutral voice. "But he never mentioned you, sir." She appeared doubtful and suspicious.

Everyone, even Geoffrey, was taken aback by this gaucherie, and stood or sat in silence. Geoffrey turned red. Mr. Holland said, very gently: "I have heard of your father, my dear, and I have read all his wonderful books, but we never met. Besides, perhaps I am not as famous as Arabella infers."

"Perhaps," agreed Melissa, with appalling frankness.

Melissa, whose sensibilities had not been blunted by social contacts, began to be acutely aware of the currents in this room. Her mother had once remarked that men were kinder than women, and Melissa had scoffed at this. But now she wondered whether it were not true. She felt nothing but interest, admiration and cordiality on the part of the gentlemen. Of course, it was only because of Geoffrey. Yet one side of her spirit warmed, as a body is warmed when it is turned towards a fire. The other side remained frozen. That was the side turned to the ladies. She felt a distinct malignance flowing from that ugly long-faced woman in black who leaned so languidly against the arm of her chair, who had such lank, oily, brown hair, and kept giving that young man near the fire such mutely intense glances. She felt amusement from Mesdames Eldridge and Holland, pallid hatred from Mrs. Bertram, and venom from Arabella. She was frightened anew, surprised, and then humiliated. They were laughing at her; they thought her ugly and ridiculous. She lifted her chin haughtily, turned her head from them, and encountered the passionate gaze of the young man before her.

Amazed, she could not look away. For the first time, she was aware that he was singularly handsome and that he was admiring her. He was not pretending, she could see that. She was absorbed in his admiration, and now she felt the bright smoothness of her hair, her white neck, the jewels at her throat, the soft caress of the silk against her skin, the length of her thighs. A long warm tremor ran over her body. She stared at the young man eagerly, only faintly doubtful now. She had tucked the disgraceful boots under the fluted edge of her skirt; she gave the hem a swift and furtive glance to see whether the boots had revealed themselves, like a hidden sin, then she returned to the marvelling contemplation of the young man's admiration.

He, in turn, was fascinated by this unique young creature and her evident wonder. A connoisseur of women, he understood, by intuition, a great deal about Melissa. Here was no swooning, pampered, artificial fool of a woman, artfully aware of the effects she created, corrupt, vain and shallow. She was as clear, cold and fresh as a spring river pouring down from white mountains into a virgin valley. She was as untouched as new snow. She was like a white young birch-tree in unfathomed forests. All sorts of extravagant similies rushed through the young man's mind. From Arabella's conversation prior to Melissa's entrance, he had learned of Melissa's background, and had feared a blue-stocking. Well, there was nothing about the girl to dispel that apprehension. She had the intelligent woman's clear, steadfast eyes, her broad white brow, her air of dignity, reserve and consciousness. Ravel, understanding women, knew that a man's approach to a woman of intellect was not by way of admiration of her brains. She could be won only by implied and outrageously frank devotion to her physical charms. Yet, he reflected, there was something else here, which he had never encountered before. He began to think that the way to Melissa was not only through open admiration.

He became very excited, and now he was enormously stirred. He recognized the first emotions of "true, real love." There was the thrill of infatuation, the excitement, the stir, the warmth. But these were hugely magnified, as they had never been magnified before. There was another thing, and that was a kind of heavy sadness. Infatuated, not only by Melissa but by his own unique emotions, he looked in urgent silence at the girl, and she gazed back at him, fascinated by what she saw in his eyes.

Involuntarily, she asked a question which only a Melissa would ask, and she asked it abruptly: "What do you do?"

Fortunately, everyone else was engaged in polite conversation and did not hear this. Ravel did not find it strange. Nothing about Melissa was strange to him now. He answered, with a rare simplicity: "I am a poet. Of a sort."

Mrs. Littlefield, who could return from the most engrossing scandal at the sound of her beloved Ravel's voice, immediately turned her head. She smiled at Melissa in her shadowy, malevolent fashion, looked at Ravel adoringly. "'Of a sort,' my darling?" she asked, raising her brows. "How can you speak so disparagingly of your wonderful work?" She looked at Melissa. "My dear boy is one of America's great poets, as yet unrecognized by an insensate public but some day to blaze like a new star in our literary heavens."

Melissa was startled. A poet. Earnestly she scrutinized Ravel, and he returned her scrutiny with an expression of somber ardor, which, for the first time in his life, was not affected. Now he was filled with a strange and powerful tenderness, a kind of hunger.

"A poet," repeated Melissa, almost inaudibly. "My father often said that a poet was the only true interpreter of life."

Ravel experienced a sensation oddly akin to humility and shame.

"I am afraid, then, that I am not a real poet," he said. "I have done nothing significant in my writing. I should say I am a spinner of sugary phrases and light superficialities. I have had it in my mind for a long time to write a great dramatic poem about Orpheus and Eurydice—" He paused. "I think I shall write it, now," he added, very softly.

But Melissa, naturally, inferred nothing from this; to her it was a bare statement of fact. Her pale blue eyes became animated, they flashed with the cold and undefiled passion of her mind. "How wonderful that would be!" she exclaimed. "Yes, you must write it!"

Her voice, with its clear, strong intonations, captured the attention of the others, and every face turned to her. But she did not see them. She saw only Ravel. Her whole face had kindled. There was a breathlessness about her. Bewitched, Ravel could only look at the girl.

It was at this moment that dinner was announced. The gentlemen offered their arms to the ladies, who rose with a long rustle of silk. Melissa stood among them, like a marvelously carved statue of blue ice, iridescent and sparkling. She took Geoffrey's arm, and walked beside him into the dining-room.

CHAPTER 30

THE DARK WARMTH and subdued light of the dining-room startled Melissa almost as much as the golden dazzle of the drawing-room had done. She saw the dark masses of crimson roses and green leaves in the center of the lace-covered table, the candles blazing in the silver candelabra at each end, the glimmer of polished silver on the side-boards, the faint gleam and sparkle of fine glass in the cupboards, the fire on the hearth which sent its scarlet waves over ceiling and panelled wall. As this was Geoffrey's wedding-night, he placed Melissa at his right, while Arabella still sat in her old place of authority at the foot of the table. Tomorrow, she knew, Melissa would occupy that place—that green, blank-faced chit with the red hands!

Ravel Littlefield sat beside Melissa. He had become unaccountably silent. He watched Melissa frankly surveying the room, her mouth opened slightly as if in wonder. He saw, for the first time, the mauve stains of fatigue under her eyes. He saw also that when she glanced at Geoffrey it was with that childlike indifference which a very young girl accords an adult. He speculated on this. Once, Geoffrey smiled at his bride, and she smiled back, with a child's awkward uneasiness. Certainly it was not the smile of a woman in love, or that of a wife; Ravel became very thoughtful, and then, curiously elated. His intuition, always acute and super-sensitive, informed him of many things long before his conscious mind caught up, like a heavy-footed animal trying to keep pace with a winged bird.

While his intuition informed him clearly of many things, the other gentlemen, and the ladies, too, sensed something wrong, in a diffused sort of way. By this time, not even Mrs. Littlefield or Mrs. Bertram believed that anything furtive or indelicate was behind this unheralded wedding; their perplexity was all the greater for not having an ugly explanation to fasten upon. The gentlemen reflected that, had Dunham been a poor man and this a girl of suddenly inherited wealth, and a booby to boot, the explanation would not have been difficult. But the reverse was true. Certainly the girl was handsome, but even more certainly she did not look upon her new husband with that delightful and blushing shyness traditionally expected. She hardly looked at him at all, not even with shrinking. She did not seem to be very much aware of anyone else, either. Unless—and now more than one eye sharpened—it was of that blackguard, Ravel Littlefield.

A marriage dinner was expected to be gay. But all at once, even the most interested voice became silent. A kind of dim disquiet spread from the table to the farthest corners of the room. The sound of the soft-footed servants grew loud; the clink of silver was startling; the crackle of the fire became intolerable. Geoffrey was carving the roast with unusual meticulousness, as if he wished the task to last indefinitely so that he need not look up. The guests watched him as if their lives depended upon their complete attention. They felt the presence of the speechless girl in their midst; out of the corner of their eyes they saw her blue rigidity, the pale shine of her hair, the sparkle of her jewels. She oppressed them by her very presence, though they did not know why.

Involuntarily, Geoffrey glanced up and looked squarely at his wife. The silver tools remained suspended in his hands while he looked at her as if only she were in this room. And it came to him that he was wrong, and had always been wrong, about her, that he had been confused by certain conventionalities of behavior which he had not known he had accepted. He had thought her a narrow and beleaguered child, a foolish if beloved girl, of intolerant and obstinate opinions, deluded by a dream that never was, confounded by her own illusions. In a way, that was true, but as she sat there beside him, among his friends, so much apart, so forever and ever much apart, he saw, in her enormous and undefiled simplicity, the human soul as it had been created, unreconciled and eternally alone. All the others about her, the whole world about her, had also been so created, but, in their terror and cowardice, they had built up about them a whole illusion of society, of phrases and noises, of grotesque businesses and empty acceptance, of morals and lip-services, of lies and attitudes and conventions, of modes and manners, of what-is-done and what-is-not-done, of proper posturings and styles and idioms—all—to hide the terrible truth from themselves: That they were alone and could never be companioned.

None of this had corrupted Melissa, because she had never encountered it. But Geoffrey thought: Even when she encounters it, will not hurt her. She has, in herself, a tragic human dignity which noise and fearful customs have destroyed in everyone else, including myself. We try desperately to drink dead sand in the delusion that it is living water. Melissa knows she is alone, that is why she has majesty. We refuse to acknowledge it, and that is why we are noisy and miserable animals.

Arabella thought, malignantly: There she sits, that odious creature, like a graven image, with not the slightest expression on her face! Oh, it is not possible that I must endure this! Surely, I shall wake up in a little while and discover it is a nightmare!

Ravel thought: This is Eurydice, who has lived so long among shadows that she is blind to the sunlight, and turns back from the world. He thought: I love her.

He looked at Geoffrey, who was gazing at his wife, and the others, also aware of Geoffrey's motionlessness, looked at him. The servants paused, and stared likewise, becoming conscious of a strong, strange current in the room, running towards their new mistress, who seemed not to see or hear anything. This unfathomable tension lasted only a moment or two, yet to almost everyone it seemed to last for a long and unendurable time.

Ravel thought: I hate him. I hated him the moment I saw him, the gross and insensate fool.

Geoffrey finished the carving and gravely deposited the red meat on the plates near his hand. The guests watched him, relieved, though they did not know why. Then Ravel said, in an amused voice: "Dunham, I have just finished reading a book which your house published recently, and which I understand is extraordinarily successful, though God knows why, unless it be because of the general imbecility of the American public."

Geoffrey smiled. "I assume you are referring to Mrs. Lydia Bainbridge's *Lady Cecily's Secret Heart?* Yes, it is very successful. It will balance our ledgers this year, especially as we pirated it from England and don't have to pay royalties to the authoress."

He added, raising his brows, and looking at Ravel with a disagreeable smile: " 'Imbecility of the American public'?"

Ravel always prided himself on a calm and judicial detachment from the coarser passions of lesser men, such as anger and petty irascibilities. But now he could not control a quite healthy umbrage against Geoffrey, a certain powerful if obscure combativeness.

He tried to speak tolerantly: "Perhaps I was a little hasty in making that remark. I should, rather, have expressed resentment that you publishers serve the American people in the name of literature such unmitigated trash."

Geoffrey glanced at the servant beside him, and said concisely: "Mr. Littlefield will now have some cabbage."

Ravel turned a fiery red, but he still smiled at his host. Geoffrey, having completed the carving, inclined his head courteously toward the younger man. Everyone listened eagerly. Mr. Littlefield, remembering his wife's careful coaching, said to himself: Bad taste, all this. But he felt that he was about to enjoy himself.

Geoffrey said: "There will be better books when there are better readers. When the public no longer buys 'trash,' as you call it, we shan't publish it. We are business men, and we merely supply the demand."

Ravel's angry color faded, and he gave Geoffrey a long, politely offensive stare. "And I accuse you of debasing the public's taste—for money, in spite of your apologia. Haven't you any sense of responsibility towards the people of America? Are you publishers unaware of the fact that men can be corrupted by unscrupulous panderers to their bestial tastes?"

"That," said Geoffrey, consideringly, "is nonsense, and only idiots, poets, and transcendental idealists believe it. They, like Rousseau, believe that it is man's institutions and environment which are vile, not man. As well accuse a man's reflection of wickedness, or frivolity, or stupidity, and not the man who casts it in the mirror. What the people buy, and want, is the reflection of their taste, or their desires, or their souls, if you will. Publishers, like any other businessmen, merely, as I said before, supply the demand." He turned to Mr. Eldridge, whose round rosy face had become grave and intent. "What have you got to say about this, Eldridge, you are also a publisher?"

Mr. Eldridge pondered, his childlike blue eyes unusually sober and thoughtful. Everyone felt the strange and urgent hostility between Geoffrey and Ravel, and now every eye and ear was turned towards them, oblivious of Melissa. Had they looked at the girl, they would have seen that she had lost her immobile appearance, her far abstraction, and that she was now listening with painful attention, her hands clenched together in the folds of her gown, and that she was gazing fixedly at her husband and at Ravel.

Mr. Eldridge spoke in a tone very different from his usual jovial one: "I agree with Dunham, Ravel. Some—misguided —people think there are more good books unprinted than printed, and that publishers deny a hearing to talented un-knowns, preferring the third-rate drivellings of known and established writers. That is absurd. Many bad books are pub-lished—yes—but only for the want of better. Every publisher shouts with delight on the rare occasion when a good manu-script comes to his desk, whoever the writer. After all," and because he was a very kindly man he gave Ravel a mollifying smile, "publishers have no aversion to money, and we always hope to find the happy combination of a good book and a good sale."

"But you would not publish a good book, if you thought it would not sell well?" said Ravel with contempt. "You would deny the people a book of worth, merely because it might not bring you profitable returns."

Mr. Eldridge's forehead, made only for amiability, had difficulty in wrinkling. He shook his head. "My dear boy, if a book is 'good,' it will sell. I doubt whether any book of considerable excellence has died for want of readers, or of cash. You are talking in paradoxes. As the Greeks said, what is good survives. If a book, or anything else, is bad, it will not survive. So 'good' and 'acceptance' are practically the same thing, with perhaps a few, very rare exceptions."

Melissa whispered passionately: "No, you are wrong!" But no one heard her. Everyone was deliciously absorbed in the sight of Ravel's suffused face, Geoffrey's cynical smile, and Mr. Eldridge's obvious distress at being forced into an argument which had powerful undercurrents he could not name or analyze.

Geoffrey said, in a deliberately patronizing and hypocritical voice: "It would appear that Ravel has been unsuccessful in marketing his wares. I should be glad to look them over, Ravel, if you'd care to send them to me."

Ravel bowed elaborately to his host. His eyes were furious, though he said negligently: "Oh, I am afraid they would not fill your coffers, Dunham."

"That would be unfortunate," said Geoffrey, with an air of regret. "I like, love, and cherish money, because it gives me time to do some of the things I want to do. Do you remember what Aristotle said: 'Money is a guarantee that we may have what we want, in the future.' Every sensible man respects, and desires, money. Eldridge, did I ever mention to you the letter Thomas Macaulay once wrote my father? Very interesting. He wrote: 'I am not fond of money or anxious about it. But—every day shows me more and more strongly how necessary a competence is to a man who desires to be either great or useful.' Of course, such a desire is held contemptible by our more delicate souls." He smiled at Ravel affectionately.

Mrs. Littlefield bridled, and cast a deeply loving glance at Ravel, in acknowledgment of the compliment dear Geoffrey had paid him. But she was startled to see her beloved son's face so black, as he stared at Geoffrey. Alarmed, she looked at the others. Her husband was smiling in a very odious fashion; Mrs. Eldridge (whom she, Mrs. Littlefield, had "never really liked") was smiling also, in a scarcely less offensive fashion. The Bertrams were silent, but palely hard of lip, and were tossing their heads pointedly. Mr. Holland and his lady sat in grave silence, very attentive, but neutral. No one appeared to hear Geoffrey's compliment, nor to understand it. Mrs. Littlefield's bewildered eye touched Melissa. She was freshly startled. The girl appeared about to leap from her seat; she was bent forward, and her whole face was wildly intolerant and expressive. There is something here I do not quite understand, thought Mrs. Littlefield in confusion.

Ravel said, in an oddly stifled voice, which contrasted with his fixed smile: "I deny that I am a 'delicate' soul. It is only that I have a high respect for the arts and think they ought not to be debased merely for money. Probably you would call me sentimental, Dunham. I notice that there is a general tendency to sneer at everything beautiful and call it sentimentality. Doubtless because of the war, for war generally re-creates bestiality in men and blunts them to finer things. But let us return to Mrs. Bainbridge's delightful opus: *Lady Cecily's Secret Heart*. Would you, under any circumstances, call that art?"

Geoffrey laid a fresh slice of meat on Melissa's plate, though she had hardly touched the food already upon it. He felt vaguely her wild and intense interest. He had never liked Ravel Littlefield, but the younger man had amused him with his airs and his languors and his gallant attentions to the ladies. Privately, he thought Ravel a popinjay and jackanapes, a determined blackguard, and had dismissed him as irrelevant as well as absurd. But, all at once, in the last few moments, he had been inspired by a strong enmity for his guest, something suspiciously like hatred. His momentary silence, as he gave Melissa another slice of meat, was caused by his acute surprise at his own passions. He had had many similar arguments with other men, and had not usually been emotionally involved, even when listening to the most ridiculous statements. He would always take time to enlighten the layman very kindly as to the intricacies of the publishing business, and the discussion usually ended in an atmosphere of mutual esteem.

But now he felt his gorge rising against his guest, and a quite primitive desire to get up and knock Ravel out of his chair and, quite probably, kick him. His surprise quickened; he saw that his big fingers had clenched over the handle of the knife, and he felt the thick and furious blood in his throat and face. His instincts, he reflected, were certainly on the rampage, and for no discernible reason except that he had mildly disliked Ravel Littlefield and was impatient at the latter's maudlin opinions on publishing!

Baffled at his own sensations, and still trying to rationalize them, he answered Ravel: "What do you mean by 'art'? What

is not art to you might be art to someone else. To paraphrase
an old poem:

> "If it be not art to me,
>   What care I what art it be?"

"What is wrong with *Lady Cecily's Secret Heart?* It's a
thumping good love story, and that is of universal interest to
all people. A touch of—indiscretion here and there—a good
love scene—a dramatic moment or two when the misguided
lady is discovered in a compromising position by her husband—what more would a reader want, especially when the
book is well-written, as novels go?" He gave Ravel an unpleasant smile. "After all, the average reader is not unin-
terested in whether or not the hero and heroine go to bed
together."

At this indelicate remark, every lady, with the exception of
Melissa and Mrs. Eldridge, felt it incumbent upon herself to
utter a faint gasp and cover her mouth with shocked fingers.
The remark flew by Melissa's ears like an inconsequential
breeze, so aroused was she, so trembling with her passionate
desire to cry out against Geoffrey's demeaning remarks regarding the sacred world of books. Mrs. Eldridge, however, joined
in the hearty laughter of the gentlemen, and she was immediately followed in her mirth by Mrs. Holland.

"Your language, sir," said Ravel.

"Oh, h—, I mean, nonsense!" said Geoffrey. "Women are
really much more earthy than men, and only pretend to be
shocked because we expect them to be. Ladies, I do not expect you to be shocked by anything said around this table, so
you may relax and be your very intelligent natural selves."

The ladies laughed uncertainly, wondering whether to be
offended or complimented. While they considered, Ravel continued the argument with his host, and attention was again
drawn to the two infuriated faces of the contestants.

"You said something about the war 'debasing' art, Ravel,"
said Dunham. "But wasn't it Homer who said the arts languish
in days of peace, and rise to their most brilliant crescendo in
days of war? But then, you would not know about that, would
you? When we were fighting the South, you were abroad, I
believe, snug in Paris. Now, I am not impugning your pa-
triotism. In fact, I should like to commend you on your common-sense."

Ravel half rose in his chair. Alarmed, the others turned
towards him, but Geoffrey only smiled. Mr. Eldridge said

hastily: "Ravel, I am afraid this argument is degenerating into a brawl. Perhaps I can clarify what Dunham means——"

"Sit down, you damn fool," said Mr. Littlefield, in a tone of harsh authority. "Remember your manners."

Ravel sat down. He became very pale. He said, quietly: "It is not I who have forgotten my manners."

Geoffrey suddenly felt considerably more good-natured. "No offense," he remarked. "But I'm touchy on the subject of books, Ravel. Shall we discontinue the argument?"

"No, if you please. Unless I bore anybody?" Ravel's eyes travelled swiftly about the table. The ladies ardently disclaimed any sensation of ennui. The gentlemen said, of course not, but perhaps the ladies would prefer—. The ladies urgently said that they did not "prefer—." It was all so interesting. It quite broadened the mind, added Mrs. Littlefield. It was most enlightening, observed Mrs. Bertram.

Melissa said nothing. She stared at Ravel, and he felt her impetuousness spurring him on, as if what he would say was the only thing of importance to her. It was as if she had taken his arm and was pressing it; she had no concealments. Her eagerness blazed from her. It became very necessary to him not to disappoint her, and so it was as if he were her spokesman when he said:

"It is an old story, this, of the neglect of a truly great artist in favor of the cheap and trashy and sensational scribbler. I should be disparaging your intelligence, Dunham, if I thought you did not secretly agree with me. In a way, I see your point of view," and he smiled disarmingly. "You are a businessman. May I diverge for a moment and remark that it is regrettable that art needs businessmen? (Or does it?) As a businessman, you need customers, and you supply the customers with what they demand. But suppose, for a moment, that a businessman, a publisher, decided that he would publish no more tripe, and that his list should contain nothing but the finest in literature? What would happen then? I say that the public would buy good literature, for want of bad."

"And I say that publishers would soon find themselves bankrupt," replied Geoffrey, with open contempt for this childish reasoning. "You can't sell the public what it doesn't want." He paused, and smiled. "By the way, who is to set up the standard as to what is good and what is bad in literature? What is the measuring rod? I say it is what the people acclaim or ignore. There is no other standard but man himself." He smiled again, nastily. "Would you be able to say, with conviction, that your own taste was impeccable, that you were competent to judge?"

"I think I am competent, in a small way, to judge poetry," answered Ravel steadily.

Geoffrey sighed. "It was only recently that Shelley was admitted to be a poet. Now no one can get enough of him. He was called a rhymster only a short time ago."

Before Ravel could speak again, Geoffrey asked: "We are going to publish three of Balzac's books this year. What do you think of Balzac, Ravel?"

Ravel sensed a trap. Geoffrey's face was too bland. But he said uncertainly: "I think France has produced no finer writer in his generation." He added: "I congratulate you on your coming venture."

He knew it had been a trap when Geoffrey smiled broadly. The older man laid down his knife and fork, felt in an inner pocket and brought out a newspaper clipping. He showed it to his guests as a magician shows a rabbit he has just lifted from a hat. "This," he said, "is a criticism of Balzac by one of Paris's most distinguished critics. It was sent to me recently and arrived only today in the post. My chief editor, who violently dislikes Balzac, thought I ought to see it, as a deterrent to my plan for publishing Balzac. Occasionally my editor has an attack of 'art,' too. Let me see: yes, it was printed in *Le Temps*. My French is rather a cumbersome thing, so I shall translate slowly. Let me see—

"'Balzac was a literary prostitute of the first order, and cannot, under any circumstances, be considered an artist. Did he write from inspiration, from a divine moving of the spirit? No! He wrote for money! Let him need a new house, or a new fence, or a new piece of land, let the money-lenders be hot on his trail, or let him wish for jewels, objets d'art, furniture for another of his apartments, or to buy a wardrobe for a *petit ami*, and immediately he sat down and dashed off two or three of his execrable novels a year to satisfy his base cravings! Is that art? Is that dedication? Is that seeking the lonely stars to shine upon the soul? No, that is degradation. The only comfort which comes to your critic's heart is the realization that this popular so-called writer's fame will not survive the test of time, that his vulgar scribblings will be used only to stuff up rat-holes in the benighted dens of those who buy his works. A book written for money is a book destined for death.'"

Geoffrey folded the clipping in a complete silence. He bowed, and smiled at Ravel. "I congratulate you upon your literary taste, which is so at variance with this famous critic's."

Ravel's mortification was complete. Anything he might say now would only tumble him deeper into the trap. His father was grinning; the Eldridges were smiling broadly; Mr. and Mrs. Holland, being kindly folk, were embarrassed in sympathy. Mrs. Littlefield was staring at Geoffrey with malevolence. But Melissa, full of fierceness, regarded Geoffrey with flashing eyes. She exclaimed:

"It isn't a new story when an artist is misunderstood even by eminent critics! You have taken an unfair advantage, sir!" Her voice, unrestrained, rushed out vehemently: "I wish to bring to your attention my father's own distinguished works. The critics unanimously acclaim him a great scholar, a great writer and artist. There is no dissenting voice, yet, in spite of the praises heaped upon him by the critics, an obdurate and stupid people, unlettered and ignorant, refuse to buy his books in any quantity." Her agitation and fury choked her; she leaned stiffly forward in her chair towards her husband, and her face glowed with anger. "Or am I not to believe that my father's books have sold as poorly as you have always claimed!"

Now there was silence and everyone, including Ravel, was bathed in complete embarrassment at Melissa's raw crude passion, ingenuous but atrocious bad manners, and the implied insult she had flung at Geoffrey. Had she stood up and began to hurl dinnerware about, had she become drunk, they could not have been more outraged and ashamed. Even Mr. Holland and his wife, gentle and tolerant though they were, were distressed. Arabella gasped, then her eyes gleamed with a small and vicious triumph as she furtively studied the faces of her guests. She glanced at her brother, who was a study, and the gleam of triumph slid over her features.

Moment after moment went by, filled with the loud fast breath of poor Melissa, until at last, becoming aware, even in her passion, of averted eyes and shut mouths, she subsided in her seat. Her heart was beating tumultuously; slowly, it calmed. She had never before cared for, nor considered, the reaction of herself upon others, but now it was borne in upon her that everyone adjudged her disgraceful, beneath contempt, and that in some obscure and baffling way she had hurt Geoffrey. But what had she done? She had merely joined an argument which seemed to her more important than anything in the world, for what could be more important than books? Did these fools believe women had no minds, that they should not speak? That must be it! Her indignation struggled to rise, then collapsed. No, it was something else. She was accustomed, at home, to break fiercely into speech, to argue heatedly whenever she desired, to declare herself roundly, and no one had thought it unnatural. So what was wrong with these strangers? Had she done something reprehensible?

The silence became unbearable. The guests finished, with great care, the last morsels on their plates, Geoffrey motioned with his head to a servant to refill the wine glasses. Melissa's throat was dry. She looked at her husband, and blurted out: "Did I say something I ought not to have said?"

Later, Mrs. Littlefield observed to her husband that Arabella had saved the situation with immense magnanimity and finesse by rising and saying to the ladies: "Shall we leave the gentlemen to their cheroots and wine?"

The gentlemen rose and waited for the ladies to rise, which they did with a creak and rustle of silk. Melissa sat dumbly, staring at Geoffrey with confused pleading and bewilderment, for he had not answered her nor looked at her. The ladies, gathering in a cluster at the door, waited for her. Geoffrey said, quietly: "Will you join the ladies, Melissa?" And still he did not turn his eyes in her direction. He was very pale. And there Melissa sat, under the gaze of the ladies, under the noses of the gentlemen, twisting a length of her gown between damp and trembling fingers.

Then she said, faintly: "Why should I join the ladies? I don't want to. I think I shall go to bed. I'm very tired."

Again, Arabella gasped, very loudly and theatrically, and touched her lips with her handkerchief. The gentlemen were nonplussed. Geoffrey could not help smiling a little, in spite of his anger and humiliation. He came to Melissa and offered her his arm. "Of course, my dear," he said, gently. "I am sure our guests will excuse you."

She rose awkwardly, and took his arm. What should she do next? The situation called for something graceful in the way of regrets. But she did not know what to do or to say. At home, she would merely have left the room, and there would have been no questions. But in this alien environment something was obviously expected, and she did not know what it was. So, hurriedly, and in a loud tone, she exclaimed: "Good night!" She looked at all those closed and avid faces, heard the murmurs of the gentlemen and, louder, the silence of the ladies. She tried to smile. She added: "I am sure we shall see you in the morning."

The ladies blushed, the gentlemen coughed softly. Melissa, on the arm of her husband, stumbled to the doorway. The ladies parted to clear the exit. Then Geoffrey released his arm and said gravely: "Good night, Melissa."

She stood there, exposed, alone and baffled, under the embarrassed scrutiny of all eyes. She could think of nothing. She gathered up her skirts and, final ignominy, all saw her great shabby boots under the silk. She turned and fled.

The ladies, mercifully chatting of other matters, followed Arabella. The gentlemen sat down, and a servant closed the door. Amiable conversation was picked up by Mr. Eldridge, tossed to Mr. Littlefield, to Mr. Bertram, to Ravel. He picked it up gracefully. Geoffrey could not speak for several moments. Then he looked up to encounter Ravel's sardonic smile, and for a moment he wanted to kill Melissa.

CHAPTER 31

RACHEL WAS SITTING by the fire in Melissa's bedroom, sewing swiftly and delicately on the brown velvet destined for tomorrow, when the door burst open and Melissa rushed in with a great noise. Startled, Rachel let the velvet slide from her knees, she stood up and stared at Melissa.

"Is there something you wish, Mrs. Dunham?" she asked, noting Melissa's hot eyes and air of disorder and rout. What ever had happened to the poor young lady now? She watched in stupefaction as Melissa ran to the dressing-table and began to throw off her jewels with wild haste. "What is the matter, ma'am?" asked the girl in distress, approaching Melissa. "Do you wish to change your jewelry?"

Melissa turned her head jerkily over her shoulder and cried: "No, of course not! I'm just going to bed, that's all, Rachel. I'm tired."

Dumfounded, Rachel glanced at the gilt clock on the mantelpiece. It was hardly half-past ten. She saw that Melissa's hands were shaking. The girl was unpinning her hair, and it suddenly fell in a heavy uncoiling length down her back. "But Mrs. Dunham, they are just starting the music downstairs," faltered Rachel. It was all very confusing. Melissa, in spite of her feverish color, was apparently in the best of health. One did not leave one's guests; it was not done even for such a reason as sudden indisposition. And especially not on one's wedding night. Her bewilderment grew as she stood beside Melissa, who was struggling with the buttons of the blue gown. Automatically, Rachel assisted. The white flesh under her finger tips was hot.

Melissa jerked away at the girl's touch. "I can manage, Rachel. And what are you doing here, anyway? Why aren't you in bed?"

"Why, ma'am, I am supposed to remain here until you come, to assist you, no matter what the time," said Rachel.

"Oh, what nonsense!" cried Melissa. "Do you mean," she continued, arrested in her haste by the outrageous idea, "that if I didn't arrive until midnight, or later, you'd just sit here, yawning and tired, until I came?"

"Why, certainly, ma'am. That is my duty."

"Nonsense!" exclaimed Melissa, roundly. "You just leave here at once and go to bed, Rachel."

Rachel's confusion mounted. She glanced hopefully at the door, expecting Mr. Dunham. But the door remained blandly closed. Melissa had reached an acute stage in her undressing, and was waiting impatiently for Rachel to leave. She had seated herself on a stool and had taken off her boots, which she now tossed aside with a clatter. Her hot agitation was growing, and this was so intense a contrast with her frozen misery and dumbness of the morning that Rachel was alarmed.

"Ma'am, what is wrong?" asked the girl, impulsively. She let herself drop on the edge of the chair she had vacated, and fumbled absently with the heap of brown velvet beside it. "Has something happened?" she added, hoping that Melissa would not consider her impertinent.

But Melissa did not think Rachel impertinent in the least. Her snobbery was not social, but intellectual, and as she considered Rachel seriously she felt an immense confidence in her servant and an inexplicable desire to unburden herself and find an answer to the puzzling events of the night. She lifted her hands from her stocking, and clenched them in her shimmering lap. She appeared very young and bewildered and vaguely frightened, on her stool, with her hair on her shoulders, her cheeks very pink, and her eyes very wide and baffled.

"Rachel," she said, "I have done something terrible downstairs, but I don't know what it is. Anyway, they are all stupid and obtuse, and they bored me horribly. Except Mr. Littlefield. Who is a poet," she added, with a touch of enthusiasm. "He understood. I'm sure he did, but they were all so shocked, and it was all so tiresome, and they were all so dull, that I am afraid he was infected by them. I wouldn't have cared, but Mr. Dunham was hurt, in some way." She pushed the hair back from her forehead, and frowned, and sighed. "No one explained. I thought Mr. Dunham would be glad when I joined the dinner conversation, for I felt that he thought me very tedious, just stitting there and not finding anything to say. So I joined the conversation."

Oh, dear, thought Rachel. And what did the poor young lady say?

She clasped her hands on her knees, and her queer affection for Melissa made her round dark eyes soft and receptive. She waited.

Melissa was becoming excited and baffled again. "They were talking about books, and publishing, and the indifference of people to classic works of art, Rachel. Mr. Dunham caught Mr. Littlefield in an argument about Balzac." She paused. "What do you think of Balzac, Rachel? My father thought him an impossible scribbler, and meretricious."

"I am sure Mr. Balzac, then, must be a very poor sort of gentlemen," said Rachel. "He cannot have been a man of breeding," she went on, wondering what "scribbler" and "meretricious" might mean. But she made her voice disapproving, to match the scorn on Melissa's face. Apparently she had said the right thing, though Melissa remarked: "Well, I don't know or care whether he was a gentleman or not. That doesn't matter. It is his books which matter. The man is unimportant. The point is, has he contributed anything of immortal value to the world, or is he just a passing sensation?"

"Only time will tell," said Rachel sententiously, and with intuitive genius.

Melissa nodded vigorously, pleased. "Naturally, time is the test of all things. But there are definite signs, just now, that the man's works are of no value. My father pointed them out to me, and his judgment was always infallible." Her mouth saddened, then she lifted her head proudly.

"Well," she said, "I do not condemn Mr. Littlefield too severely for his admiration for Balzac. Even the best minds can be dazzled and led astray, temporarily, in the face of public clamor, which, of course, cannot be trusted in the least. But Mr. Dunham quite caught him in a trap, and it was most inconsiderate. Moreover, the argument was fallacious. I wished to set Mr. Dunham to rights, and mentioned my father's works, how poorly they had been received by the people. I also mentioned that I did not quite believe this. I've had a suspicion for some time that his works sold better than reported by Mr. Dunham, and I shall suggest, tomorrow, that Mr. Dunham make a personal investigation of his account books. Chicanery is not unknown in the publishing business, Rachel," added Melissa, darkly. "I believe Mr. Dunham, himself, is being cheated, in his own offices."

Rachel was not following all this very clearly, but she caught enough of the import to be aghast. "Oh, ma'am," she murmured, "did you actually say someone was cheating Mr. Dunham?"

Melissa considered acutely, staring into space. Then she bit her lip. "I am very sorry," she said, uncertainly. She stared again. "However, I only expressed my opinion. Everyone has a right to his opinion."

She pulled off her stockings, and flung them from her. Then, becoming aware of Rachel's silence, she exclaimed defensively: "How can they be so sensitive and absurd? Mr. Dunham, too? I thought he was a man of sense. Is it forbidden to express an opinion? Must one always watch one's words? Such hypocrisy! No wonder the world is filled with liars and mendacious rascals! I, for one, will never subscribe to such mealymouthed conventions. Besides, I didn't say outright that anyone was cheating, least of all, Mr. Dunham."

"Then what happened, ma'am?"

"Oh, it was all so ridiculous! I saw I had, in their opinion, done something outrageous. What does one do then? Why, one removes oneself. It is simple. So I said I was going to bed, and that I didn't want to join the ladies. Why should I have 'joined the ladies'? They are all very stupid, I am sure that I should have found their conversation tiresome, and why should anyone allow himself to be bored by anyone else? Life is too short, as my father used to say. He would say that if you found yourself in tedious company you owed it to yourself and to your integrity to withdraw. So, I did."

Oh, heavens, sighed Rachel to herself. She moistened her lips, said gently and bravely: "But ma'am, that—that isn't customary. A lady is supposed to remain with her guests, and not to leave them."

"But they aren't *my* guests," said Melissa, with sharp simplicity. "I don't know them. I didn't invite them. They were here when I came. They are Arabella's friends. Let her entertain them. What have I to do with it?"

"But you are mistress of this household now, ma'am," ventured Rachel, seeing that Melissa had no idea that her maid was "impudent," or was "forgetting her place."

Melissa was appalled. "Ought I to have remained, Rachel? Honestly, now? Ought I to have gone into the drawing-room, with those odious dull females, as was suggested? What a waste of time! How absurd! When there are so many important things to do!"

She was outraged at the very thought. But her eyes, fixed on Rachel, were uncertain and troubled. "If you are right, and I cannot think you are, then Mr. Dunham must be very annoyed with me."

"There are certain social customs, ma'am," said Rachel, full of pity. She had an impulse to go to Melissa and kiss her, an impulse which immediately shocked her.

Melissa looked at her boots and stockings. "Ought I to go down at once, then?"

"I think it would only make matters worse, ma'am," sighed Rachel, with a vision of Melissa suddenly rushing back into the drawing-room where the ladies were doubtless avidly enjoying themselves at the poor girl's expense.

"It is a quandary," said Melissa, frowning. Then she was vexed again. "How foolishly matters are handled here! I foresee a very entertaining life for me," she added, with gloom. Her face hardened. "Well, I shall do no more than is necessary. No one can ask more. I have my own life to live, and I have work to do." She was full of vigor again, she glanced at the white-and-gold chest which held her father's manuscripts. "I must be becoming hypocritical. I told them, and you, that I was going to bed. That is untrue. I have no intention of going to bed. I am going to work."

"You told the guests you were going to bed?" faltered Rachel. She colored faintly. "On your wedding night, ma'am? What did Mr. Dunham say?"

"Nothing at all," replied Melissa, missing the implication entirely. "Naturally, he could not leave with me, for, as you said, they are his guests." She was proud of her new knowledge of etiquette. "Even though he complained to me today that Arabella was the one who really invited them, not he. But it would have been rude for the host, however involuntarily he was host, to walk off and leave his sister alone to entertain these tiresome people."

Rachel had been well grounded in the subject of social usage, and now, listening to Melissa, she felt dazed. Here was a young woman, obviously well-bred and of good family, educated and patrician, speaking in the accents of the best drawing-rooms, and yet she was as ignorant of custom as a baby in arms. It was not to be understood. Her arguments, too, were so crystalline, so forthright and simple, that it was hard to meet them with conventional objections. She would not have comprehended in the least. I must teach her, thought Rachel, for her own sake, poor young lady. What innocence!

Melissa was now tired of the subject, which she considered petty and time-wasting. She had work to do. Never had she felt so wide awake, so urgent and clear-minded. She could work for hours!

"Do go to bed, Rachel," she said, starting up. "I want to get undressed, and then I shall sit at that desk, yonder, and get to work. I have wasted enough time as it is, and it is desperately necessary for me to complete my father's manuscripts."

"You are going to work, ma'am? Now?" asked Rachel, incredulously. A young and ingenuous bride going to bed, to await her bridegroom with blushings and trepidation, was not too out of the ordinary, but a bride who, on her wedding night, fled to her bedroom for the sole purpose of working, was not to be accepted by a sane mind.

"Certainly, I am going to work. I've idled away enough time," said Melissa, eyeing her maid with open impatience. Whatever she had thought that afternoon in her tub was completely forgotten now, her single-hearted intent fixed only on one object. She was incapable of harboring more than one idea at a time. She was like a sword with a single edge, incapable of cutting in more than one direction. "Do run along, Rachel. How can I undress if you linger here?"

Still disoriented and incredulous, Rachel said: "But I am supposed to help you undress, ma'am, to lay out your nightdress, and to put away your gown."

"Oh, how nonsensical!" cried Melissa. "Am I ill, or a cripple? And why should you, a woman, do such degrading things for me, another woman, quite capable of taking care of herself? Am I a parasite, a sybarite?" She paused. "Do you mean," she added, disbelievingly, "that other women permit such services, debasing alike to the servant and to the one served?"

"It is customary, ma'am, if a lady can afford a personal maid," answered Rachel, wearily.

"Well, I shall certainly not permit it," said Melissa, roundly. "Go away at once, Rachel. You look very tired. Heat a glass of milk for yourself, put in plenty of loaf sugar, and go to bed. It will help you get a good night's sleep."

Rachel glanced at the fire. "If you will permit it, ma'am, I should like to remain here and finish this dress, and replenish the fire when you need it."

"Will you go away?" exclaimed Melissa, angrily. "Of course,

you mustn't stay here. I couldn't work with you in the room.
And there's plenty of coal. I can throw on some more, if I
need it. Besides, this room is too hot. Heat stultifies the
mind."

Rachel, in silence, went to a chest, brought out a foam
of lace and silk and ribbons and laid it on Melissa's bed.
"What's that?" demanded the girl, approaching.

"Your nightgown, of course, ma'am."

Scornfully, and with an exclamation, Melissa lifted up the
delicate cloud and held it at arm's length. "This? I never
heard of such a thing! The room will grow too cold, later
on, and I should get lung fever. So flimsy and ridiculous.
Do women actually wear such things? Where are my flannel
nightgowns, Rachel?"

Rachel faltered: "Why, Mr. Dunham told me to throw them
away, ma'am."

Melissa colored, with anger and embarrassment. "He saw
them, Rachel? You showed my nightgowns to him?"

"No, Mrs. Dunham. He opened the chest and inspected
them, himself."

"How dared he! Why, this is outrageous! How could he
have brought himself to invade my privacy?" Melissa's embarrassment was gone. She was full of umbrage at Geoffrey's
calm insolence.

Rachel said nothing. Melissa flung the nightgown disdainfully onto the bed. Then she became aware of Rachel's
distress. A little warmth, unique and strange, touched her
hard young heart. It was all too amusing and absurd, but
apparently one could hurt by saying the most natural things,
and she saw hurt in Rachel's dark little face.

"Oh, Rachel, if you think it best, I shall wear the silly
thing, though if I have a cold tomorrow, and a dreadful sore
throat, we shall know who is to blame. But all those ribbons!" she went on, looking contemptuously at the nightgown.
"I shall never manage the ribbons." She had another thought.
"My woolen dressing gown. Where is it?"

Sighing, Rachel produced a dressing gown of thin blue
wool and lace, and quietly laid it beside the nightgown.
The two young women contemplated the garments in a profound silence. Then they looked at each other. Simultane-
ously, they smiled, then began to laugh a little. Melissa's
laughter came rustily and awkwardly, then with a quicker
rush, almost gay and childlike.

She then literally pushed Rachel from the room. She
undressed quickly, piling the pretty clothing carelessly on

a chair, and pushed the boots under the rungs. She found her carpet slippers and, with a sigh of relief, thrust her feet into them. Then, scowling, she put on the nightgown. It fell in a cloud about her, clinging to her body. She awkwardly tied the ribbons, straightened the lace. The foolish thing had no weight or substance or warmth. She glanced in the mirror, and was arrested at the lovely reflection. She bent and peered closer. Her hair flowed about her, her flesh gleamed through the silk. She huriedly pulled on the blue wool gown. It was too short, but it was surprisingly warm. Forgetting everything, Melissa suddenly ran to the chest where her father's manuscripts lay, retrieved the precious papers, and heaped them on the pretty gold-and-white desk. Impatiently, she laid various crystal and porcelain articles on the floor, put out her sturdy ugly pens, pencils and ink-pot. She sat and stared at the manuscript, and then at the pile of reference books near her feet. Absently, she caught up her hair and braided it with tense fingers. Her mind had already left this room and this house, and all that it contained. The long braid fell down her back; she bent over the manuscript and the note-books, pen in hand. She began to write.

Now there was no sound in the room but that of the pen and the crackling fire. But outside it had begun to storm and a wind hurled itself savagely against the closed shutters. Sparks flew up the chimney. Music sounded softly downstairs. Melissa was oblivious.

This manuscript of Charles Upjohn's dealt with the philosophers of a certain phase of the Athenian Republic. Charles had considered that a sterile era. He quoted Machiavelli: "Republics have a longer life and enjoy better fortune than principalities, because they can profit by their greater internal diversity. They are the better able to meet emergencies." Charles took cold but strong offense at this. "Republics," said his notes, "produce nothing but hypocritical equality. No sensible man believes that equality is possible, for equality, put into practice, is an outrage to nature herself. The majority of men are born for obscurity and death. They have no function in life except to serve the superior man. Under aristocratic governments, this is accepted and acknowledged, and so, under such governments, we see the full flowering of the arts, their purest expression and essence, uncorrupted, uncoarsened and undefiled by the common touch. But Republics, admitting, as they do, the common man into all the precincts of the arts, encourage him to enter with his smell of offal, his dirt of averageness, his mud of mediocrity. He carries with him, also, the potential thunderbolt of anarchy, which can destroy the sacred temples. The distortion of the doctrine spreads to the lesser facets of life, so that eventually the servant protests at serving, leisure is curtailed for the superior man, who alone can envision the perfect civilization, and the drab dust of enforced neglect sifts over the pillared walls and the white colonnades."

Melissa copied rapidly. How true, dear Papa, she thought, remembering the guests downstairs. Then she paused. But her father was not speaking derisively of those people who had leisure and education, fine homes and rich clothing. No, he was not speaking derisively of them. He was speaking for them! She knew that surely, with a kind of surprised sickness. Those he was attacking were such as Rachel, Rachel with the kind brown eyes and the worn little hands, Rachel, servant to her inferiors.

Melissa dropped her pen slowly from her fingers, and stared blindly before her. The queerest thoughts rushed into her mind—questioning, confused and amorphous thoughts. She glanced down at the manuscript. She read: "There are some who, like myself, believe that universal literacy would mean the epicedium of culture."

No, thought Melissa, you are wrong, Papa. It is only that the wrong people, that too few people, have an opportunity for culture. Had Rachel been born among gentlefolk of means, or even gentlefolk without means, she might have displayed a mind of considerable stature. I've seen intelligence and understanding in her eyes. There is something wrong with your whole thesis, Papa.

The flight of her ideas became more confused, more rapid. She reread her father's last sentence, and suddenly it had to her a cruel, lofty and stupid ring. Something like violent protest struggled in her mind, and a strange and fierce contempt. She recalled so many things her father had said, so many quotations from men like himself, men who believed that art remained art only so long as it was protected and hidden from the people. To these men it was a secret language; it had a secret code and handclasp. It was a marble cloister, a hidden city on a forbidden hill. Once entered by the masses of mankind, and it was no longer art, because it was comprehensible. That was their belief: That art must necessarily be obscure, precious, exquisitely inscrutable and impenetrable, incapable, by its very nature, of being translated into common speech. A book which was enjoyed by the many was unworthy of the interest of the superior man, who understood that because of its wide acceptance it was not art. A poem which the masses might repeat with love, was not truly a poem. Music adored by the mob was ludicrous, it was not music. A statue worshipped by common men was a common thing.

Greatly agitated, Melissa jumped to her feet and began to walk up and down the room, her gown flowing behind her as if in a high wind. What did the jeweled phrase matter, if it expressed nothing but its own sparkle? What potency was there in an artist who was interested only in art, as a thing in itself, and did not use it to make articulate the urgent but formless thoughts of other men? An artist who painted an unfathomable picture, whose meaning was not immediately and simply obvious, was a pretentious dauber, no matter what his skill. Music preoccupied only with its own intricacy, its own mathematical and convoluted perfection, was not music, however perfect its technique.

Melissa, stunned by her own heretical and lawless thoughts, stood before the fire, twisting her fingers together. She heard the wind outside, and it was like a shout. She turned her head nervously, and started. She thought someone had entered the room. But no one was there. Her thoughts began to ebb away, and now her mind became slowly empty and cold, and very tired.

Something has happened to me, she thought. Something very wrong. It is all this strangeness and excitement. This house. I have no right in this house. Everything has lost its clarity for me, in this house. Oh, I know where I got these thoughts I have been indulging. They are only an echo of what Mr. Dunham said tonight, when he made fun of Mr. Littlefield and held him up to the contempt of his superficial guests. Am I so weak, then, that I can let a callous man's greedy ideas obscure my father's ideals, a gross man's sentiments besmirch my father's inviolate convictions? Who is right, he or my father? He lives in luxury; my father lived in self-ordained poverty, because he preferred integrity to wealth, honor, to the prostituting of his genius in the open market place. My father was right, as he always was right.

She glanced about the lovely silent room, and hated it. She hated its delicate bright colors, its shine of gilt and white and crystal and silver. She hated the very fire on the hearth. All at once, she remembered Ravel Littlefield, and something stirred in her like a surge of gratitude and happiness. If only Papa had known him, she thought.

Resolutely, she returned to the desk and continued with

her work. The music downstairs died away, lost in wind and silence. The fire burned low, flickered on the hearth. The pen scratched furiously. Note after note was coordinated smoothly. Melissa forgot her uneasy sense that someone was in the room with her watching remorselessly. Now peace and contentment filled her. The little clock chimed on and on, and she did not hear it.

A faint click reached her buried consciousness of her surroundings, and she started. Geoffrey Dunham was entering the room through his dressing-room, and he stood there silently, closing the door behind him. He wore a long gown of maroon silk, tied with a silken cord, and there were slippers on his feet.

Melissa looked over her shoulder at him, the pen in her hand. She did not move. She was pale with exhaustion, and her eyes were glazed. It was some moments before she could orient herself, before she could become fully aware of where she was and of the presence of this man whom she had completely forgotten.

Slowly, she turned in her chair, pushing away a long strand of hair which had fallen over her forehead. She stared at Geoffrey numbly; her eyes travelled from his quietly smiling face to his feet. Then she jumped to her own feet and clutched the back of the chair, and her mouth opened soundlessly.

"What on earth are you doing, Melissa?" asked Geoffrey. He came slowly into the room, stopped at the hearth. He looked at the desk, and his brows moved quickly. But he made no comment, though he understood. "It is getting very cold in here. Why haven't you put some coals on the fire?" He lifted the scuttle, tossed coals on the last pink embers, stirred the grate vigorously. A crackling and a burst of sparks rewarded him. He picked up the bellows and worked them. Melissa watched him, still clutching the chair.

All at once, she became aware that her blue robe had fallen away from her nightgown. She caught it swiftly and furtively together. Geoffrey was looking at her again. She smiled, and the smile made him frown a little, it was so terror-stricken and so pathetic, so desperately pleading.

"I've been working on my father's notes," she stammered. "I forgot the time." She glanced at the clock. "It is almost two," she added feebly. "I think I'll go to bed. I'm very tired."

Geoffrey said nothing. He just stood on the hearth and studied her, and his face darkened. Then, very slowly and deliberately, he walked towards her. She watched him come, and he saw the widening and too-brilliant stare of her eyes. She did not retreat, nor move, nor even shrink. He stopped now, before her. Then, still moving slowly as if not to startle her, he put his hands on her shoulders.

They looked at each other. He felt her agonized stiffness. Her eyes did not leave his; the iris had dwindled to a tiny glittering blackness of fear. Yet the poor foolish girl did not wince or try to free herself. She only waited.

A long time seemed to pass. Then Geoffrey took his hands from her shoulders. She stood where he had released her. He turned away from her, went back to the fire, stood and looked down at it. She would not let herself breathe more easily, nor relax her distraught tightness of muscle and body. She could only watch him in dread.

Geoffrey regarded the fire steadily and thoughtfully, as if he had forgotten her. She saw his profile, meditative and unreadable, with the firelight flickering on it. His hands were in his pockets. The dark red of his robe shimmered in a watery pattern. Melissa's hands, aching from their clutch on the back of the chair, only tightened. So long as she did not move, did not speak, did not let go, nothing would happen. She had only to be very still like this, breathing only shallow breaths, not looking away from this terrible stranger who called himself her husband and called her his wife. She had only to regard him steadily and fixedly, like this, and he could do nothing but go away.

Geoffrey continued to study the fire. Oh, go, go! cried Melissa in herself. She was becoming aware of his bigness, his strength, and her terror became more alive and threatening. She swallowed slowly and carefully, to control it. There was a huge dry lump in her throat. If he came back to her, if he touched her again, she would collapse; she knew this. But what could she do?

Geoffrey turned his head and looked at her once more, but he made no movement towards her. She smiled convulsively. Geoffrey looked away quickly. Then he began to speak, in a very quiet and gentle voice:

"Don't be frightened, Melissa. You may sit down."

"Yes," she whispered. Still keeping her eyes on him, she sat down, sideways, on the chair.

"Melissa," he went on, after a long moment, and thoughtfully studying the fire, "I told you today that you mustn't ever be afraid of me, or of anything in this house. I want you to remember that. There is nothing here to frighten you, and there never will be. Why are you frightened, now?"

She tried to speak, but the lump choked her. Then her voice came in a dry rustle: "I'm not afraid."

"Good." Geoffrey smiled somberly. He added steadily: "Did you think I would force myself on you, poor child?"

Melissa was silent. Geoffrey waited, not turning to her. Then he added impatiently: "You are a fool, Melissa. I'm your husband, and I want you. I am a man. Or didn't you know? And you are a woman. You never knew that, did you? But all this doesn't alter the case. I won't force you. Try to remember that."

She said, incredibly, and he could not believe his ears: "Thank you."

He wanted to laugh.

He said: "Well, then. Good night, Melissa."

He turned to her with a friendly smile, as though he were trying to keep from laughing. "Good night," he repeated.

"Good night," she replied.

He went to the door of his dressing-room, opened it, passed through, and closed the door behind him.

For a long time Melissa sat where she was. The clock chimed. The whole house was completely silent. There was no sound but the wind. Then Melissa moved her cramped alert body and a great sigh rushed past her lips; she dropped her head on the back of the chair. She began to tremble violently. The fire died down, and now the chill of the room struck her. She stood up, pushing against the chair, and staggered slightly. She looked at the closed door. She went to it along the stretch of the room and her eyes fixed themselves on the handle. She turned it involuntarily. It was locked.

Her hand dropped from the handle. But she remained standing against the door. Slowly, like a glacier moving over fields and meadows, a sudden and nameless desolation crept over the girl, a sudden sense of abandonment, of yearning and misery. She had no words for its overpowering anguish, for its profound sickness, for its sorrow. She was cold with it, paralyzed with it. She touched the handle again, wondering vaguely at her own huge pain, not understanding it, only suffering it.

After a very long time, shivering and exhausted, she crept into her bed and blew out the light. When, in the darkness, she felt the tears on her face, she was amazed, and said aloud in a voice of distressed wonder: "What is the matter with me?"

CHAPTER 32

IT WAS only eight o'clock the next morning when the Upjohns' decrepit farm wagon lumbered, rattled and groaned to the door of the Dunham house.

The wind had increased at dawn, and now the white countryside boiled and smoked and pillars of airy white particles swirled in high columns off the earth, like ghosts gyrating, spiraling, twisting, and fleeing. The wind caught up the blue vapor from the chimneys and sent it flooding and swirling like water over the red roof. Here and there, the torn blue sky rushed out between radiant white clouds, and the sun blazed down in an unbearable cataract of incandescent light over the white hills and fields.

A very tall and burly young man in a farmer's rough clothing and heavy jacket and woolen cap clambered to the ground, tied up the ancient nag, and went purposefully to the gleaming door of the house. Resolutely, he lifted the knocker, let it fall. The clear loud echo started back at him from the shining emptiness of the land. After some long moments, the door opened, and James, blinking, shrugging his shoulders into his newly donned coat, looked out distrustfully. He frowned at the young man, and was about to speak indignantly about back doors, when the young man said in his deep voice: "I am Andrew Upjohn. I wish to see my sister, Mrs. Dunham."

As Andrew was rarely seen in the countryside, James had not recognized him, but now the man flung open the door and politely requested the visitor to enter. He said: "I do not think Mrs. Dunham has arisen as yet, sir, but I will see."

"Oh, Melissa is certain to be up," replied Andrew. There was about him the same clean, strong simplicity which marked his sister and had marked his mother.

"Would you please wait in the library?" asked James. Andrew immediately went into the library, where he surprised a pretty maid just finishing her dusting and the cleaning of the hearth. She fled with blushes, but not without astonishment, at the entrance of this farmer.

Andrew slowly circled the room, scanning the titles of

the books. He seemed preoccupied. He fished absently in his pocket, pulled out a deplorable corncob pipe, stuffed it with tobacco, lit it, without stopping his inspection of the books. He wandered to the windows, looked out, puffed, narrowed his eyes. He began to hum abstractedly and tonelessly to himself.

He heard the swift rush of feet on the stairway, then Melissa burst into the room. Andrew turned, and examined his sister acutely in the very instant of her entrance. He saw she was wearing her old brown frock, that her hair was bundled up in her usual careless fashion, that she was as disheveled and unkempt as always. Andrew felt an angry rush of disappointment. Melissa was married; she was now doubtless a wife in fact as well as in name. Andrew did not know exactly what he had expected, but it was certain that he had not expected to see his sister in such a garb, and with such an untouched and virginal air. Then, he became conscious that her color was much better and, though she still gave the impression of a wind-blown figure-head, there was less strain in her eyes. I don't know what's happened to her, thought Andrew, but it evidently wasn't much. Well, even a little is something, I suppose. But can anything really touch Melissa at all?

"Oh, Andrew!" cried Melissa, with more eagerness than she had ever displayed. She held out her hands to him and came to him quickly. She put her hands on his shoulders, and kissed his cheek almost hungrily. Andrew was startled. He did not remember ever having been kissed by Melissa before. He patted her shoulder awkwardly, held his pipe behind his back.

"There, there, old girl," he said, uneasily catching a note of hysteria in her voice. "How are you? I was going along this way and thought I ought to stop in to see you." His shrewd eyes searched her face; he saw, with relief, that the gray shadows had left the hollows of her cheeks, and now, incredulously, but with pleasure, he detected a faint scent in her hair and on her flesh.

Brother and sister smiled at each other in the sudden self-consciousness of shy and austere people who distrust emotion in themselves or in others. "Oh, sit down, Andrew, please," said Melissa, somewhat breathlessly. "I am so glad to see you. Have you had breakfast?" Suddenly she glanced about her vaguely. "I suppose there's breakfast," she added doubtfully.

"I've had my breakfast, but I'll bet anything you haven't,"

said Andrew, cautiously lowering himself into a leather chair.
He had removed his woolen mittens. His big-knuckled hands
were red with cold. He held them to the fire.

"No, I haven't," replied Melissa. "I suppose it's too early
for the others. I forgot all about breakfast."

How like Melissa that was! Andrew again felt sharp disappointment. He studied his sister searchingly. "What have
you been doing, Melly? It seems you are up hours before
anyone else." (Where the hell was Dunham? It was odd that
a man should be unaware that his bride had left his bed
at crack of dawn, and it was even odder that a bride should
be up this early.)

"Yes, I have been up since half-past seven," answered
Melissa, without the slightest trace of embarrassment. Andrew
was confounded, but his mouth fell open idiotically when
Melissa went on: "I've been working on Papa's books."

Andrew was speechless. The old fanatical light was in
Melissa's eyes again, he observed, with a sinking sensation.
She was fishing hurriedly in the pocket of her skirt, and she
brought out a crumpled piece of paper. She unfolded it with
considerable crackling, while Andrew stared. She said: "I
have just finished a translation from Horace, which I have
decided to use as foreword in the book, because it seems
to me so appropriate for Papa. I'll read it to you.

Then, while Andrew still stared at her in an unbelieving
daze, Melissa read rapidly, in Latin:

> "Exegi monumentum aere perennius
> regalique situ pyramidum altius,
> quod non imber edax, non Aquilo impotens
> possit diruere, aut innumerabilis
> annorum series et fuga temporum.
> Non omnis moriar."

Her voice, sonorous and exultant, tender and strong, rang
out in the silent library, which was suddenly flooded by the
white winter sunlight. Andrew's mouth was still agape. He
could say nothing. Melissa smiled at him with almost passionate triumph. "Does that not seem perfect, Andrew, as
a foreword, as an epitaph, for Papa?"

Slowly, Andrew lifted his hand, rubbed his reddened forehead. He ran a finger around the neck of his woolen scarf,
and breathed loudly. Melissa remained blissfully blind to
these manifestations of intense discomfiture and perplexity.

Melissa was still smiling at him. "I know your Latin was

ever very good, dear Andrew," she said, with that blazing
nd exalted expression still bright on her face, "so I'll trans-
ate it for you." Incredibly, she believed Andrew's silence
ne of embarrassment because he had been unable to follow
er Latin. "Well, no matter, Andrew," she continued, "Latin
s a serious study in itself, I shall translate it as best I can.
Naturally, one misses the more subtle meanings in transla-
ion." She frowned at the piece of rumpled paper, then
ranslated:

"I have raised a monument more lasting than bronze,
   Loftier than the royal peak of pyramids;
   No biting storm can bring it down,
   No impotent north wind, nor the unnumbered series
   Of the years, nor the swift course of time.
   I shall not wholly die."

She looked at Andrew intensely, waiting for his comment.
Now all his face was red, suffused with complete discomfiture.
"I suppose it does very well," he commented, in a stifled
oice.
"Oh, Andrew, it is perfect!" she cried.
How often he had seen this look on her face, after a
ession with their father! He had hoped never to see it again,
ut there it was and he could not understand.
He could not help himself; the words came involuntarily:
"Where is Dunham—your husband?"
Melissa looked blank. "Geoffrey? I suppose he is still sleep-
ng. I haven't seen him," she said.
Andrew stood up abruptly. "You haven't seen him?" he
xclaimed.
"No." She was puzzled. "Is there something wrong,
ndrew?"
Something wrong! Why, God damn it, everything is wrong,
nd that poor simple creature just sits there and stares at
e like an imbecile! Andrew's mouth opened, then closed,
pened, then closed again, and now he was crimson. This
as the old Melissa, unaware of anything except the thought
he was thinking, single-minded as always, obsessed as he
ad hoped never to see her obsessed again. Andrew felt
ick. He began to have a glimmering, and again anger stirred
n him.
"He must have been tired," Melissa was incredibly going
n. "So, naturally, he would still be asleep. They all go to
ed late and sleep late," she added, disdainfully. Then she

paused. Andrew watched her in silence. All at once, a sharp wave of color ran over her face, seemed to fill her very eyes. Her hands lifted, dropped. The color ebbed, left her very pale. Now she looked at the fire.

Andrew came closer to her. "Melly," he said with quiet urgency, "tell me: Is anything wrong? Things don't sound right to me——"

"I assure you everything is all right, Andrew," said Melissa with an effort, and almost inaudibly.

Andrew made a helpless gesture. "I—I don't understand, Melly. I thought Dunham would take care of you—help you—" He stopped, unable to go on, in the inarticulate manner of people who speak rarely and only when they have something to say, and who find it almost impossible to express their emotions.

Melissa was silent. She lifted a fold of her brown frock, let it fall. She murmured: "He is very good to me. I—I think I am beginning to trust him. Of course," she added, in a louder tone, "there were some things he said last night, before his guests, with which I disagreed very strongly, just as Papa would have disagreed. But I hope to change his opinion in the future." Again she stopped, then repeated: "He is very good to me. I had a pretty gown last night, Andrew. It was blue. I'd like you to see it."

Not a nightgown, evidently, thought Andrew with bitterness. He sat down heavily, and regarded his sister with grim concentration.

"Melly," he said quietly, "I came here this morning to find out if you were quite—well, and happier."

She lifted her eyes and gave him a quick, surprised look, reluctantly moved. "Thank you, dear Andrew," she said. "That was very kind of you. I—I am well. Naturally, I cannot be very happy, under the circumstances."

"What circumstances?" asked Andrew, quickly, hoping for a clue.

Melissa sighed. The miserable gray shadows were under her strong cheekbones again. "You, Andrew, and Phoebe. I try not to think too much about it, but I cannot forget that you have sacrificed yourselves. Because we had no money, and you were both too proud to accept any from Mr. Dunham."

So, that is how she has rationalized it! Andrew did not know what to say. While he was trying to find words, he lit his pipe again, which had gone out. Clouds of smoke obscured his face. He waved them away with his hand. He leaned towards her, and she saw his eyes, a hard, bitter blue.

"Listen to me, Melly. You must listen, for I think your life depends upon it, and all your future, and any happiness you can have. It is very important, Melly I want you to understand," he said, in a slow, weighted voice, "that you are deceiving yourself. I am not too 'proud' to accept money, if I need it, and want it. But I neither need it nor want it, from anybody. I did not 'sacrifice' myself. I tell you again, as I told you yesterday, that I only want the land. I have wanted it all my life. For the first time since I can remember, I am happy, because I am a farmer now."

But Melissa did not believe it. She only gazed at him somberly, and slightly shook her head.

"For God's sake, Melissa," he pleaded. "Try to understand. You've built up a completely false premise in that narrow mind of yours. You think you are always right. You are almost always entirely wrong. You are one of the most intolerant and pig-headed people I have ever known."

Melissa's pale lips tightened with that old granite expression he remembered, and the young man was dismayed. How could one reach such a closed brain, impervious to anything it did not want to believe? If Melissa were a stupid woman, it would be easier to understand. But she was a woman of intellect—Andrew inhaled slowly. I might be wrong. It is very possible she is stupid, as only the learned can be stupid.

Andrew took his pipe from his mouth and regarded it grimly. "Melissa, do you remember how you and my father tried to make me take an interest in poetry? I resisted it always, if you remember. But there was a poem of Pope's, which expresses what I've always felt about the land. I don't remember the name, but it goes like this:

"Happy the man, whose wish and care
 A few paternal acres bound,
 Content to breathe his native air
 In his own ground."

The young man looked at his sister, and waited. But her expression was dark and obdurate. And now he saw that she was suffering. He went on resolutely:

"Whose herds with milk, whose fields with bread,
 Whose flocks supply him with attire;
 Whose trees in summer yield him shade,
 In winter, fire.

"Blest, who can unconcernedly find
Hours, days, and years slide soft away
In health of body, peace of mind,
    Quiet by day;

"Sound sleep by night; study and ease
Together mixed, sweet recreation,
And innocence, which most does please,
    With meditation.

"Thus let me live, unseen, unknown;
Thus unlamented let me die;
Steal from the world, and not a stone
    Tell where I lie."

His voice, unconsciously rising in passion in the measures of the poem, filled the sunlit library, and his eyes burned with an emotion alien to Melissa. After he had finished, she put her hand for a moment to her own eyes, and let it drop.

"Yes, Andrew," she said, as if in anguish. " '—Live, unseen, unknown.' 'Unlamented.' '—Not a stone tell where I lie.' That is what I wished to save you from. That is what I could have saved you from, had it not been for your pride." She drew a deep breath. "You cannot make me believe that any human creature of intelligence prefers to 'steal from the world' like a pauper, a beggar, a faceless being, unmarked and unhonored. You are your father's son. It is impossible for me to conceive that the son of such a man prefers obscurity, the lightless soil, ugly labor, and namelessness."

Andrew stood up, hopelessly, but heavily angered. "You can't 'conceive' of anything, can you, Melissa, but your own conceptions? They are fixed, immutable. They only are the truth. That is what you believe. But you are wrong. I never thought you stupid. But I am afraid you are. You are so damned intolerant, and that is because you are the worst sort of egotist. I don't remember who it was, but it was some old Frenchman who said: 'We ought not to be so vain and imagine that others are anxious to have a look at us, and to esteem us.' My God, Melissa, you are so infernally conceited! Do you actually think the world waits, breathless, for your words of wisdom, or that it gives a damn for Father's books, or for anyone else's?"

In the extremity of his desire to make his sister understand, he had made the most eloquent and the longest speech of his life. He was of a tenacious character. He had insulted her vehemently, for her own sake, in order to awaken her. But she sat there dumbly, in a real agony, and without the slightest sign of anger. It is no use, he thought, desperately.

Melissa wrung her hands together. "Oh, don't, Andrew," she whispered. "I do understand. You want me to be happy, and so you are pretending that all is well with you, and with Phoebe, so that I may have no regrets."

Andrew pressed his big, carved lips together, and breathed heavily through his nose. He spoke with the calmness of impotent rage: "Melissa, I plead with you not to be an infernal fool. Listen to me: I am going to marry Judge Farrell's granddaughter, Miriam McDowell, the girl who was widowed in the war. You have seen her often, I know—the child who used to sit on the log fence and watch you and Father walking in the fields."

Wretched as she was, Melissa had a sudden memory of a little girl perched on a log fence one early summer twilight, when the last bird sang in the sky and a melancholy tide of lavender and pale rose swept over the earth. The trees of the woods stood in blurred violet shadow beyond the sloping meadows; the hills had turned a dark purple against a sky of somber fire. Melissa had seen the child on the fence, and the wide curiosity in the big black eyes, before Charles had become aware of her. He was regarding the silent sky dreamily; the last bird had fallen from it in a descending arc of faint song. Charles had said: "How much more poignant is the death of day, than its birth! How much more meaningful, though the meaning is the delusion of our emotions, really, and twilight has no more significance than dawn. It is our imagination which colors a colorless universe, and gives to life a pattern." He sighed, smiled his sweet and whimsical smile, as if he chided himself tenderly for his own exquisite emotions, as one chides a lovable child. "But Melissa, my love," he had added in a wounded voice, "you are not listening to me."

"I'm looking at that horrid child sitting over there, Papa, staring at us like an impertinent crow," replied Melissa, in her loud and hectoring voice. She imperiously fluttered her hand at little Miriam. "Run along, girl. This is our property."

"Ah, yes," said Charles, annoyed. "Old Farrell's granddaughter. What a quite unprepossessing little creature. What long—er—limbs, and thin body. A veritable young scarecrow. What are those black ropes hanging over her shoulders? Ah, yes, her hair. I was never fond of dark hair; it does not look delicate on a female. It is obvious the little one is not marked by brains, which are necessary in a female devoid of beauty."

"You are trespassing, child," said Melissa, angry because the girl continued to sit on the fence, dangling her long legs in their soiled pantalettes and swinging her feet. The clarity of the heliotrope twilight made her small face very white, expressionless and still. "How can you be so odious?" Melissa demanded, when the girl did not move but only stared at Charles and herself as if they were strange and fantastic creatures from another world. All at once Melissa became aware of her patched gingham frock, her worn hands, her bedraggled hair, her muddy boots, and of her father in his cloak, his gray head bare to the skies, and of the cane he flourished delicately in his hand. An obscure fury rushed upon Melissa, and she took a menacing step towards Miriam. Miriam only swung her legs thoughtfully, and Melissa stopped a few feet away.

"I'm not trespassing," said Miriam with a note of contempt in her child's voice. "This is Grandpa's fence, anyway. I was just looking at you. Folks say you and your papa are crazy, and I wanted to see." She regarded Melissa reflectively. "I guess you are, too," she added, with satisfaction.

Then, with a hoot of raucous laughter, she had swung her legs over the fence, and run off over the darkening fields, her laughter a long, unendurable streamer flying behind her.

That had been eight years ago. And now Andrew was going to marry that frightful little creature with the long black ropes over her thin shoulders. Melissa said, in anguish: "Oh, Andrew. Oh, no, Andrew!"

"Yes, Melissa," he replied firmly. "I am. I've loved Miriam for years, even before she married poor Jim McDowell, but I didn't have the sense to speak for her. But I did, yesterday afternoon. We are going to be married just as soon as possible, and the two farms, the Judge's and mine, are going to be merged, for Miriam is the Judge's only heir, and he approves of the match. So, you see, Melissa, I am not 'averse' to money, and am very glad that Miriam has a good, healthy dowry, and if I had wanted to borrow money from Dunham I should have done so, without 'pride.' I have returned to the farm, and am marrying Miriam, because I wish to, and only because I wish to. And there's Phoebe: she is doing what she always wanted to do, and not because of some transcendental idea you think she is cherishing."

Melissa stood up, sick with her pain. It was now as strong as it had been yesterday, and sharper. She gazed at her brother with such misery that he was both freshly angered and newly compassionate.

"Oh, for God's sake, Melissa!" he exclaimed. "Why the hell don't you sleep with Dunham, and wake up?"

Melissa put her hands to her throat. Andrew furiously snatched at his woolen cap and mittens, pulled on his rough woolen jacket, wound his knitted scarf about his throat. His small blue eyes sparkled irately. Then, without another word, he swung about and lumbered rapidly towards the door. Geoffrey Dunham stood there, leaning against the wall in an attitude which suggested that he had been standing so, and listening, for a considerable time.

Andrew stopped abruptly, falling back on his heels. Color surged into his large rugged face. He seemed to choke. "Why you—you—popinjay!" he spluttered, helpless for a word which would express his full embarrassment, rage, disappointment and fear for his sister, and his disgust for this man. "What did you marry her for?"

Geoffrey looked grave. "Andrew," he said, putting out his hand. But Andrew knocked it aside, and rushed from the room. A moment later the door slammed behind him.

Melissa put her hands over her eyes and began to weep silently. Geoffrey went to her slowly. She murmured: "Oh, what shall I do, what shall I do?"

"Do about what?" asked Geoffrey, coldly.

Melissa, at this, dropped her hands with abruptness. Geoffrey was standing apart from her and wore such a detached and indifferent air that she was struck. She stared at him with the open bewilderment of a child, and again that strange misery and desolation of the night before returned to her. She stammered: "About Andrew and Phoebe." She searched his face with intense anxiety, but the anxiety was not for her brother or for her sister. It was something else, something which could not be explained, and it made her feel forsaken and deserted, and terribly alone.

A dog had folowed Geoffrey. He smiled at the animal, bent over and pulled its ears. He spoke to it affectionately. Melissa watched his caressing hands and, all at once, she reasonlessly hated the dog with its maudlin eyes and adoring expression. Noticing Melissa at last, it bristled and growled, sensing what neither Melissa nor Geoffrey had recognized.

"I don't like dogs," said Melissa nervously. The silly and mindless thing, licking its master's hands in devotion and servility! She could not look away from Geoffrey's big strong fingers, and when they stroked the dog's neck and back she shivered and glanced away, a unique and indescribable thrill running over her body.

"Well, I like dogs," said Geoffrey, with finality. He said: "It's all nonsense, you know, about Andrew and Phoebe. I thought that was all settled yesterday." He paused. "Did you sleep well? I don't suppose you did, or you'd not be up so early."

"I've been working on Papa's books again." She was alarmed at the sound of her own voice, it was so faint and hoarse. She remembered suddenly the scene last night, and was sick with mortification and pain; again, she wondered at these things. Without volition, she moved closer to Geoffrey, and she heard her own foolish words with a kind of astonishment, for she had not willed them, and they were so pleading: "I think this is Papa's best."

"Good," said Geoffrey, and she detected the falseness in his hearty voice. "But don't work too hard on it just yet. Remember, these are still the holidays." He whistled to the dog, who was regarding Melissa with savage hostility. "Come on, old fellow," he said, and he went away.

Melissa stood alone in the quiet library, with the sun shining on the books and dappling the long draperies. The house was very quiet still, though she heard a distant door open. She went to a window, dragging herself as if overwhelmingly tired. A blaze of white and cobalt blue met her eyes. Far down below, she saw her old home, a bleak mar on the landscape. Again, to her mingled outrage and surprise, she found that she was crying, that the sick wretchedness and pain were engulfing her.

She struggled to control herself. Then, horrified, as the sobs rose in her throat, she turned and ran from the room, and up the stairs, her head bent. She burst into her bedroom, and the sobs broke from her. Rachel was tidying up the room and she looked at her mistress, dumfounded.

Melissa threw herself into a chair, uncaring now for anything or anybody. As usual, she could not find her handkerchief. She fumbled at her skirts and applied the edge of her petticoat to her eyes and face. Rachel watched her with anxiety and sympathy. Then she said, timidly: "Mrs. Dunham, may I help you?" She opened a drawer and brought out some scented kerchiefs. She went to Melissa and held them out dumbly. Melissa snatched at them and dabbed roughly at her tears.

Rachel could not help it; she knelt beside the chair, and then, careless of her "station," she put her arms about her mistress and drew down the bedraggled head onto her shoulder. She said nothing, but her hands were tender.

Melissa, as if astounded or bewildered, remained stiff for a little while; then, all at once, she fell into Rachel's arms and wept with complete abandonment and despair, as only the strong and the narrow can weep.

CHAPTER 33

GEOFFREY TAPPED at Melissa's door, then entered. Rachel was putting the final touches to the hem of the brown velvet, while Melissa, bootless, stood on a stool like a mannequin. She was very stiff and careful, moving at Rachel's slight tuggings like an obedient child. The brown velvet, golden in the folds, encased her stately figure tenderly and perfectly. She was in the act of trying to pull up the shirred bodice, complaining of its lowness and arguing with Rachel, when Geoffrey came in. She was in profile to him, and had been so vehemently engrossed with the argument that Geoffrey heard her last words: "But I tell you, Rachel, this is indecent! Moreover, the exposure would give me lung fever. I shouldn't dare bend—" She stopped, became aware of Geoffrey, and turned red with embarrassment. Her hand flew to her breast in a gesture infinitely touching and virginal.

But Geoffrey apparently noticed nothing. He stood at a little distance and admired the dress. The color slowly left Melissa's face, and he saw how haggard she was. Her eyes were swollen and very pink, and her lips parched. She was not aware of it, but she listened to Geoffrey's comments with a kind of intense anxiety and eagerness. Then she said.: "This is so time-wasting, but Rachel tells me I cannot wear the blue dress twice in succession." Her voice was timid, and she dropped her head. Her breast glowed with pale pearly tints in the winter light.

"Oh, certainly, that would never do!" said Geoffrey, gravely. "It is absolutely forbidden a lady to wear a gown twice running. That is the worst of social errors. One might suspect she has nothing else to wear."

"Foolish," commented Melissa, faintly. "Besides, everyone knows you have a lot of money—Geoffrey." She said his name almost inaudibly, with a slowness that only Rachel could interpret. She added, in a louder voice: "Of course, this dress is warmer than the blue, but not half so pretty. But it is very nice," she continued, as if afraid she had offended him, "and I thank you very much."

The desk, and a nearby chair, were littered with papers and notebooks. They were incongruous in this charming room, with the crystal glittering and the silver sparkling, and all the colors as fresh as dawn.

"You did not come down to luncheon," said Geoffrey, sitting down where he had a clear view of the proceedings and could offer his opinion.

"I had a headache," said Melissa quickly, then her expression became annoyed. "No, I didn't. I was just—just—" She stopped, and her mouth trembled. She looked down at Rachel imploringly.

"Mrs. Dunham felt indisposed," said the maid, with a respectful smile at Geoffrey.

"Yes, indisposed," said Melissa, with her new eagerness. "And I wanted to do some more work, on Papa's book. I had a tray, though. Rachel brought it."

"Not too polite," said Geoffrey idly. "Our guests wondered."

Melissa forgot everything in a return of her old exasperation. "I shouldn't think they'd mind. After all, they don't know me, and I have nothing in common with them. I came only yesterday, and how could they be interested in me, or I in them? We are strangers."

Geoffrey, too, was exasperated, but for another reason. Then he could not help smiling.

"They are interested in you because you are my wife," he said, "and because you are their hostess, and because they expect to see you often over a period of many years." He watched Melissa's blank face for a moment, then went on: "You do not seem to like the prospect."

"No," said Melissa, "I do not." She considered the matter judicially, and again Geoffrey had to suppress a smile. "They are not the kind I should choose as friends. Except, perhaps, Mr. Littlefield. The poet."

"Ravel?" Irritated, Geoffrey sat up. "That limpid-eyed scoundrel and poseur? I am surprised at you, Melissa. I thought you had more discernment. The man's an actor, and a poor one at that. A parasite. And a poet!"

The old stern and censorious look flashed over Melissa's face. "There is nothing wrong with being a poet, sir."

"Well, perhaps not a real poet——"

"Such as Henry Wadsworth Longfellow?" suggested

Melissa with such passionate scorn that she stepped down from the stool, the hem of the velvet gown a glittering mass of pins. "Such banality, such syrupy triviality, such superficial sugariness—!"

"Edgar Allan Poe thinks highly of him," said Geoffrey, amused.

"Another so-called poet of no consequence! How Papa and I used to laugh at his pretensions! And you quote a man like that, on the subject of poetry!"

"You probably have a low opinion of Whitman, also?" said Geoffrey.

Melissa flushed with intense indignation. "That low poet-aster! That coarse and obscene brute!" She stood before Geoffrey, all cold violence. "Surely, sir, you do not call these men poets? I cannot believe it of you!"

"We should be happy to publish Mr. Longfellow," said Geoffrey. "He has promised us a book of ballads. Now, Melissa, whom do you consider a poet? I am really interested."

"Mr. St. John Edmonds! Papa thought his poetry in the best Greek tradition, excellent metres, sonorous rhythm——"

"Never heard of him."

"No! Because he is beyond the comprehension of fools and triflers!"

Rachel gasped softly. At the sound, Melissa jerked her head over her shoulder and encountered the girl's shocked eyes. Melissa swung her head back in Geoffrey's direction. "I didn't mean to be rude," she said, quickly, perplexed. "Rachel thinks I have said something rude. Oh, what nonsense! This having to watch everything one says, and not being honest."

"By all means, let us be honest, and let the sensibilities crash where they may," said Geoffrey, genially. "I hope you will be a little hypocritical this afternoon. We are all invited to look at Arabella's collection of the paintings she has done during the past six months. In her studio upstairs."

Melissa had never heard of Arabella's "art," and the idea was so novel to her, so astounding, that she gaped. "She paints—Arabella?" she exclaimed, incredulous.

Geoffrey stood up, and shrugged. "So she claims. But then, as a fool and a trifler, I am no judge. However, it seems she has a reputation, of a sort. You might be interested." He smiled, and the smile could be called nothing less than wickedly gleeful as he thought of Melissa's comments. Serve Arabella right. "On second thought, you need not be hypo-critical, my love. Artists always vehemently declare they want an honest opinion."

"I shall be very glad, indeed, to give it," said Melissa in a stately tone. But she appeared abstracted. She could not quite associate Arabella with paint and canvases. "You mean she really paints—things?" she asked, dubiously. "What things?"

"Oh, landscapes, flowers, the dogs," Geoffrey made a large gesture. "Anything that suddenly has a 'mood.'"

Melissa's pale gilt brows drew together in increasing perplexity.

"Like Courbet?" she asked. "Papa took me to New York, just after the war. There were two of Courbet's paintings on display. A colorful nude, painted while he was still in his Paris art school, and another. Very chiaroscuro. Papa remarked on the effect of great exaltation in his work; quite revolutionary, too. One caught the profound impression of an extraordinary mood. Arabella is of the same school, perhaps?"

"Oh, doubtless, the same school," said Geoffrey, with an evil smile.

"How very interesting!" cried Melissa, her former opinion of Arabella doing a handspring. "How little one knows of others! And how unjust one can be!"

Geoffrey knew that this naïve generosity should not be greeted with a burst of laughter, so he hurried towards the door, calling over his shoulder, in a curiously muffled voice, that the exhibition was to be at four o'clock.

Melissa mounted the stool again. She was quite excited. "I could never have imagined it! Would you have thought it, Rachel?"

Rachel tugged at the hem, and Melissa turned. "I have heard that Mrs. Shaw paints upstairs," she said.

"You have seen her work?"

"Oh, no, ma'am, none of the servants are permitted there."

"No? How silly. But then artists are very shy." The thought of shyness in connection with Arabella freshly amazed Melissa, and she felt remorse. "One never knows," she mumbled, with wide eyes. She forgot Geoffrey. She forgot her pain. Her single mind was fast rushing after Arabella, and there was nothing else. It was half-past two. She urged Rachel on with the gown.

But fast as Rachel worked, it was slightly after four o'clock before the gown's alterations had been completed. The hem covered the awful boots. Rachel had fastened the last velvet button when Geoffrey entered, bringing with him a string of golden-brown topazes, ear-rings to match, a bracelet of topazes and diamonds, and a ring. Melissa snatched them impatiently from Geoffrey's hands and put them on, herself, without glancing in the mirror. She was so excited over the prospect of the exhibition that some color had returned to her cheeks and lips, and she was less haggard.

Geoffrey made some admiring comment, but Melissa would have no wasting of time. She took Geoffrey's arm and strode beside him down the corridor to the stairs leading to the third floor. He said, trying to slow her down somewhat: "I have sent Andrew and Phoebe invitations for dinner on New Year's Eve, Melissa. As they are in mourning, they will not remain for the later festivities and the champagne, and you will be excused for the same reason."

"Oh, they won't come," said Melissa positively.

"On the contrary, they have already accepted."

This, Melissa could not believe, and her arguments were vehement and hectoring as she accompanied Geoffrey upstairs. He had to quiet her at the door of Arabella's studio.

The guests were already assembled in the great cold room, where the canvases on display were ranged on easels along the walls to catch the bleak north light. The large windows, undraped and bare, looked down from an immense height on the desolate white slopes below and on the distant woods and hills. Far to the west, over a range of hills, the sun was standing in a crimson lake of fire, and the sanguine reflection flooded into the room.

The guests slowly circled about, in utter silence, inspecting one painting after another. Arabella accompanied them, Arabella in lavender satin and lace and diamonds, her painted countenance beaming archly and modestly as she explained each canvas. The entrance of Geoffrey and his dreadful wife interrupted her, and for a moment her pale eyes were malignant. Startled at the sudden stopping of her flow of talk, the guests turned to find the cause, and they regarded Melissa with intent scrutiny, to see what changes the consummation of her odd marriage had made in her. Ravel Littlefield, in the background, looked at her piercingly and with a strange intensity.

But Melissa saw no one but Arabella. She left Geoffrey's side and almost ran to her sister-in-law. She exclaimed: "Oh, Arabella, I did not know you were an artist! This is truly wonderful!"

Arabella was taken aback. She stared up at Melissa's austere face, so unusually animated now. She gave the girl a twisted and remote smile. "So it seems that you do not know everything, my dear?" she said, in a gracious tone, with a jeeringly condescending insinuation. "I can hardly believe it." She brushed Melissa's cheek with her tinted lips, standing on tiptoe to accomplish this. "I trust you have recovered from your indisposition of last night?"

"I wasn't indisposed," said Melissa, confused. "I just did not care to remain any longer. So I went upstairs and began my work on Papa's books. I worked almost all night."

My God, thought Geoffrey. He dared not glance at any of his guests, who were suddenly and passionately interested. In fact, they began to congregate about Melissa. Ravel Littlefield's expression was one of the utmost enjoyment. He stood near Melissa, and his eyes danced, first on Geoffrey, and then on Geoffrey's wife. All the ladies' faces were a study, and Mrs. Littlefield worked her livid lips as if tasting a rare morsel.

Arabella said, kindly, her eyes dwelling with exaggerated fondness upon Melissa, who suddenly felt something peculiar in the atmosphere: "You must not work so hard, my dear Melissa. You worked all night, you say? Whenever did you sleep?"

Melissa paused. Slowly, her perplexed gaze wandered from one listening face to the other. Then she said, simply: "From about half-past two until half-past seven. The manuscript must be completed for summer publication and there is a lot to do."

Even kind little Mrs. Holland exchanged glances with Mrs. Eldridge, and the two ladies colored up to their eyebrows in a desperate effort to suppress their mirth. There was not a sound in the room; every man and woman stood as if turned into a statue. Every eye was directed upon Melissa.

Geoffrey stepped to the girl's side, lifted her hand and placed it upon his arm. "And now, my love," he said, "shall we join the Philistines and give our attention to the works of art so carefully arranged for our inspection?"

"The Philistines?" began Melissa. But Geoffrey was drawing her with him to the first painting. The others, giving one another eloquent and furtive looks, followed. Arabella smiled. She resembled a plump shark more than ever.

CHAPTER 34

GEOFFREY DUNHAM had quickly, if painfully, learned that the best defense against the voracious and male-volent interest which poor Melissa's ingenuous blunders aroused in the unsympathetic and conventional was a bland, blank face and an air of natural acceptance. It had taken him only twenty-four hours of squirming mortification, half-laughing and half-infuriated amusement, to learn this. Once let enemies, or even friends, learn that Melissa could dis-comfit him or appall him, and he might as well hide his wife and himself somewhere and let the world mercifully forget. Taking Melissa and everything she did and said with matter-of-factness, disarmed, or, at least, kept comment in careful whispers behind his back.

He did not miss the fact that his guests congregated closely around and about him and Melissa as they slowly toured the room, with Arabella condescending to explain to the heathen the finer nuances of her paintings. She had always suspected that Geoffrey considered her art a frivolous and unimportant pursuit, of value only for keeping her out of mischief, as he said, but she knew that he had enough politeness not to be too frank before her guests. As for Melissa, she dis-counted the girl entirely. Among her friends, Arabella felt strong and invulnerable. She only hoped that Melissa had enough sense not to blazon forth her ignorance. And then, she hoped she did not have that much sense. It would be another punishment for Geoffrey.

Arabella held a pointer in her hand and her voice was high and unctuous as she explained. Geoffrey and Melissa kept abreast of her, and Arabella's eye flickered hatingly on her beloved brown velvet, now altered to fit this hoyden and fool. Ravel Littlefield, flanked by his stepmother, stood be-hind Melissa. Arabella's dear friends, the gray and shadowy Bertrams, listened attentively and with concentrated frowns to her every word, and attested to their admiration with low murmurs. Mr. Holland, the artist, and his wife, tried

not to let their courteous faces reveal what they thought.
As they were kind people, each prayed silently that, for
Geoffrey's sake, Melissa would be temporarily stricken dumb.
Mr. Littlefield was bored; he wandered away to a window,
where he gloomily played with his keys and cursed the snow-
bound country. Mrs. Eldridge loved her fun, and quite maliciously hoped that Melissa would be candid in her harsh,
childlike way, and Mr. Eldridge, who knew that his wife
loved a joke, watched her anxiously. The ladies' skirts rustled
softly over the bare floor; the gentlemen's heels clacked
leisurely, Arabella's saccharine tones went on and on.

Ravel Littlefield stood where he could watch Melissa's face.
For a while, he saw only its drawn pallor and the rough
chapped spots high on her broad cheekbones. He saw her
pale dry lips and the bruised circles under her eyes, and
knew that she had been crying. She walked jerkily and
nervously, sometimes stumbling on the hem of the velvet
dress. Ravel did not understand this tenderness he felt whenever he glanced at the girl's rigid profile, this aching desire
to touch her hand and comfort her. She seemed entirely unconscious of everyone in the room; her whole attention, in
her usual fanatical and intense way, was given to the paintings. Poor, poor child, thought Ravel. She hasn't the slightest
sense of humor; everything has "meaning" for her, and God
help anything which she believes violates the standard she
has set up for herself and for others. What touching egotism,
what appalling humorlessness, the poor darling! And then
he looked at her half-exposed breast, which she had forgotten, and saw how the stark northern glare brought out its
marble contours and pearly high-lights.

Arabella had no sense of design, or of proportion, or of
the subtleties of composition and color. She had a slight
talent, but this was overwhelmed by pretentiousness. Had
she confined herself to the pretty and obvious, she might
have pleased the unfastidious. But she did not confine herself.
If she painted a still-life of fruit and flowers, she must give
it a "mood." She must suggest something eerie, significant
or fantastic, so catching the light on a yellow banana, for
instance, that it became a glaring and bilious triangle. A
drooping rose, and its bud, did not remain a rose and a bud;
they must imply melancholy and tragedy. In principle, this
was intriguing and thought-arresting. In Arabella's hands,
it became ludicrous. Moreover, her lack of real skill which,
under prettiness, might have been hidden, became embar-
rassingly clear, as did her shallowness and affection. As she

had no depth of character, her "moods" were banal and full of cheap artifice.

Melissa moved along slowly with Geoffrey, and now no one spoke, not even the murmurous Bertrams. Everyone listened for the queer Melissa's comments, if she was to make any. For it was obvious that she was seething with potential comments. Her face had become more rigid and austere than ever, but, oddly, its usual expression of closed and silent sternness had given way to a kind of fierce, pent animation as she stared with concentration at every painting. This animation could be felt rather than seen, and so violent was it, in spite of her silence, that it attracted the attention even of Mr. Littlefield, who came back to the group and hovered on the edge of it like a quick and interested beetle.

Moment by moment, Melissa's furious agitation increased. Now it was becoming increasingly apparent in her high jerky steps, the swift sweep of her pale blue eyes over the canvases, the tenseness of her long white throat. She would bend her head and stare strongly at a painting, then throw it back stiffly. There was a kind of excitement about her now. Arabella's attention was finally caught by this, and her voice died away. Like the others, she fell into a trance of waiting for Melissa to speak, for it was evident that the poor girl would explode at any moment. She had snatched away her hand from Geoffrey's arm, and in some manner had been able to shut herself in a circle of isolation.

No one else knew it, but Melissa felt as if she were accompanied by her father. From the first moment her eye had fallen upon the pictures, she had heard his soft, regretful, yet satirical voice, and so profound was the impression that she really believed he was there with her, inspecting Arabella's work. She heard him say: "But what horrors, my dear Melissa! What outrageous presumption in this woman, that she dare take up the sacred palette and disfigure innocent canvases! I implore you to look at that leprous vase containing three scabrous gilt bulrushes. What is this shameless woman trying to say? But she really says nothing, expresses nothing but her conceit, her ridiculous absence of knowledge of the simplest fundamentals. Mood? She has nothing to express but petty vanity and foolish sentimentality. Why, she cannot even draw! Does it not amuse you?"

Really horrible, thought Melissa, outraged at Arabella's presumption. What dreadful coloring, what out-of-scale drawing! Papa, are these people serious, who are looking at these things in respectful silence or murmuring politely? How can they be such liars, such fools? They are not ignorant, surely. Why, they are really laughing at her! Yes, they are laughing.

It was at this moment that Melissa snatched her hand from Geoffrey's arm, but the action was purely reflex, for with her knowledge of the hidden and malicious amusement of the others she felt a wild hard thrill of pain which she did not recognize as a virgin and novel attack of compassion. Her anger boiled up against them, and against her father, whose gentle laughter she felt keenly. She was sure she could see his long scholar's face, the glint of his hooded blue eyes, his languid and pedantic smile, and the graceful movement of his delicate hand as if he were imploring that these monstrous paintings be removed at once from his sensitive and affronted sight.

Melissa's blind fury mounted, and she felt a stamp of hatred on her heart, as agonizing and hot as a brand. Suddenly, she turned her back on the paintings and faced the others in a commotion and swirl of brown velvet skirts and crackling petticoats. Her eyes sparkled with intemperate rage and she was very white. Violence blew about her, so that her hair seemed to flow back from the harsh angles of her face. Her breath was disordered and vehement. She faced them all, and, among them, she faced her father, in resolute indignation.

Bewitched, the guests and Geoffrey and Arabella stared back at her.

She made an abrupt and unrestrained gesture, and cried out: "I know what you are all thinking! You are thinking that these paintings are frightful! You know that they have neither design, composition nor artistic meaning! You know what they are, and yet all you can do is to smile in yourselves and ridicule these things by exchanging silent glances with one another; and then you lie, and lie, and induce this poor woman to believe that you think she is a real artist! Oh, what liars you are, what hypocrites!"

Her gestures became wilder, more distracted and uncouth, in the faces of the others, who looked at her in utter stupefaction. They could not stir nor speak. No one glanced at Arabella. Geoffrey, paralyzed, gaped at his wife disbelievingly, forgetting for once to be bland and natural. The Bertrams became grayer with pallid affront and astonishment; Mrs. Littlefield opened her leaden mouth with the faintest of gasps; the Hollands appeared greatly distressed; the Eldridges, like Geoffrey, merely gaped. But Ravel, after the first incredulity, began to smile with a kind of sardonic tenderness and moved a step closer to the embattled Melissa, and there was about him a protective alertness. Mr. Littlefield, after the stupefaction of everyone had lasted for several moments, gave a queer little grunt, whether of entertainment or disgust no one knew.

Melissa's normally colorless face was suddenly deluged with hot fire. Recklessly, scornfully, she exclaimed, with another of her crude and distraught gestures:

"I know how you are secretly mocking this poor woman! And you must have been mocking her for years. You pretend to be genteel and educated people. Yet not once, I am sure, have you tried to point out to her her errors, to correct her faults. No, you were content to be amused by them, to laugh behind her back, to show your superiority. But there is one thing you have forgotten," and she paused to glare at them bitterly, "you have forgotten that she really has the urge to paint, to create, and that in itself is a sacred thing, no matter how feeble. Before that, if you had hearts, you would have been respectful and sober."

She swung upon the grimacing Arabella, who started back from her with an expression of extreme loathing and hatred which the aroused girl did not see. "Pay no heed to them, Arabella!" cried the rampant young woman. "You have very little, but it is more than any of these pretentious fools have, and you should be proud."

Arabella drew in her painted lips with a sucking sound and her eyes slid over the faces of her friends. Ravel was grinning, but he was regarding Melissa as if he were both hugely entertained and inordinately touched. The Bertrams' stare had shifted to their clasped hands; the Hollands were slowly drifting away; the Eldridges had begun to smile; Mrs. Littlefield, catching Arabella's eye, moved towards her friend and stood by her side. Geoffrey said nothing; he appeared abstracted. And then Mr. Littlefield began to chuckle uncontrollably.

Geoffrey spoke for the first time, and sternly and loudly: "Melissa, you will please go to your room."

Melissa, even in her aroused state, heard him, and she literally jumped. She turned upon him: "Geoffrey! You must tell them I am right! You must defend your sister against their ridicule; you owe it to her!"

Geoffrey visibly controlled himself. "I said, Melissa, you are to go to your room."

Melissa abruptly became very still and rigid. She regarded him with her customary searching and zealous intensity, as if doubting what she had heard and wanting only to be certain she had comprehended.

Then her face changed, became young and bewildered again. "I have said something wrong, Geoffrey?" she asked. "I do not understand."

Geoffrey did not answer. He went to the door, opened it, held it open significantly. Melissa flashed a dazed and questioning glance at the others. All looked studiously away from her, except Ravel, who smiled half sadly, half humorously, into her eyes. In the very act of turning away, she was caught by this smile, and studied it with open and singular fascination. She took a step towards him, as a child moves towards a comforting hand. Then her eyes filled with tears, she caught up her skirts, and, with bent head, she hurried out of the studio. She did not glance at Geoffrey as she passed him, but for a moment or two he watched her flight, until she disappeared down the stairway in the gathering winter dusk.

The bedroom was empty but Rachel had lit two delicate candelabra on the mantel-piece, and the fire crackled warmly in the increasing twilight. Melisa flung herself in a chair. Her breath came fast and hot; something hurt her chest. She put her hand to it. Her eyes were blinded with mist. She wiped it away with the back of her other hand.

In some incomprehensible way, she had affronted and outraged Geoffrey. What had he said to her yesterday? That she must not shame the memory of her father. Now her mind became confused, her thoughts riotous and chaotic. She could not think. She could only feel her bemused and frantic pain and a sudden and unusual loneliness. She did not recognize it as loneliness, for she had never been really lonely before. But there was such an emptiness and darkness in her now, and a new suffering, which was not grief as she had known it. However, when she remembered her outburst in the studio, she exclaimed aloud: "But I was right! Why, then, did they look so and why did Geoffrey tell me to leave?" Her voice dropped mournfully: "Poor Arabella. But I am here now, and they shall not mock you, not ever again."

She felt, in her pity, that she loved Arabella, and Arabella, incongruously, began to take on, in the poor girl's thoughts, the character and the defenselessness of Phoebe. Because there were such ardent depths in her cold nature, Melissa lacked much insight and judgment, and was totally unable to compromise or to consider.

"Oh, they shall not hurt you again, the gross and insensitive creatures!" said Melissa, her loneliness swallowed up in her indignation. She sat upright in her chair and beat her velvet knees with her clenched fists. But the pain in her heart did not diminish, and she would not think of her father.

She wanted to talk to somebody; she must talk to somebody! She jumped to her feet and ran to the bell-rope. Rachel would come, and listen comprehendingly to the story. There was a desperate hunger in Melissa now, a deepening of her pain. But her hand had only reached for the rope when the door opened and Geoffrey entered.

Melissa's hand fell to her side. Now, as she saw him, as he closed the door slowly behind him and stood against it, looking at her silently, the nameless pain suddenly swelled up in her like a conflagration. Almost without volition, she took several rapid steps towards him, and then stopped, halted by his grim silence, by the hard and piercing expression of his small gray eyes. Her hands drew together convulsively, and her fingers intertwined with an aching tightness.

Geoffrey, still without speaking, went to the fireside, took a taper and held it to the tip of his cheroot. "May I?" he asked coldly.

"Why not?" replied Melissa faintly, a shadow of her old confusion passing over her pain.

Geoffrey lit his cheroot, puffed at it a few moments, while Melissa continued to watch him from her corner. He said: "May I sit down?"

"Why, certainly," she murmured. "Why should you ask, in your own house?"

Geoffrey sat down in a chair facing her. He seemed about to speak in comment on her last remark, then apparently decided it was no use and that the ensuing argument would only tend to confuse him, himself. But his expression became a little less grim, though his eyes remained cold.

"Melissa," he said, in a conversational tone, "I am having a hard time trying to decide whether you are extraordinarily stupid or extraordinarily malignant. Perhaps you can tell me. I think I should prefer to hear that you are extraordinarily stupid. It is less dangerous, I think."

Melissa was astounded. She came from the corner with her old and stately majesty, so natural and unassumed. Then she stood by the fireplace opposite her hubsand and looked down at him in utter bafflement. "Malignant?" she said. Then she was single-heartedly outraged. "I would not waste

my time being malignant! I have always thought malignancy
the height of stupidity!"

"You have a point there," said Geoffrey, after a moment's
study of her, and with a lessening of his inflexible hardness.

"Besides, why should you consider me malignant?" cried
Melissa. "What right have you to entertain this libelous
opinion?"

Geoffrey sighed, as if now everything had become too
confused and hopeless. Melissa was staring down at him,
her pale strong face so powerfully innocent and uncorrupted,
so carved by the firelight into planes of marble and fire,
that Geoffrey was fascinated and momentarily forgot what
he had been saying.

Now Melissa's voice became peremptory: "I think you
should explain yourself, sir."

"That is my intention, Melissa. That is why I came. Would
you mind sitting down? It is a strain on the back of my
neck, looking up at you."

Stiffly, Melissa sat down in the "lady's" chair opposite
him and fixed her eyes upon him formidably. Yet those eyes
were not as assured and arrogant as usual. The long bronze
lashes blinked vulnerably.

"I want you," said Geoffrey slowly, deciding he would
proceed better if he looked only at his cheroot, "to consider
your appalling and incredible outburst up in Arabella's
studio a short time ago. I know you have lived a monkish
life, my dear, with practically no concept of the world outside your father's house and your father's study, but I have
always believed that a woman of good blood and good
family was instinctively a lady, no matter how immured a
life she might have led. I thought, in short, that there were
certain instinctive social manners. It seems I was wrong,
doesn't it?"

Melissa considered this with the fanatical closeness she
gave to everything offered for her consideration. Then she
said: "I don't think there are 'instinctive' manners or customs.
They are only products of an artificial, if necessary, civilized
order. I use the word 'necessary' advisedly, and only tentatively. In a wild and allegedly barbaric society, our customs would seem absurd and we should be faced by another
order of behavior which we, in turn, might find equally
ridiculous. Our concept is built up on unnatural acceptances—"

"Yes, yes, I quite understand," said Geoffrey hastily. He
rubbed his forehead, as if tired.

"For instance," went on Melissa, warming, "infanticide is

regarded as intolerable and evil in modern society. Why?
Because we have not felt the pressure of economic deter-
minism and necessity. You would not consider the Romans a
barbaric or uncivilized people, though Papa often thought
they were. Yet there came a time of such huge and onerous
taxes, such pressure of population, such burdens upon individual families, that infanticide was not only countenanced,
it was even approved, under certain circumstances."

She paused, and waited for Geoffrey's comment. But he
was utterly silent. Melissa added: "But what has infanticide
got to do with me?"

"I was not aware we were talking about that," said Geoffrey, wearily. "You brought up the subject, which seems to
me an extraordinary one—under our circumstances." He
waited for Melissa's reaction to this. None came. She continued to regard him expectantly.

Suddenly, Geoffrey wanted to burst out laughing. But he
controlled himself with such an effort that his face swelled
and turned crimson. Melissa thought he had become enraged,
and she said quickly: "How am I stupid, or malignant? In
what way was my 'outburst' either 'appalling' or 'incredible'?"
She became excited. "Because I recognized, and condemned,
the lying hypocrisy of your guests, who were ridiculing your
poor sister secretly, and not really trying to help her at all?
Is it wrong to attack such things? I call it dishonest not to!"

"Melissa," said Geoffrey, "have you ever heard of politeness, of good manners?"

" 'Good manners'!" she repeated, scornfully, her whole face
blazing. "What have good manners got to do with the matter?"

"Well, then," said Geoffrey, feeling he had been somehow
entangled with masses of slippery wet rope, "what do you
call good manners?"

"Being honest, unpretentious, just, and upright."

"I notice you do not include kindness in your list."

"Kindness?" Melissa frowned. "Do you consider it kindness
for them to so deceive your sister that she believes she is
a great artist, and thus continues to provide them with food
for mirth?" She paused. Geoffrey, more and more baffled, did
not answer. Melissa's face changed. "How was I unkind?"

"You were unkind to Arabella, strange as it may seem,"
said Geoffrey, beginning to wonder just what they were talking about now.

This amazed Melissa, and she sprang to her feet with her
old vehemence. "You are wrong! I was only protecting her
against those people—and my father!"

The last words came from her on a surge of emotion, and so stupefied the girl herself that she flung up the back of her hand against her lips and looked over it at Geoffrey with dilated eyes.

Geoffrey, in an electric silence, sat upright in his chair. All his grimness and severity had gone. He regarded Melissa with her own strong attention. He said, very softly: "Your father, my love?"

Melissa dropped her hand. She had become very pale, and her eyes drooped with exhaustion. She fumbled for her chair, and sat down. She rested her elbows on her knees, and, folding her arms, looked at the fire. She whispered: "I ought not to have said that. I don't know why I did. But somehow, when I was in that studio, it seemed to me that Papa was there, too, among those people, and laughing at Arabella with them. It—it became intolerable to me. I was so dreadfully sorry for Arabella then, and enraged at—at everybody. I think I even hated——"

She rubbed both hands strongly and fiercely over her face, then averted her head. "You are right," she murmured. "I ought not to have felt that way towards those people, and especially not towards Papa. I think that, under the circumstances, it is well he is dead. He would despise me, and he would be so hurt."

Geoffrey stood up and went to her. He put his hand very gently on the top of her head, and she started. Then she stared up at him. She could not understand the expression in his eyes, the moved look on his face.

"My darling," he said, "you were quite right. It is I who am wrong."

She could not speak. Her mouth shook. She sat very still, as if she hoped he would not take his hand from her head. When he did so, she sighed heavily.

"The trouble," Geoffrey went on, "is that we have a false conception of kindness. We forget that integrity might be more important. We have come such a long way from our honest childhood that we have distorted true values. We take offense when an honorable man expresses, without malice, his uncorrupted opinion."

"I did not mean to offend Arabella," said Melissa. "And I cannot believe she thinks so. I meant only to protect her."

She pushed herself to her feet. "I think I shall go at once and explain to her."

"Melissa," began Geoffrey, but before he could say anything more Melissa had run from the room.

CHAPTER 35

ELLIS, ARABELLA'S MAID, was putting cold wet cloths to her mistress' inflamed eyes and expressing her unctuous sympathy, while Arabella moaned in the most pathetic way and relaxed weakly on her chaise-longue.

"It is certainly a wicked shame, Mrs. Shaw, ma'am," said Ellis, wringing out another cloth, which was perfumed with eau de cologne, "to humiliate you so, and embarrass you before those elegant people. But rest assured, ma'am, none condemns you. I know you have their sympathy. But how intolerable, ma'am! How atrocious! How undeserved!"

Arabella sobbed, but carefully lifted a curl from under the cloth. "O Ellis, it is too frightful! That I should be humiliated in the very house where I was born, and under such circumstances, and by such a creature! My poor brother. Save your sympathy, Ellis, do, pray. Save it for Mr. Dunham, who needs it. Who am I but a glorified housekeeper, the humble gatherer of crumbs, the unwanted, the unloved, the unthanked? But Mr. Dunham, Ellis, is a great publisher, a man of renown, influential and revered. It is he who will bear the burden, and all the laughter." She pushed aside the cloth, and her face twisted viciously. "Yes, yes, it is he who is suffering, not I. I weep for him."

Ellis clasped her hands tragically, and rolled up her eyes. "Mr. Dunham! It is unthinkable. It is not my place, ma'am, to criticize Mr. Dunham's choice, nor to express my poor opinion. That would be presumptuous. But, ma'am," and the sly-lipped maid thrust her clasped hands vehemently against her breast, "I am a human being. I have my thoughts! No one can take that right away from me!"

It was at this affecting moment that Melissa burst into the room, hair quite shaggy, her velvet skirts boiling with haste. She saw Arabella on the chaise-longue and rushed towards her, exclaiming: "Mrs. Shaw! Arabella! I must talk to you. I must explain——"

She became conscious of Ellis then, and stopped. Her light

and penetrating eyes, which at times could see so clearly, saw now, in a sudden flash of insight, especially when the maid smirked and ducked her head respectfully. Melissa was seized by a strong dislike for the woman. She said coldly: "I should like to be alone with your mistress, please."

Arabella retired behind her cloth, and groaned. She said, feebly: "Do not leave me, Ellis, do not leave me alone! I command it."

The simple Melissa was exasperated. "But why, Arabella? I wish to talk to you privately." She paused, feeling for words. "I—I think the matter is—delicate. At any rate," she continued, in a clear voice, "it's none of this woman's business!"

Ellis, moving meekly, wrung out another cold cloth, removed the other, and revealed Arabella's blotched and haggard face, the eyes shut, the mouth drooping with an expression of mortal suffering. Melissa stared, then she said impatiently: "Oh, Arabella! What a fuss you are making. You surely don't care what those people think, do you? You surely don't think I meant to insult you, or anything?" Her voice was incredulous.

Arabella moaned, and disappeared behind the fresh cloth. "Oh, ma'am, do not give way, I implore you," said Ellis, and scurried for the smelling-salts. She applied them under the cloth, and again the moans issued forth. Ellis dropped to her knees and began to chaff her mistress' hands, her head bent in anxious distress. Melissa watched these proceedings, quite disconcerted, but with increasing impatience.

"It's nonsense," she said, but with uncertainty. The room reeked of eau de cologne; the fire roared hotly; the candles flickered. "There's no air in here," suggested Melissa, glancing hopefully at the drawn curtains. "You'd feel better——"

"Oh, no, ma'am," said Ellis, glancing over her shoulder at Melissa. "Mrs. Shaw is so sensitive that the slightest cool breeze disturbs her. And her poor hands are so cold and trembling."

"But why?" demanded Melissa. "The whole thing isn't the least bit important, and I can't see why you are taking on so, Arabella. At the worst, your guests will think—" she groped for the proper expression—"they will think I have no manners. Yes, that's it: they'll think I have no manners. I'm not polite. Besides," she continued, "they know I told them the truth, and that ought to shame them and make them hold their tongues."

This logical solution quite pleased the girl, and she smiled tentatively at the cloths, which again were agitated with moans, much feebler now.

"What's the matter with her?" Melissa demanded of Ellis. "It can't be that she's really upset about what I said about her—her paintings. That's so ridiculous. Does she often have the vapors like this?" she added, intrigued but austerely disapproving. Then again, in Melissa's thought, Arabella became the defenseless Phoebe, who had so much sensibility and must be protected, and with impulsive sincerity she cried: "Oh, I'm so sorry! I never meant to hurt you, truly, Arabella."

She approached closer to Arabella. "Do put that silly cloth aside, Arabella, and try to answer me."

The cloth did not move, but from behind it came a wan and sepulchral murmur: "My poor brother, my dear brother."

"You want Geoffrey?" asked Melissa, eager to be of assistance. "Shall I go for him?"

At this formidable sugestion, Arabella let the cloth drop and again showed her face. Her eyes, in spite of their swollen lids, fixed themselves upon Melissa with such virulence that she stepped back instinctively, quite agape with astonishment and fully expecting some kind of violence from her sister-in-law. She could not believe it when Arabella's voice came, quivering, blurred, shaking with compassionate tears:

"My poor brother. How is he going to endure all this? What mortification for him, what distress of mind!" Her voice trembled with love and pity.

Melissa stared. "What do you mean?" She stopped, to give all her attention to Arabella's words, and she was nonplussed for several moments. Then her face cleared. "You mean about—up in your studio, Arabella. Oh don't trouble yourself about that. Geoffrey quite understood. I've just had a talk with him, so you have no need to worry."

There was a sudden and profound silence in the room. Arabella now regarded Melissa with unfeigned indignation, open rage and balefulness. Ellis sighed, and collapsed on a stool near her mistress' feet.

"I mean," said Melissa, stepping back another pace, "that Geoffrey is not very much concerned about your guests' opinions. I don't think he regards those people very highly, anyway."

There was another silence. Then, with her glinting and evil eyes not looking away from Melissa, Arabella said: "Ellis, please bring—Mrs. Dunham—a chair. I think we must have a talk."

"What about?" demanded Melissa. "There is nothing to talk about. I only wanted you to know I was sorry if I hurt your feelings, Arabella, and that you need not fear that Geoffrey is angry." But she sat down on the chair, which was now bumping against the back of her knees. She flashed Ellis an irritable look, then gave her attention to Arabella.

Arabella lay back against her cushions. She had assumed a tragic expression, and closed her eyes, as if even speaking in a half-whisper exhausted her:

"You misunderstand me, Melissa. Because, I fear, you are incapable of comprehension. It is not your fault, however. I pity, not blame." She picked her words cautiously, remembering Geoffrey. Again her voice quivered, and she composed her mouth to express compassion for Melissa herself. "I have known you a long time, my dear Melissa. I remember you as a baby, a child, a young girl, and now— as a woman no longer young. I understand everything. I know the life you led with your father. Your mother and I often discussed it, she with tears and suffering."

Melissa turned scarlet. She started to rise from her chair, then reseated herself. Her color left her as swiftly as it had come. In stifled tones, she said: "I do not believe my mother discussed me with you. She was incapable of that." She had a swift vision of her mother, and the novel pain she had felt that afternoon stabbed her fiercely; she felt it with bemused astonishment, wondering what it was. "My mother," she continued, and now her own voice shook, "would never discuss family matters with outsiders. It was her code, and she instilled that very strongly in all of us." She thought, vaguely: I did not say that it was a lie. That would have been impolite and unmannerly, even if she is not speaking the truth. I must tell Geoffrey that I did not call his sister a liar. He will be pleased.

Arabella gave no indication that she had heard. She lay back against her cushions in an attitude of gentle agony and misery.

"What do you—think—my mother told you about Papa and me?" asked Melissa, the palms of her hands sweating.

Arabella moved her head in a weak gesture of negation, her eyes still closed: "Confidences are sacred with me. I cannot betray them. I can only say, Melissa, that I know all about you and am wrung with pity, so that I do not blame you. How could you learn civilized and constrained deportment, or genteel manners, shut away in that house, in your father's study, among all those dusty books? Who was there to teach you delicacy of speech, modesty, elegance, restraint, the gestures and voice and speech of a true lady? No one. You lived immured, shut away from the world and its realities, its cultivated breeding, its savoir faire. You know nothing of the ways of urbane politeness, of fashion, of refined custom. That is my world, and the world of my brother, whom you have married."

Her last words fell into an abyss of silence, as she had intended. She lifted her lids just sufficiently to observe Melissa.

Then Melissa said, almost inaudibly: "I do not think that world you speak of is so important to Geoffrey. If it were, he would not have married me."

Arabella did not speak for several moments. She was on dangerous ground now, and she dared not say openly what she wished to say. This odious, this dreadful monster was quite capable of running, tattling, to Geoffrey, if she, Arabella, said anything too outright.

So Arabella sighed deeply and eloquently, and said nothing.

Melissa waited. "You think that Geoffrey is shamed by me because I do not know the customs of his world?" she asked, with great earnestness. "You think I am embarrassing to him, and humiliate him, with my lack of knowledge of what is politely done or not done? You think he ought not to have married me?"

Arabella sighed again, louder than ever. She quivered: "It is you who have said that, Melissa, not I. I beg you to remember that. Ellis, you have heard Mrs. Dunham say that, and not I? You could bear witness?"

Ellis nodded, sucking in her mouth meekly. Melissa gave an impatient gesture. "But, whether you said it or not, Arabella, you mean that?"

Arabella put her hand to her eyes, then let her head drop farther back on her pillows. "I refuse to answer that question, Melissa. You have no right to press me. And you have no right to make unauthorized assertions."

Melissa got up very slowly, as if enormously tired, and went to the shrouded window. She put up her hand as if to draw the curtains; then, remembering Ellis' protest, she let her hand drop. But she stood and stared heavily at the lavishly patterned draperies. She said, in a low tone: "Geoffrey has known me since I was a child. I am nothing new to him. He knew my studious life with my father. There was nothing hidden from him. He knew it all when he agreed to marry me!"

"Agreed to marry you?" Arabella forgot her stricken languors, and sat upright. She looked, startled, at Ellis, who smirked. Arabella's face changed. She began to smile excitedly. "My brother 'agreed' to marry you, Melissa? Whatever do you mean?"

Not turning, and speaking lifelessly, Melissa said: "I asked him to marry me, so I could help Phoebe and Andrew, with his money."

"Ah," murmured Arabella. She sank back against her cushions. She could not believe her luck. She genuinely trembled now with passionate hatred and delight. Ellis clapped her hands silently, and mistress and maid exchanged a gleaming look.

Melisa slowly came back to her chair. But she did not sit down. She stood behind the chair and held it with straining fingers.

"You see," she said simply, "we did not wish to borrow the money from Geoffrey. So I said I would marry him, if he wished."

Arabella was too astute a woman, and she had known of Geoffrey's infatuation too long, to let herself be deceived. She saw it all very clearly. However, she forced herself to burst into very realistic tears, and flung her hands over her streaming eyes. Ellis jumped up, and bent over her mistress, wringing her own hands.

"Oh, my poor brother!" cried Arabella. "My gallant, my noble, my self-sacrificing brother! I canot endure it! I have suffered too much, this is more than I can bear!" She sobbed aloud. "He had such a friendship for Charles Upjohn! He would have done anything for his children, in Charles' name! My poor brother!"

"You mean to say he married me for Papa's sake?" whispered Melissa. Even her lips were white now.

Arabella's sobs became more anguished. She writhed on her cushions. Then she almost screamed: "I did not say that! It was you who said that, you who ought to know!"

Melissa put her hand to her forehead. There was something which Geoffrey had said to her once, after her father had died. She tried to remember. But just when it seemed that she would remember, that the very words were shaping themselves in her brain, her father's face, vivid and smiling, floated before her and shut them away. Yet, if she could remember, this confusion and diffused agony would leave her, she knew.

"I don't know anything," She stammered, in answer to Arabella. "I—am—afraid—I—don't—know—anything, not anything at all."

Then she turned and went silently out of the room.

"Be sure the door is shut, Ellis," whispered Arabella, suddenly ceasing to weep. "But first look to see if that awful creature is listening, outside."

Ellis tiptoed to the door, and suddenly opened it. But the hall outside was empty. She caught a glimpse of Melissa disappearing into her own room. She closed the door.

"Ellis," said Arabella exultantly, "I have been trying to discover how we could get rid of that jape, that hobbledehoy, that hideous female. And now I think I have found the way!"

CHAPTER 36

MELISSA sat alone at one of the windows of her bedroom in the darkening night. The cold hard moon, a thin glittering sphere, rolled in a black sky over the marble silence below. Bare trees stood in tangled webs of black shadow on the stark whiteness of the slopes, that undulated in slow and rigid dunes down to the valley. The hills were ghostly shadows against the sky; at a long distance a few twinkling lights like fallen stars testified to far neighbors.

The cold, the stillness, the silence, seemed, to Melissa, to be part of her own mind and desolate emotions. The house about her, warm, filled with soft lights and fires, did not exist for her now; she was not in it, nor part of it, nor did she feel it about her. She was part of the desolation outside, and alone in it, and utterly lost, as if she were dead and completely exiled from life and voices and warm faces. The moon shone on the angles and planes of her quiet face, in the dark pits of her eyes, on the still carved outlines of her lips.

The grief she had known for her father, devastating as it was, had been a wild hot grief, full of despair, denial and bitterness. But this frozen agony in her heart was infinitely more terrible, for it was without a name. It was simply there. One thought kept recurring to her: I must go away, and at once. But immediately the frozen agony tightened in her chest, became so unendurable that her physical strength fell away and left her progressively weaker and more broken. In all her life she had no memory of such pain before, it was beyond comprehension or comparison, and of such dimensions that she could not even begin to discover its identity or meaning.

There were soft sounds in the house as the guests prepared for dinner, but Melissa did not hear them. Namelessly bereaved and solitary, she could only sit by the window, like one who mourns for life itself. The firelight flickered behind her; the candles wavered gently. She neither saw nor felt them. Over and over, she relived the scene with Arabella, and Arabella's voice came back to her in sick echoes.

Finally, one thought took possession of her: Papa wanted me to marry Geoffrey. Poor Papa. He thought he would provide for all of us in that way. Papa would not want me to go away. Yet I must do so. But first, I must be certain that neither Phoebe nor Andrew needs me. Then, when this is all settled, I shall remove myself—from Geoffrey's life. For it is perfectly evident that I am shaming and disgracing him, and that I am a contemptible burden hung about his neck. Had he not known that Papa wished it, he would never have married me; he married me for Papa's sake, and out of pity, and because there was nothing else he could do to help all of us.

She had not cried before, but now she uttered a dry sob of pure anguish, and pressed her fingers to her eyes. But there were no tears at all, only this devouring and bottomless pain. She thought: In the meantime, I can spare him as much as possible, and shame him as little as I can. I will do my best, until it is time for me to go away, to let him forget all the Upjohns and relieve him of his burden.

She heard a knock on her door, and mechanically called: "Come in." Her voice hurt her throat. Rachel entered and, though she was surprised to see her mistress sitting by the window in such lonely desolation, she said cheerfully: "Good evening, Mrs. Dunham. I have just finished your new dinner dress. It is time to prepare for dinner. Mr. Dunham wishes me to remind you that everyone is going on a moonlight sleighing party, later."

Melissa rose silently. She glanced at the gown, formerly Arabella's, on the bed. The hurt in her throat was like a knife. She said: "Rachel, I cannot go down to dinner. I should embarrass him—Mr. Dunham—again. If you do not mind, you may bring me a tray; though if it is a trouble, please do not bother. And I cannot go on that party. I am afraid I am very tired."

Rachel, anxious now, came closer to the girl, and her eyes flickered swiftly over her mistress' face. She murmured: "I will bring you a tray, ma'am. You do look very tired indeed. And I will take your excuses to Mr. Dunham. Would you like to go to bed now?"

But Melissa was gazing at her with that directness which so many found disconcerting. "Rachel, am I so frightful, so impossible? What do you truly think of me, Rachel?"

"I think you are a great lady, Mrs. Dunham," answered Rachel, wrenched with compassion, "a truly great lady."

Melissa sighed. "That is very kind of you, Rachel, but I am afraid it is not true. I am beginning to see that I have no right in this house at all."

Rachel risked boldness. "Mr. Dunham does not think so, ma'am."

"Oh, he does! He married me because my father wished him to help me, and my brother and sister."

"He told you so, Mrs. Dunham?"

The naïve Melissa replied: "No, but I learned this today from—from someone who knows."

Rachel's indignant thoughts rushed accurately to Arabella. She came even closer to Melissa. "I do not know who could have told you this, ma'am, but it is not true. You are a great lady, and have elegance and presence. Perhaps—perhaps you do not know all the ways of the grand world, but they are easy to learn."

Melissa shook her head. "I fear not. Well, it does not matter. I have work to do, and that is the only thing that is important. I am afraid that I forgot that during the past hour or two. Yes," she continued, with a faint brightening of her white face, "work is most important! My father always told me that. He said it was of more worth than any other human aspiration or emotion, that it was the cure for any sickness."

Rachel dubiously considered this. Work was necessary, yes, but to regard it as the greatest human good seemed to her a very outrageous folly. Work in itself was a pointless and onerous thing. If it brought esteem, a respectable savings account, independence, then it had tangible value and should be endured with honest grace. But to substitute work, voluntarily, for more important matters revolted Rachel.

"I think Mr. Dunham would prefer you to go down to dinner, and then to the sleighing party, ma'am," she offered.

Melissa shook her head again. "No, Rachel. You see, the sooner I complete my father's manuscripts the sooner I shall have money, and then Mr. Dunham will be free of me!"

A trick of the moonlight, and her own emotions, gave her face a sudden desperate animation and mobility. Rachel saw it was useless for her to argue with her mistress when in this condition. So she merely drew the curtains, and allowed herself a moment or two of fierce anger against Arabella. The poor, poor lady! If she, Rachel, had ever seen a woman closer to hysteria than this young woman, she could not remember the occasion. Her one desire now was to pacify and soothe Melissa, and opposition, she saw, was not the way.

She lit a few lamps, and the room filled with gentle light. Rachel induced Melissa to remove her gown, which was crumpled now, and to replace it with a green velvet peignoir recruited from Arabella's wardrobe. Her narrow mind focussed intently on the work she must do, Melissa docilely allowed herself to be seated and to eat the food which Rachel later brought her. Rachel also conveyed Geoffrey's regrets. At this, Melissa lifted her head.

"That was all, Rachel?" asked Melissa faintly.

Rachel hesitated. Geoffrey had received the news coolly as he sat with his guests in the "Yellow Room." It was evident that the news annoyed him and that he considered the message from Melissa as the capricious behavior of a child. He, too, had asked: "That was all?"

Rachel had falteringly enlarged on Melissa's indisposition, which Geoffrey did not believe in the least, and his displeasure increased. But he had dismissed the girl and turned to his guests to continue the conversation she had interrupted.

"I believe Mr. Dunham really wished you to join him at dinner and go on the party, ma'am."

"Oh, no!" said Melissa, vehemently. "It will please him better if I stay out of sight. At least, until I know what to do and say, even if it is all lies. But," she added, looking up with her long grave glance at Rachel, "I think I should be glad even to tell lies, if it saves him embarrassment."

Rachel found this so piteous that she hurried away and pretended to be deeply engaged in something at a distant chest. She herself was full of seething emotion, blind anger, and pity. She remembered the titters among the servants all that day. It was an open secret among them all that Mr.

Dunham had slept alone on his wedding night, and that his wife was "queerer" than anyone had ever suspected. Only Rachel and James had kept apart from the snickering gossip and conjectures. Ellis had been there. Some innate caution kept Rachel and James from insulting Ellis when she had intimated, vaguely, some portentous scene which had taken place in her mistress' room, during which the new Mrs. Dunham had shown herself "in her true colors." It was too terrible to remember, she had said, when avidly pressed for details. "But time will tell," she had added, with a sententious nod of her head. Later, James whispered to Rachel: "If we keep quiet, we may learn something of advantage. Forewarned is forearmed, as they say."

Rachel prepared Melissa's bed, shook up the fire, laid out the nightgown. Though she had hardly touched her tray, Melissa could eat no more. She dismissed Rachel with less peremptory words than she had used the night before, and with a sudden aching loss watched the girl leave the room.

She went to her desk and began to work. It was an enormous effort for her to begin. The pen felt heavy and dull in her hand. She could not concentrate upon the papers before her. For the first time in her life her head began to pound with long strokes of pain. She rubbed her throbbing temples with her fingers, without relief. Then she heard the jingling of bells outside, and voices, and laughter. She ran to the window and pushed aside a drapery. There were sleighs outside, and horses whose breath rose in silvery vapor under the moon, and the figures of men and women emerging from the house in a flood of light. Then, while Melissa watched, the sleighs filled, and went hissing and belling down the low slopes. Geoffrey's dogs, barking, followed the cavalcade for a little distance.

When she returned slowly to the desk, the room seemed very still and empty to Melissa. She tried to work. It was impossible. Vaguely, she searched through the books she had brought, for something to read. But she turned from them, sickened. They had taken on, for her, a dry and dusty age, a meaninglessness, and she pushed them away hopelessly. But she must have something to read in bed, before going to sleep. She knew she could not sleep just now.

She remembered the library downstairs. There were many books there, she recalled. Surely, among them, there was some historical volume, a classic, which she had not yet read. One, perhaps, which might help her with her father's work. She was suddenly relieved, as if a weight had been taken from her shoulders, and dimly pleased. One must not waste time, not even when one could not work.

She opened her door, and peered distrustfully down the long, lighted corridor. But no one was about; she heard no voice, not even that of a servant. She crept down the carpeted stairs, clinging to the balustrade, holding up her green velvet skirts. The "Yellow Room," and the rooms beyond it, were in darkness, though last embers flickered on the hearths. Only the library showed a single light, shining in a diffused circle on the many books on the walls. Here a fire crackled warmly, as if freshly stirred.

Letting go of her skirts, Melissa ran swiftly into the library, her eyes fixed on the illuminated books. She reached up for one, examined it, replaced it contemptuously when she saw it was one of Mr. Dickens' inconsequential and paltry novels, and took down another. It appeared, at first glance, to be a "serious" work, then this, too, was revealed as "only a novel" by another man as trivial as Mr. Dickens. She had nothing but disdain for Mr. Thackeray, whose *Vanity Fair* had been written obviously and shamelessly for "entertainment." As if the sacred Word dared be prostituted to such abandoned use; and, worse, that such desecration should be condoned! There was no excuse at all, Papa had often said, for a book that offered only laughter, vulgar interest, diversion and amusement for an idle hour. All books should be soberly dedicated to the solution of human problems, edification, instruction or meditation. "Let the people go to halls of low comedy and cheap music, or to popular plays, for their mindless distractions," Charles had often said. "Literature is a somber and meaningful thing, and cheapjacks like Dickens and Thackeray should be denied a place on the shelves of thoughtful people, true and serious students of humanity, and those who understand that the Word has a peculiar and significant duty to men. Let those who use it, use it in solemnity of heart and soul!"

"I never cared much for Thackeray, either," said a voice behind Melissa. "A very superficial man. A buffoon, like Dickens, and one equally ephemeral."

Melissa started so violently that the book she held fell to the floor with a crash. She swung about, to look into the gravely smiling face of Ravel Littlefield.

CHAPTER 37

RAVEL CASUALLY bent over and picked up the book. He replaced it on the shelf in the most matter-of-fact and easy manner, while Melissa, her face red, clutched the green velvet peignoir tightly about her, conscious of her casual dress, her disheveled hair and ink-stained hands.

Ignoring her confusion, Ravel said gravely: "I am so glad you came down, Mrs. Dunham. I was having a very tedious hour here, alone."

"I didn't know you were here, or I should not have come," replied Melissa bluntly. Then she stammered: "Oh, no, I did not mean that as it sounds! I mean, I'd not have disturbed you!"

"On the contrary," replied Ravel, with quiet enthusiasm, "you have relieved my tedium. You see, I have a headache tonight, and was in no mood for festivities. Very distrait. Not ill enough to retire, not well enough to cavort, especially when the temperature is so unfriendly outside. I suppose you find yourself in the same case?"

"Well, yes," answered Melissa slowly. "Perhaps not exactly. I just felt that no one cared whether I went or not, and, then, I am always making the most dreadful mistakes."

Ravel was offering her a leather chair near the fire and, forgetting her state of dress, she sat down mechanically. The haggard look began to recede from her face. But Ravel knew he must move delicately. He began to scan the books on the shelves, gave a rueful smile, shook his head. "I confess I find nothing worth while or of interest to me here," he said, pretending that he had not heard Melissa's last remark. "I was reading a criticism of Mr. Dickens only recently, by a very famous and serious New York critic who openly declared that Mr. Dickens was not a writer but only a vulgar story-teller. No reality in his work, no depth. His prolific pen proves that he cannot be counted among those rare souls whom we call geniuses.

"It is is impossible to write a serious book in less than two or three years of long and arduous toil, soul-searching struggle, solemn contemplation and reflection. Mr. Dickens is, therefore, not a writer of any importance to this generation, or to the generations to come. The very prodigality of his works, the constant easy flow, the profusion of his chapters and his involved phrases, the effortless abundance, all betray the mark of the superficial scribbler, the writer of no consequence, the entertainer, whose name will be forgotten with his death, if not before." Ravel turned to Melissa. "That is the judgment of reputable critics. I quote them practically verbatim, Mrs. Dunham."

His remarks had given Melissa time to forget her confusion and dismay and to take her self-engrossed mind from her own problems. Before Ravel had half finished, she had forgotten herself and was listening with that absorbed seriousness so characteristic of her.

Ravel, a very subtle man, understood Melissa with extraordinary acuteness. The way to that beleaguered heart, that cold hard innocence, was not through physical channels but through the bookish and intellectual mind, which was at once so strong in her and so ingenuous. He believed that her ice-bound emotions could be released by abstract words only, that she was immune to human temptations as other women knew them.

Melissa considered what he had said, sitting primly and stiffly on the edge of her chair, the green velvet making her long throat seductively white and pure. It also enhanced the fragile gilt of her hair, and threw sea-colored lights into her eyes. Ravel thought he had never seen a woman so tempting, so desirable, so lovely, and his tenderness made his handsome face soft and hushed. He came closer to her, and looked down at her. She studied him thoughtfully, no coquetry in her manner, no coy shrinking or flirtation. He was, to her, a human being who had made it clear that he shared her own, and her father's, opinions, and was therefore to be trusted. Ravel sighed, half with impatience, half with amusement. He saw that he might roll his limpid eyes, show off his profile and his shoulders, and strike the most classic attitudes, yet they would not entice or interest Melissa in the least. This both intrigued and exasperated him. Here was a woman who was truly a woman, with the features, the breasts, the hair, the throat, the curves of an adorable female, yet anyone less female he had never seen in his life.

Ravel, in his eloquent and soothing voice, continued for a few moments to expound on the despicable Dickens and Thackeray, then he said: "Dear Mrs. Dunham, I am delighted to have the opportunity tonight of telling you of my profound admiration and reverence for your father's work. Books of authentic genius. Documents of a superior and immortal mind."

Immediately, Melissa became faintly animated, and she smiled, showing the beautiful even whiteness of her teeth. He had never seen her smile before and he was struck by its shy, pure charm, its open and virginal quality. Fascinated, he came even closer to her. Yes, this was certainly Eurydice; lines of his projected poem rushed suddenly into his mind, perfectly formed and faultless.

She did not thank him conventionally for his kind opinion of her father, for she took it for granted that any man of sensibility and learning would have this opinion as a matter of course. But she said, to his great confusion: "What did you think of the third volume, Mr. Littlefield? There was some controversy about that, between Papa and—and Geoffrey."

Ravel's sharp ear caught the sudden low dropping of her voice as she spoke her husband's name, but he could not interpret it. Besides, he was embarrassed. He had never read any of Charles' books, for the simple reason that he had never heard of them. But he could not withdraw now, so he said, with reverent enthusiasm: "Absolutely perfect, dear Mrs. Dunham! But not to be compared, even in perfection, with the fourth." He fervently prayed that there had been a fourth. When he saw Melissa nod gravely, he sighed with profound relief.

"What was the controversy about the third?" he asked hastily, to forestall any insistence by Melissa that he enlarge upon the comparison, with details.

"Geoffrey thought the volume too—too scholarly," said Melissa, censoriously. "I did not concur, though Papa listened. Papa did not agree that his chapter on Aristophanes demanded copious quotations from the plays, for Papa believed that the reading public would be misled by the apparent frivolousness of some of them. It was Papa's belief that only the true scholar knew that the plays were really not comedies at all but subtle tragedies full of despair and suffering. The average reader would not know that, or even the average scholar, and Papa did not wish to degrade Aristophanes, nor to popularize the plays for the benefit of the light-minded. He used to say: 'Imagine Aristophanes in the playhouses of New York! What desecration!' But Geoffrey insisted that whole acts be incorporated in the book." Melissa paused, and frowned. "Finally, Papa compromised, but only to the extent of quoting excerpts in the original Greek. Geoffrey was very annoyed, but Papa was adamant."

For some reason, Ravel wanted to laugh out loud, but he controlled himself. "That certainly would prevent the 'lightminded' from understanding," he said.

Melissa nodded vigorously. "Papa and I worked very carefully on the excerpts. To make sure, we eliminated some of the lighter speeches and moments, even from the original Greek." She added: "The first edition, of course, contained the plays in the original, but the second edition—and Papa was furious and threatened to withdraw the book from circulation—had an English translation appended. I advised him then to find another publisher."

"But he remained with Dunham?"

"Yes. I think it was a question of loyalty, on Papa's part. He had always published through that house."

Ravel was no fool. He might be pretentious when it came to "literature" and his own special province, "poetry," but even he had moments of honest clarity when he confessed to himself that he was secretly envious of the success of less "dedicated" writers. So he understood that "Papa's loyalty" was due to Papa's knowledge that probably no one else but Dunham would publish his works. And why Dunham did publish them might have been baffling unless one looked hard and long at Melissa. It was an interesting subject.

Ravel sat down near Melissa and gave her that absorbed and profound attention which no other woman had been able to resist. Melissa, too, found it irresistible, but not for the same reasons. She thought it was reverence for her father, and she was moved and deeply grateful. The pain in her heart had almost disappeared. She sat back in her chair, and smiled again at Ravel, that touching smile which had fascinated him before.

Very softly, humbly, he began to tell her of his projected poem about Eurydice. He was so genuinely stirred by this girl, so inspired by her, that whole sonorous stanzas came easily to his mind, and he spoke them aloud. Never had he composed with such fervor, such perfection, such ease. He was at once astounded at himself and enormously excited. At moments, he saw only Melissa's eyes, and it was to those eyes that he recited. And there were other moments when he cursed inwardly that he did not have pen and paper handy to put down these singing metaphors, these shining stanzas.

But for the time, it was enough that Melissa was leaning breathlessly toward him, that her hands were clasped fiercely on her knees, that her eyes were glowing, that her whole face was illuminated with delight and passion. Once or twice she cried out as if in ecstasy, and this spurred him on. They were lost in their mutual raptures; they did not remember where they were. The fire fell lower, the lamps flickered. Not a servant came near them. They were not aware that the room was becoming colder, and that the wind of the night was striking heavily against the windows. They were certainly not aware of the fact that Ellis, sent by her indisposed mistress to fetch a book, stood near the threshold, but hidden, and was listening with avid interest.

At length, Ravel was actually exhausted and burned out by the fires of his inspiration. He felt spent but mysteriously peaceful and full of happiness. Long after he had become silent, Melissa could only sit there and look at him with that deep glow in her eyes, a shy smile on her lips. And he returned her look with tender and gratified excitement, for Ravel, at once intimate and remarkably sincere. The young woman's innocent and uninhibited ardor and emotional admiration enhanced the high esteem in which he always held himself, and if he had not already loved her, he would have loved her now for this ingenuous and completely pure flattery.

Women had flattered him with their love and their adoration of his face and figure and manners. No one, he reflected ruefully for a moment, had ever flattered him for his "mind." No one, with the exception of fat beldames, ladies (very serious) of more or less certain age and frustrated emotions, and women like Arabella and Mrs. Bertram, who "devoted their lives to art." But really valuable women—that is, women fair of face and body and luminous with youth—had little knowledge of or use for poetry or for earnest and important literature of any kind. It was his one vain regret. He had always dreamed of a beautiful young woman who would admire him as a poet and not merely as a man with a face.

And now here was such a woman, beautiful and young, who listened to his impromptu poetry in a kind of shining bemusement and joy. She listened to him and looked at him as a man, too. That was evident by the expression of her eyes and the moist vividness of her lips.

It was at this point that something cold blew over Ravel, and he leaned forward the better to see Melissa. That shy smile: Why, it was the smile of a very young girl, a girl of eight or ten or twelve, perhaps. It was not the smile of a woman at all. It was not even the coy smile of green puberty. It was, Ravel reflected with sudden bitterness, "a breastless smile." Those eyes, too, though deep and intense, were the eyes of a young child unaware of life and men. I would bet, thought Ravel, with increasing bitterness, that she believes babies are found under cabbages, or, if they are not, that it is very bad taste. I haven't the slightest doubt that she can quote whole acts by Aristophanes, but what that ribald Greek was implying she wouldn't have the faintest idea.

Ravel thought female ignorance "very damn boring." Give him the rose-cheeked peach but never the hard-fibered young apple, even if the peach might be somewhat overripe. For a moment, as he studied Melissa, he felt a definite impatience and revulsion. She was not a young girl, yet she was as smooth, and possibly as sour and juiceless, as that apple still hanging on the bough.

His inspection, at a polite distance, of the female body, was always circumspect and without obviousness. But he saw he need not be so delicate with Melissa. Quite cooly, he ran his eyes nimbly over her major points of interest, and now it was only with impatience. Yet he smiled a little. Again, he felt tenderness, and amusement, and a sudden excitement. He was certain that, once having seduced her mind, he could proceed with the seduction of something infinitely more desirable and rewarding.

Melissa was saying, and Ravel came back from his musings with a start: "When your poem is published, Mr. Littlefield, I hope you will send me a copy."

Ravel said, with heavy emphasis on the bitterness: "I am sure, dear Mrs. Dunham, that no publisher will be interested. I don't write poems for the empty-headed masses. They would not understand, and would not buy them, and so there would be no profit for the publisher."

"I know!" exclaimed Melissa, with answering anger. "They prefer to let the true poet, the true writer, starve to death in his garret!"

Ravel had a sudden vision of his very elegant New York establishment, and as he was sometimes a man of reason and humor, as well as a poet, he felt some sheepishness.

"To think that genius should be at the mercy of tradesmen!" cried Melissa.

Ravel suddenly remembered that his father was a cheesemonger, and that it was to good healthy cheese, eaten by masses of people with enjoyment, that he owed his establishment, his leisure, his ladies, his excellent tailor, and the money in his pocket. But, he reflected, if Melissa wished to see the shadow of gaunt emaciation on his cheeks, it would do no harm at all. He sighed heavily, let his hands sag wearily between his broadcloth knees. A very fine diamond ring glittered on one of his white fingers. He was sure that Melissa saw neither the broadcloth nor the ring.

While Melissa stared at him, rapt, seeing him clothed in shabbiness, with the aureole of the "true, serious poet" shining about his well-barbered and exquisitely curling head, Ravel became aware of tinkling bells outside, and voices. He jumped to his feet, and said, in a lowered voice: "Mrs. Dunham, I believe the party is returning." It would be extremely embarrassing to have his host, and the other guests, enter this library and find him tête-à-tête with his hostess, whose green velvet peignoir had long since parted quite heedlessly and shamelessly, revealing the nightgown underneath.

Melissa, still bemused, stood up. She caught Ravel's meaning glance, looked down, snatched the robe about her. Without a word of goodbye, she fled out of the room, and he heard her footsteps rushing up the stairs just as the gay company reëntered the house.

When she burst into her own room, she was wild with excitement, her whole mind electric and thrumming. She threw herself into a chair, then stood up and ran to her desk. Her earlier lethargy and dullness had gone. Why, she could write for hours now, without weariness! And all because of her wonderful conversation with Mr. Littlefield, who had so inspired her, so recharged her with energy and pride. He had justified her faith in her father; he had made work meaningful for her again.

While she scribbled furiously, opened and shut books, Ellis, standing panting before her mistress, her hand on her breast, was saying: "Mrs. Shaw, ma'am, she was right on my heels! I thought she'd catch me any moment, she came that fast when the master and the other gentlemen and ladies came in. Flew like the culprit she was."

Arabella had listened to her maid's story with avidity and delight, though she had felt a momentary fury and incredulous rage at the thought of Ravel's engrossment with that impossible zany. But she knew Ravel's reputation well. It was not possible that he thought Melissa handsome! It was not possible he was really interested in her. However, to Ravel

Littlefield, a woman was a woman. If only he lived in Mid-field, he might be used to ruin Melissa and thus remove her forever from this house! But every tiniest piece of evidence could be used to destroy her, and Arabella was grateful.

"I have you as a witness, Ellis," she said, solemnly, and prepared to go to bed in comparative satisfaction.

PART THREE

CHAPTER 38

ANDREW AND HIS YOUNG WIFE, the former Miriam
McDowell, came slowly away from the barns, where they had
been anxiously brooding over Miriam's favorite mare, which
had been suffering from some obscure illness. They left the
barnyard; then, as the June night was so lovely, they strolled
together over the long lawns that surrounded the old gray
house where they lived with Judge Farrell, and went aimlessly
but contentedly towards the river. Andrew smoked his pipe;
Miriam's slender dark arm was linked affectionately in his.
Her small head, ruffled and black in the moonlight, reached
hardly to his massive shoulder, which she occasionally pressed
with her slender brown cheek.

Andrew smiled down at her with a deeper emotion that he
could ever express. To Miriam, the adjective "spry" could be
applied most aptly, yet it was not a hard and cricket-like spry-
ness; it was a gay and lively thing, quick and light, yet very
shrewd and intelligent. There were, as the Judge, her grandfather often said: "No flies on Merry." There were some who
thought her a trifle shrewish and somewhat caustic of tongue,
but her friends saw the clear bright sparkle in her black eyes,
the flash of her open smile. She might indeed on occasion have
a wounding point to her tongue, but it was never a cruel point,
and never used in malice. She loved satire, and was usually
so full of humorous quips that she kept the ordinarily impassive Andrew in a happy mood.

Miriam had a neat little figure, and the narrowest waist in
the township, for she was a small woman. Her tiny brown
hands were incessantly busy about the house, and during the
day her voice could be heard moving from room to room, ad-
vising the "hired girl" and commenting freely upon everything.
Like many small women, she was never blowsy or untidy,
preferring, in winter, smooth brown or gray bombazine well-
cut and plain, and, in summer, pleasant little frocks of flowered batiste for the evenings, and light silks for special oc-

casions. Not for Miriam the enormous new bustles, gathers, ruffles and drapes. Everything must be well-sewed and without ostentation or vulgarity.

As they strolled nearer the river, Andrew looked down fondly at his light-footed little wife, who hardly seemed to touch the grass as she walked beside him. The flood of moonlight made her small triangular face curiously elfin and alive. It bleached away its warm brown and rose tint, and left her very expressive mouth dark and mysterious. Andrew thought: There is nothing, ever, dull or heavy or oppressive about Merry. She will always laugh, always have common-sense, and will always have a shrewd remark to throw into the face of solemnity. Particularly, self-conscious and precious solemnity. Merry might make hilarious epigrams, but she would never be guilty of an intellectual profundity. And for these things Andrew, remembering his father and Melissa, was passionately grateful.

Then, as always, when he thought of Melissa, he was uneasy. He tried to shake off the uneasiness by looking at the moon-flooded earth and sky. Everything was so vivid tonight, and accompanied by such a warm, rushing wind, that the torn shadows of the trees danced and flew over the dark earth as vividly as if the sun were shining upon them. Every leaf sparkled with nimble silver; the blown grass, too, flowed in pale silver under the moon. The old roofs behind them seemed bathed in bright water. Rail fences stood sharp and clean against backgrounds of illuminated meadows and fields. When they reached the banks of the narrow river, they found it running in tumultuous silver and brilliant blackness. They stood on the low banks and listened to the frogs saluting the night, and to the softly loud murmurs of grass and tree in the wind. Now that the dew had fallen, the earth gave up a rich strong scent, at once peaceful and voluptuous, so that Andrew felt both contented and disturbed. He bent his large head and kissed Miriam's hair, which blew against his lips.

He and Miriam had been married four months now, and they had been the only four months of his life when he had felt resolved and happy and certain of himself. The two adjoining farms, the Upjohns' and the Farrells', had become one. The old Upjohn house, battered, lean and gray, stood deserted on its disheveled lawns. It was Andrew's intention to raze the house and its crumbling out-buildings very shortly. But he so hated that house that he could not, as yet, bring himself to enter it and examine its contents for salvage. There were too many memories there of misery and frustration, of hating

faces, of averted eyes, of silent turmoil, distrust and wretchedness. It pained him too much to remember his mother. He
would turn from the thought of his father with such a somber
disgust and revulsion that he could hardly endure it. But
Melissa haunted him, and he did not wish to be haunted by
Melissa. Sometimes he forced himself to share the opinion of
the countryside: that Melissa had "done very well for herself,"
and that as the wife of Geoffrey Dunham she occupied a magnificent and invulnerable position and had all that her heart
desired.

Miriam always seemed to know what her young husband
was thinking. She leaned lightly against him, and said: "I have
tried again, about Melissa, Andy. I drove up to see her today.
She was very polite, but absent-minded, as usual. But I will
say that her manners have improved. She informed me that
dear Arabella"—and Miriam's mobile lips twisted sardonically
—"was instructing her daily in elegant deportment. If so, I
must congratulate dear Arabella. Melissa's hands are now very
smooth and white, and she doesn't stride any more, though
she'll never mince correctly, and she has dropped her voice
down a couple of octaves and doesn't shout. She very carefully
pretended that she was delighted to see me, and said so in
the most civil words. Lesson number two, apparently, in 'how
to greet an unexpected and undesired guest.' She even remembered, and only a few minutes too late, to invite me for
tea, and when it came, she served it without doing any greater
harm that cracking a saucer and rattling the silver once or
twice. Arabella has taught her how to put her feet together
nicely, and how to lift her little finger elegantly, and how to
bore a guest to the final exquisite degree by not saying anything in the least startling and never offering any original
remark." Miriam paused. "I think I prefer the old, outrageous
Melissa, but this one, if much duller, is definitely easier on the
nervous system."

"In other words," Andrew remarked gloomily, "Melissa has
become lifeless."

"No, I should not say that. I should say, rather, that she is
becoming a lady." Miriam laughed, not too kindly. "And nothing is worse than a great lady's company, for more than ten
minutes."

"But does she seem well? She was not at home when I
called to see her on Tuesday, nor on last Friday, nor the week
before that, on a Thursday."

Miriam glanced up at him sharply but furtively, and then
looked away. Was it possible that Andrew was still ignorant

of what was almost common gossip these days? Miriam thoughtfully put back her blowing hair, and frowned to herself. She, for one then, would not under any circumstances tell Andrew this piece of scandal, if, indeed, in the case of Melissa, it could possibly be a scandal. Scandal and Melissa simply could never come into juxtaposition, no matter how hard gossipers might try.

"Melissa," said Miriam carefully, "takes long walks—by herself, I understand. She walked frequently with your father, if I remember, and so I suppose she haunts the places where they used to wander and discuss the Universe. I understand that she has almost finished one of his books now, and is working steadily on it."

Andrew said, with more gloom: "I thought marriage might rid Melissa of all that. But it seems I was mistaken. But tell me: how does she seem?"

"Rather too silent," admitted Miriam. "But then, we hardly know each other, and, as you know, she has never accepted our invitations to come here. We have nothing in common. She is very polite now, but still stares at me distrustfully, and with a kind of bitterness. She asked about you, and listened eagerly, and when I told her you were happy and busy she looked at me as if she 'knew' I was lying. Then, too, she is rather pale and still and very abstracted, and keeps turning her head as if she were listening or waiting for someone. I should say she is tired. But very elegant in all those fine silks and satins and laces and ribbons, and her hair so smooth. I never knew Melissa was so handsome."

Andrew sighed impatiently. He said: "I'd like to kick Dunham. What is wrong with him? Melissa is his wife, but he shows no interest in her, from what I hear. He comes home hardly twice a month now. I saw him last six weeks ago, when Phoebe was married."

He remembered Phoebe's marriage. Phoebe, when she had married her Johnnie Barrett from Judge Farrell's house, had been all pink smiles and dimples. It had been a small and pleasant wedding, with Phoebe in white satin and veiling, supplied by Andrew, and with a small string of real pearls given her by Geoffrey Dunham in the name of himself and the bride's sister. Geoffrey had attended, but not Melissa, a fact which was well-noted and commented upon throughout the countryside.

Miriam was, in turn, remembering Melissa as she had been today, with such a thin sad face and mournful eyes. She had sat with her hands folded in her lap listlessly. She had worn a very splendid suit of pearl-colored poplin, with a vest of magenta silk, the skirt trimmed with rows of magenta velvet, and her hair had been rolled back from her face and caught in a net trimmed with magenta ribbon. Cerise jewels had glittered in her ears, and her slippers had been tied with magenta ribbon to match the ones in the net. Melissa had entertained her guest in the small sitting-room beyond the drawing-rooms, and the walls of soft yellow and gray, the carpet of pale magenta and yellow and blue, had set off her costume and had made her hair brighter. Yet, in spite of all this splendor and beauty, Miriam had sensed the sadness in her husband's sister, her abstraction and remoteness. The hard clean angles of her face were so sharp and prominent, and her eyes, never of too intense a blue, had appeared faded and dead.

Miriam had commented delicately on the beauty of Melissa's costume, and for the first time Melissa had shown some faint animation. "Geoffrey chose it," she said, and then she had colored. She smoothed a row of magenta velvet with a fingertip, then subsided again. "I wore it last Saturday," she remarked. "We expected him to come home. But he did not. He wrote that he might come home today, and that is why I am wearing it now." Her voice sank. "But it is almost six o'clock and, had he arrived at Midfield, he would have been home by this time. Unless," and she regarded Miriam anxiously, "the train is late? You do not know whether the train is late?"

Miriam remembered hearing the train just before arriving at this house, and so she regretfully shook her head. Melissa had made no comment. The tea-tray had arrived then, and Melissa had conducted herself quite adequately during the serving. She betrayed no animosity towards the girl who had seduced her brother from the study of law, but she had displayed no interest either. It was evident that, to her, Miriam was a nonentity, one to be treated politely but certainly not with warmth or solicitude. Miriam was not at all important, not a dependent to be instructed, not a woman with whom to converse, and decidedly not a friend.

Miriam confided part of this to Andrew, who bent, picked up a stone, and threw it into the moonlit water. "Just like Melly," he commented. "She can show less interest in other human beings than anyone else alive. Sometimes I wonder whether she really is alive. It's not just Father's death. She was always like that. No one else but Father and herself existed in all the world, which to her was just a sprawling mass of soulless maggots."

He threw another stone. "I don't know," he mumbled. "It

seems hopeless. It is too lonely up there, with old Arabella. And Melly is incapable of making friends. She sees no one, and won't visit anyone. And I thought there would be a change."

Miriam watched the moon dissolving in the black water. She said, carefully: "The only visitors they have are Arabella's two or three friends in Midfield, and they are too old for Melissa and doubtless as little interested in her as she in them. The only one who could possibly amuse her is that very handsome Mr. Littlefield who took the old Kenfrew house for the summer, where, I understand, he is writing reams of poetry."

"Oh, Melissa would not be interested, even casually, in such a popinjay," said Andrew. "I am sure he isn't what she would call a 'serious' poet. He is too strong on the haberdashery, and uses scent, I have heard, and, besides, he doesn't look like Papa."

"But he does visit the Dunham house quite often, for tea, and sometimes dines with the ladies," said Miriam, cautiously. She glanced up at her husband's face, which expressed nothing but dissatisfaction with his sister. "I hear, too, that he and Melissa sometimes walk together along the river, and have been seen, even after dark, wandering around the countryside."

Andrew appeared a little interested now, then became gloomy again. "I doubt it. Nothing could stir up Melissa or make her look at another human being as if he were alive. If those two do talk, it's doubtless about Papa's books, and that would be very dull for an elegant jackanapes like Littlefield, if what I've seen of him is any indication."

There is more than one innocent in the Upjohn family, reflected Miriam. She pressed her cheek against her husband's arm and laughed a little. "Just imagine a scandal about Melissa and Mr. Littlefield!" she said. "Wouldn't that be delightful?"

"It would be impossible," replied Andrew, laughing in return.

They walked slowly home together. They found old Judge Farrell reading under a lamp in the small library of the ancient house.

CHAPTER 39

"HALLO! HALLO!" said the Judge, putting aside his
Farm Journal and giving his granddaughter and Andrew an
affectionate grin. "How's the mare?"

"I think she will live. The sores on her leg seem to be healing," replied Andrew. He sat down near the Judge, and the
old chair groaned and shivered under his huge bulk. He pulled
out his pipe and filled it, and, as he did so, he glanced around
the great shabby room. Yes, he reflected, as he had often reflected before, it was shabby, much shabbier than the interior
of his old home and had none of the mouldering treasures of
his mother's "parlor." Yet it had a casualness, this room, a
warmth, a blowsiness, a haphazard grouping for comfort, a
kind of peacefulness and homely ugliness which had endeared
itself to the young and lonely man. Judge Farrell was a rich
man, yet no imported rug lay on the polished maple flooring,
which had been laid for strength rather than grace; the planks
were thin, wide, short or long, as the carpenter had sawed
them, but they gave a charm to the room. Here and there
colorful rag-rugs had been scattered, of various shapes and
sizes. All the furniture was home-made and of maple: rockers,
square, round or octagon tables, sofas and foot-stools, these
boasted no padding save the chintz cushions Miriam had made
for them, chintz so faded that their pattern was a blurred tint
of mingled green and brown. The Judge, himself, had lined
the knotted pine walls with book-shelves, and all were bulging with scores of volumes well-worn and unmatched. The
small-paned little windows had been hung with the same
chintz that covered the cushions, and every table had its brass
or china lamp, or, quite often, a plain, glass, ungarnished
lamp ordinarily used in kitchens. The immense fieldstone fireplace was cold now, but heaps of ashes still lay there, "to
make a bed for the fire in winter," as the Judge said. Over it
were crossed two of the Judge's pet guns. The room was bare
of ornament which served no purpose, yet in some manner it
managed to be delightful.

All the rest of the house was furnished in a similar manner. It certainly had no elegance, no treasures, no real beauties. Yet Andrew thought it the most beautiful house in the world, for here were always laughter, good-temper, kindness, hearty food and vigorous voices. Here for the first time in his life, he felt he had a home.

Judge Farrell, that astute old man, watched Andrew as the younger man's slow, heavy gaze of content wandered about the room. He then glanced at Miriam, who had settled down to knitting nearby, and the two, who loved each other with much devotion, smiled with affectionate understanding and significance.

The Judge said: "No regrets, eh, Andy? Still find farming what you wanted?"

Andrew replied, with quiet but almost vehement firmness: "It is, indeed, Judge. I never knew, before, what it was to be happy. I always wanted to farm. It isn't just the farming, though. It is something else. In a way, I suppose, I have found myself." He was not a young man given to rhetoric, and he flushed at what he considered his extravagance of language.

The Judge nodded thoughtfully, and sucked on his pipe. They all listened to the shrilling of crickets under the moon. The Judge said: "Hot again, tomorrow. The crickets always know." Then he added: "There's something about the land which makes a man stand honestly on his own feet. Maybe it's because he's alone. There's nothing so bad for cluttering up a man's thoughts as having his fellow-man around all the time. Not being able to get away from him. Mind, I'm not saying that every man should be a solitary, or a monk, and that that's the only way to his own salvation. But he's got to breathe air some other man isn't breathing at the same time if he's to be a prideful soul on his own, full of dignity and integrity."

"I know," said Andrew, in a low voice. He looked steadfastly at his old friend, and waited. The Judge refilled his pipe, with deep thoughtfulness.

"The trouble is, when a lot of men get together, and make a city, they begin to interfere with one another. That's natural. There's nothing else for them to do! They violate, cajole and support one another, because they've got to do something to fill in the time. So, either out of boredom, or with the best intentions in the world, they deprive one another of freedom. Eventually, such big conglomerations of men destroy liberty for other men; they can't help it. They've got to have law, and there was never a law passed that didn't deprive someone of liberty. A free world begins with each individual, but that individual can't be free if when he's getting around he keeps stumbling all over other men, or if he never gets away from the sound of their voices. If the world is to be free, it must be free for every man, free for himself and in himself."

Andrew said nothing. But he thought: That was the trouble with Melissa and me. We had no freedom. No one could give it to us, though someone had deprived us of it. I had to free myself. Melly has to free herself. Yes, men can deprive other men of freedom, but only a man, himself, can give himself liberty.

The Judge chuckled. "Man is a dangerous animal. My God, they call the rattlesnake dangerous, and the tiger, and the wolf. But folks are a combination of them all, with a few brains thrown in to help them make the most of their endowments! But when a man is out on the land he is less dangerous than he is anywhere else. He's usually kind of religious, too, and that helps keep down his natural instincts. I've always thought that the function of religion is to make man harmless; and it works, in the country. But the city, as far as I can see, doesn't seem very keen on religion. So, in the city, where God isn't much at home, the function of law is to compel man to remain harmless. And because men naturally don't like laws imposed from outside by other men, city folk are more dangerous than country-folk, who usually have their consciences in good repair."

They listened for a while to the crickets and the frogs and the warm wind in the trees outside. Then the Judge said softly: "It was country-folk who discovered God, and it was shepherds on the hill-side who saw the angels. But city folk substitute men for God, and theories for men. And somehow, if a man comes to believe in his own theories very hard, he comes to hate other men who don't share them, and plots how to kill them for being so ornery and stubborn. Theories don't grow on the land. They grow only in the cities."

The sprightly Miriam stood up, and kissed her grandfather soundly. She looked at the faces of the two men, and laughed a little. "Oh, don't look so sober and gloomy, my dears. It is so peaceful here. We have just had an awful war, and we shan't have another very soon, I am sure, in spite of the nasty cities."

The Judge returned her kiss fondly, and tried to smile. "My dear, I'm not afraid for you, or even for Andrew. But I am afraid for your children's children, and their children. Don't smile. No, I am wrong. Smile, my love. And keep your children on the land, if you can."

CHAPTER 40

THE LATE JULY day steamed and fumed in heat. There was no escape from it, either under the trees or in the darkened house. There was no escape in the gardens, the long halls, the shuttered library. A hot and invisible vapor seemed to rise from the bronzed earth and exhale from the fluttering dusty rags of the bent trees.

To the weary Melissa, July was like a young thin man with a bold smile and hot eyes, wandering over the earth in the heat of the sun. He was a vagabond, sometimes noisy in thunder, with rages both brief and violent. He raised dust at his passing, and everything withered and choked at his touch. He turned the grass brown, and dried up the little brooks, leaving gravel and stone behind. He breathed his blasting breath over the hills, and burnished them. His shadow quivered in waves of heat over the fields and stood against the sky like a flame. He struck at unwary heads with the flat of his smoldering sword, and drove dogs, panting, into violet shadows. He scattered the heavy dust on the trees, and made them droop before him. He ran before August like a sheet of fire.

Never had she known so weary and hopeless a July as this, and so empty and purposeless a one, in spite of the progress she was making on her father's manuscript. Nevertheless, she was incapable of halting what she had once begun. The days were empty, yes, and the nights were sleepless with the amorphous pain that always dogged her now, yet never had she had so few free moments she could call her own, and never had life seemed so pointless and arid. Her father had said that work was the cure for all evil and all misery, and that the busy man whose mind was occupied was the healthy and contented man. If so, Melissa would reflect, she ought to be the happiest of women instead of the most wretched. A vast uneasiness seemed to be part of her, and all about her, and no amount of work and occupation could drive it away. Work aggravated it for her, enhanced her suffering. Sometimes she thought: If only I had a little time to sit down and think, and be alone, without work!

Each afternoon, Arabella gave her a lesson in etiquette and deportment. The lessons sometimes took hours. It appeared to Melissa that the more tired she was, the more harried and exhausted, the longer the lessons. This afternoon, for instance, Arabella had been drilling the girl on the proper manner for a hostess who is receiving guests. A heavy book had been placed on her head, in order that she learn to walk stiffly, erectly, and with majestic care. Then, with this impediment, Melissa must move across the long floor of the library, stop at the door, extend her hand, smile carefully, and say: "How delightful that you could come, Mrs. Smith! I welcome you to our home."

The library shutters and the closed draperies could not keep the heat from the library. The leather chairs had been shrouded in muslin; the crimson, blue and brown of the books were only a dim glimmer in the dusk. The rugs had been rolled up for the summer, and the floor, in spite of the half-twilight, ached glitteringly in Melissa's throbbing eyes. Arabella reclined on a muslin-covered sofa, while Ellis sat beside her, moving a palm-leaf fan slowly back and forth over her mistress' painted face, and occasionally dropping a little eau de cologne on a fresh kerchief for Arabella's refreshment. The heavy lemonish odor sickened Melissa, whose own face was wet and deathly pale with heat and exhaustion. There was little fresh air in the great library; little thin pencils of burning light somehow escaped through the shutters and draperies and stuck on Melissa's eyes like visible streaks of pain. She could not avoid them. Sometimes she closed her eyes in momentary protection, but she saw the streaks change to burning green and blue against the darkness of her lids.

"Dear me, Melissa," sighed Arabella, with an eloquently despairing look at Ellis, "I am afraid you will never eliminate that jerky stride. Perhaps there is something wrong with your—limbs. A certain impossible length, quite unfeminine, I am afraid. And gentlemen, I have discovered, do like petite females. It is so disconcerting," she continued, when Melissa stopped half way across the floor, and turned her head in Arabella's direction, "for a gentleman to find himself looking directly into a lady's eyes, instead of onto properly downcast lids several inches below him."

"I am not as tall as Geoffrey," said Melissa, in a dull voice. "Nor as tall as Mr. Littlefield."

Arabella glanced at Ellis, who smirked. Arabella moistened her lips with the tip of her tongue, and her eyes gleamed. "But there are not many gentlemen as tall as Geoffrey and Ravel," remarked Arabella. "And few women as tall as you. Well, we must accept the defects of nature as we humbly accept her gifts. We might mourn our fate, and long for beauty and charm and manner, but if we do not have them we must cultivate, instead, more subdued advantages."

Melissa lifted the book from her head, stood in silence in the middle of the room, holding the book in her hand. She opened it lifelessly, glanced at its pages without seeing them. Then she closed it, let her arm drop heavily. She was very thin now. The white dimity dress, embroidered in blue pansies and tied with blue ribbons, was limp and crushed, for she could not learn to sit neatly and carefully. Her hair was damp; a long lock lay wetly across her forehead. Even her eyes seemed to have faded, become quite colorless, and her mouth had no color at all. Her facial bones, always flaring and sharp and angular, had become more pronounced, so that in repose her face resembled a mask of dull tragedy, fleshless and petrified.

Arabella went on, sighing gustily: "It does appear to me, Melissa, that you deliberately resist all my efforts to teach you. But perhaps I am unkind. It is possible that you simply cannot learn, and for that you cannot be blamed, I suppose." She waited a moment for Melissa to comment, but Melissa was silent. Arabella said, with soft insinuation: "But doubtless Mr. Littlefield does not find you gauche. He probably respects your mind. Tell me: What did you two converse about this morning, when you two walked through our woods?"

Ellis sat upright, and fixed her stealthy eyes on Melissa. Melissa swung the book listlessly at her side, but she was grateful for Arabella's interest, and for the ceasing of the depressing comments on her social stupidity. "We were discussing the play, *Hippolytus*, by Euripides," she said, with her usual simplicity. "There was that diatribe against women, spoken by Hippolytus, in which he says:

> " 'He smarts the less
> In whose high seat is set a Nothingness,
> A woman naught availing. Worst of all
> The wise deep-thoughted! Never in my hall
> May she sit throned who thinks and waits and sighs!' "

Ellis put her hand to her mouth to suppress a titter. But Melissa did not hear her. She was regarding Arabella almost eagerly. "Mr. Littlefield thought Hippolytus very shallow and foolish," she said. "But, of course, he had been disillusioned. No man would really prefer a fool of a woman. A man of mind prefers a woman of mind."

"Does Ravel consider you a woman of mind, dear Melissa?" asked Arabella with gentle slyness.

Melissa stared at her with a return of her old haughty outrage. "I consider that a very silly question, Arabella! Mr. Littlefield is a great genius, a magnificent and original poet. He would not waste his time with a woman he thought a dolt and an idiot. I have never been considered either," she added proudly, and for a moment the old arrogance lifted her chin. "Mr. Littlefield is dedicating his poetic saga to me. It is the story of Eurydice, the wife of Orpheus, who returned from the dead."

Arabella turned scarlet under her paint with suppressed mirth. "Does Ravel consider that you have returned from the dead, Melissa?" she said, when she could speak without laughing.

Melissa was puzzled. She said, slowly: "I don't know what you mean, Arabella. But," she added, after thoughtfully considering Arabella's words, "I am afraid you are too literal." However, something that dully ached in her was stung, and now it smarted like a touch of poison. She had to remind herself that Arabella was a frivolous and trivial woman, of no mind at all, even if she so pathetically considered herself an artist. She had probably not heard of Euripides, and Melissa reproached herself that she had debased the noble Greek tragedian by speaking his name to Arabella. It was sacrilege. "Mr. Littlefield is not using me as a model for Eurydice, Arabella. I am afraid you do not understand. He is merely dedicating his great work to me, because of what little inspiration I have been able to give him." Melissa's voice was stiff and cold.

"How nice that you have inspired him!" exclaimed Arabella, with enthusiasm.

"Oh, I have contributed nothing, nothing," protested the ingenuous Melissa. But she looked at Arabella with youthful kindness, and blushed faintly. "But it is so helpful to an artist to discuss his work with a sympathetic mind. It helps him to view his work objectively, and stimulates his thoughts. There was a certain passage with which Mr. Littlefield has been struggling, and which has caused him much suffering.

The thought was there, but the meaning remained obscure and unresolved. We discussed it yesterday, and this morning he told me that my suggestions had helped him to clarify the meaning without interfering with the metre. For a time, the two had remained incompatible."

The two women before her, one reclining, the other sitting, gazed at her with ophidian intentness. Their eyes glimmered in the dusk, but did not move away from the girl.

"Papa often had the same difficulty," Melissa went on. "There was a certain passage from *The Furies*, the play by Aeschylus, which Papa understood instinctively had another meaning from the one accepted by the vulgar. The meaning was very clear in the original Greek, but when it was translated into English it had an entirely different significance from the one popularly accepted. Papa and I discussed it for hours and days. We came to the conclusion that it was best not to translate it literally, and we worked on an original translation which did not disturb the metre. Papa was criticized rather sternly for this by a certain critic, but the others declared that Papa's translation was far superior, if not literal." She went on eagerly: "I understand that several scholars now use Papa's translation of that particular passage, and they always add a foot-note giving him the credit. I do not remember anything that ever gave Papa such pleasure."

Her whole face glowed, became almost supernaturally beautiful in its clear emaciation and earnestness. She pushed back her damp hair, and smiled at Arabella. "Would you like to hear both translations, Arabella?" she asked. "Then you could compare them."

Arabella hastily snatched at the handkerchief which Ellis extended to her. She tapped it over her eyes, and sighed. "Not just now, dear Melissa," she pleaded, with a wan glance at the girl. "Besides, we must go on with the lesson. But it is so nice to hear that you and Ravel are such friends. It might be very lonely for him in Midfield without you."

"Yes, he admitted that," said Melissa, seriously. "And I consider it my duty to help him as much as possible. In many ways, he replaces Papa, for me. I am sure I should die of loneliness and strangeness were it not for Mr. Littlefield." And now her face clouded and darkened, and became haggard with her secret pain. "Geoffrey comes home so seldom. He is always gone to New York or Boston."

Arabella abruptly pushed aside Ellis' fanning hand, and sat upright on her sofa. She regarded Melissa with unusual and unblinking fixity. Fear, amazement and horror turned her so white that her rouge became islands of brick-pink on a skin the color of a fish's belly. She saw Melissa in a kind of fierce illumination, every feature distinct, every expression exaggerated. She said to herself: My brother! Why, the drab loves him! She dares to love him!

Arabella's nails lacerated her palms as this terrifying truth struck her. Did Geoffrey know? Did Melissa know? If they did, then everything was lost, and she, Arabella, must pack her bags and go at once. The hope of sending Melissa away, of driving her away, of thrusting her out in disgrace and ruin, had been Arabella's only hope and sustenance these past months. During all this time she had, with more force than subtlety (but then, one did not need to use subtlety with the ingenuous Melissa), been impressing upon the girl that she, Melissa, was hopelessly stupid in social manners, completely devoid of elegance and breeding, and an embarrassment to her husband, his house, and his guests. Many times, quite crudely, Arabella had hinted that the marriage had been most unwise, and was a burden to her brother which gallantry and honor forbade him to discard. She had made considerable of his frequent absences, and his infrequent returns home. The fact that he had been much worried by the post-war threat of economic collapse in the nation generally and in the publishing business in particular, and that he was personally searching for new and inspiring authors in many cities, had been carefully hidden by Arabella from the young wife.

Arabella had been quite clever in keeping Geoffrey and Melissa from any tête-à-têtes. If any threatened, she had always managed interruptions. Whenever Geoffrey was at home, there was always a guest or two for dinner. She had been much cheered by the fact that Geoffrey had shown no particular desire to be alone with his wife, that he had manifested a very hopeful indifference to her. He was invariably kind, but absent-minded, and displayed towards her an attitude reminiscent of that of an adult in the presence of a child. And Ellis had reported to her mistress that there was no exchange of confidence or conversation between the two after they had retired. In fact, Geoffrey seemed to have forgotten Melissa, and when she spoke to him, which was seldom voluntarily, he would glance at her with a startled, if patient, air. In consequence, the girl's remarks became less and less, and a whole dinner would pass without any comment from her. Arabella indeed had had reason to hope.

But now she remembered other things which she had sensed subconsciously and which only now came clearly and horrifyingly to her memory. She remembered that during entire dinners Melissa would sit and look only at Geoffrey. that in spite of guests, even in spite of Ravel Littlefield, who sedulously tried to engage her in small intimate talk, she seemed only to see Geoffrey. Arabella remembered that Melissa had become more and more silent as the months passed, and that, when Geoffrey left the room for any reason, the pale tired eyes would follow him and would glance repeatedly at the door, as if watching for his return. And when he did return, a pallid animation would pass over her face, and she would move slightly to the edge of the chair, a tenseness in her body and her hands clenched together, as if she were about to speak. But Geoffrey invariably ignored her, and finally she would sink back and the dull apathy would envelop her again.

Arabella, who was a very clever woman, understood quite well that Melissa would never be guilty of any intrigue even with so handsome a rogue as Ravel Littlefield. It would not be honor or virtue which would restrain her. It was simply that she was incapable of such a thing, and this Arabella understood completely. In truth, only Arabella had known anything of real value about Melissa, and now her knowledge was complete, if terrible.

In order to compromise Melissa, she had, during Geoffrey's absences, thrown Ravel and Melissa together constantly. The appearance of evil, Arabella understood, was quite sufficient. The upper classes of Midfield knew Ravel well by acquaintance and by reputation. It was necessary only to arrange things which seemingly threw guilt on Melissa. No one, later, would ever believe any of her protests; it was enough that she was seen with Ravel under compromising circumstances. As for Ravel, he cooperated ardently enough in the scheme, and though never a word on the subject passed between him and Arabella, they understood each other perfectly.

Thus far, Arabella had moved with perspicacity and astuteness. Never did she mention Ravel and Melissa to her friends and guests. But her insinuations, her sad expressions, her gestures of futility and anxiety, had been enough. She gained quite a reputation among her friends for loyalty and devotion, for keeping the scandalous tales from her brother. For, this time, Arabella had resolved, the tales should not come from her, but from others, and Geoffrey would have no accusations to throw furiously in her face, nor would he be able to call her a liar. On the contrary, when he demanded whether these things he had finally heard were true, and she admitted them, she would plead her loyalty to him and to his wife, her first utter disbelief in the stories, and her resolve to keep silent "for your sake, my love and in the hope that matters would adjust themselves and that Melissa would come to her senses and spare you pain and disgrace." If he should accuse her of anything at all, it would be of forbearance and long-suffering, and a too-tender regard for him.

Arabella, knowing Geoffrey's long love for Melissa, had been puzzled at first by his apparent indifference, in spite of his chronic worry over the state of the country, and the publishing business. (She knew, too, that many of his investments in the South had been utterly lost.) She was not to blame for finally reaching the conclusion that Geoffrey's incredible infatuation for the girl had finally subsided. And she had believed that Melissa, herself, had no desire for Geoffrey, and that the marriage had, in a way, been an enforced one.

Everything had gone entirely to her satisfaction. She had decided that some way of precipitating a climax must be brought about soon. Ravel was showing signs of ardent impatience and, knowing him, she knew that he would not wait much longer, in spite of Melissa's inability to see him as a lover. But whether he succeeded or not, Arabella's work was done. Again, the appearance of evil was enough.

And now, on the very verge of victory, this dreadful creature, by expression, word, intonation and gesture, had shown that she unconsciously loved her husband. Melissa, herself, apparently, did not know this for she had had no experience of love except for her father. She did not, herself, recognize what she felt. At all costs, it must remain hidden from her, and from Geoffrey.

Paralyzed, Arabella could only stare at Melissa, seeing everything clearly and fully for the first time, and feeling a rising frenzy of terror gathering in herself.

She said, hoarsely but with weight: "Gentlemen do not remain away from their homes for so long without due cause, Melissa."

Melissa opened her mouth to answer, and then she saw Arabella's tiny gray eyes fixed upon her meaningly. Slowly, a miserable color ran over her stark cheekbones. She said, however: "What would be the cause of Geoffrey's frequent absences, Arabella?" And her own eyes returned Arabella's regard with fortitude.

Arabella sighed, indicated to Ellis that she might resume her fanning. "My dear Melissa," she said wearily, "how can

I answer that? If you do not know, who else can know? Am I Geoffrey's wife? Am I his hostess, who should make his home pleasant with friends and companionship? Does he expect agreeable and witty conversation from me, the art of entertainment, feminine laughter and gaiety, elegant deportment and social graces? No, he does not expect these things from me."

Melissa said slowly: "He does not expect them from me, either. He knew I was not like that. Yet he married me." She paused, and rubbed the back of her hand against her damp forehead. "There have been times when I truly believe he married me out of pity and loyalty to my father, and when I think this, I feel that I must leave when I have completed Papa's work and have some money of my own."

Arabella's heart beat high with renewed hope, and she smiled. "Dear Melissa, that is a decision you must reach, yourself." Then, remembering what Melissa had just said, her reaction became stronger and more exultant. "You are a woman of pride, Melissa, and I admire you for it. There are times when females are placed in a most untenable position from which pride alone can rescue them. Feebler creatures remain supine, and in a state of constant humiliation. Worse, they make miserable those who, by reason of generosity or sentimentality, have become their victims."

Melissa said straightly: "You think, then, that I should go, Arabella? You think it would be best for Geoffrey?"

At this, a sudden fierce and almost delirious force of will pushed the words to Arabella's very lips: "Yes, go, go at once, and never return!" But while her tongue was in the act of forming them, she caught them back. She trembled with the struggle. She had only to speak, to urge, and the house would be rid of this slut in an hour, and forever. But in the very midst of her furious desire to accomplish this at once, caution again held Arabella back. Geoffrey would search for the creature, if only for the sake of his own curiosity or pride. And then her own share in the flight would be revealed; it would be the end of her. No, as always, she must be cautious, even if it took time, the most precious time of all.

She said, in a shaking voice, while her eyes glittered in the duskiness of the library: "I know nothing, Melissa, as I have told you before. I know only what you yourself have said. What little I know has been communicated to me by you. And it is too little. You, yourself, must judge what is best for Geoffrey, and whether you should go or not."

Melissa felt slightly dazed. She wondered, vaguely, what

she had told Arabella; she was certain she had told her nothing. Yet she was confronted, by Arabella's own words, with the evidence. She remembered that for a long time her mind had felt heavily confused and numbed. Doubtless, she had communicated to Arabella, in a desperate effort to name them and discover their source, something of her constant sickness of anguish and anonymous longing. Had she mentioned this burning hunger that was always with her, and which had taken the meaning and purpose out of life? Arabella was staring at her now with a kind of accusation and affront.

"You look doubtful, Melissa," she said, aggrieved and indignant. "Yet you, yourself, have told me what I know, which, though small, is very significant. If you have forgotten then I, in charity, will forget also."

"I think," said Melissa, bluntly, "that I have said only that I am very wretched, and very sad and hopeless, and that I do not know why."

Arabella was silent for a few moments. She pressed her scented kerchief to her lips, and then said from behind it: "It is strange, but I observed that in my brother, also, though a sister's sensibilities may be too exaggerated."

"You think he is miserable?"

Arabella shrugged, with an air of exasperation. "Melissa," she said, with heavy patience, "I think nothing. I do not even reflect on what you often tell me. The relationships between a man and his wife are too delicate for an outsider. I want you to remember this clearly, Melissa," and again her eyes fixed themselves strongly on the girl, "that I have never discussed Geoffrey with you voluntarily, that I have never passed an opinion on the subject of your relationship with him even though you have repeatedly urged me to, that I have refused to be embroiled in your conjectures, and that everything you have said about Geoffrey and your own feelings have come from you without promptings from me. I demand that you remember all this."

She waited. Melissa regarded her dully. Then the girl said: "I do not know why you should be so agitated, Arabella. What you have said is quite true. You have never expressed an opinion on the subject, though I have asked you for advice. And I do not see why you think it so important that I remember this."

Arabella smiled. "It is not important. You are too excited, Melissa. But now, shall we continue with the lesson in properly greeting a guest at the threshold?"

She was so elated, that a good color of her own appeared under the rouge. She added, with humor: "But you may remember, if you wish, that I have tried to improve your manners and your deportment. That may please Geoffrey, in the future." Her face changed, became almost evil. "He might even give me an allowance in return, as a reward for my selfless efforts and for my time and strength."

She would not have said this had she not been so elated, so certain of approaching success, for she was not a woman who spoke impulsively. Besides, she was remembering that only three weeks ago her brother had refused to give her the money she had requested for some frippery which he did not think necessary but which had been very dear to her heart, and she felt a sudden stab of hatred and resentment.

Melissa, in spite of her misery, was startled. "You mean, Arabella, that Geoffrey does not give you any money?"

Caution tried to hold Arabella back, but her grievances were too strong. She exclaimed, wallowing in her mortification even before this senseless creature: "No, he gives me nothing! He pays my bills, but I have not a single copper to call my own! I have less than my servants. Your husband, Melissa, is not a generous man, or a kind one."

Melissa studied her in earnest surprise, her pale brows drawn together in her old uncompromising frown. Arabella nodded somberly, as if Melissa had questioned her. Her plump and raddled face, with the incongruous sharp beak of a nose, the round, tooth-filled mouth, the sharp granite-like eyes, took upon itself an expression of long-suffering resignation and quiet martyrdom. Even the puffs of light, gray-streaked hair over her wrinkled forehead acquired for Melissa a kind of subtle pathos, as did the lined fat neck, the fat bosom under the light green faille bodice, the short outstretched body on the divan. Incredibly, Arabella became the defenseless and exploited Phoebe again.

Money, in the Upjohn household, had been a sort of community property. It was there, in small quantities, and equally shared by anyone who needed it, or it was not there. In either case, Melissa had believed, it was a matter of unimportance. Even when Amanda had spoken of it bitterly, no one had paid much heed to her comments. Melissa had considered Amanda's remarks as only the outpourings of an acid and disagreeable temperament, calculated to disturb her father and to distract him from his work.

That anyone should withhold money from another, deliberately, especially when it was as plentiful as it was in this household, puzzled and angered Melissa. It was plentiful indeed, this money, and its plenitude ought to have been shared with anyone in the household who needed it at a particular moment. Melissa concentrated intently on this new phase of money, and became more and more baffled and indignant.

"But Geoffrey has plenty of money," she protested. "Why should there be any question of your having it when you need it, Araeblla?"

"I have tried to tell you, my dear. Geoffrey is tight-fisted with everyone but himself. Moreover, I suspect he delights in keeping others in a state of subservience and mortifying dependence. Has he ever given you any money?"

Melissa glanced away. "I have never asked for any," she replied, stiffly. "I have not needed it." She added: "But I cannot understand why you should not have what you need and want." She looked at Arabella again. Her narrow and literal mind could sometimes be illuminated by the wide and brilliant glare of insight, and as she studied Arabella acutely her intuition told her many things. "It is wrong, wrong!" she exclaimed, vehemently, as her insight broadened and she began to understand. "He has no right to do this thing to you! It is not only the money; it is the prideful independence of the human spirit which he has attacked. I am sure you would be a different woman, Arabella, had not this humiliation been forced upon you!"

Again, Arabella sat up, and this time her face became ugly with affront.

"And what do you mean by that, Madam?" she asked, while Ellis, delighted, listened closely.

Melissa was confused by Arabella's expression, and by her tightly furious voice.

"I meant no offense," she stammered. "I only meant that you might have been a kinder and more charitable woman, a better woman, a less embittered one, one more inclined to gentleness—" She paused, appalled at what she had said in her simple integrity. It was an indication of the subtle change which had been at work in her for six months that she could be appalled at what she had said. Before her marriage to Geoffrey, such remarks would have seemed to her entirely natural and honest and to be expected. "I hope I have not offended you, Arabella. I sometimes express things clumsily."

" 'Clumsily' is a vast understatement," replied Arabella, with a swift and vicious smile. "You see, Melissa, the reason why I so often lose hope about you. There are times when I feel that my task is completely hopeless, my work in vain. I have done my best, but I am afraid it will always be impossible to make a lady of you, to fit you for the position which has been—thrust—upon you." She scrutinized Melissa with long and cold cruelty. "So, you consider me uncharitable, embittered, ungentle and unkind, do you?"

Melissa was silent. She wrung a fold of the dimity in her damp fingers. Fear did not come to her often, but now, for some nameless reason, she felt afraid. She did not yet recognize hatred and implacability when she saw them. The sick and ominous oppression of the spirit which so afflicted her these days fell on her like a great darkness again. I should really go away at once, she thought. My presence is a constant wretchedness to him, my inability to learn keeps him from his own home.

Arabella saw the spectral mask of the girl's face in the gloom, and she sensed her depression with exultation.

"I am afraid that Geoffrey is going to be very angry with me when he discovers how little I have been able to help you, my dear Melissa," she said sadly, after several moments had passed.

"He should not be angry," said Melissa, almost inaudibly. "You have done your best. The fault lies with me."

The enormous clock in the hall struck four sonorous notes in the hot dim silence.

Arabella sighed. "Well," she murmured, with a swift glance of elation at Ellis, "it is four o'clock. Is not your sister expected at half-past for tea, Melissa? If so, I would suggest changing your gown and brushing your hair, in preparation."

"Oh, Phoebe does not care what I look like. It is very unimportant," said Melissa wearily.

"My dear Melissa! You see how little you have absorbed of what I have tried to teach you! A lady is always well-groomed and well-dressed to receive any visitor at all, is always scented and fresh—even if the visitor be only her own sister! Never would a lady present herself to the view in a disheveled and—" she glanced over at Melissa and elaborately winced, "—in a coarsely perspiring condition!"

Melissa immediately got to her feet and hastened towards the door. Arabella let her reach the threshold, then called thinly and tiredly: "Melissa. Do you not remember what I have taught you to say when you leave the room?"

Melissa turned slowly. There was a movement along her white throat as she swallowed. She said, in a lifeless tone:

'Pray excuse me, Arabella. I beg your permission to retire."

Arabella smirked, replied in a theatrical tone: "Indeed, Melissa, the permission is granted, but do not deprive us of your company too long."

"I shall return immediately," said Melissa, obediently following the routine of her lesson. Then she went out with the precipitate swiftness of an embarrassed child.

Arabella and Ellis waited until they could no longer hear Melissa's footsteps, then they buried their faces in their hands and shrilled with mirth and triumph.

CHAPTER 41

RACHEL WAS already waiting for Melissa when her mistress entered with a slow and heavy step and a heart-sick face. The maid had laid out for her a light summer tea-gown of chocolat-au-lait-colored silk, with streamers of green silk trimmed with airy black lace, a confection newly sent from New York and guaranteed to have been created by Worth. Melissa had been taking a novel interest in clothing lately, and Rachel was dismayed now when the girl only glanced dully at the gown as Rachel held it up for her inspection.

"Tell me, Rachel, why is it necessary to lie and tell a guest that you are delighted to see her when you are not?" asked Melissa, so absently that Rachel was aware that she hardly heard her own words.

"It is an accepted social custom, Mrs. Dunham," replied Rachel, anxiously studying Melissa's pallor and the lines about her pale mouth. "You would not say: 'Mrs. Jones, I am not delighted to see you, but please come in just the same'?"

She hoped to amuse Melissa, and indeed Melissa did smile, but so faintly that it only added to the deep misery of her eyes.

"Well," said Melissa, "I don't think it honest, or even kind, to express delight when you are not delighted and the guest is probably interrupting an interesting afternoon or evening of work or quiet solitude. I think it is enough to invite the guest in. Then, if she is a woman of sensibility, she will soon learn that she is intruding, and will take herself off, and everyone will be more comfortable. It saves your own time, and the guest's, for she will then go to another house where she will indeed be welcome."

"It is not possible always to be honest," said Rachel, non-plussed as usual when faced with Melissa's inflexible logic.

A slight animation returned to Melissa's eyes. "Why not? Do you know, I think that we'd have fewer wars, and certainly would make fewer enemies, and society would be set on a firmer basis, if we were always uncompromisingly honest. My father was a completely honest man, and I surely believe he had no enemies and was respected by all, because he refused to prevaricate even in the interests of a false politeness."

She sat down suddenly, overcome with the unbearable weight of her depression. She leaned her elbow on the arm of the chair, and dropped her head in her hand. "I am so tired," she murmured.

Rachel stood with the gown in her arms, and could not speak. She could only look at her mistress with aching compassion and love. She knew, and guessed at the cause of, the chronic and overpowering agony that was breaking down the high and intolerant spirit of Melissa, that had taken away her old arrogant certitude of mind and conviction. Such agony, Rachel knew, was too vast and enormous for words of comfort. An outsider was powerless to help. A kind of spiritual disintegration was taking place in Melissa, and the force that would reintegrate it into a new and happier pattern was not coming to her rescue. Rachel felt a fierce anger against Geoffrey, and a bafflement.

Melissa had no friends, in this household, but James and Rachel. Melissa instinctively felt the derision and hostility of the other servants, and shrank from their services and their presence. This seemed most terrible to Rachel: that Melissa should be demonstrating fear before eyes both friendly and hostile. And Rachel understood that, to Melissa, fear was a new and unrecognized emotion, as was the more powerful anguish that beset her every moment.

Had Melissa's suffering been less deep, been even faintly self-understood or articulate, Rachel would have been able to help her with argument, reason and comfort. But it was a mute and gigantic anguish, too immense for any consolation or sympathy. Rachel could only convey her love and understanding by smiles, by a murmur, by a touch, by a great gentleness. She knew the gossip of the countryside and the household about Melissa and Ravel Littlefield, and once or twice she had wanted to warn her mistress. But one glance at that strong and uncomprehending face, and Rachel fell into impotent silence again. Melissa would not understand.

She just would not understand in the least, and her bewilderment and incredulity might force her to drive Rachel from her.

"May I help you get dressed, Mrs. Dunham?" asked Rachel, in a moved voice.

Melissa wearily lifted her head. "In just a moment, Rachel," she replied. She glanced at her desk, and sighed. "So much work to be done, and I must waste time on a tea-party."

"But, Mrs. Dunham, it was you, was it not, who extended the invitation?"

Melissa stared at her emptily. "Oh, that doesn't matter. We never stood on ceremony at home."

Rachel was concerned. "I think Mrs. Shaw might object," she ventured. "She is very rigid about social manners. She would think it necessary for you to be present at a tea for your sister, Mrs. Dunham."

Melissa nodded. "I suppose you are right, Rachel. No wonder Arabella considers me hopeless. I never remember." She stood up and let Rachel unbutton her frock. She had become accustomed to these services and thought no more of them. Besides, the maid's touch soothed her like the touch of a friend. Rachel felt the cold and clammy flesh under her finger-tips, and again she ached with pity.

"I think, if we hurry, that I might have fifteen minutes or more to work," said Melissa, as Rachel assisted her to dress.

Rachel turned her towards the mirror. "This new gown is so becoming, Mrs. Dunham," she said admiringly. "The turquoise necklace and ear-rings and bangles will go excellently with the green silk streamers. And I think you should wear the green silk net over your hair, with the black bows, to match the black lace."

Melissa glanced into the mirror. "Nothing," she said, despairingly, "will ever make me passable in appearance. I have such an ugly face and such pale lifeless hair, and I am too tall and thin. But, then, I should not be distressed at all this. I have had my body for twenty-six years, and Papa often pointed out to me that, though I am not pleasing to look at, I at least had intelligence. Though I am beginning to doubt this, too."

Rachel's mouth compressed itself into a straight line. "You are a beautiful lady, Mrs. Dunham," she said, as she had said a hundred times before without impressing Melissa. Again Melissa shook her head impatiently and commented: "You are very kind, Rachel, but you know it is not true. No wonder Mr. Dunham cannot bear to look at me."

"I remember the evening of the day you married Mr. Dunham," said Rachel. "You wore a blue silk frock. If you remember, ma'am, he said that you were very beautiful. And you believed him, then."

"Yes, I did. I was a fool. He was only trying to be kind. I ought to have known." She allowed Rachel to brush and twist up her long hair. "Arabella has made me see myself as I am. She has done her best for me, to change me, but it is no use."

Rachel listened grimly. Her mouth opened once or twice, then she closed it. But finally she said: "Mrs. Shaw is getting old, ma'am, and I have heard it said that elderly ladies do not like young and handsome ones."

Melissa turned on her in outrage. "Rachel! How cruel of you to say that! Arabella has spent endless hours with me in an effort to teach me graces and manners and elegances! She has chosen my gowns, my laces, my ribbons, my—silks. Even you have commented on their beauty and costliness, and how they become me. How can you be so unkind?"

Rachel knew it was hopeless, so she did not reply.

Melissa, now dressed, glanced at the clock on the white mantel. It was only twenty minutes past four. Forgetting Rachel, she ran, rustling, to her desk, determined to use the last precious moments for work on her father's almost completed manuscript. She sat down, and hastily pulled a bundle of papers from a lower drawer. She had not as yet gone through these thoroughly, though a former cursory glance had convinced her that these notes were merely redundant and contained little of what had not already been enlarged upon and included in the finished portion of the manuscript. In a moment, she was completely engrossed, rapidly skimming over page after page. She saw that many of the notes were old, for Charles had meticulously dated each one at the top. Apparently he had intended them for earlier books, then had laid them aside to be included in later ones, not caring to discard them completely. Some of them bore dates as early as 1859 and 1860, and were worn and dog-eared.

Rachel watched her mistress helplessly. The poor young creature, with her pale thin face and slender worn hands! How busily she turned the pages and laid them aside, and how reverently she handled them. She was so engrossed that she might have been lifted bodily into a different and remote world, where no one could touch her. It was a face in a trance, a dedicated face, lost to any human contact. The bright sunlight that flooded the lovely room lay on her head as it would lie on curved gold, and made the turquoises on white neck and in white ears glow like illuminated green metal.

Melissa came upon a shorter sheet of paper. It was dated March 15, 1860. Apparently it had been crushed, tossed aside, then smoothed out, reread, and finally discarded. Whole sentences had been crossed out, others added above. Melissa studied it, puzzling over the faded writing. She glanced at the date again. Above it, she saw the words: "Midfield, State of Pennsylvania," and below it: "Dear Geoffrey." It was a letter, then. How had it come to be included in the papers? It was most obviously the first draft of a letter written to Geoffrey, and had only accidentally found its way into the bundle of notes. But perhaps her father had reason to keep the draft, after all. He often kept copies of important letters to his publishers, or to critics, or to other scholars. Melissa looked through it hastily, trying to find the reason for its preservation. It was some moments before the full import of the letter came to her.

"Dear Geoffrey," Charles had written, "I have your letter of the first, and I am deeply moved by it, and by its implications of your regard for a member of my family, and your concern for her. But, as I wrote you before, when you hinted at matters more boldly expressed in your last letter, it is impossible. The girl has been well-schooled by me; she is far better educated than you realize, and if I were not an understanding friend of yours, and did not sense the kindness that prompted your letter, I might take serious offense. I do know, however, your attachment to my family, and, I humbly understand, to myself. I feel compassion in your letter. I am a proud man, and I resent compassion in others, particularly when I do not need pity or generosity, and when the girl certainly does not need it. If I should send her to the school you suggest, and on your bounty, she would most surely be driven out of her very precariously balanced mind. She is not only incurably unworldly, but she suffers from fantasies and delusions, as only a father can know, and from which only a loving and suffering father can derive so complete a despair. Imagine her in the company of graceful and handsome young females! The imagination recoils at the thought. She is not only unprepossessing by nature, but, I confess with anguish, is strangely stupid and obtuse. Consider, too, her lack of charm of face and figure, afflictions which would cause her wretchedness in contrast with others more blessed and fortunate. I have considered all these things from her earliest childhood, and have kept her with me to shield her from the world and its inevitable thrusts. And now you suggest that I expose her to all manner of agonies! You will recall that we have had many conversations on this very subject before and that, out of my own understanding of the motives that inspired you, I have expressed my gratitude for your pity for the girl and for your desire to aid her. Believe me, should I ever, in a weak moment, consent, you would long and sadly rue the day."

The crushed letter lay in Melissa's hands, and slowly all its letters and all its lines began to dance before her in a kind of wavering fire. The fire seemed to enter her brain, to fill it with a dazzling empty light of numbness and overpowering shock. She had no thoughts at all, no sensation but a sort of utter and devastating paralysis of emotional reaction. Even her fingers, holding the letter, turned numb and senseless. She read and reread the paper over and over, some phrases rising from it like brilliant swords to strike at her eyes. Somewhere, something was beating like wild drums, and somewhere, someone was screaming on one prolonged note. But she felt nothing, though that disembodied creature nearby began to feel a horrible nausea and an unendurable agony creeping through the deadness.

She sat there. From some far distance she heard the faint echo of a voice: "Mrs. Dunham, ma'am, you have only five minutes more. I think I heard Mrs. Barrett's rig come up the drive."

Melissa carefully smoothed the letter with her cold fingers, and reread it. Sweat had started out all over her, icy and sickening. A great pain had pierced her head and her breast. She put the letter down, stood up, and faced Rachel. "Oh, no," she said, very calmly and quietly. Her eyes, however, pierced Rachel in a penetrating frenzy. "It isn't true, Rachel. He didn't mean me, did he? He must be referring to Phoebe. Though it is still so unkind—that about her having no—no intelligence—" Her voice began to fail, and she struggled with it, so that it emerged from her throat as a croak. "You have seen Phoebe, my sister, haven't you, Rachel? Is she not very beautiful? Phoebe is a poet, too—" And then she stopped, and could not speak again. But she looked at Rachel with her great pale eyes as if she were dying.

"Mrs. Dunham!" cried Rachel, terrified. She ran to Melissa and caught her by the arms. "You are ill, ma'am. What is wrong?" In affright, Rachel stared at her mistress' face.

Melissa stood very still. "There is nothing wrong with me," she said, uttering every word precisely and carefully. "Nothing at all. It is the heat. I have never known such heat before in July. Where is my kerchief, Rachel?"

But Rachel produced her own handkerchief, and with trembling hands wiped away the sweat from Melissa's forehead and upper lip. She wished she might dart away for the smelling-salts, for help, but Melissa's whole appearance was so terrible, so stricken, so wild, in spite of her calmness, that the girl was afraid she might fall to the floor.

"Please read the letter, Rachel," said Melissa. "You will see my father means Phoebe. It is so unjust— Phoebe must never know. It would hurt her immeasurably. Phoebe used to write the most wonderful poetry. I had such hopes for her. And now it is all over. But it is still unkind, and cruel of Papa. Phoebe must never know——"

She held the letter out to Rachel, who, still holding Melissa by one hand, took the letter and read it slowly. Most of the words were unintelligible to her, but she caught the meaning, and she gasped. She wanted to crush the hideous thing in her hand, to throw it down and stamp on it, and she was filled with hatred for a dead man she had never seen or known.

"No," said Rachel, her own voice breaking, "Mrs. Barrett must never know. It is cruel, indeed. But fathers don't always know about their own children, do they, ma'am? And, besides, it is possible that Mr. Upjohn wanted to—to keep his daughters with him. Kind of like jealousy, ma'am. I've heard fathers sometimes do outrageous things, keeping their daughters from suitors and—and—benefactors."

"It was indeed kind of Mr. Dunham," said Melissa, frowning like one in profound and only half-conscious shock. "It was kind, wasn't it, Rachel?"

"Oh, surely, very kind, ma'am," said Rachel. She held Melissa's arms, and gently pressed her down into a chair. Then she darted to the dressing-table, found the smelling-salts, returned to Melissa, and put the opened bottle under the girl's nose. But Melissa did not turn aside, or cough, as the pungent fumes struck her nostrils. She merely sat like stone, looking emptily before her, her arms fallen heavily over the arms of the chair.

"Phoebe," said Melissa, "had a truly great imagination. Perhaps Papa did not realize that, in full. Mama always monopolized Phoebe, and kept her so busy. Papa must have thought Phoebe rather tiresome and ordinary. I did, too, until I saw her poems. And Papa thought them excellent and extraordinary, also. Rachel, what is the date of that letter? March 15, 1860. That was before the war. That was eight years ago. Yes, yes, of course. Phoebe was twelve years old then. At the school-girl's age. She was ready for school." Her voice died again. But she gazed at Rachel with those enormous and fainting eyes, so numbly pleading, so desperate.

"Just at the school-age, yes, ma'am," murmured Rachel, in growing distress. Again she wiped the sweat from Melissa's forehead.

"Phoebe must never know. It would hurt her immeasurably," repeated Melissa with stony emphasis. "She would never forgive Papa. She could not bear to live, if she knew of this letter. There—there would be nothing left to live for, Rachel. There is nothing ever left to live for, when—when the heart has been struck like this, and all the faith and the dreams are gone, and everything is so very empty."

"I think Mrs. Barrett has much character, ma'am," replied Rachel. "Unkind letters never hurt very much, in the long run, especially when they are prompted by jealousy and deliberate misunderstanding."

"Oh, Papa was not jealous, nor did he misunderstand," said Melissa, in a loud and childlike tone of denial. "But that was before he knew about Phoebe's poems, of course. After he had read them, he would not have written such a letter."

"Mrs. Dunham, will you not lie down, and let me tell Mrs. Barrett and Mrs. Shaw that you are indisposed?" pleaded Rachel, almost in tears.

Melissa seemed to see Rachel for the first time. She shook her head, as if outraged. "Oh, no, Rachel, that would never do at all. That would be very impolite. Arabella has often told me that a lady must receive her invited guests, no matter how ill she may be. Only death, Arabella said, could be an excuse for such discourtesy. Rachel, I do feel very ill, though. I think I might feel this way if I were dying——"

However, she pushed aside Rachel's hands, and stood up. She absently smoothed the black lace on her breast, and pushed up the ruffled sleeves. She appeared to be half asleep, moving mechanically. She pressed her hands against the wings of hair on her temples. "I really must go down," she said, in her curious, slow tone of emphasis. "Phoebe would be disturbed. She might wonder. She must never know, and if I did not go down she might come up here, and even see the letter."

She glanced behind her at the desk. She turned and thrust the letter into the sheaf of notes. Now she began to shiver so violently that she almost staggered. Rachel watched her with helpless alarm.

"Why not destroy the letter, Mrs. Dunham? Then you could be sure that no one would ever see it."

"Oh, no," answered Melissa, seriously, "that would be very wrong. Everything of Papa's is important."

She turned heavily, and then, as if she had forgotten Rachel entirely and was walking in the numbness of complete sleep, she moved slowly towards the door, and went out.

The long staircase lay before her, a shadowy darkness falling down into bottomless space. She held to the balustrade very tightly, and went downwards, step by step. Her knees were strangely fluid and jelly-like. There was no air anywhere. Melissa found it difficult to breathe. Though she moved so slowly, her heart was beating in her breast and throat and temples in swift hard strokes of intolerable pain. Her head swam; there was no feeling in her feet and she had to grope in a swirling mist.

She did not know that Rachel stepped down beside her, hands ready to catch her if she fell.

CHAPTER 42

ARABELLA HAD INVITED Phoebe to the comparatively cool and tree-shaded quiet of the terrace behind the house, where enormous elms had tangled their branches together against the intense blue of the summer sky. The slabs of gray stones that formed the floor of the terrace were outlined with green moss. Great urns of flowers stood at the corners, burning reds and blues and greens in the sheltered and aqueous light. Masses of flowering vines climbed up the posts which supported the roof of the terrace. Here were comfortable chairs filled with cushions, a hammock, several tables of ornamental iron. The view that lay beyond was of bright gardens smoldering in the hot sunshine, of intense green lawns, a distant fountain over which pigeons hovered, and a small white statue or two on a pedestal. Beyond the gardens was a pond on which water-lilies grew, and in which, at night, a chorus of frogs lifted itself to the moon and the stars.

Though none of the Upjohns could claim any affection

from Arabella, the latter sometimes regarded Phoebe with a slight fondness. Unlike the other Upjohns, Arabella would reflect pleasantly, Phoebe was no freak, had no peculiarities, no strangeness of character, no odd ways, none of the long and somber taciturnities which made Andrew a formidable presence, no sudden hard intuitivenesses which had made Amanda, his mother, a companion able to inspire uneasy suspicions, no elegant affectations like Charles', which had been all the more irritating because one suspected that he knew they were such. Phoebe was no fool, and she had, in Arabella's estimation, a normal and human maliciousness towards those more fortunate in a solid, worldly sense, a bent for gossip, a healthy interest in clothes, and in the scandals of Midfield, and a pleasure in the afflictions of envied others. All this was understandable to Arabella, and she enjoyed Phoebe's visits, especially now that Phoebe was safely married to a prosperous young farmer, well-dressed and socially acceptable. And because Arabella enjoyed the superiority of compassion, she could gaze on Phoebe affectionately and meditate on what a wretched life the poor girl must have led among the queer Upjohns.

Moreover, Arabella strongly suspected that Phoebe despised and ridiculed her sister, which fact gave Phoebe a warm charm in her eyes.

Phoebe, however, had a charm of her own on this hot July day. Clad in rose-sprinkled dimity tied with rose-colored ribbons, with a rose-laden wide, flat straw hat on her golden head, pink streamers flowing over her young shoulders, and black sandals tied with more pink ribbons on her dainty crossed feet, she was a most delightful vision of young freshness and beauty. Always plump, her few weeks of marriage had increased her flesh, so that her face was a mass of rosy dimples, smiles and flashes of blue from sprightly eyes. Released from the strain of her ominous home, she had revealed a new gaiety and liveliness, enhanced by the malice of her laughing remarks and a natural shrewd wit. She loved her new husband, her well-built, secure house, the rich acres of the farm, her pretty clothing, her rig, which was her own, the two servants who waited upon her sedulously, and her position as a rising and sensible young matron in Midfield. She was always content and happy until she visited the lofty splendors of the Dunham house and looked enviously at the "yellow" room, the immense library, the park-like grounds, and felt all the luxury which only great wealth can impart to any establishment. She was apt to return home in a peevish mood, full of condemnations of her dull sister and commiserations for both Geoffrey and Arabella, who must always be afflicted by the gaunt and Gothic presence of Melissa.

John Barrett usually felt very uneasy about Phoebe after these visits. After them, she was often discontented, petulant, hard to please, captious and faintly whining. As he was a simple-minded young man, very kind and upright, it never occurred to him that Phoebe was simply envious and resentful of her sister's good fortune. He thought, merely, that Melissa must have upset his darling, and his sentiments towards his sister-in-law would take on reproachfulness and annoyance. On the occasion of his few meetings with Melissa, he would demonstrate a silent surliness foreign to his real nature, and Melissa shrank from him and became even more silent in his presence. She resented him for his "rape" of little Phoebe, and considered that he had "forced" an intolerable marriage upon her because of the Upjohn penury; in consequence, she regarded the young man with bitter repulsion. However, whenever she discovered him eyeing her with somber distrust and unfriendliness, she would feel a sad thrill of bewilderment.

Neither Phoebe nor John had, as yet, heard the local gossip about Melissa and Ravel Littlefield, and this was evidence of the delicacy of their friends. Arabella, who had made Phoebe comfortable, regarded her speculatively. She was a clever woman, and though she well knew Phoebe's sentiments towards her sister, she suspected that there was a kind of clannishness among the Upjohns which outsiders would attack at their peril. There might come a day when that clannishness would disappear. But today was not the time. It was coming close, in Phoebe, but it was still not the time. So Arabella smiled fondly upon her young visitor, and complimented her upon her dress and her ability to remain fresh and bright on such a day. Phoebe responded to this with gratification, and artlessly informed Arabella of the price of the gown, the hat and the ribbons. She swung a rose-colored velvet reticule by its ribbons, and thought of the comfortable sum of money it contained and the lace-trimmed linen handkerchief delicately scented and her heavy bunch of household keys. The girl smiled happily; then, with a sudden frown, she glanced at the open terrace door.

"Where can Melly be?" she asked, pettishly.

"I'm sure I don't know," sighed Arabella patiently. "She knew the time of your arrival. I am certain her maid also kept her informed."

It annoyed Phoebe that Melissa—horrid, silly old Melly—

should have a personal maid. Moreover, it was incongruous.
Stupid old Melly, who often forgot to wash her dirty, ink-
stained hands, with a maid of her own to dress and furbish
her and comb her hair! It was not easy for Phoebe to endure
this. She, who was so very pretty, so conscious of the amenities and the elegances, so natural a mistress of all this grandeur, had not been considered a moment by Geoffrey Dunham. For some strange and still baffling reason, he had chosen
Melissa, who would forever be a shame and a burden to him.
The months of Melissa's marriage had not improved her, given
her gracefulness or presence, nor did she ever appear aware
of the magnificence which surrounded her and the loftiness
of her position. Phoebe could feel the symptoms of her old
irritation arising in her, and it was really too warm a day
to be imposed on in this manner. She repeated: "Where can
she be? But Melly was always that way. Completely indifferent
to the obligations she might have towards others. She was ever
selfish, dear Arabella, and you must find her a trial."

But Arabella was not to be inveigled into making any remark which might later be used against her. She had had
one or two disconcerting experiences in the past, when, stimulated by some remark of a friend, she had expressed sympathy,
later to find herself quoted viciously by the "friend" without
the preliminary explanation of the confidences which had pro-
voked her observations. Whatever she might say of Melissa
now, would quite possibly be repeated by Phoebe as comment
out of the blue and out of Arabella's own odious nature. So
Arabella merely smiled a long-suffering and eloquent smile
and shrugged.

"I do not envy you, dear Arabella," goaded Phoebe, irritated at the older woman's silence, and dissatisfied by the
smile that said everything but was yet unquotable. "I had
twenty years of Melly, so you can imagine."

Again Arabella smiled. She was beginning to enjoy herself,
quite understanding Phoebe's irritation. "It is not my place
to comment on anything," she said. But she waited expectantly.

Phoebe brooded on her sister. It was intolerable for one
as stupid as Melissa to have been blessed in this fashion, to
have been given all these rich opportunities. It was part of
the cruel inconsistencies of fate, which always seemed to give
the best fortune to the most unworthy, to heap honors on the
doltish and witless and to deny them to the meritorious, to
pour wealth into the hands of those who could not properly
exploit it and to withhold it from the competent and shrewd.

It was wrong, wrong! It never occurred to Phoebe, as it never occurred to thousands like her commonplace self, that Melissa and her kind might have talents and characters which drew honors and fortune naturally, and that there is a wisdom in fate not discernible to the ordinary run of humanity. It was just her undeserved good luck, thought Phoebe. I was just less lucky than this silly fool.

The dimity frock, the beribboned pretty hat, and the rose-velvet reticule no longer pleased Phoebe. She thought of her own home, and its tidy gardens, with discontent and envy. Why could Johnnie not have had the position, wealth and prestige of Geoffrey Dunham, Johnnie who was so much more deserving? Oh, it was intolerable! She loved Johnnie, and hated Geoffrey for the injustice of fate. What was the difference between Johnnie, wise, kind, sweet Johnnie, and that arrogant and gross-faced Geoffrey Dunham? None at all, except that Geoffrey had inherited an unearned fortune!

Arabella saw the pettish frown on Phoebe's pretty face, and guessed at much of her thoughts. So she said: "Have you seen the lovely rope of pearls which Geoffrey recently gave your sister? They belonged to my mother. And there is a diamond necklace, too, with diamond bangles to match, and a magnificent diamond ring. Melissa has not yet worn them, but then, we have not had a grand party this year. She will probably wear them in October."

Phoebe listened with angry awe. She pressed her pink lips together so tightly that the color disappeared. She said, ill-naturedly: "I am sure Melissa will not appreciate these things. She never cared for the gowns and jewels which other females find delightful. Her whole world was Papa, and books, and musty dead languages," Suddenly, she giggled. "It was such a waste, too. Papa always made the most subtle fun of Melly, right in front of her, so that even a zany would have seen. But she never saw in the least. She has no humor, no sense of proportion."

Arabella, though soothed by these confidences, glanced cautiously at the door. "I think I hear Melissa," she warned.

"I hope she heard me," replied Phoebe, sullenly, but she dropped her voice. She listened to the slow and dragging footsteps crossing the flagged sun-room inside. Then Melissa appeared on the threshold, and Phoebe, arranging her lips in a tight little smile of sisterly superiority, turned towards her. Her glance was immediately caught by the handsome new gown and the jewels, and her own dimity frock became the cheap gingham of a farm-wife. But, a moment later, the

envious glance fixed itself in surprise on Melissa's face, and
even Phoebe's small hard heart was struck by Melissa's
ghastly pallor and by the still anguish in the dazed eyes. A
suppressed concern rose in her, and her own rich color faded
in a new anxiety.

She stood up quickly and went towards Melissa. "Melly!"
she exclaimed. "Are you ill?"

Melissa stopped, and looked down at her little sister. The
expression of sightless fixity did not fade for several moments,
and she did not speak. Phoebe took her hand; it was heavy
and ice-cold, and she dropped it hastily. Arabella, also caught
by the strangeness about Melissa, ceased fanning her plump
countenance, and sat very straight in her chair, her fan
suspended in the air.

Melissa just stood there, tall and thin and silent, with the
face and eyes of a stricken and speechless ghost. A hot breeze
stirred the black lace on her gown, and ruffled the lace on her
breast. But she did not appear to be breathing. There was
something corpse-like about her which affrighted Phoebe and
made her step back a pace or two.

"What is wrong, Melly dear?" she faltered. She repeated:
"Are you ill?"

For the first time, Melissa seemed to be aware of her sister.
She glanced about her dazedly, and even started a little. Her
white lips moved in the faint parody of a smile. Her hands
lifted slightly, then dropped.

She said, in an unnaturally loud slow voice, as if she were
deaf: "No, I am not ill. It was the heat. I think it was the
heat."

Now her eyes focussed upon Phoebe. The younger girl
could not understand their expression, for it was urgent and
piercing and desperate. Moreover, they did not see Arabella,
who was listening intently.

"Phoebe," said Melissa. "did Papa once think of sending
you away to school, when you were a little girl? Please think,
Phoebe, think very clearly, and try to remember."

Phoebe was struck dumb by this extraordinary question.
Bewildered, she looked at Arabella. Her rosy lips parted in
astonishment.

She stammered: "Why, Melly, whatever do you mean? And
what does it matter if he did or did not? What a queer question!"

Melissa's hand darted out and caught Phoebe's plump,
warm white arm in a strong grip. "You must answer me,
Phoebe," she said. "You don't know what it means to me."

Phoebe could not believe her own ears, nor the evidence of her astounded eyes. But something warned her that she must not pull away nor answer Melissa lightly. There was some terribleness here, some agony, some horror, which all her instincts recognized, even if her mind could not encompass them and their meaning.

She said, soothingly: "Why, Melissa. I don't know why you should ask this, or why it should seem important to you." Her pretty brows drew together in an earnest desire to concentrate. Then she smiled, and dimpled. "I think I do remember something about it. Yes, I was very young, but I remember. Mama wanted me to go away to school, I believe, and she and Papa discussed it, and then there was no money." Her own face cleared, and she laughed softly. "I did so want to go. But Mama said there was no money for clothes and books, even if there had been enough for the board and tuition. So nothing more was said or done about it."

Arabella thought: Is the fool mad? Why does it appear a matter of life-and-death to her? Why does she stare at Phoebe like that, as if she were trying to probe the girl's brain? And what a ridiculous scene! She has no self-control, no manners, and all my work, as I long suspected, has been a waste of time. How often I have taught her how to greet a guest, how to suppress vulgar emotion, and what to say! Yet she just stands there like a great gaunt dolt fresh from the plow and the fields.

Melissa dropped her hand from Phoebe's arm. Some of the rigidity left her face and body. She sagged a little, as if intolerably exhausted. The gray of shock began to recede from her mouth and the shadow of shock lessened in her eyes.

She murmured: "Poor little Phoebe."

No one answered her or spoke. In spite of the hot sunlight and the flowers and the distant splash of the fountain, the terrace held something pent and ominous.

Then Phoebe said: "Oh, it doesn't matter in the least, Melly. But what made you ask this?"

Melissa drew a deep breath, like a heavy sigh. "There was a letter Papa had written to someone— I found it today."

Again, Phoebe frowned in perplexity. "But what does it matter? And why should it concern you so?"

"I think," said Melissa, as if she had not heard the questions, "that some way should have been found to send you. It was very wrong. Yes, it was very wrong."

Phoebe, in spite of her envy and her chronic detestation of Melissa, was touched. She sighed sweetly. "Please do not think so. It does not matter now. I am sure it is all for the best, though at the time it was a great disappointment. But, Melly, do sit down. You look so tired. The heat has given you the vapors." She scrutinized her sister anxiously. She had always thought Melissa quite insane, but she had thought it maliciously. Now she considered the possibility with real alarm and sympathy.

She took Melissa's arm, and Melissa let herself be led to a chair like an obedient and stupefied child. She sat down, but her eyes did not leave Phoebe's face. They had a dull, drowned look about them, though now the expression of shock was completely gone from them. Arabella watched curiously.

She said: "Dear Melissa, how extraordinary you are! And how seriously you take everything! It is not that important, as Phoebe has told you."

Melissa suddenly clasped her hands tightly together. She turned to Arabella and gazed at her like one in a painful trance. She said: "Oh yes, it is important! You don't know how important! No one knows. You see, when I read that letter," she added simply, "I thought I was going to die."

Arabella stared, and Phoebe also. They were both speechless with astonishment. Phoebe flashed Arabella a glance of fear, and Arabella pursed her lips.

Arabella finally said: "You do take things to heart in the most amazing way, Melissa, things which are of no consequence to others who are less—emotional."

Melissa was silent. She looked down at her twisted hands. After a long time, she murmured: "I thought I was going to die."

"How extravagant!" cried Arabella, with a light, contemptuous laugh. "I did not know you were so attached to your sister, Melissa."

Phoebe moved a step closer to Melissa, as if to protect her against Arabella's scorn. Phoebe was only an ordinary girl, and could not understand or know unusual things. But she felt, again, that something terrible had stricken Melissa, and that her sister had been in some mysterious danger.

She put her hand gently on Melissa's shoulder, greatly moved by what she believed her sister's concern for her. She actually knew a pang of remorse for her own malevolences to Melissa in the past. She said, tenderly: "But, darling Melissa, it does not matter, believe me. You should not be so upset. I came to see you today, and now you have alarmed me."

Arabella, remembering that a hostess should be tactful,

rang the silver bell near her hand on an iron table. "Let us have tea," she said. "Tea will refresh us all, I hope. I am sure that Melissa's—singular—conduct can be explained by the heat."

A part of Melissa's mind recalled the many long lessons it had learned. She said mechanically: "Yes, let us have our tea." She regarded her sister confusedly. "I was late. I am very sorry. How are you, Phoebe?"

"It is of no consequence," said Phoebe. She had sat down now, perched on the edge of her chair. She studied Melissa acutely. This was all very queer. Of course, poor old Melly always had the strangest ideas, and became agitated over the most outlandish things. Phoebe remembered that her sister, in reading over a newly published book of her father's, had come upon a slight error in the translation of a poem. The error, of course, had been the printer's. Not one scholar in ten thousand would have observed it, and not one in twenty thousand, unless he was a confirmed pedant, would have cared. But Melissa had been thrown into a veritable frenzy over the error. She had raved and stamped, and had breathed fire. Even Charles had been amazed at her passion. She had insisted upon writing Geoffrey, demanding not only the dismissal of the blasphemous printer but a long and detailed apology and correction to be printed in a separate pamphlet and sent to the few hundred purchasers of the book. Whatever Geoffrey, full of amusement, had written in reply, Phoebe had never known, but apparently it was a facetious answer, belittling the importance of the error, for Melissa had displayed fresh frenzy and rage and had denounced Geoffrey as a "gross and incompetent publisher, a buffoon, a despoiler of scholarship, a jape who had no regard for learning." Geoffrey, declared Melissa bitterly, was in a universal conspiracy to destroy the sanctity of scholarly learning in America and to reduce the American people to a state little above complete illiteracy. She had not calmed down for many weeks, and she had written Geoffrey again, three times, in the most virulent terms.

Thinking of this, Phoebe was again irritated by the silliness of her sister. Her novel concern for Melissa died away. There she sat, as always, with that blankness on her haggard face, a face which expressed nothing at all, except, perhaps, the blankness of the mind behind it. Phoebe again scanned the lovely Worth creation. How magnificent such a gown would be on her own dainty figure! Green was her favorite color, and those cascades of fragile black lace set it off deliciously.

Those turquoises, too, on the golden chain set with tiny pearls, hung about Melissa's neck incongruously. That long, thin white neck, like the neck of a goose! Nothing could arouse any life in the pale, lightless hair, either. Phoebe caressed one of her own vivid, bright ringlets, and her envy filled her with resentment. She had only one consolation: Melissa was growing more ugly every day.

It was just like stupid old Melly to be thrown into a tizzy because, long ago, one of the family had been denied an education she had not in the least wanted. It was all settled neatly now, in Phoebe's thoughts, and the nagging irritation could increase, unimpeded.

Melissa sat, her emaciated fingers locked together, and stared at the floor of the flagged terrace. The tea arrived. Arabella suggested that Melissa pour. She did so, mechanically. This time she did not drop a single spoon, though she spilled sugar. Arabella sighed, with resignation, after a telling glance at Phoebe.

Melissa, because of her mutenesses, her lack of interest in the company, had an oppressive effect on any conversation anywhere. She had this effect now. It was no use trying to ignore her Gothic presence, though Phoebe and Arabella tried valorously. It was like attempting to conduct conversation in a light vein in the company of an embarrassing corpse.

"Have you seen the last issue of *Godey's?*" asked Arabella. She had looked at Melissa significantly, calling attention to the little cakes on the silver salver, which ought to be offered Phoebe. But Melissa had not noticed, though she was now staring directly at the salver. So Arabella did the honors. She went on: "There is a velvet mantle, called The Metternich. It can be of any color, though bottle-green and crimson are much favored. It is trimmed around with a wide guipure lace, criss-crossed up the back, and carried down the front of the wrap. Jet and crochet ornaments are arranged in with the lace. I understand it is very soignée, and very new. I think I shall order it, in bottle-green."

"Yes," said Phoebe, momentarily forgetting the depressing figure of her sister. "I saw that issue. But I preferred the gray cloth paletot, slit on each side and at the back. The openings, if you remember, dear Arabella, are caught together with bands of bead trimming. Then there are epaulets and a very full trimming formed of crochet and bugles. The entire wrap is bound with black velvet. Worth suggests a violet poplin dress and violet velvet bonnet, trimmed with black lace and pink roses, to set off the wrap."

"I liked that exceedingly, too!" cried Arabella, enthusiastically. "Do order it, darling Phoebe! It should be very fetching, with your figure. Do you know that we have much the same proportions? There are times when it is very pleasing to be petite."

Phoebe surveyed Arabella's plump and tightly-laced figure and was annoyed at the comparison with her own dainty form. How stupid of Arabella to find the slightest resemblance. But she answered amiably: "Yes, it is so unfashionable, and so without style, to be tall. Amazonian, and unfeminine!"

They both glanced at Melissa's long body sitting so rigidly in the chair. They hoped she had caught the allusion. They were, however, disappointed. Melissa was not aware of them, or of their conversation. A vast and glaring emptiness filled her head. That emptiness shimmered, and darts of pain ran through her eyes and through all her body. A sense of swimming giddiness pervaded her. Sometimes the chair swayed under her and she had to grip the arms to keep from falling forward. A lump, like a stone, was in her throat. It shut off her breath and paralyzed her chest. There was a dry sick taste of metal in her mouth. Through it all pounded the deep and speechless old anguish, but stronger now, and more threatening. All at once, she was overpowered with her illness, and once again her face was bathed in a cold dampness.

But she could not think. She had not a single thought. She tried to grasp floating impressions that fluttered through her brain. But they were fog and mist.

"Tell me, dear Melissa," said Phoebe, in a voice like a kittenish purr, "what have you ordered from New York for the autumn?"

Melissa did not answer. She had not heard. Then she picked up the untouched tea and held the tepid liquid against her lips. She put it down abruptly. She became conscious of the silence about her, which was suddenly ripped open by the raucous scream of a chorus of locusts. She blinked as the hot sunlight stung her eyes. Then she saw Arabella and Phoebe looking at her, and she started, as if surprised to find them about her, and herself on the terrace.

Phoebe smirked. She repeated her question in a rallying tone meant to amuse Arabella. Melissa listened with piteous attention. She said, slowly: "I haven't ordered anything. Ought I to?"

"It is customary," said Arabella, lightly. "However, my

dear, if you wish, I shall order for you, as usual. If you would only indicate a preference."

"I think, a brown cloak, of wool," said poor Melissa, trying to smile and to be part of the conversation. If only that strange agony would lift and let her breathe! If only these two would not look at her, or, if looking at her, their eyes would be less piercing and hostile. She wanted to placate them, to urge them to accept her. She suddenly caught up the salver of cakes and thrust them quickly at Phoebe. Phoebe shook her head, smiling. "I have had too many as it is," she said. She gave Arabella a suppressed glance of mirth.

"A brown wool cloak!" exclaimed Arabella, lifting her hands in a gesture of horror. "My dear girl, how horrid! A cloak for a servant girl. Or are you trying to economize? So unnecessary. I am sure that Geoffrey would be much pleased if you displayed better taste, and less thrift."

Geoffrey. The agony suddenly ran over Melissa like a drowning wave. Again, her face changed, became desperate and very still. She swallowed with visible effort, while the two other women, caught by her expression, gazed at her with fresh astonishment.

"Geoffrey does not care," said Melissa, hoarsely. "It does not matter to him whether I wear a brown shawl or a velvet wrap. I rarely see him. I wore the yellow dress, with the violet ribbons. Rachel said it was pretty. But he did not notice it. Rachel arranged my hair quite becomingly too. It took a long while. There was a rose in it, over the ear. He never saw it."

She turned her eyes from one woman to the other, as if supplicating them. But they were honestly speechless. She stood up, and the tea-cup before her, shaken from the table, fell with a crash to the floor.

"I think," she said, rather wildly, "that I must lie down. It is the heat. I cannot bear it."

And she swung about, upsetting her chair with another loud crash, and ran away into the house.

For a long time there was silence on the terrace. Phoebe had turned quite pale. Her fingers plucked at the clasp of her reticule. She had caught her under lip between her little white teeth. Then she looked at Arabella directly.

"What is wrong with my sister?" she asked, and her voice was clear and sharp in the summer warmth.

Arabella, who had become ugly with hate and fear, tried to smile.

"I do not know, my dear," she replied, sadly. "But do I

need to tell you that she is no queerer than when she lived with you in your old home?"

Phoebe did not answer. She glanced at the open door through which Melissa had disappeared. She had an impulse to go in search of her sister. But she immediately shrank from the idea. The whole day was already spoiled. Melissa's vapors were enough to make anyone distraught. And she, Phoebe, was feeling somewhat strange and indisposed herself these last few days. There was no use in aggravating her condition. She caught her breath, and all at once her eyes began to shine musingly. She forgot Melissa.

CHAPTER 43

WHENEVER RAVEL LITTLEFIELD met Melissa, it was with uneasiness and misgivings. He, unlike Melissa, was not in the least ingenuous. He had known that open meetings, within sight of the whole countryside, could lead to but one result—scandal and gossip. In order to protect Melissa, he had hinted that a little discretion might be in order, but Melissa had only stared at him blankly, not understanding in the least.

"Why should we not walk together, and talk, when we wish?" she had demanded. Her tired eyes had been clear and puzzled, and somewhat annoyed. But Ravel, after his first impatience, understood that no explanations would do more than baffle Melissa, and his reluctant tenderness for her grew steadily. She was so incredibly honest.

Hers, he saw, was not a deliberate and righteous honesty, sternly and dutifully chosen out of a conviction that it was correct, high-minded, or likely to serve as an "example." Such honesty, he reflected, was hypocritical. Rather, hers was an honesty which could be nothing else but itself, which could not conceive of anything else, and thus it had majesty and grandeur. He could see very well why such integrity would inspire the ridicule of fools, the superior smiles of the pseudosophisticates, the exchange-of-glances between those who mistook truth for naïveté. It had power—the power of complete innocence.

So great was that power, that Ravel tried to convince himself that Melissa's innocence made her invulnerable even to slander and lies and scandal, that when he walked with her a kind of invisibility attached itself to them. He really knew better than this, but Melissa had hypnotized him against his own good judgment and knowledge of the world. Moreover, unconsciously, he knew that scandal might in the end be his best ally in his determination to have Melissa, not for a few days or months, but for always. If matters reached a state where she would be compelled to leave her husband it would be only what Ravel, himself, now wanted.

It had, at first, alarmed and frightened him when he discovered that he loved Melissa, not lightly, not with mere physical fascination, not even with much passion. He loved her with a love he had not believed possible; he had not believed it existed, or could exist, between men and women. This love made him feel at once humble and strong, cleansed and invincible, tender and protective. He soon saw that it also made the thought of life without Melissa completely intolerable, and that was why he was so disturbed.

A wise man, he knew, cared about many things, but cared for nothing very much. Emotions, uncontrolled, were the enemies of a serene and happy and enjoyable existence. It was agreeable to love, but it was wiser not to love too much or too well. A man had his life to plan, whether that life was of work or of pleasure, and emotional storms could well wreck the nicety of accomplishment and joy. To permit love to make everything else quite without significance was the mark of a fool.

He could not understand why he loved Melissa with such violent force and exclusiveness. He had thought her beautiful and desirable. But the world is full of beautiful and desirable women. She had excited him, but he had often been excited before. She had no charm or fascination of manner, no gaiety (and gaiety was his first demand in a woman), no little arts and graces and coquetries. In short, she was, in many ways, a neutral creature, almost sexless. Beyond the mere modelling of her face, her coloring, and her figure, she had few feminine lovelinesses. She knew nothing of reality and, while this might be charming in a child, it could be wearisome in a woman. Even in love, there must be a realistic contact between men and women, a mutual exchange of impressions. Her range of conversation was very limited. Let talk stray beyond the world of books, poetry, literature and the exact meaning of language, and Melissa became blank and con-taught her to assume an expression of polite attention. But fused, though Ravel observed that someone had recently there were times when she forgot to be polite, and presented a stony exterior very disconcerting to a gentleman (even if he was a poet) who had other interests besides the ones Melissa considered ought to occupy, exclusively, the minds of adult human beings.

She was not interested in the turbulent post-war world, the terrors of the Southern Reconstruction, wars, personalities and people. When Ravel tried to discuss them, she would listen with impatience for him to have done. She thought it all very trivial, and Ravel, who prided himself on his conversation, would be quite infuriated. She was actually unsure who had succeeded Lincoln. Ravel had no liking for a blue-stocking, and he preferred stupidity in a really beautiful woman, yet he found himself disappointed and frustrated in Melissa, because she actually knew nothing at all. He knew her intellect; he wished she might exercise it on something else besides the monotonous subjects she appeared to believe were the only ones worthy of discussion. Sometimes he laughed at himself. Here was a desirable woman, and for the first time in his life he wished such a woman would talk to him like a man and like a friend! As an intelligent man, he delighted in paradoxes so long as they did not touch him personally.

He found himself hating Charles Upjohn. Charles Upjohn was always present when Ravel was with Melissa.

At first, he encouraged Melissa to talk about her father, for he saw that was the one vulnerable spot through which he could reach her chambered nautilus of a heart. He had only to mention a man who was dead (and yet who seemed, in the presence of Melissa, forbodingly alive) and Melissa would become eloquent, awkwardly passionate, and fanatical. Her pale, rather deep-set eyes would sparkle, take on a swift blueness; her colorless skin would flush delicately; her rough gestures would assume the compelling drama of a really aroused and ardent spirit. In short, her static rigidity would be broken up, like strong waters breaking through a crust of dull ice. In the beginning, Ravel was fascinated by this phenomenon, and out of curiosity he would speak almost exclusively of Charles Upjohn. He gathered, from the rush of Melissa's words, that Charles was the noblest scholar of them all, a man of complete perfections, kind, exquisite, delightful in conversation, excellent in learning, a creation in which God Himself would take the most awed and respectful pleasure. No one could surpass him in the choice of the felicitous phrase, the poetry of his language, the beauty of his paragraphs, the irrefutable soundness of his ideas, his logic and his knowledge.

So great was Melissa's eloquence upon the subject that Ravel, who again knew better, began to feel himself subtly hypnotized into believing what she told him. He even wished, in the beginning, that he might have known such a wonder and sat at his feet. But natural human jealousy and skepticism made him question Melissa closely upon matters other than Charles' prodigious learning and genius. In her innocence, Melissa revealed more than she ever consciously suspected or knew. Finally, a really accurate picture of Charles began to develop in Ravel's mind, and he was disgusted, and alarmed for Melissa.

Not only was Charles a constant intruder when they were together, but he was an intruder both evil and petty, wanton and deformed, sinister and mean, jealous and exigent. He was a man of power, but it was a power of extreme and twisted littleness. He had superimposed himself on Melissa's imagination, had seduced her reason, had made grotesque her vision, knew, because he was a frustrated man ruled by hatred. could destroy. And he had done all this, Ravel intuitively had imprisoned her in a tower which only a major convulsion Nothing else but hatred could have impelled any man to take over the sovereignty of any other soul, and to cripple it so terribly. Ravel suspected also that the hatred which had destroyed Charles Upjohn was a hatred for the world which had denied him eminence and fame. But the world was invulnerable. Charles had fallen back on the only domain he had, his family, and he had poured out on that family the full if impotent measure of his will-to-power, his lust for destruction.

It was apparent that the others had finally escaped. Melissa alone had not. Why? She was a woman of character and inherent strength. Only love could make a victim of such a woman. She had loved her father without reservation and with awful completeness, and so had delivered herself up to him.

If Ravel had heard, somewhere, of two people like himself and Melissa, if he had heard of a man who seriously felt himself beginning to grapple with a dead man for a woman's soul, he would have laughed with amusement. He would have said such a man had, to be very charitable, no sense of humor. Yet he was not laughing now.

He sent to New York for copies of Charles' writings. He read them closely, for it was necessary to understand a thing in order to hate it constructively. He was, himself, no mean scholar, and there were times when he admired, involuntarily, this minute and precise scholarship. And then he saw its essential pedantry, its narrowness and conceit, its enormous egotism and dogmatic self-love. Ravel had always detested the pedant. Charles was its archetype. He was the pedant enamored of the word, the gelid and quivering snail in its drab shell. And, like all pedants, he was potentially dangerous.

That such a man might take possession of one like Melissa was understandable. But complete understanding only increased the horror of the thing. Sometimes Ravel felt paralyzed. There was nothing he could do, that was immediately evident. Unlike Geoffrey, it never occurred to him that only Melissa could save Melissa, and that if Melissa were left alone, in silence and in contemplation, she must inevitably be awakened by the rising clamor of heretofore self-suppressed knowledge. The healing of any madness, Geoffrey knew, came from self-realization, from meditation and reflection. The human mind, if only it had quiet, tended to health. Let the trampling be ended, and the grass of fruitful thoughts would struggle to life again and cover all scars with greenness.

Ravel had become a man whom he had always found even more absurd than the man abjectly in love: a man who believed that the woman he desired was married to an obdurate and stupid husband from whom her lover must rescue her at all costs. Incredibly, for Ravel, he saw himself as Melissa's deliverer. He had forgotten everything he had ever known. There was nothing for him in the world now but Melissa and the poem he was writing, and this was coming more and more to be a heroic saga of her own bewitched and sleeping self.

It was to be the one poem he ever wrote that was to bring him fame. But he never thought of fame now. He thought only of Melissa.

They met very frequently at the Dunham house. The old friendship between Arabella and Ravel had become stronger, and both knew why. During Geoffrey's absence, Ravel dined at least twice a week with the two lonely women in the great house, and summer afternoons often found him on the terrace with them, drinking tea. But he met Melissa alone, in a spot which had become their favorite haunt, usually at sundown.

This spot was in a sharp bend of the river, where a grove of willows leaned over the water and trailed their green fingers in their own reflections. Two or three flat, sun-warmed stones were conveniently grouped together in a place where drooping boughs laced themselves into a canopy against the hot sky. This left Ravel and Melissa hidden from anyone who strolled nearby on the banks above, while leaving a clear and open view of the river before them and the distant banks beyond and of occasional small craft bobbing on the brilliant water. Only the sounds of wind and river and birds moved about them, and these enhanced their privacy and isolation. If the spot had a tendency to be somewhat dank, and if insects showed a predilection for their company, neither knew nor cared.

Ravel was not entirely sure why Melissa met him here and why she was always waiting for him. He was not even sure that she did wait for him. She had found this place herself, and when he came he would usually discover her reading or making notes, utterly absorbed in what she was doing. When she heard his step, she would glance up vaguely, smile only a little, and wait for him to sit down beside her. There were times when she actually seemed slightly annoyed at his interruption of her work and thoughts. He had only one consolation. She no longer was shy with him, or awkward and painfully embarrassed. She accepted him. His intuition, almost feminine, assured him that in this he had made an enormous gain.

At first, she had merely tolerated him. But now he had become that best and dearly beloved friend, an ear. If Ravel had had any iota of his old sense of humor left, he would have found his new rôle ridiculous, he who had charmed all women with his conversation, his bons mots, his flattery, his eloquence. But an ear for Melissa he had become. He had known this must be his rôle, and though he had entered it reluctantly and artfully in the beginning, he played it now with passionate interest and fascination. He might be bored with Melissa's incessant talk of books and her father, but he was delighted with her ingenuousness, her lofty and bizarre comments upon a world about which she knew nothing, and by her opinions, which were invariably fanatical, fantastic and arrogant.

Moreover, he found that her very presence excited him, brought streams of thought to his own mind as he listened to her firm remarks and opinions. He could not understand this; certainly he never engaged in spirited controversy with Melissa, for he knew it would be useless. Nor did she permit him to tell her anything of the world he knew, for to her that world did not exist, or, if existing, it was not important. But he had only to sit beside her and watch the movement

of her faintly colored and strongly carved lips, to catch a
beam of light which made her eyes suddenly and vividly
blue, to see her breast rise on a sudden vehemence, or her large
white hands lift in a quick and heroic gesture, and a pattern of
beautiful words would form in his thoughts.

He had forgotten his old tricks of presenting his profile for
her admiration, for he saw that she did not notice it. He
never flattered her; he flattered her father. He never struck
an attitude, for that would only confuse her. His approach to
her was as an audience only. His hope was that he would
become indispensable to her in that rôle, and all the signs
were encouraging. Now she would greet him with every indication of pleasure, in her reserved fashion. The fact that
she still did not see him as a man and a potential lover sometimes disturbed and infuriated him. However, he was certain
that he had only to wait. He had some hope: once or twice
when he had made some particularly acute remark she had
turned her head and had listened to him as if strangely entranced, and she had not quoted her father in reply.

She did not speak of Geoffrey and, as a man experienced in
the ways of women, Ravel could not but think that she had
some guilty thoughts on the subject of her husband. The
young man did not know that she came to him in her hunger
and loneliness, and that she found comfort in him for her
misery and pain.

Still, she remained an enigma to him, not because she
concealed anything but because she had nothing to conceal.
Such a human being was mysterious, and new to Ravel's
experience.

He found her waiting for him tonight. She did not hear
him at first. She sat on the stone, under a canopy of willows,
and her brown linen frock was the color of fallen leaves.
She was staring at the river, upon which lay a wide flood of
sunset light. There was a loneliness about that empty light
on the waters; there was a desolation about the woman on
the stone, her arms folded on her knees, her face in shadow.
Ravel stood a moment and watched her. He no longer
marvelled at the fierce surge of emotion he always felt when
he saw her, it had become too familiar.

It was late July, but the sunset on the river, the silence
of the spot, the attitude of Melissa on the stone, suggested the
coming of mournful autumn. A wind lifted a fold of her
brown frock, blew it against her ankles. She did not stir.
A lock of her hair fluttered against her cheeks. She did not put
it back. Now the shadow moved, and he saw the white angles

of her face, the drawn and frozen suffering of her mouth.

He had never seen her like this even when she did not suspect he was close by. When alone, Melissa was usually very still, sunken in her own thoughts. But there was about her this evening less stillness than the quietude of despair. This made him exclaim, as if in protest and alarm: "Melissa!"

She turned her head slowly, and saw him. She watched him come to her. Then she said: "I was thinking of my mother. I haven't thought of my mother for a long time."

Though he was accustomed to her simplicities and unpredictability, he felt that odd disorientation which she frequently inspired in him. He sat down beside her, and tried to smile. He flicked a bit of mold from his impeccable pantaloons, and ruefully gave a moment's attention to the mud on his polished boots. He then turned his attention to Melissa.

"Your mother? She has not been dead for very long, has she? I suppose you miss her very much, poor child." He did not recall that he had ever heard Melissa mention her mother before, and he became curious. Arabella had once told him of the hostility between mother and daughter, and the cause of it. So Ravel studied Melissa, and added: "But why think of sad things, if it can be avoided?"

"Oh, I am not sad," replied Melissa, sighing. "At least, I do not think so. It is just that I feel very strange, thinking of Mama tonight, Ravel."

She had only recently, and unconsciously, begun to call him by his first name, and it never failed to excite him. He drew a little closer to her. Matters had not progressed to the point where he had ever taken her hand or indulged in any other intimacies. Yet her look and her air of desolation just now made him take her hand; the gesture was not premeditated, nor did he watch for her reaction. It was an impulsive gesture, and a kind one, and she appeared grateful for the touch of comfort. At least, she did not pull her hand away from him. As for Ravel, when he held it and felt its coldness and lassitude, he forgot for a moment everything else, and could only feel that ancient wonder of the lover, and his tender delight.

She watched him like a child, as he rubbed her fingers to bring warmth to them. Evening had not cooled the heat of the day, yet her hand was very cold and there was no color in the fingertips. Ravel concentrated on them, and was inordinately happy when they flushed pink under his manipulations. He looked at Melissa's interested face, and he came still closer to her. Then she was no longer interested. Her hand lay in his, unresisting.

"I keep remembering my mother. I don't think I am sad about her," she repeated. "Yet it is very strange. She was very lonely when she died." She stared at Ravel, as if surprised. "I never thought of that before—that Mama was lonely. Why should she have been lonely? We were all at home. Phoebe was her great favorite, and she was proud of Andrew. It has just occurred to me that Andrew is very like Mama. I never believed that before. Yes," she added, startled, "Andrew is very like Mama. He has her quietness and firmness. In a way, they were both incorruptible."

This amazed her. "Why should I say that, Ravel? There was nothing to corrupt them. No one attempted, ever, to corrupt them. So why should they have seemed incorruptible? No one gives that impression unless someone, somewhere, has tried to corrupt him. I don't quite know what I am talking about," she continued, and she rubbed her forehead with her free hand, as if confused. "I only know that they both had that manner of bitter integrity and resistance. And when I remember it, I am sorrowful, in a way I cannot explain, as one would be sorry about something strong which had been assaulted and which had resisted attack."

Ravel understood, where Melissa did not. He was stirred, and full of pity. He could not find anything to say.

"I never liked my mother," said Melissa, simply. "I believe she made my father very unhappy. But now I am beginning to see that it was not because she was malevolent, as I once thought, but because she did not understand him. And it has come to me that perhaps Papa did not understand Mama, either. She wanted things for her children which he did not think were important and which were not really important. She wanted the farm, and she wanted Papa to supervise it properly so it would keep us in comfort. But Papa hated the farm, and he wished only to leave it and have done with it. And Mama did not appreciate what a great genius my father was. But still, she was very lonely. I feel her loneliness now, as if it were my own."

As usual, Ravel wished that Melissa might display a little more versatility in conversation. He was tired of her family. He knew Andrew now, and thought him dull beyond consideration. He had met Phoebe, and recognized her at once. As for Charles, it sometimes seemed incredible to Ravel that he never met this man, for by now he knew him as well as he had ever known anyone. But he had heard little, if anything, from Melissa about Amanda, and he forgot to be bored, and even became interested.

He did not know what made him say it, but he said: "I think you must be very like your mother, Melissa."

She turned on him with a startling abruptness and something like a fierce, concentrated glare. "Why should you say that? Who spoke of it to you? It is not true! You must not believe it."

Ravel was nonplussed at this sudden emotional storm. He regarded Melissa closely. There was a flare of color on her cheek-bones and her eyes were flashing.

He said, quickly: "I don't know why I said it, Melissa. You may call it intuition, if you will. I never saw your mother. No one has told me much about her. Yet," he added, "I feel you are like her."

"No!" exclaimed Melissa. She pressed the palms of her hands together. "It is not true. There is a physical resemblance, I confess. I have had to see that myself. We have the same coloring, the same height. But beyond that, there was nothing."

Disconcertingly then, she forgot him, as she often did. She appeared to shrink together; the very dimensions of her body lessoned, drew together, as if she had become chilled. "Had I been my father's wife, I should have understood him," she said.

But you tried to be his wife, my poor child, thought Ravel. And he encouraged you in your attempt, for his own amusement. Ravel looked at Melissa's hands, and it did not seem possible to him that he had held one of them only a moment ago. They had become remote, not human hands but like the hands of the dead. They had taken on a kind of transparency and fragile outline. This frightened him.

"But why think of what is past?" he said, quickly.

She looked at him seriously, with her childlike earnestness. "I don't know," she replied. "But it has become very important to me. There is something I am trying to remember, to understand. Sometimes I have very strange thoughts." She continued to regard him steadily. "You said, a few days ago, that you would soon finish your poem. Is it finished now?"

He had become accustomed to the suddenness with which she changed subjects. In another woman, he would have thought this duplicity or a desire to conceal something. But he knew that in some way, which would probably always be obscure to him, her question was linked with what she had previously been saying. He was relieved.

"I am polishing the last twenty lines. When they are

finished, I shall read them to you. You remember, you did not like the last line."

"No. It was colorless. 'The drowning moon lost self and image in the sea.' The death of Orpheus should end on a more wild and sonorous note. He mourned Eurydice, so that all the rocks and the waters sang and mourned loudly, in echoing answer. Your line is too muted, too weary. It is like an old, tired man mourning, not a young man."

But what do you know of youth? thought Ravel. What do you know of mourning, you poor child, who have never loved?

Suddenly, Melissa was animated, with a strained and desperate animation. Her voice became hurried: "When one has lost what one has loved, then there is no silence in the heart. There is a terrible pain, so loud that there is no other sound at all but grief. Everything seems to grieve with you; everything seems to cry back, and takes on distorted shapes of agony."

Ravel said nothing. She is speaking of that damned fraud, her father, he thought with sudden disgust. But something else made him acutely uneasy, made him look at Melissa with a new sharpness.

He said: "You must have loved your father beyond imagining, Melissa."

She sat still, without turning or moving, for what was a considerable time. Then she said faintly: "My father? Oh, yes, my father. I grieved very much for him."

Abruptly, and unaffectedly, she thrust her hand into the bosom of her frock and pulled out a crumpled paper which had been carefully folded. She held it in her hand and gazed at Ravel with eyes that were vivid with suffering.

"This is a copy of a letter which my father wrote to Geoffrey a long time ago. It is apparently an answer to a letter which Geoffrey had written him suggesting that Papa send Phoebe to school. Read it. You will then see how very kind Geoffrey is. I thought him a very coarse and unfeeling man. And now I am miserable because I thought that."

Accustomed as Ravel was to swift changes of subjects when he was talking with Melissa, he could not help being startled at her last words. Moreover, the conversation had taken a disagreeable turn. He and Melissa never talked of Geoffrey. It had been tact on his part: what it was on Melissa's, he was never quite certain. Yet now she had thrust the name of her husband into Ravel's notice, like a child suddenly presenting an obnoxious toad it had recently captured. Ravel reflected briefly on the subject of inconvenient husbands, and the thought was not pleasant. But he took the letter with a sensation of ennui. He was not interested in Phoebe, and he was certainly not interested in discovering how "kind" was the man whom he intended to rob of a very peculiar wife at the earliest possible moment. For one instant the realistic Ravel found the whole situation distasteful and ludicrous, and he wondered why he remained here on this uncomfortable stone with insects buzzing about his head. But the moment scuttled away swiftly. He had found love to be too engrossing and too delightful to allow realism to smear it with its dirty finger.

Holding the letter very gingerly, he began to read carelessly. Then he read closely and with profound interest. The light on the water began to dim. The willows crowded closer in their darkening isolation. The sound of the river reverberated more strongly in the approaching twilight.

Ravel read and reread the letter. He was a man who had long ago forgotten ever to be sickened by any manifestation of the enormities of human nature. If he was told a tale of guile or of evil, of contemptible novelty or treachery, he would laugh and find it all very amusing. But he did not find this amusing.

He thoughtfully refolded the letter. He could not yet look at Melissa. He was afraid. It did not seem possible to him that she had deceived herself. Yet, when he finally turned to her, he was not sure. He looked into her eyes, and then glanced away again. He could not bear what he had seen. That imploring, that supplicating, expression was more than he could endure. She knows, he thought, but she will not let herself know yet. She wants me to reassure her. Is it a good thing for me to do so? Would it not be better for her to see that I know the truth, and to acknowledge it?

"You see how kind Geoffrey was," Melissa was saying, and her voice was low and hoarse and questioning. He heard the pleading note, so desperate and urgent, and he could not resist it.

"Yes, it was very kind," he said gently. His handsome face became grim and hard.

He heard Melissa draw a deep breath, as if she had been rescued from intolerable anguish. Now her voice was steadier: "It was wrong of Papa not to let Phoebe go to school. He could have repaid Geoffrey later. He was wrong, too, about Phoebe. But then, I also was wrong. Neither of us could have suspected, in the beginning, that she had so much talent."

Ravel was silent. He put the letter down on the stone between himself and Melissa. He could not bring himself to place it in her hand. He stared down at it. His face was no longer suave and charming. He knew all the uglinesses but, to him, this was the ugliest thing he had ever known. He watched Melissa pick up the letter tenderly and thrust it back into her bodice. He thought of it there, between her white breasts, and his hands tightened into fists.

"It was because Geoffrey was so kind that he married me," he heard Melissa say. He glanced up swiftly, disbelieving. Melissa nodded. "Yes," she said. "He tried to help all of us, for Papa's sake. But Andrew was too proud. He married that dreadful girl, and Phoebe married John Barrett. I was the only one left who needed help, and so he married me. And that is why I must go away soon, to relieve him of the burden."

With a stunned sensation Ravel realized that the moment for which he had been waiting all these months had finally come. Yet he could not move. He could only sit there and stare incredulously at Melissa. Her face stood out in the quickening twilight like a sharp white mask, its shadowy hollows poignant and luminous. Her eyes, full of torment and simple revelation, looked into his.

And then Ravel knew all there was to know. He resisted the knowledge violently and with an enraged and defeated passion which he had not thought it possible for him to feel. In a real and frantic effort to deny what he knew, he lost all sense of proportion. He was sickened with the loss that confronted him. He knew the first desolation of his life, his first furious grief, and he would not accept it. All at once, he felt the emptiness about him, the loneliness and bereavement, and he knew what it was to recognize the face of his own intolerable sorrow.

He took Melissa's arms in his hands and pulled her so close to him that their faces almost touched. She tried to draw away, but he held her strongly.

"Yes, Melissa," he said, "you must go away, and very soon. Will you go away with me, tomorrow?"

His hands gripped her flesh. He wanted to kiss her, to cover her mouth with his in a frenzy of desire and misery. If she would only go with him, tonight, tomorrow, she herself might never know what he knew. This was his only hope. He shook her almost savagely, hating her for the restraint he put on himself.

"Tonight, Melissa? Tomorrow?"

She did not try to pull away now. He saw the swimming blue of her eyes, steadfast and still.

"You think I should go?" she said, and her breath was full in his face.

"Yes, you should go. There is no one here who loves you." He stopped. He could not cry out to her of his own love, not yet. "There is no one who wants you, Melissa. Let me help you."

He appreciated fully the fantastic qualities of this whole situation. Now his rage against what he knew became frantic. Yet it had a quality of unreality.

"I will take you away, my dear. To New York. We shall be happy, I promise you. Tomorrow?"

Melissa closed her eyes and leaned back against his gripping hands. Her face became as quiet as it would be in death. But she said quite clearly: "You are very kind. I have no friends, anywhere. But you must know many people. You could help me get a position of some kind. Perhaps there is a publisher you know, for whom I could read, or a family who desire a governess."

Ravel's grip on her arms loosened. Then his hands dropped. He regarded her for a long, very quiet, moment. He knew it was no use. He knew it was no use even when he denied it and would not accept it. If he was to gain anything, he thought, he must not tell her. That was his only hope. But, with a stark premonition, he understood that he really had no hope, that he could never reach her. He shook his head slowly. There must be a way. There was no such a thing as inevitability.

"I'll help you, Melissa," he said. But his voice was lifeless.

She stood up, slowly and heavily, and he stood up also. They faced each other in the falling light, a space between them.

In spite of himself, he could not stop himself from making one last effort. He said, pleadingly: "Melissa, look at me. Do you see nothing, nothing at all?"

The gray shadow of exhaustion had fallen over her face. Through it, she peered at him uncertainly.

"I don't know what you mean," she said, confusedly. "I see you. You are my friend. At least, I believe you are my friend."

Ravel did not speak. "It is getting late," he said at last, knowing that she was watching him uncertainly.

They went away, side by side, through the clustering willows. They reached the spot where they usually parted. Here, Ravel said: "How shall I know when you wish to leave?" He spoke dully.

"I have only a few pages more to write," replied Melissa.

"I can complete it in a day or two. I will let you know in time."

Dimly, she sensed something was wrong. But she did not know what it was. She waited for him to speak. He could only look at her in silence. And then, he turned away and left her.

It took Ravel two days to accept the fact that everything was hopeless, that he could expect nothing. It was the longest and most bitter struggle of his life. On Friday, very quietly, without the knowledge even of the avid townsfolk, he packed his belongings and went away. He did not write Melissa, to tell her of his going, for in some manner he knew that she would not care, would not even wonder at his absence.

CHAPTER 44

GEOFFREY RETURNED HOME suddenly and unexpectedly on Saturday evening, on the last train from Philadelphia. A heavy rain was falling, after a recent thunderstorm. Before entering the house, he glanced up at the windows of the apartments which he occupied with Melissa. They were dark. Melissa had evidently gone to bed. Geoffrey was somewhat relieved. He wished to have a talk with his sister, and he entered his bedroom as quietly as possible, so that Melissa might not know he had returned.

He had come home on an impulse. For the past few months he had been filled with a restless depression and a feeling that he could not come to grips with affairs, either in his business or his personal life. It was like encountering spiderwebs in the dark. He was not a man to be thankful that crises had been delayed, or might never occur. He believed in crises. Without them, existence tended to become stale and null, like brackish backwaters.

He had been watching Melissa unobtrusively for a long time. He now believed that a crisis should be precipitated. So, after he had washed his hands and face, he went to his sister's apartments. He knew she was still up.

Arabella greeted him with every display of affectionate surprise. He looked at her sharply, without appearing to do so. She was sitting by an open window, reading one of the novels which his firm had recently published and which he found contemptible. But it was to her taste, he knew. It was, unfortunately, to the taste of much of the American reading public, the taste of middle-aged women especially. Arabella was dressed in a peignoir of many-ruffled mauve silk and lace, which cast a yellowish light on her face, and emphasized her wrinkles. She had touched up her hair again, so that the faded and graying strands he had observed a month ago were now completely gone in a haze of brass. Geoffrey noted that she was growing fatter, and that her tiny gray eyes were more metallic and penetrating than ever. He saw them, above her happy smile. He kissed her painted cheek, holding his breath against the effluvium of attar-of-roses which pervaded her immediate vicinity.

Though he protested that it was late and that he had dined in Philadelphia, she insisted that he must have tea. She put aside her book and ordered tea, and he drank it to please her, and they talked inconsequentially, and the heavy rain rumbled on outside. The trees swayed in the rain, whose sound could be heard through the open window.

Arabella again expressed her pleasure in his unexpected return. "We grow so dull here, in the summer," she confided. She waited. He did not ask about his wife. He turned the tea-cup in his hand, his head bent. Arabella's eyes narrowed upon him. She had, at one time, only disliked him. Now, because he had so humiliated and debased her, she hated him. She hated his broad thick shoulders, the angle of his dark cheek and chin, the big strength of his hands, the heaviness of his mouth. To her, they embodied all her mortifications and bitterness, all her resentment, the injustices of her life. She smiled tenderly when he lifted his head and looked at her.

He was, in some ways, a naïf man. He knew he held the whip-lash over his sister. Knowing that without him she would be a pauper, and that he had complete power over her, he believed she would not dare lift a hand against Melissa, that she would obey him in everything he asked for his wife. He had great faith in power, and so he had come to trust Arabella in anything which pertained to Melissa. She dared not, he believed, do anything but help Melissa, and himself.

He said: "How is Melissa?"

He had asked this question of her on the occasion of each of his visits, and she answered him as she had always answered him: "Very well, indeed. She is doing splendidly with her lessons. Very docile and eager to learn. And happier, I do believe. Yes, she grows happier each day."

He frowned, put down his cup. "I thought, the last two times, that she was paler and more quiet than usual."

"Oh, dear Geoffrey, what an imagination you have! You must remember that the summer has been an uncommonly trying one. Besides, Melissa has been working every day on her father's book. Really, you must leave her alone, my love. As you once said, she must find the way herself. I truly believe she is finding it. There are times when she seems very thoughtful, and uncertain."

As this agreed with Geoffrey's own opinions and beliefs, he nodded his head. Nevertheless, he was somewhat uneasy. "I have asked her many times to come with me to Philadelphia or New York, for music and the art galleries. But she has always refused." He paused, for this was a delicate subject. "Now, I intend to go to Europe soon. I want her to go with me. I shall insist that she go."

Arabella felt suddenly ill. She said, quickly: "Oh, Geoffrey, you must not press her! She has been so content all this summer, so peaceful and friendly. You remember, I urged you to let her be, not to be importunate or insistent. We agreed that Melissa must be quiet, that she must become accustomed to her new home, that she must have long, tranquil periods in which to forget her old life and miseries and to free herself from the incubus of her father. She is doing so well now. Why not merely suggest to her that you would like her to accompany you, that you wish her to consider it?"

Geoffrey was silent. His face had darkened. Then he said: "I have left her alone for months. I have, for her own sake, not intruded myself upon her. I have hardly spoken to her, convinced that it was best to let her make her own advances. But she has not made them. I can't wait any longer, Bella. I must take matters into my own hands. I have a feeling it is dangerous to let matters drift as they have been drifting. We have been married seven months. In that time, Melissa must have found herself or she never will, without outside help. I have waited long enough. I intend to offer, or force, that help."

Arabella clenched her hands together desperately under the mauve ruffles. A sick sweat broke out under her rouge, and smarted.

"Geoffrey," she pleaded, "for Melissa's sake, merely suggest Europe. If she refuses, let her remain here quietly. She is happier. I swear. She is becoming accustomed to the house, to the routine, to the peace and comfort. She and I have become very affectionate friends. She defers to my opinion and is learning many things in a truly commendable way. A few months longer, and I am sure that she will have recovered both mental and physical health and will be prepared to welcome you home with every manifestation of wifely devotion."

"You think she is still afraid of me?" asked Geoffrey.

Arabella hesitated, then said sadly: "Yes, I believe so. But it is becoming less, that fear. Occasionally, she mentions your name without her usual shrinking. Oh, Geoffrey, do not press her! Believe me, I speak from full knowledge. It would be dangerous."

She was so terrified that her voice rang with complete sincerity, and Geoffrey was impressed by it. He stood up, patted her shoulder. "I shall think about what you have said, Bella. But I can promise no more than that."

"You need promise me nothing," said Arabella, aware of the desperation in her voice, and attempting to cover it with a fond smile. "It is your affair, and Melissa's. I speak only from affection for both of you. I am a woman, and I understand a woman's heart, even so strange a one as that poor girl's. She has not recovered completely from her father's death, but time is doing its long healing. I am her confidante now, and she tells me many things. I can say with conviction that the influence her father had over her is diminishing. By forcing matters, you would only antagonize her. Once or twice I have spoken of Charles, and immediately she bristled and became fanatical again. Now I let her broach the subject herself, and listen in silent sympathy. I do not speak of you, but I have observed that she has, lately, on a few occasions, mentioned your name. That is a very good omen, dear Geoffrey. Let time do for you what precipitation will not do."

Geoffrey considered this thoughtfully for a few moments. He was a little cheered by what his sister had said. Moreover, it sounded sensible to him. However, he could not rid himself of a sense of uneasiness and doubt. He touched his sister's cheek, smiled, and announced that he had some work to finish in the library and that he would see her in the morning.

Arabella had contemplated going to bed before her brother's arrival, but now she was sleepless. She sat for a long time, distractedly plotting and discarding each plot as it presented itself. What if Melissa consented to accompany Geoffrey to Europe? What if she now had come to a realization of her own suppressed emotions with regard to her husband? Then, for Arabella, everything was over. Hour after hour, she sat in her chair, full of hatred and fear and wretchedness. If only Geoffrey had not returned so soon! Ravel was still Arabella's only hope, and it was a hope dwindling away very fast. Even when morning approached, Arabella could not sleep.

Though it was now very late, Geoffrey went to the library and unpacked his briefcase of manuscripts and other papers, spread them before him, and picked up his pen. But, though he was pressed for time, it was impossible to begin work. He refilled his whiskey glass repeatedly. The rain and the wind had ceased. He listened to the lonely cry of the crickets, to the scream of an owl. He could smell the hot wet earth and the scent of evergreens dripping with moisture. When in the city, he remembered these things with nostalgia. But now the night silences and the intermittent wild sounds only increased his restlessness.

There was much to annoy and worry him lately, but nothing imminent and urgent enough for him to grasp and analyze. Though he had persuaded himself that matters concerning her would soon be settled, Melissa was the chronically uneasy background of all his thoughts. He refused to think of her actively, but concentrated on other things connected with his business affairs and annoyances.

He was not a man normally given to strong patriotic impulses, and his interest in the late war had not been overwhelming and enthusiastic. But he had lately been thinking that America was too much preoccupied with British writers, and that England, though ostensibly regarded with bitterness, more particularly in the North, still had a mysterious fascination for Americans. When he complained that America was not producing writers who really expressed American life and strength and vitality, he was reproachfully referred to Holmes, Longfellow, Whittier and Lowell. Even when he pointed out that these merely imitated British writers and poets, his audience was not convinced. They did not understand his reference to "spirit." Geoffrey had published several of Dickens' books, and admired them conservatively, but the worship of Mr. Dickens in America irritated him. Harpers had published the English Collins' novels, and *Lothair*, by Disraeli, had sold prodigiously. Reade's assinine novels had commanded large royalties. The worst of the English novelists could depend on a huge American public, as could Hugo, Björnson and Turgenev. But, Geoffrey argued, these did nothing to explain

America to Americans, and that, in these days of national restlessness and uncertainty and confusion, was the enormous need. America needed a vision, an interpretation, a translator. She needed them, but she was not getting them. The time had arrived for Americans to produce a literary art peculiarly their own, full of the strength, the passion and all the powerful loveliness which was America.

Some of his friends advised him, cynically, to be content with his profits. It was advice which, only a short time ago, he would have given other publishers. He had had no patience with that romantic "itch" which impelled some publishers to believe they had a "mission" and to take their business seriously. Now he found himself suffering from the same condition, and could not laugh himself out of it. It was not enough for him that younger Americans were now engrossed with the great English scientists and essayists such as Darwin, Spencer, Huxley and Tyndall. Surely, somewhere, there lived men who could express American philosophies. He had not found them. There was Emerson, of course, but in a nation of incredible Anglophiles, who considered everything home-grown as distinctly unfashionable and unworthy of serious study, Emerson was not as popular as Huxley.

In short, even the American writers of worth and genius were still influenced by English writers and modes, methods of thought and approach. It sometimes surprised Geoffrey that he was forced to remember that Edgar Allan Poe was an American. To him, Poe was more English than American, in sentiment and spirit and expression.

Though Geoffrey was making large profits from such American books as Elizabeth Stuart Phelps' sentimental and eclectic novels, and the maundering tracts of T. S. Arthur and the sweet idiocy of Theodore Tilton's tales, the fact remained that no American writer of great stature was indicating his existence. Perhaps, he thought, the reason for the popularity of saccharine trash by American writers in America was because the American women were almost the sole patrons of novels. American men still did not realize that it was not effeminate to appreciate, admire and support literary artists. In truth, there was an alarming and growing indication that American men considered any form of art to be effeminate and left to the women.

Geoffrey was resisting a new form of writing which had become popular after the war, and that was the cheap "dime novel" with yellow covers and gory titles. The Far West had come into vogue, an incredible West which had never existed.

Mr. Eldridge had succumbed to the lure of profits, and was now happily pouring out "yellowbacks" in enormous profusion. He argued that many of them truly recorded the hell-raising adventures of pioneers and woodsmen, and should be appreciated for that fact. But to Geoffrey they were not the literature he wished for America. The theme was good, but the writing was execrable.

Moreover, he had come to the conclusion that the book trade, itself, needed reorganization. If he published books in the spring, they were conveyed to auction rooms on lower Broadway in New York, where publishers, like cheap auctioneers, sold stock on consignment, and later hoped for the best in slow national distribution. The subscription system, which Geoffrey detested, further enlarged the purses and reputations of foreign authors, because it necessarily must concentrate on famous writers to the hurt of any aspiring American author.

Slowly, two novel ideas presented themselves to Geoffrey: retailers and advertising. There were some of his colleagues, particularly in conservative Boston, who lifted horrified hands at the mere thought of advertising "literature" as one would advertise furniture, stoves, horses and chinaware. But Geoffrey began to understand that if vast areas of the country were to be made acquainted with books of any kind they must first be approached by advertising. Such advertising would introduce still unknown American writers of worth to a public that knew only foreign writers by way of the subscription system. Better still, it would make books of all kinds accessible to the American people.

As publishers were not immune to the cupidity affecting other human beings, they were also averse to the idea of allowing retailers to take a cut on their profits. They preferred the system, much more contemptible to Geoffrey than the thought of retailers, whereby they auctioned off their publications. Though he had long ago become accustomed to human inconsistencies, he could still marvel at this attitude. He finally came to the conclusion that it was no mere reverence for literature which made his colleagues shudder at "commercialism," but sheer timidity at atttempting the new, and avarice.

He was determined, at whatever risk, to begin advertising wherever a newspaper was published, or a monthly periodical. He determined, too, to engage the services of retailers. There was still another way of acquainting Americans far from large cities with books of all kinds, and that was the private circulating library. The idea was not new; there were at least r thousand such libraries in existence. Geoffrey decided that their numbers must be increased. He, himself, would sponsor at least one hundred more, in remote outposts and in the smaller towns of the West and South.

Only by such methods would the hopeful, if still unpublished, American writers obtain the audience they deserved, and Americans become truly literate.

In pursuit of these ideas, he had spent much of the past months in traveling over the country, talking with newspaper proprietors and the owners of national periodicals. They were willing to accept his money for advertising, but laughed at him behind his back. He knew this, and merely shrugged. Most of these gentlemen were avaricious, and had no objection to taking his dollars, but he found in them, too, that curious phenomenon: the belief that "literature" was too sacred for the touch of the dirty hand of advertising.

He had engaged, and set up in business, a few retailers in distant towns and cities, men quite happy to agree to his propositions but also quite doubtful of their success. They listened respectfully when he said: "Create an audience for American writers, and they will appear, I have no doubt." But they did not believe him.

He had pursued any trail, however faint, which he thought might lead him to a future American writer of stature and importance. Lately, he had come upon some copies of the San Francisco *Alta California*, which contained some amusing and vivid letters contributed by one "Mark Twain." In them he thought he detected a virile and living spirit, distinctly and exclusively American, with no overtones of British influence. But when he had written to the paper for the author's address, he was informed that Mr. Twain had embarked on the steamship *Quaker City* for a tour of the Mediterranean. He was supplied with the itinerary by the obliging newspaper, and he had decided to follow Mr. Twain and try to induce him to write a book or two for publication.

He had read only a few of the letters but, by some mysterious intuition, he felt that he had come on a fat quarry, one of importance and power, and expressive of America. He intended to sail within two weeks. His passage was already engaged. He also intended to take Melissa with him.

These, then, were the problems and hazards occupying him tonight. He had many plans, but he knew the danger and possible loss inherent in them. Sometimes, as he paced up and down, he accused himself of being a "damned sentimentalist." But he could not shake off his intuitive convictions, nor could he really believe himself a fool. There was something strong and stirring in America. It needed a voice. He believed that he had found one such voice. America needed many. Even if they involved new methods and novel approaches which might be successfully resisted, he was willing to wager all his fortune on his hopes and his ideas. It was worth tr ng. He intended to try.

The ultimate problem was Melissa. He returned with impatience and determination to the thought of his wife. The girl had had time enough. If she was not ready, then he must leave her, for she would never be ready. When he had married her, he had had moments when he believed that he had done a stupid and foolish thing. It was time to determine whether it had indeed been stupid and foolish, or whether there was some hope for Melissa and himself. In either event, he had decided, he must force a crisis and submit to the outcome.

It was useless to try to work. He replaced his papers, blew out the lights, and went up to bed. James came in to help him undress and to prepare him for the night. Geoffrey thought such service a "damned lot of nonsense" but it appeared to give James satisfaction and pleasure. On such occasions, Geoffrey was accustomed to discussing casual matters with James in a friendly and jocular way, exchanging jokes, gossip and comments. But tonight, though they had not seen each other for almost a month, Geoffrey was silent and preoccupied. Had he been observant, he would have noticed that James was not communicative but went about his duties in a markedly mournful fashion.

Though ostentatious, the mournfulness was not assumed. James had decided that when he next saw his master he would hint to him of Melissa and her unhappiness, quoting Rachel copiously. But how was it possible, he asked himself, to tell an employer that his wife was miserable, subtly and not so subtly persecuted and bedevilled by her husband's sister, that she was fast reaching the breaking point, and that her husband was an obtuse fool who did not see what was shouting at him under his very nose? James, however diplomatic, could see no way of informing Geoffrey of all this in a delicate yet unmistakable manner. In spite of the intimacy and familiarity which Geoffrey frequently encouraged in his servants, James well knew that he was a capricious and brutal man and that, for all his genial air of democracy, there were barriers he would not allow to be crossed. Once or twice, in his earlier days, encouraged by a hearty friendliness, James had crossed that barrier, and he would never forget, he reminded himself, the devastating results. Geoffrey might not be "a gentleman," but there were times when he acted as viciously as if he had been one. Worst of all, one never knew when he would suddenly decide to be "gentry." He never indicated when this metamorphosis was about to take place, and so it was all very disconcerting.

But, though Geoffrey was preoccupied, he finally became aware of James' heavy silence and sad countenance. He did not want, tonight, to hear any account of any indisposition conceivably being suffered by his man. He contemplated being a gentleman and ignoring James, but both this and James began very shortly to irritate him. He got into bed and looked at his man impatiently.

"Well, James, what is it? What's wrong with you? You've the face of an undertaker."

James was immediately frightened. He first decided to deny that anything was wrong, and tried to assume a more cheerful expression. He had come to the conclusion that there was no way in which he could "speak" to Geoffrey, except obliquely.

"It's just that Mrs. Dunham's maid, Rachel, has had to go to Pittsburgh, sir, for a few days, to care for a sister who has become ill."

"Oh," said Geoffrey. He regarded James thoughtfully. "You miss the girl, eh? Sweet on her?"

James blushed. "Well, you could call it that, sir, if you wish. But it's because Mrs. Dunham misses Rachel. She'd come to rely on her, if I may say it."

Geoffrey did not believe this. He could not imagine Melissa "relying" on anyone. Moreover, why Melissa's temporary loss of Rachel, who, Geoffrey was certain, was of no importance to Melissa, should sadden James, was quite beyond Geoffrey's comprehension. But James was looking at him steadily, if fearfully, and Geoffrey's interest was vaguely aroused.

"Well, the girl will be back soon," he said tentatively. "And I'm sure that Mrs. Dunham can care for herself for a few days."

"But Mrs. Dunham is unhappy—about it," replied James clumsily.

"Unhappy, eh?" Geoffrey thought this over. He did not know whether to be pleased or displeased that Melissa found the loss of a servant distressing. Again, he could not credit it. Knowing Melissa's painful reserve, her terror of strangers, her inability to make friends, it was not possible to believe that the absence of a girl she had known only in a servile capacity should upset her. Melissa had the arrogance of her type of mind: she would be entirely unaware of the existence of anyone who could not share her interests.

Geoffrey found it all very absurd. He yawned, and lay down. "If Mrs. Dunham is unhappy over her brief loss, James, she will soon be happy again, eh?"

There was nothing James could say. He only sighed in answer, turned down the lamps, and crept away. Geoffrey, irritated again, watched him go. Then he closed his eyes and tried to sleep.

But he could not sleep. All at once, the door that separated his apartments from Melissa's became vivid and sentient to him. It was the only thing in the room, an insistent presence. He turned his back to it and thumped his pillows. Then, slowly, he became angry. He thought of Melissa sleeping soundly and obliviously behind that door, and suddenly she seemed to him an obdurate and silly fool, and one quite hopeless to change. How many nights had he slept like this, alone, with the locked door between him and his wife! How many times had she sat at the table with himself and Arabella, mute and pale, starting if he spoke to her, and replying, if she replied at all, in a faint stammer! If anything, her aversion and fear in his presence had increased these last months. Not even his hypocritical questions about her "confounded work" brought forth a reply that could be regarded as remotely sensible or interested. She was becoming whiter and thinner, even if less fanatical and domineering in opinion.

The night was very quiet now, and Geoffrey's thoughts became louder and more extravagant. It was hopeless. The girl was miserable, completely wretched. He had done a ridiculous thing in marrying her. She would never want him; she would never be at home in this house. She had her existence here, but she *lived* in that lean and barren house down the hill, with her dead father and his dead and dusty books. What an idiot, he, Geoffrey, had been, thinking that he could rescue her from a malevolent and exigent ghost! She had not even begun to comprehend that she needed rescuing. She would have been far happier had she remained in her old home, where she could sit in familiar surroundings and live in that empty and soundless world of her own.

I will try once more, thought Geoffrey. If she refuses to go with me, I shall be forced to make other arrangements. She can return to her father and all his damned works, and I will give her a small income. If she will accept it. But she will have to accept it. She has no other choice.

He had come to his decision. But still he could not sleep. He kept seeing Melissa's white face and long gilt hair, and the lost look in her eyes.

Melissa, too, was sleepless. She had heard Geoffrey's arrival. While he was with Arabella, and even later, when she had heard him go downstairs, she had lain rigid in bed. She had heard him return, and then his voice and the sounds of his preparations for bed. She had listened with an enormous intensity, as if she possessed nothing but ears.

Then there was only silence behind that door, silence that became full of tumult. After a long while, Melissa slipped from her bed and went to the door. She pressed her hand to it, as Amanda had once pressed her hand to her daughter's door, and with a similar anguish. Then, slowly slipping down beside it, Melissa crouched in the warm darkness, and now it was her cheek that was pressed to the wood, pressed so strongly and so urgently that the bones of her face protested.

She finally fell asleep in that position. She dreamed that she had opened the door, that she had gone to Geoffrey, crying: "I love you! I love you!" And he had held out his hand to her in the darkness, and she saw the shadow of it in the darkness. She had taken his hand, and had held it convulsively to her breast, and had burst into tears.

She awoke. It was still dark. The tears were wet on her cheeks. She understood now. But she understood also that she could no longer remain in this house where she was unloved and unwanted, where she had been taken in in an indifferent if generous pity.

She crept into bed, and held a pillow in her arms, clutching it passionately, sobbing into it, as if she could get from it some consolation, some tenderness, so great was her need, so terrible her sorrow and despair.

CHAPTER 45

GEOFFREY WAS ANNOYED to discover, when awakening after a very short sleep, that he had overslept. He had wanted to see Melissa at breakfast time. But now James brought him a tray, and found his master in a very bad mood indeed. During the night James had decided that he must speak, even at the risk of losing his post, but one look at Geoffrey's dark sullen face made his courage run away like a mouse. He served Geoffrey in silence, helped him to dress.

Geoffrey went downstairs and found his sister in the morning-room, arranging flowers. Her rouge was harsh in the early light, and her morning-robe of green tissue faille, floating with panels, was entirely too young for her, and enhanced the false brassiness of her hair. Her sharp eyes took in Geoffrey's mood, and she said cheerily: "Good morning, dear Geoffrey. Is it not pleasant today? I do believe the hot weather has abated a little."

She fluttered up to him archly, and pinned a rose-bud to his coat. The tendrils of her hair tickled his chin, and he lifted his head, trying not to be freshly irritated.

"Where is Melissa?" he asked abruptly. "I especially want to see her this morning and to have a talk with her."

Arabella concentrated upon the delicate matter of adjusting the rosebud. Then she stood off and surveyed her handiwork with pride. But her heart began to beat unevenly. She smiled at the flower, put her head to one side, and said absently: "She often walks in the morning, after breakfast, and sometimes meets Ravel for one of their everlasting talks about the most absurd things."

She went back to her vases and to the heaps of flowers on the table. Her hands shook. Geoffrey knew that Ravel was a new, if temporary, neighbor. He had often, on his visits home, invited the younger man to this house. He had, in a way, even begun to like him, or at least to be amused by him, for Ravel had lately lost his facetious mannerisms and poses. But this was the first he had heard of Melissa showing any interest in him. He was surprised, and he smiled a little, which was not exactly the reaction Arabella had expected. After a few moments, she glanced up, and when she saw that smile she could have struck him with the bouquet she held.

"Well, well," he said jocularly, trying to readjust himself to the vision of Melissa actually talking to someone, actually walking with a stranger. "What can she find in that jackanapes to interest her? You mean, Arabella, that she sees him often and alone? How did he manage that?"

Arabella sat down abruptly, full of rage. She smiled sweetly. She said; "Oh, yes indeed, she often sees him alone." The time for complete caution was gone. She looked at Geoffrey's amused face, and hated him. Yet she did not dare

go too far. "I believe he is writing a poem on which he con-
sults her frequently."

Geoffrey burst out laughing, and with the laughter his
black mood disappeared. "How typical of Melissa!" he exclaimed. (The fool! The dear fool!) "No doubt she gives him
the benefit of her classical education, with her usual severity
and insistence on perfection."

"I believe," said Arabella, in a stifled voice, "that he is
writing a poem which he is to dedicate to her. Melissa told me
that."

Geoffrey considered this, and was more and more amused.
"He told me about the poem, and I generously offered to read
it when he had finished it. So he is dedicating it to Melissa!
This is very interesting, indeed, very rich. And it is also
good news, for it shows that Melissa is slowly coming out of
her shell, poor girl." He bent to sniff at a flower-filled vase.
"When does she return from these edifying walks?"

"There is no particular time," said Arabella, heavy with her
defeat and fury. She tried once more: "We both know dear
Melissa, of course. But I have heard whispers from others;
there is some thought that Melissa is a trifle indiscreet in
being seen so regularly with Ravel along the river."

"What nonsense!" said Geoffrey, still pleased at the thought
of Melissa emerging from her solitariness. "Let the old women
wag their heads. Can you imagine Melissa, dear Arabella,
having an intrigue with anyone? If she wanders around with
that popinjay, and listens to his poems, she has no more
intention of being improper than has a young child."

"Oh, of course, dear Geoffrey!" cried Arabella. She waited,
still hoping that she had planted an ugly idea in her brother's
mind. But he only mused on what he had heard, then laughed
again, his hateful, boisterous laugh. She said: "I do think,
though, that you might suggest to Melissa that she see Ravel
less often. It does no good to inspire gossip."

"I shall do nothing of the kind! Ravel is evidently good for
Melissa; though, knowing Ravel, I wonder how he came to
find her interesting. She is definitely not the type for him.
But he is probably bored to death in Midfield. Bella, can you
imagine anyone who knew Melissa even slightly, believing in
any such gossip about her?"

"Certainly not!" said Arabella, her voice shaking with her
emotions. "It is all very silly."

Geoffrey strolled towards the door. His sister watched him
go. He whistled softly, and glanced through the windows at
the warm, bright sun. "Not going to church, eh?" he said.

"No, dear Geoffrey. If you remember, I never go on the Sundays you are home. We see you so seldom as it is."

He was in a mood to be touched by this. "Well, I am afraid that you won't see much of me today, however. I am going to work in the library. When Melissa returns, will you send her in to me? We are going to discuss the European matter."

Arabella waited until he had left the room, then she flung the scissors violently from her and began to cry. She had tried, and it had been useless. She had lost everything. She had not the faintest doubt but that he would succeed with Melissa, and that her own life was over. Perhaps, though, Geoffrey would give her an allowance and let her go away to Philadelphia to live, among her friends, or perhaps he would buy her a small house in Midfield. She wiped her wet eyes and looked at the sunshine streaming through the windows. The great house was fragrant and silent about her. Her home! This was the house in which she had been born, which she loved and cherished, which was part of herself! How could she bear to leave it, to give it up to a slut and a drab, a fool and a dolt?

Her tears came faster, and she wept as she had never wept before.

CHAPTER 46

GEOFFREY WORKED busily on the copy for Mr. Dickens' latest novel. It was a bundle of London newspapers containing all the installments of the story, which was to be published in book form in the spring. Geoffrey's chief editor had scrawled disparaging remarks in the margins, for he was no admirer of the writer. Geoffrey deleted the scribblings, or, in reply, wrote some sarcastic remark.

He became so absorbed that he did not know how time was passing. Then, when he glanced up, to rub his aching eyes, he saw Melissa standing mutely on the threshold, a thick sheaf of papers in her hand.

He was so startled that he did not rise. Suddenly, he knew that she had been there a long time. She had been standing there and looking at him while he worked, watching him in her curious still silence. Only fear could inspire such muteness, such timidity, and Geoffrey became angry. Why was she so pale and thin, and why was there so much speechless misery in her eyes? Was he so abominable, so repulsive, so fear-inspiring, that he could bring her to such a pass? All his resentment of the night, his sense of hopelessness, his angry resignation, returned in full force and, with them, an intense depression and pain.

He said, without greeting her by so much as a single word or smile: "Why do you stand there, Melissa, like a dummy? Why don't you come in? Why didn't you indicate you had returned, like a sensible person?"

For a moment longer she stood there. He sat behind his desk, his cold eyes fixed upon her, and in them she thought she saw derision and impatience. She looked at him and she felt that something flowed out of her towards him in a wild and frenzied current of anguish and longing, and this made any word she attempted to say die off in her throat. She toyed with the papers in her hand. She became even whiter, if possible. Her hair was disordered. Her mouth had fallen open a trifle, and there was a pinched blueness about it.

Geoffrey, more and more angered and hurt, said sarcastically: "Well, come in. I want to talk to you, Melissa if you can spare time from these poetic excursions with Ravel, about which I have just heard."

Melissa said, in the faintest of voices: "I didn't see Ravel today."

"Come in, come in!" said Geoffrey impatiently, throwing aside his pen. "Apparently, though, you find his company more congenial than mine. You couldn't have been unaware that I had returned, yet you went in search of that grandiloquent poet rather than greet me."

"I had something to tell him," whispered Melissa. But Geoffrey only heard the dry rustle of the sound, and he was too incensed to care. He watched her move heavily towards him across the floor. She did not take her eyes from his face. They were enormously widened and abnormally bright and fixed. Then she was standing before him, in front of the desk.

They regarded each other in a thick silence. The sunlight poured over the books on the walls and made a tangled pattern on the floor. Birds cheeped in the trees outside; a soft wind fluttered the draperies. At this closer range, Geoffrey studied Melissa's face. When she would be on her death-bed she would have such a face and wear such an expression of suffering and torment. He wanted to get up and go to her, to hold her in his arms, and the impulse was so strong that his whole body stiffened. But he would only frighten her the more, only send her fleeing from him in complete terror. He remembered the night of their marriage, and his promise. Because of his own pain, his rage against her increased, and his compassion. He must be very patient, and kind. But he had already a foreboding of defeat and despondency.

Then, without looking away from him—she seemed to be hypnotized—she thrust the sheaf of manuscript at him and said feebly: "I've completed Papa's book. It is all here. I hope you may admire it as it deserves."

His face tightened and darkened ominously. He regarded her steadily. Then he took up the manuscript. How was he going to speak to her? What was he to say? He had no words at all with which to approach that tortured mind and reason with it. Sightlessly, he began to ruffle the carefully written pages of the manuscript. He even read a phrase or two, in the first section. It was obvious that old Charles had not improved, that his writings were as pedantic and solemn and without interest as they had always been.

With a motion of his hand he put the book aside. "Why do you not sit down, Melissa?" he asked coldly. He began to rise, as if to offer her the chair beside him, but she sat down with such haste that he stopped. So, he thought, it's come to such a pass that she is terrified at the very idea of my even approaching her. Certainly her expression and features had, in the last moment or two, become more haggard and drawn. But why did she stare at him so strangely, as if the poor girl was nothing but eyes? Did she believe she had to watch him like this, so that any move of his might not escape her besieged notice? He began to feel the full force of her anguish and dread.

"There are some things I wish to talk with you about," he began, in as neutral a tone as possible.

She lifted one hand in a jerky and distracted gesture. "You haven't really looked at Papa's book," she stammered. "I wish you would. It—it is very important to me."

He was about to refuse brusquely, and then he thought that he would oblige her and give her a little time in which to lose her panic in his presence. So, with a motion that was not free of exasperation and contempt, he pulled the manuscript towards him again and flipped through some pages towards the close, never unconscious for a moment of her piercing and distraught eyes.

Every page was neat and perfect, written in her clear, angular hand. Geoffrey's mind was too preoccupied to allow him to concentrate, and it was his intention merely to pretend to read. But then a phrase or two began to penetrate his consciousness, and he found himself reading with the true editor's attention.

In the summary comparing modern scientists and philosophers with the ancient Greek, there were several quotations from Darwin and Huxley. Then Melissa had written:

"There are some new voices rising just now, especially among the philosopher-scientists, who are rediscovering 'Nature' and who shout that man is merely a beast and that he can live happily only when conducting himself in accordance with his bestial instincts which, the modern scientist solemnly assures us, are really moral impulses. Let us consider the bestial nature and its instincts. The natural instincts of the beast are murder, destructiveness, cruelty, promiscuity, and even cannibalism. Man's social, civilized, and acquired virtues, not instincts, are respect for life, constructiveness, kindness, religion, morality, and a regard for his fellow-creatures. These are the virtues which our exponents of 'instinct' would have us believe are not only unnatural, but that, because they are unnatural, they frustrate the instinctual beast and pervert him. But I say that men progress not by following the instincts of their true natures but by suppressing them, and that civilized man rises in direct ratio to his successful self-repression. Civilization is the determined frustration of instinct, from within and without, and the more frustration, the more peace, art, science, poetry and literature, the more ethics, brotherly love, wisdom and charity. The history of man, painful and bloody, is the history of his triumph over his instinctual nature, and the decline of civilizations is the history of the resurgent conquest of man by his instincts."

Is it possible that Charles, who hated all men, really wrote this? Geoffrey thought. It is not like him. It is not the sustained cry of the man who lusted for power over those he despised. Had he, towards the last, changed? If so, what had changed him? Geoffrey read and reread this paragraph, and his doubt grew, and his excitement. He looked up quickly at Melissa, and said:

"This paragraph"—and he read it aloud—"I like it very much. But it does not sound like Charles. You took it direct from his notes, Melissa?"

She was still staring at him, and then, not looking away from him, her pale lips moved, and she said: "It is not exactly as Papa wrote it. But it is what he meant. He had written something else, hastily and incompletely, and so I gave it the meaning he had intended."

Her voice was dry and harsh, as if something were wounding her intolerably. But Geoffrey hardly heard the tone. He thought: "Ah!" He said: "Can you remember just what it was that he said, Melissa?"

She half whispered: " 'The perversion of modern man lies in the frustration of those impulses which in the past have made him the conqueror of the weak and the healthful destroyer of the unfit.' "

Geoffrey leaned back in his chair, his big brown hands on the manuscript. He gazed at Melissa as intensely as she gazed at him. He thought: "I see. Charles was a devil and a swine to the last." How could Melissa have misunderstood this final malignant cry of a hating man who knew, in the end, that he had been defeated and that not even his victory over the two who loved him was enough? Melissa had never misunderstood her father before, either deliberately or unconsciously. But she had misunderstood him now, unconsciously and completely. Something had changed her. Something loud and protesting in her had disputed Charles' malevolence, had changed poison into bread. At the last, her own innocent and passionate instinct for truth and nobility had obliterated the evil falseness which had been her father. Geoffrey smiled inwardly, with grimness. If Charles possibly were still living, his ghost must be impotently cursing his daughter.

Geoffrey returned to the book. He read swiftly, phrase by phrase. And then he began to see that a new and brilliant style had been superimposed here and there on Charles' dull and pedestrian notes. It was possible to pick out what Charles had intended and what Melissa had interpreted. The book was a duet in which dry viciousness and clear high challenge took part—a song of affirmation, a protest against ugliness.

Again, Geoffrey put aside the manuscript. Melissa was searching his face with painful earnestness. "Papa's notes were not quite complete," she faltered, thinking that he found the manuscript disappointing. "It is not his fault. Perhaps I coordinated them poorly, and expanded them carelessly. Papa always edited the completed manuscript and often obliterated what I had written. Sometimes I was very stupid. I hope you will take that into consideration—Geoffrey."

Her voice had become urgent and frightened.

"I am taking it all into consideration, Melissa," he said, very gently. "You misinterpret what I am thinking. I consider this Charles' best book. I hope you have notes for another."

A startling thought occurred to him. He leaned towards Melissa, and his eyes narrowed incredulously. Was it possible that this girl herself had the powerful gift of expressive writing? Yes, it was possible! It was more than possible: it was obvious! Once or twice, when reading Charles' former books, Geoffrey had come upon paragraphs and phrases which had rung like golden bells in a murky darkness, which had been like a flash of sunlight bursting into a jungle—a perfection of simile and expression, new and fresh and pure, which certainly could not have originated in Charles. These had given his books a certain fascinating quality. The reader floundered through page after page of pedantry, acid cynicism and stagnation, for the unexpected reward of what, Geoffrey now realized, could only have been Melissa's work. Perhaps even Charles had recognized this shining and unconscious majesty, and had instinctively understood that it alone made his own work acceptable. This, possibly, had increased his malignance towards his daughter, and, out of his unconfessed envy and resentment, he had been goaded to treat her with increasing, but always subtle, venom.

Because Charles' notes had not been entirely completed, and because he was not alive to edit them mercilessly, Melissa's gift had been unhampered. What could she not do working alone? It was incredible. It opened up possibilities which the editor in Geoffrey sensed with amazement and excitement.

He wanted to say to Melissa: "Whatever merit lay in your father's books was because of your own writing, your own noble simplicity, your capacity for choosing the freshest and most acute words. You strung together many facts which he had given you, dull and often erroneous, and made them into a string of pearls. Your father was nothing but a poor and malevolent fraud who victimized you. You are free of him now, to do what you wish and to go where you wish."

But, though he had half planned, while he had lain sleepless, to say something like this to Melissa, he now knew that he could not say it. She was still her father's victim. He tested his depressed conviction by saying: "When you work on your father's next book, Melissa, I hope to see more of your own writing and interpretation in it. You do as well, if not better, alone."

He was sure he was right when Melissa's stark face flushed and her mouth settled into rigid lines. She said: "No, you are wrong. This book, and the others I shall compile from Papa's notes, will all be very inferior to his own work when he was alive."

Now she looked at him without fear, her head lifted proudly. But he saw her emaciation, the piteous and meager angle of her cheeks and chin, the thinness of her neck. He glanced at the manuscript and leaned back in his chair, forgetting everything else but this poor girl he had married. He had been enraged with her last night, and had prepared to attack her with brutal words today. But he had no anger now, only compassion and love. Had he actually thought, last night, that he would have it out with her today and then, if necessary, put her aside, and forget her? He could never forget Melissa. A dozen of her younger faces flashed over this one of hers as she sat opposite him, so stiffly, her hands clenched in her lap, and each was more touching and desirable than the other. He could no more put her aside and forget her than he could put aside and forget his own arm, or his eyes, or stop the beating of his heart.

He had known, from the very beginning, that she could never really be his wife unless she were freed from her father. But there was little indication that she had been freed; there was every evidence that her enslavement had grown stronger. Charles dead was Charles more formidable than ever. Geoffrey slowly found and lit a cheroot. His polite request for permission was answered by Melissa with only an absent lift of a hand, as if she had not fully heard him.

He did not know what to say to her! He had no words at all. He rubbed his chin and stared at her in complete and wretched bafflement. And she looked back at him, with the nameless anguish in her eyes, like a suffering animal that has no voice.

Finally he said lamely: "Do you find it lonely here, Melissa?"

She answered abstractedly: "No. I have my work, and Arabella—teaches—me. It is very hard for Arabella. I try, but I do not learn what Arabella calls the 'social graces' very well. There are times when I am very stupid."

"Nonsense," said Geoffrey. "What do those 'manners' matter?" But he knew even while he said this that neither he nor Melissa was paying attention to what he was saying. There was something else in the room, pent and tragic, which could not be explained. He had the formless but urgent conviction that the answer lay in the pale and exhausted eyes that never left his face.

Melissa spoke again, and he had to concentrate to hear what she said, for her voice was faint. "I often think of how kind you have been to me, to all of us. I know that you did this because of your attachment to my father and your friendship for him. There isn't any way we—I—can repay you. If there were, I would do—anything. Instead, I have received so much, and have given nothing in return. I am a burden to you, and a stranger in this house—" She could not go on. Her voice broke, as though tears would follow. But her eyes only became more feverishly bright.

Geoffrey was dumfounded. All at once he felt a sudden flood of joy and incredulity. He exclaimed: "Melissa!" and got to his feet.

But she was speaking: "There is just one thing I'd like to ask you, Geoffrey, please."

He stood there, wanting to rush around the desk and take her in his arms, but something in the quality of her voice stopped him. He leaned his knuckles on the desk and bent towards her. "Yes, my dear?" he said gently.

Her pinched nostrils moved as she drew in a quick breath. "Geoffrey, did Papa ever write you about any suggestion of yours to send Phoebe away to school?"

Astonished, Geoffrey could only regard her in silence. Then he sat down. After a moment or two, he said slowly: "Phoebe? No. Not Phoebe, Melissa."

He was frightened at the way her face seemed to shrink and become smaller. But she did not look away from him. "Not Phoebe?" She paused. Then she stood up. "Was it I, Geoffrey?"

Still unable to understand why she should have changed so ominously and why there was about her such a tragic stillness, Geoffrey said: "Your mother and I, Melissa, once discussed the possibility of your going away to some good school. Then I wrote your father." He remembered Charles' letter, very suddenly, and his mouth tightened.

Melissa saw this. She stood there and gazed at him steadfastly. She had become very quiet.

"And Papa did not think it—advisable?" She spoke very calmly.

Geoffrey answered: "No, he did not think it advisable." He hesitated. "It seems that he considered your presence, and services to him, indispensable." He spoke the lie deliberately.

"I thought it was I. I knew it all the time," said Melissa, with that strange quietness. "I was not really deceived."

"What do you mean, Melissa?" asked Geoffrey quickly. He stood up again. They were almost eye to eye now. Melissa said: "Somewhere—I do not remember—I heard that you wanted to send either Phoebe or me to school. Perhaps Mama told me. I do not remember. It—it just occurred to me. It was very kind of you."

Geoffrey said nothing. He was too engrossed with Melissa's appearance. She was so calm, so very quiet, and her face was a blank whiteness under her hair.

Then Geoffrey said, uncertainly: "Well, it is unimportant, isn't it." He paused. "Melissa, I wanted to talk to you about something really important."

"Yes." She appeared attentive enough; yet Geoffrey had the curious and alarming idea that she was not really aware of what he was saying. He thought: She is terribly ill. Something has happened to her. He went on swiftly: "Melissa, I believe that everything that has happened to you this year has been too much for you. I think you need a change. I am going to Europe, to find a promising American author. I want you to come with me."

Then there was utter silence in the library. Melissa did not turn aside, or drop her eyes. She still faced him, without moving, as if blind or unconscious.

"Italy, France, England, Austria, Germany, Holland," said Geoffrey, in a stumbling voice. "You've never seen them, Melissa. I want you to come with me."

She did not speak. But now her hands began to move aimlessly as she held her arm stiffly at her sides. Geoffrey's attention was suddenly caught by their movements: each finger flexed and sprang out from the palm with a mechanical precision which was like the motions of a marionette. Fascinated, he watched the bloodless and machine-like flexing and unbending of these fingers, for nothing else about Melissa moved. Her motionlessness was like that of a stone.

He thought: Can she be so agitated at the thought of going away with me? If so, then it is all useless.

Still watching her hands, he said: "I know you must have time to consider. But I want you to think it over very carefully, Melissa. I'll be away a long time. I want you with me. You promise that you'll consider it?"

"Oh, yes," she said, very softly, speaking the first lie of her life. "Oh, yes, Geoffrey."

She must get away. She must get away very fast. There was such a thick and sickening darkness before her eyes, a mist in which Geoffrey's face floated like a disembodied mask and through which his voice came from a far distance. She must leave before she dropped before him, and died. She must leave before she began to scream with intolerable agony. She backed away from the desk, a little at a time.

Puzzled, and overwhelmingly alarmed, Geoffrey made a motion to follow her, then stopped. Was that terror, in her eyes, again? He could not decide, but he knew it was something frightful. If he should touch her, come near her, God only knew what she would do. He stood still, and could only watch her with grim pain.

She had almost reached the threshold of the library now, moving backwards. Once there, she smiled at him, the wildest smile he had ever seen. She said, quite clearly: "Thank you, Geoffrey. Thank you."

Geoffrey did not answer. She stood there in the arch of the doorway, like some tormented ghost, all eyes and whiteness and terrible smile. Then she was gone. But Geoffrey continued to stand there, looking at the empty doorway.

CHAPTER 47

IT WAS a long time after Melissa had left him before Geoffrey could resume his work. A dozen times or more he stood up, with an impulse to go to her. But then he would sit down. He could not forget her white smile, strange and distraught, as she had stood on the threshold and thanked him. Thanked him for what? Yet there had been a kind of strong passion in her voice, a wildness. He thought about this, drumming his fingers on the desk. There was something here which was escaping him but which it was most necessary for him to remember and to understand. He had spoken to her of Europe, and she had promised to consider it. She had not refused, hastily and completely, as he had expected her to do. This had surprised and delighted him. Yet he was not delighted now. There was something wrong. Something was out of key, and its import was ominous.

He shook his head. There was no fathoming Melissa. But he could not rid himself of the vague and disturbing suspicion that something was being held before him which he ought to be able to see. Over and over, he forced himself to remember that she had not refused him, that she had given him her promise. But why did she fear him so? For the first time it came to him that perhaps it was not fear he had seen in her eyes, but something else.

"Nonsense," he said aloud. "The girl has always been afraid of practically everything. Yet she said she would think about going to Europe, and she knew I must have her decision soon."

He became impatient with himself and picked up the bundle

of newspapers he had been reviewing. His eye touched Charles' manuscript. He looked at it with somber bitterness. Then he pushed it aside with a gesture of loathing and contempt. You haven't won yet, you old devil, he thought. There was a look about Melissa today which makes me think you have lost.

He worked for at least two hours, making notes and comments, and writing out a memorandum for his editor. The latter, especially when he was suffering an acute attack of "art," held Mr. Dickens in high disfavor and disdain. Geoffrey found it easier not to argue but to write out memoranda and his decision.

James tiptoed into the library with a message, a telegram from the station. It was from Philadelphia, from Geoffrey's editor, and it informed him that the editor had knowledge that Mr. Dickens himself would be in the city for a few hours early the next day, for a speaking engagement, on the way to New York. If Geoffrey was serious about publishing Mr. Dickens' next book, despite the contemptible things the author had said about America after his last visit, then it might be well for Geoffrey to see the gentleman personally.

"James, I have to leave on the six o'clock train," said Geoffrey, folding up the newspapers. "What time is it? Five? Order the carriage for me and get my bag ready. Mrs. Shaw and Mrs. Dunham are in the house, I presume."

"Mrs. Shaw is on the terrace, I believe," said James uneasily. "But I thought I saw Mrs. Dunham leave the house about half an hour ago."

"Oh, one of her walks!" said Geoffrey with annoyance. "Well, when does she usually return?"

"Sometimes it is seven o'clock or later," replied James, dubiously. He stared at Geoffrey, and hesitated. "Mrs. Dunham is a great walker, sir."

"So I've heard," said Geoffrey. "I've got to leave, and it's damnable if I must go without seeing her. She wouldn't have gone to church, eh?"

James tried to smile humorously. "Oh no, sir, definitely not. Mrs. Dunham has expressed herself frequently to Rachel on the subject of church. Rachel gathered Mrs. Dunham does not approve of it."

Geoffrey had a quick vision of Melissa arrogantly enlarging on the subject of religion. He could see all her gestures, hear her clear and fanatical voice. He laughed. What a child it was. Then, a moment later, he was angry with her.

He went in search of his sister. Arabella was gravely reading what Geoffrey saw was some edifying tome suitable for the Sabbath. She had, also, dressed herself in a thin black silk, to match her reading matter. Her eyes were red, he saw, when she self-consciously removed her spectacles. Had he felt less annoyed just now he would have asked why she had been crying, but the necessity not to ask made him irritable. With hardly forty-five minutes in which to drive to Midfield and catch his train, he had no time for women's tears. So he said abruptly:

"I've got to leave, and at once, Bella. A matter of importance. No, I really must go. There was a telegram. Where is Melissa?"

"Melissa?" asked Arabella, in a tone of wonderment. She searched his face sharply. She could read in it nothing but irritation. But for some reason her despondent spirits rose, and she smiled eagerly. "I thought Melissa was with you."

"I haven't seen her for hours," replied Geoffrey impatiently. "Does she often go off like this, without a word to anyone?"

Arabella closed her book with hands unaccountably trembling. She did not remove her fixed gaze from Geoffrey. But her voice was very casual and indulgent: "Oh, yes, quite often. There are times when I suspect that Melissa does not know it is polite to leave word. She is so—engrossed." She paused. Geoffrey did not seem happy, or content, or triumphant. He was only a large, hurried and irate man. "Ravel's poem has, I hear, reached a significant state, very acute. At least, that is what Melissa tells me." Her smile became maternal, but she watched him.

"Damn Ravel!" said Geoffrey. Then he was silent. He looked at his sister. She smiled serenely at him, and her reddened eyes glinted with sly malice. There was an utter quiet, now, on the terrace.

Then, very slowly, an ugliness crept into Geoffrey's expression as he looked at his sister with a rising hatred. He said, almost softly: "Don't be malicious, Bella, and childish. I don't know what you are trying to say, but you know it is a lie. You know that as well as I do."

Arabella stood up, her book falling to the floor. Tears rushed to her eyes. "Geoffrey! I do not understand you! What do you mean, speaking to me so? What have I done? Is there to be no peace between us, undisturbed by suspicions and cruelty? I have said nothing! I have done nothing, except to be kind to the miserable girl you in your folly have married, except to be her friend, and to display a sisterly affection for her." She pressed her kerchief to her eyes, and turned away from him

with a very loud and dramatic sob. "It is no use!" she exclaimed. "I am continually misunderstood and abused, and
the vilest motives are attributed to me! It is more than I can
bear."

Fuming, Geoffrey stood and listened to her. He felt a fool.
He had no time to be sorry for his sister, though he had the
impulse and was angrily ashamed of himself. He said: "Bella,
don't be ridiculous. I'm sorry if I've offended you." He waited.
But Arabella's sobs racked her with increasing vehemence.
Geoffrey pulled out his watch, and groaned. He put it back.
What had Arabella said, in truth? Nothing. Nothing more than
she had said this morning. He had imagined a viciousness in
her smile.

He said, with more impatience: "Do stop caterwauling a
moment, please. I've said I am sorry. I haven't the time for
lavish apologies. You must accept this or not, as you wish."

Arabella's sobs slowly lessened. She wiped her eyes. She
said, her back to him. "I accept your apology, Geoffrey. After
all, I have accepted so many, haven't I? One more is of no
moment."

"You make me sound like an execrable brute," remarked
Geoffrey. "You aren't much of a martyr, really, Bella. You can
be quick with your own abuse. Well, never mind. I must go
at once. But I shall return the middle of the week. Please tell
Melissa that I must have her answer then."

Arabella caught her breath. She stood in silence, still turned
from him. But her eyes stared before her with a sudden intense glow. Then it was not too late! Everything was not yet
lost; she still had time. The gardens swam before her in a
dazzle of light and brilliance. Slowly she turned about and
faced Geoffrey, and her face was illuminated. She stretched
out her hands to him in a wide gesture.

"Dear Geoffrey! Are we not very foolish, brother and
sister, quarrelling so absurdly! We shall forget it, shall we
not?"

He took her hands. They were damp and hot. She beamed
at him with an expression he could not read. But the minutes were running out very fast, so he kissed her, patted her
shoulder, called her a fool, and himself a bigger one. She
passionately denied that he was guilty of any folly, and
accused herself of being a silly and sensitive female. He
must forgive her, he truly must.

On this fond note, she went with him to the doorway where
the carriage waited. She waved to him as long as she could
see him. There was no one about, when the carriage was

out of sight, and Arabella executed a few capers which could have been called nothing but a frenzied dance of joy.

Then she ran into the house, calling for Ellis, and her voice was shrill with excitement and glee.

CHAPTER 48

LONG BEFORE the sun struck the river, the milky mists began to rise, cool and spectral, from the water. As the darkness rushed away over the hills, the sky also became milky, streaked with opaline colors, and the birds cried out. The east sprang into flame and threw a vivid pink light over the river, a strong breeze turned every tree white in its passing, died down, and the earth exhaled her long, sweet breath. Moment by moment the shadow, like a tide retreating, crept away from hollows and banks and stones, and each object lost its nebulous outline and became sharp and clean with morning. The willows bowed their green fountains; the ferns dripped moisture. And now the sun struck the tops of the highest trees in a rain of golden light.

The long night was gone. Melissa saw the approach of morning, from where she sat on the wide flat stone with her black shawl huddled over her shoulders. A small canvas bag lay near her feet. It had lain there all night, as she had sat there all night, unmoving. It contained a few of the coarse things she had brought to Geoffrey's house: her comb and brush, a muslin nightgown and petticoat and other garments, and a pair of cotton stockings. The stained brown frock she wore had been her own, and the damp boots. Her hand was bare of the ring Geoffrey had given her.

She was very still and quiet, as she watched the sunlight flow over the river. Her sleepless eyes gazed before her, not stirring. Her arms were folded on her knees. Her pale mouth was as motionless as a mouth that slept. Her attitude was not one of resignation or despair; everything about her was spent and tranquil, as if she had done with all suffering and could suffer no more.

She had come here the evening before, to meet Ravel, after leaving Geoffrey's house. Never once had he failed to come, though she often had failed to appear. But there had been an agreement between them that, no matter what happened, they would meet here on Sunday evenings. So she had come. She had waited numbly all through the summer twilight. The moon had come up, had invaded the field of stars. It had floated overhead, had wheeled down the long dark slope of the sky, had falllen into the pale cavern of the west. But Ravel had not come to meet Melissa, and he would never come again. She had known that for hours. He was gone.

She had come to meet him, for he had promised to help her, to take her away to find work and life in Philadelphia or New York. She had never doubted that he would give her that help. She had no money of her own. She had nothing but what she had left behind, and this bag that she had brought with her.

She had not been able to think at all until midnight, when the anesthetic of pain had lifted and complete awareness had fallen upon her. Then, she had not noticed the passing of the hours. She had not moved from this position in which she now sat. She had not been conscious that she was alone by the river in the night chill and damp. She had been thinking and feeling as she had never thought or felt before, with a terrible, calm reality and acceptance, without the self-delusion of a lifetime of innocence, without a single strong emotion or fierce denial. She had seen all that she had always refused to see, and she saw it in the clear hard light of a passionless agony.

Had she been less than she was, she would have cried out in self-pity and maudlin protest. She would have seen herself as a piteous victim of betrayal. She would have tried to the last to find some protective delusion, would have found in an utter and abandoned despair some consolation and relief. In the vision of herself, unwanted, despised, homeless and friendless, there would have been the comfort of self-conscious martyrdom. But Melissa was not of this breed. She blamed nobody, not even her father. She accepted what she had to accept, and her anguish was without voice or tears.

She knew how frightful her betrayal had been, and she studied it with detachment and with emptiness, and with all the intellectual thoroughness of which she was capable. Like a judge, unmoved by superficial emotions, she saw herself and her father, and she knew all the evil that he had been, and what he had done to her. All through the night, she had held his letter to Geoffrey in her hand. It was like evidence against him, but it was quiet evidence, not to be offered vehemently but as a fact to be accepted. She had read and reread it, until she could not read any longer. For a moment or two, she had cried out wildly against Charles' description of her. And then she knew he had lied, that he had always lied. Now memories had come back, vivid and irrefutable, a whole lifetime of evidence against Charles, evidence she had suppressed because to have looked at it clearly would once have been unendurable, would have destroyed the whole world for her. But he had indeed destroyed the world for her, after all, she told herself quietly. There was nothing left. Her reason for living was gone; it had never really existed. It had all been a lie and an illusion. She had not been necessary to Charles, except that he had needed someone to hate. He had hated Amanda, and Andrew, and Phoebe, but they had not loved him as she, Melissa, had loved him, so that to the last he had been impotent to harm them as he had harmed her.

Melissa saw herself as she had been in her father's house and, for a little, agony had given way to a profound contempt, a cold disgust. She did not denounce herself; she merely looked at herself as one looks in a fully revealing mirror, and would not turn away. She had been a fool and an idiot, as Charles had said in his letter to Geoffrey, and she had deserved his disdain. It was not possible, she reflected, to hate someone, and have that one fawn upon you, without complete loathing. Amanda had known of that loathing, and had warned her daughter. Phoebe and Andrew had known; Phoebe had thrown the knowledge in her sister's face; Andrew had tried to tell her. She had even, in turning suddenly, often caught swift glints in Charles' own eyes, had seen his faint and derisive half-smile. She had been uneasy after these occasions, though the uneasiness had been without a name. But it had all been there for her to see. Nothing, really, but herself, had concealed from her the full evil of her father. She had been an egotistic fool. If she had been a victim, she had been an eager one, willing, even anxious to be deceived, because she had had in her mind a picture of herself, trenchant, consequential, valuable, absolutely necessary to a man of tremendous import to the world.

But even then she did not denounce herself. She merely accepted what she saw. She did not hate Charles. She called up his face, the sound of his voice, his eyes, his thin marbled hands, his gestures, his smiles and quiet laughter, and she felt no rage against him. She felt nothing at all. Then she let all that he had been sink into the ground and be lost forever. There was not even one last call to him, begging him to deny the truth she knew. He was dead. He had, in fact, she said to herself, never really existed as she had known him, and so, for her, he now had no reality. What he had really been was no part of her. It never had been a part. She had been a prisoner, but she herself had built the prison and had locked herself in.

She remembered all her father's books, and it seemed that they lay open before her. She read page after page, chapter after chapter. And then she said to herself: He was a poseur and a fraud, a miserable digester of other men's thoughts and scholarships, without originality, without color or grandeur, without validity. He knew it. Mama knew it; even Phoebe and Andrew knew it. But I did not know it.

Geoffrey, she thought, knew all about Papa and me. Now, for the first time, heat flowed into her cold face and she felt a twist of pure torment. How could he help despising me, the grovelling thing I was, the blind and stupid thing? Yet he thought he could help me, out of pity he even married me. But pity is not enough. It was Mama who asked him to help me, knowing me for an idiot beyond hope. And he thought that through me he could help my sister and brother. Did I not ask him to marry me? I must never forget that.

She put her chilled hands to her cheeks, and bit her lips in her pain and humiliation.

Arabella was right; she had always been right. She, Melissa, had been a shame and a burden to a man who had known everything and had yet been kind. He was free of her now. She would never disgrace or humiliate him again. She would never let him see her again, and he would forget what she was and what she had done to him.

When she reached this stage in her thoughts, she dropped her head on her knees and sat very still. There was agony in her now, not impersonal, but emotionless, wild and enormous, more awful than any pain she had ever known, even the pain of her father's death.

And now it was morning, and something had shifted, and she saw the world as it really was, without the shadow of Charles falling across it, and the shadow of all her delusions. I am nothing, she said to herself clearly. I must understand it, and never forget it. I must go on from this place, alone. It is a lonely and terrible place, but I have brought myself to it. The world was like a cold and heavy stone in her hands.

She got up. Her body was without feeling and she had to catch the trunk of a willow to save herself from falling. "I am very tired," she said aloud. "I must find a place to rest and sleep a little before I can decide what I must do."

She moved through the grove of willows, carrying her bag. She was exhausted with shock, and she staggered a little. But all the thoughts that had filled her mind during the night were retreating, leaving behind only that complete emptiness. She crept along the hedges of fields; no one saw her. Once, she caught a glimpse of a distant farmer and she shrank back into the woods.

Then, far away, she saw the house where she had been born, and moved towards it, seeing only its barren and abandoned outline against the sky.

The tall lean gray house seemed to see Melissa's slow and dragging progress towards it. It had been sleeping throughout the night, but it had now become sentient, alive, gathering itself together to watch her with a strange and sinister vigilance. Seven months of desertion had cast age upon its age; it had become a derelict, witchlike and haunted. The high and dusty grass had grown up about it, and as Melissa stumbled through the grass it rattled under her feet, brittle and crackling, filling the air with a pungent odor. Its dust clung to her skirts, her dragging shawl, her boots, and once, unseeing, she stirred up a flock of yellow butterflies, which fluttered in her gaunt face and then went spinning off over the grass.

The flagged walk was overgrown. Some old rose-bushes of Amanda's tore at Melissa's skirts; a few tattered flowers, wizened and almost odorless, clung to the forlorn plants. The old pump had rusted; not a drop of water fell from its spout. Approaching the door, Melissa was startled by a toad hopping dryly near it, and she found herself trembling. She climbed the two sagging steps; in their interstices was green mold. All about lay a profound yet ominous silence, swimming in the hot and brazen light of morning. Even the shadows, sharp and black, seemed breathless with the gathering heat.

No one had bothered to lock the door. It was as if everyone had fled the place, not caring whether a homeless tramp entered here, or any other marauder. Melissa turned the rusted handle; the door fell open before her with a loud and groaning noise. Here was the hallway; the mirror facing the door was so clouded with dust that Melissa's image in it was the image of a ghost. She stood on the threshold of Amanda's "parlor." On the hearth lay the feathery ashes of old fires, and through the blurred windows the sun shone, misty and smothering. All Amanda's precious old furniture had been powdered with a gritty grayness; the lamps were entangled in swaying webs.

She turned back to the hall. The old clock had lost its voice, and stood mute and dead, its face almost obliterated. She went up the steep stairs, and her footsteps echoed. She passed the closed doors of the bedrooms, and it was like passing the rooms of the dead. She reached the door of the study, and opened it with a hand that was cold and un-hesitating.

She entered the study, looked about her with quiet and careful eyes. Her father's couch was there, his books, his desk, his tables, his favorite chair, her own footstool on which she had sat at his feet. But everything had fallen into decay, silent and remorseless. It was the room of a man who had died, who had never existed.

Melissa stood there for a long time. In this room she had been robbed of the living world, of laughter and of youth, of love and joy, of music and hope. She had thought of it as a place where she had truly lived. She saw it now as the place where she had been murdered.

Now a sick and awful bitterness rose up in her against Charles. Now she saw that what he had done to her had been deliberate and, therefore, unpardonable. Had he done what he had done in ignorance or stupidity, or even in bottomless egotism, she could have forgiven him. But he had done it in full knowledge, and knew why he was doing it. Even if his hatred had been a strong and powerful hatred rising out of a great and defeated mind, he could still have been forgiven, even pitied. But he had done it out of little-ness, out of malice, cunningly, and with secret laughter. Even in her bitterness she still could not hate him, but she despised him. "Such a small victory," she said aloud. "Yet it could satisfy him."

The house drew about her, as if to clutch and hold her forever, and it was full of Charles. She closed the door, and went across the narrow hallway to her mother's room. The pitiless sun drove through the unshuttered windows upon the shrouded bed, the grayed furniture, the worn, patched hang-ings.

"Mama," said Melissa, softly and clearly. She closed the door behind her, and approached the bed. "O Mama," she

said, and put her hands on the counterpane. A cloud of
dust rose, but Melissa did not see nor care. Here she had
been born; here her mother had died. In the room the silence
deepened, but it seemed to hold at bay the inimical silence
of the rest of the house, the ghost that listened behind the
door with a gently inclined head and a derisive smile. Peace
and tenderness were in the room, like a breathing presence,
like a voice of comfort and protection.

Melissa put down her bag and shawl. Her hands and face
were smeared with dust, and now tears made paths of whiteness down her cheeks. She lay upon the bed, hopeless and
quiet. The fixed pain began to retreat from her. Everything
became foggy and unreal. She closed her eyes, and fell into
the darkness of a shocked sleep.

CHAPTER 49

MELISSA WOKE suddenly, and completely, in a gray
and swimming twilight full of heavy silence. She was
drenched with sweat, prostrated with heat. There was an
ominous and waiting quality in the house, but that quality
was also beyond the house.

She lay in her mother's bed, and her mind was sharp
and clear. She stared up at the dimming ceiling without
lifting her hand or moving her painful body. But there was
no pain in her mind, only that vast emptiness of emotion
which had ended the night. She had turned her back upon
a world that never was, a world that had been compounded
of lies and illusions. She had, in a way, died. But all was still
chaos before her. No new world of substance or hope or
promise had formed, upon which she could set her foot and
travel on. Did it exist, that new world, she thought, or was
that, too, an illusion? Was there nothing at all, only this
sustained blankness, this untenanted formlessness, this
vacuity? If so, it would soon be easy to lose all reality, to
question whether one lived or not. Terror lay in that question.

Her thoughts began to circle in vague patterns of dread
and despair. Loneliness filled her, but such a loneliness as
she had never known in all her life.

She sat up in bed and pushed back her loosened wet hair.
It clung stickily to her cheeks and forehead and neck. Now

her head swam, and she had to bend forward to retain consciousness. When the sensation passed, she was panting feebly but swiftly. Then she sat, holding onto the mattress with tight fingers, and tried to bring her thoughts to order, to consider the immediate future.

If there was no world ready-made and unshakable, then she had to make one for herself. She had no money, she told herself steadily. She had no home except this, and it had become a place of horror from which she wanted to run in fear. She had no friends, no one who wanted her. She had never, in all her twenty-six years, asked help for herself. But now she must ask for help, not in shame, but simply because she needed it. Surely, she thought, there was no need of shame when one truly needed help, any more than there was shame in a drowning man crying for rescue.

Whom could she ask? Andrew? He would be glad to help her. Phoebe? Ah, yes, Phoebe, her sister! It was more natural for a sister to help a sister than for a brother to help a sister. Then, too, Phoebe had been so kind the other day, so solicitous. Despite the illusions from which she had been so shockingly delivered only recently, in poor Melissa's mind Phoebe's pretty dimpled face rose up ringed with tender light. Melissa had yet to learn that in discarding major illusions minor ones had an irritating, if not dangerous, tendency to remain behind, like seeds, ready to grow into greater ones and again swamp the mind with a jungle-growth. She thought she had no self-deceptions left. In the vast unheaval that had taken place in her, surely no lie or credulity had survived.

I must take one step at a time, she told herself severely. My first step must be to wash my face and hands. It is possible that the pump still works. The room became dimmer. A light. No, not a light! It might be seen—by someone, somehow.

She struggled from the bed, and the floor up-ended, but she caught a bed-post and rigidly forced her body to remain upright. A loud sound of gasping filled the room. She said, aloud, and slowly, as to an hysterical fool: "Be still. Be quiet." Now the beat of heavy wings that seemed to be in herself subsided under the force of her will.

She crept down the stairs to the pump outside the door. A rusted bucket still remained under the spout. She lifted the handle of the pump and worked it. The creaking tore at the darkening silence. After some moments, dull and reluctant water trickled forth, became stronger, then gushed. She let the bucket fill, plunged her hands into it, splashed water over her face. She gasped as the cold wetness stung her and dripped in her hair. She wiped herself with her petticoat, in her old, forgotten habit.

Now she did not feel so ill, so weak and broken. A little strength returned to her. Standing in the deep grass, under the brightening stars, she unfastened her hair, clumsily re-braided it, and pinned it as neatly as possible around her head. She did not look about her. She did not look towards the long and distant slope in the direction of Geoffrey's house. That, too, had become part of the world which never was and which she must never let herself remember. She did not look at the house where she had been born, and in which so much of her had died. That, too, was behind her. She would never enter it again.

She set out across the wet dark fields towards Phoebe's home, which she had not once entered. The grass was thick with dew. Heat lightning flashed momentarily across the sky, revealed the mountainous shapes of hills, and drenched the hushed trees in livid light. Crickets shrilled all about her. From nearby woods owls hooted. She saw and heard nothing. All her mind was bent towards seeing Phoebe.

Brambles caught at her skirts and nettles stung her ankles. She passed a farmhouse, and a dog barked fiercely. Cattle and horses stamped in fat barns. Now a muttering of thunder came from the hills. Melissa went on. She was not conscious of time. She had no thought but Phoebe, the shelter her sister would give her, and the rest, while she gathered her strength to deal with the new world which had not yet formed for her. It would not be long. She was certain of that. A few days, a week, of peace and quiet, of long, dreamless sleep. Perhaps Phoebe would give her some money, so that she might go to Philadelphia and find a position, or any kind of work. Or perhaps Phoebe might let her remain in her house; she would learn household tasks, and be of use. She wanted nothing now but an opportunity to be truly useful, without illusions and stupidities, or her former grandiose ideas of importance. There was no longing in her for her former state of self-deception, only horror and disgust and contempt.

It might have been an hour, or even more, before a dim bulk rose before her, with rectangles of yellow light flaring in it. It was Phoebe's house. Melissa was forced to rest at the gate, leaning against it. A dog came rushing out of the night, barking and snarling. He caught a fold of her dress.

She beat him off, without fright, with impatience only. He caught another fold and tugged at it, growling. But she opened the gate and went inside the garden, the dog struggling to hold her back. The uproar he made must have aroused someone within, for the door was suddenly flung open, and a hoarse female voice called: "Bill! Bill, what is it?" A stout shadow stood in the doorway.

The light fell full upon Melissa, and she must have been a strange sight, bedraggled and disheveled, with the dog wrenching at the hem of her rumpled skirts, her hair, loosened again, falling in braids over her shoulders. She came up the garden path with difficulty, her face stark and white in the lamplight, her eyes shining with preternatural brightness. The shadow in the doorway stepped back in alarm.

Though Susie Whitehall, Phoebe's maid-of-all-work, knew Melissa by sight, as did everyone in the township, she could not at first recognize this wild torn woman as the sister of her mistress. So, in stupefaction, she merely stood and watched Melissa approach, the dog clinging grimly to her. It was not until Melissa stumbled up the white stone steps that Susie came to life and shouted furiously at the dog to release the girl. The dog, bewildered at this, snarled one last defiance and slunk away, but remained at a distance, his eyes shining in the dark.

Susie caught at Melissa's arm, for it was obvious that the girl was about to collapse. "Dear me, ma'am, I didn't know you!" exclaimed Susie, drawing Melissa into the lamplit parlor of the comfortable farmhouse. "Of all things! Here, do sit down, and let me put this footstool under your feet, ma'am."

In the excitement, Susie forgot what was now common knowledge in Midfield. As she was a kindly, middle-aged woman, her first thought was to help Melissa. But now, as she stood beside the soiled and distracted young woman, staring down at her in utter astonishment, her broad rough face flushed crimson. Whatever was Mrs. Dunham doing here, here in her sister's house, when everyone knew that she had run away with that young Mr. Ravel Littlefield with whom she had been carrying on the whole summer to the shame of all honest folk? Now curiosity began to excite Susie, and she wet her lips avidly. What had happened to Mrs. Dunham? Had her fancy man abandoned her?

Melissa sat in the mahogany and red-plush chair, the lamplight striking her vividly and revealing her stark and haggard face, her sunken eyes and falling hair. She saw nothing of the solid bourgeois comfort of this big room, the black wallpaper with its red roses and brilliant green leaves, the heavily carved chairs and tables, the red, green and yellow china lamps, the Brussels carpeting on the polished floor, the crimson draperies at the tall windows. She had begun to rub the soiled palms of her hands together, over and over, as if cold. She looked about her almost frantically. "Susie, where is my sister?" she asked, in a faint voice. "I must see my sister at once. Please call her."

Susie hesitated, more excited than ever. She said: "Oh, ma'am, Mrs. Barrett was quite—upset—today! It was terrible." She paused, significantly.

But Melissa appeared not to have grasped the significance. She said: "Phoebe is never really ill. And I must see her. Tell her I am here."

"Yes, ma'am," replied Susie, in a solemn and portentous voice, and beginning to back away. "But I doubt she'll see you. She is in bed, with vinegar cloths and smelling-salts, and must be quiet, Mr. Barrett said." She stopped, and waited for Melissa's comment, for some guilty flush, for some discomfiture. But Melissa had forgotten her. She had folded her hands in her lap, and sat motionless, her head bent. She had not heard or understood a word.

Baffled, Susie left the room, leaving Melissa alone in her exhaustion and silence. Melissa began to forget where she was. The queer swimming sensation had returned to her. Everything wavered before her, as if seen through water, and the beat of monstrous wings was all about her again. Her whole body numbed; her senses were unconscious of their surroundings, so that she neither saw nor heard. It was a long time before she became aware that someone had cried out, more than once, in a shrill and furious voice. She was so tired that it took an enormous effort of the will to lift her head.

Phoebe was standing before her, Phoebe, a pretty and enraged fury in a crimson silk peignoir, her yellow ringlets blowing on her shoulders, her tear-stained eyes dancing with anger and hatred, her little white fists clenched at her sides.

From some far distance, Melissa heard her cries: "How dare you come to my house, you slut? How dare you creep back here, like a dog? After all the shame you've brought on your innocent family, and the disgrace? I'll never live it down, never, never, that my sister ran away with a strange man, abandoning her home and her husband!"

Very slowly Melissa pushed herself to her feet, but one

hand retained hold of the back of the chair, to keep from falling.

She said: "Phoebe."

With a dramatic gesture, Phoebe recoiled from her, and with so much exaggeration that under other circumstances it would have been absurd. Phoebe wrapped her gown about her as if to protect herself from pollution, and regarded her sister with pure malignance.

"Don't you dare touch me! Don't you dare speak my name! Why, you're nothing but a loathsome Thing! I knew you'd do something like this, some day, to dishonor your family. I knew it all the time. But no one else knew about you—except Papa. He knew! He knew all the time. How he laughed at you, behind your back! He must have known all about you. He hated you." She paused, her eyes, for all their tearstains, glittering with something monstrously like glee and delight. "Did you know that? He hated you."

Melissa pushed herself upright, and stood very tall and quiet, full of dignity, her hands clasped together.

"I know," she said gently.

But the satisfaction of hatred and envy in Phoebe was now so rich and full and delicious that she did not hear what her sister had said. Her heart swelled with a voluptuous delight, as if, long hungering, it was being fed.

"You thought you were the world to him, that you meant something to him, and all the time he despised you, and made fun of you with little smiles when you weren't looking, and he would rub the side of his nose with his finger. Why, you weren't important to him at all, except that you amused him. He couldn't help being amused. You were so stupid. You never knew you were stupid, did you? You thought you were a learned blue-stocking, and all the time you were only a fool."

"I know," whispered Melissa. Her pale and shining eyes fixed themselves upon her sister.

Now the joy and fulfilment made Phoebe's breath come short and fast, and filled her with frenzy. She pointed her finger derisively at Melissa, and actually gave a skip or two, her ringlets bouncing.

"Look at you now! Look at your dirt, you shameless creature, you abandoned woman! Look at you, and all your pretenses! You and your books! You and your grand marriage, and your servants, and a rich husband, and your handsome frocks! You and your trickery, deceiving Geoffrey Dunham into marrying you, heavens know how! Why, you're nothing but a drab and an imbecile. You always were; I knew it, even when you swept about the house, all haughty and serious, with a pen in your hair, and your hands stained with ink. How dared you marry Geoffrey? How dared you have the effrontery to think you could be a fine lady—you baggage? How I've wanted to laugh in your face when you trailed around in the handsome frocks and gowns he bought you, with jewels on your hands and around your dirty neck! Sometimes it was more than I could endure, just looking at you, and I had to run home, time after time, so I could laugh in peace."

She shivered with such pure delight that she caught her hands together and clasped them against her chin. Her eyes studied Melissa with jubilation, and what she saw made her give another exuberant skip.

"You had no right to marry poor Geoffrey!" she cried.

"I know," said Melissa again, and this time clearly.

Phoebe stood and looked at her. If she did not skip again, her eyes did, with distilled malice.

"Oh, you do?" she cried, mockery dancing in her voice.

"Yes," said Melissa.

Phoebe laughed out loud, and clapped her hands together.

"How consoling that will be to him now, since you have been deceiving him all summer with Ravel Littlefield, and then ran off with him! How pleasant it will make him feel, realizing at last that he ought never to have married you!"

But Melissa had moved. She had certainly not taken a step backward or forward; she had not swayed nor changed her towering and rigid posture. Yet, in some way, she had changed, and stirred.

"Phoebe," she said, steadfastly, "what do you mean, about deceiving Geoffrey all summer, with Ravel. I don't understand." She paused, and now her white face blazed. "You don't mean—but you never believed that, did you? You, Phoebe, my sister?"

Wonder filled her, and disbelief. Her light brows drew together in stern incredulity.

Phoebe was aghast at this effrontery. "You have the temerity to deny it, to lie to me, to pretend, you odious hussy? You dare insult me like that? Why, the whole township was watching and laughing, pitying Geoffrey, condemning you! Everyone waited for this to happen. No!" she exclaimed, enraged, "I did not know! I was protected from knowing, because my friends were merciful. Andrew did not know, and for the same reason. But now I know that everyone else knew. Tonight, Susie told me what has been common knowledge for months—"

Melissa was silent. Her eyes did not leave Phoebe's face. Piercing and inflexible, they scrutinized her, as if seeing her for the first time. Phoebe, about to burst into a fresh tirade of abuse, stopped. Something about her sister vaguely alarmed her.

"Yes," said Melissa, at last. "I see that you believe it. I see that you want to believe it. Why, Phoebe?"

If Phoebe had taken a moment to consider, or if she had been less exultant, she might not have said what she did say. But she cried out, in fierce exultation: "Because I hate you! Because I've always hated you!"

Then, the very sound of these ugly words made her put the fingers of her right hand quickly against her lips, as if to recall them. Her eyes remained vengeful, but some of the glitter of malice faded from them.

"I see," said Melissa. There was no emotion in her voice. She still gazed at her sister. She sighed. "Does Andrew believe it, too? But no, he does not hate me."

Shame, and something else which she refused to recognize, made Phoebe say loudly and vehemently: "If he does not hate you, he must, now. Arabella sent for my Johnnie, with a message telling him what you had done. She also sent a message to Andrew. They are both up at the Dunham house, this minute, hearing all the details. A family conclave!" she added, her mouth twisting contemptuously. "And I suppose she's sent for Geoffrey."

She paused. "My advice to you is to leave at once and never to let anyone see you again. If Geoffrey finds you, he will probably kill you."

But Melissa seemed to be meditating. Even her bedraggled skirts, her fallen hair, her stained face and scratched hands could not detract from her somber dignity and abstraction. There was no sound in the room now. Melissa had forgotten Phoebe. She was deep in some desolate world of her own. Phoebe watched her intently. There was something strange about this fool and slut now, something untouchable and invulnerable. Something that made a curious pang run through Phoebe, like a quick slash of pain. This made her say, with a savage defensiveness: "What else could we believe, after you ran off with him? There was nothing else to believe."

Melissa slowly looked up, and regarded her sister almost thoughtfully.

"I suppose not. Though, if you had loved me, Phoebe, as I loved you, you would never have believed it."

"Love!" cried Phoebe, struck again with pain. "You never loved anyone in all your life but yourself."

Melissa shook her head. "You are quite wrong. I loved—Papa. And I love Geoffrey."

Phoebe drew in her breath. She could not speak.

"But he does not love me, and I was a burden to him, and an embarrassment, and so I decided to go away and let him forget me." Melissa spoke slowly and calmly. "Ravel had promised to help me find work or a position in New York or Philadelphia. I have no money, no means at all. He was to give me what assistance I needed, because he was my friend."

Phoebe was still silent. But now the hot flush of joy and excitement left her cheeks. She did not want to believe it; she tried not to believe it. Yet, all at once, she knew that Melissa was speaking the truth. She knew also that, in spite of what she had said, in spite of her rapture and exultation over her sister's "fall," she had not believed it, not even when Johnnie had told her, not even when Susie had informed her, in hushed, shocked tones, of what all the township had seen and suspected.

There was a hard lump in Phoebe's throat now, and a sickness in her heart. She took a step towards Melissa, and asked, insistently:

"Well, why didn't you *go* with him?" She tried to bring back the old malevolent delight, but succeeded only for a moment. "Or did he discard you, after all?"

Melissa sighed again, and the sound was all desolation. "I went to meet him, down by the river. He did not come. I waited all night, and then I knew he would never come again. And now I know. He loved me, and he knew I'd never love him. It was no use at all. So, he went away, without me."

She lifted her hands from her sides, dropped them again in a moving and eloquent gesture. "I seem to know so many things I never knew before. I didn't know, until this very minute, that Ravel loved me. I am very sorry. I'm afraid I never really saw Ravel, at any time, either as a man or as a human being. He was just someone I could talk to, and with; I was very lonely. I was grateful that there was someone with whom I could speak. It is very strange, but I seem only now, for the first time, to see Ravel."

Phoebe had no words with which to make any comment. She could not look away from her sister.

Melissa smiled, the strangest, saddest smile.

"There are so many things I did not know yesterday, but which I know today. It seems impossible that I was the fool you know I was. But I was indeed a fool. It is too late, of course. Everything has, I see, always been too late."

Phoebe tried to speak again, but her tongue lay heavy and numb in her mouth.

Melissa said: "Do you remember, Phoebe, the day I asked you whether Geoffrey had once wanted to send you away to school? I asked you that because I found an old draft of a letter Papa had written to Geoffrey. I thought he meant you." She smiled again. "I was such a fool. I dared not believe the truth."

She put her hand inside her stained bodice and drew out the letter. She held it out to Phoebe, whose face had changed. The younger woman hesitated, then she stepped towards her sister and took the letter. She read it quickly.

She had so small and petty a soul that she could exclaim immediately: "How could you insult me by thinking Papa meant me? 'Stupid'! 'Fantasies'! All the rest of it! I was never like that, and you knew it, yet still you could think Papa meant me!" Her voice rose shrilly in indignation.

She stopped abruptly. Melissa was still smiling that mournful and enigmatic smile. "You are right, Phoebe, it was an insult to think that. Anyone could have seen Papa meant me. I knew it at once, but I dared not let myself believe it."

Phoebe was silent. She held out the letter to Melissa, as if it were a repugnant thing, and her gesture was honest. Her mouth had lost its cruelty; her eyes were uncertain and troubled. Melissa shook her head. "No, Phoebe, I do not want it. Destroy it, if you wish. But I never want to see it, or to remember it, again."

Phoebe laid the paper on a table near at hand. She said sullenly:

"Why did you come here tonight, to me, after what you had done? Because you know what you have done, and you admitted, yourself, that you had intended to run away with Mr. Littlefield, and would have done so, had he come for you."

Melissa looked at her, and said clearly and simply: "I thought you might give me shelter, and help me, and let me rest a little, until I could discover what I must do."

Phoebe was still sullen, despite the increasing pain in her heart. She thought: Why should I feel like this, when none of it is my fault, when stupid old Melissa has brought it all down on herself? And disgraced us all, and made us the laughing-stock of the whole countryside?

She opened her mouth to speak, but Melissa had turned away and was going to the door. She had reached it, had opened it, when Phoebe cried impulsively:

"What are you going to do? Where are you going?"

"I don't know yet. It is of no importance," replied Melissa, without glancing back. She closed the door gently behind her.

Phoebe was alone in the room now, with all the comfort of her ugly but pleasant parlor about her, and the soft lamplight. She stood for a long time in the center of the room, her yellow brows frowning and thoughtful. Her eyes wandered helplessly. Her breast hurt with a dull and throbbing pain. Then she saw her father's letter, lifted it, reread it. She flung it from her with disgust, and said aloud: "Monster!"

Now she started. She stared at the door through which her sister had gone. She ran to it, tripping over her flounces. She flung them aside. She tore open the door, ran down the stone steps, shouting: "Melissa! Melissa, come back!"

But only the climbing moon was outside, whitening the trees, and the night. The dog, barking, rushed towards his mistress. His barking became more excited as she called into the darkness with hopelessness and frenzy.

Melissa walked aimlessly away from the house to which she had gone for protection and help, and from which she had been turned away. She walked for a long time, her head hanging, her arms lax at her sides. Her step was very slow and dragging.

Again, her mind was blank and empty, and there was no feeling in her, no memory. She had already forgotten Phoebe. There was no sight in her eyes, no hearing in her ears. She did not even say to herself: There is nowhere for me to go. She only wandered on, mechanically, under the moon, through fields and pastures sleeping and still.

Finally, sheer exhaustion made her stop. She had come to the river and was standing beside it, the water almost at her feet. Mud sucked at her boots. The river's voice was loud as surf; a wind had blown up, and it bent the trees and tore at them. The lightning, which had died down, now began to flash fiercely again, glimmering on the water like steel, and the river answered the fateful thunder. No rain had fallen as yet, but the earth breathed its disturbed breath to the night and the wind.

Melissa looked about her dazedly, pushing the tangled hair

from her face. For the first time since she had left her sister's house, full sanity returned to her, clearing her mind of the silent chaos that had possessed it. She began to tremble, and shivered. Suddenly a frightful pain attacked her, a pain compounded of grief and sorrow and despair. She was standing beside a willow. She put her arm about it, she pressed her face to the warm bark. She hugged it to her breast as if it were alive and comprehending, and she was utterly lost and desolate, seeking for comfort in a most terrible world.

At last, she grew very quiet. She rubbed her wet eyes and cheeks childishly with the back of her hands. She looked steadily about her. There was nothing, nothing at all. There was no other world to which she could go. Everything was without meaning. Her face changed, in the stormy moonlight. Firmly, she took a step closer to the water, the sticky mud sucking at her heels. She did not waver or hesitate for a moment. She went down into the water, step by step. After the first shock of cold, she became numb. It was as though her legs dissolved slowly into the water; she could not even feel the sloping bottom under her feet. The current tugged at her thighs, rose to her waist. It swirled under her breasts, embraced them.

CHAPTER 50

"YOU DO NOT BELIEVE IT? You dare to insinuate, Andrew Upjohn, that I am a liar?" Arabella almost screamed. "Look at this, then. Here is the letter she left, found this morning in her room! Read it for yourself."

The library was fully lighted, as if alerted for an emergency. The windows stood open to the hot night, there was the sullen mutter of thunder beyond, the flash of lightning and the cry of the crickets. Arabella, clothed in heavy, funereal black, appropriate to the awful occasion, sat opposite the two young men before her, and sobbed loudly.

Andrew looked at the letter in Arabella's outthrust hand. He sat, the huge and somber young man, in Geoffrey's chair, his pipe cold in his fingers. Under the sun-bronze of his skin a paleness glimmered; there were great beads of sweat on his forehead. But, otherwise, he showed no emotion, except by the grimness of his big mouth. He had changed very hastily from his overalls and sweat-stained shirt. His shirt was white and clean, but he had not bothered with a cravat or a coat, in his hurry to respond to Arabella's urgent summons. His brown and pillar-like neck was exposed; a pulse throbbed in it, like a small heart. His little dark-blue eyes expressed nothing.

Near him sat Johnnie Barrett, Phoebe's husband, also summoned by Arabella. He was a silent, brown young man, slighter and smaller than Andrew, but strangely like him, except that his thin face was normally gentler, less crag-like, and more sensitive. Tonight, his usual gentleness had given way to a fixed grimness. He looked slowly from Arabella to Andrew. He was very fond of his brother-in-law. They had much in common, beyond the relationship that existed by marriage. They had the countryman's means of slow and silent communication. Johnnie had never liked Melissa. But now his brown eyes were uncertain. They said to Andrew: It is not true. It cannot be true. Do not believe it.

They were redolent of the fields and the barns, these young men. They sat before Arabella, and she hated their impassive silence, their "stupid" obduracy. She hated their calm and their patience and the way they looked at her, with the long and motionless serenity that had come to them from the earth. They were like trees or stones, she thought furiously. They were without life, imagination or understanding. Johnnie had not yet spoken at all. Andrew had only said: "It is not true."

But Arabella now had a letter in her hand. Her small gray eyes glittered in their swollen redness, and there was exultation in them, and triumph. She fluttered the paper at Andrew, and exclaimed: "Read it! It was addressed to my brother, but when it was brought to me, after it was discovered that Melissa had not been home all night, I felt it my duty to open it, in order to notify Geoffrey, if necessary. I immediately dispatched a telegram to him. He will doubtless be home on the midnight train. What? You do not wish to read it? Then I shall read it to you both."

She looked at Andrew, who had not moved to take the letter. He was staring at Arabella attentively, with the most curious glint in his eyes. She gave a short hard laugh, and tossed her head. With elaboration, she unfolded the letter, and read aloud:

"'Geoffrey, I have gone to join Ravel Littlefield. He has promised to help me, either in Philadelphia or New York. When I know where I am to be, I shall ask you to send me the rest of my belongings, my father's books and papers. I should have told you today that I was going, but I did not wish to annoy you. And something had hurt me beyond any imagining. You will be glad to know that I have gone. You have been so very kind, but I have nothing to give you in return. I want to thank you; I had no words for thanks today.' " It was signed: "Melissa."

Arabella read it all, dramatically, and with a flourish. When she had finished, she glanced up vindictively at the two young men. But they still sat unmoving, watching her. Their obdurate expressions had not changed, except that Andrew appeared strangely and subtly stirred. Johnnie now looked only at Andrew, as if awaiting his explanation. Neither spoke.

Arabella smiled. She folded the letter, placed it carefully on the table beside her, and gave a deep and mournful sigh. "Neither you, Andrew, nor you, Johnnie, nor the whole countryside, could have been unaware of what has been transpiring between Melissa and Ravel Littlefield. You cannot have been so stupid. It was common knowledge."

"Was it?" said Andrew quietly.

Arabella was outraged. "Certainly it was! It was the talk of the whole township! If you have not heard, Andrew, then someone was sentimentally protecting you, for, after all, she is your sister."

"Did Geoffrey know? Had you told him before this?" asked Andrew, still very quietly.

"I?" Arabella cried out that syllable in righteous disbelief. "Was I the one to deal my brother such a blow? Was I to be the one to announce his dishonor and his shame? I would rather have died! He knew nothing. I hoped he need never know anything. I thought the shameless girl might come to her senses. In truth, I even believed, until this morning, that there was really nothing serious between her and Ravel. I thought it a foolish, but harmless, summer interlude, in spite of all the evidence to the contrary, in spite of her constant and frequent meetings with Ravel, in spite of——"

"In spite of everything, believing what you believed, you let him come to this house?" Andrew's voice was suddenly like the thrust of a broad-sword. Arabella shrank before it. She tried to look away from the eyes fixed upon her so steadily now, so ruthlessly, and with such contempt.

She stammered: "I tell you, I thought it was nothing."

"You knew it was nothing. You know it is still nothing," said Andrew. "You are not a stupid woman, Arabella. You know all about Melissa. You have read that letter, many times over,

I know. You know as well as I know that if Melissa has really gone with Littlefield, she will not sleep with him."

Arabella flung the back of her hand against her eyes, and the rings on her fingers flashed as she did so. "How dare you speak so lewdly to me!" she cried. "And I to be insulted in my own house, as if no tragedy had come upon us here, no disgrace and no dishonor? My brother! My poor brother!"

"You evade everything I say to you," said Andrew, without raising his voice. "You are very clever. But you thought you might compromise Melissa. You have always hated and resented her. So you encouraged Littlefield to come here. Somehow, you must have known he was attracted to her, though Melissa probably never saw him as a man. You hoped something like this might happen. Melissa never said anything to me, but I'll wager you made her life wretched, that you tried to drive her away. It is all very clear to me. I have no proof but my own inner convictions. I may be wrong. But I do not think so."

Though no one was looking at Johnnie Barrett, he nodded his head solemnly.

Andrew's voice was still calm, but louder now: "She might have been happy, but for you. But for you, she might have found her way to peace and happiness. I don't care what the letter says. You are reading lies into it. To me, it isn't lying. Something broke my sister's heart, and you helped to break it. Something drove her out of this house, and I think you are part of it."

Arabella's hand fell slowly from her eyes. Her raddled paint was blotches of brick-colored grease on her cheeks. Her mouth gaped, showing the rounded rows of yellow teeth within. Her eyes glittered with hatred and rage.

She said, with slow emphasis and quietness: "You are a fool. All the Upjohns were fools. Your father was a miserable pretender, and you know it. Melissa was little more than an idiot, and you know that, too. Yet I tried to help her. I did all in my power to give her some small polish and grace, so that my brother need no longer be ashamed of her—as indeed he was. I chose her frocks and gowns. I taught her manners every day. I have my own servants as witnesses. I was kind to her, though she was always impossible. For this, I receive your vituperation, your insults. No matter. It is over now. It is finished."

Andrew stood up, ponderously. He went to the cold fireplace and looked down at it thoughtfully. He was still pale, under his brownness, but his expression was moved and somber.

"No," he said, not turning to Arabella, "it is not over. It is not finished. There is too much to explain. Dunham's infrequent returns here. Melissa's open wretchedness. Where she has gone. What she is doing now. Your own part in all this. There is too much to be explained. And I shall find the explanation." He added, with rough gentleness, as if to himself: "Poor Melly."

Now he turned to Arabella. His eyes were sharp spots of blue fire. His big hands knotted. He did not move, but she sat upright in her chair, catching her breath in quick and abject fear.

"I am not such a fool as you believe me," he said. "I am not such a fool as to believe your lies. I know all about you. I shall come back here, tomorrow, and see Dunham, if he has arrived. I shall tell him everything I know or suspect."

He said to Johnnie Barrett, who was rising slowly: "Come on, Johnnie. This isn't a place for clean and decent men to be in, just now."

In utter silence, the young men left the library. They had reached the door when they heard a whispering sound behind them. They turned, to see James, Geoffrey's man. Andrew scowled at him, but James put his finger eagerly to his lips, and then said in a loud and courteous voice: "This way, gentlemen, please. I believe your horses are tethered to the post near the door? Ah, yes, please allow me."

The little man accompanied them outside and carefully drew the door closed behind him. Andrew no longer scowled. By the light of the storm-wracked moon and the intermittent lightning, he eyed James with a sudden interest. James bent towards him and whispered hastily:

"I have tried to tell the master, but there did not seem to be the opportunity or the words, Mr. Upjohn. I wanted to tell him how wretched Mrs. Dunham was in this house while he was away. The madam, Mrs. Shaw, made her life a misery, sir. Yes, a misery," and he nodded his head with vehemence, and his prominent eyes glared in his small face. "You'll not quote me direct, sir, but when you see the master, you'll tell him that you—you've heard Mrs. Shaw tried to drive the poor young lady from the house, telling her she was a burden and a shame to Mr. Dunham?"

"I see," said Andrew softly, his dark face grim in the lightning.

James nodded, over and over. "This'd not happened—today

—Mr. Upjohn, if Mrs. Dunham's maid, Rachel, had been at home. But she's in Pittsburgh. The only friend Mrs. Dunham had in this house. It's pitiful, sir. Every day, there was lessons in manners and deportment, and every day Mrs. Dunham was told she was a—a fool, sir, and would never learn to take her place in society with Mr. Dunham."

Andrew and Johnnie Barrett looked at each other in silence.

James glanced apprehensively at the door behind him. He came closer to Andrew, and whispered hoarsely: "Rachel told me. The poor young lady had found a copy of a letter her father had written to Mr. Dunham many years ago. It called her stupid, and many worse things, sir. The young lady persuaded herself it meant her sister, your lady, Mr. Barrett, sir. But I think she knew, all the time."

Andrew's face changed. But he could not speak. Then he said, in a voice that shook: "Melly. Poor Melly."

James retreated towards the door. He said, with sudden hushed passion: "I don't believe it, sir! I don't believe the poor young lady went off with Mr. Littlefield!" He tore open the door and ran inside, closing it behind him.

The two young men in complete and somber silence got on their horses and rode away down the long gravel paths of the estate. The windless and rainless thunder and lightning rolled and flashed all about them. Night stood on the earth, hot and oppressive, and the branches of trees swooped over their heads.

Johnnie Barrett was never much given to comment, but now he said: "That is an old bitch."

"I knew. Someway, I knew," answered Andrew, in a low voice. His hands tightened on the reins. "I blame myself, in a way. I ought to have taken more interest in poor Melly. But she irritated me, probably because I pitied her and didn't know how to help her. And now it's too late." He paused. "No, it's not too late. If we only knew where she was! I believe that little man. She never went off with Littlefield. That was either to put Dunham off the trail—which means that Melly is brighter and more sly than I think she is—or she decided against it at the last minute. But she's not gone away with him," he added positively.

Johnnie's thoughts were deep, if slow. "Andy, you've got to admit that Melissa was a queer one. Like a child, if you see what I mean. She never knew anything. People, grown-up people, could do anything they wanted with Melly. I didn't know her well, but all at once I know that's true. People could tell her anything and she'd believe it, especially if she trusted them. She couldn't lie, and so she couldn't believe others could. You once said she was suspicious. But I don't think she was, except as a calf is suspicious, or a young deer. But if someone got her confidence, or she believed in 'em, she'd swaller anything."

"Yes," said Andrew, looking at his brother-in-law with new respect, "she'd 'swaller' anything. That's been the whole trouble, all her life, with Melly. She's older than I am, but she's an innocent, if there ever was one."

They cantered more quickly now, towards Johnnie's house. There was a long silence between them. Then Andrew said an extraordinary thing, in a loud, compassionate and wondering tone: "D'you know, Johnnie, the trouble with Melly is that she is—she is what they call 'pure.' And that's a bad business in this world." He added, with bitter urgency: "Christ! If I only knew where she was!"

They did not speak until they came within sight of Johnnie's house. Then Johnnie reined in his horse, and spoke awkwardly: "Look here, Andy. I can't handle this—I mean, Phoebe. Had hysterics, when she was told. All about your sister disgracin' and dishonorin' us, and such damn foolishness. Phoebe's a nice girl, but she's got some wrong idees, and I've been a-workin' on 'em, and maybe I'm gettin' somewheres. I don't know. A good girl, but she got her share of gettin' twisted by your dad. Anyways," said Johnnie, pleadingly, "I'd take it as a favor if you'd come in a minute and quiet Phoebe down, tell her what you think about your sister. She sets quite a store by you."

Andrew had the natural horror of the male for female hysterics. He was about to refuse. But he liked Johnnie. He hesitated only a moment, then went on in with his brother-in-law.

Phoebe, waiting and weeping in the "parlor," heard the jingle of their harness. She flew to the door, and with a cry of joy she saw the flickering of the lanterns they carried. She ran out onto the steps to meet them, throwing out her arms in a distraught and tragic gesture.

"Johnnie! Andy! Did you see Melissa? She was here! I wouldn't take her in, and now she's gone. O Johnnie, Andy, you've got to find Melissa!"

Melissa had once read, in an old French tale, of a suicide. The author had gone into great detail as to the mental and emotional state of the suicide in the process of causing his own death. It had been very gruesome, vivid and minute.

The suicide had reflected profoundly on his anguish, and on the despair which had finally led to this end. Never had his mind been so acute, so well-ordered, so meticulous in functioning. But the author, of course, had never attempted suicide. He had never known that a man about to take his life thinks nothing at all, has no emotions in the final moment, no feelings, no passions. He is a blind organism going unconsciously towards extinction, and if he has any sensation it is merely of a faint but pervading relief, such as one feels when escaping pain under an anesthetic.

Never in her life, not even during sleep, had Melissa been so devoid of any mental or emotional reactions. There was nothing in her but a black blindness and unawareness. She was the utter negation of all passion. She had not gone into the water deliberately. The powerful wish-to-die, which lies at the foot of the tree of life like the primordial soil which paradoxically nourishes it, had taken complete possession of her. The tree had fallen; only the soil remained, covering up the faded branches, the rotting trunk. She had gone into the water without knowing why, driven by profound and instinctive impulses. For the first time in her life, instinct, rather than reason, however grotesque, had taken over the final decision.

She saw nothing, felt nothing. The water rose to her chin; the river's current caught and tugged at her heavy clothing. Her feet went, obediently, down and down. Now the water lapped at her lips, coldly.

An unusually sharp flare of lightning lit up the river all about her. It struck her eyes, and she blinked, and started instinctively. It was this last protective reflex of her body which suddenly woke her, momentarily, to where she was and what she was doing.

The torn moonlight glimmered over the water, silvered ridges on the flowing blackness. She heard, in her ears, the water's loud voice, like the voice of an urgent multitude. She stood still, bracing herself against the current which urged her on. Slowly she turned her head and saw the waste behind, beside and before her. She stood and resisted for a long time, looking and realizing.

She thought: What am I doing? What brought me into the river? When did I go down into it? And then, after a blank and absorbed moment: Am I such a coward, then? Am I such a fool?

Something within her, black, deep, abysmal, had betrayed her. She had read, with scholarly detachment, about "instinct."

But she did not realize that it was instinct that had betrayed her now, and that neither cowardice nor courage had brought her to the very edge of death. She felt only an enormous and bitter scorn of herself, a passionate contempt. It was not a sudden love for life, or a desire for it, which made her slowly turn about, carefully search for a footing on the muddy floor of the river, and move towards the shore again. It was only a devastating disgust.

She had no plans at all. Her only desire, now, was to reach land, to be free of the loathsome thing which had brought her into the water.

The water reluctantly receded from her, fell back to her shoulders, to her breasts, to her waist, to her hips. Her long loose hair was drenched; her clothing clung to her numbed body like wet stone. Slimy waterweeds draped themselves like gleaming ropes over her shoulders, had twined themselves about her arms. In the moonlight, her face was white and set and still, and strangely old.

Now the water had fallen to her knees. She went on, doggedly, though each moment was a crucial grim struggle against the desire to lie down and rest, with the water covering her in complete forgetfulness. The water fell to her ankles.

It was then that she saw lanterns flickering madly along the shore, running up and down the fern-covered banks, lighting up the lower branches of the threshing trees. It was then that she heard men's voices calling her desperately, mingling with the thunder. She did not answer until she had climbed the bank, until she had thrown back her dripping hair, and then her voice came strong and loud against the wind.

A lantern came running up to her, and behind it she saw the face of her brother. The lantern stopped abruptly, then swung towards her.

Later, Andrew told himself that he would never forget the sight of his sister, who had just risen out of the river. He would never forget the sight of her in the stormy moonlight, with her pale hair glimmering and drowned, with her clothing carved about her, with her face, deathly and fixed, turned towards him, the moon-torn black water behind her.

He had dropped the lantern, then, and had run the last few steps. But he was not quick enough. She fell at his feet before he could catch her.

CHAPTER 51

FOR AT LEAST half an hour, Geoffrey had not spoken at all. He had just walked back and forth, up and down the library, with measured steps as though he was completely occupied with his own thoughts. Even his sister had stopped talking and weeping loudly, and now huddled in her chair dabbing at the acid tears which kept oozing from her eyes.

The great grandfather clock in the hall boomed three times. The threatening storm had blown itself away long ago. Now the stars were wheeling and dimming, and the darkness had become tense with the soundless quality of waiting. It was still too early for the morning birds. The earth held her breath, and the moon sank.

For the past three hours everything that could be said had been said by Arabella, in the brightly lit library which poured its lamplight onto the dark lawns and trees outside. Arabella was completely exhausted. Even her triumph, her high elation and almost delirious joy, had subsided before her weariness. She had talked, and Geoffrey had said very little. He had walked into the house at midnight, had given his bag, hat, cane and gloves to James, had gone directly into the library, where his sobbing sister had been waiting for him, and had said one word only: "Yes?"

He had known it was about Melissa, though Arabella, naturally, had not, in her telegram, mentioned the name of his wife, and had only urged his immediate return. He had sat in the train, unseeing. He had known that some calamity was waiting to be told him at home, that it concerned Melissa and Melissa only. He had not allowed himself to think, though a thousand times during the short journey he had seen Melissa mysteriously dead, mysteriously ill, vanished. He had asked nothing of the coachman who met him. It was all Melissa. He had no sooner stepped inside the house than he knew that Melissa was gone, not dead, but gone completely. And so he had said: "Yes?"

The last of Arabella's rouge had melted away in her excited tears, and her elaborate coiffure had become a heap of agitated strings. She had sent Ellis away. She had wanted only to sit and think, until Geoffrey returned. Fear, exultation, anxiety, dread, and hope, had alternately assailed her. There were times when she wanted to get up and fly from the house; other times when she longed only for her bed; still other times when every nerve, sinew and muscle in her body seemed tense and drawn beyond endurance. When she heard Geoffrey's step she had been stricken with terror, and she had caught Melissa's letter and crushed it in her hand.

As Geoffrey came across the room towards her, she had looked at his face, unable to speak. He was white and drawn, and there was a blue shadow about his nostrils and lips. She had held out the letter to him, speechlessly. He had taken it, but before reading it he had looked at her steadily for a long and inscrutable moment.

He read it, slowly and carefully, standing there before his sister. Then he folded it neatly and put it away in his pocket. His expression had not changed in the least, had become neither enraged nor saddened. He said: "And now? Tell me all about it."

She had told him, finally finding words that gushed and splattered forth hysterically, that became a mixture of orderly explanation, furious denunciation of Melissa, hypocritically sympathetic tirades against him for his folly in marrying "the drab," protestations of her own innocence in the affair, confessions that she had heard "tales" but had refused to believe them, and her own torment when the letter had been brought to her in the morning. As she talked, she gained confidence, and her gestures became dramatic, even theatrical in their extravagance. She mouthed, demonstrated her own shocked expression of disbelief when she had first read the letter, rolled her eyes and clasped her hands passionately together to show him her second reaction, repeated her crushed denials to Ellis, imitated Ellis attempting to comfort her, threw herself back in her chair and closed her eyes to show him how she had fainted when she finally began "to realize," rose to her feet and tragically pressed her hands against her bosom to exhibit her gathering shock of the morning, collapsed again in her chair, and burst into fresh tears.

Geoffrey had not moved or spoken during all this fine repetition of her earlier emotions and actions. He had only watched her, with a curious deadness in his eyes. Then he had said: "Yes." He had taken out Melissa's letter again, and had reread it. He sat down, regarded his sister unmovingly, without speaking.

Something cold ran over Arabella's body. To divert his attention from herself, she cried: "As I told you, Geoffrey, this has been going on all summer! Whispers came to me, but I refused to believe them. Whoever would have thought it of Melissa? I knew she walked with Ravel; it was not possible not to know it. But I thought it mere friendliness, loneliness, if you will. He had gained her confidence, though I blame him less than I blame her. They often mentioned that they had been together along the river and in the woods, but in so open and, I now see, so guileful a manner, that I could not suspect in the least!"

"But you did suspect," said Geoffrey, very quietly. "Before I went away on Sunday night, if you remember, you intimated something. So, you did suspect. And, suspecting, you allowed that filthy rascal to dine at this house regularly, you entertained him at my table. Why, Arabella? I think I know."

He had stood up then, and had begun that endless walking up and down the room. Arabella, stunned, watched him for a little, then she burst out:

"I tell you, I did not suspect! Oh, I began to think it indiscreet! Did I not suggest to you a few days ago that you speak to Melissa? Think, Geoffrey," and now her face glared with relief. "Think! You will remember that I told you!"

But he did not answer her. He walked up and down, his head bent, his hands clasped behind him.

She continued, her voice thick and urgent with fear of him: "It was not until last week that I became seriously concerned, and that is why I spoke to you. Until then I thought it nothing, and when I heard whispers I was only angry. I believed in Melissa. I always thought her sly and stupid, and did not conceal my opinion from you, but I never thought for a moment that she could be guilty of such perfidy, such dishonor, such shamelessness. I have known her all her life; it was not possible, I thought, that she could be so."

"No," said Geoffrey, "it was not possible."

Arabella could not speak; she had no words in answer to this.

Geoffrey repeated, as if to himself: "It was not possible. It still is not possible. I do not believe it."

Arabella found her voice, trembling and faint: "I find it easier to believe now. You knew Charles Upjohn. You knew he was a liar, and disingenuous. You knew he was deceitful and treacherous, artful and false. You often hinted to me of these things. Melissa is his daughter. There have been times during the past months when I have discerned the more odious of his traits in her, though less prettily concealed. She does not have his arts and his poses. But she has his nature. I saw that, at last."

"Charles," repeated Geoffrey, and paced up and down.

If only he would say something sensible, something enraged and brutal! If even he would begin to accuse her, Arabella! She could endure anything but this quietness of his, this calm and thoughtfulness. She could endure even this, if he had shown signs of being openly stricken or outraged, or full of hatred for his wife. But it was not possible to bear the sight of his expressionless face, with only the blueness around the nostrils and mouth to testify to any inner emotion. For beyond that one reference, he had said nothing about Ravel, had not mentioned his name again.

And then she knew that he did, in spite of his denial, believe that his wife had betrayed him, had run away with another man. He was trying, she saw, to discover why, to learn how such a one as Melissa had come to this pass, and how Melissa, the silent and intolerant and fearful of strangers, had managed to interest herself in Ravel to the point of running away with him.

Arabella was very astute. Geoffrey *was*, indeed, thinking this. He could not understand. He felt no hatred for Melissa, no anger, no bitterness or disgust. He had completely forgotten Ravel as an intimate part of this whole affair. He only wanted to know. Melissa seemed to stand before him, mute and grave, following him with her eyes. He went back and back, into her childhood, to the very first day when he had seen her. Step by step, he recalled all the years of watching her grow, of loving her, of understanding her, pitying her, plotting for her. Never once had she shown a single equivocal trait, uttered a word which was not in accord with her nature or which did not grow out of it. There were times when she had been enigmatical, even to him, but this had been part of her very innocence, not to be measured by sophisticated or subtle standards or understood by those who compared everyone with the accepted average. Never, to Geoffrey, had she seemed obscure, in the full meaning of the term, never consciously ambiguous or questionable. Subtlety, assumed or natural, had been beyond her.

So, with the facts he had, there was no understanding what had happened. It could only be that he did not have all the facts.

He stopped before Arabella and ruthlessly questioned her. But first he warned her, in an oddly moderate tone, that this was the one time in her life when she must not lie. Looking, terrified, into his eyes, she knew, indeed, that she must not lie. She dared not tell him all the truth. But she could suppress part of it.

He went over the months since he had married Melissa; sometimes he went over certain weeks, and then even over certain days. An hour went by, another, and still the terrible questions went on, and still Arabella, growing more exhausted, more frightened, more weak, answered. A few times she became hysterical and begged to be allowed to go to bed, crying that it was half-past one, two o'clock, half-past two. But Geoffrey appeared not to have heard. He waited until she became comparatively calm, then went on with the questioning.

Slowly, in spite of Arabella's evasions, a picture was forming before him, a picture of a lonely, heart-broken, bewildered girl, alternately retiring into her solitariness and emerging for those accursed "lessons." The old picture of her becoming reconciled, of taking an interest in her new life, of trying to adjust herself resolutely, began to fade, though he felt that there was still some truth in it, somewhere. He could not completely discard the old picture, but it began to merge with the new one, giving Melissa another dimension. Arabella dared not lie, but she did not spare Melissa. She exaggerated the girl's rudeness, her boorishness, her inability to understand the finer points of civilized deportment, her inadvertent and innocent insults to her sister-in-law. Once or twice, in spite of everything, Geoffrey almost smiled, bleakly. But he could not convince himself that Melissa's struggles with her "lessons" had impelled her to run away with Ravel. That was too grotesque, even for Melissa. Something, somewhere, was being left out, in this whining narrative. The skeleton was being shown him, but the flesh was still not visible. And so the questioning went on.

In her hatred and malice, Arabella launched into an attack on Phoebe, the girl's malevolence towards her sister, her envy, her small and mean remarks. Andrew's neglect was gone into thoroughly. Nothing was spared by Arabella which might deflect Geoffrey's dangerous closeness to the real meat of the affair. She could feel him searching, prodding, almost touching. There were wild moments when she thought she would not care if he found it, so tormented was she by now, so shocked with terror. Nothing could be worse than this remorseless questioning. She had only one comfort: Melissa was gone, and with Ravel, and, even if found and questioned, would not be able to say, distinctly and truthfully, that her sister-in-law had suggested that she leave this house forever, that she was a burden and a shame in it, and a disgrace to the man who had unfortunately married her.

Secure in this knowledge, and congratulating herself on her subtlety, Arabella became calmer, and her terror lessened. For a while she could answer Geoffrey without a stammer, without evasion.

Everything finally came back to the one thing sure: Melissa had been seen with Ravel in many places during the summer, and she had gone off with him. The facts were there, and there was her letter. But Geoffrey knew, more surely with each tick of the clock, that something vital was missing. For he was now remembering Sunday afternoon, when Melissa had come to him with her father's manuscript, and he was remembering her strange manner, her wildness, her incoherence, her queer questions and glances. But there was a hiatus in his memory. He could not remember what she had asked him. He could not rid himself of the conviction that the clue lay in whatever she had asked.

Moment by moment, his old compassion for Melissa returned with increasing strength and, with it, his love and tenderness for her. He could not, as yet, envision Melissa with Ravel. It was impossible. He could only feel desolation and misery, and a grim determination to uncover the torturing answer to the whole thing. It was not time for plans, for action. These would come later.

He was no longer questioning Arabella. He could not remember when he had last spoken or when she had last answered him. He had been pacing up and down forever, while Arabella sniffled softly in her chair and dabbed at her eyes. The clock had boomed three, a long time ago, and there was no sound after it but the sound of his footsteps, up and down, back and forth.

Arabella watched him malignantly. Why, he did not seem aware that he had been dishonored, betrayed, and disgraced! This might have been only a serious illness of Melissa's, which was concerning him! Had he no shame, no pride, no self-respect? Was he so contemptible that he cared nothing for the blight on his name, his father's name? Now outrage stirred Arabella, and her swollen eyes flashed at him vindictively.

She broke the crushing silence in a loud if wavering voice: "Geoffrey, is it possible that you've forgotten the most important thing in this whole affair, the flagrant ignominy that creature has brought to this house, the house where we were born, where our parents lived and died? How dare you overlook that! How dare you forget! Have you no sense of honor, no sense of shame? But no! If you had had any of these, you'd never have married her, never have humiliated me with her presence, never have allowed her to enter these doors!"

In her agitation and hatred and vengefulness she sprang to her feet and confronted him as he turned in his pacing and returned to the spot where she stood. He stopped, and looked at her in silence, at her distorted face, furious gestures, mouthings.

He said, without any emotion at all: "I seem to have forgotten something, I admit. And I think it concerns you, Arabella. Somewhere, somehow, whether you know it or not, you have the key to everything. But I think you know it."

His eyes hypnotized her, her arms fell to her sides and her mouth sagged. He came a little closer to her. He said, almost gently: "What is it, Arabella? You know, don't you?"

She retreated a step from him, but he followed her, with a white cold excitement. Then she stopped, and cried out:

"I know nothing but what I have told you!"

"You are a liar," he said, in a neutral tone that had something deadly in it. "You know, and soon I shall know, too. That will be the end of you in this house, Bella."

She could not speak, but now she began to pant in the extremity of her malevolence, wrestling with her hatred for him and the memory of her old humiliations. Her head began to hum and throb with a loud and twisting noise. She wanted to kill him. She wanted to see him fall dead at her feet. She wanted to strike at him so violently that he would never recover.

"Yes!" she exclaimed, "there is something! You are right. I would never have told you, but I can, now, since it is too late! Late, too late! The drab dared to love you, Geoffrey! At the last, before she disgraced you, she dared to love you."

She began to laugh, showing the round yellow ridges of the teeth in her ovalled mouth. Her laughter filled the library with an obscene sound.

"She didn't know it herself, dear Geoffrey. I discovered it only a short time ago. She thought you didn't care about her, and because I knew what she was and what she was already doing with Ravel Littlefield, I refused to enlighten her. I wanted her out of this house, because I knew all about her. That, Geoffrey, is what I know."

He only stood there and looked at her, and it was this lack

of expression in him, this lack of reaction, this lack of fury, which goaded her in into madness:

"I am glad, glad to be able to tell you this now, for it is some consolation to me after the years of humiliation you inflicted upon me, your callousness, your miserliness, your brutality! Do you think I have forgotten a single one of your insults, your sneers, your contemptuous remarks about everything I did, said, wore? Did you think I was less than human, Geoffrey? No, I was human, and I could not forget. And that is why I am glad this thing has happened to you. It is a just judgment."

The rush of her memories exalted her and she acquired a kind of ugly dignity, in spite of her mockery, in spite of her hideous smiles. Because she had struck him in the one spot in which he was vulnerable, she was no longer afraid of him. He might stand there and just look at her with a quiet dead face, but she knew she had struck him and that he had felt it. She knew he believed her. That would be his punishment.

She said, still smiling: "That, I think, is why she went away with Ravel. Because she thought you did not want her, that you were tired of her and regretted your marriage."

He said nothing, did nothing. Arabella waited. They faced each other in silence. Then, very slowly, Arabella's smile faded; her face changed, became old and dwindled and full of wrinkles. All at once she was a tired and elderly woman, worn out by secret miseries and heart-burnings, by frustrations and petty despairs, by posings and artfulnesses, by pretensions and piteous hypocrisy. She no longer cared about anything. She wanted only to sleep and to forget. She wanted to force out from her this new sick pain, this illness, which might have been called remorse.

"I am sorry, Geoffrey," she said faintly. "It is true, and I am sorry now. If I could have back the time, it might be different. I'd have told you, before it was too late. If I am guilty, you also are guilty, and you must forgive me."

Geoffrey began to shake his head from side to side, ponderously, almost helplessly. "Yes," he said. And then again: "Yes."

She could not stand it. She burst into tears and ran out of the room, and he heard her sobs as she rushed up the stairs beyond.

The clock struck four. Now the sky outside the library windows began to turn gray as pearl, and the birds cried out in a multitude of voices. It was silent in the house. The house was like a soundless shell, impervious and shut against the tumult of the awakening earth. The black and distant hills began slowly to be outlined with pale rosy fire. The lamps in the library became raucous in their yellowness and, to the eyes of the man who sat in their light, were ringed in desolation.

He did not move, or even smoke. He sat, with his weighted arms heavy on the arms of his chair, and looked at the lamps.

Melissa, he thought. And over and over again: Melissa.

There was something he could do, and he would do it. He would find Melissa. He had no feeling against Ravel, not the slightest stir of rage or jealousy, because he was certain now that Melissa had not only not betrayed him but that she was incapable of betraying him. He was becoming more sure, and this frightened him, that Ravel probably did not know where Melissa was.

But where could Melissa have gone? To the best of his knowledge, she had no money, no friends. Could she have gone to her sister, her brother? But surely, if that were so, they would have told him or sent him some word. Yet he could not rid himself of the conviction that Phoebe or Andrew might be able to give him some help. In a little while he would go to them. But, before that, he must find some solution for Melissa and himself.

Yet, though his whole mind was filled with Melissa, there was someone else even closer, more imminent, almost more real. Charles Upjohn. Exhaustion, suffering, pain, had temporarily removed from Geoffrey reason and common sense. He felt the exultant presence of Charles Upjohn in this very room. He believed that he need only stare steadily at a certain spot and he would see his old enemy as he had seen him in life, gently smiling, his thin delicate head tilted, his large pale eyes gleaming in the fading lamplight, his slender shoulders bowed under his cloak. He did not want to see Charles, for he was afraid of the surge of hatred that would rise up in him. He did not want to see that scholarly and reflective face, which hid so much malignity, so much petty yet potent evil. If there was a villain in all this, it was old Charles, Charles who lived because he still influenced Melissa and could make his presence so felt to Geoffrey. Yes, it was Charles who was the villain, who had always been the villain, who had almost destroyed, if he had not actually destroyed, Melissa, and with her, her husband. His presence had been corruption; he had lived in his family like a stealthy disease. Geoffrey could hear the echo of his voice, insidious, melting, most touching and melliflous, and everything he had ever said had been a lie, and everything he had touched had been polluted. If there is danger in a stupid man, thought Geoffrey, there is even greater danger in an intelligent man if that man be both ego-tistic and frustrated and if his aspirations are greater than his abilities.

The clock struck five. It was long past the time for ghosts to vanish. But Charles Upjohn did not vanish. He became more and more imminent. Geoffrey in his exhausted state, thought that he heard soft footfalls in the room, a murmur, a rustle as of paper.

He stood up suddenly. He went to his desk and withdrew from it the manuscript Melissa had given him on Sunday. He held it in his hand, and smiled. He carried it to the hearth, laid it on the dead ashes. He struck a light and applied it to the heap of papers. The flame caught, snatched hungrily at the food offered it, leapt upwards triumphantly. But its light was a thin and spectral one, for now the first fiery rays of the rising sun soared into the room.

Geoffrey stood and watched the burning manuscript. In a little while he would go upstairs and find all of Charles' papers, and they would join these, and then, perhaps, Charles would finally die. He would see himself dying on this hearth, and it would be too much for him.

Geoffrey had the conviction that not only he but Charles himself was watching this rite of exorcism, and that they watched it together and knew it was the end.

The dawn came into the library brighter and clearer, and the lamps flickered. Now the sun touched the lower shelves of the books, brought out the pattern of the carpet. The manu-script blackened on the hearth; fragments were caught in the draft and rushed up the chimney. With them went the ghost of Charles Upjohn, and Geoffrey knew that he was finally alone.

The house began to come alive with the distant footsteps and murmurs of servants. But Geoffrey stood by the hearth. In spite of his desolation and fear for Melissa, a curious peace had come to him.

It was then that he heard a loud knocking at the door, a peremptory knocking. He went to answer it, not running, but with the sure conviction that it was news of Melissa. When he opened the door, he saw Andrew, Andrew with a gray, drawn face and grim eyes.

"We've found Melissa," said the young man, without pre-liminary greeting. "I found her coming out of the river, last night. She's at my house. I think you'd better come."

CHAPTER 52

IF THERE IS ANYTHING more terrible than an army with swords, it is innocence, thought Geoffrey Dunham. The romanticists might find this fact a source of inspiration, of poetry, of music and painting. But the awful truth remained that the innocent are very frequently not only a source of danger to themselves, but to others. For innocence is often armed with ruthlessness and fanaticism and can be the fountain-head of corruption and calamity, and of its own death.

Even in his present state of peace and happiness and hope for the future, he could think this, somberly and with detachment, because he knew that unless Melissa's profound innocence could be modified there would be no peace, happiness or hope for her or for him in the years to come.

He had just come from the room where Melissa lay, in the house of her brother. She was sleeping. The doctor had said that she was suffering from intense shock and exposure but her naturally hardy constitution would preserve her from any lasting effects and would help her to recover rapidly.

Geoffrey still did not know exactly what had brought Melissa to this pass. The whole story had been told him, partly by the sobbing and remorseful Phoebe, who had shown him Charles' letter, partly by Andrew, partly by Arabella, and a little by Melissa herself. In all these was discernible the outer architecture of the truth. But the deeper and more inaccessible truth lay in Melissa, and in Melissa alone. She had been victimized, derided, rejected and vilified, and though Geoffrey could not yet bring himself to forgive those who had done these things to Melissa, he had to admit that it was she, herself, who had exposed herself to attack, and who, by her very nature, had awakened the more brutish instincts of her enemies against her. Charles had not completely submerged his wife; he had been more or less impotent against Phoebe and Andrew. Only in Melissa had he found the total and ready victim, blindly eager to be used and destroyed. This did not excuse either Charles or Arabella, or the hard-hearted who had had no pity upon her. In fact, this was further condemnation of them. But Melissa, because of her intrinsic innocence, had not been able to defend herself, and thus her innocence had been a weakness and a danger rather than a virtue. If there was truth in the theory that the murdered is in part guilty for the crime of his murderer, then Melissa was in part guilty for the evil that had been Charles Upjohn, and the aggravated malice that had been aroused in Arabella.

Geoffrey thought of all the heroes and martyrs who had been hanged, crucified, burned, beheaded and beaten to death throughout man's horrible history. Their assassins were despised, and remembered with hatred. But, in truth, the heroes and martyrs were also responsible, because they had been unable to see that there might be another point of view besides their own, however noble, and that if man is to endure the proximity of his brother without killing or being killed by him, he must learn to compromise and to consider the other side of the question.

Melissa did not, Geoffrey knew, share many of the instincts and jejune impulses of the rest of humanity, but she did share one, and to an overpowering degree, the desire for clear-cut issues. The stronger the desire for such issues, the more sinister the man, and the more intrinsically stupid, Geoffrey was convinced, not matter how intelligent he was considered. The beginning of wisdom, then, was to understand that there are no clear-cut issues anywhere, nothing which one can absolutely accept to the exclusion of anything else. Those who did not know this were the most dangerous men on earth, more dangerous even than those who believed nothing at all. Out of these came the fanatics who lighted the auto-da-fes, who hung the gibbets with man-flesh, who inspired pogroms, who instigated and encouraged wars and died in them fervently, who incited man to tear at the throat of his brother. Intense belief in anything very often excited hallucinations in the victim, and if sometimes those hallucinations gave rise to great poetry and acts of selfless heroism, they also gave rise to the calamities which periodically almost destroy mankind.

The more Geoffrey considered Melissa's problem, the more apprehensive he grew. His only relief, when the problem became too exigent, was to remember the morning, two days ago, when he had gone into her bedroom and had seen her lying, white, spent and unconscious, on her bed. Miriam, Andrew's wife, was beside her, her competent brown hands ministering to the poor girl, while the Judge had hovered distressedly in the doorway, and the doctor packed up his bag.

Somewhere, in the room beyond, Phoebe was weeping, unconsoled by her husband who was as yet too shocked and too outraged by his wife's part in this tragedy to do anything to comfort her.

Geoffrey had taken the chair indicated by Miriam, and had sat down beside Melissa. He had looked at her for a long time. She might have been dead, as she lay there, her closed eyelids dark and bruised, her mouth carved and bloodless, her cheeks sunken. Her long silver-gilt hair had been braided neatly by Miriam, and lay on her pillows. The warm bricks, wrapped in flannel, which had been placed at her feet and against her body, had not yet warmed her or brought life back into that poor, tormented mind.

Geoffrey's love and compassion had risen to such heights they were actually a torture. He had longed to take Melissa in his arms, but the doctor had refused to allow him even to touch her. He must wait until she awoke naturally.

She did not awaken until long past noon. By this time, Phoebe had been partially forgiven by Johnnie, and sometimes tiptoed timidly into the room to look at her sister, and to avoid Geoffrey's eyes. How he must hate her, she thought. But Geoffrey did not hate her. She was only a silly, malicious and envious young woman; in short, she was human. He did not hate his sister; for the first time in his life, he did not even dislike her. For she, too, was human, and had he not once told himself that, being human himself, nothing human was alien to him? One might rail against the vices of humanity, detest them in exalted moments, hate and loathe them. Nevertheless, the fact remained that these were the natural instincts of man. Only centuries of unremitting effort would avail against man's instincts. The Church understood this, however the lofty theorists might cry that man's instinctual nature was his best and that man was naturally "good." The Church stood as an enemy against man's inherent bestiality, and though Geoffrey, in the past, had smiled at dogma and what he called "cant," he understood, now, that these could be powerful spells against the evil that was born in humanity and which had projected an objective reality of confusion, hatred, and intolerance upon a whole world.

Melissa awoke without any preliminary moan, sigh, or restlessness. She merely opened her eyes. There was no confusion in them, no bewilderment or pain. She saw Geoffrey beside her, and she lay and looked at him steadfastly, not lifting her hand, or moving. She accepted his presence. He bent over her and took her hand; it was cold but relaxed. Then she smiled faintly, and said, in quite a normal voice: "I tried and tried to remember what it was you once said to me, Geoffrey. It was terribly necessary for me to remember, but I had forgotten."

Geoffrey could not speak; he could only wait. He was alone with her now. She did not try to take her hand out of his. The fingers began to twine about his fingers as simply and trustfully as a child's. Her light brows drew together for an instant, and then her smile grew stronger, a smile he had never seen before. In fact, he was not sure that he had ever seen Melissa smile, and the phenomenon was all the more remarkable and engrossing to him.

She said: "I remember now what it was. You said you loved me."

He made his own smile humorous and indulgent. "So, you forgot it! That is nice to know."

But Melissa, as he ought to have remembered, had no sense of humor at all. She became agitated.

"Oh, how stupid you must think me! How can you ever forgive such stupidity!"

He said quickly: "Now, Melissa, you take everything too seriously. You are not in the least stupid." His voice changed, and he said gently: "You never really forgot, you know. It was in your mind all the time. I knew it was there. Just as I know you love me, too. If I had not known it, I should never have married you," he added with magnificent mendacity.

When he saw the sudden white brilliance that rushed over her face then, he thought he could not bear it. Her head moved weakly towards him on the pillow, and he got up and quite simply bent over her and kised her mouth. As he did so, he could see into the pale blue depths of her eyes, innocent, marvelling, full of tears. He sat down on the edge of her bed and lifted her in his arms. Her head fell against his shoulder. But she could not look away from him.

"Geoffrey," she said, and then over and over again: "Geoffrey."

When Phoebe and Miriam, aroused by the sound of voices, tiptoed into the room they found Melissa asleep in her husband's arms, like an infant, her cheek pressed against his chest, both her hands holding one of his. Geoffrey did not see them enter. He held Melissa close to him, his lips on her hair.

She had asked no questions. She had made no explanations. To her innocence, everything was possible, everything acceptable.

Later, when Melissa slept again after meekly eating the hot soup which Geoffrey fed her, Arabella came in, fearfully. She was ready for anything except Geoffrey's kind greeting. She could not believe it. She began to cry, to upbraid herself. Geoffrey led her outside into the hot mauve twilight, where they could be alone. The dark lavender hills stood against a background of fire, and a long purple peace floated over the fields and meadows.

"Don't cry, Arabella," said Geoffrey. He took his sister's arm, and for the first time in his life he felt pity for her, even fondness. "It's all over. I think it's about time, don't you, that we should understand each other? You were quite right about me. I've been something of a swine to you. I'm sorry, I truly am. Late as it is, you must try to forgive me."

This excited Arabella beyond control. She accused herself of all manner of crimes, against him and Melissa. She confessed her plot of the past months, her hatred for "poor Melissa," her determination to get her out of her brother's house, her envy and malice and resentment. Geoffrey listened without comment. If Arabella expected him to show anger, to denounce her, she was happily disappointed. He listened very gravely and attentively. And he knew that he, too, was guilty, guilty of the misery and humiliation which had driven his sister to such cruelty and ruthlessness.

He said, when her sobs would not let her continue: "Well, Arabella, I suppose it is partly my fault. It goes back more years than I like to remember. Shall we try to forget all of it, you and I; shall we promise each other never to speak of it again?"

"But Geoffrey," she said, timidly, allowing him to dry her tears, "you surely will not want me in your house, after this? You surely will want me to go away?"

"Nonsense. Of course not. What should we do without you? You know that insofar as household knowledge is concerned, Melissa is practically a child. And I have a feeling she won't improve very much. And what when the children come? Who will guide and help them, treat them in a common-sense fashion, instruct and discipline them? Melissa? Bella, don't you find the thought a little ridiculous?"

Arabella looked at him in disbelief, hardly daring to believe that he spoke seriously. But he was smiling at her, inviting her to smile at Melissa with his own indulgent tenderness. And so she began to smile, tremulously. She said: "Oh, Geoffrey."

She began to see herself with several as yet nameless little children at her knee, listening to their childish lessons, listening to their Sunday-school texts. She heard their pretty babble; she saw herself comfortably, and relievedly, growing gray and stout, a lace cap on her head and a white fichu crossed crisply on her plump bosom. The children would listen to her with adoration, awed by her wisdom and gentleness and patience. This touching and delightful picture made fresh tears come to her eyes. She could even see Melissa in the background, Melissa with a book in her hand, gratefully watching Arabella's "way" with the children, and thankful that someone was relieving her of a task that would doubtless bore her.

There would, of course, be one child named Geoffrey, who would early show a genius for art. She would take him, and him alone, up to her studio. She would show him her canvases. She would teach him to paint. She saw him as a man, saying: "All the homage I receive, all the fame I have acquired, is due to my saintly aunt, Arabella Shaw, of immortal memory." But no. That would not be entirely satisfactory. Arabella swiftly deleted the "immortal memory," and added: "Who is standing at my side, faithful and patient as always." She saw the admiring and reverent faces of a whole multitude, and her heart swelled.

There would be at least one little girl with golden hair and a grave face, whose triumphs in Philadelphia and New York society would be the result of her aunt's impeccable taste and guidance. She saw herself supervising brilliant weddings. She heard the wedding march, as the white brides, with bent heads, walked by the sides of their husbands down the flowered aisles of some great cathedral. The brides blushed, and dropped their eyes. But as they passed their aunt they looked up, and their first smiling glance of love was for her, and for her alone, in passionate acknowledgment.

Geoffrey, unaware of these delicious visions, was saying: "And, of course, there must be a special and liberal allowance for you, for yourself and no one or nothing else. I ought to have done that in the beginning."

"Oh, Geoffrey," said Arabella, weakly, only half listening, and still absorbed in her dreams.

"I'm not going to say," added Geoffrey, "that we shan't have, from time to time, new and unique difficulties with Melissa. I know her too well. But I am trusting to your patience, Bella, and to your kindness. We must never forget what her life has been, and we must make allowances."

Arabella felt herself capable of dealing with a hundred Melissas' oddities. "Do I not know and remember that dreadful Charles Upjohn!" she cried. "How can I ever forget what he did to that poor child! I shall never forgive him."

"Don't think of him, Bella. I promise you he has gone, and gone forever. I drove out his ghost last night. He'll never bother Melissa again."

She stared at him. But he was not smiling.

CHAPTER 53

THE NEXT MORNING Geoffrey had a long talk with Andrew, and with his friend, Judge Farrell, while Miriam and Phoebe helped Melissa to prepare for her return to her home.

"The first thing I am going to do," said Andrew grimly, "is to pull down that damned old house. We'll start, almost immediately, before the crops are ready. Every stick and stone will come down. I ought to have done it months ago. Melissa could see it any time she wished, and as long as it's there, she'll remember my father." He paused. "She remembers him now, with disgust, but that's almost as bad as the other way she remembered him."

Geoffrey was surprised at the younger man's subtlety. He nodded his head. "I'm going to take her on a—delayed—honeymoon," he said. "We're going to Europe. You can take down the old eyesore while we are gone."

"No," said Andrew positively, "I'm going to start tomorrow. You won't be leaving for at least two weeks." He added: "And there'll be no piece of furniture, not even a saucer or a cup, a book or a chair, to remind her. It all goes."

"Why not burn the whole damn thing down?" asked the Judge, with humor. "Simpler."

Geoffrey laughed and then was amused to see Andrew in his forthright way so reminiscent of Melissa considering the idea. Humor, thought Geoffrey, was not a conspicuous Upjohn trait. Only Charles had had it in any measure at all.

Geoffrey expressed with frankness to both of his sympathetic friends his deep concern about Melissa. "If she were younger," he said, "the problem would not be such a source of anxiety to all who care for her. Ordinarily healthy children learn early that man is naturally 'evil,' a murderer and a liar and they accept this fundamental truth as they accept the food they eat and the air they breath. By the time they reach maturity they have incorporated this knowledge in their own minds and have made compromises, steadily adjusting themselves to their own natures and to the very similar natures of other men. Unless they become either saints or politicians, they give no particular thought to it, neither lamenting it nor plotting to use it unduly."

The Judge nodded soberly, while Andrew listened in intent silence.

"But Melissa," continued Geoffrey, "is no longer young. The full nature of man has been revealed to her at a time when she is not young enough to digest and forget it, to accept it as one of the irrefutable facts of life. It was revealed to her when she possessed both the awful innocence of a child and the maturity and insight of an intelligent human being. Her well-developed mind is incapable of forgetting as a child normally forgets. Moreover, though a young child does not reflect, and so cannot comment to himself on his own nature, Melissa not only can see but inevitably will meditate upon what she sees. I am afraid this will be a constant source of misery to her."

"Well," said the Judge, after thoughtfully considering this, "I can see that you're going to have your hands full, Dunham. I don't envy you. But it is something, I suppose, to have a woman like Melissa as a wife."

Geoffrey sighed. "I don't know. If Melissa could be thrown into such disruption, such despair and agony, upon her first real contact with the world and the nature of men, then she is due for successive and steadily more devastating shocks. Worse, she possesses an inflexibility of temperament, a fanatical inability to compromise. Sometimes, in spite of everything, I am afraid that she will be constantly besieged and embattled. This does not argue very well for her own peace of mind."

Andrew said, with firmness: "Melissa was always a fighter. I don't think you ought to worry too much. Melissa without a fight for something or other on her hands would be miserable. I know."

Geoffrey laughed. "Yes, I see. And they'll always be fanatical fights. I suppose I ought to try to find harmless subjects for her to fight over."

"I think," said the Judge, "that the only hope for the girl will be to convince her that her latest opinion cannot possibly be the true and final one, that there are no fixed verities anywhere in the universe. Try to get her to doubt what her senses reveal to her, help her to be uncertain about any positive judgment of her own, and I think everything will be all right. Of course, it would be her salvation could she develop a sense of humor, but I suppose that is too much to expect."

Geoffrey laughed again. "Sometimes I wonder whether the development of a sense of humor, with its ability to compromise, is not the final corruption of man."

Phoebe came out, still avoiding meeting Geoffrey's eyes, and announced that Melissa was ready to go home. Arabella, too, had arrived in the Dunham carriage, and was waiting.

Geoffrey went into the large, old-fashioned bedroom, trying to cover, with a smile, his anxiety over Melissa. She was waiting for him, dressed in the clothing Arabella had brought: a soft, pale-blue poplin gown with cascades of white lace at breast and elbows. A broad yellow straw hat had been tied on her head, and her hands were gloved. There was a quiet and tranquil air about her, subdued and meditative. When Geoffrey entered, her white face became illuminated with that new look of hers, a shy yet fixed adoration which made her tired eyes kindle with brilliance. This always disconcerted Geoffrey while it delighted him. He began to wonder whether it was a good thing for Melissa to have transferred her fanaticism to himself. It imposed too impossible a burden on a mere human being. It had in it, for Melissa, the potentiality of pain, disillusionment and distress.

He sat down beside her and took both her hands in his. He leaned towards her, no longer smiling, but very grave:

"My darling, I am taking you home now. You are going to be very happy there, with me. You believe that, don't you?"

"Yes, yes, Geoffrey," she said, and her hands clung to his.

He sighed. "Melissa, I must talk to you before we leave. It is very important. You know, now, that you were wrong about many things and had formed dangerous opinions which almost destroyed you?"

"Yes." She spoke simply and fully. "I was wrong. I was so very wrong about dear little Phoebe, and Arabella. They are so good. I never knew people could be so kind."

Geoffrey frowned. "Melissa, listen to me closely. Phoebe and Arabella have not changed in the least. They are neither better nor worse than they were a week ago, a month ago, a year ago, or when they were born. If you continue to think them angels, formerly unjustly maligned by you, you are going to have plenty of shocks. I want you to remember this: Accept everybody just as he or she is. Demand from them nothing impossible in kindness, virtue, generosity, sympathy or wisdom. At the present moment, you think I am all perfec-

"Yes." She looked at him steadily. "It sounds very confusing though."

"It is. That's what makes life so unpredictable and interesting. Try to understand, darling. The trouble was that your first world remained, inflexibly, the one in which you spent twenty-five years of your life without discarding an illusion or an opinion. Be determined, then, not to make the same mistake again, or you will inevitably be condemned to a chronic unhappiness. You are too young for that. Such a state is reserved for the old, or for the stupid, who let their minds harden in a matrix of ideas from which they cannot, or will not, permit themselves to be freed. You are not old, and you are not stupid."

Melissa became agitated. "Am I to have no opinions, no convictions at all?" she demanded, with a touch of her old arrogant impatience.

He was very pleased at this. "Yes, indeed. Have opinions and convictions all over the premises, like the trees in a jungle, if you wish. But don't let yourself get the idea that these are the right ones, the irrefutable ones, the ultimate ones. Doubt, Melissa." He smiled at her. "Doubt like hell."

She laughed, suddenly and spontaneously, and he thought he had never heard so good a sound, so cleansing and so full of hope.

Now he put her to the test of the lessons he had been trying to teach her. "What are your thoughts about your father, Melissa?"

Her face changed abruptly, became pinched and quiet. She drew her hands away from his, twisted the gloved fingers together. He waited for some time before she spoke.

"My father. At first, I could not bear the thought of him. I made my whole mind empty of him. Then I was disgusted, and I hated him. When I remembered his face and his voice, it seemed more than I could bear. But now I think I am beginning to see that he was very miserable, that he was cheated, not by others but by his own limitations. He had wonderful aspirations. He did not have the ability to realize them in actual performance. And so I am very sorry for him. Sometimes I am so sorry that I can hardly endure it."

It was much more than Geoffrey could ever have expected. He took her hands again, and stood up, pulling her to her feet. They looked at each other for a long moment.

Then Geoffrey said: "I think we can go home now, darling."

tion. If you continue to think that, you are going to suffer, and that might embitter you and turn you against the whole world. We are all just human beings. You have no right to expect anything very much from anybody."

She listened with absorbed attention. Her face became somewhat sad. "Yes, I see," she said in a low tone. But there was uncertainty in her. She added: "I don't believe you'll ever hurt or disillusion me, Geoffrey."

"That is sweet of you, and I am touched," he said with sincerity. "But you are quite wrong, my love. I shall hurt you often and even more often I shall disillusion you. I shan't be able to help it. Sometimes it will be my fault, sometimes yours. And, in the natural course of events, you'll wound me, too, and sometimes we shan't like each other in the least. There may be rare moments when we'll even hate each other. None of this can injure the love between us, if we remember that we have all the faults of humanity in common."

She was silent. Geoffrey waited a moment, then said: "Melissa, I can't imagine anything worse for you and for me than for you to transfer to me the old unthinking worship you had for your father, your old belief that the one you love is beyond vice or malice or cruelty, your old conviction that the one you love is all wisdom and perfection. I don't want that from you, Melissa. I only want you to love me, to understand me as much as you can, to forgive me very frequently. You'll have need to do all of these, and I, also, shall have need for them in my life with you."

"I'd die rather than hurt you!" she cried.

"No, Melissa. You'll hurt me, and you won't die. And there is another thing: "I'd like you to learn to laugh. Do you know, love, that I've never heard you laugh?"

She began to smile, and then, to his delight and astonishment, she actually laughed, though with uncertainty and shyness.

After a little, he said: "At the moment, you are sure that the new world waiting for you is going to be all light and joy and peace. You are wrong. You must not get any fixed notions about the world, in any way, any idea that what you see today or tomorrow or the next year is immutable. The intelligent human being passes constantly from old worlds to new, constantly discarding, renewing and inventing illusions. Mind, no less than external nature, is always in flux. So you must be prepared to shed your erroneous illusions and opinions, day by day, with complete flexibility. Do you follow me, my dear?"